The Mystery of Marie Rogêt

and Other Tales

Edgar Allan Poe

ALMA CLASSICS

ALMA CLASSICS
an imprint of

ALMA BOOKS LTD
60 High Street
Wimbledon Village
London SW19 5EE
United Kingdom
www.almaclassics.com

Represented by:
Authorised Rep Compliance Ltd
Ground Floor
71 Lower Baggot Street
Dublin, D02 P593
Ireland
www.arccompliance.com

For the publication details of the individual stories in this collection see the relevant note to each title

This edition first published by Alma Classics in 2026

Cover: Nathan Burton

Printed in Great Britain by CPI Group (UK) Ltd, Croydon CR0 4YY

MIX
Paper | Supporting responsible forestry
FSC® C013604
FSC www.fsc.org

ISBN: 978-1-84749-941-7

Contents

The Mystery of Marie Rogêt

and Other Tales

THE UNPARALLELED ADVENTURE OF ONE HANS PFAALL*

With a heart of furious fancies,
  Whereof I am commander,
With a burning spear and a horse of air,
To the wilderness I wander.
      – Tom O'Bedlam's Song*

By late accounts from Rotterdam, that city seems to be in a high state of philosophical excitement. Indeed, phenomena have there occurred of a nature so completely unexpected – so entirely novel, so utterly at variance with preconceived opinions – as to leave no doubt on my mind that long ere this all Europe is in an uproar, all physics in a ferment, all reason and astronomy together by the ears.

It appears that on the — day of ——— (I am not positive about the date), a vast crowd of people, for purposes not specifically mentioned, were assembled in the great square of the Exchange in the well-conditioned city of Rotterdam.* The day was warm – unusually so for the season: there was hardly a breath of air stirring – and the multitude were in no bad humour at being now and then besprinkled with friendly showers of momentary duration, that fell from large white masses of cloud profusely distributed about the blue vault of the firmament. Nevertheless, about noon, a slight but remarkable agitation became apparent in the assembly: the clattering of ten thousand tongues succeeded – and, in an instant afterward, ten thousand faces were upturned towards the heavens, ten thousand pipes descended simultaneously from the corners of ten thousand mouths, and a shout, which could be compared to nothing but the roaring of Niagara, resounded long, loudly and furiously through all the city and through all the environs of Rotterdam.

The origin of this hubbub soon became sufficiently evident. From behind the huge bulk of one of those sharply defined masses of cloud already mentioned was seen slowly to emerge into an open area of blue space a queer, heterogeneous but apparently solid substance, so oddly shaped, so whimsically put together, as not to be in any manner comprehended and never to be sufficiently admired by the host of sturdy burghers who stood open-mouthed below. What could it be? In the name of all the devils in Rotterdam, what could it possibly portend? No one knew, no one could imagine, no one – not even the burgomaster Mynheer* Superbus von Underduk – had the slightest clue by which to unravel the mystery. So, as nothing more reasonable could be done, everyone to a man replaced his pipe carefully in the corner of his mouth and, maintaining an eye steadily upon the phenomenon, puffed, paused, waddled about and grunted significantly – then waddled back, grunted, paused and finally... puffed again.

In the mean time, however, lower and still lower towards the goodly city, came the object of so much curiosity and the cause of so much smoke. In a very few minutes it arrived near enough to be accurately discerned. It appeared to be... yes!... it *was* undoubtedly a species of balloon – but surely no *such* balloon had ever been seen in Rotterdam before. For who, let me ask, ever heard of a balloon manufactured entirely of dirty newspapers? No man in Holland certainly – yet here, under the very noses of the people, or rather at some distance *above* their noses, was the identical thing in question, and composed, I have it on the best authority, of the precise material which no one had ever before known to be used for a similar purpose. It was an egregious insult to the good sense of the burghers of Rotterdam. As to the shape of the phenomenon, it was even still more reprehensible – being little or nothing better than a huge fool's cap turned upside down. And this similitude was regarded as by no means lessened when, upon nearer inspection, the crowd saw a large tassel depending from its apex, and, around the upper rim or base of the cone, a circle of little instruments resembling sheep bells, which kept up a continual tinkling to the tune of 'Betty Martin'* – but still worse. Suspended by blue ribbons to the end of this fantastic machine, there hung, by way of car, an enormous drab beaver hat, with a brim superlatively broad and a hemispherical crown with a black band and a silver buckle. It is, however, somewhat remarkable that many citizens of Rotterdam swore to having seen the same hat repeatedly before – and indeed the whole assembly seemed to regard it with eyes of familiarity, while the vrow* Grettel Pfaall, upon sight of it, uttered an exclamation of joyful surprise, and declared it to be the identical hat of her goodman himself. Now, this was a circumstance the more to be observed as Pfaall, with three companions, had actually disappeared from Rotterdam about five years before in a very sudden and unaccountable manner, and up to the date of this narrative all attempts at obtaining intelligence concerning them had failed. To be sure, some bones which were thought to be human, mixed up with a quantity of odd-looking rubbish, had been lately discovered in a retired situation to the east of the city, and some people went so far as to imagine that in this spot a foul murder had been committed, and that the sufferers were in all probability Hans Pfaall and his associates. But to return.

The balloon (for such no doubt it was) had now descended to within a hundred feet of the earth, allowing the crowd below a sufficiently distinct view of the person of its occupant. This was in truth a very singular somebody. He could not have been more than two feet in height, but this altitude, little as it was, would have been sufficient to destroy his equilibrium and tilt him over the edge of his tiny car but for the intervention of a circular rim reaching as high as the breast, and rigged onto the cords of the balloon. The body of the little man was more than proportionally broad, giving to his entire figure a rotundity highly absurd. His feet, of course, could not be seen at all. His hands were enormously large. His hair was grey, and collected into a queue behind. His nose was prodigiously long, crooked and inflammatory, his eyes full, brilliant and acute; his chin and cheeks, although wrinkled with age, were broad, puffy and double – but of ears of any kind there was not a semblance to be discovered upon any portion of his head. This odd little gentleman was dressed in a loose surtout of sky-blue satin, with tight breeches to match fastened with silver buckles at the knees. His vest was of some bright-yellow material; a white taffety cap was set jauntily on one side of his head – and, to complete his equipment, a blood-red silk handkerchief enveloped his throat and fell down in a dainty manner upon his bosom, in a fantastic bow knot of supereminent dimensions.

Having descended, as I said before, to about one hundred feet from the surface of the earth, the little old gentleman was suddenly seized with a fit of trepidation, and appeared disinclined to make any nearer approach to terra firma. Throwing out, therefore, a quantity of sand from a canvas bag, which he lifted with great difficulty, he became stationary in an instant. He then proceeded, in a hurried and agitated manner, to extract from a side pocket in his surtout a large morocco pocketbook. This he poised suspiciously in his hand, then eyed it with an air of extreme surprise, and was evidently astonished at its weight. He at length opened it and, drawing therefrom a huge letter sealed with red sealing wax and tied carefully with red tape, let it fall precisely at the feet of the burgomaster, Superbus von Underduk. His Excellency stooped to take it up. But the aeronaut, still greatly discomposed, and having apparently no further business to detain him in Rotterdam, began at this moment to make busy preparations for departure – and it being necessary to discharge a portion of ballast to enable him to reascend, the half-dozen bags which he threw out, one after another, without taking the trouble to empty their contents, tumbled, every one of them, most unfortunately upon the back of the burgomaster, and rolled him over and over no less than half a dozen times, in the face of every individual in Rotterdam. It is not to be supposed, however, that the great Underduk suffered this impertinence on the part of the little old man to pass off with impunity. It is said, on the contrary, that during each of his half-dozen circumvolutions he emitted no less than half a dozen distinct and furious whiffs from his pipe, to which he held fast the whole time with all his might, and to which he intends holding fast (God willing) until the day of his decease.

In the mean time, the balloon arose like a lark, and, soaring far away above the city, at length drifted quietly behind a cloud similar to that from which it had so oddly emerged, and was thus lost for ever to the wondering eyes of the good citizens of Rotterdam. All attention was now directed to the letter, the descent of which, and the consequences attending thereupon, had proved so fatally subversive of both person and personal dignity to His Excellency, Von Underduk. That functionary, however, had not failed, during his circumgyratory movements, to bestow a thought upon the important object of securing the epistle, which was seen, upon inspection, to have fallen into the most proper hands, being actually addressed to himself and Professor Rubadub in their official capacities of president and vice-president of the Rotterdam College of Astronomy. It was accordingly opened by those dignitaries upon the spot, and found to contain the following extraordinary, and indeed very serious, communication:

To Their Excellencies Von Underduk and Rubadub, president and vice-president of the States' College of Astronomers in the city of Rotterdam.

Your Excellencies may perhaps be able to remember an humble artisan, by name Hans Pfaall, and by occupation a mender of bellows, who, with three others, disappeared from Rotterdam about five years ago, in a manner which must have been considered unaccountable. If, however, it so please Your Excellencies, I, the writer of this communication, am the identical Hans Pfaall himself. It is well known to most of my fellow citizens that for the period of forty years I continued to occupy the little square brick building at the head of the alley called Sauerkraut, in which I resided at the time of my disappearance. My ancestors have also resided therein time out of mind – they, as well as myself, steadily following the respectable and indeed lucrative profession of mending of bellows – for, to speak the truth, until of late years, that the heads of all the people have been set agog with politics, no better business than my own could an honest citizen of Rotterdam either desire or deserve. Credit was good, employment was never wanting, and there was no lack of either money or goodwill. But, as I was saying, we soon began to feel the effects of liberty and long speeches, and radicalism, and all that sort of thing. People who were formerly the best customers in the world had now not a moment of time to think of us at all. They had as much as they could do to read about the revolutions and keep up with the march of intellect and the spirit of the age. If a fire wanted fanning, it could readily be fanned with a newspaper, and, as the government grew weaker, I have no doubt that leather and iron acquired durability in proportion – for, in a very short time, there was not a pair of bellows in all Rotterdam that ever stood in need of a stitch or required the assistance of a hammer. This was a state of things not to be endured. I soon grew as poor as a rat, and, having a wife and children to provide for, my burdens at length became intolerable, and I spent hour after hour in reflecting upon the most convenient method of putting an end to my life. Duns,* in the mean time, left me little leisure for contemplation. My house was literally besieged from morning till night. There were three fellows in particular who worried me beyond endurance, keeping watch continually about my door, and threatening me with the law. Upon these three I vowed the bitterest revenge, if ever I should be so happy as to get them within my clutches – and I believe nothing in the world but the pleasure of this anticipation prevented me from putting my plan of suicide into immediate execution, by blowing my brains out with a blunderbuss. I thought it best, however, to dissemble my wrath, and to treat them with promises and fair words, until, by some good turn of fate, an opportunity of vengeance should be afforded me.

One day, having given them the slip and feeling more than usually dejected, I continued for a long time to wander about the most obscure streets without object, until at length I chanced to stumble against the corner of a bookseller's stall. Seeing a chair close at hand for the use of customers, I threw myself doggedly into it, and, hardly knowing why, opened the pages of the first volume which came within my reach. It proved to be a small pamphlet treatise on speculative astronomy, written either by Professor Encke of Berlin* or by a Frenchman of somewhat similar name. I had some little tincture of information on matters of this nature, and soon became more and more absorbed in the contents of the book – reading it actually through twice before I awoke to a recollection of what was passing around me. By this time it began to grow dark, and I directed my steps towards home. But the treatise (in conjunction with a discovery in pneumatics, lately communicated to me as an important secret by a cousin from Nantes) had made an indelible impression on my mind, and, as I sauntered along the dusky streets, I revolved carefully over in my memory the wild and sometimes unintelligible reasonings of the writer. There are some particular passages which affected my imagination in an extraordinary manner. The longer I meditated upon these, the more intense grew the interest which had been excited within me. The limited nature of my education in general, and more especially my ignorance on subjects connected with natural philosophy, so far from rendering me diffident of my own ability to comprehend what I had read or inducing me to mistrust the many vague notions which had arisen in consequence, merely served as a further stimulus to imagination – and I was vain enough, or perhaps reasonable enough, to doubt whether those crude ideas which, arising in ill-regulated minds, have all the appearance, may not often in effect possess all the force, the reality and other inherent properties of instinct or intuition.

It was late when I reached home, and I went immediately to bed. My mind, however, was too much occupied to sleep, and I lay the whole night buried in meditation. Arising early in the morning, I repaired eagerly to the bookseller's stall, and laid out what little ready money I possessed in the purchase of some volumes of mechanics and practical astronomy. Having arrived at home safely with these, I devoted every spare moment to their perusal, and soon made such proficiency in studies of this nature as I thought sufficient for the execution of a certain design with which either the Devil or my better genius had inspired me. In the intervals of this period, I made every endeavour to conciliate the three creditors who had given me so much annoyance. In this I finally succeeded – partly by selling enough of my household furniture to satisfy a moiety* of their claim, and partly by a promise of paying the balance upon completion of a little project which I told them I had in view, and for assistance in which I solicited their services. By these means (for they were ignorant men) I found little difficulty in gaining them over to my purpose.

Matters being thus arranged, I contrived, by the aid of my wife and with the greatest secrecy and caution, to dispose of what property I had remaining, and to borrow, in small sums, under various pretences, and without giving any attention (I am ashamed to say) to my future means of repayment, no inconsiderable quantity of ready money. With the means thus accruing, I proceeded to procure, at intervals, cambric muslin, very fine, in pieces of twelve yards each; twine; a lot of the varnish of caoutchouc;* a large and deep basket of wickerwork, made to order; and several other articles necessary in the construction and equipment of a balloon of extraordinary dimensions. This I directed my wife to make up as soon as possible, and gave her all requisite information as to the particular method of proceeding. In the mean time I worked up the twine into a network of sufficient dimensions; rigged it with a hoop and the necessary cords; and made purchase of numerous instruments and materials for experiment in the upper regions of the upper atmosphere. I then took opportunities of conveying by night, to a retired situation east of Rotterdam, five iron-bound casks, to contain about fifty gallons each, and one of a larger size; six tin tubes, three inches in diameter, properly shaped and ten feet in length; a quantity of *a particular metallic substance, or semi-metal*, which I shall not name, and a dozen demijohns of *a very common acid*. The gas to be formed from these latter materials is a gas never yet generated by any other person than myself – or at least never applied to any similar purpose. I can only venture to say here that it is *a constituent of azote*, so long considered irreducible, and that its density is about 37.4 times *less than that of hydrogen*. It is tasteless, but not odourless; burns, when pure, with a greenish flame; and is instantaneously fatal to animal life. Its full secret I would make no difficulty in disclosing but that it of right belongs (as I have before hinted) to a citizen of Nantes, in France, by whom it was conditionally communicated to myself. The same individual submitted to me, without being at all aware of my intentions, a method of constructing balloons from the membrane of a certain animal, through which substance any escape of gas was nearly an impossibility. I found it however altogether too expensive, and was not sure, upon the whole, whether cambric muslin with a coating of gum caoutchouc was not equally as good. I mention this circumstance because I think it probable that hereafter the individual in question may attempt a balloon ascension with the novel gas and material I have spoken of, and I do not wish to deprive him of the honour of a very singular invention.

On the spot which I intended each of the smaller casks to occupy respectively during the inflation of the balloon, I privately dug a small hole – the holes forming in this manner a circle twenty-five feet in diameter. In the centre of this circle, being the station designed for the large cask, I also dug a hole of greater depth. In each of the five smaller holes, I deposited a canister containing fifty pounds, and in the larger one a keg holding one hundred and fifty pounds, of cannon powder. These – the keg and canisters – I connected in a proper manner with covered trains; and, having let into one of the canisters the end of about four feet of slow match,* I covered up the hole and placed the cask over it, leaving the other end of the match protruding about an inch, and barely visible beyond the cask. I then filled up the remaining holes and placed the barrels over them in their destined situation.

Besides the articles above enumerated, I conveyed to the depot, and there secreted, one of M. Grimm's improvements upon the apparatus for condensation of the atmospheric air.* I found this machine, however, to require considerable alteration before it could be adapted to the purposes to which I intended making it applicable. But, with severe labour and unremitting perseverance, I at length met with entire success in all my preparations. My balloon was soon completed. It would contain more than forty thousand cubic feet of gas – would take me up easily, I calculated, with all my implements, and, if I managed rightly, with one hundred and seventy-five pounds of ballast into the bargain. It had received three coats of varnish, and I found the cambric muslin to answer all the purposes of silk itself, being quite as strong and a good deal less expensive.

Everything being now ready, I exacted from my wife an oath of secrecy in relation to all my actions from the day of my first visit to the bookseller's stall; and promising, on my part, to return as soon as circumstances would permit, I gave her what little money I had left and bade her farewell. Indeed I had no fear on her account. She was what people call "a notable woman", and could manage matters in the world without my assistance. I believe, to tell the truth, she always looked upon me as an idle body, a mere makeweight – good for nothing but building castles in the air – and was rather glad to get rid of me. It was a dark night when I bade her goodbye – and, taking with me as aides-de-camp the three creditors who had given me so much trouble, we carried the balloon, with the car and accoutrements, by a roundabout way, to the station where the other articles were deposited. We there found them all unmolested, and I proceeded immediately to business.

It was the first of April.* The night, as I said before, was dark; there was not a star to be seen, and a drizzling rain, falling at intervals, rendered us very uncomfortable. But my chief anxiety was concerning the balloon – which, in spite of the varnish with which it was defended, began to grow rather heavy with the moisture; the powder also was liable to damage. I therefore kept my three duns working with great diligence, pounding down ice around the central cask and stirring the acid in the others. They did not cease, however, importuning me with questions as to what I intended to do with all this apparatus, and expressed much dissatisfaction at the terrible labour I made them undergo. They could not perceive (so they said) what good was likely to result from their getting wet to the skin merely to take a part in such horrible incantations. I began to get uneasy, and worked away with all my might, for I verily believe the idiots supposed that I had entered into a compact with the Devil, and that, in short, what I was now doing was nothing better than it should be. I was, therefore, in great fear of their leaving me altogether. I contrived, however, to pacify them by promises of payment of all scores in full as soon as I could bring the present business to a termination. To these speeches they gave, of course, their own interpretation – fancying, no doubt, that at all events I should come into possession of vast quantities of ready money – and provided I paid them all I owed, and a trifle more, in consideration of their services, I dare say they cared very little what became of either my soul or my carcass.

In about four hours and a half I found the balloon sufficiently inflated. I attached the car, therefore, and put all my implements in it: a telescope; a barometer, with some important modifications; a thermometer; an electrometer; a compass; a magnetic needle; a seconds watch; a bell; a speaking trumpet, etc., etc., etc.; also a globe of glass, exhausted of air and carefully closed with a stopper – not forgetting the condensing apparatus, some unslacked lime,* a stick of sealing wax, a copious supply of water and a large quantity of provisions such as pemmican,* in which much nutriment is contained in comparatively little bulk. I also secured in the car a pair of pigeons and a cat.

It was now nearly daybreak, and I thought it high time to take my departure. Dropping a lighted cigar on the ground, as if by accident, I took the opportunity, in stooping to pick it up, of igniting privately the piece of slow match, the end of which, as I said before, protruded a little beyond the lower rim of one of the smaller casks. This manoeuvre was totally unperceived on the part of the three duns – and, jumping into the car, I immediately cut the single cord which held me to the earth, and was pleased to find that I shot upwards with inconceivable rapidity, carrying with all ease one hundred and seventy-five pounds of leaden ballast, and able to have carried up as many more. As I left the earth, the barometer stood at thirty inches, and the centigrade thermometer at 19°.

Scarcely, however, had I attained the height of fifty yards, when, roaring and rumbling up after me in the most tumultuous and terrible manner, came so dense a hurricane of fire and gravel and burning wood and blazing metal and mangled limbs that my very heart sunk within me, and I fell down in the bottom of the car, trembling with terror. Indeed, I now perceived that I had entirely overdone the business, and that the main consequences of the shock were yet to be experienced. Accordingly, in less than a second, I felt all the blood in my body rushing to my temples, and, immediately thereupon, a concussion, which I shall never forget, burst abruptly through the night, and seemed to rip the very firmament asunder. When I afterwards had time for reflection, I did not fail to attribute the extreme violence of the explosion, as regarded myself, to its proper cause: my situation directly above it, and in the line of its greatest power. But at the time I thought only of preserving my life. The balloon at first collapsed, then furiously expanded, then whirled round and round with sickening velocity, and finally, reeling and staggering like a drunken man, hurled me over the rim of the car, and left me dangling, at a terrific height, with my head downward, and my face outward, by a piece of slender cord about three feet in length which hung accidentally through a crevice near the bottom of the wickerwork, and in which, as I fell, my left foot became most providentially entangled. It is impossible – utterly impossible – to form any adequate idea of the horror of my situation. I gasped convulsively for breath… a shudder resembling a fit of the ague agitated every nerve and muscle in my frame... I felt my eyes starting from their sockets... a horrible nausea overwhelmed me... and at length I lost all consciousness in a swoon.

How long I remained in this state it is impossible to say. It must, however, have been no inconsiderable time, for when I partially recovered the sense of existence, I found the day breaking, the balloon at a prodigious height over a wilderness of ocean, and not a trace of land to be discovered far and wide within the limits of the vast horizon. My sensations, however, upon thus recovering, were by no means so replete with agony as might have been anticipated. Indeed, there was much of madness in the calm survey which I began to take of my situation. I drew up to my eyes each of my hands, one after the other, and wondered what occurrence could have given rise to the swelling of the veins and the horrible blackness of the fingernails. I afterwards carefully examined my head, shaking it repeatedly and feeling it with minute attention, until I succeeded in satisfying myself that it was not, as I had more than half suspected, larger than my balloon. Then, in a knowing manner, I felt in both my breeches pockets, and, missing therefrom a set of tablets and a toothpick case, endeavoured to account for their disappearance – and, not being able to do so, felt inexpressibly chagrined. It now occurred to me that I suffered great uneasiness in the joint of my left ankle, and a dim consciousness of my situation began to glimmer through my mind. But – strange to say! – I was neither astonished nor horror-stricken. If I felt any emotion at all, it was a kind of chuckling satisfaction at the cleverness I was about to display in extricating myself from this dilemma – and never for a moment did I look upon my ultimate safety as a question susceptible of doubt. For a few minutes I remained wrapped in the profoundest meditation. I have a distinct recollection of frequently compressing my lips, putting my forefinger to the side of my nose and making use of other gesticulations and grimaces common to men who, at ease in their armchairs, meditate upon matters of intricacy or importance. Having, as I thought, sufficiently collected my ideas, I now, with great caution and deliberation, put my hands behind my back and unfastened the large iron buckle which belonged to the waistband of my pantaloons. This buckle had three teeth, which, being somewhat rusty, turned with great difficulty on their axis. I brought them, however, after some trouble, at right angles to the body of the buckle, and was glad to find them remain firm in that position. Holding within my teeth the instrument thus obtained, I now proceeded to untie the knot of my cravat. I had to rest several times before I could accomplish this manoeuvre; but it was at length accomplished. To one end of the cravat I then made fast the buckle, and the other end I tied, for greater security, tightly around my wrist. Drawing now my body upwards, with a prodigious exertion of muscular force I succeeded, at the very first trial, in throwing the buckle over the car and entangling it, as I had anticipated, in the circular rim of the wickerwork.

My body was now inclined towards the side of the car, at an angle of about forty-five degrees, but it must not be understood that I was therefore only forty-five degrees below the perpendicular. So far from it, I still lay nearly level with the plane of the horizon, for the change of situation which I had acquired had forced the bottom of the car considerably outwards from my position, which was accordingly one of the most imminent peril. It should be remembered, however, that when I fell, in the first instance, from the car, if I had fallen with my face turned towards the balloon instead of turned outwardly from it, as it actually was – or if, in the second place, the cord by which I was suspended had chanced to hang over the upper edge instead of through a crevice near the bottom of the car – I say it may be readily conceived that in either of these supposed cases I should have been unable to accomplish even as much as I had now accomplished, and the disclosures now made would have been utterly lost to posterity. I had therefore every reason to be grateful – although, in point of fact, I was still too stupid* to be any thing at all, and hung for perhaps a quarter of an hour in that extraordinary manner without making the slightest further exertion, and in a singularly tranquil state of idiotic enjoyment. But this feeling did not fail to die rapidly away, and thereunto succeeded horror and dismay and a sense of utter helplessness and ruin. In fact, the blood so long accumulating in the vessels of my head and throat, and which had hitherto buoyed up my spirits with delirium, had now begun to retire within their proper channels, and the distinctness which was thus added to my perception of the danger merely served to deprive me of the self-possession and courage to encounter it. But this weakness was, luckily for me, of no very long duration. In good time came to my rescue the spirit of despair, and, with frantic cries and struggles, I jerked my way bodily upwards, till at length, clutching with a vice-like grip the long-desired rim, I writhed my person over it and fell headlong and shuddering within the car.

It was not until some time afterwards that I recovered myself sufficiently to attend to the ordinary cares of the balloon. I then, however, examined it with attention, and found it, to my great relief, uninjured. My implements were all safe, and, fortunately, I had lost neither ballast nor provisions. Indeed, I had so well secured them in their places that such an accident was entirely out of the question. Looking at my watch, I found it six o'clock. I was still rapidly ascending, and the barometer gave a present altitude of three and three quarter miles. Immediately beneath me in the ocean lay a small black object, slightly oblong in shape, seemingly about the size of a domino, and in every respect bearing a great resemblance to one of those toys. Bringing my telescope to bear upon it, I plainly discerned it to be a British ninety-four-gun ship, close-hauled* and pitching heavily in the sea with her head to the WSW. Besides this ship, I saw nothing but the ocean and the sky and the sun, which had long arisen.

It is now high time that I should explain to Your Excellencies the object of my voyage. Your Excellencies will bear in mind that distressed circumstances in Rotterdam had at length driven me to the resolution of committing suicide. It was not, however, that to life itself I had any positive disgust, but that I was harassed beyond endurance by the adventitious miseries attending my situation. In this state of mind, wishing to live, yet wearied with life, the treatise at the stall of the bookseller, backed by the opportune discovery of my cousin of Nantes, opened a resource to my imagination. I then finally made up my mind. I determined to depart, yet live – to leave the world, yet continue to exist – in short, to drop enigmas, I resolved, let what would ensue, to force a passage, if I could, *to the moon*. Now, lest I should be supposed more of a madman than I actually am, I will detail, as well as I am able, the considerations which led me to believe that an achievement of this nature, although without doubt difficult and full of danger, was not absolutely, to a bold spirit, beyond the confines of the possible.

The moon's actual distance from the earth was the first thing to be attended to. Now, the mean or average interval between the *centres* of the two planets is 59.9643 of the earth's equatorial radii, or only about 237,000 miles. I say "the mean or average interval", but it must be borne in mind that the form of the moon's orbit being an ellipse of eccentricity amounting to no less than 0.05484 of the major semi-axis of the ellipse itself, and the earth's centre being situated in its focus, if I could in any manner contrive to meet the moon in its perigee,* the above-mentioned distance would be materially diminished. But, to say nothing at present of this possibility, it was very certain that, at all events, from the 237,000 miles I would have to deduct the radius of the earth, say 4,000, and the radius of the moon, say 1,080 – in all 5,080 – leaving an actual interval to be traversed, under average circumstances, of 231,920 miles. Now this, I reflected, was no very extraordinary distance. Travelling on the land has been repeatedly accomplished at the rate of sixty miles per hour – and indeed a much greater speed may be anticipated. But, even at this velocity, it would take me no more than 161 days to reach the surface of the moon. There were, however, many particulars inducing me to believe that my average rate of travelling might possibly very much exceed that of sixty miles per hour – and, as these considerations did not fail to make a deep impression upon my mind, I will mention them more fully hereafter.

The next point to be regarded was one of far greater importance. From indications afforded by the barometer, we find that, in ascensions from the surface of the earth, we have, at the height of 1,000 feet, left below us about one thirtieth of the entire mass of atmospheric air; that at 10,600 we have ascended through nearly one third; and that at 18,000, which is not far from the elevation of Cotopaxi,* we have surmounted one half the material – or, at all events, one half the *ponderable** body of air incumbent upon our globe. It is also calculated that at an altitude not exceeding the hundredth part of the earth's diameter – that is, not exceeding eighty miles – the rarefaction would be so excessive that animal life could in no manner be sustained, and, moreover, that the most delicate means we possess of ascertaining the presence of the atmosphere would be inadequate to assure us of its existence. But I did not fail to perceive that these latter calculations are founded altogether on our experimental knowledge of the properties of air and the mechanical laws regulating its dilation and compression in what may be called, comparatively speaking, *the immediate vicinity* of the earth itself – and, at the same time, it is taken for granted that animal life is and must be essentially *incapable of modification* at any given unattainable distance from the surface. Now, all such reasoning, and from such data, must of course be simply analogical. The greatest height ever reached by man was that of 25,000 feet, attained in the aeronautic expedition of Messieurs Gay-Lussac and Biot.* This is a moderate altitude, even when compared with the eighty miles in question – and I could not help thinking that the subject admitted room for doubt and great latitude for speculation.

But, in point of fact, an ascension being made to any given altitude, the ponderable quantity of air surmounted in any *farther* ascension is by no means in proportion to the additional height ascended (as may be plainly seen from what has been stated before), but in a ratio constantly decreasing. It is therefore evident that, ascend as high as we may, we cannot, literally speaking, arrive at a limit beyond which *no* atmosphere is to be found. It *must exist*, I argued – although it *may* exist in a state of infinite rarefaction.

On the other hand, I was aware that arguments have not been wanting to prove the existence of a real and definite limit to the atmosphere beyond which there is absolutely no air whatsoever. But a circumstance which has been left out of view by those who contend for such a limit seemed to me, although no positive refutation of their creed, still a point worthy very serious investigation. On comparing the intervals between the successive arrivals of Encke's comet at its perihelion,* after giving credit, in the most exact manner, for all the disturbances due to the attractions of the planets, it appears that the periods are gradually diminishing – that is to say, the major axis of the comet's ellipse is growing shorter in a slow but perfectly regular decrease. Now, this is precisely what ought to be the case if we suppose a resistance experienced from the comet from an extremely *rare ethereal medium* pervading the regions of its orbit. For it is evident that such a medium must, in retarding the comet's velocity, increase its centripetal by weakening its centrifugal force. In other words, the sun's attraction would be constantly attaining greater power, and the comet would be drawn nearer at every revolution. Indeed, there is no other way of accounting for the variation in question. But again – the real diameter of the same comet's nebulosity is observed to contract rapidly as it approaches the sun and dilate with equal rapidity in its departure towards its aphelion. Was I not justified* in supposing, with M. Valz,* that this apparent condensation of volume has its origin in the compression of the same ethereal medium I have spoken of before, and which is dense in proportion to its vicinity to the sun? The lenticular-shaped phenomenon, also called "the zodiacal light",* was a matter worthy of attention. This radiance, so apparent in the tropics, and which cannot be mistaken for any meteoric lustre, extends from the horizon obliquely upwards, and follows generally the direction of the sun's equator. It appeared to me evidently in the nature of a rare atmosphere extending from the sun outwards, beyond the orbit of Venus at least, and I believed indefinitely farther. Indeed, this medium

I could not suppose confined to the path of the comet's ellipse, or to the immediate neighbourhood of the sun. It was easy, on the contrary, to imagine it pervading the entire regions of our planetary system, condensed into what we call atmosphere at the planets themselves, and perhaps at some of them modified by considerations purely geological – that is to say, modified or varied in its proportions (or absolute nature) by matters volatilized from the respective orbs.

Having adopted this view of the subject, I had little further hesitation. Granting that on my passage I should meet with atmosphere *essentially* the same as at the surface of the earth, I conceived that, by means of the very ingenious apparatus of M. Grimm, I should readily be enabled to condense it in sufficient quantity for the purposes of respiration. This would remove the chief obstacle in a journey to the moon. I had indeed spent some money and great labour in adapting the apparatus to the object intended, and confidently looked forward to its successful application, if I could manage to complete the voyage within any reasonable period. This brings me back to the *rate* at which it would be possible to travel.

It is true that balloons, in the first stage of their ascensions from the earth, are known to rise with a velocity comparatively moderate. Now, the power of elevation lies altogether in the superior gravity of the atmospheric air compared with the gas in the balloon – and, at first sight, it does not appear probable that, as the balloon acquires altitude and consequently arrives successively in atmospheric strata of densities rapidly diminishing – I say, it does not appear at all reasonable that, in this its progress upwards, the original velocity should be accelerated. On the other hand, I was not aware that, in any recorded ascension, a *diminution* had been proved to be apparent in the absolute rate of ascent; although such should have been the case, if on account of nothing else, on account of the escape of gas through balloons ill constructed and varnished with no better material than the ordinary varnish. It seemed, therefore, that the effect of such escape was only sufficient to counterbalance the effect of the acceleration attained in the diminishing of the balloon's distance from the gravitating centre. I now considered that, provided in my passage I found the medium I had imagined, and provided it should prove to be *essentially* what we denominate "atmospheric air", it could make comparatively little difference at what extreme state of rarefaction I should discover it – that is to say, in regard to my power of ascending – for the gas in the balloon would not only be itself subject to similar rarefaction (in proportion to the occurrence of which, I could suffer an escape of so much as would be requisite to prevent explosion), but, *being what it was*, would at all events continue specifically lighter than any compound whatever of mere nitrogen and oxygen. Thus there was a chance (in fact, there was a strong probability) that, *at no epoch of my ascent, I should reach a point where the united weights of my immense balloon, the inconceivably rare gas within it, the car and its contents should equal the weight of the mass of the surrounding atmosphere displaced* – and this will be readily understood as the sole condition upon which my upward flight would be arrested. But, if this point were even attained, I could dispense with ballast and other weight to the amount of nearly three hundred pounds. In the mean time, the force of gravitation would be constantly diminishing, in proportion to the squares of the distances, and so, with a velocity prodigiously accelerating, I should at length arrive in those distant regions where the force of the earth's attraction would be superseded by that of the moon.

There was another difficulty, however, which occasioned me some little disquietude. It has been observed that, in balloon ascensions to any considerable height, besides the pain attending respiration, great uneasiness is experienced about the head and body, often accompanied with bleeding at the nose, and other symptoms of an alarming kind, and growing more and more inconvenient in proportion to the altitude attained.* This was a reflection of a nature somewhat startling. Was it not probable that these symptoms would increase until terminated by death itself? I finally thought not. Their origin was to be looked for in the progressive removal of the *customary* atmospheric pressure upon the surface of the body and consequent distention of the superficial blood vessels – not in any positive disorganization of the animal system, as in the case of difficulty in breathing, where the atmospheric density is *chemically insufficient* for the due renovation of blood in a ventricle of the heart. Unless for default of this renovation, I could see no reason, therefore, why life could not be sustained even in a *vacuum* – for the expansion and compression of chest commonly called breathing is action purely muscular, and the cause, not the effect, of respiration. In a word, I conceived that, as the body should become habituated to the want of atmospheric pressure, these sensations of pain would gradually diminish – and to endure them while they continued, I relied with confidence upon the iron hardihood of my constitution.

Thus, may it please Your Excellencies, I have detailed some, though by no means all, the considerations which led me to form the project of a lunar voyage. I shall now proceed to lay before you the result of an attempt so apparently audacious in conception – and, at all events, so utterly unparalleled in the annals of mankind.

Having attained the altitude before mentioned – that is to say, three miles and three quarters – I threw out from the car a quantity of feathers, and found that I still ascended with sufficient rapidity: there was, therefore, no necessity for discharging any ballast. I was glad of this, for I wished to retain with me as much weight as I could carry, for the obvious reason that I could not be *positive* either about the gravitation or the atmospheric density of the moon. I as yet suffered no bodily inconvenience, breathing with great freedom and feeling no pain whatever in the head. The cat was lying very demurely upon my coat, which I had taken off, and eyeing the pigeons with an air of nonchalance. These latter being tied by the leg to prevent their escape, were busily employed in picking up some grains of rice scattered for them in the bottom of the car.

At twenty minutes past six o'clock, the barometer showed an elevation of 26,400 feet, or five miles to a fraction. The prospect seemed unbounded. Indeed, it is very easily calculated by means of spherical geometry how great an extent of the earth's area I beheld. The convex surface of any segment of a sphere is, to the entire surface of the sphere itself, as the versed sine of the segment to the diameter of the sphere. Now, in my case, the versed sine – that is to say, the *thickness* of the segment beneath me – was about equal to my elevation, or the elevation of the point of sight above the surface. "As five miles, then, to eight thousand" would express the proportion of the earth's area seen by me. In other words, I beheld as much as a sixteen-hundredth part of the whole surface of the globe. The sea appeared unruffled as a mirror – although, by means of the telescope, I could perceive it to be in a state of violent agitation. The ship was no longer visible, having drifted away, apparently to the eastward. I now began to experience, at intervals, severe pain in the head, especially about the ears – still, however, breathing with tolerable freedom. The cat and pigeons seemed to suffer no inconvenience whatsoever.

At twenty minutes before seven, the balloon entered a long series of dense cloud, which put me to great trouble by damaging my condensing apparatus and wetting me to the skin – this was, to be sure, a singular *rencontre*,* for I had not believed it possible that a cloud of this nature could be sustained at so great an elevation. I thought it best, however, to throw out two five-pound pieces of ballast, reserving still a weight of one hundred and sixty-five pounds. Upon so doing, I soon rose above the difficulty, and perceived immediately that I had obtained a great increase in my rate of ascent. In a few seconds after my leaving the cloud, a flash of vivid lightning shot from one end of it to the other, and caused it to kindle up throughout its vast extent like a mass of ignited charcoal. This, it must be remembered, was in the broad light of day. No fancy may picture the sublimity which might have been exhibited by a similar phenomenon taking place amid the darkness of the night. Hell itself might then have found a fitting image. Even as it was, my hair stood on end while I gazed afar down within the yawning abysses, letting imagination descend and stalk about in the strange vaulted halls and ruddy gulfs and red ghastly chasms of the hideous and unfathomable fire. I had indeed made a narrow escape. Had the balloon remained a very short while longer within the cloud – that is to say, had not the inconvenience of getting wet determined me to discharge the ballast – my destruction might, and probably would, have been the consequence. Such perils, although little considered, are perhaps the greatest which must be encountered in balloons. I had by this time, however, attained too great an elevation to be any longer uneasy on this head.

I was now rising rapidly, and by seven o'clock the barometer indicated an altitude of no less than nine miles and a half. I began to find great difficulty in drawing my breath. My head, too, was excessively painful – and, having felt for some time a moisture about my cheeks, I at length discovered it to be blood, which was oozing quite fast from the drums of my ears. My eyes also gave me great uneasiness. Upon passing the hand over them, they seemed to have protruded from their sockets in no inconsiderable degree – and all objects in the car, and even the balloon itself, appeared distorted to my vision. These symptoms were more than I had expected, and occasioned me some alarm. At this juncture, very imprudently, and without consideration, I threw out from the car three five-pound pieces of ballast. The accelerated rate of ascent thus obtained carried me too rapidly, and without sufficient gradation, into a highly rarefied stratum of the atmosphere, and the result had nearly proved fatal to my expedition and to myself. I was suddenly seized with a spasm which lasted for more than five minutes, and even when this, in a measure, ceased, I could catch my breath only at long intervals and in a gasping manner – bleeding all the while copiously at the nose and ears, and even slightly at the eyes. The pigeons appeared distressed in the extreme, and struggled to escape, while the cat mewed piteously and, with her tongue hanging out of her mouth, staggered to and fro in the car as if under the influence of poison. I now too late discovered the great rashness of which I had been guilty in discharging the ballast, and my agitation was excessive. I anticipated nothing less than death, and death in a few minutes. The physical suffering I underwent contributed also to render me nearly incapable of making any exertion for the preservation of my life. I had, indeed, little power of reflection left, and the violence of the pain in my head seemed to be greatly on the increase. Thus I found that my senses would shortly give way altogether, and I had already clutched one of the valve ropes with the view of attempting a descent, when the recollection of the trick I had played the three creditors, and the possible consequences to myself should I return, operated to deter me for the moment. I lay down in the bottom of the car, and endeavoured to collect my faculties. In this I so far succeeded as to determine upon the experiment of losing blood. Having no lancet, however, I was constrained to perform the operation in the best manner I was able, and finally succeeded in opening a vein in my left arm with the blade of my penknife. The blood had hardly commenced flowing when I experienced a sensible relief, and, by the time I had lost about half a moderate basinful, most of the worst symptoms had abandoned me entirely. I nevertheless did not think it expedient to attempt getting on my feet immediately, but, having tied up my arm as well as I could, I lay still for about a quarter of an hour. At the end of this time I arose, and found myself freer from absolute *pain* of any kind than I had been during the last hour and a quarter of my ascension. The difficulty of breathing, however, was diminished in a very slight degree, and I found that it would soon be positively necessary to make use of my condenser. In the mean time, looking towards the cat, who was again snugly stowed away upon my coat, I discovered to my infinite surprise that she had taken the opportunity of my indisposition to bring into light a litter of three little kittens. This was an addition to the number of passengers on my part altogether unexpected, but I was pleased at the occurrence. It would afford me a chance of bringing to a kind of test the truth of a surmise – which, more than anything else, had influenced me in attempting this ascension. I had imagined that the *habitual* endurance of the atmospheric pressure at the surface of the earth was the cause, or nearly so, of the pain attending animal existence at a distance above the surface. Should the kittens be found to suffer uneasiness *in an equal degree with their mother*, I must consider my theory in fault – but a failure to do so I should look upon as a strong confirmation of my idea.

By eight o'clock I had actually attained an elevation of seventeen miles above the surface of the earth. Thus it seemed to me evident that my rate of ascent was not only on the increase, but that the progression would have been apparent in a slight degree even had I not discharged the ballast which I did. The pains in my head and ears returned, at intervals, with violence, and I still continued to bleed occasionally at the nose, but upon the whole I suffered much less than might have been expected. I breathed, however, at every moment with more and more difficulty, and each inhalation was attended with a troublesome spasmodic action of the chest. I now unpacked the condensing apparatus, and got it ready for immediate use.

The view of the earth, at this period of my ascension, was beautiful indeed. To the westward, the northward and the southward, as far as I could see, lay a boundless sheet of apparently unruffled ocean, which every moment gained a deeper and deeper tint of blue. At a vast distance to the eastward, although perfectly discernible, extended the islands of Great Britain, the entire Atlantic coasts of France and Spain, with a small portion of the northern part of the continent of Africa. Of individual edifices not a trace could be discovered, and the proudest cities of mankind had utterly faded away from the face of the earth.

What mainly astonished me, in the appearance of things below, was the seeming concavity of the surface of the globe. I had, thoughtlessly enough, expected to see its real *convexity* become evident as I ascended, but a very little reflection sufficed to explain the discrepancy. A line dropped from my position perpendicularly to the earth would have formed the perpendicular of a right-angled triangle, of which the base would have extended from the right angle to the horizon, and the hypotenuse from the horizon to my position. But my height was little or nothing in comparison with my prospect. In other words, the base and hypotenuse of the supposed triangle would, in my case, have been so long, when compared to the perpendicular, that the two former might have been regarded as nearly parallel. In this manner, the horizon of the aeronaut appears always to be *upon a level* with the car. But as the point immediately beneath him seems, and is, at a great distance below him, it seems of course also at a great distance below the horizon. Hence the impression of concavity – and this impression must remain until the elevation shall bear so great a proportion to the prospect that the apparent parallelism of the base and hypotenuse disappears.

The pigeons about this time seeming to undergo much suffering, I determined upon giving them their liberty. I first untied one of them, a beautiful grey-mottled pigeon, and placed him upon the rim of the wickerwork. He appeared extremely uneasy, looking anxiously around him, fluttering his wings and making a loud cooing noise, but could not be persuaded to trust himself from the car. I took him up at last and threw him to about half a dozen yards from the balloon. He made, however, no attempt to descend as I had expected, but struggled with great vehemence to get back, uttering at the same time very shrill and piercing cries. He at length succeeded in regaining his former station on the rim, but had hardly done so when his head dropped upon his breast, and he fell dead within the car. The other one did not prove so unfortunate. To prevent his following the example of his companion, and accomplishing a return, I threw him downwards with all my force, and was pleased to find him continue his descent with great velocity, making use of his wings with ease, and in a perfectly natural manner. In a very short time he was out of sight, and I have no doubt he reached home in safety. Puss, who seemed in a great measure recovered from her illness, now made a hearty meal of the dead bird, and then went to sleep with much apparent satisfaction. Her kittens were quite lively, and so far evinced not the slightest sign of any uneasiness.

At a quarter past eight, being able no longer to draw breath without the most intolerable pain, I proceeded forthwith to adjust around the car the apparatus belonging to the condenser. This apparatus will require some little explanation, and Your Excellencies will please to bear in mind that my object, in the first place, was to surround myself and the car entirely with a barricade against the highly rarefied atmosphere in which I was existing, with the intention of introducing within this barricade, by means of my condenser, a quantity of this same atmosphere sufficiently condensed for the purposes of respiration. With this object in view, I had prepared a very strong, perfectly airtight but flexible gum-elastic bag.* In this bag, which was of sufficient dimensions, the entire car was in a manner placed. That is to say, it (the bag) was drawn over the whole bottom of the car, up its sides, and so on, along the outside of the ropes, to the upper rim or hoop where the network is attached. Having pulled the bag up in this way and formed a complete enclosure on all sides and at bottom, it was now necessary to fasten up its top or mouth by passing its material over the hoop of the network – in other words, between the network and the hoop. But if the network were separated from the hoop to admit this passage, what was to sustain the car in the mean time? Now, the network was not permanently fastened to the hoop, but attached by a series of running loops or nooses. I therefore undid only a few of these loops at one time, leaving the car suspended by the remainder. Having thus inserted a portion of the cloth forming the upper part of the bag, I refastened the loops – not to the hoop, for that would have been impossible, since the cloth now intervened – but to a series of large buttons affixed to the cloth itself, about three feet below the mouth of the bag, the intervals between the buttons having been made to correspond to the intervals between the loops. This done, a few more of the loops were unfastened from the rim, a further portion of the cloth introduced, and the disengaged loops then connected with their proper buttons. In this way it was possible to insert the whole upper part of the bag between the network and the hoop. It is evident that the hoop would now drop down within the car, while the whole weight of the car itself, with all its contents, would be held up merely by the strength of the buttons. This, at first sight, would seem an inadequate dependence, but it was by no means so, for the buttons were not only very strong in themselves, but so close together that a very slight portion of the whole weight was supported by any one of them. Indeed, had the car and contents been three times heavier than they were, I should not have been at all uneasy. I now raised up the hoop again within the covering of gum elastic, and propped it at nearly its former height by means of three light poles prepared for the occasion. This was done, of course, to keep the bag distended at the top and to preserve the lower part of the network in its proper situation. All that now remained was to fasten up the mouth of the enclosure – and this was readily accomplished by gathering the folds of the material together and twisting them up very tightly on the inside by means of a kind of stationary tourniquet.

In the sides of the covering thus adjusted round the car had been inserted three circular panes of thick but clear glass, through which I could see without difficulty around me in every horizontal direction. In that portion of the cloth forming the bottom was likewise a fourth window, of the same kind, and corresponding with a small aperture in the floor of the car itself. This enabled me to see perpendicularly down, but having found it impossible to place any similar contrivance overhead, on account of the peculiar manner of closing up the opening there, and the consequent wrinkles in the cloth, I could expect to see no objects situated directly in my zenith. This, of course, was a matter of little consequence, for, had I even been able to place a window at top, the balloon itself would have prevented my making any use of it.

About a foot below one of the side windows was a circular opening, three inches in diameter, and fitted with a brass rim adapted in its inner edge to the windings of a screw. In this rim was screwed the large tube of the condenser, the body of the machine being, of course, within the chamber of gum elastic. Through this tube a quantity of the rare atmosphere circumjacent being drawn by means of a vacuum created in the body of the machine, was thence discharged, in a state of condensation, to mingle with the thin air already in the chamber. This operation being repeated several times, at length filled the chamber with atmosphere proper for all the purposes of respiration – but in so confined a space it would, in a short time, necessarily become foul and unfit for use from frequent contact with the lungs. It was then ejected by a small valve at the bottom of the car – the dense air readily sinking into the thinner atmosphere below. To avoid the inconvenience of making a total vacuum at any moment within the chamber, this purification was never accomplished all at once, but in a gradual manner – the valve being opened only for a few seconds, then closed again, until one or two strokes from the pump of the condenser had supplied the place of the atmosphere ejected. For the sake of experiment, I had put the cat and kittens in a small basket and suspended it outside the car to a button at the bottom, close by the valve, through which I could feed them at any moment when necessary. I did this at some little risk, and before closing the mouth of the chamber, by reaching under the car with one of the poles before mentioned, to which a hook had been attached. As soon as dense air was admitted in the chamber, the hoop and poles became unnecessary, the expansion of the enclosed atmosphere powerfully distending the gum elastic.

By the time I had fully completed these arrangements and filled the chamber as explained, it wanted only ten minutes of nine o'clock. During the whole period of my being thus employed, I endured the most terrible distress from difficulty of respiration, and bitterly did I repent the negligence (or rather foolhardiness) of which I had been guilty of putting off to the last moment a matter of so much importance. But having at length accomplished it, I soon began to reap the benefit of my invention. Once again I breathed with perfect freedom and ease – and, indeed, why should I not? I was also agreeably surprised to find myself, in a great measure, relieved from the violent pains which had hitherto tormented me. A slight headache, accompanied with a sensation of fullness or distention about the wrists, the ankles and the throat, was nearly all of which I had now to complain. Thus it seemed evident that a greater part of the uneasiness attending the removal of atmospheric pressure had actually *worn off*, as I had expected, and that much of the pain endured for the last two hours should have been attributed altogether to the effects of a deficient respiration.

At twenty minutes before nine o'clock – that is to say, a short time prior to my closing up the mouth of the chamber – the mercury attained its limit, or ran down, in the barometer (which, as I mentioned before, was one of an extended construction). It then indicated an altitude on my part of 132,000 feet, or five-and-twenty miles, and I consequently surveyed at that time an extent of the earth's area amounting to no less than the three-hundred-and-twentieth part of its entire superficies. At nine o'clock, I had again lost sight of land to the eastward, but not before I became aware that the balloon was drifting rapidly to the NNW. The ocean beneath me still retained its apparent concavity, although my view was often interrupted by the masses of cloud which floated to and fro.

At half-past nine, I tried the experiment of throwing out a handful of feathers through the valve. They did not float as I had expected, but dropped down perpendicularly, like a bullet, en masse, and with the greatest velocity – being out of sight in a very few seconds. I did not at first know what to make of this extraordinary phenomenon, not being able to believe that my rate of ascent had, of a sudden, met with so prodigious an acceleration. But it soon occurred to me that the atmosphere was now far too rare to sustain even the feathers; that they actually fell, as they appeared to do, with great rapidity; and that I had been surprised by the united velocities of their descent and my own elevation.

By ten o'clock I found that I had very little to occupy my immediate attention. Affairs went on swimmingly, and I believed the balloon to be going upwards with a speed increasing momently, although I had no longer any means of ascertaining the progression of the increase. I suffered no pain or uneasiness of any kind, and enjoyed better spirits than I had at any period since my departure from Rotterdam, busying myself now in examining the state of my various apparatus and now in regenerating the atmosphere within the chamber. This latter point

I determined to attend to at regular intervals of forty minutes, more on account of the preservation of my health than from so frequent a renovation being absolutely necessary. In the mean while, I could not help making anticipations. Fancy revelled in the wild and dreamy regions of the moon. Imagination, feeling herself for once unshackled, roamed at will among the ever-changing wonders of a shadowy and unstable land. Now there were hoary and time-honoured forests and craggy precipices and waterfalls tumbling with a loud noise into abysses without a bottom. Then I came suddenly into still noonday solitudes, where no wind of heaven ever intruded, and where vast meadows of poppies and slender lily-looking flowers spread themselves out a weary distance, all silent and motionless for ever. Then again I journeyed far down away into another country where it was all one dim and vague lake, with a boundary line of clouds. But fancies such as these were not the sole possessors of my brain. Horrors of a nature most stern and most appalling would too frequently obtrude themselves upon my mind and shake the innermost depths of my soul with the bare supposition of their possibility. Yet I would not suffer my thoughts for any length of time to dwell upon these latter speculations, rightly judging the real and palpable dangers of the voyage sufficient for my undivided attention.

At five o'clock p.m., being engaged in regenerating the atmosphere within the chamber, I took that opportunity of observing the cat and kittens through the valve. The cat herself appeared to suffer again very much, and I had no hesitation in attributing her uneasiness chiefly to a difficulty in breathing – but my experiment with the kittens had resulted very strangely. I had expected, of course, to see them betray a sense of pain, although in a less degree than their mother, and this would have been sufficient to confirm my opinion concerning the habitual endurance of atmospheric pressure. But I was not prepared to find them, upon close examination, evidently enjoying a high degree of health, breathing with the greatest ease and perfect regularity, and evincing not the slightest sign of any uneasiness. I could only account for all this by extending my theory, and supposing that the highly rarefied atmosphere around might perhaps not be, as I had taken for granted, chemically insufficient for the purposes of life, and that a person born in such a medium might possibly be unaware of any inconvenience attending its inhalation – while, upon removal to the denser strata near the earth, he might endure tortures of a similar nature to those I had so lately experienced. It has since been to me a matter of deep regret that an awkward accident, at this time, occasioned me the loss of my little family of cats and deprived me of the insight into this matter which a continued experiment might have afforded. In passing my hand through the valve with a cup of water for the old puss, the sleeve of my shirt became entangled in the loop which sustained the basket, and thus, in a moment, loosened it from the button. Had the whole actually vanished into air, it could not have shot from my sight in a more abrupt and instantaneous manner. Positively, there could not have intervened the tenth part of a second between the disengagement of the basket and its absolute disappearance with all that it contained. My good wishes followed it to the earth – but of course I had no hope that either cat or kittens would ever live to tell the tale of their misfortune.

At six o'clock, I perceived a great portion of the earth's visible area to the eastward involved in thick shadow, which continued to advance with great rapidity, until, at five minutes before seven, the whole surface in view was enveloped in the darkness of night. It was not, however, until long after this time that the rays of the setting sun ceased to illumine the balloon – and this circumstance, although of course fully anticipated, did not fail to give me an infinite deal of pleasure. It was evident that, in the morning, I should behold the rising luminary many hours at least before the citizens of Rotterdam, in spite of their situation so much farther to the eastward – and thus, day after day, in proportion to the height ascended, would I enjoy the light of the sun for a longer and a longer period. I now determined to keep a journal of my passage, reckoning the days from one to twenty-four hours continuously, without taking into consideration the intervals of darkness.

At ten o'clock, feeling sleepy, I determined to lie down for the rest of the night – but here a difficulty presented itself, which, obvious as it may appear, had escaped my attention up to the very moment of which I am now speaking. If I went to sleep as I proposed, how could the atmosphere in the chamber be regenerated in the interim? To breathe it for more than an hour, at the furthest, would be a matter of impossibility – or, if even this term could be extended to an hour and a quarter, the most ruinous consequences might ensue. The consideration of this dilemma gave me no little disquietude – and it will hardly be believed that, after the dangers I had undergone, I should look upon this business in so serious a light as to give up all hope of accomplishing my ultimate design and finally make up my mind to the necessity of a descent. But this hesitation was only momentary. I reflected that man is the veriest slave of custom, and that many points in the routine of his existence are deemed *essentially* important which are only so *at all* by his having rendered them habitual. It was very certain that I could not do without sleep – but I might easily bring myself to feel no inconvenience from being awakened at intervals of an hour during the whole period of my repose. It would require but five minutes at most to regenerate the atmosphere in the fullest manner – and the only real difficulty was to contrive a method of arousing myself at the proper moment for so doing. But this was a question which, I am willing to confess, occasioned me no little trouble in its solution. To be sure, I had heard of the student who, to prevent his falling asleep over his books, held in one hand a ball of copper, the din of whose descent into a basin of the same metal on the floor beside his chair served effectually to startle him up if, at any moment, he should be overcome with drowsiness. My own case, however, was very different indeed, and left me no room for any similar idea – for I did not wish to keep awake, but to be aroused from slumber at regular intervals of time. I at length hit upon the following expedient – which, simple as it may seem, was hailed by me, at the moment of discovery, as an invention fully equal to that of the telescope, the steam engine or the art of printing itself.

It is necessary to premise that the balloon, at the elevation now attained, continued its course upwards with an even and undeviating ascent, and the car consequently followed with a steadiness so perfect that it would have been impossible to detect in it the slightest vacillation. This circumstance favoured me greatly in the project I now determined to adopt. My supply of water had been put on board in kegs containing five gallons each, and ranged very securely around the interior of the car. I unfastened one of these, and, taking two ropes, tied them tightly across the rim of the wickerwork from one side to the other, placing them about a foot apart and parallel, so as to form a kind of shelf, upon which I placed the keg, and steadied it in a horizontal position. About eight inches immediately below these ropes, and four feet from the bottom of the car, I fastened another shelf – but made of thin plank, being the only similar piece of wood I had. Upon this latter shelf, and exactly beneath one of the rims of the keg, a small earthen pitcher was deposited. I now bored a hole in the end of the keg over the pitcher, and fitted in a plug of soft wood, cut in a tapering or conical shape. This plug I pushed in or pulled out as might happen, until, after a few experiments, it arrived at that exact degree of tightness at which the water, oozing from the hole and falling into the pitcher below, would fill the latter to the brim in the period of sixty minutes. This, of course, was a matter briefly and easily ascertained by noticing the proportion of the pitcher filled in any given time. Having arranged all this, the rest of the plan is obvious. My bed was so contrived upon the floor of the car as to bring my head, in lying down, immediately below the mouth of the pitcher. It was evident that, at the expiration of an hour, the pitcher, getting full, would be forced to run over, and to run over at the mouth, which was somewhat lower than the rim. It was also evident that the water thus falling from a height of more than four feet could not do otherwise than fall upon my face, and that the sure consequence would be to waken me up instantaneously, even from the soundest slumber in the world.

It was fully eleven by the time I had completed these arrangements, and I immediately betook myself to bed, with full confidence in the efficiency of my invention. Nor in this matter was I disappointed. Punctually every sixty minutes was I aroused by my trusty chronometer, when, having emptied the pitcher into the bunghole of the keg and performed the duties of the condenser, I retired again to bed. These regular interruptions to my slumber caused me even less discomfort than I had anticipated – and when I finally arose for the day, it was seven o'clock, and the sun had attained many degrees above the line of my horizon.

APRIL 3RD. I found the balloon at an immense height indeed, and the earth's convexity had now become strikingly manifest. Below me in the ocean lay a cluster of black specks, which undoubtedly were islands. Overhead, the sky was of a jetty black, and the stars were brilliantly visible – indeed, they had been so constantly since the first day of ascent. Far away to the northward, I perceived a thin, white and exceedingly brilliant line, or streak, on the edge of the horizon, and I had no hesitation in supposing it to be the southern disc of the ices of the Polar Sea. My curiosity was greatly excited, for I had hopes of passing on much farther to the north, and might possibly, at some period, find myself placed directly above the Pole itself. I now lamented that my great elevation would, in this case, prevent my taking as accurate a survey as I could wish. Much, however, might be ascertained.

Nothing else of an extraordinary nature occurred during the day. My apparatus all continued in good order, and the balloon still ascended without any perceptible vacillation. The cold was intense, and obliged me to wrap up closely in an overcoat. When darkness came over the earth, I betook myself to bed, although it was for many hours afterwards broad daylight all around my immediate situation. The water clock was punctual in its duty, and I slept until next morning soundly, with the exception of the periodical interruption.

APRIL 4TH. Arose in good health and spirits, and was astonished at the singular change which had taken place in the appearance of the sea. It had lost, in a great measure, the deep tint of blue it had hitherto worn, being now of a greyish-white and of a lustre dazzling to the eye. The convexity of the ocean had become so evident that the entire mass of the distant water seemed to be tumbling headlong over the abyss of the horizon, and I found myself listening on tiptoe for the echoes of the mighty cataract. The islands were no longer visible – whether they had passed down the horizon to the south-east, or whether my increasing elevation had left them out of sight, it is impossible to say. I was inclined, however, to the latter opinion. The rim of ice to the northward was growing more and more apparent. Cold by no means so intense. Nothing of importance occurred, and I passed the day in reading, having taken care to supply myself with books.

APRIL 5TH. Beheld the singular phenomenon of the sun rising while nearly the whole visible surface of the earth continued to be involved in darkness. In time, however, the light spread itself over all, and I again saw the line of ice to the northward. It was now very distinct, and appeared of a much darker hue than the waters of the ocean. I was evidently approaching it, and with great rapidity. Fancied I could again distinguish a strip of land to the eastward, and one also to the westward, but could not be certain. Weather moderate. Nothing of any consequence happened during the day. Went early to bed.

APRIL 6TH. Was surprised at finding the rim of ice at a very moderate distance, and an immense field of the same material stretching away off to the horizon in the north. It was evident that if the balloon held its present course, it would soon arrive above the frozen ocean, and I had now little doubt of ultimately seeing the Pole. During the whole of the day I continued to near the ice. Towards night the limits of my horizon very suddenly and materially increased, owing undoubtedly to the earth's form being that of an oblate spheroid, and my arriving above the flattened regions in the vicinity of the Arctic Circle. When darkness at length overtook me, I went to bed in great anxiety, fearing to pass over the object of so much curiosity when I should have no opportunity of observing it.

APRIL 7TH. Arose early, and, to my great joy, at length beheld what there could be no hesitation in supposing the Northern Pole itself. It was there, beyond a doubt, and immediately beneath my feet, but – alas! – I had now ascended to so vast a distance that nothing could with accuracy be discerned. Indeed, to judge from the progression of the numbers indicating my various altitudes, respectively, at different periods, between six a.m. on the second of April and twenty minutes before nine a.m. of the same day (at which time the barometer ran down), it might be fairly inferred that the balloon had now, at four o'clock in the morning of April the seventh, reached a height of *not less*, certainly, than 7,254 miles above the surface of the sea. This elevation may appear immense, but the estimate upon which it is calculated gave a result in all probability far inferior to the truth. At all events, I undoubtedly beheld the whole of the earth's major diameter; the entire northern hemisphere lay beneath me like a chart orthographically projected – and the great circle of the Equator itself formed the boundary line of my horizon. Your Excellencies may, however, readily imagine that the confined regions hitherto unexplored within the limits of the Arctic Circle, although situated directly beneath me, and therefore seen without any appearance of being foreshortened, were still, in themselves, comparatively too diminutive and at too great a distance from the point of sight to admit of any very accurate examination. Nevertheless, what could be seen was of a nature singular and exciting. Northwardly from that huge rim before mentioned (and which, with slight qualification, may be called the limit of human discovery in these regions), one unbroken, or nearly unbroken sheet of ice continues to extend. In the first few degrees of this its progress, its surface is very sensibly flattened, farther on depressed into a plane, and finally, becoming *not a little concave*, it terminates, at the Pole itself, in a circular centre sharply defined, whose apparent diameter subtended at the balloon an angle of about sixty-five seconds,* and whose dusky hue, varying in intensity, was at all times darker than any other spot upon the visible hemisphere, and occasionally deepened into the most absolute blackness. Farther than this, little could be ascertained. By twelve o'clock the circular centre had materially decreased in circumference, and by seven p.m. I lost sight of it entirely, the balloon passing over the western limb of the ice and floating away rapidly in the direction of the Equator.

APRIL 8TH. Found a sensible diminution in the earth's apparent diameter, besides a material alteration in its general colour and appearance. The whole visible area partook in different degrees of a tint of pale yellow, and in some portions had acquired a brilliancy even painful to the eye. My view downward was also considerably impeded by the dense atmosphere in the vicinity of the surface being loaded with clouds, between whose masses I could only now and then obtain a glimpse of the earth itself. This difficulty of direct vision had troubled me more or less for the last forty-eight hours, but my present enormous elevation brought closer together, as it were, the floating bodies of vapour, and the inconvenience became, of course, more and more palpable in proportion to my ascent. Nevertheless, I could easily perceive that the balloon now hovered above the range of great lakes in the continent of North America, and was holding a course, due south, which would soon bring me to the tropics. This circumstance did not fail to give me the most heartfelt satisfaction, and I hailed it as a happy omen of ultimate success. Indeed, the direction I had hitherto taken had filled me with uneasiness, for it was evident that, had I continued it much longer, there would have been no possibility of my arriving at the moon at all, whose orbit is inclined to the ecliptic at only the small angle of 5° 8' 48". Strange as it may seem, it was only at this late period that I began to understand the great error I had committed in not taking my departure from earth at some point *in the plane of the lunar ellipse.*

APRIL 9TH. Today the earth's diameter was greatly diminished, and the colour of the surface assumed hourly a deeper tint of yellow. The balloon kept steadily on her course to the southward, and arrived, at nine p.m., over the northern edge of the Mexican Gulf.

APRIL 10TH. I was suddenly aroused from slumber, about five o'clock this morning, by a loud, crackling and terrific sound, for which I could in no manner account. It was of very brief duration, but, while it lasted, resembled nothing in the world of which I had any previous experience. It is needless to say that I became excessively alarmed, having in the first instance attributed the noise to the bursting of the balloon. I examined all my apparatus, however, with great attention, and could discover nothing out of order. Spent a great part of the day in meditating upon an occurrence so extraordinary, but could find no means whatever of accounting for it. Went to bed dissatisfied, and in a state of great anxiety and agitation.

APRIL 11TH. Found a startling diminution in the apparent diameter of the earth, and a considerable increase, now observable for the first time, in that of the moon itself, which wanted only a few days of being full. It now required long and excessive labour to condense within the chamber sufficient atmospheric air for the sustenance of life.

APRIL 12TH. A singular alteration took place in regard to the direction of the balloon, and, although fully anticipated, afforded me the most unequivocal delight. Having reached, in its former course, about the twentieth parallel of southern latitude, it turned off suddenly, at an acute angle, to the eastward, and thus proceeded throughout the day, keeping nearly, if not altogether, in the *exact plane of the lunar ellipse*. What was worthy of remark, a very perceptible vacillation in the car was a consequence of this change of route – a vacillation which prevailed, in a more or less degree, for a period of many hours.

APRIL 13TH. Was again very much alarmed by a repetition of the loud crackling noise which terrified me on the tenth. Thought long upon the subject, but was unable to form any satisfactory conclusion. Great decrease in the earth's apparent diameter, which now subtended from the balloon an angle of very little more than twenty-five degrees. The moon could not be seen at all, being nearly in my zenith. I still continued in the plane of the ellipse, but made little progress to the eastward.

APRIL 14TH. Extremely rapid decrease in the diameter of the earth. Today I became strongly impressed with the idea that the balloon was now actually running up the line of apsides* to the point of perigee – in other words, holding the direct course which would bring it immediately to the moon in that part of its orbit the nearest to the earth. The moon itself was directly overhead, and consequently hidden from my view. Great and long-continued labour necessary for the condensation of the atmosphere.

APRIL 15TH. Not even the outlines of continents and seas could now be traced upon the earth with distinctness. About twelve o'clock I became aware, for the third time, of that appalling sound which had so astonished me before. It now, however, continued for some moments, and gathered intensity as it continued. At length – while, stupefied and terror-stricken, I stood in expectation of I knew not what hideous destruction – the car vibrated with excessive violence, and a gigantic and flaming mass of some material which I could not distinguish came with a voice of a thousand thunders, roaring and booming by the balloon. When my fears and astonishment had in some degree subsided, I had little difficulty in supposing it to be some mighty volcanic fragment ejected from that world to which I was so rapidly approaching – and, in all probability, one of that singular class of substances occasionally picked up on the earth and termed "meteoric stones" for want of a better appellation.

APRIL 16TH. Today, looking upwards as well as I could, through each of the side windows alternately, I beheld, to my great delight, a very small portion of the moon's disc protruding, as it were, on all sides beyond the huge circumference of the balloon. My agitation was extreme; for I had now little doubt of soon reaching the end of my perilous voyage. Indeed, the labour now required by the condenser had increased to a most oppressive degree, and allowed me scarcely any respite from exertion. Sleep was a matter nearly out of the question. I became quite ill, and my frame trembled with exhaustion. It was impossible that human nature could endure this state of intense suffering much longer. During the now brief interval of darkness, a meteoric stone again passed in my vicinity, and the frequency of these phenomena began to occasion me much apprehension.

APRIL 17TH. This morning proved an epoch in my voyage. It will be remembered that, on the thirteenth, the earth subtended an angular breadth of twenty-five degrees. On the fourteenth this had greatly diminished; on the fifteenth a still more rapid decrease was observable; and, on retiring for the night of the sixteenth, I had noticed an angle of no more than about seven degrees and fifteen minutes. What, therefore, must have been my amazement, on awakening from a brief and disturbed slumber, on the morning of this day, the seventeenth, at finding the surface beneath me so suddenly and wonderfully *augmented* in volume as to subtend no less than thirty-nine degrees in apparent angular diameter! I was thunderstruck! No words can give any adequate idea of the extreme, the absolute horror and astonishment with which I was seized, possessed and altogether overwhelmed. My knees tottered beneath me... my teeth chattered... my hair started up on end. "The balloon, then, had actually burst!" These were the first tumultuous ideas which hurried through my mind: "The balloon had positively burst!... I was falling... falling with the most impetuous, the most unparalleled velocity! To judge from the immense distance already so quickly passed over, it could not be more than ten minutes, at the furthest, before I should meet the surface of the earth and be hurled into annihilation!" But at length reflection came to my relief. I paused; I considered; and I began to doubt. The matter was impossible. I could not in any reason have so rapidly come down. Besides, although I was evidently approaching the surface below me, it was with a speed by no means commensurate with the velocity I had at first conceived. This consideration served to calm the perturbation of my mind, and I finally succeeded in regarding the phenomenon in its proper point of view. In fact, amazement must have fairly deprived me of my senses, when I could not see the vast difference, in appearance, between the surface below me and the surface of my mother earth. The latter was indeed over my head, and completely hidden by the balloon, while the moon – the moon itself in all its glory – lay beneath me, and at my feet.

The stupor and surprise produced in my mind by this extraordinary change in the posture of affairs was perhaps, after all, that part of the adventure least susceptible of explanation. For the *bouleversement** in itself was not only natural and inevitable, but had been long actually anticipated as a circumstance to be expected whenever I should arrive at that exact point of my voyage where the attraction of the planet should be superseded by the attraction of the satellite – or, more precisely, where the gravitation of the balloon towards the earth should be less powerful than its gravitation towards the moon. To be sure I arose from a sound slumber, with all my senses in confusion, to the contemplation of a very startling phenomenon, and one which, although expected, was not expected at the moment. The revolution itself must, of course, have taken place in an easy and gradual manner, and it is by no means clear that, had I even been awake at the time of the occurrence, I should have been made aware of it by any *internal* evidence of an inversion – that is to say, by any inconvenience or disarrangement either about my person or about my apparatus.

It is almost needless to say that, upon coming to a due sense of my situation and emerging from the terror which had absorbed every faculty of my soul, my attention was, in the first place, wholly directed to the contemplation of the general physical appearance of the moon. It lay beneath me like a chart – and although I judged it to be still at no inconsiderable distance, the indentures of its surface were defined to my vision with a most striking and altogether unaccountable distinctness. The entire absence of ocean or sea, and indeed of any lake or river or body of water whatsoever, struck me, at first glance, as the most extraordinary feature in its geological condition. Yet, strange to say, I beheld vast level regions of a character decidedly alluvial, although by far the greater portion of the hemisphere in sight was covered with innumerable volcanic mountains – conical in shape, and having more the appearance of artificial than of natural protuberances. The highest among them does not exceed three and three quarter miles in perpendicular elevation, but a map of the volcanic districts of the Campi Phlegræi* would afford to Your Excellencies a better idea of their general surface than any unworthy description I might think proper to attempt. The greater part of them were in a state of evident eruption, and gave me fearfully to understand their fury and their power, by the repeated thunders of the miscalled meteoric stones, which now rushed upward by the balloon with a frequency more and more appalling.

APRIL 18TH. Today I found an enormous increase in the moon's apparent bulk – and the evidently accelerated velocity of my descent began to fill me with alarm. It will be remembered that, in the earliest stage of my speculations upon the possibility of a passage to the moon, the existence, in its vicinity, of an atmosphere dense in proportion to the bulk of the planet had entered largely into my calculations – this too in spite of many theories to the contrary, and, it may be added, in spite of a general disbelief in the existence of any lunar atmosphere at all. But, in addition to what I have already urged in regard to Encke's comet and the zodiacal light, I had been strengthened in my opinion by certain observations of Mr Schröter, of Lilienthal.* He observed the moon when two days and a half old, in the evening soon after sunset, before the dark part was visible, and continued to watch it until it became visible. The two cusps appeared tapering in a very sharp, faint prolongation, each exhibiting its furthest extremity faintly illuminated by the solar rays before any part of the dark hemisphere was visible. Soon afterwards, the whole dark limb became illuminated. This prolongation of the cusps beyond the semicircle, I thought, must have arisen from the refraction of the sun's rays by the moon's atmosphere. I computed, also, the height of the atmosphere (which could refract light enough into its dark hemisphere to produce a twilight more luminous than the light reflected from the earth when the moon is about 32° from the new) to be 1,356 Paris feet;* in this view, I supposed the greatest height capable of refracting the solar ray to be 5,376 feet. My ideas upon this topic had also received confirmation by a passage in the eighty-second volume of the *Philosophical Transactions*, in which it is stated that, at an occultation of Jupiter's satellites, the third disappeared after having been about 1" or 2" of time indistinct, and the fourth became indiscernible near the limb.*

Upon the resistance, or, more properly, upon the support of an atmosphere existing in the state of density imagined, I had of course entirely depended for the safety of my ultimate descent. Should I then, after all, prove to have been mistaken, I had in consequence nothing better to expect, as a finale to my adventure, than being dashed into atoms against the rugged surface of the satellite. And, indeed, I had now every reason to be terrified. My distance from the moon was comparatively trifling, while the labour required by the condenser was diminished not at all, and I could discover no indication whatever of a decreasing rarity in the air.

APRIL 19TH. This morning, to my great joy, about nine o'clock, the surface of the moon being frightfully near and my apprehensions excited to the utmost, the pump of my condenser at length gave evident tokens of an alteration in the atmosphere. By ten, I had reason to believe its density considerably increased. By eleven, very little labour was necessary at the apparatus, and at twelve o'clock, with some hesitation, I ventured to unscrew the tourniquet – when, finding no inconvenience from having done so, I finally threw open the gum-elastic chamber and unrigged it from around the car. As might have been expected, spasms and violent headache were the immediate consequences of an experiment so precipitate and full of danger. But these and other difficulties attending respiration, as they were by no means so great as to put me in peril of my life, I determined to endure as I best could, in consideration of my leaving them behind me momently in my approach to the denser strata near the moon. This approach, however, was still impetuous in the extreme – and it soon became alarmingly certain that, although I had probably not been deceived in the expectation of an atmosphere dense in proportion to the mass of the satellite, still I had been wrong in supposing this density, even at the surface, at all adequate to the support of the great weight contained in the car of my balloon. Yet this *should* have been the case, and in an equal degree as at the surface of the earth, the actual gravity of bodies at either planet supposed in the ratio of the atmospheric condensation. That it *was not* the case, however, my precipitous downfall gave testimony enough; *why* it was not so can only be explained by a reference to those possible geological disturbances to which I have formerly alluded. At all events, I was now close upon the planet, and coming down with the most terrible impetuosity. I lost not a moment, accordingly, in throwing overboard first my ballast, then my water kegs, then my condensing apparatus and gum-elastic chamber, and finally every article within the car. But it was all to no purpose. I still fell with horrible rapidity, and was now not more than half a mile from the surface. As a last resource, therefore, having got rid of my coat, hat and boots, I cut loose from the balloon *the car itself*, which was of no inconsiderable weight – and thus, clinging with both hands to the network, I had barely time to observe that the whole country, as far as the eye could reach, was thickly interspersed with diminutive habitations, ere I tumbled headlong into the very heart of a fantastical-looking city, and into the middle of a vast crowd of ugly little people, who none of them uttered a single syllable or gave themselves the least trouble to render me assistance, but stood, like a parcel of idiots, grinning in a ludicrous manner and eyeing me and my balloon askant, with their arms set akimbo. I turned from them in contempt, and, gazing upwards at the earth so lately left, and left perhaps for ever, beheld it like a huge, dull copper shield, about two degrees in diameter, fixed immovably in the heavens overhead and tipped on one of its edges with a crescent border of the most brilliant gold. No traces of land or water could be discovered, and the whole was clouded with variable spots and belted with tropical and equatorial zones.

Thus, may it please Your Excellencies, after a series of great anxieties, unheard-of dangers and unparalleled escapes, I had, at length, on the nineteenth day of my departure from Rotterdam, arrived in safety at the conclusion of a voyage undoubtedly the most extraordinary and the most momentous ever accomplished, undertaken or conceived by any denizen of earth. But my adventures yet remain to be related. And indeed Your Excellencies may well imagine that, after a residence of five years upon a planet not only deeply interesting in its own peculiar character, but rendered doubly so by its intimate connection, in capacity of satellite, with the world inhabited by man, I may have intelligence for the private ear of the States' College of Astronomers of far more importance than the details, however wonderful, of the mere voyage which so happily concluded. This is, in fact, the case. I have much – very much which it would give me the greatest pleasure to communicate. I have much to say of the climate of the planet; of its wonderful alternations of heat and cold; of unmitigated and burning sunshine for one fortnight, and more than polar frigidity for the next; of a constant transfer of moisture by distillation like that *in vacuo*,* from the point beneath the sun to the point the farthest from it; of a variable zone of running water; of the people themselves; of their manners, customs and political institutions; of their peculiar physical construction; of their ugliness; of their want of ears, those useless appendages in an atmosphere so peculiarly modified; of their consequent ignorance of the use and properties of speech; of their substitute for speech in a singular method of intercommunication; of the incomprehensible connection between each particular individual in the moon with some particular individual on the earth – a connection analogous with, and depending upon, that of the orbs of the planet and the satellite, and by means of which the lives and destinies of the inhabitants of the one are interwoven with the lives and destinies of the inhabitants of the other; and, above all, if it so please Your Excellencies, above all, of those dark and hideous mysteries which lie in the outer regions of the moon – regions which, owing to the almost miraculous accordance of the satellite's rotation on its own axis with its sidereal revolution about the earth, have never yet been turned (and, by God's mercy, never shall be turned) to the scrutiny of the telescopes of man. All this, and more – much more – would I most willingly detail. But, to be brief, I must have my reward. I am pining for a return to my family and to my home, and as the price of any further communications on my part – in consideration of the light which I have it in my power to throw upon many very important branches of physical and metaphysical science – I must solicit, through the influence of your honourable body, a pardon for the crime of which I have been guilty in the death of the creditors upon my departure from Rotterdam. This, then, is the object of the present paper. Its bearer, an inhabitant of the moon, whom I have prevailed upon and properly instructed to be my messenger to the earth, will await Your Excellencies' pleasure, and return to me with the pardon in question – if it can, in any manner, be obtained.

I have the honour to be, etc., Your Excellencies' very humble servant,

HANS PFAALL

Upon finishing the perusal of this very extraordinary document, Professor Rubadub, it is said, dropped his pipe upon the ground in the extremity of his surprise, and Mynheer Superbus von Underduk, having taken off his spectacles, wiped them and deposited them in his pocket, so far forgot both himself and his dignity as to turn round three times upon his heel in the quintessence of astonishment and admiration. There was no doubt about the matter: the pardon should be obtained. So at least swore, with a round oath, Professor Rubadub, and so finally thought the illustrious Von Underduk as he took the arm of his brother in science and, without saying a word, began to make the best of his way home to deliberate upon the measures to be adopted. Having reached the door, however, of the burgomaster's dwelling, the professor ventured to suggest that as the messenger had thought proper to disappear – no doubt frightened to death by the savage appearance of the burghers of Rotterdam – the pardon would be of little use, as no one but a man of the moon would undertake a voyage to so vast a distance. To the truth of this observation the burgomaster assented, and the matter was therefore at an end. Not so, however, rumours and speculations. The letter, having been published, gave rise to a variety of gossip and opinion. Some of the over-wise even made themselves ridiculous by decrying the whole business as nothing better than a hoax. But hoax, with these sort of people, is, I believe, a general term for all matters above their comprehension. For my part, I cannot conceive upon what data they have founded such an accusation. Let us see what they say.

Imprimis. That certain wags in Rotterdam have certain especial antipathies to certain burgomasters and astronomers.

Secondly. That an odd little dwarf and bottle conjuror,* both of whose ears, for some misdemeanour, have been cut off close to his head, has been missing for several days from the neighbouring city of Bruges.

Thirdly. That the newspapers which were stuck all over the little balloon were newspapers of Holland, and therefore could not have been made in the moon. They were dirty papers – very dirty – and Gluck, the printer, would take his Bible oath to their having been printed in Rotterdam.

Fourthly. That Hans Pfaall himself, the drunken villain, and the three very idle gentlemen styled "his creditors", were all seen, no longer than two or three days ago, in a tippling house in the suburbs, having just returned, with money in their pockets, from a trip beyond the sea.

Lastly. That it is an opinion very generally received, or which ought to be generally received, that the College of Astronomers in the city of Rotterdam, as well as other colleges in all other parts of the world – not to mention colleges and astronomers in general – are, to say the least of the matter, not a whit better, nor greater, nor wiser than they ought to be.

NOTE. Strictly speaking, there is but little similarity between the above sketchy trifle and the celebrated 'Moon Story' of Mr Locke, but, as both have the character of *hoaxes* (although the one is in a tone of banter, the other of downright earnest), and as both hoaxes are on the same subject, the moon – moreover, as both attempt to give plausibility by scientific detail – the author of 'Hans Pfaall' thinks it necessary to say, in *self-defence*, that his own *jeu d'esprit* was published, in the *Southern Literary Messenger*, about three weeks before the commencement of Mr L.'s in the New York *Sun*.* Fancying a likeness which, perhaps, does not exist, some of the New York papers copied 'Hans Pfaall' and collated it with the "Moon Hoax" by way of detecting the writer of the one in the writer of the other.

As many more persons were actually gulled by the "Moon Hoax" than would be willing to acknowledge the fact, it may here afford some little amusement to show why no one should have been deceived – to point out those particulars of the story which should have been sufficient to establish its real character. Indeed, however rich the imagination displayed in this ingenious fiction, it wanted much of the force which might have been given it by a more scrupulous attention to facts and to general analogy. That the public were misled, even for an instant, merely proves the gross ignorance which is so generally prevalent upon subjects of an astronomical nature.

The moon's distance from the earth is, in round numbers, 240,000 miles. If we desire to ascertain how near, apparently, a lens would bring the satellite (or any distant object), we, of course, have but to divide the distance by the magnifying or, more strictly, by the space-penetrating power of the glass. Mr L. makes his lens have a power of 42,000 times. By this divide 240,000 (the moon's real distance), and we have five miles and five sevenths as the apparent distance. No animal at all could be seen so far – much less the minute points particularized in the story. Mr L. speaks about Sir John Herschel's perceiving flowers (the *Papaver rhoeas*,* etc.), and even detecting the colour and the shape of the eyes of small birds. Shortly before, too, he has himself observed that the lens would not render perceptible objects of less than eighteen inches in diameter – but even this, as I have said, is giving the glass by far too great power. It may be observed, in passing, that this prodigious glass is said to have been moulded at the glasshouse* of Messrs Hartley and Grant, in Dumbarton – but Messrs H. and G.'s establishment had ceased operations for many years previous to the publication of the hoax.

On p. 13, pamphlet edition, speaking of "a hairy veil" over the eyes of a species of bison, the author says: "It immediately occurred to the acute mind of Dr Herschel that this was a providential contrivance to protect the eyes of the animal from the great extremes of light and darkness to which all the inhabitants of our side of the moon are periodically subjected." But this cannot be thought a very "acute" observation of the doctor's. The inhabitants of our side of the moon have, evidently, no darkness at all, so there can be nothing of the "extremes" mentioned. In the absence of the sun, they have a light from the earth equal to that of thirteen full unclouded moons.

The topography throughout, even when professing to accord with Blunt's Lunar Chart,* is entirely at variance with that or any other lunar chart, and even grossly at variance with itself. The points of the compass, too, are in inextricable confusion, the writer appearing to be ignorant that, on a lunar map, these are not in accordance with terrestrial points, the east being to the left, etc.

Deceived, perhaps, by the vague titles, Mare Nubium, Mare Tranquillitatis, Mare Fœcunditatis,* etc., given to the dark spots by former astronomers, Mr L. has entered into details regarding oceans and other large bodies of water in the moon – whereas there is no astronomical point more positively ascertained than that no such bodies exist there. In examining the boundary between light and darkness (in the crescent or gibbous moon) where this boundary crosses any of the dark places, the line of division is found to be rough and jagged – but, were these dark places liquid, it would evidently be even.

The description of the wings of the man-bat on p. 21 is but a literal copy of Peter Wilkins's account of the wings of his flying islanders.* This simple fact should have induced suspicion at least, it might be thought.

On p. 23, we have the following: "What a prodigious influence must our thirteen-times-larger globe have exercised upon this satellite when an embryo in the womb of time, the passive subject of chemical affinity!" This is very fine – but it should be observed that no astronomer would have made such remark, especially to any journal of science, for the earth, in the sense intended, is not only thirteen, but forty-nine times *larger* than the moon. A similar objection applies to the whole of the concluding pages, where, by way of introduction to some discoveries in Saturn, the philosophical correspondent enters into a minute schoolboy account of that planet – this to the *Edinburgh Journal of Science*!*

But there is one point, in particular, which should have betrayed the fiction. Let us imagine the power actually possessed of seeing animals upon the moon's surface – what would *first* arrest the attention of an observer from the earth? Certainly neither their shape, size, nor any other such peculiarity, so soon as their remarkable *situation*. They would appear to be walking with heels up and head down in the manner of flies on a ceiling. The *real* observer would have uttered an instant ejaculation of surprise (however prepared by previous knowledge) at the singularity of their position – the *fictitious* observer has not even mentioned the subject, but speaks of seeing the entire bodies of such creatures, when it is demonstrable that he could have seen only the diameter of their heads!

It might as well be remarked, in conclusion, that the size, and particularly the powers of the man-bats (for example, their ability to fly in so rare an atmosphere – if, indeed, the moon have any), with most of the other fancies in regard to animal and vegetable existence, are at variance, generally, with all analogical reasoning on these themes – and that analogy here will often amount to conclusive demonstration. It is, perhaps, scarcely necessary to add that all the suggestions attributed to Brewster* and Herschel, in the beginning of the article, about "a transfusion of artificial light through the focal object of vision", etc., etc., belong to that species of figurative writing which comes, most properly, under the denomination of "rigmarole".

There is a real and very definite limit to optical discovery among the stars – a limit whose nature need only be stated to be understood. If, indeed, the casting of large lenses were all that is required, man's ingenuity would ultimately prove equal to the task, and we might have them of any size demanded. But, unhappily, in proportion to the increase of size in the lens (and, consequently, of space-penetrating power) is the diminution of light from the object by diffusion of its rays. And for this evil there is no remedy within human ability, for an object is seen by means of that light alone which proceeds from itself, whether direct or reflected. Thus the only "*artificial*" light which could avail Mr Locke would be some artificial light which he should be able to throw... not upon the "focal object of vision", but upon the real object to be viewed – to wit: *upon the moon*. It has been easily calculated that, when the light proceeding from a star becomes so diffused as to be as weak as the natural light proceeding from the whole of the stars in a clear and moonless night, then the star is no longer visible for any practical purpose.

The Earl of Rosse telescope, lately constructed in England,* has a speculum with a reflecting surface of 4,071 square inches, the Herschel telescope having one of only 1,811. The metal of the Earl of Rosse's is 6 feet diameter; it is 5 ½ inches thick at the edges, and 5 at the centre. The weight is 3 tons. The focal length is 50 feet.

I have lately read a singular and somewhat ingenious little book, whose title page runs thus: "L'HOMME DANS LA LVNE: OV LE VOYAGE CHIMERIQVE fait au Monde de la LVNE, nouuellement découuert par DOMINIQVE GONZALES, Aduanturier Espagnol, autrement dit LE COVRRIER VOLANT. Mis en nostre Langue, Par I.B.D. A Paris, Chez FRANÇOIS PIOT, prés la Fontaine de Saint Benoist; Et chez I. GVIGNARD, au premier pilier de la grand' Salle du Palais, proche les Consultations,* M. DC. XLVIII.", pp. 176.

The writer professes to have translated his work from the English of one Mr D'Avisson (Davidson?), although there is a terrible ambiguity in the statement. "I'en ay eu," says he "l'Original de Monsieur D'AVISSON, Medecin, des mieux versez qui soient aujourd'huy dans la connoissance des belles Lettres, & sur tout de la Philosophie naturelle. Ie luy ay cette obligation entre les autres, de m'auoir non seulement mis en main ce Liure en Anglois, mais encore le Manuscrit du sieur THOMAS D'ANAN, Gentilhomme Escossois, recommandable pour sa Vertu, sur la Version duquel i'aduoüe que i'ay tiré le plan de la mienne."*

After some irrelevant adventures, much in the manner of *Gil Blas*,* and which occupy the first thirty pages, the author relates that, being ill during a sea voyage, the crew abandoned him, together with a Negro servant, on the island of Saint Helena. To increase the chances of obtaining food, the two separate, and live as far apart as possible. This brings about a training of birds, to serve the purpose of carrier pigeons between them. By and by these are taught to carry parcels of some weight – and this weight is gradually increased. At length the idea is entertained of uniting the force of a great number of the birds, with a view to raising the author himself. A machine is contrived for the purpose, and we have a minute description of it, which is materially helped out by a steel engraving. Here we perceive the Señor* Gonzales, with point ruffles and a huge periwig, seated astride something which resembles very closely a broomstick, and borne aloft by a multitude of wild swans (*ganzas*) who had strings reaching from their tails to the machine.

The main event detailed in the Señor's narrative depends upon a very important fact, of which the reader is kept in ignorance until near the end of the book. The *ganzas*, with whom he had become so familiar, were not really denizens of Saint Helena, but of the moon. Thence it had been their custom, time out of mind, to migrate annually to some portion of the earth. In proper season, of course, they would return home – and the author, happening one day to require their services for a short voyage, is unexpectedly carried straight up, and in a very brief period arrives at the satellite. Here he finds, among other odd things, that the people enjoy extreme happiness; that they have no *law*; that they die without pain; that they are from ten to thirty feet in height; that they live five thousand years; that they have an emperor called Irdonozur; and that they can jump sixty feet high when, being out of the gravitating influence, they fly about with fans.

I cannot forbear giving a specimen of the general *philosophy* of the volume.

"I must now declare to you," says the Señor Gonzales, "the nature of the place in which I found myself. All the clouds were beneath my feet – or, if you please, spread between me and the earth. As to the stars, *since there was no night where I was, they always had the same appearance – not brilliant, as usual, but pale, and very nearly like the moon of a morning.* But few of them were visible, and these ten times larger (as well as I could judge) than they seem to the inhabitants of the earth. The moon, which wanted two days of being full, was of a terrible bigness.

"I must not forget here that the stars appeared only on that side of the globe turned towards the moon, and that the closer they were to it, the larger they seemed. I have also to inform you that, whether it was calm weather or stormy, I found myself *always immediately between the moon and the earth*. I was convinced of this for two reasons: because my birds always flew in a straight line, and because whenever we attempted to rest, *we were carried insensibly around the globe of the earth*. For I admit the opinion of Copernicus, who maintains that it never ceases to revolve *from the east to the west*, not upon the poles of the equinoctial, commonly called the poles of the world, but upon those of the zodiac,* a question of which I propose to speak more at length hereafter, when I shall have leisure to refresh my memory in regard to the astrology which I learnt at Salamanca when young, and have since forgotten."*

Notwithstanding the blunders italicized, the book is not without some claim to attention, as affording a naive specimen of the current astronomical notions of the time. One of these assumed that the "gravitating power" extended but a short distance from the earth's surface, and, accordingly, we find our voyager "carried insensibly around the globe", etc.

There have been other "voyages to the moon", but none of higher merit than the one just mentioned. That of Bergerac* is utterly meaningless. In the third volume of the *American Quarterly Review* will be found quite an elaborate criticism upon a certain "journey" of the kind in question* – a criticism in which it is difficult to say whether the critic most exposes the stupidity of the book or his own absurd ignorance of astronomy. I forget the title of the work, but the *means* of the voyage are more deplorably ill conceived than are even the *ganzas* of our friend the Señor Gonzales. The adventurer, in digging the earth, happens to discover a peculiar metal for which the moon has a strong attraction, and straightway constructs of it a box which, when cast loose from its terrestrial fastenings, flies with him, forthwith, to the satellite. 'The Flight of Thomas O'Rourke'* is a *jeu d'esprit* not altogether contemptible, and has been translated into German. Thomas, the hero, was in fact the gamekeeper of an Irish peer, whose eccentricities gave rise to the tale. The "flight" is made on an eagle's back, from Hungry Hill, a lofty mountain at the end of Bantry Bay.

In these various brochures the aim is always satirical, the theme being a description of lunarian customs as compared with ours. In none is there any effort at *plausibility* in the details of the voyage itself. The writers seem, in each instance, to be utterly uninformed in respect to astronomy. In 'Hans Pfaall' the design is original, inasmuch as regards an attempt at *verisimilitude*, in the application of scientific principles (so far as the whimsical nature of the subject would permit) to the actual passage between the earth and the moon.

MESMERIC REVELATION*

Whatever doubt may still envelop the *rationale* of mesmerism, its startling *facts* are now almost universally admitted. Of these latter, those who doubt are your mere doubters by profession – an unprofitable and disreputable tribe. There can be no more absolute waste of time than the attempt to *prove*, at the present day, that man, by mere exercise of will, can so impress his fellow as to cast him into an abnormal condition of which the phenomena resemble very closely those of *death*, or at least resemble them more nearly than they do the phenomena of any other normal condition within our cognizance; that, while in this state, the person so impressed employs only with effort, and then feebly, the external organs of sense, yet perceives with keenly refined perception, and through channels supposed unknown, matters beyond the scope of the physical organs; that, moreover, his intellectual faculties are wonderfully exalted and invigorated; that his sympathies with the person so impressing him are profound; and, finally, that his susceptibility to the impression increases with its frequency, while, in the same proportion, the peculiar phenomena elicited are more extended and more *pronounced*.

I say that these – which are the laws of mesmerism in its general features – it would be supererogation to demonstrate, nor shall I inflict upon my readers so needless a demonstration today. My purpose at present is a very different one indeed. I am impelled, even in the teeth of a world of prejudice, to detail, without comment, the very remarkable substance of a colloquy occurring between a sleepwaker* and myself.

I had been long in the habit of mesmerizing the person in question (Mr Vankirk), and the usual acute susceptibility and exaltation of the mesmeric perception had supervened. For many months he had been labouring under confirmed phthisis,* the more distressing effects of which had been relieved by my manipulations – and on the night of Wednesday the fifteenth instant,* I was summoned to his bedside.

The invalid was suffering with acute pain in the region of the heart, and breathed with great difficulty, having all the ordinary symptoms of asthma. In spasms such as these he had usually found relief from the application of mustard to the nervous centres, but tonight this had been attempted in vain.

As I entered his room, he greeted me with a cheerful smile, and although evidently in much bodily pain, appeared to be mentally quite at ease.

"I sent for you tonight," he said, "not so much to administer to my bodily ailment, as to satisfy me concerning certain psychal* impressions which, of late, have occasioned me much anxiety and surprise. I need not tell you how sceptical I have hitherto been on the topic of the soul's immortality. I cannot deny that there has always existed, as if in that very soul which I have been denying, a vague half-sentiment of its own existence. But this half-sentiment at no time amounted to conviction. With it my reason had nothing to do. All attempts at logical enquiry resulted, indeed, in leaving me more sceptical than before. I had been advised to study Cousin.* I studied him in his own works as well as in those of his European and American echoes. The *Charles Elwood* of Mr Brownson,* for example, was placed in my hands. I read it with profound attention. Throughout I found it logical, but the portions which were not *merely* logical were unhappily the initial arguments of the disbelieving hero of the book. In his summing up it seemed evident to me that the reasoner had not even succeeded in convincing himself. His end had plainly forgotten his beginning, like the government of Trinculo.* In short, I was not long in perceiving that if man is to be intellectually convinced of his own immortality, he will never be so convinced by the mere abstractions which have been so long the fashion of the moralists of England, of France and of Germany. Abstractions may amuse and exercise, but take no hold on the mind. Here upon earth, at least, philosophy, I am persuaded, will always in vain call upon us to look upon qualities as things. The will may assent – the soul, the intellect, never.

"I repeat, then, that I only half felt, and never intellectually believed. But latterly there has been a certain deepening of the feeling, until it has come so nearly to resemble the acquiescence of reason that I find it difficult to distinguish between the two. I am enabled, too, plainly to trace this effect to the mesmeric influence. I cannot better explain my meaning than by the hypothesis that the mesmeric exaltation enables me to perceive a train of ratiocination which, in my abnormal existence, convinces, but which, in full accordance with the mesmeric phenomena, does not extend, except through its *effect*, into my normal condition. In sleepwaking, the reasoning and its conclusion – the cause and its effect – are present together. In my natural state, the cause vanishing, the effect only, and perhaps only partially, remains.

"These considerations have led me to think that some good results might ensue from a series of well-directed questions propounded to me while mesmerized. You have often observed the profound self-cognizance evinced by the sleepwaker – the extensive knowledge he displays upon all points relating to the mesmeric condition itself – and from this self-cognizance may be deduced hints for the proper conduct of a catechism."

I consented of course to make this experiment. A few passes threw Mr Vankirk into the mesmeric sleep. His breathing became immediately more easy, and he seemed to suffer no physical uneasiness. The following conversation then ensued (V. in the dialogue representing the patient, and P. myself).

P. Are you asleep?
V. Yes… no – I would rather sleep more soundly.
P. (*After a few more passes*) Do you sleep now?
V. Yes.
P. How do you think your present illness will result?
V. (*After a long hesitation, and speaking as if with effort*) I must die.
P. Does the idea of death afflict you?
V. (*Very quickly*) No – no!
P. Are you pleased with the prospect?
V. If I were awake, I should like to die, but now it is no matter. The mesmeric condition is so near death as to content me.
P. I wish you would explain yourself, Mr Vankirk.
V. I am willing to do so, but it requires more effort than I feel able to make. You do not question me properly.
P. What then shall I ask?
V. You must begin at the beginning.
P. The beginning! But where is the beginning?
V. You know that the beginning is GOD. (*This was said in a low, fluctuating tone, and with every sign of the most profound veneration.*)
P. What, then, is God?
V. (*Hesitating for many minutes*) I cannot tell.
P. Is not God spirit?
V. While I was awake, I knew what you meant by "spirit", but now it seems only a word – such, for instance, as truth, beauty – a quality, I mean.

P. Is not God immaterial?

V. There is no immateriality – it is a mere word. That which is not matter, is not at all – unless qualities are things.

P. Is God, then, material?

V. No. (*This reply startled me very much.*)

P. What, then, is he?

V. (*After a long pause, and mutteringly*) I see – but it is a thing difficult to tell. (*Another long pause.*) He is not spirit, for he exists. Nor is he matter, *as you understand it*. But there are *gradations* of matter of which man knows nothing – the grosser impelling the finer, the finer pervading the grosser. The atmosphere, for example, impels the electric principle, while the electric principle permeates the atmosphere. These gradations of matter increase in rarity or fineness, until we arrive at a matter *unparticled*... without particles... indivisible... *one* – and here the law of impulsion and permeation is modified. The ultimate or unparticled matter not only permeates all things, but impels all things – and thus *is* all things within itself. This matter is God. What men attempt to embody in the word "thought" is this matter in motion.

P. The metaphysicians maintain that all action is reducible to motion and thinking, and that the latter is the origin of the former.

V. Yes; and I now see the confusion of idea. Motion is the action of *mind*, not of *thinking*. The unparticled matter, or God, in quiescence, is (as nearly as we can conceive it) what men call "mind". And the power of self-movement (equivalent in effect to human volition) is, in the unparticled matter, the result of its unity and omniprevalence – *how*, I know not, and now clearly see that I shall never know. But the unparticled matter, set in motion by a law or quality existing within itself, is thinking.

P. Can you give me no more precise idea of what you term "the unparticled matter"?

V. The matters of which man is cognizant escape the senses in gradation. We have, for example, a metal, a piece of wood, a drop of water, the atmosphere, a gas, caloric, electricity, the luminiferous ether. Now, we call all these things "matter", and embrace all matter in one general definition – but in spite of this, there can be no two ideas more essentially distinct than that which we attach to a metal and that which we attach to the luminiferous ether. When we reach the latter, we feel an almost irresistible inclination to class it with spirit, or with nihility. The only consideration which restrains us is our conception of its atomic constitution – and here, even, we have to seek aid from our notion of an atom as something possessing, in infinite minuteness, solidity, palpability, weight. Destroy the idea of the atomic constitution and we should no longer be able to regard the ether as an entity – or, at least, as matter. For want of a better word, we might term it "spirit". Take, now, a step beyond the luminiferous ether, conceive a matter as much more rare than the ether as this ether is more rare than the metal, and we arrive at once (in spite of all the school dogmas) at a unique mass – an unparticled matter. For although we may admit infinite littleness in the atoms themselves, the infinitude of littleness in the spaces between them is an absurdity. There will be a point – there will be a degree of rarity at which, if the atoms are sufficiently numerous, the interspaces must vanish, and the mass absolutely coalesce. But the consideration of the atomic constitution being now taken away, the nature of the mass inevitably glides into what we conceive of spirit. It is clear, however, that it is as fully matter as before. The truth is, it is impossible to conceive spirit, since it is impossible to imagine what is not. When we flatter ourselves that we have formed its conception, we have merely deceived our understanding by the consideration of infinitely rarefied matter.

P. There seems to me an insurmountable objection to the idea of absolute coalescence, and that is the very slight resistance experienced by the heavenly bodies in their revolutions through space – a resistance now ascertained, it is true, to exist in *some* degree, but which is, nevertheless, so slight as to have been quite overlooked by the sagacity even of Newton. We know that the resistance of bodies is, chiefly, in proportion to their density. Absolute coalescence is absolute density. Where there are no interspaces, there can be no yielding. An ether, absolutely dense, would put an infinitely more effectual stop to the progress of a star than would an ether of adamant or of iron.

V. Your objection is answered with an ease which is nearly in the ratio of its apparent unanswerability... As regards the progress of the star, it can make no difference whether the star passes through the ether *or the ether through it*. There is no astronomical error more unaccountable than that which reconciles the known retardation of the comets with the idea of their passage through an ether, for, however rare this ether be supposed, it would put a stop to all sidereal revolution in a very far briefer period than has been admitted by those astronomers who have endeavoured to slur over a point which they found it impossible to comprehend. The retardation actually experienced is, on the other hand, about that which might be expected from the *friction* of the ether in the instantaneous passage through the orb. In the one case, the retarding force is momentary and complete within itself – in the other, it is endlessly accumulative.

P. But in all this – in this identification of mere matter with God – is there nothing of irreverence? (*I was forced to repeat this question before the sleepwaker fully comprehended my meaning.*)

V. Can you say *why* matter should be less reverenced than mind? But you forget that the matter of which I speak is, in all respects, the very "mind" or "spirit" of the schools, so far as regards its high capacities, and is, moreover, the "matter" of these schools at the same time. God, with all the powers attributed to spirit, is but the perfection of matter.

P. You assert, then, that the unparticled matter, in motion, is thought.

V. In general, this motion is the universal thought of the universal mind. This thought creates. All created things are but the thoughts of God.

P. You say, "in general".

V. Yes. The universal mind is God. For new individualities, *matter* is necessary.

P. But you now speak of "mind" and "matter" as do the metaphysicians.

V. Yes – to avoid confusion: when I say "mind", I mean the unparticled or ultimate matter; by "matter" I intend all else.

P. You were saying that "for new individualities matter is necessary".

V. Yes, for mind, existing unincorporate, is merely God. To create individual thinking beings, it was necessary to incarnate portions of the divine mind. Thus man is individualized. Divested of corporate investiture, he were God. Now, the particular motion of the incarnated portions of the unparticled matter is the thought of man – as the motion of the whole is that of God.

P. You say that divested of the body man will be God?

V. (*After much hesitation*) I could not have said this – it is an absurdity.

P. (*Referring to my notes*) You *did* say that "divested of corporate investiture man were God".

V. And this is true. Man thus divested *would be* God – would be unindividualized. But he can never be thus divested – at least never *will be*, else we must imagine an action of God returning upon itself, a purposeless and futile action. Man is a creature. Creatures are thoughts of God. It is the nature of thought to be irrevocable.

P. I do not comprehend. You say that man will never put off the body?

V. I say that he will never be bodiless.

P. Explain.

V. There are two bodies – the rudimental and the complete, corresponding with the two conditions of the worm and the butterfly.* What we call "death" is but the painful metamorphosis. Our present incarnation is progressive, preparatory, temporary. Our future is perfected, ultimate, immortal. The ultimate life is the full design.

P. But of the worm's metamorphosis we are palpably cognizant.

V. *We*, certainly – but not the worm. The matter of which our rudimental body is composed is within the ken of the organs of that body – or, more distinctly, our rudimental organs are adapted to the matter of which is formed the rudimental body, but not to that of which the ultimate is composed. The ultimate body thus escapes our rudimental senses, and we perceive only the shell which falls, in decaying, from the inner form – not that inner form itself – but this inner form, as well as the shell, is appreciable by those who have already acquired the ultimate life.

P. You have often said that the mesmeric state very nearly resembles death. How is this?

V. When I say that it resembles death, I mean that it resembles the ultimate life – for when I am entranced, the senses of my rudimental life are in abeyance, and I perceive external things directly, without organs, through a medium which I shall employ in the ultimate, unorganized life.

P. Unorganized?

V. Yes – organs are contrivances by which the individual is brought into sensible relation with particular classes and forms of matter, to the exclusion of other classes and forms. The organs of man are adapted to his rudimental condition, and to that only: his ultimate condition, being unorganized, is of unlimited comprehension in all points but one: the nature of the volition of God – that is to say, the motion of the unparticled matter. You will have a distinct idea of the ultimate body by conceiving it to be entire brain. This it is *not* – but a conception of this nature will bring you near a comprehension of what it *is*. A luminous body imparts vibration to the luminiferous ether. The vibrations generate similar ones within the retina – these again communicate similar ones to the optic nerve. The nerve conveys similar ones to the brain – the brain, also, similar ones to the unparticled matter which permeates it. The motion of this latter is thought, of which perception is the first undulation. This is the mode by which the mind of the rudimental life communicates with the external world; and this external world is, to the rudimental life, limited, through the idiosyncrasy of its organs. But in the ultimate, unorganized life, the external world reaches the whole body (which is of a substance having affinity to brain, as I have said), with no other intervention than that of an infinitely rarer ether than even the luminiferous – and to this ether, in unison with it, the whole body vibrates, setting in motion the unparticled matter which permeates it. It is to the absence of idiosyncratic organs, therefore, that we must attribute the nearly unlimited perception of the ultimate life. To rudimental beings, organs are the cages necessary to confine them until fledged.

P. You speak of rudimental "beings". Are there other rudimental thinking beings than man?

V. The multitudinous conglomeration of rare matter into nebulae, planets, suns and other bodies which are neither nebulae, suns nor planets is for the sole purpose of supplying pabulum for the idiosyncrasy of the organs of an infinity of rudimental beings. But for the necessity of the rudimental, prior to the ultimate life, there would have been no bodies such as these. Each of these is tenanted by a distinct variety of organic, rudimental thinking creatures. In all, the organs vary with the features of the place tenanted. At death, or metamorphosis, these creatures, enjoying the ultimate life – immortality – and cognizant of all secrets but *the one*, act all things and pass everywhere by mere volition: indwelling not the stars, which to us seem the sole palpabilities, and for the accommodation of which we blindly deem space created, but that SPACE itself – that infinity of which the truly substantive vastness swallows up the star-shadows, blotting them out as nonentities from the perception of the angels.

P. You say that, "but for the *necessity* of the rudimental life", there would have been no stars. But why this necessity?

V. In the inorganic life, as well as in the inorganic matter generally, there is nothing to impede the action of one simple *unique* law – the Divine Volition. With the view of producing impediment, the organic life and matter (complex, substantial and law-encumbered) were contrived.

P. But again – why need this impediment have been produced?

V. The result of law inviolate is perfection, right, negative happiness. The result of law violate is imperfection, wrong, positive pain. Through the impediments afforded by the number, complexity and substantiality of the laws of organic life and matter, the violation of law is rendered, to a certain extent, practicable. Thus pain, which in the inorganic life is impossible, is possible in the organic.

P. But to what good end is pain thus rendered possible?

V. All things are either good or bad by comparison. A sufficient analysis will show that pleasure, in all cases, is but the contrast of pain. *Positive* pleasure is a mere idea. To be happy at any one point, we must have suffered at the same. Never to suffer would have been never to have been blessed. But it has been shown that, in the inorganic life, pain cannot be – thus the necessity for the organic. The pain of the primitive life of earth is the sole basis of the bliss of the ultimate life in heaven.

P. Still, there is one of your expressions which I find it impossible to comprehend – "the truly *substantive* vastness" of infinity.

V. This, probably, is because you have no sufficiently generic conception of the term "*substance*" itself. We must not regard it as a quality, but as a sentiment – it is the perception, in thinking beings, of the adaptation of matter to their organization. There are many things on the earth which would be nihility to the inhabitants of Venus – many things visible and tangible in Venus which we could not be brought to appreciate as existing at all. But to the inorganic beings, to the angels, the whole of the unparticled matter is substance – that is to say, the whole of what we term "space" is to them the truest substantiality, the stars meantime, through what we consider their materiality, escaping the angelic sense, just in proportion as the unparticled matter, through what we consider its immateriality, eludes the organic.

As the sleepwaker pronounced these latter words in a feeble tone, I observed on his countenance a singular expression which somewhat alarmed me, and induced me to awake him at once. No sooner had I done this than, with a bright smile irradiating all his features, he fell back upon his pillow and expired. I noticed that in less than a minute afterwards his corpse had all the stern rigidity of stone. His brow was of the coldness of ice. Thus, ordinarily, should it have appeared only after long pressure from Azrael's hand.* Had the sleepwaker, indeed, during the latter portion of his discourse been addressing me from out the region of the shadows?

THE THOUSAND-AND-SECOND TALE OF SCHEHERAZADE*

Truth is stranger than fiction.
– Old saying

Having had occasion, lately, in the course of some oriental investigations, to consult the *Tellmenow Isitsöornot*, a work which (like the *Zohar* of Simeon Jochaides)* is scarcely known at all, even in Europe, and which has never been quoted, to my knowledge, by any American (if we except, perhaps, the author of the "Curiosities of American Literature")* – having had occasion, I say, to turn over some pages of the first-mentioned very remarkable work, I was not a little astonished to discover that the literary world has hitherto been strangely in error respecting the fate of the vizier's daughter, Scheherazade, as that fate is depicted in the *Arabian Nights* – and that the denouement there given, if not altogether inaccurate, as far as it goes, is at least to blame in not having gone very much further.

For full information on this interesting topic, I must refer the inquisitive reader to the *Isitsöornot* itself – but, in the mean time, I shall be pardoned for giving a summary of what I there discovered.

It will be remembered that, in the usual version of the tales, a certain monarch, having good cause to be jealous of his queen, not only puts her to death, but makes a vow, by his beard and the Prophet, to espouse each night the most beautiful maiden in his dominions, and the next morning to deliver her up to the executioner.

Having fulfilled this vow for many years to the letter, and with a religious punctuality and method that conferred great credit upon him as a man of devout feelings and excellent sense, he was interrupted one afternoon (no doubt at his prayers) by a visit from his grand vizier, to whose daughter, it appears, there had occurred an idea.

Her name was Scheherazade, and her idea was that she would either redeem the land from the depopulating tax upon its beauty or perish, after the approved fashion of all heroines, in the attempt.

Accordingly, and although we do not find it to be leap year (which makes the sacrifice more meritorious), she deputes her father, the grand vizier, to make an offer to the king of her hand. This hand the king eagerly accepts (he had intended to take it at all events, and had put off the matter from day to day, only through fear of the vizier) – but, in accepting it now, he gives all parties very distinctly to understand that, grand vizier or no grand vizier, he has not the slightest design of giving up one iota of his vow or of his privileges. When, therefore, the fair Scheherazade insisted upon marrying the king, and did actually marry him despite her father's excellent advice not to do anything of the kind – when she would and did marry him, I say, willy-nilly, it was with her beautiful black eyes as thoroughly open as the nature of the case would allow.

It seems, however, that this politic damsel (who had been reading Machiavelli, beyond doubt), had a very ingenious little plot in her mind. On the night of the wedding, she contrived, upon I forget what specious pretence, to have her sister occupy a couch sufficiently near that of the royal pair to admit of easy conversation from bed to bed – and, a little before cock-crowing, she took care to awaken the good monarch, her husband (who bore her none the worse will because he intended to wring her neck on the morrow) – she managed to awaken him, I say (although, on account of a capital conscience and an easy digestion, he slept well), by the profound interest of a story (about a rat and a black cat, I think) which she was narrating (all in an undertone, of course) to her sister. When the day broke, it so happened that this history was not altogether finished, and that Scheherazade, in the nature of things, could not finish it just then, since it was high time for her to get up and be bowstrung* – a thing very little more pleasant than hanging, only a trifle more genteel!

The king's curiosity, however, prevailing, I am sorry to say, even over his sound religious principles, induced him for this once to postpone the fulfilment of his vow until next morning, for the purpose and with the hope of hearing that night how it fared in the end with the black cat (a black cat, I think it was) and the rat.

The night having arrived, however, the lady Scheherazade not only put the finishing stroke to the black cat and the rat (the rat was blue), but before she well knew what she was about, found herself deep in the intricacies of a narration having reference (if I am not altogether mistaken) to a pink horse (with green wings) that went, in a violent manner, by clockwork, and was wound up with an indigo key. With this history the king was even more profoundly interested than with the other – and, as the day broke before its conclusion (notwithstanding all the queen's endeavours to get through with it in time for the bowstringing), there was again no resource but to postpone that ceremony as before for twenty-four hours. The next night there happened a similar accident with a similar result, and then the next, and then again the next – so that, in the end, the good monarch, having been unavoidably deprived of all opportunity to keep his vow during a period of no less than one thousand and one nights, either forgets it altogether by the expiration of this time, or gets himself absolved of it in the regular way, or (what is more probable) breaks it outright, as well as the head of his father confessor. At all events, Scheherazade, who, being lineally descended from Eve, fell heir, perhaps, to the whole seven baskets of talk, which the latter lady, we all know, picked up from under the trees in the garden of Eden* – Scheherazade, I say, finally triumphed, and the tariff upon beauty was repealed.

Now, this conclusion (which is that of the story as we have it upon record) is, no doubt, excessively proper and pleasant, but, alas, like a great many pleasant things, is more pleasant than true – and I am indebted altogether to the *Isitsöornot* for the means of correcting the error. "*Le mieux*," says a French proverb, "*est l'ennemi du bien*"* – and, in mentioning that Scheherazade had inherited the seven baskets of talk, I should have added that she put them out at compound interest until they amounted to seventy-seven.

"My dear sister," said she, on the thousand-and-second night (I quote the language of the *Isitsöornot* at this point, verbatim), "my dear sister," said she, "now that all this little difficulty about the bowstring has blown over, and that this odious tax is so happily repealed, I feel that I have been guilty of great indiscretion in withholding from you and the king (who, I am sorry to say, snores – a thing no gentleman would do) the full conclusion of 'Sinbad the Sailor'. This person went through numerous other and more interesting adventures than those which I related – but the truth is, I felt sleepy on the particular night of their narration, and so was seduced into cutting them short – a grievous piece of misconduct, for which I only trust that Allah will forgive me. But even yet it is not too late to remedy my great neglect – and as soon as I have given the king a pinch or two in order to wake him up so far that he may stop making that horrible noise, I will forthwith entertain you (and him, if he pleases) with the sequel of this very remarkable story."

Hereupon the sister of Scheherazade, as I have it from the *Isitsöornot*, expressed no very particular intensity of gratification, but the king, having been sufficiently pinched, at length ceased snoring, and finally said "Hum!" and then "Hoo!", when the queen, understanding these words (which are no doubt Arabic) to signify that he was all attention and would do his best not to snore any more – the queen, I say, having arranged these matters to her satisfaction, re-entered thus, at once, into the history of Sinbad the Sailor:

"'At length, in my old age,'" (these are the words of Sinbad himself as retailed by Scheherazade) "'at length, in my old age, and after enjoying many years of tranquillity at home, I became once more possessed with a desire of visiting foreign countries – and one day, without acquainting any of my family with my design, I packed up some bundles of such merchandise as was most precious and least bulky, and, engaging a porter to carry them, went with him down to the seashore to await the arrival of any chance vessel that might convey me out of the kingdom into some region which I had not as yet explored.

"'Having deposited the packages upon the sands, we sat down beneath some trees, and looked out into the ocean in the hope of perceiving a ship, but during several hours we saw none whatever. At length I fancied that I could hear a singular buzzing or humming sound – and the porter, after listening awhile, declared that he also could distinguish it. Presently it grew louder, and then still louder, so that we could have no doubt that the object which caused it was approaching us. At length, on the edge of the horizon, we discovered a black speck, which rapidly increased in size until we made it out to be a vast monster, swimming with a great part of its body above the surface of the sea. It came towards us with inconceivable swiftness, throwing up huge waves of foam around its breast, and illuminating all that part of the sea through which it passed with a long line of fire that extended far off into the distance.

"'As the thing drew near, we saw it very distinctly. Its length was equal to that of three of the loftiest trees that grow, and it was as wide as the great hall of audience in your palace, O most sublime and munificent of the caliphs. Its body, which was unlike that of ordinary fishes, was as solid as a rock, and of a jetty blackness throughout all that portion of it which floated above the water, with the exception of a narrow blood-red streak that completely begirdled it. The belly, which floated beneath the surface, and of which we could get only a glimpse now and then as the monster rose and fell with the billows, was entirely covered with metallic scales, of a colour like that of the moon in misty weather. The back was flat and nearly white, and from it there extended upwards of six spines, about half the length of the whole body.

"'This horrible creature had no mouth that we could perceive, but, as if to make up for this deficiency, it was provided with at least fourscore of eyes, that protruded from their sockets like those of the green dragonfly and were arranged all around the body in two rows, one above the other, and parallel to the blood-red streak, which seemed to answer the purpose of an eyebrow. Two or three of these dreadful eyes were much larger than the others, and had the appearance of solid gold.

"'Although this beast approached us, as I have before said, with the greatest rapidity, it must have been moved altogether by necromancy, for it had neither fins like a fish nor web feet like a duck, nor wings like the seashell which is blown along in the manner of a vessel – nor yet did it writhe itself forward as do the eels. Its head and its tail were shaped precisely alike – only, not far from the latter, were two small holes that served for nostrils, and through which the monster puffed out its thick breath with prodigious violence, and with a shrieking, disagreeable noise.

"'Our terror at beholding this hideous thing was very great, but it was even surpassed by our astonishment when, upon getting a nearer look, we perceived upon the creature's back a vast number of animals about the size and shape of men, and altogether much resembling them, except that they wore no garments (as men do), being supplied (by nature, no doubt) with an ugly uncomfortable covering, a good deal like cloth, but fitting so tight to the skin as to render the poor wretches laughably awkward, and put them apparently to severe pain. On the very tips of their heads were certain square-looking boxes, which, at first sight, I thought might have been intended to answer as turbans, but I soon discovered that they were excessively heavy and solid, and I therefore concluded they were contrivances designed, by their great weight, to keep the heads of the animals steady and safe upon their shoulders. Around the necks of the creatures were fastened black collars (badges of servitude, no doubt), such as we keep on our dogs, only much wider and infinitely stiffer, so that it was quite impossible for these poor victims to move their heads in any direction without moving the body at the same time – and thus they were doomed to perpetual contemplation of their noses, a view puggish and snubby in a wonderful if not positively in an awful degree.

"'When the monster had nearly reached the shore where we stood, it suddenly pushed out one of its eyes to a great extent, and emitted from it a terrible flash of fire, accompanied by a dense cloud of smoke, and a noise that I can compare to nothing but thunder. As the smoke cleared away, we saw one of the odd man-animals standing near the head of the large beast with a trumpet in his hand, through which (putting it to his mouth) he presently addressed us in loud, harsh and disagreeable accents, that, perhaps, we should have mistaken for language, had they not come altogether through the nose.

"'Being thus evidently spoken to, I was at a loss how to reply, as I could in no manner understand what was said – and in this difficulty I turned to the porter, who was near swooning through affright, and demanded of him his opinion as to what species of monster it was, what it wanted and what kind of creatures those were that so swarmed upon its back. To this the porter replied, as well as he could for trepidation, that he had once before heard of this sea beast; that it was a cruel demon, with bowels of sulphur and blood of fire, created by evil genii as the means of inflicting misery upon mankind; that the things upon its back were vermin, such as sometimes infest cats and dogs, only a little larger and more savage; and that these vermin had their uses, however evil – for, through the torture they caused the beast by their nibblings and stingings, it was goaded into that degree of wrath which was requisite to make it roar and commit ill, and so fulfil the vengeful and malicious designs of the wicked genii.

"'This account determined me to take to my heels, and, without once even looking behind me, I ran at full speed up into the hills, while the porter ran equally fast, although nearly in an opposite direction, so that, by these means, he finally made his escape with my bundles, of which I have no doubt he took excellent care – although this is a point I cannot determine, as I do not remember that I ever beheld him again.

"'For myself, I was so hotly pursued by a swarm of the men-vermin (who had come to the shore in boats) that I was very soon overtaken, bound hand and foot, and conveyed to the beast, which immediately swam out again into the middle of the sea.

"'I now bitterly repented my folly in quitting a comfortable home to peril my life in such adventures as this – but regret being useless, I made the best of my condition, and exerted myself to secure the goodwill of the man-animal that owned the trumpet, and who appeared to exercise authority over his fellows. I succeeded so well in this endeavour that, in a few days, the creature bestowed upon me various tokens of its favour, and in the end even went to the trouble of teaching me the rudiments of what it was vain enough to denominate its language – so that, at length, I was enabled to converse with it readily, and came to make it comprehend the ardent desire I had of seeing the world.

"'*Washish squashish squeak, Sinbad, hey-diddle diddle, grunt unt grumble, hiss, fiss, whiss*,' said he to me, one day after dinner – but I beg a thousand pardons, I had forgotten that Your Majesty is not conversant with the dialect of the Cock-neighs (so the man-animals were called – I presume because their language formed the connecting link between that of the horse and that of the rooster). With your permission, I will translate. '*Washish squashish*,' and so forth... that is to say, 'I am happy to find, my dear Sinbad, that you are really a very excellent fellow; we are now about doing a thing which is called circumnavigating the globe – and since you are so desirous of seeing the world, I will strain a point and give you a free passage upon the back of the beast.'"

When the lady Scheherazade had proceeded thus far, relates the *Isitsöornot*, the king turned over from his left side to his right and said:

"It is, in fact, *very* surprising, my dear queen, that you omitted, hitherto, these latter adventures of Sinbad. Do you know I think them exceedingly entertaining and strange?"

The king having thus expressed himself, we are told, the fair Scheherazade resumed her history in the following words:

"Sinbad went on in this manner with his narrative. 'I thanked the man-animal for its kindness, and soon found myself very much at home on the beast, which swam at a prodigious rate through the ocean – although the surface of the latter is, in that part of the world, by no means flat, but round like a pomegranate, so that we went (so to say) either uphill or downhill all the time.'"

"That, I think, was very singular," interrupted the king.

"Nevertheless, it is quite true," replied Scheherazade.

"I have my doubts," rejoined the king, "but, pray, be so good as to go on with the story."

"I will," said the queen. "'The beast,' continued Sinbad, 'swam, as I have related, uphill and downhill until, at length, we arrived at an island, many hundreds of miles in circumference, but which, nevertheless, had been built in the middle of the sea by a colony of little things like caterpillars.'"*

"Hum!" said the king.

"'Leaving this island,' said Sinbad," (for Scheherazade, it must be understood, took no notice of her husband's ill-mannered ejaculation) "'leaving this island, we came to another where the forests were of solid stone, and so hard that they shivered to pieces the finest-tempered axes with which we endeavoured to cut them down.'"*

"Hum!" said the king, again – but Scheherazade, paying him no attention, continued in the language of Sinbad.

"'Passing beyond this last island, we reached a country where there was a cave that ran to the distance of thirty or forty miles within the bowels of the earth, and that contained a greater number of far more spacious and more magnificent palaces than are to be found in all Damascus and Baghdad. From the roofs of these palaces there hung myriads of gems, like diamonds, but larger than men – and in among the streets of towers and pyramids and temples there flowed immense rivers as black as ebony, and swarming with fish that had no eyes.'"*

"Hum!" said the king.

"'We then swam into a region of the sea where we found a lofty mountain, down whose sides there streamed torrents of melted metal, some of which were twelve miles wide and sixty miles long* – while from an abyss on the summit issued so vast a quantity of ashes that the sun was entirely blotted out from the heavens, and it became darker than the darkest midnight, so that when we were even at the distance of a hundred and fifty miles from the mountain, it was impossible to see the whitest object, however close we held it to our eyes.'"*

"Hum!" said the king.

"'After quitting this coast, the beast continued his voyage until we met with a land in which the nature of things seemed reversed – for we here saw a great lake, at the bottom of which, more than a hundred feet beneath the surface of the water, there flourished in full leaf a forest of tall and luxuriant trees.'"*

"Hoo!" said the king.

"'Some hundred miles further on brought us to a climate where the atmosphere was so dense as to sustain iron or steel, just as our own does feathers.'"*

"Fiddle-de-dee," said the king.

"'Proceeding still in the same direction, we presently arrived at the most magnificent region in the whole world.* Through it, there meandered a glorious river for several thousands of miles. This river was of unspeakable depth, and of a transparency richer than that of amber. It was from three to six miles in width, and its banks, which arose on either side to twelve hundred feet in perpendicular height, were crowned with ever-blossoming trees and perpetual sweet-scented flowers that made the whole territory one gorgeous garden – but the name of this luxuriant land was "the Kingdom of Horror", and to enter it was inevitable death.'"

"Humph!" said the king.

"'We left this kingdom in great haste, and, after some days, came to another, where we were astonished to perceive myriads of monstrous animals with horns resembling scythes upon their heads. These hideous beasts dig for themselves vast caverns in the soil, of a funnel shape, and line the sides of them with rocks, so disposed one upon the other that they fall instantly when trodden upon by other animals, thus precipitating them into the monsters' dens, where their blood is immediately sucked, and their carcasses afterwards hurled contemptuously out to an immense distance from "the caverns of death".'"*

"Pooh!" said the king.

"'Continuing our progress, we perceived a district with vegetables that grew not upon any soil, but in the air.* There were others that sprang from the substance of other vegetables;* others that derived their substance from the bodies of living animals;* and then again, there were others that glowed all over with intense fire;* others that moved from place to place at pleasure;* and, what is still more wonderful, we discovered flowers that lived and breathed and moved their limbs at will, and had, moreover, the detestable passion of mankind for enslaving other creatures and confining them in horrid and solitary prisons until the fulfilment of appointed tasks.'"*

"Pshaw!" said the king.

"'Quitting this land, we soon arrived at another in which the bees and the birds are mathematicians of such genius and erudition that they give daily instructions in the science of geometry to the wise men of the empire. The king of the place having offered a reward for the solution of two very difficult problems, they were solved upon the spot, the one by the bees, and the other by the birds – but the king keeping their solution a secret, it was only after the most profound researches and labour, and the writing of an infinity of big books during a long series of years that the men-mathematicians at length arrived at the identical solutions which had been given upon the spot by the bees and by the birds.'"*

"Oh my!" said the king.

"'We had scarcely lost sight of this empire when we found ourselves close upon another, from whose shores there flew over our heads a flock of fowls a mile in breadth and two hundred and forty miles long, so that, although they flew a mile during every minute, it required no less than four hours for the whole flock to pass over us – in which there were several millions of millions of fowls.'"*

"Oh fie!" said the king.

"'No sooner had we got rid of these birds, which occasioned us great annoyance, than we were terrified by the appearance of a fowl of another kind, and infinitely larger than even the rocs* which I met in my former voyages – for it was bigger than the biggest of the domes on your seraglio, O most munificent of caliphs. This terrible fowl had no head that we could perceive, but was fashioned entirely of belly, which was of a prodigious fatness and roundness, of a soft-looking substance, smooth, shining and striped with various colours. In its talons, the monster was bearing away to his eyrie in the heavens a house from which it had knocked off the roof, and in the interior of which we distinctly saw human beings, who, beyond doubt, were in a state of frightful despair at the horrible fate which awaited them. We shouted with all our might, in the hope of frightening the bird into letting go of its prey, but it merely gave a snort or puff, as if of rage, and then let fall upon our heads a heavy sack which proved to be filled with sand!'"*

"Stuff!" said the king.

"'It was just after this adventure that we encountered a continent of immense extent and prodigious solidity, but which, nevertheless, was supported entirely upon the back of a sky-blue cow that had no fewer than four hundred horns.'"*

"*That*, now, I believe," said the king, "because I have read something of the kind before, in a book."

"'We passed immediately beneath this continent (swimming in between the legs of the cow), and, after some hours, found ourselves in a wonderful country indeed, which, I was informed by the man-animal, was his own native land, inhabited by things of his own species. This elevated the man-animal very much in my esteem – and, in fact, I now began to feel ashamed of the contemptuous familiarity with which I had treated him, for I found that the man-animals in general were a nation of the most powerful magicians, who lived with worms in their brain* – which, no doubt, served to stimulate them by their painful writhings and wrigglings to the most miraculous efforts of imagination.'"

"Nonsense!" said the king.

"'Among the magicians were domesticated several animals of very singular kinds – for example, there was a huge horse whose bones were iron and whose blood was boiling water. In place of corn, he had black stones for his usual food – and yet, in spite of so hard a diet, he was so strong and swift that he would drag a load more weighty than the grandest temple in this city, at a rate surpassing that of the flight of most birds.'"*

"Twattle!" said the king.

"'I saw also, among these people, a hen without feathers, but bigger than a camel; instead of flesh and bone, she had iron and brick; her blood, like that of the horse (to whom, in fact, she was nearly related), was boiling water, and like him she ate nothing but wood or black stones. This hen brought forth very frequently a hundred chickens in the day – and, after birth, they took up their residence for several weeks within the stomach of their mother.'"*

"Fal-lal!" said the king.

"'One of this nation of mighty conjurors created a man out of brass and wood and leather, and endowed him with such ingenuity that he would have beaten at chess all the race of mankind with the exception of the great caliph Harun al-Rashid.* Another of these magi constructed (of like material) a creature that put to shame even the genius of him who made it – for so great were its reasoning powers that, in a second, it performed calculations of so vast an extent that they would have required the united labour of fifty thousand fleshy men for a year.* But a still more wonderful conjuror fashioned for himself a mighty thing that was neither man nor beast, but which had brains of lead, intermixed with a black matter like pitch, and fingers that it employed with such incredible speed and dexterity that it would have had no trouble in writing out twenty thousand copies of the Koran in an hour – and this with so exquisite a precision that in all the copies there should not be found one to vary from another by the breadth of the finest hair. This thing was of prodigious strength, so that it erected or overthrew the mightiest empires at a breath – but its powers were exercised equally for evil and for good.'"*

"Ridiculous!" said the king.

"'Among this nation of necromancers, there was also one who had in his veins the blood of the salamanders – for he made no scruple of sitting down to smoke his chibouc in a red-hot oven until his dinner was thoroughly roasted upon its floor.* Another had the faculty of converting the common metals into gold without even looking at them during the process.* Another had such a delicacy of touch that he made a wire so fine as to be invisible.* Another had such quickness of perception that he counted all the separate motions of an elastic body while it was springing backward and forward at the rate of nine hundred millions of times in a second.'"*

"Absurd!" said the king.

"'Another of these magicians, by means of a fluid that nobody ever yet saw, could make the corpses of his friends brandish their arms, kick out their legs, fight or even get up and dance at his will.* Another had cultivated his voice to so great an extent that he could have made himself heard from one end of the earth to the other.* Another had so long an arm that he could sit down in Damascus and indite a letter at Baghdad – or indeed at any distance whatsoever.* Another commanded the lightning to come down to him out of the heavens, and it came at his call, and served him for a plaything when it came. Another took two loud sounds, and out of them made a silence. Another constructed a deep darkness out of two brilliant lights.* Another made ice in a red-hot furnace.* Another directed the sun to paint his portrait, and the sun did.* Another took this luminary* with the moon and the planets, and, having first weighed them with scrupulous accuracy, probed into their depths and found out the solidity of the substance of which they are made. But the whole nation is, indeed, of so surprising a necromantic ability that not even their infants, nor their commonest cats and dogs, have any difficulty in seeing objects that do not exist at all, or that for twenty millions of years before the birth of the nation itself had been blotted out from the face of creation.'"*

"Preposterous!" said the king.

"'The wives and daughters of these incomparably great and wise magi,'" continued Scheherazade, without being in any manner disturbed by these frequent and most ungentlemanly interruptions on the part of her husband, "'the wives and daughters of these eminent conjurors are everything that is accomplished and refined – and would be everything that is interesting and beautiful but for an unhappy fatality that besets them, and from which not even the miraculous powers of their husbands and fathers has, hitherto, been adequate to save. Some fatalities come in certain shapes, and some in others – but this of which I speak has come in the shape of a crotchet.'"*

"A what?" said the king.

"'A crotchet,'" said Scheherazade. "'One of the evil genii who are perpetually upon the watch to inflict ill has put it into the heads of these accomplished ladies that the thing which we describe as personal beauty consists altogether in the protuberance of the region which lies not very far below the small of the back. Perfection of loveliness, they say, is in the direct ratio of the extent of this hump. Having been long possessed of this idea, and bolsters being cheap in that country, the days have long gone by since it was possible to distinguish a woman from a dromedary—'"

"Stop!" said the king. "I can't stand that, and I won't. You have already given me a dreadful headache with your lies. The day, too, I perceive, is beginning to break. How long have we been married?... My conscience is getting to be troublesome again. And then that dromedary touch – do you take me for a fool? Upon the whole, you might as well get up and be throttled."

These words, as I learn from the *Isitsöornot*, both grieved and astonished Scheherazade – but, as she knew the king to be a man of scrupulous integrity and quite unlikely to forfeit his word, she submitted to her fate with a good grace. She derived, however, great consolation (during the tightening of the bowstring) from the reflection that much of the history remained still untold, and that the petulance of her brute of a husband had reaped for him a most righteous reward in depriving him of many inconceivable adventures.

THE MYSTERY OF MARIE ROGÊT*

A SEQUEL TO 'THE MURDERS IN THE RUE MORGUE'

Es giebt eine Reihe idealischer Begebenheiten, die der Wircklichen parallel läuft. Selten fallen sie zusammen. Menschen und Zufälle modificiren gewöhnlich die idealische Begebenheit, so dass sie unvollkommen erscheint und ihre Folgen gleichfalls unvollkommen sind. So bey der Reformation. Statt des Protestantism kam das Lutherthum hervor.

There are ideal series of events which run parallel with the real ones. They rarely coincide. Men and circumstances generally modify the ideal train of events, so that it seems imperfect, and its consequences are equally imperfect. Thus with the Reformation; instead of Protestantism came Lutheranism.

– Novalis, *Moralische Ansichten**

There are few persons, even among the calmest thinkers, who have not occasionally been startled into a vague yet thrilling half-credence in the supernatural, by *coincidences* of so seemingly marvellous a character that, as *mere* coincidences, the intellect has been unable to receive them. Such sentiments – for the half-credences of which I speak have never the full force of *thought* – such sentiments* are seldom thoroughly stifled unless by reference to the doctrine of chance, or, as it is technically termed, the "calculus of probabilities". Now this calculus is, in its essence, purely mathematical – and thus we have the anomaly of the most rigidly exact in science applied to the shadow and spirituality of the most intangible in speculation.

The extraordinary details which I am now called upon to make public will be found to form, as regards sequence of time, the primary branch of a series of scarcely intelligible *coincidences* whose secondary or concluding branch will be recognized by all readers in the late murder of MARY CECILIA ROGERS at New York.

When, in an article entitled 'The Murders in the Rue Morgue', I endeavoured, about a year ago, to depict some very remarkable features in the mental character of my friend, the Chevalier C. Auguste Dupin,* it did not occur to me that I should ever resume the subject. This depicting of character constituted my design – and this design was thoroughly* fulfilled in the wild* train of circumstances brought to instance Dupin's idiosyncrasy. I might have adduced other examples, but I should have proven no more. Late events, however, in their surprising development, have startled me into some further details, which will carry with them the air of extorted confession. Hearing what I have lately heard, it would be indeed strange should I remain silent in regard to what I both heard and saw so long ago.

Upon the winding-up of the tragedy involved in the deaths of Madame L'Espanaye and her daughter, the Chevalier dismissed the affair at once from his attention and relapsed into his old habits of moody reverie. Prone, at all times, to abstraction, I readily fell in with his humour – and, continuing to occupy our chambers in the Faubourg Saint-Germain, we gave the future to the winds and slumbered tranquilly in the present, weaving the dull world around us into dreams.

But these dreams were not altogether uninterrupted. It may readily be supposed that the part played by my friend in the drama at the Rue Morgue had not failed of its impression upon the fancies of the Parisian police. With its emissaries, the name of Dupin had grown into a household word. The simple character of those inductions by which he had disentangled the mystery never having been explained even to the prefect or to any other individual than myself, of course it is not surprising that the affair was regarded as little less than miraculous, or that the Chevalier's analytical abilities acquired for him the credit of intuition. His frankness would have led him to disabuse every enquirer of such prejudice, but his indolent humour forbade all further agitation of a topic whose interest to himself had long ceased. It thus happened that he found himself the cynosure* of the policial eyes – and the cases were not few in which attempt was made to engage his services at the prefecture. One of the most remarkable instances was that of the murder of a young girl named Marie Rogêt.

This event occurred about two years after the atrocity in the Rue Morgue. Marie, whose Christian and family name will at once arrest attention from their resemblance to those of the unfortunate "cigar girl",* was the only daughter of the widow Estelle Rogêt. The father had died during the child's infancy, and from the period of his death until within eighteen months before the assassination which forms the subject of our narrative the mother and daughter had dwelt together in the Rue Pavée-Saint-Andrée,* Madame there keeping a *pension*, assisted by Marie. Affairs went on thus until the latter had attained her twenty-second year, when her great beauty attracted the notice of a perfumer, who occupied one of the shops in the basement of the Palais Royal, and whose custom lay chiefly among the desperate adventurers infesting that neighbourhood. Monsieur Le Blanc* was not unaware of the advantages to be derived from the attendance of the fair Marie in his perfumery, and his liberal proposals were accepted eagerly by the girl, although with somewhat more of hesitation by Madame.

The anticipations of the shopkeeper were realized, and his rooms soon became notorious through the charms of the sprightly grisette. She had been in his employ about a year when her admirers were thrown into confusion by her sudden disappearance from the shop. Monsieur Le Blanc was unable to account for her absence, and Madame Rogêt was distracted with anxiety and terror. The public papers immediately took up the theme, and the police were upon the point of making serious investigations when, one fine morning, after the lapse of a week, Marie, in good health but with a somewhat saddened air, made her reappearance at her usual counter in the perfumery. All enquiry, except that of a private character, was of course immediately hushed. Monsieur Le Blanc professed total ignorance, as before. Marie, with Madame, replied to all questions that the last week had been spent at the house of a relation in the country. Thus the affair died away, and was generally forgotten, for the girl, ostensibly to relieve herself from the impertinence of curiosity, soon bade a final adieu to the perfumer and sought the shelter of her mother's residence in the Rue Pavée-Saint-Andrée.

It was about three years* after this return home that her friends were alarmed by her sudden disappearance for the second time. Three days elapsed, and nothing was heard of her. On the fourth, her corpse was found floating in the Seine,* near the shore which is opposite the Quartier of the Rue Saint-Andrée, and at a point not very far distant from the secluded neighbourhood of the Barrière du Roule.*

The atrocity of this murder (for it was at once evident that murder had been committed), the youth and beauty of the victim, and, above all, her previous notoriety, conspired to produce intense excitement in the minds of the sensitive Parisians. I can call to mind no similar occurrence producing so general and so intense an effect. For several weeks, in the discussion of this one absorbing theme, even the momentous political topics of the day were forgotten. The prefect made unusual exertions, and the powers of the whole Parisian police were, of course, tasked to the utmost extent.

Upon the first discovery of the corpse, it was not supposed that the murderer would be able to elude for more than a very brief period the inquisition which was immediately set on foot. It was not until the expiration of a week that it was deemed necessary to offer a reward – and even then this reward was limited to a thousand francs. In the mean time the investigation proceeded with vigour, if not always with judgement, and numerous individuals were examined to no purpose – while, owing to the continual absence of all clue to the mystery, the popular excitement greatly increased. At the end of the tenth day, it was thought advisable to double the sum originally proposed – and, at length, the second week having elapsed without leading to any discoveries, and the prejudice which always exists in Paris against the police having given vent to itself in several serious *émeutes*,* the prefect took it upon himself to offer the sum of twenty thousand francs "for the conviction of the assassin", or, if more than one should prove to have been implicated, "for the conviction of any one of the assassins". In the proclamation setting forth this reward, a full pardon was promised to any accomplice who should come forward in evidence against his fellow – and to the whole was appended, wherever it appeared, the private placard of a committee of citizens offering ten thousand francs in addition to the amount proposed by the prefecture. The entire reward thus stood at no less than thirty thousand francs, which will be regarded as an extraordinary sum when we consider the humble condition of the girl and the great frequency, in large cities, of such atrocities as the one described.

No one doubted now that the mystery of this murder would be immediately brought to light. But although, in one or two instances, arrests were made which promised elucidation, yet nothing was elicited which could implicate the parties suspected, and they were discharged forthwith. Strange as it may appear, the third week from the discovery of the body had passed, and passed without any light being thrown upon the subject, before even a rumour of the events which had so agitated the public mind reached the ears of Dupin and myself. Engaged in researches which absorbed our whole attention, it had been nearly a month since either of us had gone abroad* or received a visitor, or more than glanced at the leading political articles in one of the daily papers. The first intelligence of the murder was brought us by G——— in person. He called upon us early in the afternoon of 13th July 18—, and remained with us until late in the night. He had been piqued by the failure of all his endeavours to ferret out the assassins. His reputation – so he said with a peculiarly Parisian air – was at stake. Even his honour was concerned. The eyes of the public were upon him – and there was really no sacrifice which he would not be willing to make for the development of the mystery. He concluded a somewhat droll speech with a compliment upon what he was pleased to term "the tact of Dupin", and made him a direct and certainly a liberal proposition, the precise nature of which I do not feel myself at liberty to disclose, but which has no bearing upon the proper subject of my narrative.

The compliment my friend rebutted as best he could, but the proposition he accepted at once, although its advantages were altogether provisional. This point being settled, the prefect broke forth at once into explanations of his own views, interspersing them with long comments upon the evidence – of which latter we were not yet in possession. He discoursed much, and beyond doubt learnedly, while I hazarded an occasional suggestion as the night wore drowsily away. Dupin, sitting steadily in his accustomed armchair, was the embodiment of respectful attention. He wore spectacles during the whole interview, and an occasional glance beneath their green glasses sufficed to convince me that he slept not the less soundly, because silently, throughout the seven or eight leaden-footed hours which immediately preceded the departure of the prefect.

In the morning, I procured at the prefecture a full report of all the evidence elicited, and, at the various newspaper offices, a copy of every paper in which, from first to last, had been published any decisive information in regard to this sad affair. Freed from all that was positively disproved, this mass of information stood thus.

Marie Rogêt left the residence of her mother, in the Rue Pavée-Saint-Andrée, about nine o'clock in the morning of Sunday, June 22nd, 18—. In going out, she gave notice to a Monsieur Jacques Saint-Eustache,* and to him only, of her intention to spend the day with an aunt who resided in the Rue des Drômes.* The Rue des Drômes is a short and narrow but populous thoroughfare, not far from the banks of the river, and at a distance of some two miles, in the most direct course possible, from the *pension* of Madame Rogêt. Saint-Eustache was the accepted suitor of Marie, and lodged, as well as took his meals, at the *pension*. He was to have gone for his betrothed at dusk and to have escorted her home. In the afternoon, however, it came on to rain heavily – and, supposing that she would remain all night at her aunt's (as she had done under similar circumstances before), he did not think it necessary to keep his promise. As night drew on, Madame Rogêt (who was an infirm old lady, seventy years of age) was heard to express a fear "that she should never see Marie again" – but this observation attracted little attention at the time.

On Monday it was ascertained that the girl had not been to the Rue des Drômes, and when the day elapsed without tidings of her, a tardy search was instituted at several points in the city and its environs. It was not, however, until the fourth day from the period of disappearance that anything satisfactory was ascertained respecting her. On this day (Wednesday 25th June), a Monsieur Beauvais* – who, with a friend, had been making enquiries for Marie near the Barrière du Roule, on the shore of the Seine which is opposite the Rue Pavée-Saint-Andrée – was informed that a corpse had just been towed ashore by some fishermen, who had found it floating in the river. Upon seeing the body, Beauvais, after some hesitation, identified it as that of the perfumery girl. His friend recognized it more promptly.

The face was suffused with dark blood, some of which issued from the mouth. No foam was seen, as in the case of the merely drowned. There was no discoloration in the cellular tissue. About the throat were bruises and impressions of fingers. The arms were bent over on the chest, and were rigid. The right hand was clenched, the left partially open. On the left wrist were two circular excoriations, apparently the effect of ropes, or of a rope in more than one volution. A part of the right wrist, also, was much chafed, as well as the back throughout its extent, but more especially at the shoulder blades. In bringing the body to the shore, the fishermen had attached to it a rope, but none of the excoriations had been effected by this. The flesh of the neck was much swollen. There were no cuts apparent, or bruises which appeared the effect of blows. A piece of lace was found tied so tightly around the neck as to be hidden from sight; it was completely buried in the flesh, and was fastened by a knot which lay just under the left ear. This alone would have sufficed to produce death. The medical testimony spoke confidently of the virtuous character of the deceased. She had been subjected, it said, to brutal violence. The corpse was in such condition, when found, that there could have been no difficulty in its recognition by friends.

The dress was much torn and otherwise disordered. In the outer garment, a slip, about a foot wide, had been torn upward from the bottom hem to the waist, but not torn off. It was wound three times around the waist, and secured by a sort of hitch in the back. The dress immediately beneath the frock was of fine muslin, and from this a slip eighteen inches wide had been torn entirely out – torn very evenly and with great care. It was found around her neck, fitting loosely and secured with a hard knot. Over this muslin slip and the slip of lace the strings of a bonnet were attached, the bonnet being appended. The knot by which the strings of the bonnet were fastened was not a lady's, but a slip or sailor's knot.

After the recognition of the corpse, it was not, as usual, taken to the morgue (this formality being superfluous), but hastily interred not far from the spot at which it was brought ashore. Through the exertions of Beauvais, the matter was industriously hushed up as far as possible; and several days had elapsed before any public emotion resulted. A weekly paper,* however, at length took up the theme; the corpse was disinterred, and a re-examination instituted, but nothing was elicited beyond what has been already noted. The clothes, however, were now submitted to the mother and friends of the deceased, and fully identified as those worn by the girl upon leaving home.

Meantime, the excitement increased hourly. Several individuals were arrested and discharged. Saint-Eustache fell especially under suspicion – and he failed, at first, to give an intelligible account of his whereabouts during the Sunday on which Marie left home. Subsequently, however, he submitted to Monsieur G——— affidavits accounting satisfactorily for every hour of the day in question. As time passed and no discovery ensued, a thousand contradictory rumours were circulated, and journalists busied themselves in *suggestions*. Among these, the one which attracted the most notice was the idea that Marie Rogêt still lived – that the corpse found in the Seine was that of some other unfortunate. It will be proper that I submit to the reader some passages which embody the suggestion alluded to. These passages are *literal* translations from *L'Étoile*,* a paper conducted, in general, with much ability.

> Mademoiselle Rogêt left her mother's house on Sunday morning, June 22nd, 18—, with the ostensible purpose of going to see her aunt, or some other connection, in the Rue des Drômes. From that hour, nobody is proved to have seen her. There is no trace or tidings of her at all. […] There has no person whatever come forward, so far, who saw her

> at all, on that day, after she left her mother's door. [...] Now, though we have no evidence that Marie Rogêt was in the land of the living after nine o'clock on Sunday, June 22nd, we have proof that, up to that hour, she was alive. On Wednesday noon, at twelve, a female body was discovered afloat on the shore of the Barrière du Roule. This was, even if we presume that Marie Rogêt was thrown into the river within three hours after she left her mother's house, only three days from the time she left her home – three days to an hour. But it is folly to suppose that the murder, if murder was committed on her body, could have been consummated soon enough to have enabled her murderers to throw the body into the river before midnight. Those who are guilty of such horrid crimes choose darkness rather than light. [...] Thus we see that if the body found in the river *was* that of Marie Rogêt, it could only have been in the water two and a half days, or three at the outside. All experience has shown that drowned bodies, or bodies thrown into the water immediately after death by violence, require from six to ten days for decomposition to take place to bring them to the top of the water. Even where a cannon is fired over a corpse and it rises before at least five or six days' immersion, it sinks again, if let alone.* Now, we ask, what was there in this case to cause a departure from the ordinary course of nature? [...] If the body had been kept in its mangled state on shore until Tuesday night, some trace would be found on shore of the murderers. It is a doubtful point, also, whether the body would be so soon afloat even were it thrown in after having been dead two days. And, furthermore, it is exceedingly improbable that any villains who had committed such a murder as is here supposed would have thrown the body in without weight to sink it, when such a precaution could have so easily been taken.

The editor here proceeds to argue that the body must have been in the water "not three days merely, but at least five times three days", because it was so far decomposed that Beauvais had great difficulty in recognizing it. This latter point, however, was fully disproved. I continue the translation.

> What, then, are the facts on which M. Beauvais says that he has no doubt the body was that of Marie Rogêt? He ripped up the gown sleeve, and says he found marks which satisfied him of the identity. The public generally supposed those marks to have consisted of some description of scars. He rubbed the arm and found *hair* upon it,

> something as indefinite, we think, as can readily be imagined – as little conclusive as finding an arm in the sleeve. M. Beauvais did not return that night, but sent word to Madame Rogêt, at seven o'clock on Wednesday evening, that an investigation was still in progress respecting her daughter. If we allow that Madame Rogêt, from her age and grief, could not go over (which is allowing a great deal), there certainly must have been someone who would have thought it worthwhile to go over and attend the investigation, if they thought the body was that of Marie. Nobody went over. There was nothing said or heard about the matter in the Rue Pavée-Saint-Andrée that reached even the occupants of the same building. M. Saint-Eustache, the lover and intended husband of Marie, who boarded in her mother's house, deposes that he did not hear of the discovery of the body of his intended until the next morning, when M. Beauvais came into his chamber and told him of it. For an item of news like this, it strikes us it was very coolly received.

In this way the journal endeavoured to create the impression of an apathy on the part of the relatives of Marie inconsistent with the supposition that these relatives believed the corpse to be hers. Its insinuations amount to this: that Marie, with the connivance of her friends, had absented herself from the city for reasons involving a charge against her chastity; and that these friends, upon the discovery of a corpse in the Seine somewhat resembling that of the girl, had availed themselves of the opportunity to impress the public with the belief of her death. But *L'Étoile* was again overhasty. It was distinctly proved that no apathy such as was imagined existed; that the old lady was exceedingly feeble, and so agitated as to be unable to attend to any duty; that Saint-Eustache, so far from receiving the news coolly, was distracted with grief, and bore himself so frantically that M. Beauvais prevailed upon a friend and relative to take charge of him and prevent his attending the examination at the disinterment. Moreover, although it was stated by *L'Étoile* that the corpse was reinterred at the public expense, that an advantageous offer of private sepulture was absolutely declined by the family and that no member of the family attended the ceremonial – although, I say, all this was asserted by *L'Étoile* in furtherance of the impression it designed to convey, yet *all* this was satisfactorily disproved. In a subsequent number of the paper,* an attempt was made to throw suspicion upon Beauvais himself. The editor says:

> Now, then, a change comes over the matter. We are told that on one occasion, while a Madame B—— was at Madame Rogêt's house, M. Beauvais, who was going out, told her that a gendarme was expected there, and she, Madame B——, must not say anything to the gendarme until he returned, but let the matter be for him. [...] In the present posture of affairs, M. Beauvais appears to have the whole matter locked up in his head. A single step cannot be taken without M. Beauvais, for, go which way you will, you run against him. [...] For some reason, he determined that nobody shall have anything to do with the proceedings but himself, and he has elbowed the male relatives out of the way, according to their representations, in a very singular manner. He seems to have been very much averse to permitting the relatives to see the body.

By the following fact, some colour was given to the suspicion thus thrown upon Beauvais. A visitor at his office, a few days prior to the girl's disappearance, and during the absence of its occupant, had observed a *rose* in the keyhole of the door, and the name "Marie" inscribed upon a slate which hung near at hand.

The general impression, so far as we were enabled to glean it from the newspapers, seemed to be that Marie had been the victim of a gang of desperadoes – that by these she had been borne across the river, maltreated and murdered. *Le Commerciel*,* however, a print of extensive influence, was earnest in combating this popular idea. I quote a passage or two from its columns:

> We are persuaded that pursuit has hitherto been on a false scent, so far as it has been directed to the Barrière du Roule. It is impossible that a person so well known to thousands as this young woman was should have passed three blocks without someone having seen her – and anyone who saw her would have remembered it, for she interested all who knew her. It was when the streets were full of people that* she went out. [...] It is impossible that she could have gone to the Barrière du Roule or to the Rue des Drômes without being recognized by a dozen persons – yet no one has come forward who saw her outside of her mother's door, and there is no evidence, except the testimony concerning her *expressed intentions*, that she did go out at all. Her gown was torn, bound round her and tied – and by that the body was carried as a bundle. If the murder had been committed at the Barrière du Roule, there would have been no necessity for any such arrangement. The fact that the body was found

> floating near the Barrière is no proof as to where it was thrown into the water. [...] A piece of one of the unfortunate girl's petticoats, two feet long and one foot wide, was torn out and tied under her chin around the back of her head, probably to prevent screams. This was done by fellows who had no pocket handkerchiefs.*

A day or two before the prefect called upon us, however, some important information reached the police, which seemed to overthrow, at least, the chief portion of *Le Commerciel*'s argument. Two small boys, sons of a Madame Deluc,* while roaming among the woods near the Barrière du Roule, chanced to penetrate a close thicket, within which were three or four large stones forming a kind of seat with a back and footstool. On the upper stone lay a white petticoat; on the second, a silk scarf. A parasol, gloves and a pocket handkerchief were also here found. The handkerchief bore the name "Marie Rogêt". Fragments of dress were discovered on the brambles around. The earth was trampled, the bushes were broken, and there was every evidence of a struggle. Between the thicket and the river, the fences were found taken down, and the ground bore evidence of some heavy burden having been dragged along it.

A weekly paper, *Le Soleil*,* had the following comments upon this discovery – comments which merely echoed the sentiment of the whole Parisian press.

> The things had all evidently been there at least three or four weeks; they were all mildewed down hard with the action of the rain, and stuck together from mildew. The grass had grown around and over some of them. The silk on the parasol was strong, but the threads of it were run together within. The upper part, where it had been doubled and folded, was all mildewed and rotten, and tore on its being opened. [...] The pieces of her frock torn out by the bushes were about three inches wide and six inches long. One part was the hem of the frock, and it had been mended – the other piece was part of the skirt, not the hem. They looked like strips torn off, and were on the thorn bush, about a foot from the ground. [...] There can be no doubt, therefore, that the spot of this appalling outrage has been discovered.

Consequent upon this discovery, new evidence appeared. Madame Deluc testified that she keeps a roadside inn not far from the bank of the river, opposite the Barrière du Roule.* The neighbourhood is secluded

– particularly so. It is the usual Sunday resort of blackguards from the city, who cross the river in boats. About three o'clock in the afternoon of the Sunday in question, a young girl arrived at the inn, accompanied by a young man of dark complexion. The two remained here for some time. On their departure, they took the road to some thick woods in the vicinity. Madame Deluc's attention was called to the dress worn by the girl, on account of its resemblance to one worn by a deceased relative. A scarf was particularly noticed. Soon after the departure of the couple, a gang of miscreants made their appearance, behaved boisterously, ate and drank without making payment, followed in the route of the young man and girl, returned to the inn about dusk and recrossed the river as if in great haste.

It was soon after dark, upon this same evening, that Madame Deluc, as well as her eldest son, heard the screams of a female in the vicinity of the inn. The screams were violent but brief. Madame D. recognized not only the scarf which was found in the thicket, but the dress which was discovered upon the corpse. An omnibus driver, Valence,* now also testified that he saw Marie Rogêt cross a ferry on the Seine, on the Sunday in question, in company with a young man of dark complexion. He, Valence, knew Marie, and could not be mistaken in her identity. The articles found in the thicket were fully identified by the relatives of Marie.

The items of evidence and information thus collected by myself from the newspapers, at the suggestion of Dupin, embraced only one more point – but this was a point of seemingly vast consequence. It appears that, immediately after the discovery of the clothes as above described, the lifeless or nearly lifeless body of Saint-Eustache, Marie's betrothed, was found in the vicinity of what all now supposed the scene of the outrage. A phial labelled "laudanum", and emptied, was found near him. His breath gave evidence of the poison. He died without speaking. Upon his person was found a letter, briefly stating his love for Marie, with his design of self-destruction.

"I need scarcely tell you," said Dupin, as he finished the perusal of my notes, "that this is a far more intricate case than that of the Rue Morgue – from which it differs in one important respect. This is an *ordinary*, although an atrocious, instance of crime. There is nothing peculiarly *outré* about it. You will observe that, for this reason, the mystery has been considered easy, when, for this reason, it should have been considered difficult of solution. Thus, at first, it was thought unnecessary to offer a reward. The myrmidons of G——— were able at once to comprehend how and why such an atrocity *might have been* committed. They could picture to their imaginations a mode (many modes) and a motive (many motives) – and because it was not impossible that either of these numerous modes and motives *could* have been the actual one, they have taken it for granted that one of them *must*. But the ease with which these variable fancies were entertained, and the very plausibility which each assumed, should have been understood as indicative rather of the difficulties than of the facilities which must attend elucidation. I have before observed that it is by prominences above the plane of the ordinary that reason feels her way, if at all, in her search for the true, and that the proper question in cases such as this is not so much 'What has occurred?' as 'What has occurred that has never occurred before?' In the investigations at the house of Madame L'Espanaye,* the agents of G——— were discouraged and confounded by that very *unusualness* which, to a properly regulated intellect, would have afforded the surest omen of success, while this same intellect might have been plunged in despair at the ordinary character of all that met the eye in the case of the perfumery girl, and yet told of nothing but easy triumph to the functionaries of the prefecture.

"In the case of Madame L'Espanaye and her daughter, there was, even at the beginning of our investigation, no doubt that murder had been committed. The idea of suicide was excluded at once. Here, too, we are freed, at the commencement, from all supposition of self-murder. The body found at the Barrière du Roule was found under such circumstances as to leave us no room for embarrassment upon this important point. But it has been suggested that the corpse discovered is not that of the Marie Rogêt for the conviction of whose assassin, or assassins, the reward is offered, and respecting whom, solely, our agreement has been arranged with the prefect. We both know this gentleman well. It will not do to trust him too far. If, dating our enquiries from the body found, and thence tracing a murderer, we yet discover this body to be that of some other individual than Marie – or if, starting from the living Marie, we find her, yet find her unassassinated – in either case we lose our labour, since it is Monsieur G——— with whom we have to deal. For our own purpose, therefore, if not for the purpose of justice, it is indispensable that our first step should be the determination of the identity of the corpse with the Marie Rogêt who is missing.

"With the public the arguments of *L'Étoile* have had weight – and that the journal itself is convinced of their importance would appear from the manner in which it commences one of its essays upon the subject. 'Several of the morning papers of the day,' it says, 'speak of the *conclusive* article in Monday's *Étoile*.' To me, this article appears conclusive of little beyond the zeal of its inditer. We should bear in mind that, in general, it is the object of our newspapers rather to create a sensation – to make a point – than to further the cause of truth. The latter end is only pursued when it seems coincident with the former. The print which merely falls in with ordinary opinion (however well founded this opinion may be) earns for itself no credit with the mob. The mass of the people regard as profound only him who suggests *pungent contradictions* of the general idea. In ratiocination, not less than in literature, it is the *epigram* which is the most immediately and the most universally appreciated. In both, it is of the lowest order of merit.

"What I mean to say is that it is the mingled epigram and melodrame of the idea that Marie Rogêt still lives, rather than any true plausibility in this idea, which have suggested it to *L'Étoile* and secured it a favourable reception with the public. Let us examine the heads of this journal's argument, endeavouring to avoid the incoherence with which it is originally set forth.

"The first aim of the writer is to show, from the brevity of the interval between Marie's disappearance and the finding of the floating corpse, that this corpse cannot be that of Marie. The reduction of this interval to its smallest possible dimension becomes thus, at once, an object with the reasoner. In the rash pursuit of this object, he rushes into mere assumption at the outset. 'It is folly to suppose,' he says, 'that the murder, if murder was committed on her body, could have been consummated soon enough to have enabled her murderers to throw the body into the river before midnight.' We demand at once, and very naturally, *why*? Why is it folly to suppose that the murder was committed *within five minutes* after the girl's quitting her mother's house? Why is it folly to suppose that the murder was committed at any given period of the day? There have been assassinations at all hours. But, had the murder taken place at any moment between nine o'clock in the morning of Sunday and a quarter before midnight, there would still have been time enough 'to throw the body into the river before midnight'. This assumption, then, amounts precisely to this: that the murder was not committed on Sunday at all – and, if we allow *L'Étoile* to assume this, we may permit it any liberties whatever. The paragraph beginning 'It is folly to suppose that the murder, etc.' – however it appears as printed in *L'Étoile* – may be imagined to have existed actually *thus* in the brain of its inditer: 'It is folly to suppose that the murder, if murder was committed on the body, could have been committed soon enough to have enabled her murderers to throw the body into the river before midnight – it is folly, we say, to suppose all this, and to suppose at the same time (as we are resolved to suppose) that the body was *not* thrown in until *after* midnight' – a sentence sufficiently inconsequential in itself, but not so utterly preposterous as the one printed."

"Were it my purpose," continued Dupin, "merely to *make out a case* against this passage of *L'Étoile*'s argument, I might safely leave it where it is. It is not, however, with *L'Étoile* that we have to do, but with the truth. The sentence in question has but one meaning, as it stands, and this meaning I have fairly stated – but it is material that we go behind the mere words for an idea which these words have obviously intended and failed to convey. It was the design of the journalist to say that, at whatever period of the day or night of Sunday this murder was committed, it was improbable that the assassins would have ventured to bear the corpse to the river before midnight. And herein lies, really, the assumption of which I complain. It is assumed that the murder was committed at such a position, and under such circumstances, that *the bearing it* to the river became necessary. Now, the assassination might have taken place upon the river's brink or on the river itself – and, thus, the throwing the corpse in the water might have been resorted to at any period of the day or night as the most obvious and most immediate mode of disposal. You will understand that I suggest nothing here as probable, or as coincident with my own opinion. My design, so far, has no reference to the facts of the case. I wish merely to caution you against the whole tone of *L'Étoile*'s *suggestion* by calling your attention to its *ex parte** character at the outset.

"Having prescribed thus a limit to suit its own preconceived notions, having assumed that, if this were the body of Marie, it could have been in the water but a very brief time, the journal goes on to say:

> All experience has shown that drowned bodies, or bodies thrown into the water immediately after death by violence, require from six to ten days for sufficient decomposition to take place to bring them to the top of the water. Even when a cannon is fired over a corpse and it rises before at least five or six days' immersion, it sinks again if let alone.

"These assertions have been tacitly received by every paper in Paris, with the exception of *Le Moniteur*.* This latter print endeavours to combat that portion of the paragraph which has reference to 'drowned bodies' only, by citing some five or six instances in which the bodies of individuals known to be drowned were found floating after the lapse of less time than is insisted upon by *L'Étoile*. But there is something excessively unphilosophical in the attempt on the part of *Le Moniteur* to rebut the general assertion of *L'Étoile* by a citation of particular instances militating against that assertion. Had it been possible to adduce fifty instead of five examples of bodies found floating at the end of two or three days, these fifty examples could still have been properly regarded only as exceptions to *L'Étoile*'s rule until such time as the rule itself should be confuted. Admitting the rule (and this *Le Moniteur* does not deny, insisting merely upon its exceptions), the argument of *L'Étoile* is suffered to remain in full force, for this argument does not pretend to involve more than a question of the *probability* of the body having risen to the surface in less than three days – and this probability will be in favour of *L'Étoile*'s position until the instances so childishly adduced shall be sufficient in number to establish an antagonistical rule.

"You will see at once that all argument upon this head should be urged, if at all, against the rule itself – and for this end we must examine the *rationale* of the rule. Now, the human body, in general, is neither much lighter nor much heavier than the water of the Seine – that is to say, the specific gravity of the human body, in its natural condition, is about equal to the bulk of fresh water which it displaces. The bodies of fat and fleshy persons with small bones, and of women generally, are lighter than those of the lean and large-boned, and of men – and the specific gravity of the water of a river is somewhat influenced by the presence of the tide from sea. But, leaving this tide out of question, it may be said that *very* few human bodies will sink at all, even in fresh water, *of their own accord*. Almost anyone, falling into a river, will be enabled to float if he suffer the specific gravity of the water fairly to be adduced in comparison with his own – that is to say, if he suffer his whole person to be immersed with as little exception as possible. The proper position for one who cannot swim is the upright position of the walker on land, with the head thrown fully back and immersed, the mouth and nostrils alone remaining above the surface. Thus circumstanced, we shall find that we float without difficulty and without exertion. It is evident, however, that the gravities of the body and of the bulk of water displaced are very nicely balanced, and that a trifle will cause either to preponderate. An arm, for instance, uplifted from the water, and thus deprived of its support, is an additional weight sufficient to immerse the whole head, while the accidental aid of the smallest piece of timber will enable us to elevate the head so as to look about. Now, in the struggles of one unused to swimming, the arms are invariably thrown upwards, while an attempt is made to keep the head in its usual perpendicular position. The result is the immersion of the mouth and nostrils, and the inception, during efforts to breathe while beneath the surface, of water into the lungs. Much is also received into the stomach, and the whole body becomes heavier by the difference between the weight of the air originally distending these cavities and that of the fluid which now fills them. This difference is sufficient to cause the body to sink, as a general rule, but is insufficient in the cases of individuals with small bones and an abnormal quantity of flaccid or fatty matter. Such individuals float even after drowning.

"The corpse, being supposed at the bottom of the river, will there remain until, by some means, its specific gravity again becomes less than that of the bulk of water which it displaces. This effect is brought about by decomposition or otherwise. The result of decomposition is the generation of gas distending the cellular tissues and all the cavities, and giving the *puffed* appearance which is so horrible. When this distension has so far progressed that the bulk of the corpse is materially increased without a corresponding increase of *mass* or weight, its specific gravity becomes less than that of the water displaced, and it forthwith makes its appearance at the surface. But decomposition is modified by innumerable circumstances, is hastened or retarded by innumerable agencies – for example, by the heat or cold of the season, by the mineral impregnation or purity of the water, by its depth or shallowness, by its currency or stagnation, by the temperament of the body, by its infection or freedom from disease before death. Thus it is evident that we can assign no period, with anything like accuracy, at which the corpse shall rise through decomposition. Under certain conditions this result would be brought about within an hour – under others, it might not take place at all. There are chemical infusions by which the animal frame can be preserved *for ever* from corruption – the bichloride of mercury is one. But, apart from decomposition, there may be, and very usually is, a generation of gas within the stomach from the acetous fermentation of vegetable matter (or within other cavities from other causes) sufficient to induce a distension which will bring the body to the surface. The effect produced by the firing of a cannon is that of simple vibration. This may either loosen the corpse from the soft mud or ooze in which it is imbedded, thus permitting it to rise when other agencies have already prepared it for so doing, or it may overcome the tenacity of some putrescent portions of the cellular tissue, allowing the cavities to distend under the influence of the gas.

"Having thus before us the whole philosophy of this subject, we can easily test by it the assertions of *L'Étoile*. 'All experience shows,' says this paper, 'that drowned bodies, or bodies thrown into the water immediately after death by violence, require from six to ten days for sufficient decomposition to take place to bring them to the top of the water. Even when a cannon is fired over a corpse and it rises before at least five or six days' immersion, it sinks again if let alone.'

"The whole of this paragraph must now appear a tissue of inconsequence and incoherence. All experience does *not* show that 'drowned bodies' *require* from six to ten days for sufficient decomposition to take place to bring them to the surface. Both science and experience show that the period of their rising is, and necessarily must be, indeterminate. If, moreover, a body has risen to the surface through firing of cannon, it will *not* 'sink again if let alone' until decomposition has so far progressed as to permit the escape of the generated gas. But I wish to call your attention to the distinction which is made between 'drowned bodies' and 'bodies thrown into the water immediately after death by violence'. Although the writer admits the distinction, he yet includes them all in the same category. I have shown how it is that the body of a drowning man becomes specifically heavier than its bulk of water, and that he would not sink at all except for the struggles by which he elevates his arms above the surface and his gasps for breath while beneath the surface – gasps which supply by water the place of the original air in the lungs. But these struggles and these gasps would not occur in the body 'thrown into the water immediately after death by violence'. Thus, in the latter instance, *the body, as a general rule, would not sink at all* – a fact of which *L'Étoile* is evidently ignorant. When decomposition had proceeded to a very great extent – when the flesh had in a great measure left the bones – then, indeed, but not *till* then, should we lose sight of the corpse.

"And now what are we to make of the argument that the body found could not be that of Marie Rogêt because, three days only having elapsed, this body was found floating? If drowned, being a woman, she might never have sunk – or, having sunk, might have reappeared in twenty-four hours or less. But no one supposes her to have been drowned – and, dying before being thrown into the river, she might have been found floating at any period afterwards whatever.

"'But,' says *L'Étoile*, 'if the body had been kept in its mangled state on shore until Tuesday night, some trace would be found on shore of the murderers.' Here it is at first difficult to perceive the intention of the reasoner. He means to anticipate what he imagines would be an objection to his theory, viz. that the body was kept on shore two days, suffering rapid decomposition – *more* rapid than if immersed in water. He supposes that, had this been the case, it *might* have appeared at the surface on the Wednesday, and thinks that *only* under such circumstances it could so have appeared. He is, accordingly, in haste to show that it *was not* kept on shore – for, if so, 'some trace would be found on shore of the murderers'. I presume you smile at the *sequitur*.* You cannot be made to see how the mere *duration* of the corpse on the shore could operate to *multiply traces* of the assassins. Nor can I.

"'And, furthermore, it is exceedingly improbable,' continues our journal, 'that any villains who had committed such a murder as is here supposed would have thrown the body in without weight to sink it, when such a precaution could have so easily been taken.' Observe, here, the laughable confusion of thought! No one – not even *L'Étoile* – disputes the murder committed *on the body found*. The marks of violence are too obvious. It is our reasoner's object merely to show that this body is not Marie's. He wishes to prove that *Marie* is not assassinated – not that the corpse was not. Yet his observation proves only the latter point. Here is a corpse without weight attached. Murderers, casting it in, would not have failed to attach a weight. Therefore it was not thrown in by murderers. This is all which is proved, if anything is. The question of identity is not even approached, and *L'Étoile* has been at great pains merely to gainsay now what it has admitted only a moment before. 'We are perfectly convinced,' it says, 'that the body found was that of a murdered female.'

"Nor is this the sole instance, even in this division of his subject, where our reasoner unwittingly reasons against himself. His evident object, I have already said, is to reduce, as much as possible, the interval between Marie's disappearance and the finding of the corpse. Yet we find him *urging* the point that no person saw the girl from the moment of her leaving her mother's house. 'We have no evidence,' he says, 'that Marie Rogêt was in the land of the living after nine o'clock on Sunday, June 22nd.' As his argument is obviously an *ex parte* one, he should, at least, have left this matter out of sight, for had anyone been known to see Marie, say on Monday or on Tuesday, the interval in question would have been much reduced, and, by his own ratiocination, the probability much diminished of the corpse being that of the grisette. It is nevertheless amusing to observe that *L'Étoile* insists upon its point in the full belief of its furthering its general argument.

"Reperuse now that portion of this argument which has reference to the identification of the corpse by Beauvais. In regard to the *hair* upon the arm, *L'Étoile* has been obviously disingenuous. M. Beauvais, not being an idiot, could never have urged, in identification of the corpse, simply *hair upon its arm*. No arm is *without* hair. The *generality* of the expression of *L'Étoile* is a mere perversion of the witness's phraseology. He must have spoken of some *peculiarity* in this hair. It must have been a peculiarity of colour, of quantity, of length or of situation.

"'Her foot,' says the journal, 'was small – so are thousands of feet. Her garter is no proof whatever – nor is her shoe, for shoes and garters are sold in packages. The same may be said of the flowers in her hat. One thing upon which M. Beauvais strongly insists is that the clasp on the garter found had been set back to take it in. This amounts to nothing, for most women find it proper to take a pair of garters home and fit them to the size of the limbs they are to encircle rather than to try them in the store where they purchase.' Here it is difficult to suppose the reasoner in earnest. Had M. Beauvais, in his search for the body of Marie, discovered a corpse corresponding in general size and appearance to the missing girl, he would have been warranted (without reference to the question of habiliment at all) in forming an opinion that his search had been successful. If, in addition to the point of general size and contour, he had found upon the arm a peculiar hairy appearance which he had observed upon the living Marie, his opinion might have been justly strengthened – and the increase of positiveness might well have been in the ratio of the peculiarity, or unusualness, of the hairy mark. If, the feet of Marie being small, those of the corpse were also small, the increase of probability that the body was that of Marie would not be an increase in a ratio merely arithmetical, but in one highly geometrical, or accumulative. Add to all this shoes such as she had been known to wear upon the day of her disappearance, and, although these shoes may be 'sold in packages', you so far augment the probability as to verge upon the certain. What of itself would be no evidence of identity becomes, through its corroborative position, proof most sure. Give us, then, flowers in the hat corresponding to those worn by the missing girl, and we seek for nothing further. If only *one* flower, we seek for nothing further – what then if two or three, or more? Each successive one is multiple evidence – proof not *added* to proof, but *multiplied* by hundreds or thousands. Let us now discover, upon the deceased, garters such as the living used, and it is almost folly to proceed. But these garters are found to be tightened, by the setting back of a clasp, in just such a manner as her own had been tightened by Marie shortly previous to her leaving home. It is now madness or hypocrisy to doubt. What *L'Étoile* says in respect to this abbreviation of the garter's being an usual occurrence shows nothing beyond its own pertinacity in error. The elastic nature of the clasp-garter is self-demonstration of the *unusualness* of the abbreviation. What is made to adjust itself must of necessity require foreign adjustment but rarely. It must have been by an accident, in its strictest sense, that these garters of Marie needed the tightening described. They alone would have amply established her identity. But it is not that the corpse was found to have the garters of the missing girl, or found to have her shoes, or her bonnet, or the flowers of her bonnet, or her feet, or a peculiar mark upon the arm, or her general size and appearance – it is that the corpse had each, and *all collectively*. Could it be proved that the editor of *L'Étoile* really entertained a doubt, under the circumstances, there would be no need, in his case, of a commission *de lunatico inquirendo*.* He has thought it sagacious to echo the small talk of the lawyers, who, for the most part, content themselves with echoing the rectangular* precepts of the courts. I would here observe that very much of what is rejected as evidence by a court is the best of evidence to the intellect. For the court, guiding itself by the general principles of evidence – the recognized and *booked** principles – is averse from swerving at particular instances. And this steadfast adherence to principle, with rigorous disregard of the conflicting exception, is a sure mode of attaining the *maximum* of attainable truth in any long sequence of time. The practice, *in mass*, is therefore philosophical – but it is not the less certain that it engenders vast individual error.*

"In respect to the insinuations levelled at Beauvais, you will be willing to dismiss them in a breath. You have already fathomed the true character of this good gentleman. He is a *busybody*, with much of romance and little of wit. Anyone so constituted will readily so conduct himself, upon occasion of *real* excitement, as to render himself liable to suspicion on the part of the over-acute or the ill-disposed. M. Beauvais (as it appears from your notes) had some personal interviews with the editor of *L'Étoile*, and offended him by venturing an opinion that the corpse, notwithstanding the theory of the editor, was, in sober fact, that of Marie. 'He persists,' says the paper, 'in asserting the corpse to be that of Marie, but cannot give a circumstance, in addition to those which we have commented upon, to make others believe.' Now, without readverting to the fact that stronger evidence 'to make others believe' could *never* have been adduced, it may be remarked that a man may very well be understood to believe, in a case of this kind, without the ability to advance a single reason for the belief of a second party. Nothing is more vague than impressions of individual identity. Each man recognizes his neighbour, yet there are few instances in which anyone is prepared to *give a reason* for his recognition. The editor of *L'Étoile* had no right to be offended at Mr Beauvais's unreasoning belief.

"The suspicious circumstances which invest him will be found to tally much better with my hypothesis of *romantic busybodyism* than with the reasoner's suggestion of guilt. Once adopting the more charitable interpretation, we shall find no difficulty in comprehending the rose in the keyhole; the 'Marie' upon the slate, the 'elbowing the male relatives out of the way', the 'aversion to permitting them to see the body', the caution given to Madame B—— that she must hold no conversation with the gendarme until his return (Beauvais's) – and, lastly, his apparent determination 'that nobody should have anything to do with the proceedings except himself'. It seems to me unquestionable that Beauvais was a suitor of Marie's, that she coquetted with him, and that he was ambitious of being thought to enjoy her fullest intimacy and confidence. I shall say nothing more upon this point – and, as the evidence fully rebuts the assertion of *L'Étoile* touching the matter of *apathy* on the part of the mother and other relatives – an apathy inconsistent with the supposition of their believing the corpse to be that of the perfumery girl – we shall now proceed as if the question of *identity* were settled to our perfect satisfaction."

"And what," I here demanded, "do you think of the opinions of *Le Commerciel*?"

"That, in spirit, they are far more worthy of attention than any which have been promulgated upon the subject. The deductions from the premises are philosophical and acute – but the premises, in two instances at least, are founded in imperfect observation. *Le Commerciel* wishes to intimate that Marie was seized by some gang of low ruffians not far from her mother's door. 'It is impossible,' it urges, 'that a person so well known to thousands as this young woman was should have passed three blocks without someone having seen her.' This is the idea of a man long resident in Paris – a public man – and one whose walks to and fro in the city have been mostly limited to the vicinity of the public offices. He is aware that he seldom passes so far as a dozen blocks from his own bureau without being recognized and accosted. And, knowing the extent of his personal acquaintance with others and of others with him, he compares his notoriety with that of the perfumery girl, finds no great difference between them and reaches at once the conclusion that she, in her walks, would be equally liable to recognition with himself in his. This could only be the case were her walks of the same unvarying methodical character and within the same *species* of limited region as are his own. He passes to and fro, at regular intervals, within a confined periphery abounding in individuals who are led to observation of his person through interest in the kindred nature of his occupation with their own. But the walks of Marie may, in general, be supposed discursive.* In this particular instance, it will be understood as most probable that she proceeded upon a route of more than average diversity from her accustomed ones. The parallel which we imagine to have existed in the mind of *Le Commerciel* would only be sustained in the event of the two individuals traversing the whole city. In this case, granting the personal acquaintances to be equal, the chances would be also equal that an equal number of personal rencounters would be made. For my own part, I should hold it not only as possible, but as very far more than probable, that Marie might have proceeded, at any given period, by any one of the many routes between her own residence and that of her aunt without meeting a single individual whom she knew or by whom she was known. In viewing this question in its full and proper light, we must hold steadily in mind the great disproportion between the personal acquaintances of even the most noted individual in Paris and the entire population of Paris itself.

"But whatever force there may still appear to be in the suggestion of *Le Commerciel* will be much diminished when we take into consideration *the hour* at which the girl went abroad. 'It was when the streets were full of people,' says *Le Commerciel*, 'that she went out.' But not so. It was at nine o'clock in the morning. Now, at nine o'clock of every morning in the week, *with the exception of Sunday*, the streets of the city are, it is true, thronged with people. At nine on Sunday, the populace are chiefly within doors *preparing for church*. No observing person can have failed to notice the peculiarly deserted air of the town from about eight until ten on the morning of every Sabbath. Between ten and eleven the streets are thronged, but not at so early a period as that designated.

"There is another point at which there seems a deficiency of *observation* on the part of *Le Commerciel*. 'A piece,' it says, 'of one of the unfortunate girl's petticoats, two feet long and one foot wide, was torn out and tied under her chin, and around the back of her head, probably to prevent screams. This was done by fellows who had no pocket handkerchiefs.' Whether this idea is or is not well founded we will endeavour to see hereafter, but by 'fellows who have no pocket handkerchiefs' the editor intends the lowest class of ruffians. These, however, are the very description of people who will always be found to have handkerchiefs even when destitute of shirts. You must have had occasion to observe how absolutely indispensable, of late years, to the thorough blackguard has become the pocket handkerchief."

"And what are we to think," I asked, "of the article in *Le Soleil*?"

"That it is a vast* pity its inditer was not born a parrot – in which case he would have been the most illustrious parrot of his race. He has merely repeated the individual items of the already published opinion, collecting them, with a laudable industry, from this paper and from that. 'The things had all evidently been there,' he says, 'at least three or four weeks, and there can be *no doubt* that the spot of this appalling outrage has been discovered.' The facts here restated by *Le Soleil* are very far indeed from removing my own doubts upon this subject, and we will examine them more particularly hereafter in connection with another division of the theme.

"At present we must occupy ourselves with other investigations. You cannot fail to have remarked the extreme laxity of the examination of the corpse. To be sure, the question of identity was readily determined, or should have been – but there were other points to be ascertained. Had the body been in any respect *despoiled*? Had the deceased any articles of jewellery about her person upon leaving home? If so, had she any when found? These are important questions utterly untouched by the evidence – and there are others of equal moment which have met with no attention. We must endeavour to satisfy ourselves by personal enquiry. The case of Saint-Eustache must be re-examined. I have no suspicion of this person, but let us proceed methodically. We will ascertain beyond a doubt the validity of the affidavits in regard to his whereabouts on the Sunday. Affidavits of this character are readily made matter of mystification. Should there be nothing wrong here, however, we will dismiss Saint-Eustache from our investigations. His suicide, however corroborative of suspicion, were there found to be deceit in the affidavits, is, without such deceit, in no respect an unaccountable circumstance, or one which need cause us to deflect from the line of ordinary analysis.

"In that which I now propose, we will discard the interior points of this tragedy, and concentrate our attention upon its outskirts. Not the least usual error, in investigations such as this, is the limiting of enquiry to the immediate, with total disregard of the collateral or circumstantial events. It is the malpractice of the courts to confine evidence and discussion to the bounds of apparent relevancy. Yet experience has shown, and a true philosophy will always show, that a vast, perhaps the larger portion of truth arises from the seemingly irrelevant. It is through the spirit of this principle, if not precisely through its letter, that modern science has resolved to *calculate upon the unforeseen*. But perhaps you do not comprehend me. The history of human knowledge has so uninterruptedly shown that to collateral or incidental or accidental events we are indebted for the most numerous and most valuable discoveries that it has at length become necessary, in any prospective view of improvement, to make not only large, but the largest allowances for inventions that shall arise by chance, and quite out of the range of ordinary expectation. It is no longer philosophical to base upon what has been a vision of what is to be. *Accident* is admitted as a portion of the substructure. We make chance a matter of absolute calculation. We subject the unlooked-for and unimagined to the mathematical formulae of the schools.

"I repeat that it is no more than fact that the *larger* portion of all truth has sprung from the collateral – and it is but in accordance with the spirit of the principle involved in this fact that I would divert enquiry, in the present case, from the trodden and hitherto unfruitful ground of the event itself to the cotemporary* circumstances which surround it. While you ascertain the validity of the affidavits, I will examine the newspapers more generally than you have as yet done. So far, we have only reconnoitred the field of investigation, but it will be strange indeed if a comprehensive survey such as I propose of the public prints will not afford us some minute points which shall establish a *direction* for enquiry."

In pursuance of Dupin's suggestion, I made scrupulous examination of the affair of the affidavits. The result was a firm conviction of their validity, and of the consequent innocence of Saint-Eustache. In the mean time, my friend occupied himself, with what seemed to me a minuteness altogether objectless, in a scrutiny of the various newspaper files. At the end of a week, he placed before me the following extracts.

> About three years and a half ago, a disturbance very similar to the present was caused by the disappearance of this same Marie Rogêt from the *parfumerie* of Monsieur Le Blanc in the Palais Royal. At the end of a week, however, she reappeared at her customary *comptoir*,* as well as ever, with the exception of a slight paleness not altogether usual. It was given out by Monsieur Le Blanc and her mother that she had merely been on a visit to some friend in the country – and the affair was speedily hushed up. We presume that the present absence is a freak of the same

nature, and that, at the expiration of a week, or perhaps of a month, we shall have her among us again. – *Evening Paper*, Monday, June 23*

An evening journal of yesterday refers to a former mysterious disappearance of Mademoiselle Rogêt. It is well known that, during the week of her absence from Le Blanc's *parfumerie*, she was in the company of a young naval officer, much noted for his debaucheries. A quarrel, it is supposed, providentially led to her return home. We have the name of the Lothario in question, who is at present stationed in Paris, but for obvious reasons forbear to make it public. – *Le Mercurie*, Tuesday Morning, June 24*

An outrage of the most atrocious character was perpetrated near this city the day before yesterday. A gentleman, with his wife and daughter, engaged, about dusk, the services of six young men, who were idly rowing a boat to and fro near the banks of the Seine, to convey him across the river. Upon reaching the opposite shore, the three passengers stepped out, and had proceeded so far as to be beyond the view of the boat when the daughter discovered that she had left in it her parasol. She returned for it, was seized by the gang, carried out into the stream, gagged, brutally treated and finally taken to the shore at a point not far from that at which she had originally entered the boat with her parents. The villains have escaped for the time, but the police are upon their trail, and some of them will soon be taken. – *Morning Paper*, June 25*

We have received one or two communications, the object of which is to fasten the crime of the late atrocity upon Mennais* – but as this gentleman has been fully exonerated by a legal inquiry, and as the arguments of our several correspondents appear to be more zealous than profound, we do not think it advisable to make them public. – *Morning Paper*, June 28*

We have received several forcibly written communications, apparently from various sources, and which go far to render it a matter of certainty, that the unfortunate Marie Rogêt has become a victim of one of the numerous bands of blackguards which infest the vicinity of the city upon Sunday. Our own opinion is decidedly in favour of this supposition. We shall endeavour to make room for some of these arguments hereafter. – *Evening Paper*, Tuesday, June 30*

> On Monday, one of the bargemen connected with the revenue service saw an empty boat floating down the Seine. Sails were lying in the bottom of the boat. The bargeman towed it under the barge office. The next morning it was taken from thence without the knowledge of any of the officers. The rudder is now at the barge office. – *Le Diligence*, Thursday, June 26*

Upon reading these various extracts, they not only seemed to me irrelevant, but I could perceive no mode in which any one of them could be brought to bear upon the matter in hand. I waited for some explanation from Dupin.

"It is not my present design," he said, "to *dwell* upon the first and second of these extracts. I have copied them chiefly to show you the extreme remissness of the police, who, as far as I can understand from the prefect, have not troubled themselves in any respect with an examination of the naval officer alluded to. Yet it is mere folly to say that between the first and second disappearance of Marie there is no *supposable* connection. Let us admit the first elopement to have resulted in a quarrel between the lovers and the return home of the betrayed. We are now prepared to view a second *elopement* (if we know that an elopement has again taken place) as indicating a renewal of the betrayer's advances rather than as the result of new proposals by a second individual – we are prepared to regard it as a "making-up" of the old *amour* rather than as the commencement of a new one. The chances are ten to one that he who had once eloped with Marie would again propose an elopement, rather than that she to whom proposals of elopement had been made by one individual should have them made to her by another. And here let me call your attention to the fact that the time elapsing between the first ascertained and the second supposed elopement is a few months more than the general period of the cruises of our men-of-war. Had the lover been interrupted in his first villainy by the necessity of departure to sea, and had he seized the first moment of his return to renew the base designs not yet altogether accomplished – or not yet altogether accomplished by *him*? Of all these things we know nothing.

"You will say, however, that in the second instance there was no elopement as imagined. Certainly not – but are we prepared to say that there was not the frustrated design? Beyond Saint-Eustache, and perhaps Beauvais, we find no recognized, no open, no honourable suitors of Marie. Of none other is there anything said. Who, then, is the secret lover of whom the relatives (*at least most of them*) know nothing, but whom Marie meets upon the morning of Sunday, and who is so deeply in her confidence that she hesitates not to remain with him until the shades of the evening descend amid the solitary groves of the Barrière du Roule? Who is that secret lover, I ask, of whom, at least, *most* of the relatives know nothing? And what means the singular prophecy of Madame Rogêt on the morning of Marie's departure – 'I fear that I shall never see Marie again'?

"But if we cannot imagine Madame Rogêt privy to the design of elopement, may we not at least suppose this design entertained by the girl? Upon quitting home, she gave it to be understood that she was about to visit her aunt in the Rue des Drômes, and Saint-Eustache was requested to call for her at dark. Now, at first glance, this fact strongly militates against my suggestion – but let us reflect. That she *did* meet some companion and proceed with him across the river, reaching the Barrière du Roule at so late an hour as three o'clock in the afternoon, is known. But in consenting so to accompany this individual (*for whatever purpose – to her mother known or unknown*), she must have thought of her expressed intention when leaving home, and of the surprise and suspicion aroused in the bosom of her affianced suitor, Saint-Eustache, when, calling for her at the hour appointed in the Rue des Drômes, he should find that she had not been there – and when, moreover, upon returning to the *pension* with this alarming intelligence, he should become aware of her continued absence from home. She must have thought of these things, I say. She must have foreseen the chagrin of Saint-Eustache, the suspicion of all. She could not have thought of returning to brave this suspicion – but the suspicion becomes a point of trivial importance to her, if we suppose her *not* intending to return.

"We may imagine her thinking thus: 'I am to meet a certain person for the purpose of elopement, or for certain other purposes known only to myself. It is necessary that there be no chance of interruption… there must be sufficient time given us to elude pursuit… I will give it to be understood that I shall visit and spend the day with my aunt at the Rue des Drômes… I will tell Saint-Eustache not to call for me until dark – in this way, my absence from home for the longest possible period without causing suspicion or anxiety will be accounted for, and I shall gain more time than in any other manner. If I bid Saint-Eustache call for me at dark, he will be sure not to call before – but if I wholly neglect to bid him call, my time for escape will be diminished, since it will be expected that I return the earlier, and my absence will the sooner excite anxiety. Now, if it were my design to return *at all*, if I had in contemplation merely a stroll with the individual in question, it would not be my policy to bid Saint-Eustache call – for, calling, he will be *sure* to ascertain that I have played him false, a fact of which I might keep him for ever in ignorance by leaving home without notifying him of my intention, by returning before dark and by then stating that I had been to visit my aunt in the Rue des Drômes. But, as it is my design *never* to return – or not for some weeks, or not until certain concealments are effected – the gaining of time is the only point about which I need give myself any concern.'

"You have observed, in your notes, that the most general opinion in relation to this sad affair is – and was from the first – that the girl had been the victim of *a gang* of blackguards. Now, the popular opinion, under certain conditions, is not to be disregarded. When arising of itself – when manifesting itself in a strictly spontaneous manner – we should look upon it as analogous with that *intuition* which is the idiosyncrasy of the individual man of genius. In ninety-nine cases from the hundred I would abide by its decision. But it is important that we find no palpable traces of *suggestion*. The opinion must be rigorously *the public's own* – and the distinction is often exceedingly difficult to perceive and to maintain. In the present instance, it appears to me that this 'public opinion' in respect to *a gang* has been superinduced by the collateral event which is detailed in the third of my extracts. All Paris is excited by the discovered corpse of Marie, a girl young, beautiful and notorious. This corpse is found bearing marks of violence and floating in the river. But it is now made known that at the very period, or about the very period, in which it is supposed that the girl was assassinated, an outrage similar in nature to that endured by the deceased, although less in extent, was perpetrated by a gang of young ruffians upon the person of a second young female. Is it wonderful that the one known atrocity should influence the popular judgement in regard to the other unknown? This judgement awaited direction, and the known outrage seemed so opportunely to afford it! Marie, too, was found in the river – and upon this very river was this known outrage committed. The connection of the two events had about it so much of the palpable that the true wonder would have been a *failure* of the populace to appreciate and to seize it. But, in fact, the one atrocity known to be so committed is, if anything, evidence that the other, committed at a time nearly coincident, was *not* so committed. It would have been a miracle indeed if, while a gang of ruffians were perpetrating at a given locality a most unheard-of wrong, there should have been another similar gang in a similar locality, in the same city, under the same circumstances, with the same means and appliances, engaged in a wrong of precisely the same aspect at precisely the same period of time! Yet in what, if not in this marvellous train of coincidence, does the accidentally *suggested* opinion of the populace call upon us to believe?

"Before proceeding further, let us consider the supposed scene of the assassination, in the thicket at the Barrière du Roule. This thicket, although dense, was in the close vicinity of a public road. Within were three or four large stones, forming a kind of seat with a back and footstool. On the upper stone was discovered a white petticoat – on the second, a silk scarf. A parasol, gloves and a pocket handkerchief were also here found. The handkerchief bore the name 'Marie Rogêt'. Fragments of dress were seen on the branches around. The earth was trampled, the bushes were broken, and there was every evidence of a violent struggle.

"Notwithstanding the acclamation with which the discovery of this thicket was received by the press and the unanimity with which it was supposed to indicate the precise scene of the outrage, it must be admitted that there was some very good reason for doubt. That it *was* the scene, I may or I may not believe – but there was excellent reason for doubt. Had the *true* scene been, as *Le Commerciel* suggested, in the neighbourhood of the Rue Pavée-Saint-Andrée, the perpetrators of the crime, supposing them still resident in Paris, would naturally have been stricken with terror at the public attention thus acutely directed into the proper channel – and, in certain classes of minds, there would have arisen at once a sense of the necessity of some exertion to redivert this attention. And thus, the thicket of the Barrière du Roule having been already suspected, the idea of placing the articles where they were found might have been naturally entertained. There is no real evidence, although *Le Soleil* so supposes, that the articles discovered had been more than a very few days in the thicket – while there is much circumstantial proof that they could not have remained there without attracting attention during the twenty days elapsing between the fatal Sunday and the afternoon upon which they were found by the boys. 'They were all *mildewed* down hard,' says *Le Soleil*, adopting the opinions of its predecessors, 'with the action of the rain and stuck together from *mildew*. The grass had grown around and over some of them. The silk of the parasol was strong, but the threads of it were run together within. The upper part, where it had been doubled and folded, was all *mildewed* and rotten, and tore on being opened.' In respect to the grass having 'grown around and over some of them', it is obvious that the fact could only have been ascertained from the words, and thus from the recollections, of two small boys – for these boys removed the articles and took them home before they had been seen by a third party. But grass will grow, especially in warm and damp weather (such as was that of the period of the murder), as much as two or three inches in a single day. A parasol lying upon a newly turfed ground might, in a single* week, be entirely concealed from sight by the upspringing grass. And touching that *mildew* upon which the editor of *Le Soleil* so pertinaciously insists that he employs the word no less than three times in the brief paragraph just quoted, is he really unaware of the nature of this *mildew*? Is he to be told that it is one of the many classes of *fungus* of which the most ordinary feature is its upspringing and decadence within twenty-four hours?

"Thus we see, at a glance, that what has been most triumphantly adduced in support of the idea that the articles had been 'for at least three or four weeks' in the thicket is most absurdly null as regards any evidence of that fact. On the other hand, it is exceedingly difficult to believe that these articles could have remained in the thicket specified for a longer period than a single week – for a longer period than from one Sunday to the next. Those who know anything of the vicinity of Paris know the extreme difficulty of finding *seclusion*, unless at a great distance from its suburbs. Such a thing as an unexplored or even an unfrequently visited recess amid its woods or groves is not for a moment to be imagined. Let anyone who, being at heart a lover of nature, is yet chained by duty to the dust and heat of this great metropolis – let any such one attempt, even during the week days, to slake his thirst for solitude amid the scenes of natural loveliness which immediately surround us. At every second step he will find the growing charm dispelled by the voice and personal intrusion of some ruffian or party of carousing blackguards. He will seek privacy amid the densest foliage all in vain. Here are the very nooks where the unwashed* most abound – here are the temples most desecrate. With sickness of the heart the wanderer will flee back to the polluted Paris as to a less odious because less incongruous sink of pollution. But if the vicinity of the city is so beset during the working days of the week, how much more so on the Sabbath! It is now especially that, released from the claims of labour or deprived of the customary opportunities of crime, the town blackguard seeks the precincts of the town not through love of the rural, which in his heart he despises, but by way of escape from the restraints and conventionalities of society. He desires less the fresh air and the green trees than the utter *licence* of the country. Here, at the roadside inn or beneath the foliage of the woods, he indulges, unchecked by any eye except those of his boon companions, in all the mad excess of a counterfeit hilarity – the joint offspring of liberty and of rum. I say nothing more than what must be obvious to every dispassionate observer when I repeat that the circumstance of the articles in question having remained undiscovered for a longer period than from one Sunday to another in *any* thicket in the immediate neighbourhood of Paris is to be looked upon as little less than miraculous.

"But there are not wanting other grounds for the suspicion that the articles were placed in the thicket with the view of diverting attention from the real scene of the outrage. And, first, let me direct your notice to the *date* of the discovery of the articles. Collate this with the date of the fifth extract made by myself from the newspapers. You will find that the discovery followed, almost immediately, the urgent communications sent to the evening paper. These communications, although various and apparently from various sources, tended all to the same point – viz. the directing of attention to *a gang* as the perpetrators of the outrage, and to the neighbourhood of the Barrière du Roule as its scene. Now, here, of course, the suspicion is not that, in consequence of these communications or of the public attention by them directed, the articles were found by the boys – but the suspicion might and may well have been that the articles were not *before* found by the boys, for the reason that the articles had not before been in the thicket, having been deposited there only at so late a period as at the date, or shortly prior to the date of the communications, by the guilty authors of these communications themselves.

"This thicket was a singular... an exceedingly singular one. It was unusually dense. Within its naturally walled enclosure were three extraordinary stones, *forming a seat with a back and footstool*. And this thicket, so full of a natural art, was in the immediate vicinity, *within a few rods*,* of the dwelling of Madame Deluc, whose boys were in the habit of closely examining the shrubberies about them in search of the bark of the sassafras.* Would it be a rash wager – a wager of one thousand to one – that *a day* never passed over the heads of these boys without finding at least one of them ensconced in the umbrageous hall and enthroned upon its natural throne? Those who would hesitate at such a wager have either never been boys themselves or have forgotten the boyish nature. I repeat – it is exceedingly hard to comprehend how the articles could have remained in this thicket undiscovered for a longer period than one or two days – and that thus there is good ground for suspicion, in spite of the dogmatic ignorance of *Le Soleil*, that they were at a comparatively late date deposited where found.

"But there are still other and stronger reasons for believing them so deposited than any which I have as yet urged. And now let me beg your notice to the highly artificial arrangement of the articles. On the *upper* stone lay a white petticoat – on the *second*, a silk scarf; scattered around were a parasol, gloves and a pocket handkerchief bearing the name 'Marie Rogêt'. Here is just such an arrangement as would *naturally* be made by a not-over-acute person wishing to dispose the articles *naturally*. But it is by no means a *really* natural arrangement. I should rather have looked to see the things *all* lying on the ground and trampled underfoot. In the narrow limits of that bower, it would have been scarcely possible that the petticoat and scarf should have retained a position upon the stones when subjected to the brushing to and fro of many struggling persons. 'There was evidence,' it is said, 'of a struggle – and the earth was trampled, the bushes were broken' – but the petticoat and the scarf are found deposited as if upon shelves. 'The pieces of the frock torn out by the bushes were about three inches wide and six inches long. One part was the hem of the frock, and it had been mended. They *looked like strips torn off*.' Here, inadvertently, *Le Soleil* has employed an exceedingly suspicious phrase. The pieces, as described, do indeed 'look like strips torn off' – but purposely and by hand. It is one of the rarest of accidents that a piece is 'torn off' from any garment such as is now in question by the agency *of a thorn*. From the very nature of such fabrics, a thorn or nail becoming entangled in them tears them rectangularly – divides them into two longitudinal rents at right angles with each other and meeting at an apex where the thorn enters – but it is scarcely possible to conceive the piece 'torn off'. I never so knew it, nor did you. To tear a piece *off* from such fabric, two distinct forces, in different directions, will be in almost every case required. If there be two edges to the fabric – if, for example, it be a pocket handkerchief, and it is desired to tear from it a slip – then and then only will the one force serve the purpose. But in the present case the question is of a dress presenting but one edge. To tear a piece from the interior where no edge is presented could only be effected by a miracle through the agency of thorns, and no *one* thorn could accomplish it. But, even where an edge is presented, two thorns will be necessary, operating the one in two distinct directions and the other in one. And this in the supposition that the edge is unhemmed. If hemmed, the matter is nearly out of the question. We thus see the numerous and great obstacles in the way of pieces being 'torn off' through the simple agency of 'thorns' – yet we are required to believe not only that one piece, but that many have been so torn. 'And one part,' too, '*was the hem of the frock*'! Another piece was '*part of the skirt, not the hem*' – that is to say, was torn completely out, through the agency of thorns, from the unedged interior of the dress! These, I say, are things which one may well be pardoned for disbelieving – yet, taken collectedly,* they form perhaps less of reasonable ground for suspicion than the one startling circumstance of the articles having been left in this thicket at all by any *murderers* who had enough precaution to think of removing the corpse. You will not have apprehended me rightly, however, if you suppose it my design to *deny* this thicket as the scene of the outrage. There might have been a wrong *here* – or, more possibly, an accident at Madame Deluc's. But in fact this is a point of minor importance. We are not engaged in an attempt to discover the scene, but to produce the perpetrators of the murder. What I have adduced, notwithstanding the minuteness with which I have adduced it, has been with the view first to show the folly of the positive and headlong assertions of *Le Soleil*, but secondly and chiefly to bring you, by the most natural route, to a further contemplation of the doubt whether this assassination has or has not been the work of *a gang*.

"We will resume this question by mere allusion to the revolting details of the surgeon examined at the inquest. It is only necessary to say that his published *inferences*, in regard to the number of ruffians, have been properly ridiculed as unjust and totally baseless by all the reputable anatomists of Paris. Not that the matter *might* not have been as inferred, but that there was no ground for the inference – was there not much for another?

"Let us reflect now upon 'the traces of a struggle' – and let me ask what these traces have been supposed to demonstrate. A gang. But do they not rather demonstrate the absence of a gang? What *struggle* could have taken place – what struggle so violent and so enduring as to have left its 'traces', in all directions, between a weak and defenceless girl and the *gang* of ruffians imagined? The silent grasp of a few rough arms and all would have been over. The victim must have been absolutely passive at their will. You will here bear in mind that the arguments urged against the thicket as the scene are applicable, in chief part, only against it as the scene of an outrage committed by *more than a single individual*. If we imagine but *one* violator, we can conceive, and thus only conceive, the struggle of so violent and so obstinate a nature as to have left the 'traces' apparent.

"And again. I have already mentioned the suspicion to be excited by the fact that the articles in question were suffered to remain *at all* in the thicket where discovered. It seems almost impossible that these evidences of guilt should have been accidentally left where found. There was sufficient presence of mind (it is supposed) to remove the corpse – and yet a more positive evidence than the corpse itself (whose features might have been quickly obliterated by decay) is allowed to lie conspicuously in the scene of the outrage – I allude to the handkerchief with the *name* of the deceased. If this was accident, it was not the accident *of a gang*. We can imagine it only the accident of an individual. Let us see. An individual has committed the murder. He is alone with the ghost of the departed. He is appalled by what lies motionless before him. The fury of his passion is over, and there is abundant room in his heart for the natural awe of the deed. His is none of that confidence which the presence of numbers inevitably inspires. He is *alone* with the dead. He trembles and is bewildered. Yet there is a necessity for disposing of the corpse. He bears it to the river, but leaves behind him the other evidences of guilt – for it is difficult, if not impossible, to carry all the burden at once, and it will be easy to return for what is left. But in his toilsome journey to the water his fears redouble within him. The sounds of life encompass his path. A dozen times he hears or fancies the step of an observer. Even the very lights from the city bewilder him. Yet, in time, and by long and frequent pauses of deep agony, he reaches the river's brink and disposes of his ghastly charge – perhaps through the medium of a boat. But *now* what treasure does the world hold – what threat of vengeance could it hold out – which would have power to urge the return of that lonely murderer over that toilsome and perilous path to the thicket and its blood-chilling recollections? He returns *not*, let the consequences be what they may. He *could* not return if he would. His sole thought is immediate escape. He turns his back *for ever* upon those dreadful shrubberies and flees as from the wrath to come.

"But how with a gang? Their number would have inspired them with confidence – if, indeed, confidence is ever wanting in the breast of the arrant blackguard (and of arrant blackguards alone are the supposed *gangs* ever constituted). Their number, I say, would have prevented the bewildering and unreasoning terror which I have imagined to paralyse the single man. Could we suppose an oversight in one or two or three, this oversight would have been remedied by a fourth. They would have left nothing behind them – for their number would have enabled them to carry *all* at once. There would have been no need of *return*.

"Consider now the circumstance that, in the outer garment of the corpse when found, 'a slip, about a foot wide, had been torn upward from the bottom hem to the waist, wound three times round the waist and secured by a sort of hitch in the back'. This was done with the obvious design of affording a *handle* by which to carry the body. But would any *number* of men have dreamt of resorting to such an expedient? To three or four, the limbs of the corpse would have afforded not only a sufficient but the best possible hold. The device is that of a single individual – and this brings us to the fact that 'between the thicket and the river the rails of the fences were found taken down, and the ground bore evident traces of some heavy burden having been dragged along it'! But would a *number* of men have put themselves to the superfluous trouble of taking down a fence for the purpose of dragging through it a corpse which they might have *lifted over* any fence in an instant? Would a *number* of men have so *dragged* a corpse at all as to have left evident *traces* of the dragging?

"And here we must refer to an observation of *Le Commerciel* – an observation upon which I have already, in some measure, commented. 'A piece,' says this journal, 'of one of the unfortunate girl's petticoats was torn out and tied under her chin, and around the back of her head, probably to prevent screams. This was done by fellows who had no pocket handkerchiefs.'

"I have before suggested that a genuine blackguard is never *without* a pocket handkerchief. But it is not to this fact that I now especially advert. That it was not through want of a handkerchief for the purpose imagined by *Le Commerciel* that this bandage was employed is rendered apparent by the handkerchief left in the thicket – and that the object was not 'to prevent screams' appears, also, from the bandage having been employed in preference to what would so much better have answered the purpose. But the language of the evidence speaks of the strip in question as 'found around the neck, fitting loosely, and secured with a hard knot'. These words are sufficiently vague, but differ materially from those of *Le Commerciel*. The slip was eighteen inches wide, and therefore, although of muslin, would form a strong band when folded or rumpled longitudinally. And thus rumpled it was discovered. My inference is this. The solitary murderer, having borne the corpse for some distance (whether from the thicket or elsewhere) by means of the bandage *hitched* around its middle, found the weight, in this mode of procedure, too much for his strength. He resolved to drag the burden – the evidence goes to show that it *was* dragged. With this object in view, it became necessary to attach something like a rope to one of the extremities. It could be best attached about the neck, where the head would prevent its slipping off. And now the murderer bethought him, unquestionably, of the bandage about the loins. He would have used this but for its volution about the corpse, the *hitch* which embarrassed it and the reflection that it had not been 'torn off' from the garment. It was easier to tear a new slip from the petticoat. He tore it, made it fast about the neck and so *dragged* his victim to the brink of the river. That this 'bandage', only attainable with trouble and delay, and but imperfectly answering its purpose – that this bandage was employed *at all* demonstrates that the necessity for its employment sprang from circumstances arising at a period when the handkerchief was no longer attainable, that is to say, arising, as we have imagined, after quitting the thicket (if the thicket it was), and on the road between the thicket and the river.

"But the evidence, you will say, of Madame Deluc (!) points especially to the presence of *a gang* in the vicinity of the thicket, at or about the epoch of the murder. This I grant. I doubt if there were not a *dozen* gangs such as described by Madame Deluc in and about the vicinity of the Barrière du Roule at *or about* the period of this tragedy. But the gang which has drawn upon itself the pointed animadversion (although the somewhat tardy and very suspicious evidence) of Madame Deluc is the *only* gang which is represented by that honest and scrupulous old lady as having eaten her cakes and swallowed her brandy without putting themselves to the trouble of making her payment. *Et hinc illæ iræ?**

"But what is the precise evidence of Madame Deluc? 'A gang of miscreants made their appearance, behaved boisterously, ate and drank without making payment, followed in the route of the young man and girl, returned to the inn *about dusk* and recrossed the river as if in great haste.'

"Now this 'great haste' very possibly seemed *greater* haste in the eyes of Madame Deluc, since she dwelt lingeringly and lamentingly upon her violated cakes and ale – cakes and ale for which she might still have entertained a faint hope of compensation. Why, otherwise, since it was *about dusk*, should she make a point of the *haste*? It is no cause for wonder, surely, that even a gang of blackguards should make *haste* to get home when a wide river is to be crossed in small boats, when storm impends and when night *approaches*.

"I say 'approaches', for the night had *not yet* arrived. It was only *about dusk* that the indecent haste of these 'miscreants' offended the sober eyes of Madame Deluc. But we are told that it was upon this very evening that Madame Deluc, as well as her eldest son, 'heard the screams of a female in the vicinity of the inn'. And in what words does Madame Deluc designate the period of the evening at which these screams were heard? 'It was *soon after dark*,' she says. But '*soon after dark*' is at least *dark* – and 'about dusk' is as certainly daylight. Thus it is abundantly clear that the gang quitted the Barrière du Roule *prior* to the screams overheard (?) by Madame Deluc. And although, in all the many reports of the evidence, the relative expressions in question are distinctly and invariably employed just as I have employed them in this conversation with yourself, no notice whatever of the gross discrepancy has as yet been taken by any of the public journals or by any of the myrmidons of police.

"I shall add but one to the arguments against *a gang* – but this *one* has, to my own understanding at least, a weight altogether irresistible. Under the circumstances of large reward offered, and full pardon to any King's evidence,* it is not to be imagined for a moment that some member of *a gang* of low ruffians, or of any body of men, would not long ago have betrayed his accomplices. Each one of a gang, so placed, is not so much greedy of reward, or anxious for escape, as *fearful of betrayal*. He betrays eagerly and early that *he may not himself be betrayed*. That the secret has not been divulged is the very best of proof that it is, in fact, a secret. The horrors of this dark deed are known only to *one* or two living human beings, and to God.

"Let us sum up now the meagre yet certain fruits of our long analysis. We have attained the idea either of a fatal accident under the roof of Madame Deluc or of a murder perpetrated in the thicket at the Barrière du Roule by a lover or at least by an intimate and secret associate of the deceased. This associate is of swarthy complexion. This complexion, the 'hitch' in the bandage and the 'sailor's knot' with which the bonnet ribbon is tied point to a seaman. His companionship with the deceased – a gay but not an abject young girl – designates him as above the grade of the common sailor. Here the well-written and urgent communications to the journals are much in the way of corroboration. The circumstance of the first elopement, as mentioned by *Le Mercurie*, tends to blend the idea of this seaman with that of the 'naval officer' who is first known to have led the unfortunate into crime.

"And here, most fitly, comes the consideration of the continued absence of him of the dark complexion. Let me pause to observe that the complexion of this man is dark and swarthy – it was no common swarthiness which constituted the *sole* point of remembrance, both as regards Valence and Madame Deluc. But why is this man absent? Was he murdered by the gang? If so, why are there only *traces* of the assassinated *girl*? The scene of the two outrages will naturally be supposed identical. And where is his corpse? The assassins would most probably have disposed of both in the same way. But it may be said that this man lives, and is deterred from making himself known through dread of being charged with the murder. This consideration might be supposed to operate upon him now – at this late period – since it has been given in evidence that he was seen with Marie, but it would have had no force at the period of the deed. The first impulse of an innocent man would have been to announce the outrage and to aid in identifying the ruffians. This, *policy* would have suggested. He had been seen with the girl. He had crossed the river with her in an open ferry boat. The denouncing of the assassins would have appeared, even to an idiot, the surest and sole means of relieving himself from suspicion. We cannot suppose him, on the night of the fatal Sunday, both innocent himself and incognizant of an outrage committed. Yet only under such circumstances is it possible to imagine that he would have failed, if alive, in the denouncement of the assassins.

"And what means are ours of attaining the truth? We shall find these means multiplying and gathering distinctness as we proceed. Let us sift to the bottom this affair of the first elopement. Let us know the full history of 'the officer', with his present circumstances and his whereabouts at the precise period of the murder. Let us carefully compare with each other the various communications sent to the evening paper, in which the object was to inculpate *a gang*. This done, let us compare these communications, both as regards style and MS,* with those sent to the morning paper at a previous period, and insisting so vehemently upon the guilt of Mennais. And, all this done, let us again compare these various communications with the known MSS of the officer. Let us endeavour to ascertain, by repeated questionings of Madame Deluc and her boys, as well as of the omnibus driver, Valence, something more of the personal appearance and bearing of the 'man of dark complexion'. Queries, skilfully directed, will not fail to elicit, from some of these parties, information on this particular point (or upon others) – information which the parties themselves may not even be aware of possessing. And let us now trace the *boat* picked up by the bargeman on the morning of Monday 23rd June, and which was removed from the barge office, without the cognizance of the officer in attendance and *without the rudder*, at some period prior to the discovery of the corpse. With a proper caution and perseverance we shall infallibly trace this boat – for not only can the bargeman who picked it up identify it, but the *rudder is at hand*. The rudder of a sailboat would not have been abandoned, without enquiry, by one altogether at ease in heart. And here let me pause to insinuate a question. There was no *advertisement* of the picking-up of this boat. It was silently taken to the barge office and as silently removed. But its owner or employer, how *happened* he, at so early a period as Tuesday morning, to be informed, without the agency of advertisement, of the locality of the boat taken up on Monday, unless we imagine some connection with the *navy* – some personal permanent connection leading to cognizance of its minute interests, its petty local news?

"In speaking of the lonely assassin dragging his burden to the shore, I have already suggested the probability of his availing himself *of a boat*. Now, we are to understand that Marie Rogêt *was* precipitated from a boat. This would naturally have been the case. The corpse could not have been trusted to the shallow waters of the shore. The peculiar marks on the back and shoulders of the victim tell of the bottom ribs of a boat. That the body was found without weight is also corroborative of the idea. If thrown from the shore, a weight would have been attached. We can only account for its absence by supposing the murderer to have neglected the precaution of supplying himself with it before pushing off. In the act of consigning the corpse to the water, he would unquestionably have noticed his oversight, but then no remedy would have been at hand. Any risk would have been preferred to a return to that accursed shore. Having rid himself of his ghastly charge, the murderer would have hastened to the city. There, at some obscure wharf, he would have leapt on land. But the boat – would he have secured it? He would have been in too great haste for such things as securing a boat. Moreover, in fastening it to the wharf, he would have felt as if securing evidence against himself. His natural thought would have been to cast from him, as far as possible, all that had held connection with his crime. He would not only have fled from the wharf, but he would not have permitted *the boat* to remain. Assuredly, he would have cast it adrift. Let us pursue our fancies. In the morning, the wretch is stricken with unutterable horror at finding that the boat has been picked up and detained at a locality which he is in the daily habit of frequenting – at a locality, perhaps, which his duty compels him to frequent. The next night, *without daring to ask for the rudder*, he removes it. Now, *where* is that rudderless boat? Let it be one of our first purposes to discover. With the first glimpse we obtain of it, the dawn of our success shall begin. This boat shall guide us, with a rapidity which will surprise even ourselves, to him who employed it in the midnight of the fatal Sabbath. Corroboration will rise upon corroboration, and the murderer will be traced."

[For reasons which we shall not specify, but which to many readers will appear obvious, we have taken the liberty of here omitting from the MSS placed in our hands such portion as details the *following up* of the apparently slight clue obtained by Dupin. We feel it advisable only to state, in brief, that the result desired was brought to pass, and that the prefect fulfilled punctually, although with reluctance, the terms of his compact with the Chevalier. Mr Poe's article concludes with the following words. – Eds.]*

It will be understood that I speak of coincidences *and no more*. What I have said above upon this topic must suffice. In my own heart there dwells no faith in preternature. That Nature and its God are two, no man who thinks will deny. That the latter, creating the former, can at will control or modify it, is also unquestionable. I say "at will", for the question is of will and not, as the insanity of logic has assumed, of power. It is not that the Deity *cannot* modify his laws, but that we insult him in imagining a possible necessity for modification. In their origin, these laws were fashioned to embrace *all* contingencies which *could* lie in the future. With God all is *now*.

I repeat, then, that I speak of these things only as of coincidences. And further: in what I relate it will be seen that between the fate of the unhappy Mary Cecilia Rogers, so far as that fate is known, and the fate of one Marie Rogêt up to a certain epoch in her history, there has existed a parallel in the contemplation of whose wonderful exactitude the reason becomes embarrassed. I say all this will be seen. But let it not for a moment be supposed that, in proceeding with the sad narrative of Marie from the epoch just mentioned, and in tracing to its denouement the mystery which enshrouded her, it is my covert design to hint at an extension of the parallel, or even to suggest that the measures adopted in Paris for the discovery of the assassin of a grisette, or measures founded in any similar ratiocination, would produce any similar result.

For, in respect to the latter branch of the supposition, it should be considered that the most trifling variation in the facts of the two cases might give rise to the most important miscalculations, by diverting thoroughly the two courses of events – very much as, in arithmetic, an error which in its own individuality may be inappreciable produces at length, by dint of multiplication at all points of the process, a result enormously at variance with truth. And in regard to the former branch, we must not fail to hold in view that the very calculus of probabilities to which I have referred forbids all idea of the extension of the parallel – forbids it with a positiveness strong and decided just in proportion as this parallel has already been long-drawn and exact. This is one of those anomalous propositions which, seemingly appealing to thought altogether apart from the mathematical, is yet one which only the mathematician can fully entertain. Nothing, for example, is more difficult than to convince the merely general reader that the fact of sixes having been thrown twice in succession by a player at dice is sufficient cause for betting the largest odds that sixes will not be thrown in the third attempt. A suggestion to this effect is usually rejected by the intellect at once. It does not appear that the two throws which have been completed, and which lie now absolutely in the past, can have influence upon the throw which exists only in the future. The chance for throwing sixes seems to be precisely as it was at any ordinary time – that is to say, subject only to the influence of the various other throws which may be made by the dice. And this is a reflection which appears so exceedingly obvious that attempts to controvert it are received more frequently with a derisive smile than with anything like respectful attention. The error here involved – a gross error redolent of mischief – I cannot pretend to expose within the limits assigned me at present, and with the philosophical it needs no exposure. It may be sufficient here to say that it forms one of an infinite series of mistakes which arise in the path of reason through her propensity for seeking truth *in detail.*

THE ISLAND OF THE FAY*

Nullus enim locus sine genio est.*
– Servius

"*La musique*," says Marmontel, in those *Contes moraux* which, in all our translations, we have insisted upon calling *Moral Tales*, as if in mockery of their spirit,* "*la musique est le seul des talents qui jouissent de lui même – tous les autres veulent des témoins.*"* He here confounds the pleasure derivable from sweet sounds with the capacity for creating them. No more than any other *talent* is that for music susceptible of complete enjoyment where there is no second party to appreciate its exercise. And it is only in common with other talents that it produces *effects* which may be fully enjoyed in solitude. The idea which the raconteur has either failed to entertain clearly or has sacrificed in its expression to his national love of *point* is, doubtless, the very tenable one that the higher order of music is the most thoroughly estimated when we are exclusively alone. The proposition, in this form, will be admitted at once by those who love the lyre for its own sake and for its spiritual uses. But there is one pleasure still within the reach of fallen mortality – and perhaps only one – which owes even more than does music to the accessory sentiment of seclusion. I mean the happiness experienced in the contemplation of natural scenery. In truth, the man who would behold aright the glory of God upon earth must in solitude behold that glory. To me, at least, the presence not of human life only, but of life in any other form than that of the green things which grow upon the soil and are voiceless, is a stain upon the landscape – is at war with the genius of the scene. I love, indeed, to regard the dark valleys and the grey rocks, and the waters that silently smile, and the forests that sigh in uneasy slumbers, and the proud watchful mountains that look down upon all – I love to regard these as themselves but the colossal members of one vast animate and sentient whole... a whole whose form (that of the sphere) is the most perfect and most inclusive of all, whose path is among associate planets, whose meek handmaiden is the moon, whose mediate sovereign is the sun, whose life is eternity, whose thought is that of a God, whose enjoyment is knowledge, whose destinies are lost in immensity, whose cognizance of ourselves is akin with our own cognizance of the *animalculæ** which infest the brain – a being which we, in consequence, regard as purely inanimate and material much in the same manner as these *animalculæ* must thus regard us.

Our telescopes and our mathematical investigations assure us on every hand – notwithstanding the cant of the more ignorant of the priesthood – that space, and therefore that bulk, is an important consideration in the eyes of the Almighty. The cycles in which the stars move are those best adapted for the evolution, without collision, of the greatest possible number of bodies. The forms of those bodies are accurately such as, within a given surface, to include the greatest possible amount of matter – while the surfaces themselves are so disposed as to accommodate a denser population than could be accommodated on the same surfaces otherwise arranged. Nor is it any argument against bulk being an object with God that space itself is infinite, for there may be an infinity of matter to fill it. And since we see clearly that the endowment of matter with vitality is a principle – indeed, as far as our judgements extend, the *leading* principle in the operations of Deity – it is scarcely logical to imagine it confined to the regions of the minute, where we daily trace it, and not extending to those of the august. As we find cycle within cycle without end, yet all revolving around one far-distant centre which is the Godhead, may we not analogically suppose, in the same manner, life within life, the less within the greater, and all within the Spirit Divine? In short, we are madly erring, through self-esteem, in believing man, in either his temporal or future destinies, to be of more moment in the universe than that vast "clod of the valley"* which he tills and contemns, and to which he denies a soul for no more profound reason than that he does not behold it in operation.*

These fancies, and such as these, have always given to my meditations among the mountains and the forests, by the rivers and the ocean, a tinge of what the everyday world would not fail to term "fantastic". My wanderings amid such scenes have been many, and far-searching, and often solitary – and the interest with which I have strayed through many a dim deep valley or gazed into the reflected heaven of many a bright lake has been an interest greatly deepened by the thought that I have strayed and gazed *alone*. What flippant Frenchman was it who said, in allusion to the well-known work of Zimmerman, that "*la solitude est une belle chose – mais il faut quelqu'un pour vous dire que la solitude est une belle chose*"?* The epigram cannot be gainsaid, but the necessity is a thing that does not exist.

It was during one of my lonely journeyings, amid a far-distant region of mountain locked within mountain, and sad rivers and melancholy tarns* writhing or sleeping within all, that I chanced upon a certain rivulet and island. I came upon them suddenly in the leafy June, and threw myself upon the turf, beneath the branches of an unknown odorous shrub, that I might doze as I contemplated the scene. I felt that thus only should I look upon it, such was the character of phantasm which it wore.

On all sides – save to the west, where the sun was about sinking – arose the verdant walls of the forest. The little river which turned sharply in its course, and was thus immediately lost to sight, seemed to have no exit from its prison but to be absorbed by the deep-green foliage of the trees to the east – while in the opposite quarter (so it appeared to me as I lay at length and glanced upwards) there poured down noiselessly and continuously into the valley a rich golden and crimson waterfall from the sunset fountains of the sky.

About midway in the short vista which my dreamy vision took in, one small circular island, profusely verdured, reposed upon the bosom of the stream.

> So blended bank and shadow there
> That each seemed pendulous in air* –

so mirror-like was the glassy water that it was scarcely possible to say at what point upon the slope of the emerald turf its crystal dominion began.

My position enabled me to include in a single view both the eastern and western extremities of the islet – and I observed a singularly marked difference in their aspects. The latter was all one radiant harem of garden beauties. It glowed and blushed beneath the eye of the slant sunlight, and fairly laughed with flowers. The grass was short, springy, sweet-scented and asphodel-interspersed.* The trees were lithe, mirthful, erect – bright, slender and graceful – of eastern figure and foliage, with bark smooth, glossy and particoloured. There seemed a deep sense of life and joy about all – and although no airs blew from out the heavens, yet everything had motion through the gentle sweepings to and fro of innumerable butterflies, that might have been mistaken for tulips with wings.*

The other or eastern end of the isle was whelmed* in the blackest shade. A sombre yet beautiful and peaceful gloom here pervaded all things. The trees were dark in colour, and mournful in form and attitude, wreathing themselves into sad, solemn and spectral shapes that conveyed ideas of mortal sorrow and untimely death. The grass wore the deep tint of the cypress, and the heads of its blades hung droopingly, and hither and thither among it were many small unsightly hillocks, low and narrow, and not very long, that had the aspect of graves, but were not – although over and all about them the rue and the rosemary clambered. The shade of the trees fell heavily upon the water, and seemed to bury itself therein, impregnating the depths of the element with darkness. I fancied that each shadow, as the sun descended lower and lower, separated itself sullenly from the trunk that gave it birth, and thus became absorbed by the stream, while other shadows issued momently from the trees, taking the place of their predecessors thus entombed.

This idea, having once seized upon my fancy, greatly excited it, and I lost myself forthwith in reverie. "If ever island were enchanted," said I to myself, "this is it. This is the haunt of the few gentle fays who remain from the wreck of the race. Are these green tombs theirs – or do they yield up their sweet lives as mankind yield up their own? In dying, do they not rather waste away mournfully, rendering unto God, little by little, their existence, as these trees render up shadow after shadow, exhausting their substance unto dissolution? What the wasting tree is to the water that imbibes its shade, growing thus blacker by what it preys upon, may not the life of the fay be to the death which engulfs it?"

As I thus mused with half-shut eyes, while the sun sank rapidly to rest and eddying currents careered round and round the island, bearing upon their bosom large, dazzling white flakes of the bark of the sycamore – flakes which, in their multiform positions upon the water, a quick imagination might have converted into anything it pleased – while I thus mused, it appeared to me that the form of one of those very fays about whom I had been pondering made its way slowly into the darkness from out the light at the western end of the island. She stood erect in a singularly fragile canoe, and urged it with the mere phantom of an oar. While within the influence of the lingering sunbeams, her attitude seemed indicative of joy – but sorrow deformed it as she passed within the shade. Slowly she glided along, and at length rounded the islet and re-entered the region of light. "The revolution which has just been made by the fay," continued I musingly, "is the cycle of the brief year of her life. She has floated through her winter and through her summer. She is a year nearer unto death, for I did not fail to see that, as she came into the shade, her shadow fell from her, and was swallowed up in the dark water, making its blackness more black."

And again the boat appeared, and the fay – but about the attitude of the latter there was more of care and uncertainty, and less of elastic joy. She floated again from out the light and into the gloom (which deepened momently), and again her shadow fell from her into the ebony water, and became absorbed into its blackness. And again and again she made the circuit of the island (while the sun rushed down to his slumbers), and at each issuing into the light there was more sorrow about her person, while it grew feebler and far fainter and more indistinct – and at each passage into the gloom there fell from her a darker shade, which became whelmed in a shadow more black. But at length, when the sun had utterly departed, the fay, now the mere ghost of her former self, went disconsolately with her boat into the region of the ebony flood – and that she issued thence at all I cannot say, for darkness fell over all things, and I beheld her magical figure no more.

THE ASSIGNATION*

> Stay for me there! I will not fail
> To meet thee in that hollow vale.*
> (Exequy on the death of his wife,
> by Henry King, Bishop of Chichester)

Ill-fated and mysterious man – bewildered in the brilliancy of thine own imagination, and fallen in the flames of thine own youth! Again in fancy I behold thee! Once more thy form hath risen before me... not – oh! – not as thou art... in the cold valley and shadow... but as thou *shouldst be*... squandering away a life of magnificent meditation in that city of dim visions, thine own Venice – which is a star-beloved Elysium of the sea, and the wide windows of whose Palladian palaces look down with a deep and bitter meaning upon the secrets of her silent waters. Yes! I repeat it – as thou *shouldst be*. There are surely other worlds than this... other thoughts than the thoughts of the multitude... other speculations than the speculations of the sophist. Who then shall call thy conduct into question – who blame thee for thy visionary hours, or denounce those occupations as a wasting-away of life, which were but the overflowings of thine everlasting energies?

It was at Venice, beneath the covered archway there called the Ponte dei Sospiri, that I met for the third or fourth time the person of whom I speak. It is with a confused recollection that I bring to mind the circumstances of that meeting. Yet I remember – ah, how should I forget? – the deep midnight, the Bridge of Sighs, the beauty of woman and the Genius of Romance that stalked up and down the narrow canal.*

It was a night of unusual gloom. The great clock of the Piazza* had sounded the fifth hour of the Italian evening. The square of the Campanile lay silent and deserted, and the lights in the old Ducal Palace* were dying fast away. I was returning home from the Piazzetta,* by way of the Grand

Canal. But as my gondola arrived opposite the mouth of the Canal San Marco,* a female voice from its recesses broke suddenly upon the night in one wild, hysterical and long-continued shriek. Startled at the sound, I sprang upon my feet, while the gondolier, letting slip his single oar, lost it in the pitchy darkness beyond a chance of recovery, and we were consequently left to the guidance of the current which here sets from the greater into the smaller channel. Like some huge and sable-feathered condor, we were slowly drifting down towards the Bridge of Sighs, when a thousand flambeaux flashing from the windows and down the staircases of the Ducal Palace turned all at once that deep gloom into a livid and preternatural day.

A child, slipping from the arms of its own mother, had fallen from an upper window of the lofty structure into the deep and dim canal. The quiet waters had closed placidly over their victim – and, although my own gondola was the only one in sight, many a stout swimmer, already in the stream, was seeking in vain upon the surface the treasure which was to be found, alas, only within the abyss. Upon the broad black marble flagstones at the entrance of the palace, and a few steps above the water, stood a figure which none who then saw can have ever since forgotten. It was the Marchesa Aphrodite – the adoration of all Venice, the gayest of the gay, the most lovely where all were beautiful – but still the young wife of the old and intriguing* Mentoni, and the mother of that fair child, her first and only one, who now, deep beneath the murky water, was thinking in bitterness of heart upon her sweet caresses, and exhausting its little life in struggles to call upon her name.

She stood alone. Her small, bare and silvery feet gleamed in the black mirror of marble beneath her. Her hair, not as yet more than half loosened for the night from its ballroom array, clustered, amid a shower of diamonds, round and round her classical head in curls like those of the young hyacinth. A snowy-white and gauze-like drapery seemed to be nearly the sole covering to her delicate form – but the midsummer and midnight air was hot, sullen and still, and no motion in the statue-like form itself stirred even the folds of that raiment of very vapour which hung around it as the heavy marble hangs around the Niobe.* Yet – strange to say! – her large lustrous eyes were not turned downward upon that grave wherein her brightest hope lay buried, but riveted in a widely different direction! The Prison of the Old Republic* is, I think, the stateliest building in all Venice – but how could that lady gaze so fixedly upon it, when beneath her lay stifling her own child? Yon dark, gloomy niche, too, yawns right opposite her chamber window – what, then, *could* there be in its shadows, in its architecture, in its ivy-wreathed and solemn cornices, that the Marchesa di Mentoni had not wondered at a thousand times before? Nonsense!... Who does not remember that, at such a time as this, the eye, like a shattered mirror, multiplies the images of its sorrow, and sees in innumerable far-off places the woe which is close at hand?

Many steps above the marchesa, and within the arch of the watergate, stood in full dress the satyr-like figure of Mentoni himself. He was occasionally occupied in thrumming a guitar, and seemed *ennuyé** to the very death as at intervals he gave directions for the recovery of his child. Stupefied and aghast, I had myself no power to move from the upright position I had assumed upon first hearing the shriek, and must have presented to the eyes of the agitated group a spectral and ominous appearance as with pale countenance and rigid limbs I floated down among them in that funereal gondola.

All efforts proved in vain. Many of the most energetic in the search were relaxing their exertions and yielding to a gloomy sorrow. There seemed but little hope for the child (how much less than for the mother!) – but now, from the interior of that dark niche which has been already mentioned as forming a part of the Old Republican prison, and as fronting the lattice of the marchesa, a figure muffled in a cloak stepped out within reach of the light, and, pausing a moment upon the verge of the giddy descent, plunged headlong into the canal. As, in an instant afterwards, he stood with the still-living and breathing child within his grasp upon the marble flagstones by the side of the marchesa, his cloak, heavy with the drenching water, became unfastened, and, falling in folds about his feet, discovered to the wonder-stricken spectators the graceful person of a very young man with the sound of whose name the greater part of Europe was then ringing.

No word spoke the deliverer. But the marchesa! She will now receive her child... she will press it to her heart... she will cling to its little form and smother it with her caresses. Alas! *Another's* arms have taken it from the stranger – *another's* arms have taken it away and borne it afar off, unnoticed, into the palace! And the marchesa! Her lip... her beautiful lip trembles; tears are gathering in her eyes – those eyes which, like Pliny's acanthus, are "soft and almost liquid".* Yes! Tears are gathering in those eyes, and see – the entire woman thrills throughout the soul, and the statue has started into life! The pallor of the marble countenance, the swelling of the marble bosom, the very purity of the marble feet, we behold suddenly flushed over with a tide of ungovernable crimson – and a slight shudder quivers about her delicate frame, as a gentle air at Napoli about the rich silver lilies in the grass.

Why *should* that lady blush? To this demand there is no answer – except that, having left, in the eager haste and terror of a mother's heart, the privacy of her own boudoir, she has neglected to enthral her tiny feet in their slippers, and utterly forgotten to throw over her Venetian shoulders that drapery which is their due. What other possible reason could there have been for her so blushing? For the glance of those wild, appealing eyes? For the unusual tumult of that throbbing bosom? For the convulsive pressure of that trembling hand – that hand which fell, as Mentoni turned into the palace, accidentally upon the hand of the stranger? What reason could there have been for the low, the singularly low tone of those unmeaning words which the lady uttered hurriedly in bidding him adieu? "Thou hast conquered," she said, or the murmurs of the water deceived me. "Thou hast conquered... one hour after sunrise... we shall meet... so let it be!"

* * * * * * *

The tumult had subsided, the lights had died away within the palace, and the stranger, whom I now recognized, stood alone upon the flags. He shook with inconceivable agitation, and his eye glanced around in search of a gondola. I could not do less than offer him the service of my own, and he accepted the civility. Having obtained an oar at the watergate, we proceeded together to his residence, while he rapidly recovered his self-possession, and spoke of our former slight acquaintance in terms of great apparent cordiality.

There are some subjects upon which I take pleasure in being minute. The person of the stranger – let me call him by this title who to all the world was still a stranger – the person of the stranger is one of these subjects. In height he might have been below rather than above the medium size – although there were moments of intense passion when his frame actually *expanded* and belied the assertion. The light, almost slender symmetry of his figure promised more of that ready activity which he evinced at the Bridge of Sighs than of that Herculean strength which he has been known to wield without an effort upon occasions of more dangerous emergency. With the mouth and chin of a deity – singular, wild, full, liquid eyes, whose shadows varied from pure hazel to intense and brilliant jet – and a profusion of curling black hair, from which a forehead of unusual breadth gleamed forth at intervals all light and ivory – his were features than which I have seen none more classically regular, except perhaps the marble ones of the Emperor Commodus.* Yet his countenance was, nevertheless, one of those which all men have seen at some period of their lives and have never afterwards seen again. It had no peculiar, it had no settled predominant expression to be fastened upon the memory: a countenance seen and instantly forgotten – but forgotten with a vague and never-ceasing desire of recalling it to mind. Not that the spirit of each rapid passion failed, at any time, to throw its own distinct image upon the mirror of that face – but that the mirror, mirror-like, retained no vestige of the passion when the passion had departed.

Upon leaving him on the night of our adventure, he solicited me, in what I thought an urgent manner, to call upon him *very* early the next morning. Shortly after sunrise, I found myself accordingly at his palazzo, one of those huge structures of gloomy yet fantastic pomp which tower above the waters of the Grand Canal in the vicinity of the Rialto. I was shown up a broad winding staircase of mosaics into an apartment whose unparalleled splendour burst through the opening door with an actual glare, making me blind and dizzy with luxuriousness.

I knew my acquaintance to be wealthy. Report had spoken of his possessions in terms which I had even ventured to call terms of ridiculous exaggeration. But as I gazed about me, I could not bring myself to believe that the wealth of any subject in Europe could have supplied the princely magnificence which burned and blazed around.

Although, as I say, the sun had arisen, yet the room was still brilliantly lighted up. I judge from this circumstance, as well as from an air of exhaustion in the countenance of my friend, that he had not retired to bed during the whole of the preceding night. In the architecture and embellishments of the chamber, the evident design had been to dazzle and astound. Little attention had been paid to the *decora** of what is technically called *keeping,** or to the proprieties of nationality. The eye wandered from object to object, and rested upon none – neither the grotesques* of the Greek painters nor the sculptures of the best Italian days, nor the huge carvings of untutored Egypt. Rich draperies in every part of the room trembled to the vibration of low melancholy music, whose origin was not to be discovered. The senses were oppressed by mingled and conflicting perfumes, reeking up from strange, convolute censers, together with multitudinous flaring and flickering tongues of emerald and violet fire. The rays of the newly risen sun poured in upon the whole through windows, formed each of a single pane of crimson-tinted glass. Glancing to and fro in a thousand reflections from curtains which rolled from their cornices like cataracts of molten silver, the beams of natural glory mingled at length fitfully with the artificial light, and lay weltering in subdued masses upon a carpet of rich, liquid-looking cloth of Chile gold.*

"Ha ha ha!... Ha ha ha!" laughed the proprietor, motioning me to a seat as I entered the room, and throwing himself back at full length upon an ottoman. "I see," said he, perceiving that I could not immediately reconcile myself to the *bienséance** of so singular a welcome, "I see you are astonished at my apartment... at my statues... my pictures... my originality of conception in architecture and upholstery! Absolutely drunk, eh, with my magnificence? But pardon me, my dear sir," (here his tone of voice dropped to the very spirit of cordiality) "pardon me for my uncharitable laughter. You appeared so *utterly* astonished. Besides, some things are so completely ludicrous that a man *must* laugh or die. To die laughing must be the most glorious of all glorious deaths! Sir Thomas More – a very fine man was Sir Thomas More – Sir Thomas More died laughing, you remember.* Also in the *Absurdities* of Ravisius Textor, there is a long list of characters who came to the same magnificent end.* Do you know, however," continued he musingly, "that at Sparta (which is now Palæochori),* at Sparta, I say, to the west of the citadel, among a chaos of scarcely visible ruins, is a kind of *socle*, upon which are still legible the letters ΛΑΣΜ. They are undoubtedly part of ΓΕΛΑΣΜΑ. Now, at Sparta were a thousand temples and shrines to a thousand different divinities. How exceedingly strange that the altar of Laughter should have survived all the others!* But in the present instance," he resumed, with a singular alteration of voice and manner, "I have no right to be merry at your expense. You might well have been amazed. Europe cannot produce anything so fine as this, my little regal cabinet. My other apartments are by no means of the same order – mere *ultras** of fashionable insipidity. This is better than fashion – is it not? Yet this has but to be seen to become the rage – that is, with those who could afford it at the cost of their entire patrimony. I have guarded, however, against any such profanation. With one exception, you are the only human being, besides myself and my valet, who has been admitted within the mysteries of these imperial precincts since they have been bedizened* as you see!"

I bowed in acknowledgement – for the overpowering sense of splendour and perfume and music, together with the unexpected eccentricity of his address and manner, prevented me from expressing in words my appreciation of what I might have construed into a compliment.

"Here," he resumed, arising and leaning on my arm as he sauntered around the apartment, "here are paintings from the Greeks to Cimabue,* and from Cimabue to the present hour. Many are chosen, as you see, with little deference to the opinions of Virtù.* They are all, however, fitting tapestry for a chamber such as this. Here, too, are some *chefs-d'œuvre* of the unknown great – and here unfinished designs by men celebrated in their day whose very names the perspicacity of the academies has left to silence and to me. What think you," said he, turning abruptly as he spoke, "what think you of this *Madonna della Pietà*?"

"It is Guido's own!"* I said, with all the enthusiasm of my nature, for I had been poring intently over its surpassing loveliness. "It is Guido's own!… How *could* you have obtained it? She is undoubtedly in painting what the Venus is in sculpture."

"Ha!" said he thoughtfully. "The Venus?… The beautiful Venus?… The Venus of the Medici?… She of the diminutive head and the gilded hair?* Part of the left arm" – here his voice dropped so as to be heard with difficulty – "and all the right are restorations, and in the coquetry of that right arm lies, I think, the quintessence of all affectation. Give *me* the Canova!* The Apollo,* too, is a copy – there can be no doubt of it – blind fool that I am, who cannot behold the boasted inspiration of the Apollo! I cannot help – pity me! – I cannot help preferring the Antinous.* Was it not Socrates who said that the statuary found his statue in the block of marble?* Then Michelangelo was by no means original in his couplet

> *Non ha l'ottimo artista alcun concetto*
> *Ch'un marmo solo in sé non circonscriva."**

It has been (or should be remarked) that, in the manner of the true gentleman, we are always aware of a difference from the bearing of the vulgar without being at once precisely able to determine in what such difference consists. Allowing the remark to have applied in its full force to the outward demeanour of my acquaintance, I felt it, on that eventful morning, still more fully applicable to his moral temperament and character. Nor can I better define that peculiarity of spirit which seemed to place him so essentially apart from all other human beings than by calling it a *habit* of intense and continual thought pervading even his most trivial actions, intruding upon his moments of dalliance and interweaving itself with his very flashes of merriment – like adders which writhe from out the eyes of the grinning masks in the cornices around the temples of Persepolis.*

I could not help, however, repeatedly observing, through the mingled tone of levity and solemnity with which he rapidly descanted upon matters of little importance, a certain air of trepidation – a degree of nervous *unction* in action and in speech, an unquiet excitability of manner which appeared to me at all times unaccountable, and upon some occasions even filled me with alarm. Frequently, too, pausing in the middle of a sentence whose commencement he had apparently forgotten, he seemed to be listening in the deepest attention, as if either in momentary expectation of a visitor, or to sounds which must have had existence in his imagination alone.

It was during one of these reveries or pauses of apparent abstraction that, in turning over a page of the poet and scholar Politian's beautiful tragedy, *The Orfeo* (the first native Italian tragedy), which lay near me upon an ottoman, I discovered a passage underlined in pencil. It was a passage towards the end of the third act* – a passage of the most heart-stirring excitement, a passage which, although tainted with impurity, no man shall read without a thrill of novel emotion, no woman without a sigh. The whole page was blotted with fresh tears, and, upon the opposite interleaf, were the following English lines, written in a hand so very different from the peculiar characters of my acquaintance that I had some difficulty in recognizing it as his own:

Thou wast that all to me, love,
  For which my soul did pine,
A green isle in the sea, love,
  A fountain and a shrine,
All wreathed with fairy fruits and flowers –
  And all the flowers were mine.

Ah, dream too bright to last!
  Ah, starry hope that didst arise
But to be overcast!
  A voice from out the future cries,
"Onwards!" – but o'er the past
  (Dim gulf!) my spirit hovering lies,
Mute, motionless, aghast!

For alas! alas! with me
  The light of life is o'er.
"No more... no more... no more
  (Such language holds the solemn sea
To the sands upon the shore)
  Shall bloom the thunderblasted tree,
Or the stricken eagle soar!

Now all my hours are trances,
  And all my nightly dreams
Are where the dark eye glances,
  And where thy footstep gleams
In what ethereal dances,
  By what Italian streams.

Alas! for that accursed time
  They bore thee o'er the billow,
From love to titled age and crime,
  And an unholy pillow!...
From me, and from our misty clime,
  Where weeps the silver willow!

That these lines were written in English – a language with which I had not believed their author acquainted – afforded me little matter for surprise. I was too well aware of the extent of his acquirements and of the singular pleasure he took in concealing them from observation to be astonished at any similar discovery, but the place of date, I must confess, occasioned me no little amazement. It had been originally "London", and afterwards carefully overscored – not, however, so effectually as to conceal the word from a scrutinizing eye. I say, this occasioned me no little amazement, for I well remember that, in a former conversation with my friend, I particularly enquired if he had at any time met in London the Marchesa di Mentoni (who for some years previous to her marriage had resided in that city), when his answer, if I mistake not, gave me to understand that he had never visited the metropolis of Great Britain. I might as well here mention that I have more than once heard (without, of course, giving credit to a report involving so many improbabilities), that the person of whom I speak was not only by birth, but in education, an *Englishman*.

* * * * * * *

"There is one painting," said he, without being aware of my notice of the tragedy, "there is still one painting which you have not seen." And, throwing aside a drapery, he discovered a full-length portrait of the Marchesa Aphrodite.

Human art could have done no more in the delineation of her superhuman beauty. The same ethereal figure which stood before me the preceding night upon the steps of the Ducal Palace stood before me once again. But in the expression of the countenance, which was beaming all over with smiles, there still lurked (incomprehensible anomaly!) that fitful stain of melancholy which will ever be found inseparable from the perfection of the beautiful. Her right arm lay folded over her bosom. With her left she pointed downwards to a curiously fashioned vase. One small, fairy foot, alone visible, barely touched the earth – and, scarcely discernible in the brilliant atmosphere which seemed to encircle and enshrine her loveliness, floated a pair of the most delicately imagined wings. My glance fell from the painting to the figure of my friend, and the vigorous words of Chapman's *Bussy D'Ambois* quivered instinctively upon my lips:

He is up
There like a Roman statue! He will stand
Till Death hath made him marble!*

"Come," he said at length, turning towards a table of richly enamelled and massive silver, upon which were a few goblets fantastically stained, together with two large Etruscan vases fashioned in the same extraordinary model as that in the foreground of the portrait, and filled with what I supposed to be Johannisberger.* "Come," he said abruptly, "let us drink! It is early – but let us drink. It is *indeed* early," he continued musingly, as a cherub with a heavy golden hammer made the apartment ring with the first hour after sunrise. "It is *indeed* early – but what matters it? Let us drink! Let us pour out an offering to yon solemn sun which these gaudy lamps and censers are so eager to subdue!" And, having made me pledge him in a bumper, he swallowed in rapid succession several goblets of the wine.

"To dream," he continued, resuming the tone of his desultory conversation as he held up to the rich light of a censer one of the magnificent vases, "to dream has been the business of my life – I have therefore framed for myself, as you see, a bower of dreams. In the heart of Venice could I have erected a better? You behold around you, it is true, a medley of architectural embellishments. The chastity of Ionia is offended by antediluvian devices, and the sphinxes of Egypt are outstretched upon carpets of gold. Yet the effect is incongruous to the timid alone. Proprieties of place, and especially of time, are the bugbears which terrify mankind from the contemplation of the magnificent. Once I was myself a decorist,* but that sublimation of folly has palled upon my soul. All this is now the fitter for my purpose. Like these arabesque censers, my spirit is writhing in fire, and the delirium of this scene is fashioning me for the wilder visions of that land of real dreams whither I am now rapidly departing." He here paused abruptly, bent his head to his bosom and seemed to listen to a sound which I could not hear. At length, erecting his frame, he looked upwards and ejaculated the lines of the Bishop of Chichester:

> Stay for me there! I will not fail
> To meet thee in that hollow vale.*

In the next instant, confessing the power of the wine, he threw himself at full length upon an ottoman.

A quick step was now heard upon the staircase, and a loud knock at the door rapidly succeeded. I was hastening to anticipate a second disturbance, when a page of Mentoni's household burst into the room and faltered out, in a voice choking with emotion, the incoherent words, "My mistress!... My mistress!... Poisoned!... Poisoned! Oh, beautiful... oh, beautiful Aphrodite!"

Bewildered, I flew to the ottoman and endeavoured to arouse the sleeper to a sense of the startling intelligence. But his limbs were rigid, his lips were livid, his lately beaming eyes were riveted in *death*. I staggered back towards the table – my hand fell upon a cracked and blackened goblet* – and a consciousness of the entire and terrible truth flashed suddenly over my soul.

THE SYSTEM OF DOCTOR TARR AND PROFESSOR FETHER*

During the autumn of 18—, while on a tour through the extreme southern provinces of France, my route led me within a few miles of a certain *maison de santé*, or private madhouse, about which I had heard much in Paris from my medical friends. As I had never visited a place of the kind, I thought the opportunity too good to be lost, and so proposed to my travelling companion (a gentleman with whom I had made casual acquaintance a few days before) that we should turn aside for an hour or so and look through the establishment. To this he objected – pleading haste, in the first place, and, in the second, a very usual horror at the sight of a lunatic. He begged me, however, not to let any mere courtesy towards himself interfere with the gratification of my curiosity, and said that he would ride on leisurely, so that I might overtake him during the day, or, at all events, during the next. As he bade me goodbye, I bethought me that there might be some difficulty in obtaining access to the premises, and mentioned my fears on this point. He replied that, in fact, unless I had personal knowledge of the superintendent, Monsieur Maillard, or some credential in the way of a letter, a difficulty might be found to exist, as the regulations of these private madhouses were more rigid than the public hospital laws. For himself, he added, he had, some years since, made the acquaintance of Maillard, and would so far assist me as to ride up to the door and introduce me – although his feelings on the subject of lunacy would not permit of his entering the house.

I thanked him, and, turning from the main road, we entered a grass-grown bypath which, in half an hour, nearly lost itself in a dense forest, clothing the base of a mountain. Through this dank and gloomy wood we rode some two miles, when the *maison de santé* came in view. It was a fantastic chateau, much dilapidated, and indeed scarcely tenantable through age and neglect. Its aspect inspired me with absolute dread, and, checking my horse, I half resolved to turn back. I soon, however, grew ashamed of my weakness, and proceeded.

As we rode up to the gateway, I perceived it slightly open, and the visage of a man peering through. In an instant afterwards, this man came forth, accosted my companion by name, shook him cordially by the hand and begged him to alight. It was Monsieur Maillard himself. He was a portly, fine-looking gentleman of the old school, with a polished manner and a certain air of gravity, dignity and authority which was very impressive.

My friend – having presented me, mentioned my desire to inspect the establishment and received Monsieur Maillard's assurance that he would show me all attention – now took leave, and I saw him no more.

When he had gone, the superintendent ushered me into a small and exceedingly neat parlour, containing, among other indications of refined taste, many books, drawings, pots of flowers and musical instruments. A cheerful fire blazed upon the hearth. At a piano, singing an aria from Bellini,* sat a young and very beautiful woman, who, at my entrance, paused in her song and received me with graceful courtesy. Her voice was low, and her whole manner subdued. I thought, too, that I perceived the traces of sorrow in her countenance, which was excessively (although, to my taste, not unpleasingly) pale. She was attired in deep mourning, and excited in my bosom a feeling of mingled respect, interest and admiration.

I had heard, at Paris, that the institution of Monsieur Maillard was managed upon what is vulgarly termed the "system of soothing" – that all punishments were avoided; that even confinement was seldom resorted to; that the patients, while secretly watched, were left much apparent liberty; and that most of them were permitted to roam about the house and grounds in the ordinary apparel of persons in right mind.

Keeping these impressions in view, I was cautious in what I said before the young lady, for I could not be sure that she was sane – and, in fact, there was a certain restless brilliancy about her eyes which half led me to imagine she was not. I confined my remarks, therefore, to general topics, and to such as I thought would not be displeasing or exciting even to a lunatic. She replied in a perfectly rational manner to all that I said, and even her original observations were marked with the soundest good sense – but a long acquaintance with the metaphysics of *mania* had taught me to put no faith in such evidence of sanity, and I continued to practise, throughout the interview, the caution with which I commenced it.

Presently a smart footman in livery brought in a tray with fruit, wine and other refreshments, of which I partook, the lady soon afterwards leaving the room. As she departed, I turned my eyes in an enquiring manner towards my host.

"No," he said, "oh, no... a member of my family... my niece, and a most accomplished woman."

"I beg a thousand pardons for the suspicion," I replied, "but of course you will know how to excuse me. The excellent administration of your affairs here is well understood in Paris, and I thought it just possible, you know—"

"Yes, yes... say no more – or, rather, it is myself who should thank you for the commendable prudence you have displayed. We seldom find so much of forethought in young men – and, more than once, some unhappy *contretemps* has occurred in consequence of thoughtlessness on the part of our visitors. While my former system was in operation and my patients were permitted the privilege of roaming to and fro at will, they were often aroused to a dangerous frenzy by injudicious persons who called to inspect the house. Hence I was obliged to enforce a rigid system of exclusion, and none obtained access to the premises upon whose discretion I could not rely."

"While your *former* system was in operation!" I said, repeating his words. "Do I understand you, then, to say that the 'soothing system' of which I have heard so much is no longer in force?"

"It is now," he replied, "several weeks since we have concluded to renounce it for ever."

"Indeed! You astonish me!"

"We found it, sir," he said with a sigh, "absolutely necessary to return to the old usages. The *danger* of the soothing system was, at all times, appalling – and its advantages have been much overrated. I believe, sir, that in this house it has been given a fair trial, if ever in any. We did everything that rational humanity could suggest. I am sorry that you could not have paid us a visit at an earlier period, that you might have judged for yourself. But I presume you are conversant with the soothing practice – with its details."

"Not altogether. What I have heard has been at third or fourth hand."

"I may state the system, then, in general terms, as one in which the patients were *ménagés* – humoured. We contradicted *no* fancies which entered the brains of the mad. On the contrary, we not only indulged, but encouraged them – and many of our most permanent cures have been thus effected. There is no argument which so touches the feeble reason of the madman as the *reductio ad absurdum*.* We have had men, for example, who fancied themselves chickens. The cure was to insist upon the thing as a fact – to accuse the patient of stupidity in not sufficiently perceiving it to be a fact, and thus to refuse him any other diet for a week than that which properly appertains to a chicken. In this manner a little corn and gravel were made to perform wonders."

"But was this species of acquiescence all?"

"By no means. We put much faith in amusements of a simple kind, such as music, dancing, gymnastic exercises generally, cards, certain classes of books, and so forth. We affected to treat each individual as if for some ordinary physical disorder – and the word 'lunacy' was never employed. A great point was to set each lunatic to guard the actions of all the others. To repose confidence in the understanding or discretion of a madman is to gain him body and soul. In this way we were enabled to dispense with an expensive body of keepers."

"And you had no punishments of any kind?"

"None."

"And you never confined your patients?"

"Very rarely. Now and then, the malady of some individual growing to a crisis or taking a sudden turn of fury, we conveyed him to a secret cell, lest his disorder should infect the rest, and there kept him until we could dismiss him to his friends – for with the raging maniac we have nothing to do. He is usually removed to the public hospitals."

"And you have now changed all this – and you think for the better?"

"Decidedly. The system had its disadvantages, and even its dangers. It is now, happily, exploded throughout all the *maisons de santé* of France."

"I am very much surprised," I said, "at what you tell me, for I made sure that, at this moment, no other method of treatment for mania existed in any portion of the country."

"You are young yet, my friend," replied my host, "but the time will arrive when you will learn to judge for yourself of what is going on in the world, without trusting to the gossip of others. Believe nothing you hear, and only one half that you see. Now, about our *maisons de santé*, it is clear that some ignoramus has misled you. After dinner, however, when you have sufficiently recovered from the fatigue of your ride, I will be happy to take you over the house and introduce to you a system which, in my opinion, and in that of everyone who has witnessed its operation, is incomparably the most effectual as yet devised."

"Your own?" I enquired. "One of your own invention?"

"I am proud," he replied, "to acknowledge that it is – at least in some measure."

In this manner I conversed with Monsieur Maillard for an hour or two, during which he showed me the gardens and conservatories of the place.

"I cannot let you see my patients," he said, "just at present. To a sensitive mind there is always more or less of the shocking in such exhibitions – and I do not wish to spoil your appetite for dinner. We will dine. I can give you some veal *à la Menehould*,* with cauliflowers in *velouté* sauce... after that a glass of Clos de Vougeot...* then your nerves will be sufficiently steadied."

At six, dinner was announced, and my host conducted me into a large *salle à manger*,* where a very numerous company were assembled – twenty-five or thirty in all. They were, apparently, people of rank – certainly of high breeding – although their habiliments, I thought, were extravagantly rich, partaking somewhat too much of the ostentatious finery of the *vieille cour*.* I noticed that at least two thirds of these guests were ladies, and some of the latter were by no means accoutred in what a Parisian would consider good taste at the present day. Many females, for example, whose age could not have been less than seventy, were bedecked with a profusion of jewellery, such as rings, bracelets and earrings, and wore their bosoms and arms shamefully bare. I observed, too, that very few of the dresses were well made – or, at least, that very few of them fitted the wearers. In looking about, I discovered the interesting girl to whom Monsieur Maillard had presented me in the little parlour – but my surprise was great to see her wearing a hoop and farthingale, with high-heeled shoes and a dirty cap of Brussels lace, so much too large for her that it gave her face a ridiculously diminutive expression. When I had first seen her, she was attired, most becomingly, in deep mourning. There was an air of oddity, in short, about the dress of the whole party, which, at first, caused me to recur to my original idea of the "soothing system", and to fancy that Monsieur Maillard had been willing to deceive me until after dinner, that I might experience no uncomfortable feelings during the repast at finding myself dining with lunatics, but I remembered having been informed, in Paris, that the southern provincialists were a peculiarly eccentric people, with a vast number of antiquated notions – and then, too, upon conversing with several members of the company, my apprehensions were immediately and fully dispelled.

The dining room itself, although perhaps sufficiently comfortable and of good dimensions, had nothing too much of elegance about it. For example, the floor was uncarpeted – in France, however, a carpet is frequently dispensed with. The windows, too, were without curtains; the shutters, being shut, were securely fastened with iron bars applied diagonally, after the fashion of our shop shutters. The apartment, I observed, formed in itself a wing of the chateau, and thus the windows were on three sides of the parallelogram, the door being at the other. There were no less than ten windows in all.

The table was superbly set out. It was loaded with plate, and more than loaded with delicacies. The profusion was absolutely barbaric. There were meats enough to have feasted the Anakim.* Never, in all my life, had I witnessed so lavish, so wasteful an expenditure of the good things of life. There seemed very little taste, however, in the arrangements – and my eyes, accustomed to quiet lights, were sadly offended by the prodigious glare of a multitude of wax candles, which, in silver candelabra, were deposited upon the table and all about the room, wherever it was possible to find a place. There were several active servants in attendance – and, upon a large table, at the farther end of the apartment, were seated seven or eight people with fiddles, fifes, trombones and a drum. These fellows annoyed me very much, at intervals, during the repast, by an infinite variety of noises, which were intended for music, and which appeared to afford much entertainment to all present with the exception of myself.

Upon the whole, I could not help thinking that there was much of the *bizarre* about everything I saw – but then the world is made up of all kinds of persons, with all modes of thought and all sorts of conventional customs. I had travelled, too, so much as to be quite an adept at the *nil admirari** – so I took my seat very coolly at the right hand of my host, and, having an excellent appetite, did justice to the good cheer set before me.

The conversation, in the mean time, was spirited and general. The ladies, as usual, talked a great deal. I soon found that nearly all the company were well educated, and my host was a world of good-humoured anecdote in himself. He seemed quite willing to speak of his position as superintendent of a *maison de santé* – and, indeed, the topic of lunacy was, much to my surprise, a favourite one with all present. A great many amusing stories were told, having reference to the *whims* of the patients.

"We had a fellow here once," said a fat little gentleman who sat at my right, "a fellow that fancied himself a teapot – and, by the way, is it not especially singular how often this particular crotchet has entered the brain of the lunatic? There is scarcely an insane asylum in France which cannot supply a human teapot. *Our* gentleman was a Britannia-ware teapot,* and was careful to polish himself every morning with buckskin and whiting."

"And then," said a tall man just opposite, "we had here, not long ago, a person who had taken it into his head that he was a donkey – which, allegorically speaking, you will say, was quite true. He was a troublesome patient, and we had much ado to keep him within bounds. For a long time he would eat nothing but thistles – but of this idea we soon cured him by insisting upon his eating nothing else. Then he was perpetually kicking out his heels… so… so—"

"Mr De Kock! I will thank you to behave yourself!" here interrupted an old lady who sat next to the speaker. "Please keep your feet to yourself! You have spoilt my brocade! Is it necessary, pray, to illustrate a remark in so practical a style? Our friend here can surely comprehend you without all this. Upon my word, you are nearly as great a donkey as the poor unfortunate imagined himself. Your acting is very natural, as I live."

"*Mille pardons, Ma'm'selle!*" replied Monsieur De Kock, thus addressed. "A thousand pardons! I had no intention of offending. Ma'm'selle Laplace – Monsieur De Kock will do himself the honour of taking wine with you."

Here Monsieur De Kock bowed low, kissed his hand with much ceremony and took wine with Ma'm'selle Laplace.

"Allow me, *mon ami*,"* now said Monsieur Maillard, addressing myself, "allow me to send you a morsel of this veal *à la Sainte-Menehould* – you will find it particularly fine."

At this instant three sturdy waiters had just succeeded in depositing safely upon the table an enormous dish, or trencher, containing what I supposed to be the "*monstrum horrendum, informe, ingens, cui lumen ademptum*".* A closer scrutiny assured me, however, that it was only a small calf roasted whole and set upon its knees, with an apple in its mouth, as is the English fashion of dressing a hare.

"Thank you, no," I replied. "To say the truth, I am not particularly partial to veal *à la Sainte*… what is it?… for I do not find that it altogether agrees with me. I will change my plate, however, and try some of the rabbit."

There were several side dishes on the table, containing what appeared to be the ordinary French rabbit – a very delicious *morceau** which I can recommend.

"Pierre," cried the host, "change this gentleman's plate, and give him a side piece of this rabbit *au chat*."

"This what?" said I.

"This rabbit *au chat*."

"Why, thank you – upon second thoughts, no. I will just help myself to some of the ham."

There is no knowing what one eats, thought I to myself, at the tables of these people of the province. I will have none of their rabbit *au chat* – and, for the matter of that, none of their *cat au rabbit* either.

"And then," said a cadaverous-looking personage near the foot of the table, taking up the thread of the conversation where it had been broken off, "and then, among other oddities, we had a patient, once upon a time, who very pertinaciously maintained himself to be a Córdoba cheese, and went about, with a knife in his hand, soliciting his friends to try a small slice from the middle of his leg."

"He was a great fool, beyond doubt," interposed someone, "but not to be compared with a certain individual whom we all know, with the exception of this strange gentleman. I mean the man who took himself for a bottle of champagne and always went off with a pop and a fizz in this fashion."

Here the speaker, very rudely, as I thought, put his right thumb in his left cheek, withdrew it with a sound resembling the popping of a cork, and then, by a dextrous movement of the tongue upon the teeth, created a sharp hissing and fizzing which lasted for several minutes, in imitation of the frothing of champagne. This behaviour, I saw plainly, was not very pleasing to Monsieur Maillard, but that gentleman said nothing, and the conversation was resumed by a very lean little man in a big wig.

"And then there was an ignoramus," said he, "who mistook himself for a frog – which, by the way, he resembled in no little degree. I wish you could have seen him, sir" – here the speaker addressed myself – "it would have done your heart good to see the natural airs that he put on. Sir, if that man was *not* a frog, I can only observe that it is a pity he was not. His croak thus – o-o-o-o-gh… o-o-o-o-gh! – was the finest note in the world: B flat – and when he put his elbows upon the table thus, after taking a glass or two of wine, and distended his mouth thus, and rolled up his eyes thus, and winked them with excessive rapidity thus… why then, sir, I take it upon myself to say positively that you would have been lost in admiration of the genius of the man."

"I have no doubt of it," I said.

"And then," said somebody else, "then there was Petit Gaillard, who thought himself a pinch of snuff, and was truly distressed because he could not take himself between his own finger and thumb."

"And then there was Jules Desoulières, who was a very singular genius indeed, and went mad with the idea that he was a pumpkin. He persecuted the cook to make him up into pies – a thing which the cook indignantly refused to do. For my part, I am by no means sure that a pumpkin pie *à la Desoulières* would not have been very capital eating indeed!"

"You astonish me!" said I, and I looked inquisitively at Monsieur Maillard.

"Ha ha ha!" said that gentleman. "He he he!… Hi hi hi!… Ho ho ho!… Hu hu hu!… very good indeed! You must not be astonished, *mon ami* – our friend here is a wit… a *drôle*… you must not understand him to the letter."

"And then," said some other one of the party, "then there was Bouffon Le Grand – another extraordinary personage in his way. He grew deranged through love, and fancied himself possessed of two heads. One of these he maintained to be the head of Cicero, the other he imagined a composite one, being Demosthenes's from the top of the forehead to the mouth and Lord Brougham's from the mouth to the chin.* It is not impossible that he was wrong, but he would have convinced you of his being in the right, for he was a man of great eloquence.* He had an absolute passion for oratory, and could not refrain from display. For example, he used to leap upon the dinner table thus, and… and—"

Here a friend at the side of the speaker put a hand upon his shoulder and whispered a few words in his ear – upon which he ceased talking with great suddenness and sank back within his chair.

"And then," said the friend who had whispered, "there was Boullard, the teetotum.* I call him the teetotum because, in fact, he was seized with the droll but not altogether irrational crotchet that he had been converted into a teetotum. You would have roared with laughter to see him spin. He would turn round upon one heel by the hour, in this manner… so—"

Here the friend whom he had just interrupted by a whisper performed an exactly similar office for himself.

"But then," cried the old lady, at the top of her voice, "your Monsieur Boullard was a madman, and a very silly madman at best – for who, allow me to ask you, ever heard of a human teetotum? The thing is absurd. Madame Joyeuse was a more sensible person, as you know. She had a crotchet, but it was instinct with common sense, and gave pleasure to all who had the honour of her acquaintance. She found, upon mature deliberation, that by some accident she had been turned into a chicken-cock – but, as such, she behaved with propriety. She flapped her wings with prodigious effect… so… so… so… and, as for her crow, it was delicious! Cock-a-doodle-doo!… Cock-a-doodle-doo!… Cock-a-doodle-de-doo-doo-dooo-do-o-o-o-o-o-o!"

"Madame Joyeuse, I will thank you to behave yourself!" here interrupted our host, very angrily. "You can either conduct yourself as a lady should do, or you can quit the table forthwith – take your choice."

The lady (whom I was much astonished to hear addressed as Madame Joyeuse, after the description of Madame Joyeuse she had just given) blushed up to the eyebrows, and seemed exceedingly abashed at the reproof. She hung down her head, and said not a syllable in reply. But another and younger lady resumed the theme. It was my beautiful girl of the little parlour.

"Oh, Madame Joyeuse *was* a fool!" she exclaimed. "But there was really much sound sense, after all, in the opinion of Eugénie Salsafette. She was a very beautiful and painfully modest young lady who thought the ordinary mode of habiliment indecent, and wished to dress herself always by getting outside instead of inside of her clothes. It is a thing very easily done, after all. You have only to do so… and then so… so… so… and then so… so… so… and then—"

"*Mon dieu!** Ma'm'selle Salsafette!" here cried a dozen voices at once. "What *are* you about?… Forbear!… That is sufficient!… We see, very plainly, how it is done!… Hold! Hold!" – and several persons were already leaping from their seats to withhold Ma'm'selle Salsafette from putting herself upon a par with the Medicean Venus,* when the point was very effectually and suddenly accomplished by a series of loud screams, or yells, from some portion of the main body of the chateau.

My nerves were very much affected, indeed, by these yells, but the rest of the company I really pitied. I never saw any set of reasonable people so thoroughly frightened in my life. They all grew as pale as so many corpses, and, shrinking within their seats, sat quivering and gibbering with terror, and listening for a repetition of the sound. It came again – louder and seemingly nearer – and then a third time *very* loud, and then a fourth time with a vigour evidently diminished. At this apparent dying-away of the noise, the spirits of the company were immediately regained, and all was life and anecdote as before. I now ventured to enquire the cause of the disturbance.

"A mere *bagatelle*," said Monsieur Maillard. "We are used to these things, and care really very little about them. The lunatics, every now and then, get up a howl in concert – one starting another, as is sometimes the case with a bevy of dogs at night. It occasionally happens, however, that the concerto yells are succeeded by a simultaneous effort at breaking loose – when, of course, some little danger is to be apprehended."

"And how many have you in charge?"

"At present we have not more than ten altogether."

"Principally females, I presume?"

"Oh, no – every one of them men, and stout fellows too, I can tell you."

"Indeed! I have always understood that the majority of lunatics were of the gentler sex."

"It is generally so, but not always. Some time ago, there were about twenty-seven patients here – and, of that number, no less than eighteen were women – but, lately, matters have changed very much, as you see."

"Yes – have changed very much, as you see," here interrupted the gentleman who had broken the shins of Ma'm'selle Laplace.

"Yes – have changed very much, as you see!" chimed in the whole company at once.

"Hold your tongues, every one of you!" said my host, in a great rage. Whereupon the whole company maintained a dead silence for nearly a minute. As for one lady, she obeyed Monsieur Maillard to the letter, and, thrusting out her tongue, which was an excessively long one, held it very resignedly, with both hands, until the end of the entertainment.

"And this gentlewoman," said I to Monsieur Maillard, bending over and addressing him in a whisper, "this good lady who has just spoken and who gives us the cock-a-doodle-de-doo… she, I presume, is harmless – quite harmless, eh?"

"Harmless!" ejaculated he, in unfeigned surprise. "Why… why, what *can* you mean?"

"Only slightly touched?" said I, touching my head. "I take it for granted that she is not particularly… not dangerously affected, eh?"

"*Mon dieu!* What is it you imagine? This lady, my particular old friend, Madame Joyeuse, is as absolutely sane as myself. She has her little eccentricities, to be sure – but then, you know, all old women… all *very* old women… are more or less eccentric!"

"To be sure," said I, "to be sure… and then the rest of these ladies and gentlemen—"

"Are my friends and keepers," interrupted Monsieur Maillard, drawing himself up with hauteur, "my very good friends and assistants."

"What! All of them?" I asked. "The women and all?"

"Assuredly," he said. "We could not do at all without the women: they are the best lunatic nurses in the world; they have a way of their own, you know; their bright eyes have a marvellous effect – something like the fascination of the snake, you know?"

"To be sure," said I, "to be sure! They behave a little odd, eh?… They are a little *queer*, eh?… Don't you think so?"

"Odd!… Queer!… Why, do you *really* think so? We are not very prudish, to be sure, here in the south… do pretty much as we please… enjoy life, and all that sort of thing, you know…"

"To be sure," said I, "to be sure."

"And then, perhaps, this Clos de Vougeot is a little heady, you know... a little *strong*... you understand, eh?"

"To be sure," said I, "to be sure. By the by, Monsieur, did I understand you to say that the system you have adopted, in place of the celebrated 'soothing system', was one of very rigorous severity?"

"By no means. Our confinement is necessarily close, but the treatment – the medical treatment, I mean – is rather agreeable to the patients than otherwise."

"And the new system is one of your own invention?"

"Not altogether. Some portions of it are referable to Professor Tarr, of whom you have, necessarily, heard – and, again, there are modifications in my plan which I am happy to acknowledge as belonging of right to the celebrated Fether, with whom, if I mistake not, you have the honour of an intimate acquaintance."

"I am quite ashamed to confess," I replied, "that I have never even heard the name of either gentleman before."

"Good Heavens!" ejaculated my host, drawing back his chair abruptly and uplifting his hands. "I surely do not hear you aright! You did not intend to say – eh? – that you had never *heard* either of the learned Doctor Tarr or of the celebrated Professor Fether?"

"I am forced to acknowledge my ignorance," I replied. "But the truth should be held inviolate above all things. Nevertheless, I feel humbled to the dust not to be acquainted with the works of these no doubt extraordinary men. I will seek out their writings forthwith, and peruse them with deliberate care. Monsieur Maillard, you have really... I must confess it... you have *really*... made me ashamed of myself!"

And this was the fact.

"Say no more, my good young friend," he said kindly, pressing my hand, "join me now in a glass of Sauternes."*

We drank. The company followed our example without stint. They chatted... they jested... they laughed... they perpetrated a thousand absurdities... the fiddles shrieked... the drum row-de-dowed...* the trombones bellowed like so many brazen bulls of Phalaris* – and the whole scene, growing gradually worse and worse as the wines gained the ascendancy, became at length a sort of Pandaemonium *in petto*.* In the mean time, Monsieur Maillard and myself, with some bottles of Sauternes and Vougeot between us, continued our conversation at the top of the voice. A word spoken in an ordinary key stood no more chance of being heard than the voice of a fish from the bottom of Niagara Falls.

"And, sir," said I, screaming in his ear, "you mentioned something before dinner about the danger incurred in the old system of soothing. How is that?"

"Yes," he replied, "there was, occasionally, very great danger indeed. There is no accounting for the caprices of madmen – and, in my opinion, as well as in that of Doctor Tarr and Professor Fether, it is *never* safe to permit them to run at large unattended. A lunatic may be 'soothed', as it is called, for a time, but in the end he is very apt to become obstreperous. His cunning, too, is proverbial and great. If he has a project in view, he conceals his design with a marvellous wisdom – and the dexterity with which he counterfeits sanity presents to the metaphysician one of the most singular problems in the study of mind. When a madman appears *thoroughly* sane, indeed, it is high time to put him in a straitjacket."

"But the *danger*, my dear sir, of which you were speaking... in your own experience... during your control of this house... have you had practical reason to think liberty hazardous in the case of a lunatic?"

"Here?... In my own experience?... Why, I may say, yes. For example... no *very* long while ago, a singular circumstance occurred in this very house. The 'soothing system', you know, was then in operation, and the patients were at large. They behaved remarkably well – especially so – anyone of sense might have known that some devilish scheme was brewing from that particular fact, that the fellows behaved so *remarkably* well. And, sure enough, one fine morning the keepers found themselves pinioned hand and foot, and thrown into the cells, where they were attended, as if *they* were the lunatics, by the lunatics themselves, who had usurped the offices of the keepers."

"You don't tell me so! I never heard of anything so absurd in my life!"

"Fact! It all came to pass by means of a stupid fellow, a lunatic, who, by some means, had taken it into his head that he had invented a better system of government than any ever heard of before – of lunatic government, I mean. He wished to give his invention a trial, I suppose, and so he persuaded the rest of the patients to join him in a conspiracy for the overthrow of the reigning powers."

"And he really succeeded?"

"No doubt of it. The keepers and kept were soon made to exchange places. Not that exactly either, for the madmen had been free, but the keepers were shut up in cells forthwith, and treated, I am sorry to say, in a very cavalier manner."

"But I presume a counter-revolution was soon effected. This condition of things could not have long existed. The country people in the neighbourhood – visitors coming to see the establishment – would have given the alarm."

"There you are out. The head rebel was too cunning for that. He admitted no visitors at all – with the exception, one day, of a very stupid-looking young gentleman of whom he had no reason to be afraid. He let him in to see the place – just by way of variety, to have a little fun with him. As soon as he had gammoned* him sufficiently, he let him out, and sent him about his business."

"And *how* long, then, did the madmen reign?"

"Oh, a very long time indeed – a month certainly... how much longer I can't precisely say. In the mean time, the lunatics had a jolly season of it – that you may swear. They doffed their own shabby clothes and made free with the family wardrobe and jewels. The cellars of the chateau were well stocked with wine – and these madmen are just the devils that know how to drink it. They lived well, I can tell you."

"And the treatment – what was the particular species of treatment which the leader of the rebels put into operation?"

"Why, as for that, a madman is not necessarily a fool, as I have already observed – and it is my honest opinion that his treatment was a much better treatment than that which it superseded. It was a very capital system indeed: simple... neat... no trouble at all – in fact, it was delicious... it was—"

Here my host's observations were cut short by another series of yells, of the same character as those which had previously disconcerted us. This time, however, they seemed to proceed from persons rapidly approaching.

"Gracious Heavens!" I ejaculated. "The lunatics have most undoubtedly broken loose."

"I very much fear it is so," replied Monsieur Maillard, now becoming excessively pale. He had scarcely finished the sentence before loud shouts and imprecations were heard beneath the windows – and, immediately afterwards, it became evident that some persons outside were endeavouring to gain entrance into the room. The door was beaten with what appeared to be a sledgehammer, and the shutters were wrenched and shaken with prodigious violence.

A scene of the most terrible confusion ensued. Monsieur Maillard, to my excessive astonishment, threw himself under the sideboard. I had expected more resolution at his hands. The members of the orchestra – who, for the last fifteen minutes, had been seemingly too much intoxicated to do duty – now sprang all at once to their feet and to their instruments, and, scrambling upon their table, broke out, with one accord, into 'Yankee Doodle',* which they performed, if not exactly in tune, at least with an energy superhuman during the whole of the uproar.

Meantime, upon the main dining table, among the bottles and glasses, leapt the gentleman who, with such difficulty, had been restrained from leaping there before. As soon as he fairly settled himself, he commenced an oration which, no doubt, was a very capital one, if it could only have been heard. At the same moment, the man with the teetotum predilection set himself to spinning around the apartment with immense energy, and with arms outstretched at right angles with his body, so that he had all the air of a teetotum, in fact, and knocked everybody down that happened to get in his way. And now, too, hearing an incredible popping and fizzing of champagne, I discovered at length that it proceeded from the person who performed the bottle of that delicate drink during dinner. And then, again, the frog-man croaked away as if the salvation of his soul depended upon every note that he uttered. And, in the midst of all this, the continuous braying of a donkey arose over all. As for my old friend, Madame Joyeuse, I really could have wept for the poor lady, she appeared so terribly perplexed. All she did, however, was to stand up in a corner, by the fireplace, and sing out incessantly at the top of her voice, "Cock-a-doodle-de-dooooooh!"

And now came the climax – the catastrophe of the drama.* As no resistance, beyond whooping and yelling and cock-a-doodling, was offered to the encroachments of the party without, the ten windows were very speedily, and almost simultaneously, broken in. But I shall never forget the emotions of wonder and horror with which I gazed, when, leaping through these windows and down among us *pêle-mêle*,* fighting, stamping, scratching and howling, there rushed a perfect army of what I took to be chimpanzees, orang-utans or big black baboons of the Cape of Good Hope.

I received a terrible beating – after which I rolled under a sofa and lay still. After lying there some fifteen minutes, during which time I listened with all my ears to what was going on in the room, I came to some satisfactory denouement of this tragedy. Monsieur Maillard, it appeared, in giving me the account of the lunatic who had excited his fellows to rebellion, had been merely relating his own exploits. This gentleman had, indeed, some two or three years before, been the superintendent of the establishment, but grew crazy himself, and so became a patient. This fact was unknown to the travelling companion who introduced me. The keepers, ten in number, having been suddenly overpowered, were first well tarred, then carefully feathered,* and then shut up in underground cells. They had been so imprisoned for more than a month, during which period Monsieur Maillard had generously allowed them not only the tar and feathers (which constituted his "system"), but some bread and abundance of water. The latter was pumped on them daily. At length, one escaping through a sewer, gave freedom to all the rest.

The "soothing system", with important modifications, has been resumed at the chateau – yet I cannot help agreeing with Monsieur Maillard that his own "treatment" was a very capital one of its kind. As he justly observed, it was "simple... neat... and gave no trouble at all – not the least".

I have only to add that, although I have searched every library in Europe for the works of Doctor *Tarr* and Professor *Fether*, I have, up to the present day, utterly failed in my endeavours at procuring an edition.

THE LITERARY LIFE OF THINGUM BOB, ESQ.*

LATE EDITOR OF THE *GOOSETHERUMFOODLE*

BY HIMSELF

I am now growing in years, and – since I understand that Shakespeare and Mr Emmons* are deceased – it is not impossible that I may even die. It has occurred to me, therefore, that I may as well retire from the field of letters and repose upon my laurels. But I am ambitious of signalizing my abdication of the literary sceptre by some important bequest to posterity – and, perhaps, I cannot do a better thing than just pen for it an account of my earlier career. My name, indeed, has been so long and so constantly before the public eye that I am not only willing to admit the naturalness of the interest which it has everywhere excited, but ready to satisfy the extreme curiosity which it has inspired. In fact, it is no more than the duty of him who achieves greatness to leave behind him, in his ascent, such landmarks as may guide others to be great. I propose, therefore, in the present paper (which I had some idea of calling 'Memoranda to Serve for the Literary History of America') to give a detail of those important, yet feeble and tottering, first steps by which, at length, I attained the high road to the pinnacle of human renown.

Of one's *very* remote ancestors it is superfluous to say much. My father, Thomas Bob, Esq., stood for many years at the summit of his profession, which was that of a merchant barber, in the city of Smug. His warehouse was the resort of all the principal people of the place, and especially of the editorial corps – a body which inspires all about it with profound veneration and awe. For my own part, I regarded them as gods, and drank in with avidity the rich wit and wisdom which continuously flowed from their august mouths during the process of what is styled "lather". My first moment of positive inspiration must be dated from that ever-memorable epoch when the brilliant conductor of the *Gadfly*, in the intervals of the important process just mentioned, recited aloud, before a conclave of our apprentices, an inimitable poem in honour of the "Only Genuine Oil-of-Bob" (so called from its talented inventor, my father),* and for which effusion the editor of the *Fly* was remunerated with a regal liberality by the firm of Thomas Bob & Company, merchant barbers.

The genius of the stanzas to the "Oil-of-Bob" first breathed into me, I say, the divine afflatus. I resolved at once to become a great man, and to commence by becoming a great poet. That very evening I fell upon my knees at the feet of my father.

"Father," I said, "pardon me!… but I have a soul above lather. It is my firm intention to cut the shop. I would be an editor… I would be a poet… I would pen stanzas to the 'Oil-of-Bob'. Pardon me and aid me to be great!"

"My dear Thingum," replied Father (I had been christened Thingum after a wealthy relative so surnamed). "My dear Thingum," he said, raising me from my knees by the ears, "Thingum, my boy, you're a trump,* and take after your father in having a soul. You have an immense head, too, and it must hold a great many brains. This I have long seen, and therefore had thoughts of making you a lawyer. The business, however, has grown ungenteel, and that of a politician don't pay. Upon the whole you judge wisely: the trade of editor is best – and if you can be a poet at the same time (as most of the editors are, by the by), why, you will kill two birds with the one stone. To encourage you in the beginning of things, I will allow you a garret; pen, ink and paper; a rhyming dictionary; and a copy of the *Gadfly*. I suppose you would scarcely demand any more."

"I would be an ungrateful villain if I did," I replied with enthusiasm. "Your generosity is boundless. I will repay it by making you the father of a genius."

Thus ended my conference with the best of men, and, immediately upon its termination, I betook myself with zeal to my poetical labours – as upon these, chiefly, I founded my hopes of ultimate elevation to the editorial chair.

In my first attempts at composition, I found the stanzas to the "Oil-of-Bob" rather a drawback than otherwise. Their splendour more dazzled than enlightened me. The contemplation of their excellence tended, naturally, to discourage me by comparison with my own abortions, so that for a long time I laboured in vain. At length, there came into my head one of those exquisitely original ideas which now and then *will* permeate the brain of a man of genius. It was this – or, rather, thus was it carried into execution. From the rubbish of an old bookstall in a very remote corner of the town, I got together several antique and altogether unknown or forgotten volumes. The bookseller sold them to me for a song. From one of these, which purported to be a translation of one Dante's *Inferno*, I copied with remarkable neatness a long passage about a man named Ugolino, who had a parcel of brats.* From another, which contained a good many old plays by some person whose name I forget, I extracted in the same manner, and with the same care, a great number of lines about "angels" and "ministers saying grace" and "goblins damned" and more besides of that sort.* From a third, which was the composition of some blind man or other, either a Greek or a Choctaw* – I cannot be at the pains of remembering every trifle exactly – I took about fifty verses beginning with "Achilles' wrath" and "grease" and something else.* From a fourth, which I recollect was also the work of a blind man, I selected a page or two all about "hail" and "holy light" – and, although a blind man has no business to write about light, still the verses were sufficiently good in their way.*

Having made fair copies of these poems, I signed every one of them "Oppodeldoc"* (a fine sonorous name), and, doing each up nicely in a separate envelope, I dispatched one to each of the four principal magazines, with a request for speedy insertion and prompt pay. The result of this well-conceived plan, however (the success of which would have saved me much trouble in afterlife),* served to convince me that some editors are not to be bamboozled, and gave the *coup de grâce* (as they say in France) to my nascent hopes (as they say in the city of the transcendentals).*

The fact is that each and every one of the magazines in question gave Mr "Oppodeldoc" a complete using-up* in the "Monthly Notices to Correspondents". The *Humdrum* gave him a dressing after this fashion:

> "Oppodeldoc" (whoever he is) has sent us a long *tirade* concerning a bedlamite whom he styles "Ugolino", who had a great many children that should have been all whipped and sent to bed without their suppers. The whole affair is exceedingly tame – not to say *flat*. "Oppodeldoc" (whoever he is) is entirely devoid of imagination – and imagination, in our humble opinion, is not only the soul of POESY, but also its very heart. "Oppodeldoc" (whoever he is) has the audacity to demand of us, for his twattle, a "speedy insertion and prompt pay". We neither insert nor purchase any stuff of the sort. There can be no doubt, however, that he would meet with a ready sale for all the balderdash he can scribble at the office of either the *Rowdy-Dow*,* the *Lollipop* or the *Goosetherumfoodle*.

All this, it must be acknowledged, was very severe upon "Oppodeldoc" – but the unkindest cut was putting the word POESY in small caps. In those five pre-eminent letters, what a world of bitterness is there not involved!

But "Oppodeldoc" was punished with equal severity in the *Rowdy-Dow*, which spoke thus:

> We have received a most singular and insolent communication from a person (whoever he is) signing himself "Oppodeldoc" – thus desecrating the greatness of the illustrious Roman emperor so named. Accompanying the letter of "Oppodeldoc" (whoever he is) we find sundry lines of most disgusting and unmeaning rant about "angels and ministers of grace" – rant such as no madman short of a Nat Lee* or an "Oppodeldoc" could possibly perpetrate. And for this trash of trash, we are modestly requested to "pay promptly". No, sir – no! We pay for nothing of *that* sort. Apply to the *Humdrum*, the *Lollipop* or the *Goosetherumfoodle*. These *periodicals* will undoubtedly accept any literary offal you may send them – and as undoubtedly *promise* to pay for it.

This was bitter indeed upon poor "Oppodeldoc" – but, in this instance, the weight of the satire falls upon the *Humdrum*, the *Lollipop* and the *Goosetherumfoodle*, who are pungently styled "*periodicals*" (in italics, too), a thing that must have cut them to the heart.

Scarcely less savage was the *Lollipop*, which thus discoursed:

> Some *individual*, who rejoices in the appellation "Oppodeldoc" (to what low uses are the names of the illustrious dead too often applied!), has enclosed us some fifty or sixty *verses* commencing after this fashion:
>
> > Achilles' wrath, to Greece the direful spring
> > Of woes unnumbered, etc., etc., etc., etc.*
>
> "Oppodeldoc" (whoever he is) is respectfully informed that there is not a printer's devil* in our office who is not in the daily habit of composing better *lines*. Those of "Oppodeldoc" will not *scan*. "Oppodeldoc" should learn to *count*. But why he should have conceived the idea that *we* (of all others, *we*!) would disgrace our pages with his ineffable nonsense is utterly beyond comprehension. Why, the absurd twattle is scarcely good enough for the *Humdrum*, the *Rowdy-Dow*, the *Goosetherumfoodle*

> – things that are in the practice of publishing "Mother Goose's Melodies" as original lyrics. And "Oppodeldoc" (whoever he is) has even the assurance to demand *pay* for this drivel. Does "Oppodeldoc" (whoever he is) know – is he aware that we could not be paid to insert it?

As I perused this, I felt myself growing gradually smaller and smaller, and when I came to the point at which the editor sneered at the poem as "*verses*", there was little more than an ounce of me left. As for "Oppodeldoc", I began to experience *compassion* for the poor fellow. But the *Goosetherumfoodle* showed, if possible, less mercy than the *Lollipop*. It was the *Goosetherumfoodle* that said:

> A wretched poetaster, who signs himself "Oppodeldoc", is silly enough to fancy that *we* will print and *pay* for a medley of incoherent and ungrammatical bombast which he has transmitted to us, and which commences with the following most *intelligible* line:
>
> Hail, holy light, offspring of heaven first-born.*
>
> We say "most *intelligible*". "Oppodeldoc" (whoever he is) will be kind enough to tell us, perhaps, how "*hail*" can be "*holy light*". We always regarded it as *frozen rain*. Will he inform us, also, how frozen rain can be, at one and the same time, both "holy light" (whatever that is) and an "offspring"? – which latter term (if we understand anything about English) is only employed, with propriety, in reference to small babies of about six weeks old. But it is preposterous to descant upon such absurdity – although "Oppodeldoc" (whoever he is) has the unparalleled effrontery to suppose that we will not only "insert" his ignorant ravings, but (absolutely) *pay for them*!
>
> Now this is fine – it is rich! – and we have half a mind to punish this young scribbler for his egotism by really publishing his effusion *verbatim et literatim** as he has written it. We could inflict no punishment so severe – and we *would* inflict it but for the boredom which we should cause our readers in so doing.
>
> Let "Oppodeldoc" (whoever he is) send any future *composition* of like character to the *Humdrum*, the *Lollipop* or the *Rowdy-Dow*. *They* will "insert" it. *They* "insert" every month just such stuff. Send it to them. WE are not to be insulted with impunity.

This made an end of me – and as for the *Humdrum*, the *Rowdy-Dow* and the *Lollipop*, I never could comprehend how they survived it. The putting *them* in the smallest possible *minion* (that was the rub – thereby insinuating their lowness, their baseness), while WE stood looking upon them in gigantic capitals!* – oh it was *too* bitter!... it was wormwood... it was gall. Had I been either of these periodicals, I would have spared no pains to have the *Goosetherumfoodle* prosecuted. It might have been done under the Act for the "Prevention of Cruelty to Animals". As for Oppodeldoc (whoever he was), I had by this time lost all patience with the fellow, and sympathized with him no longer. He was a fool, beyond doubt (whoever he was), and got not a kick more than he deserved.

The result of my experiment with the old books convinced me, in the first place, that "honesty is the best policy", and, in the second, that if I could not write better than Mr Dante and the two blind men, and the rest of the old set, it would at least be a difficult matter to write worse. I took heart, therefore, and determined to prosecute the "entirely original" (as they say on the covers of the magazines), at whatever cost of study and pains. I again placed before my eyes, as a model, the brilliant stanzas on the "Oil-of-Bob" by the editor of the *Gadfly*, and resolved to construct an ode on the same sublime theme, in rivalry of what had already been done.

With my first line I had no material difficulty. It ran thus:

> To pen an Ode upon the "Oil-of-Bob"

Having carefully looked out, however, all the legitimate rhymes to "Bob", I found it impossible to proceed. In this dilemma I had recourse to paternal aid – and, after some hours of mature thought, my father and myself thus constructed the poem:

> To pen an Ode upon the "Oil-of-Bob"
> Is all sorts of a job.
>
> (Signed) SNOB

To be sure, this composition was of no very great length – but I "have yet to learn", as they say in the *Edinburgh Review*,* that the mere extent of a literary work has anything to do with its merit. As for the *Quarterly** cant about "sustained effort", it is impossible to see the sense of it. Upon the whole, therefore, I was satisfied with the success of my maiden attempt, and now the only question regarded the disposal I should make of it. My father suggested that I should send it to the *Gadfly* – but there were two reasons which operated to prevent me from so doing. I dreaded the jealousy of the editor – and I had ascertained that he did not pay for original contributions. I therefore, after due deliberation, consigned the article to the more dignified pages of the *Lollipop*, and awaited the event in anxiety, but with resignation.

In the very next published number, I had the proud satisfaction of seeing my poem printed at length as the leading article, with the following significant words prefixed in italics and between brackets:

> [We call the attention of our readers to the subjoined admirable stanzas on the "Oil-of-Bob". We need say nothing of their sublimity or of their pathos – it is impossible to peruse them without tears. Those who have been nauseated with a sad dose on the same august topic from the goose quill of the editor of the *Gadfly* will do well to compare the two compositions.
>
> PS: We are consumed with anxiety to probe the mystery which envelops the evident pseudonym "Snob". May we hope for a personal interview?]

All this was scarcely more than justice, but it was, I confess, rather more than I had expected – I acknowledge* this, be it observed, to the everlasting disgrace of my country and of mankind. I lost no time, however, in calling upon the editor of the *Lollipop*, and had the good fortune to find this gentleman at home. He saluted me with an air of profound respect, slightly blended with a fatherly and patronizing admiration, wrought in him, no doubt, by my appearance of extreme youth and inexperience. Begging me to be seated, he entered at once upon the subject of my poem – but modesty will ever forbid me to repeat the thousand compliments which he lavished upon me. The eulogies of Mr Crab (such was the editor's name) were, however, by no means fulsomely indiscriminate. He analysed my composition with much freedom and great ability – not hesitating to point out a few trivial defects, a circumstance which elevated him highly in my esteem. The *Gadfly* was, of course, brought upon the tapis,* and I hope never to be subjected to a criticism so searching, or to rebukes so withering, as were bestowed by Mr Crab upon that unhappy effusion. I had been accustomed to regard the editor of the *Gadfly* as something superhuman – but Mr Crab soon disabused me of that idea. He set the literary as well as the personal character of the "Fly" (so Mr C. satirically designated the rival editor) in its true light. He, the Fly, was very little better than he should be. He had written infamous things. He was a penny-a-liner, and a buffoon. He was a villain. He had composed a tragedy which set the whole country in a guffaw, and a farce which deluged the universe in tears. Besides all this, he had the impudence to pen what he meant for a lampoon upon himself (Mr Crab), and the temerity to style him "an ass". Should I at any time wish to express my opinion of Mr Fly, the pages of the *Lollipop*, Mr Crab assured me, were at my unlimited disposal. In the mean time, as it was very certain that I would be attacked in the *Fly* for my attempt at composing a rival poem on the "Oil-of-Bob", he (Mr Crab) would take it upon himself to attend, pointedly, to my private and personal interests. If I were not made a man of at once, it should not be the fault of himself (Mr Crab).

Mr Crab having now paused in his discourse (the latter portion of which I found it impossible to comprehend), I ventured to suggest something about the remuneration which I had been taught to expect for my poem by an announcement on the cover of the *Lollipop*, declaring that it (the *Lollipop*) "insisted upon being permitted to pay exorbitant prices for all accepted contributions – frequently expending more money for a single brief poem than the whole annual cost of the *Humdrum*, the *Rowdy-Dow* and the *Goosetherumfoodle* combined.

As I mentioned the word "remuneration", Mr Crab first opened his eyes, and then his mouth, to quite a remarkable extent, causing his personal appearance to resemble that of a highly agitated elderly duck in the act of quacking – and in this condition he remained (ever and anon pressing his hands tightly to his forehead, as if in a state of desperate bewilderment) until I had nearly made an end of what I had to say.

Upon my conclusion, he sank back into his seat, as if much overcome, letting his arms fall lifelessly by his side, but keeping his mouth still rigorously open, after the fashion of the duck. While I remained in speechless astonishment at behaviour so alarming, he suddenly leapt to his feet and made a rush at the bell rope – but just as he reached this, he appeared to have altered his intention, whatever it was, for he dived under a table and immediately reappeared with a cudgel. This he was in the act of uplifting (for what purpose I am at a loss to imagine) when, all at once, there came a benign smile over his features, and he sank placidly back in his chair.

"Mr Bob," he said (for I had sent up my card before ascending myself), "Mr Bob, you are a young man, I presume – *very*?"

I assented, adding that I had not yet concluded my third lustrum.*

"Ah!" he replied. "Very good! I see how it is – say no more! Touching this matter of compensation, what you observe is very just – in fact, it is excessively so. But ah... ah... the *first* contribution... the *first*, I say... it is never the magazine custom to pay for – you comprehend, eh? The truth is, we are usually the *recipients*, in such case." Mr Crab smiled blandly as he emphasized the word "recipients". "For the most part, we are *paid* for the insertion of a maiden attempt – especially in verse. In the second place, Mr Bob, the magazine rule is never to disburse what we term in France the *argent comptant** – I have no doubt you understand. In a quarter or two after publication of the article, or in a year or two, we make no objection to giving our note at nine months* – provided, always, that we can so arrange our affairs as to be quite certain of a 'burst-up'* in six. I really *do* hope, Mr Bob, that you will look upon this explanation as satisfactory." Here Mr Crab concluded, and the tears stood in his eyes.

Grieved to the soul at having been, however innocently, the cause of pain to so eminent and so sensitive a man, I hastened to apologize, and to reassure him by expressing my perfect coincidence with his views, as well as my entire appreciation of the delicacy of his position. Having done all this in a neat speech, I took leave.

One fine morning very shortly afterwards, "I awoke and found myself famous".* The extent of my renown will be best estimated by reference to the editorial opinions of the day. These opinions, it will be seen, were embodied in critical notices of the number of the *Lollipop* containing my poem, and are perfectly satisfactory, conclusive and clear – with the exception, perhaps, of the hieroglyphical marks "Sep. 15 – 1 t"* appended to each of the critiques.

The *Owl*, a journal of profound sagacity and well known for the deliberate gravity of its literary decisions – the *Owl*, I say, spoke as follows:

> The LOLLIPOP! The October number of this delicious magazine surpasses its predecessors, and sets competition at defiance. In the beauty of its typography and paper, in the number and excellence of its steel plates – as well as in the literary merit of its contributions – the *Lollipop* compares with its slow-paced rivals as Hyperion with satyr.* The *Humdrum*, the *Rowdy-Dow* and the *Goosetherumfoodle* excel, it is true, in braggadocio, but in all other points give us the *Lollipop*! How this celebrated journal can sustain its evidently tremendous expenses is more than we can understand. To be sure, it has a circulation of 100,000, and its subscription list has increased one fourth during the

> last month – but, on the other hand, the sums it disburses constantly for contributions are inconceivable. It is reported that Mr Slyass received no less than thirty-seven and a half cents for his inimitable paper on "Pigs". With Mr CRAB as editor, and with such names upon the list of contributors as SNOB and Slyass, there can be no such word as "fail" for the *Lollipop*. Go and subscribe. Sep. 15 – 1 t.

I must say that I was gratified with this high-toned notice from a paper so respectable as the *Owl*. The placing my name – that is to say, my *nom de guerre** – in priority of station to that of the great Slyass was a compliment as happy as I felt it to be deserved.

My attention was next arrested by these paragraphs in the *Toad* – a print highly distinguished for its uprightness and independence, from its entire freedom from sycophancy and subservience to the givers of dinners:

> The *Lollipop* for October is out in advance of all its contemporaries, and infinitely surpasses them, of course, in the splendour of its embellishments, as well as in the richness of its contents. The *Humdrum*, the *Rowdy-Dow* and the *Goosetherumfoodle* excel, we admit, in braggadocio, but, in all other points, give us the *Lollipop*. How this celebrated magazine can sustain its evidently tremendous expenses is more than we can understand. To be sure, it has a circulation of 200,000, and its subscription list has increased one third during the last fortnight, but, on the other hand, the sums it disburses monthly for contributions are fearfully great. We learn that Mr Mumblethumb received no less than fifty cents for his late 'Monody in a Mud Puddle'.
>
> Among the original contributors to the present number we notice (besides the eminent editor, Mr CRAB), such men as SNOB, Slyass and Mumblethumb. Apart from the editorial matter, the most valuable paper, nevertheless, is, we think, a poetical gem by "Snob" on the "Oil-of-Bob" – but our readers must not suppose from the title of this incomparable *bijou** that it bears any similitude to some balderdash on the same subject by a certain contemptible individual whose name is unmentionable to ears polite. The *present* poem 'On the Oil-of-Bob' has excited universal anxiety and curiosity in respect to the owner of the evident pseudonym, "Snob" – a curiosity which, happily, we have it in our power to satisfy. "Snob" is the *nom de plume* of Mr Thingum Bob, of this city – a relative of the great Mr Thingum (after whom he is named), and otherwise connected with the most illustrious families

> of the state. His father, Thomas Bob, Esq., is an opulent merchant in Smug. Sep. 15 – 1 t.

This generous approbation touched me to the heart – the more especially as it emanated from a source so avowedly, so proverbially pure as the *Toad*. The word "balderdash", as applied to the "Oil-of-Bob" of the *Fly*, I considered singularly pungent and appropriate. The words "gem" and "*bijou*", however, used in reference to my composition, struck me as being, in some degree, feeble. They seemed to me to be deficient in force. They were not sufficiently *prononcés** (as we have it in France).

I had hardly finished reading the *Toad* when a friend placed in my hands a copy of the *Mole*, a daily enjoying high reputation for the keenness of its perception about matters in general, and for the open, honest, above-ground style of its editorials. The *Mole* spoke of the *Lollipop* as follows:

> We have just received the *Lollipop* for October, and *must* say that never before have we perused any single number of any periodical which afforded us a felicity so supreme. We speak advisedly. The *Humdrum*, the *Rowdy-Dow* and the *Goosetherumfoodle* must look well to their laurels. These prints no doubt surpass everything in loudness of pretension, but, in all other points, give us the *Lollipop*! How this celebrated magazine can sustain its evidently tremendous expenses is more than we can comprehend. To be sure, it has a circulation of 300,000, and its subscription list has increased one half within the last week, but then the sum it disburses monthly for contributions is astoundingly enormous. We have it upon good authority that Mr Fatquack received no less than sixty-two cents and a half for his late domestic novelette, the *Dish-Clout*.*
>
> The contributors to the number before us are Mr CRAB (the eminent editor), SNOB, Mumblethumb, Fatquack and others – but, after the inimitable compositions of the editor himself, we prefer a diamond-like effusion from the pen of a rising poet who writes over the signature "Snob" – a *nom de guerre* which we predict will one day extinguish the radiance of "BOZ".* "SNOB", we learn, is a Mr THINGUM BOB, Esq., sole heir of a wealthy merchant of this city, Thomas Bob, Esq., and a near relative of the distinguished Mr Thingum. The title of Mr B.'s admirable poem is the 'Oil-of-Bob' – a somewhat unfortunate name, by the by, as some contemptible vagabond connected with the penny press has already disgusted the town with a great deal of drivel upon the same topic. There will be no danger, however, of confounding the compositions. Sep. 15 – 1 t.

The generous approbation of so clear-sighted a journal as the *Mole* penetrated my soul with delight. The only objection which occurred to me was that the terms "contemptible vagabond" might have been better written "*odious* and contemptible *wretch, villain and vagabond*". This would have sounded more gracefully, I think. "Diamond-like", also, was scarcely, it will be admitted, of sufficient intensity to express what the *Mole* evidently *thought* of the brilliancy of the 'Oil-of-Bob'.

On the same afternoon in which I saw these notices in the *Owl*, the *Toad* and the *Mole*, I happened to meet with a copy of the *Daddy-Long-Legs*, a periodical proverbial for the extreme extent of its understanding. And it was the *Daddy-Long-Legs* which spoke thus:

> The *Lollipop*! This gorgeous magazine is already before the public for October. The question of pre-eminence is for ever put to rest, and hereafter it will be excessively preposterous in the *Humdrum*, the *Rowdy-Dow* or the *Goosetherumfoodle* to make any further spasmodic attempts at competition. These journals may excel the *Lollipop* in outcry, but, in all other points, give us the *Lollipop*! How this celebrated magazine can sustain its evidently tremendous expenses is past comprehension. To be sure it has a circulation of precisely half a million, and its subscription list has increased seventy-five per cent within the last couple of days, but then the sums it disburses monthly for contributions are scarcely credible: we are cognizant of the fact that Mademoiselle Cribalittle received no less than eighty-seven cents and a half for her late valuable Revolutionary tale, entitled 'The York Town Katy-Did, and the Bunker Hill Katy Didn't'.
>
> The most able papers in the present number are, of course, those furnished by the editor (the eminent Mr CRAB), but there are numerous magnificent contributions from such names as SNOB, Mademoiselle Cribalittle, Slyass, Mrs Fibalittle, Mumblethumb, Mrs Squibalittle and, last though not least, Fatquack. The world may well be challenged to produce so rich a galaxy of genius.
>
> The poem over the signature "SNOB" is, we find, attracting universal commendation, and, we are constrained to say, deserves, if possible, even more applause than it has received. The 'Oil-of-Bob' is the title of this masterpiece of eloquence and art. One or two of our readers *may* have a *very* faint, although sufficiently disgusting recollection of a poem (?) similarly entitled, the perpetration of a miserable penny-a-liner, mendicant and cut-throat connected in the capacity of scullion, we believe,

> with one of the indecent prints about the purlieus of the city – we beg them, for God's sake, not to confound the compositions. The author of *the* 'Oil-of-Bob' is, we hear, THINGUM BOB, Esq., a gentleman of high genius and a scholar. "Snob" is merely a *nom de guerre*. Sep. 15 – 1 t.

I could scarcely restrain my indignation while I perused the concluding portions of this diatribe. It was clear to me that the yea-nay manner – not to say the gentleness, the positive forbearance, with which the *Daddy-Long-Legs* spoke of that pig, the editor of the *Gadfly* – it was evident to me, I say, that this gentleness of speech could proceed from nothing else than a partiality for the Fly – whom it was clearly the intention of the *Daddy-Long-Legs* to elevate into reputation at my expense. Anyone, indeed, might perceive with half an eye that, had the real design of the *Daddy* been what it wished to appear, it (the *Daddy*) might have expressed itself in terms more direct, more pungent and altogether more to the purpose. The words "penny-a-liner", "mendicant", "scullion" and "cut-throat" were epithets so intentionally inexpressive and equivocal as to be worse than nothing when applied to the author of the very worst stanzas ever penned by one of the human race. We all know what is meant by "damning with faint praise",* and, on the other hand, who could fail seeing through the covert purpose of the *Daddy* – that of glorifying with feeble abuse?

What the *Daddy* chose to say of the *Fly*, however, was no business of mine. What it said of myself *was*. After the noble manner in which the *Owl*, the *Toad*, the *Mole* had expressed themselves in respect to my ability, it was rather too much to be coolly spoken of by a thing like the *Daddy-Long-Legs* as merely "a gentleman of high genius and a scholar". Gentleman indeed! I made up my mind at once either to get a written apology from the *Daddy-Long-Legs* or to call it out.

Full of this purpose, I looked about me to find a friend whom I could entrust with a message to His Daddyship, and, as the editor of the *Lollipop* had given me marked tokens of regard, I at length concluded to seek assistance upon the present occasion.

I have never yet been able to account, in a manner satisfactory to my own understanding, for the *very* peculiar countenance and demeanour with which Mr Crab listened to me as I unfolded to him my design. He again went through the scene of the bell rope and cudgel, and did not omit the duck. At one period I thought he really intended to quack. His fit, nevertheless, finally subsided as before, and he began to act and speak in a rational way. He declined bearing the cartel,* however, and in fact dissuaded me from sending it at all, but was candid enough to admit that the *Daddy-Long-Legs* had been disgracefully in the wrong – more especially in what related to the epithets "gentleman and scholar".

Towards the end of this interview with Mr Crab, who really appeared to take a paternal interest in my welfare, he suggested to me that I might turn an honest penny and at the same time advance my reputation by occasionally playing Thomas Hawk for the *Lollipop*.

I begged Mr Crab to inform me who was Mr Thomas Hawk, and how it was expected that I should play him.

Here Mr Crab again "made great eyes" (as we say in Germany), but at length, recovering himself from a profound attack of astonishment, he assured me that he employed the words "Thomas Hawk" to avoid the colloquialism Tommy, which was low – but that the true idea was Tommy Hawk – or tomahawk – and that by "playing tomahawk" he referred to scalping, browbeating and otherwise using up the herd of poor-devil authors.

I assured my patron that, if this was all, I was perfectly resigned to the task of playing Thomas Hawk. Hereupon Mr Crab desired me to use up the editor of the *Gadfly* forthwith in the fiercest style within the scope of my ability, and as a specimen of my powers. This I did, upon the spot, in a review of the original 'Oil-of-Bob' occupying thirty-six pages of the *Lollipop*. I found playing Thomas Hawk, indeed, a far less onerous occupation than poetizing, for I went upon *system* altogether, and thus it was easy to do the thing thoroughly well. My practice was this. I bought auction copies (cheap) of Lord Brougham's *Speeches*,* Cobbett's *Complete Works*,* the *New Slang Syllabus*, the *Whole Art of Snubbing*, Prentice's *Billingsgate* (folio edition) and *Lewis G. Clark on Tongue*.* These works I cut up thoroughly with a curry-comb,* and then, throwing the shreds into a sieve, sifted out carefully all that might be thought decent (a mere trifle), reserving the hard phrases, which I threw into a large tin pepper castor with longitudinal holes, so that an entire sentence could get through without material injury. The mixture was then ready for use. When called upon to play Thomas Hawk, I anointed a sheet of foolscap with the white of a gander's egg. Then, shredding the thing to be reviewed as I had previously shredded the books – only with more care, so as to get every word separate – I threw the latter shreds in with the former, screwed on the lid of the castor, gave it a shake and so dusted out the mixture upon the egged foolscap, where it stuck. The effect was beautiful to behold. It was captivating. Indeed, the reviews I brought to pass by this simple expedient have never been approached, and were the wonder of the world. At first, through bashfulness – the result of inexperience – I was a little put out by a certain inconsistency, a certain air of the *bizarre* (as we say in France) worn by the composition as a whole. All the phrases did not *fit* (as we say in the Anglo-Saxon). Many were quite awry. Some, even, were upside down, and there were none of them which were not, in some measure, injured in regard to effect by this latter species of accident when it occurred – with the exception of Mr Lewis Clark's paragraphs, which were so vigorous and altogether stout that they seemed not particularly disconcerted by any extreme of position, but looked equally happy and satisfactory whether on their heads or on their heels.

What became of the editor of the *Gadfly* after the publication of my criticism on his 'Oil-of-Bob' it is somewhat difficult to determine. The most reasonable conclusion is that he wept himself to death. At all events, he disappeared instantaneously from the face of the earth, and no man has seen even the ghost of him since.

This matter having been properly accomplished, and the Furies appeased, I grew at once into high favour with Mr Crab. He took me into his confidence, gave me a permanent situation as Thomas Hawk of the *Lollipop* and, as for the present he could afford me no salary, allowed me to profit, at discretion, by his advice.

"My dear Thingum," said he to me one day after dinner, "I respect your abilities and love you as a son. You shall be my heir. When I die, I will bequeath you the *Lollipop*. In the mean time, I will make a man of you – I will, provided always that you follow my counsel. The first thing to do is to get rid of the old bore."

"Boar?" said I enquiringly. "Pig, eh?... *aper*?* (as we say in Latin) – who?... where?"

"Your father," said he.

"Precisely," I replied. "Pig."

"You have your fortune to make, Thingum," resumed Mr Crab, "and that governor of yours is a millstone about your neck. We must cut him at once." Here I took out my knife. "We must cut him," continued Mr Crab, "decidedly and for ever. He won't do – he *won't*. Upon second thoughts, you had better kick him or cane him, or something of that kind."

"What do you say," I suggested modestly, "to my kicking him in the first instance, caning him afterwards, and winding up by tweaking his nose?"

Mr Crab looked at me musingly for some moments, and then answered: "I think, Mr Bob, that what you propose would answer sufficiently well – indeed, remarkably well, that is to say, as far as it went – but barbers are exceedingly hard to cut, and I think upon the whole that, having performed upon Thomas Bob the operations you suggest, it would be advisable to blacken with your fists both his eyes very carefully and thoroughly, to prevent his ever seeing you again in fashionable promenades. After doing this, I really do not perceive that you can do any more. However... it might be just as well to roll him once or twice in the gutter, and then put him in charge of the police. Any time the next morning you can call at the watch-house and swear an assault."

I was much affected by the kindness of feeling towards me personally which was evinced in this excellent advice of Mr Crab, and I did not fail to profit by it forthwith. The result was that I got rid of the old bore and began to feel a little independent and gentlemanlike. The want of money, however, was, for a few weeks, a source of some discomfort, but at length, by carefully putting to use my two eyes and observing how matters went just in front of my nose, I perceived how the thing was to be brought about. I say "thing" – be it observed – for they tell me the Latin for it is *rem*. By the way, talking of Latin, can any one tell me the meaning of *quocunque* – or what is the meaning of *modo*?*

My plan was exceedingly simple. I bought, for a song, a sixteenth of the *Snapping Turtle* – that was all. The thing was *done*, and I put money in my purse. There were some trivial arrangements afterwards, to be sure, but these formed no portion of the plan. They were a consequence – a result. For example, I bought pen, ink and paper, and put them into furious activity. Having thus completed a magazine article, I gave it, for appellation, "FOL LOL, *by the Author of* 'THE OIL-OF-BOB'", and enveloped it to the *Goosetherumfoodle*. That journal however, having pronounced it "twattle" in the "Monthly Notices to Correspondents", I reheaded the paper "Hey-Diddle-Diddle", by THINGUM BOB, Esq., Author of the 'Ode on the Oil-of-Bob' *and* Editor of the *Snapping Turtle*". With this amendment, I re-enclosed it to the *Goosetherumfoodle*, and, while I awaited a reply, published daily, in the *Turtle*, six columns of what may be termed philosophical and analytical investigation of the literary merits of the *Goosetherumfoodle*, as well as of the personal character of the editor of the *Goosetherumfoodle*. At the end of a week, the *Goosetherumfoodle* discovered that it had, by some odd mistake, "confounded a stupid article headed 'Hey-Diddle-Diddle', and composed by some unknown ignoramus, with a gem of resplendent lustre similarly entitled, the work of Thingum Bob, Esq., the celebrated author of the 'Oil-of-Bob'." The *Goosetherumfoodle* deeply "regretted this very natural accident", and promised, moreover, an insertion of the *genuine* "Hey-Diddle-Diddle" in the very next number of the magazine.

The fact is, I *thought* – I *really* thought, I thought at the time, I thought *then*, and have no reason for thinking otherwise *now* – that the *Goosetherumfoodle did* make a mistake. With the best intentions in the world, I never knew anything that made as many singular mistakes as the *Goosetherumfoodle*. From that day I took a liking to the *Goosetherumfoodle*, and the result was I soon saw into the very depths of its literary merits, and did not fail to expatiate upon them in the *Turtle* whenever a fitting opportunity occurred. And it is to be regarded as a very peculiar coincidence – as one of those positively *remarkable* coincidences which set a man to serious thinking – that just such a total revolution of opinion, just such entire *bouleversement** (as we say in French), just such thorough *topsy-turviness* (if I may be permitted to employ a rather forcible term of the Choctaws) as happened *pro* and *con* between myself on the one part and the *Goosetherumfoodle* on the other, did actually again happen, in a brief period afterwards and with precisely similar circumstances, in the case of myself and the *Rowdy-Dow*, and in the case of myself and the *Humdrum*.

Thus it was that, by a masterstroke of genius, I at length consummated my triumphs by "putting money in my purse", and thus may be said really and fairly to have commenced that brilliant and eventful career which rendered me illustrious, and which now enables me to say, with Chateaubriand, "I have made history" – "*J'ai fait l'histoire*".*

I have indeed "made history". From the bright epoch which I now record, my actions – my works – are the property of mankind. They are familiar to the world. It is, then, needless for me to detail how, soaring rapidly, I fell heir to the *Lollipop*, how I merged this journal in the *Humdrum*, how again I made purchase of the *Rowdy-Dow*, thus combining the three periodicals – how, lastly, I effected a bargain for the sole remaining rival, and united all the literature of the country in one magnificent magazine known everywhere as the

Rowdy-Dow, Lollipop, Humdrum
and
GOOSETHERUMFOODLE

Yes – I have made history. My fame is universal. It extends to the uttermost ends of the earth. You cannot take up a common newspaper in which you shall not see some allusion to the immortal THINGUM BOB. It is Mr Thingum Bob said so, and Mr Thingum Bob wrote this, and Mr Thingum Bob did that. But I am meek and expire with an humble heart. After all, what is it, this indescribable something which men will persist in terming "genius"? I agree with Buffon – with Hogarth: it is but *diligence*, after all.*

Look at *me*!… how I laboured… how I toiled… how I wrote! Ye Gods, did I *not* write? I knew not the word "ease". By day I adhered to my desk, and at night, a pale student, I consumed the midnight oil. You should have seen me – you *should*. I leant to the right. I leant to the left. I sat forward. I sat backward. I sat *tête baissée** (as they have it in the Kickapoo),* bowing my head close to the alabaster page. And, through all, I… *wrote*. Through joy and through sorrow, I… *wrote*. Through hunger and through thirst, I… *wrote*. Through good report and through ill report, I… *wrote*. Through sunshine and through moonshine, I… *wrote*. *What* I wrote it is unnecessary to say. The *style*! – that was the thing. I caught it from Fatquack… whizz!… fizz!… and I am giving you a specimen of it now.

X-ING A PARAGRAB*

As it is well known that the "wise men" came "from the East",* and as Mr Touch-and-Go Bullet-Head* came from the East, it follows that Mr Bullet-Head was a wise man – and if collateral proof of the matter be needed, here we have it: Mr B. was an editor. Irascibility was his sole foible, for in fact the obstinacy of which men accused him was anything but his *foible*, since he justly considered it his *forte*. It was his strong point, his virtue – and it would have required all the logic of a Brownson* to convince him that it was "anything else".

I have shown that Touch-and-Go Bullet-Head was a wise man, and the only occasion on which he did not prove infallible was when, abandoning that legitimate home for all wise men, the East, he migrated to the city of Alexander-the-Great-o-Nopolis, or some place of a similar title, out West.

I must do him the justice to say, however, that when he made up his mind finally to settle in that town, it was under the impression that no newspaper, and consequently no editor, existed in that particular section of the country. In establishing the *Teapot*, he expected to have the field all to himself. I feel confident he never would have dreamt of taking up his residence in Alexander-the-Great-o-Nopolis had he been aware that, in Alexander-the-Great-o-Nopolis, there lived a gentleman named John Smith (if I rightly remember), who for many years had there quietly grown fat in editing and publishing the *Alexander-the-Great-o-Nopolis Gazette*. It was solely, therefore, on account of having been misinformed that Mr Bullet-Head found himself in Alex... suppose we call it Nopolis* "for short" – but, as he *did* find himself there, he determined to keep up his character for obst... for firmness, and remain. So remain he did – and he did more: he unpacked his press, type, etc., etc., rented an office exactly opposite to that of the *Gazette* and, on the third morning after his arrival, issued the first number of the *Alexan*... that is to say, of the *Nopolis Teapot* – as nearly as I can recollect, this was the name of the new paper.

The leading article, I must admit, was brilliant – not to say severe. It was especially bitter about things in general – and as for the editor of the *Gazette*, he was torn all to pieces in particular. Some of Bullet-Head's remarks were really so fiery that I have always, since that time, been forced to look upon John Smith, who is still alive, in the light of a salamander.* I cannot pretend to give *all* the *Teapot*'s paragraphs verbatim, but one of them runs thus:

> Oh, yes!… Oh, we perceive! Oh, no doubt! The editor over the way is a genius… Oh, my! Oh, goodness gracious!… What *is* this world coming to? *Oh, tempora! Oh, Moses!**

A philippic at once so caustic and so classical alighted like a bombshell among the hitherto peaceful citizens of Nopolis. Groups of excited individuals gathered at the corners of the streets. Everyone awaited with heartfelt anxiety the reply of the dignified Smith. Next morning it appeared as follows:

> We quote from the *Teapot* of yesterday the subjoined paragraph: "*Oh*, yes! *Oh*, we perceive! *Oh*, no doubt! *Oh*, my! *Oh*, goodness! *Oh*, tempora! *Oh*, Moses!" Why, the fellow is all O! That accounts for his reasoning in a circle, and explains why there is neither beginning nor end to him, nor to anything he says. We really do not believe the vagabond can write a word that hasn't an O in it. Wonder if this O-ing is a habit of his? By the by, he came away from down East in a great hurry. Wonder if he O's as much there as he does here? "O, it is pitiful!"*

The indignation of Mr Bullet-Head at these scandalous insinuations I shall not attempt to describe. On the eel-skinning principle,* however, he did not seem to be so much incensed at the attack upon his integrity as one might have imagined. It was the sneer at his *style* that drove him to desperation. What!… *he*, Touch-and-Go Bullet-Head!… not able to write a word without an O in it! He would soon let the jackanapes see that he was mistaken. Yes! he would let him see how much he was mistaken, the puppy! He, Touch-and-Go Bullet-Head, of Frogpondium,* would let Mr John Smith perceive that he, Bullet-Head, could indite, if it so pleased him, a whole paragraph – ay, a whole article! – in which that contemptible vowel should not *once* – not even *once* – make its appearance. But no… that would be yielding a point to the said John Smith. *He*, Bullet-Head, would make *no* alteration in his style to suit the caprices of any Mr Smith in Christendom. Perish so vile a thought! The O for ever! He would persist in the O. He would be as O-wy as O-wy could be.

Burning with the chivalry of this determination, the great Touch-and-Go, in the next *Teapot*, came out merely with this simple but resolute paragraph in reference to this unhappy affair:

> The editor of the *Teapot* has the *honour* of advising the editor of the *Gazette* that he (the *Teapot*) will take an opportunity in tomorrow morning's paper of convincing him (the *Gazette*) that he (the *Teapot*) both can and will be *his own master* as regards style, he (the *Teapot*) intending to show him (the *Gazette*) the supreme and indeed the withering contempt with which the criticism of him (the *Gazette*) inspires the independent bosom of him (the *Teapot*) by composing for the especial gratification (?) of him (the *Gazette*) a leading article, of some extent, in which the beautiful vowel – the emblem of Eternity, yet so offensive to the hyper-exquisite delicacy of him (the *Gazette*) – shall most certainly *not be avoided* by his (the *Gazette*'s) most obedient, humble servant, the *Teapot*. "So much for Buckingham!"*

In fulfilment of the awful threat thus darkly intimated rather than decidedly enunciated, the great Bullet-Head, turning a deaf ear to all entreaties for "copy", and simply requesting his foreman to "go to the d——l" when he (the foreman) assured him (the *Teapot*!) that it was high time to "go to press" – turning a deaf ear to everything, I say, the great Bullet-Head sat up until daybreak, consuming the midnight oil and absorbed in the composition of the really unparalleled paragraph which follows:

> So ho, John! How now? Told you so, you know. Don't crow, another time, before you're out of the woods! Does your mother *know* you're out? Oh, no, no!… So go home at once, now, John, to your odious old woods of Concord! Go home to your woods, old owl – go! You won't? Oh, poh, poh, John, don't do so! You've *got* to go, you know! So go at once, and don't go slow, for nobody owns you here, you know. Oh, John, John, if you *don't* go, you're no *homo** – no! You're only a fowl, an owl, a cow, a sow; a doll, a poll; a poor old good-for-nothing-to-nobody, log, dog, hog or frog come out of a Concord bog. Cool, now – cool! *Do* be cool, you fool! None of your crowing, old cock! Don't frown so – don't! Don't hollo, nor howl, nor growl, nor bow-wow-wow! Good Lord, John, how

you *do* look! Told you so, you know – but stop rolling your goose of an old poll about so, and go and drown your sorrows in a bowl!

Exhausted, very naturally, by so stupendous an effort, the great Touch-and-Go could attend to nothing further that night. Firmly, composedly, yet with an air of conscious power, he handed his MS to the devil* in waiting, and then, walking leisurely home, retired with ineffable dignity to bed.

Meantime the devil to whom the copy was entrusted ran upstairs to his "case"* in an unutterable hurry, and forthwith made a commencement at "setting" the MS "up".

In the first place, of course – as the opening word was "So" – he made a plunge into the capital-S hole and came out in triumph with a capital S. Elated by this success, he immediately threw himself upon the little-o box with a blindfold impetuosity – but who shall describe his horror when his fingers came up without the anticipated letter in their clutch? Who shall paint his astonishment and rage at perceiving, as he rubbed his knuckles, that he had been only thumping them to no purpose against the bottom of an *empty* box? Not a single little o was in the little-o hole – and, glancing fearfully at the capital-O partition, he found *that*, to his extreme terror, in a precisely similar predicament. Awe-stricken, his first impulse was to rush to the foreman.

"Sir!" said he, gasping for breath. "I can't never set up nothing without no o's."

"*What* do you mean by that?" growled the foreman, who was in a very ill humour at being kept so late.

"Why, sir, there beant an o in the office, neither a big 'un nor a little 'un!"

"What… what the d——l has become of all that were in the case?"

"*I* don't know, sir," said the boy, "but one of them ere *G'zette* devils is bin prowling 'bout here all night, and I spect *he's* gone and cabbaged 'em every one."

"Dod rot him! I haven't a doubt of it," replied the foreman, getting purple with rage. "But I tell you what you do, Bob, that's a good boy – you go over the first chance you get and hook every one of their i's and (d—n them!) their izzards."*

"Jist so," replied Bob, with a wink and a frown. "I'll be into 'em, *I'll* let 'em know a thing or two – but in de mean time, that ere paragrab? *Mus* go in tonight, you know – else there'll be the d——l to pay, and—"

"And not a *bit* of pitch hot,"* interrupted the foreman, with a deep sigh and an emphasis on the "bit". "Is it a *very* long paragraph, Bob?"

"Shouldn't call it a *wery* long paragrab," said Bob.

"Ah, well, then! Do the best you can with it! We *must* get to press," said the foreman, who was over head and ears in work. "Just stick in some other letter for o – nobody's going to read the fellow's trash anyhow."

"*Wery* well," replied Bob, "here goes it!" – and off he hurried to his case, muttering as he went: "Considdeble vell, them ere expressions, perticcler for a man as doesn't swar. So I's to gouge out all their eyes, eh? And d—n all their gizzards! Vell! this here's the chap as is just able *for* to do it." The fact is that although Bob was but twelve years old and four feet high, he was equal to any amount of fight, in a small way.

The exigency here described is by no means of rare occurrence in printing offices – and I cannot tell how to account for it, but the fact is indisputable that when the exigency *does* occur, it almost always happens that x is adopted as a substitute for the letter deficient. The true reason, perhaps, is that x is rather the most superabundant letter in the cases, or at least *was* so in the old times – long enough to render the substitution in question an habitual thing with printers. As for Bob, he would have considered it heretical to employ any other character, in a case of this kind, than the x to which he had been accustomed.

"I *shell* have to x this ere paragrab," said he to himself as he read it over in astonishment. "But it's jest about the awfulest *o*-wy paragrab I ever *did* see." So x it he did, unflinchingly, and to press it went *x-ed*.

Next morning, the population of Nopolis were taken all aback by reading in *The Teapot* the following extraordinary leader:

> Sx hx, Jxhn! Hxw nxw? Txld yxu sx, yxu knxw. Dxn't crxw, anxther time, befxre yxu're xut xf the wxxds! Dxes yxur mxther *knxw* yxu're xut? Xh, nx, nx!… Sx gx hxme at xnce, nxw, Jxhn, tx yxur xdixus xld wxxds xf Cxncxrd! Gx hxme tx yxur wxxds, xld xwl – gx! Yxu wxn't? Xh, pxh, pxh, Jxhn, dxn't dx sx! Yxu've *gxt* tx gx, yxu knxw! Sx gx at xnce, and dxn't gx slxw, fxr nxbxdy xwns yxu here, yxu knxw. Xh, Jxhn, Jxhn, if yxu *dxn't* gx, yxu're nx *hxmx* – nx! Yxu're xnly a fxwl, an xwl, a cxw, a sxw; a dxll, a pxll; a pxxr xld gxxd-fxr-nxthing-tx-nxbxdy, lxg, dxg, hxg xr frxg cxme xut xf a Cxncxrd bxg. Cxxl, nxw – cxxl! *Dx* be cxxl, yxu fxxl! Nxne xf yxur crxwing, xld cxck! Dxn't frxwn sx – dxn't! Dxn't hxllx, nxr hxwl, nxr grxwl, nxr bxw-wxw-wxw! Gxxd Lxrd, Jxhn, hxw yxu *dx* lxxk! Txld yxu sx, yxu knxw – but stxp rxlling yxur gxxse xf an xld pxll abxut sx, and gx and drxwn yxur sxrrxws in a bxwl!

The uproar occasioned by this mystical and cabalistical article is not to be conceived. The first definite idea entertained by the populace was that some diabolical treason lay concealed in the hieroglyphics, and there was a general rush to Bullet-Head's residence for the purpose of riding him on a rail* – but that gentleman was nowhere to be found. He had vanished, no one could tell how – and not even the ghost of him has ever been seen since.

Unable to discover its legitimate object, the popular fury at length subsided – leaving behind it, by way of sediment, quite a medley of opinion about this unhappy affair.

One gentleman thought the whole an X-ellent joke.

Another said that, indeed, Bullet-Head had shown much X-uberance of fancy.

A third admitted him X-entric, but no more.

A fourth could only suppose it the Yankee's design to X-press, in a general way, his X-asperation.

"Say, rather, to set an X-ample to posterity," suggested a fifth.

That Bullet-Head had been driven to an extremity was clear to all – and in fact, since *that* editor could not be found, there was some talk about lynching the other one.

The more common conclusion, however, was that the affair was, simply, X-traordinary and in-X-plicable. Even the town mathematician confessed that he could make nothing of so dark a problem. X, everybody knew, was an unknown quantity – but in this case (as he properly observed), there was an unknown quantity of X.

The opinion of Bob, the devil (who kept dark about his having "X-ed the paragrab"), did not meet with so much attention as I think it deserved, although it was very openly and very fearlessly expressed. He said that, for his part, he had no doubt about the matter at all; that it was a clear case; that "Mr Bullet-Head never *could* be persvaded fur to drink like other folks, but vas *con*tinually a-svigging o' that ere blessed XXX ale – and, as a naiteral consekvence, it just puffed him up savage, and made him X (cross) in the X-treme".

THE ANGEL OF THE ODD*

AN EXTRAVAGANZA

It was a chilly November afternoon. I had just consummated an unusually hearty dinner, of which the dyspeptic *truffe** formed not the least important item, and was sitting alone in the dining room with my feet upon the fender and at my elbow a small table which I had rolled up to the fire, and upon which were some apologies for dessert, with some miscellaneous bottles of wine, spirit and *liqueur*. In the morning I had been reading Glover's *Leonidas*, Wilkie's *Epigoniad*, Lamartine's *Pilgrimage*, Barlow's *Columbiad*, Tuckerman's *Sicily* and Griswold's "Curiosities"* – I am willing to confess, therefore, that I now felt a little stupid.* I made effort to arouse myself by aid of frequent Lafite,* and, all failing, I betook myself to a stray newspaper in despair. Having carefully perused the column of "houses to let" and the column of "dogs lost", and then the two columns of "wives and apprentices runaway", I attacked with great resolution the editorial matter, and, reading it from beginning to end without understanding a syllable, conceived the possibility of its being Chinese, and so reread it from the end to the beginning, but with no more satisfactory result. I was about throwing away in disgust

> This folio of four pages, happy work!
> Which not even critics criticize*

when I felt my attention somewhat aroused by the paragraph which follows:

> The avenues to death are numerous and strange. A London paper mentions the decease of a person from a singular cause. He was playing at "puff the dart", which is played with a long needle inserted in some

> worsted and blown at a target through a tin tube. He placed the needle at the wrong end of the tube, and, drawing his breath strongly to puff the dart forwards with force, drew the needle into his throat. It entered the lungs, and in a few days killed him.

Upon seeing this, I fell into a great rage, without exactly knowing why. "This thing," I exclaimed, "is a contemptible falsehood… a poor hoax… the lees of the invention of some pitiable penny-a-liner… of some wretched concoctor of accidents in Cockaigne.* These fellows, knowing the extravagant gullibility of the age, set their wits to work in the imagination of improbable possibilities – of odd accidents, as they term them – but to a reflecting intellect (like mine)," I added in parenthesis, putting my forefinger unconsciously to the side of my nose, "to a contemplative understanding such as I myself possess, it seems evident at once that the marvellous increase of late in these 'odd accidents' is by far the oddest accident of all. For my own part, I intend to believe nothing henceforward that has anything of the 'singular' about it."

"Mein Gott,* den, vat a vool you bees for dat!" replied one of the most remarkable voices I ever heard. At first I took it for a rumbling in my ears, such as a man sometimes experiences when getting very drunk, but, upon second thought, I considered the sound as more nearly resembling that which proceeds from an empty barrel beaten with a big stick – and, in fact, this I should have concluded it to be but for the articulation of the syllables and words. I am by no means naturally nervous, and the very few glasses of Lafite which I had sipped served to embolden me a little, so that I felt nothing of trepidation, but merely uplifted my eyes with a leisurely movement and looked carefully around the room for the intruder. I could not, however, perceive anyone at all.

"Humph!" resumed the voice as I continued my survey. "You mus pe so dronk as de pig, den, for not zee me as I zit here at your zide."

Hereupon I bethought me of looking immediately before my nose – and there, sure enough, confronting me at the table sat a personage nondescript, although not altogether indescribable. His body was a wine pipe,* or a rum puncheon,* or something of that character, and had a truly Falstaffian air.* In its nether extremity were inserted two kegs, which seemed to answer all the purposes of legs. For arms there dangled from the upper portion of the carcass two tolerably long bottles, with the necks outward for hands. All the head that I saw the monster possessed of was one of those Hessian canteens* which resemble a large snuffbox with a hole in the middle of the lid. This canteen (with a funnel on its top, like a cavalier cap slouched over the eyes) was set on edge upon the puncheon with the hole towards myself – and through this hole, which seemed puckered up like the mouth of a very precise old maid, the creature was emitting certain rumbling and grumbling noises which he evidently intended for intelligible talk.

"I zay," said he, "you mos pe dronk as de pig, vor zit dare and not zee me zit ere – and I zay, doo, you mos pe pigger vool as de goose, vor to dispelief vat iz print in de print. 'Tiz de troof – dat it iz – eberry vord ob it."

"Who are you, pray?" said I, with much dignity, although somewhat puzzled. "How did you get here? And what is it you are talking about?"

"As vor ow I com'd ere," replied the figure, "dat iz none of your pizziness... and as vor vat I be talking apout, I be talk apout vat I tink proper... and as vor who I be, vy, dat is de very ting I com'd here for to let you zee for yourzelf."

"You are a drunken vagabond," said I, "and I shall ring the bell and order my footman to kick you into the street."

"He he he!" said the fellow. "Hu hu hu! Dat you can't do."

"Can't do!" said I. "What do you mean?... I can't do what?"

"Ring de pell," he replied, attempting a grin with his little villainous mouth.

Upon this, I made an effort to get up, in order to put my threat into execution, but the ruffian just reached across the table very deliberately, and, hitting me a tap on the forehead with the neck of one of the long bottles, knocked me back into the armchair from which I had half arisen. I was utterly astounded – and, for a moment, was quite at a loss what to do. In the mean time, he continued his talk.

"You zee," said he, "it iz te bess vor zit still – and now you shall know who I pe. Look at me! Zee! I am te *Angel ov te Odd*."

"And odd enough, too," I ventured to reply. "But I was always under the impression that an angel had wings."

"Te wing!" he cried, highly incensed. "Vat I pe do mit te wing? *Mein Gott!* Do you take me vor a shicken?"

"No – oh no!" I replied, much alarmed. "You are no chicken – certainly not."

"Well, den, zit still and pehabe yourself, or I'll rap you again mid me vist. It iz te shicken ab te wing, und te owl ab te wing, und te imp ab te wing, und te head-teuffel* ab te wing. Te angel ab *not* te wing, and I am te *Angel ov te Odd*."

"And your business with me at present is... is..."

"My pizzness!" ejaculated the thing. "Vy, vat a low-bred buppy you mos pe vor to ask a gentleman und an angel apout his pizziness!"

This language was rather more than I could bear, even from an angel – so, plucking up courage, I seized a salt cellar which lay within reach and hurled it at the head of the intruder. Either he dodged, however, or my aim was inaccurate, for all I accomplished was the demolition of the crystal which protected the dial of the clock upon the mantelpiece. As for the angel, he evinced his sense of my assault by giving me two or three hard consecutive raps upon the forehead as before. These reduced me at once to submission, and I am almost ashamed to confess that either through pain or vexation there came a few tears into my eyes.

"Mein Gott!" said the Angel of the Odd, apparently much softened at my distress. "Mein Gott, te man is eder ferry dronk or ferry zorry. You mos not trink it so strong – you mos put te water in te wine. Here, trink dis, like a goot veller, und don't gry now – don't!"

Hereupon, the Angel of the Odd replenished my goblet (which was about a third full of port) with a colourless fluid that he poured from one of his hand bottles. I observed that these bottles had labels about their necks, and that these labels were inscribed "Kirschwasser".*

The considerate kindness of the angel mollified me in no little measure, and, aided by the water with which he diluted my port more than once, I at length regained sufficient temper to listen to his very extraordinary discourse. I cannot pretend to recount all that he told me, but I gleaned from what he said that he was the genius who presided over the *contretemps* of mankind, and whose business it was to bring about the *odd accidents* which are continually astonishing the sceptic. Once or twice, upon my venturing to express my total incredulity in respect to his pretensions, he grew very angry indeed, so that at length I considered it the wiser policy to say nothing at all and let him have his own way. He talked on, therefore, at great length, while I merely leant back in my chair with my eyes shut and amused myself with munching raisins and filliping the stems about the room. But, by and by, the angel suddenly construed this behaviour of mine into contempt. He arose in a terrible passion, slouched his funnel down over his eyes, swore a vast oath, uttered a threat of some character which I did not precisely comprehend and, finally, made me a low bow and departed, wishing me, in the language of the archbishop in *Gil Blas*, "*beaucoup de bonheur et un peu plus de bon sens*".*

His departure afforded me relief. The *very* few glasses of Lafite that I had sipped had the effect of rendering me drowsy, and I felt inclined to take a nap of some fifteen or twenty minutes, as is my custom after dinner. At six I had an appointment of consequence, which it was quite indispensable that I should keep. The policy of insurance for my dwelling house had expired the day before – and, some dispute having arisen, it was agreed that at six I should meet the board of directors of the company and settle the terms of a renewal. Glancing upward at the clock on the mantelpiece (for I felt too drowsy to take out my watch), I had the pleasure to find that I had still twenty-five minutes to spare. It was half-past five: I could easily walk to the insurance office in five minutes, and my usual siestas had never been known to exceed five-and-twenty. I felt sufficiently safe, therefore, and composed myself to my slumbers forthwith.

Having completed them to my satisfaction, I again looked towards the timepiece, and was half inclined to believe in the possibility of odd accidents when I found that, instead of my ordinary fifteen or twenty minutes, I had been dozing only three – for it still wanted seven-and-twenty of the appointed hour. I betook myself again to my nap, and at length a second time awoke, when, to my utter amazement, it *still* wanted twenty-seven minutes of six. I jumped up to examine the clock, and found that it had ceased running. My watch informed me that it was half-past seven – and, of course, having slept two hours, I was too late for my appointment. "It will make no difference," I said. "I can call at the office in the morning and apologize – in the mean time, what can be the matter with the clock?" Upon examining it, I discovered that one of the raisin stems which I had been filliping about the room during the discourse of the Angel of the Odd had flown through the fractured crystal, and, lodging, singularly enough, in the keyhole with an end projecting outward, had thus arrested the revolution of the minute hand.

"Ah!" said I. "I see how it is. This thing speaks for itself. A natural accident, such as *will* happen now and then!"

I gave the matter no further consideration, and at my usual hour retired to bed. Here, having placed a candle upon a reading stand at the bedhead, and having made an attempt to peruse some pages of *The Omnipresence of the Deity*,* I unfortunately fell asleep in less than twenty seconds, leaving the light burning as it was.

My dreams were terrifically disturbed by visions of the Angel of the Odd. Methought he stood at the foot of the couch, drew aside the curtains and, in the hollow, detestable tones of a rum puncheon, menaced me with the bitterest vengeance for the contempt with which I had treated him. He concluded a long harangue by taking off his funnel cap, inserting the tube into my gullet, and thus deluging me with an ocean of kirschwasser, which he poured, in a continuous flood, from one of the long-necked bottles that stood him instead of an arm. My agony was at length insufferable, and I awoke just in time to perceive that a rat had run off with the lighted candle from the stand, but *not* in season to prevent his making his escape with it through the hole. Very soon, a strong suffocating odour assailed my nostrils – the house, I clearly perceived, was on fire. In a few minutes, the blaze broke forth with violence, and in an incredibly brief period the entire building was wrapped in flames. All egress from my chamber, except through a window, was cut off. The crowd, however, quickly procured and raised a long ladder. By means of this I was descending rapidly, and in apparent safety, when a huge hog, about whose rotund stomach, and indeed about whose whole air and physiognomy, there was something which reminded me of the Angel of the Odd – when this hog, I say, which hitherto had been quietly slumbering in the mud, took it suddenly into his head that his left shoulder needed scratching, and could find no more convenient rubbing post than that afforded by the foot of the ladder. In an instant I was precipitated, and had the misfortune to fracture my arm.

This accident, with the loss of my insurance and with the more serious loss of my hair – the whole of which had been singed off by the fire – predisposed me to serious impressions, so that, finally, I made up my mind to take a wife. There was a rich widow disconsolate for the loss of her seventh husband, and to her wounded spirit I offered the balm of my vows. She yielded a reluctant consent to my prayers. I knelt at her feet in gratitude and adoration. She blushed and bowed her luxuriant tresses into close contact with those supplied me, temporarily, by Grandjean.* I know not how the entanglement took place, but so it was. I arose with a shining pate, wigless – she, in disdain and wrath, half buried in alien hair. Thus ended my hopes of the widow by an accident which could not have been anticipated, to be sure, but which the natural sequence of events had brought about.

Without despairing, however, I undertook the siege of a less implacable heart. The Fates were again propitious for a brief period – but again a trivial incident interfered. Meeting my betrothed in an avenue thronged with the elite of the city, I was hastening to greet her with one of my best considered bows when a small particle of some foreign matter, lodging in the corner of my eye, rendered me, for the moment, completely blind. Before I could recover my sight, the lady of my love had disappeared – irreparably affronted at what she chose to consider my premeditated rudeness in passing her by ungreeted. While I stood bewildered at the suddenness of this accident (which might have happened, nevertheless, to anyone under the sun), and while I still continued incapable of sight, I was accosted by the Angel of the Odd, who proffered me his aid with a civility which I had no reason to expect. He examined my disordered eye with much gentleness and skill, informed me that I had a drop in it,* and (whatever a "drop" was) took it out and afforded me relief.

I now considered it high time to die (since fortune had so determined to persecute me), and accordingly made my way to the nearest river. Here, divesting myself of my clothes (for there is no reason why we cannot die as we were born), I threw myself headlong into the current, the sole witness of my fate being a solitary crow that had been seduced into the eating of brandy-saturated corn,* and so had staggered away from his fellows. No sooner had I entered the water than this bird took it into his head to fly away with the most indispensable portion of my apparel. Postponing, therefore, for the present, my suicidal design, I just slipped my nether extremities into the sleeves of my coat and betook myself to a pursuit of the felon with all the nimbleness which the case required and its circumstances would admit. But my evil destiny attended me still. As I ran at full speed with my nose up in the atmosphere and intent only upon the purloiner of my property, I suddenly perceived that my feet rested no longer upon terra firma – the fact is, I had thrown myself over a precipice, and should inevitably have been dashed to pieces but for my good fortune in grasping the end of a long guide rope* which depended* from a passing balloon.

As soon as I sufficiently recovered my senses to comprehend the terrific predicament in which I stood, or rather hung, I exerted all the power of my lungs to make that predicament known to the aeronaut overhead. But for a long time I exerted myself in vain. Either the fool could not or the villain would not perceive me. Meantime, the machine rapidly soared, while my strength even more rapidly failed. I was soon upon the point of resigning myself to my fate and dropping quietly into the sea, when my spirits were suddenly revived by hearing a hollow voice from above, which seemed to be lazily humming an opera air. Looking up, I perceived the Angel of the Odd. He was leaning with his arms folded over the rim of the car, and with a pipe in his mouth, at which he puffed leisurely, seemed to be upon excellent terms with himself and the universe. I was too much exhausted to speak, so I merely regarded him with an imploring air.

For several minutes, although he looked me full in the face, he said nothing. At length, removing carefully his meerschaum* from the right to the left corner of his mouth, he condescended to speak.

"Who pe you," he asked, "und what der teuffel you pe do dare?"

To this piece of impudence, cruelty and affectation, I could reply only by ejaculating the monosyllable "Help!"

"Elp!" echoed the ruffian. "Not I. Dare iz te pottle – elp yourself, und pe tam'd!"

With these words he let fall a heavy bottle of kirschwasser – which, dropping precisely upon the crown of my head, caused me to imagine that my brains were entirely knocked out. Impressed with this idea, I was about to relinquish my hold and give up the ghost with a good grace, when I was arrested by the cry of the angel, who bade me hold on.

"Old on!" he said. "Don't pe in te urry – don't. Will you pe take de odder pottle, or ave you pe got zober yet and come to your zenzes?"

I made haste, hereupon, to nod my head twice – once in the negative, meaning thereby that I would prefer not taking the other bottle at present, and once in the affirmative, intending thus to imply that I *was* sober and *had* positively come to my senses. By these means, I somewhat softened the angel.

"Und you pelief, ten," he enquired, "at te last? You pelief, ten, in te possibilty of te odd?"

I again nodded my head in assent.

"Und you ave pelief in *me*, te Angel of te Odd?"

I nodded again.

"Und you acknowledge tat you pe te blind dronk and te vool?"

I nodded once more.

"Put your right hand into your left-hand preeches pocket, ten, in token ov your vull zubmizzion unto te Angel ov te Odd."

This thing, for very obvious reasons, I found it quite impossible to do. In the first place, my left arm had been broken in my fall from the ladder – and, therefore, had I let go my hold with the right hand, I must have let go altogether. In the second place, I could have no breeches until I came across the crow. I was therefore obliged, much to my regret, to shake my head in the negative – intending thus to give the angel to understand that I found it inconvenient, just at that moment, to comply with his very reasonable demand! No sooner, however, had I ceased shaking my head than…

"Go to der teuffel, ten!" roared the Angel of the Odd.

In pronouncing these words, he drew a sharp knife across the guide rope by which I was suspended, and as we then happened to be precisely over my own house (which, during my peregrinations, had been handsomely rebuilt), it so occurred that I tumbled headlong down the ample chimney and alit upon the dining-room hearth.

Upon coming to my senses (for the fall had very thoroughly stunned me), I found it about four o'clock in the morning. I lay outstretched where I had fallen from the balloon. My head grovelled in the ashes of an extinguished fire, while my feet reposed upon the wreck of a small table, overthrown, and amid the fragments of a miscellaneous dessert, intermingled with a newspaper, some broken glass and shattered bottles, and an empty jug of the Schiedam* kirschwasser. Thus revenged himself the Angel of the Odd.

MELLONTA TAUTA*

On board balloon *Skylark*, April 1,* 2848

Now, my dear friend – now, for your sins, you are to suffer the infliction of a long gossiping letter. I tell you distinctly that I am going to punish you for all your impertinences by being as tedious, as discursive, as incoherent and as unsatisfactory as possible. Besides, here I am, cooped up in a dirty balloon, with some one or two hundred of the *canaille*,* all bound on a *pleasure* excursion (what a funny idea some people have of pleasure!) – and I have no prospect of touching terra firma for a month at least. Nobody to talk to. Nothing to do. When one has nothing to do, then is the time to correspond with one's friends. You perceive, then, why it is that I write you this letter: it is on account of my ennui and your sins.

Get ready your spectacles and make up your mind to be annoyed. I mean to write at you every day during this odious voyage.

Heigho! When will any *invention* visit the human pericranium? Are we for ever to be doomed to the thousand inconveniences of the balloon? Will *nobody* contrive a more expeditious mode of progress? The jog-trot movement, to my thinking, is little less than positive torture. Upon my word, we have not made more than a hundred miles the hour since leaving home! The very birds beat us – at least some of them. I assure you that I do not exaggerate at all. Our motion, no doubt, seems slower than it actually is – this on account of our having no objects about us by which to estimate our velocity, and on account of our going with the wind. To be sure, whenever we meet a balloon, we have a chance of perceiving our rate – and then, I admit, things do not appear so very bad. Accustomed as I am to this mode of travelling, I cannot get over a kind of giddiness whenever a balloon passes us in a current directly overhead. It always seems to me like an immense bird of prey about to pounce upon us and carry us off in its claws. One went over us this morning about sunrise, and so nearly overhead that its drag rope* actually brushed the network suspending our car, and caused us very serious apprehension. Our captain said that if the material of the bag had been the trumpery varnished "silk" of five hundred or a thousand years ago, we should inevitably have been damaged. This silk, as he explained it to me, was a fabric composed of the entrails of a species of earthworm. The worm was carefully fed on mulberries – kind of fruit resembling a watermelon – and, when sufficiently fat, was crushed in a mill. The paste thus arising was called *papyrus* in its primary state, and went through a variety of processes until it finally became "silk". Singular to relate, it was once much admired as an article of *female dress*! Balloons were also very generally constructed from it. A better kind of material, it appears, was subsequently found in the down surrounding the seed vessels of a plant vulgarly called *euphorbium*, and at that time botanically termed "milkweed".* This latter kind of silk was designated as "silk-buckingham",* on account of its superior durability, and was usually prepared for use by being varnished with a solution of gum caoutchouc* – a substance which in some respects must have resembled the gutta-percha* now in common use. This caoutchouc was occasionally called "Indian rubber" or "rubber of twist", and was no doubt one of the numerous *fungi*. Never tell me again that I am not at heart an antiquarian.

Talking of drag ropes – our own, it seems, has this moment knocked a man overboard from one of the small magnetic propellers that swarm in ocean below us – a boat of about six thousand tons, and, from all accounts, shamefully crowded. These diminutive barques should be prohibited from carrying more than a definite number of passengers. The man, of course, was not permitted to get on board again, and was soon out of sight, he and his life-preserver. I rejoice, my dear friend, that we live in an age so enlightened that no such a thing as an individual is supposed to exist. It is the mass for which the true Humanity cares. By the by, talking of Humanity, do you know that our immortal Wiggins is not so original in his views of the social condition and so forth, as his contemporaries are inclined to suppose? Pundit assures me that the same ideas were put nearly in the same way about a thousand years ago by an Irish philosopher called Furrier,* on account of his keeping a retail shop for cat peltries and other furs. Pundit *knows*, you know – there can be no mistake about it. How very wonderfully do we see verified every day the profound observation of the Hindoo Aries Tottle* (as quoted by Pundit): "Thus must we say that, not once or twice, or a few times, but with almost infinite repetitions, the same opinions come round in a circle among men."*

APRIL 2ND. Spoke today the magnetic cutter in charge of the middle section of floating telegraph wires. I learn that when this species of telegraph was first put into operation by Horse,* it was considered quite impossible to convey the wires over sea, but now we are at a loss to comprehend where the difficulty lay! So wags the world. *Tempora mutantur** – excuse me for quoting the Etruscan. What *would* we do without the Atalantic telegraph? (Pundit says Atlantic was the ancient adjective.) We lay to a few minutes to ask the cutter some questions, and learnt, among other glorious news, that civil war is raging in Africa, while the plague is doing its good work beautifully both in Yurope and Ayesher. Is it not truly remarkable that, before the magnificent light shed upon philosophy by Humanity, the world was accustomed to regard war and pestilence as calamities? Do you know that prayers were actually offered up in the ancient temples to the end that these *evils* (!) might not be visited upon mankind? Is it not really difficult to comprehend upon what principle of interest our forefathers acted? Were they so blind as not to perceive that the destruction of a myriad of individuals is only so much positive advantage to the mass?

APRIL 3RD. It is really a very fine amusement to ascend the rope ladder leading to the summit of the balloon bag, and thence survey the surrounding world. From the car below you know the prospect is not so comprehensive – you can see little vertically. But seated here (where I write this), in the luxuriously cushioned open piazza of the summit, one can see everything that is going on in all directions. Just now there is quite a crowd of balloons in sight, and they present a very animated appearance, while the air is resonant with the hum of so many millions of human voices. I have heard it asserted that when Yellow or (Pundit *will* have it) Violet, who is supposed to have been the first aeronaut,* maintained the practicability of traversing the atmosphere in all directions by merely ascending or descending until a favourable current was attained, he was scarcely hearkened to at all by his contemporaries, who looked upon him as merely an ingenious sort of madman, because the philosophers (!) of the day declared the thing impossible. Really now it does seem to me *quite* unaccountable how anything so obviously feasible could have escaped the sagacity of the ancient savants. But in all ages the great obstacles to advancement in art have been opposed by the so-called "men of science". To be sure, *our* men of science are not quite so bigoted as those of old – oh, I have something *so* queer to tell you on this topic. Do you know that it is not more than a thousand years ago since the metaphysicians consented to relieve the people of the singular fancy that there existed but *two possible* *roads for the attainment of Truth*? Believe it if you can! It appears that long, long ago, in the night of Time, there lived a Turkish philosopher (or Hindoo, possibly) called Aries Tottle. This person introduced, or at all events propagated, what was termed the deductive or *a priori* mode of investigation. He started with what he maintained to be *axioms* or "self-evident truths", and thence proceeded "logically" to results. His greatest disciples were one Neuclid* and one Cant.* Well, Aries Tottle flourished supreme until the advent of one Hog, surnamed the "Ettrick Shepherd", who preached an entirely different system, which he called the *a posteriori* or *inductive*.* His plan referred altogether to sensation. He proceeded by observing, analysing and classifying facts – *instantiæ naturæ*,* as they were affectedly called – into general laws. Aries Tottle's mode, in a word, was based on *noumena** – Hog's on *phenomena*. Well, so great was the admiration excited by this latter system that, at its first introduction, Aries Tottle fell into disrepute, but finally he recovered ground and was permitted to divide the realm of Truth with his more modern rival. The savants now maintained the Aristotelian and *Baconian* roads were the sole possible avenues to knowledge. "Baconian", you must know, was an adjective invented as equivalent to Hoggian and more euphonious and dignified.

Now, my dear friend, I do assure you, most positively, that I represent this matter fairly, on the soundest authority – and you can easily understand how a notion so absurd on its very face must have operated to retard the progress of all true knowledge, which makes its advances almost invariably by intuitive bounds. The ancient idea confined investigations to *crawling*, and for hundreds of years so great was the infatuation about Hog especially that a virtual end was put to all thinking properly so called. No man dared utter a truth to which he felt himself indebted to his *Soul* alone. It mattered not whether the truth was even *demonstrably* a truth, for the bullet-headed* savants of the time regarded only *the road* by which he had attained it. They would not even *look* at the end. "Let us see the means," they cried, "the means!" If, upon investigation of the means, it was found to come under neither the category Aries (that is to say Ram) nor under the category Hog, why, then the savants went no further, but pronounced the "theorist" a fool, and would have nothing to do with him or his truth.

Now, it cannot be maintained, even, that by the crawling system the greatest amount of truth would be attained in any long series of ages, for the repression of *imagination* was an evil not to be compensated for by any superior *certainty* in the ancient modes of investigation. The error of these Jurmains, these Vrinch, these Inglitch and these Amriccans (the latter, by the way, were our own immediate progenitors), was an error quite analogous with that of the wiseacre who fancies that he must necessarily see an object the better the more closely he holds it to his eyes. These people blinded themselves by details. When they proceeded Hoggishly, their "facts" were by no means always facts – a matter of little consequence had it not been for assuming that they *were* facts and must be facts because they appeared to be such. When they proceeded on the path of the Ram, their course was scarcely as straight as a ram's horn, for they *never had* an axiom which was an axiom at all. They must have been very blind not to see this, even in their own day, for even in their own day many of the long "established" axioms had been rejected. For example: "*Ex nihilo nihil fit*";* "a body cannot act where it is not"; "there cannot exist antipodes"; "darkness cannot come out of light" – all these, and a dozen other similar propositions formerly admitted without hesitation as axioms, were, even at the period of which I speak, seen to be untenable. How absurd in these people, then, to persist in putting faith in "axioms" as immutable bases of Truth! But even out of the mouths of their soundest reasoners it is easy to demonstrate the futility, the impalpability of their axioms in general. Who *was* the soundest of their logicians? Let me see! I will go and ask Pundit and be back in a minute… Ah, here we have it! Here is a book written nearly a thousand years ago and lately translated from the Inglitch – which, by the way, appears to have been the rudiment of the Amriccan. Pundit says it is decidedly the cleverest ancient work on its topic, logic. The author (who was much thought of in his day) was one Miller, or Mill* – and we find it recorded of him, as a point of some importance, that he had a mill horse called Bentham.* But let us glance at the treatise!

Ah!… "Ability or inability to conceive," says Mr Mill, very properly, "is in no case to be received as a criterion of axiomatic truth." What *modern* in his senses would ever think of disputing this truism? The only wonder with us must be how it happened that Mr Mill conceived it necessary even to hint at anything so obvious. So far, good – but let us turn over another paper. What have we here?… "Contradictories cannot both be true – that is, cannot coexist in nature." Here Mr Mill means, for example, that a tree must be either a tree or not a tree – that it cannot be at the same time a tree and not a tree. Very well – but I ask him *why*. His reply is this (and never pretends to be anything else than this): "Because it is impossible to conceive that contradictories can both be true." But this is no answer at all, by his own showing, for has he not just admitted as a truism that "ability or inability to conceive is *in no case* to be received as a criterion of axiomatic truth"?

Now, I do not complain of these ancients so much because their logic is, by their own showing, utterly baseless, worthless and fantastic altogether, as because of their pompous and imbecile proscription of all *other* roads of Truth, of all *other* means for its attainment than the two preposterous paths – the one of creeping and the one of crawling – to which they have dared to confine the Soul that loves nothing so well as to *soar*.

By the by, my dear friend, do you not think it would have puzzled these ancient dogmaticians to have determined by *which* of their two roads it was that the most important and most sublime of *all* their truths was, in effect, attained? I mean the truth of Gravitation. Newton owed it to Kepler.* Kepler admitted that his three laws* were *guessed at*: these three laws of all laws which led the great Inglitch mathematician to his principle, the basis of all physical principle – to go behind which we must enter the Kingdom of Metaphysics – Kepler guessed, that is to say, *imagined*. He was essentially a "theorist" – that word now of so much sanctity, formerly an epithet of contempt. Would it not have puzzled these old moles too to have explained by which of the two "roads" a cryptographist unriddles a cryptograph of more than usual secrecy, or by which of the two roads Champollion directed mankind to those enduring and almost innumerable truths which resulted from his deciphering the Hieroglyphics?*

One word more on this topic and I will be done boring you. Is it not *passing* strange that, with their eternal prattling about *roads* to Truth, these bigoted people missed what we now so clearly perceive to be the great highway – that of consistency? Does it not seem singular how they should have failed to deduce from the works of God the vital fact that a perfect consistency *must* be an absolute truth? How plain has been our progress since the late announcement of this proposition! Investigation has been taken out of the hands of the ground moles and given, as a task, to the true and only true thinkers, the men of ardent imagination. These latter *theorize*. Can you not fancy the shout of scorn with which my words would be received by our progenitors, were it possible for them to be now looking over my shoulder? These men, I say, *theorize*, and their theories are simply corrected, reduced, systematized – cleared, little by little, of their dross of inconsistency – until, finally, a perfect consistency stands apparent which even the most stolid admit (because it *is* a consistency) to be an absolute and an unquestionable *truth*.

APRIL 4TH. The new gas is doing wonders, in conjunction with the new improvement with gutta-percha. How very safe, commodious, manageable and in every respect convenient are our modern balloons! Here is an immense one approaching us at the rate of at least a hundred and fifty miles an hour. It seems to be crowded with people – perhaps there are three or four hundred passengers – and yet it soars to an elevation of nearly a mile, looking down upon poor us with sovereign contempt. Still a hundred or even two hundred miles an hour is slow travelling after all. *Do* you remember our flight on the railroad across the Kanadaw continent?... Fully three hundred miles the hour – *that* was travelling. Nothing to be seen, though – nothing to be done but flirt, feast and dance in the magnificent saloons. Do you remember what an odd sensation was experienced when, by chance, we caught a glimpse of external objects while the cars were in full flight? Everything seemed unique* – in one mass. For my part, I cannot say but that I preferred the travelling by the slow train of a hundred miles the hour. Here we were permitted to have glass windows – even to have them open – and something like a distinct view of the country was attainable... Pundit says that *the route* for the great Kanadaw railroad must have been in some measure marked out about nine hundred years ago! In fact, he goes so far as to assert that actual traces of a road are still discernible – traces referable to a period quite as remote as that mentioned. The track, it appears, was *double* only – ours, you know, has twelve paths, and three or four new ones are in preparation. The ancient rails were very slight, and placed so close together as to be, according to modern notions, quite frivolous, if not dangerous in the extreme. The present width of track – fifty feet – is considered, indeed, scarcely secure enough. For my part, I make no doubt that a track of some sort *must* have existed in very remote times, as Pundit asserts, for nothing can be clearer, to my mind, than that, at some period – not less than seven centuries ago, certainly – the northern and southern Kanadaw continents were *united*: the Kanawdians, then, would have been driven by necessity to a great railroad across the continent.

APRIL 5TH. I am almost devoured by ennui. Pundit is the only conversible person on board – and he, poor soul, can speak of nothing but antiquities. He has been occupied all the day in the attempt to convince me that the ancient Amriccans *governed themselves* (did ever anybody hear of such an absurdity?) – that they existed in a sort of every-man-for-himself confederacy, after the fashion of the "prairie dogs" that we read of in fable!* He says that they started with the queerest idea conceivable, viz. that all men are born free and equal – this in the very teeth of the laws of *gradation* so visibly impressed upon all things both in the moral and physical universe. Every man "voted", as they called it – that is to say, meddled with public affairs – until at length it was discovered that what is everybody's business is nobody's, and that the "Republic" (so the absurd thing was called) was without a government at all. It is related, however, that the first circumstance which disturbed, very particularly, the self-complacency of the philosophers who constructed this "Republic" was the startling discovery that universal suffrage gave opportunity for fraudulent schemes by means of which any desired number of votes might at any time be polled, without the possibility of prevention or even detection, by any party which should be merely villainous enough not to be ashamed of the fraud. A little reflection upon this discovery sufficed to render evident the consequences, which were that rascality *must* predominate – in a word, that a republican government *could* never be anything but a rascally one. While the philosophers, however, were busied in blushing at their stupidity in not having foreseen these inevitable evils, and intent upon the invention of new theories, the matter was put to an abrupt issue by a fellow of the name of *Mob*, who took everything into his own hands and set up a despotism, in comparison with which those of the fabulous Zeros and Hellofagabaluses* were respectable and delectable. This Mob (a foreigner, by the by) is said to have been the most odious of all men that ever encumbered the earth. He was a giant in stature – insolent, rapacious, filthy; had the gall of a bullock with the heart of a hyena and the brains of a peacock. He died, at length, by dint of his own energies, which exhausted him. Nevertheless, he had his uses, as everything has, however vile, and taught mankind a lesson which to this day it is in no danger of forgetting: never to run directly contrary to the natural analogies. As for Republicanism, no analogy could be found for it upon the face of the earth – unless we except the case of the "prairie dogs", an exception which seems to demonstrate, if anything, that democracy is a very admirable form of government… for dogs.

APRIL 6TH. Last night had a fine view of Alpha Lyrae,* whose disc, through our captain's spyglass, subtends an angle of half a degree,* looking very much as our sun does to the naked eye on a misty day. Alpha Lyrae, although so *very* much larger than our sun, by the by, resembles him closely as regards its spots, its atmosphere, and in many other particulars. It is only within the last century, Pundit tells me, that the binary relation existing between these two orbs began even to be suspected. The evident motion of our system in the heavens was (strange to say!) referred to an orbit about a prodigious star in the centre of the galaxy. About this star, or at all events about a centre of gravity common to all the globes of the

Milky Way, and supposed to be near Alcyone in the Pleiades,* every one of these globes was declared to be revolving, our own performing the circuit in a period of 117,000,000 of years! *We*, with our present lights, our vast telescopic improvements, and so forth, of course find it difficult to comprehend *the ground* of an idea such as this. Its first propagator was one Mudler.* He was led, we must presume, to this wild hypothesis by mere analogy in the first instance – but, this being the case, he should have at least adhered to analogy in its development. A great central orb *was*, in fact, suggested – so far Mudler was consistent. This central orb however, dynamically, should have been greater than all its surrounding orbs taken together. The question might then have been asked: "Why do we not see it?" – *we*, especially, who occupy the mid region of the cluster, the very locality *near* which, at least, must be situated this inconceivable central sun. The astronomer, perhaps, at this point, took refuge in the suggestion of non-luminosity – and here analogy was suddenly let fall. But even admitting the central orb non-luminous, how did he manage to explain its failure to be rendered visible by the incalculable host of glorious suns glaring in all directions about it? No doubt what he finally maintained was merely a centre of gravity common to all the revolving orbs – but here again analogy must have been let fall. Our system revolves, it is true, about a common centre of gravity, but it does this in connection with and in consequence of a material sun whose mass more than counterbalances the rest of the system. The mathematical circle is a curve composed of an infinity of straight lines, but this idea of the circle – this idea of it which, in regard to all earthly geometry, we consider as merely the mathematical, in contradistinction from the practical, idea – is, in sober fact, the *practical* conception which alone we have any right to entertain in respect to those titanic circles with which we have to deal, at least in fancy, when we suppose our system, with its fellows, revolving about a point in the centre of the galaxy. Let the most vigorous of human imaginations but attempt to take a single step towards the comprehension of a circuit so unutterable! It would scarcely be paradoxical to say that a flash of lightning itself, travelling *for ever* upon the circumference of this inconceivable circle, would still *for ever* be travelling in a straight line. That the path of our sun along such a circumference, that the direction of our system in such an orbit would, to any human perception, deviate in the slightest degree from a straight line even in a million of years is a proposition not to be entertained – and yet these ancient astronomers were absolutely cajoled, it appears, into believing that a decisive curvature had become apparent during the brief period of their astronomical history, during the mere point, during the utter nothingness of two or three thousand years! How incomprehensible that considerations such as this did not at once indicate to them the true state of affairs – that of the binary revolution of our sun and Alpha Lyrae around a common centre of gravity!

APRIL 7TH. Continued last night our astronomical amusements. Had a fine view of the five Neptunian* asteroids, and watched with much interest the putting-up of a huge impost on a couple of lintels in the new temple at Daphnis in the moon. It was amusing to think that creatures so diminutive as the lunarians, and bearing so little resemblance to humanity, yet evinced a mechanical ingenuity so much superior to our own. One finds it difficult, too, to conceive the vast masses which these people handle so easily to be as light as our own reason tells us they actually are.

APRIL 8TH. Eureka! Pundit is in his glory. A balloon from Kanadaw spoke us today and threw on board several late papers – they contain some exceedingly curious information relative to Kanawdian or rather Amriccan antiquities. You know, I presume, that labourers have for some months been employed in preparing the ground for a new fountain at Paradise, the Emperor's principal pleasure garden. Paradise, it appears, has been, *literally* speaking, an island* time out of mind – that is to say, its northern boundary was always (as far back as any record extends) a rivulet, or rather a very narrow arm of the sea. This arm was gradually widened until it attained its present breadth – a mile. The whole length of the island is nine miles; the breadth varies materially. The entire area (so Pundit says) was, about eight hundred years ago, densely packed with houses, some of them twenty storeys high, land (for some most unaccountable reason) being considered as especially precious just in this vicinity. The disastrous earthquake, however, of the year 2050 so totally uprooted and overwhelmed the town (for it was almost too large to be called a village) that the most indefatigable of our antiquarians have never yet been able to obtain from the site any sufficient data (in the shape of coins, medals or inscriptions) wherewith to build up even the ghost of a theory concerning the manners, customs, etc., etc., etc., of the aboriginal inhabitants. Nearly all that we have hitherto known of them is that they were a portion of the Knickerbocker tribe* of savages infesting the continent at its first discovery by Recorder Riker, a knight of the Golden Fleece.* They were by no means uncivilized, however, but cultivated various arts and even sciences after a fashion of their own. It is related of them that they were acute in many respects, but were oddly afflicted with monomania for building what, in the ancient Amriccan, was denominated "churches" – a kind of pagoda instituted for the worship of two idols that went by the names of Wealth and Fashion. In the end, it is said, the island became, nine tenths of it, church. The women, too, it appears, were oddly deformed by a natural protuberance of the region just below the small of the back – although, most unaccountably, this deformity was looked upon altogether in the light of a beauty. One or two pictures of these singular women have, in fact, been miraculously preserved. They look very odd, *very* – like something between a turkey-cock and a dromedary.*

Well, these few details are nearly all that have descended to us respecting the ancient Knickerbockers. It seems, however, that while digging in the centre of the Emperor's garden (which, you know, covers the whole island) some of the workmen unearthed a cubical and evidently chiselled block of granite weighing several hundred pounds. It was in good preservation, having received, apparently, little injury from the convulsion which entombed it. On one of its surfaces was a marble slab with (only think of it!) *an inscription – a legible inscription*. Pundit is in ecstasies. Upon detaching the slab, a cavity appeared, containing a leaden box filled with various coins, a long scroll of names, several documents which appear to resemble newspapers, with other matters of intense interest to the antiquarian! There can be no doubt that all these are genuine Amriccan relics belonging to the tribe called Knickerbocker. The papers thrown on board our balloon are filled with facsimiles of the coins, MSS, typography, etc., etc. I copy for your amusement the Knickerbocker inscription on the marble slab:

This Cornerstone of a Monument to the
Memory of
GEORGE WASHINGTON,
Was Laid with Appropriate Ceremonies on the
19TH DAY OF OCTOBER 1847,
the anniversary of the surrender of
Lord Cornwallis
to General Washington at Yorktown,
AD 1781,
Under the auspices of the
Washington Monument Association of the
City of New York*

This, as I give it, is a verbatim translation done by Pundit himself, so there *can* be no mistake about it. From the few words thus preserved, we glean several important items of knowledge, not the least interesting of which is the fact that a thousand years ago *actual* monuments had fallen into disuse, as was all very proper, the people contenting themselves, as we do now, with a mere indication of the design to erect a monument at some future time; a cornerstone being cautiously laid by itself "solitary and alone" (excuse me for quoting the great Amriccan poet Benton!),* as a guarantee of the magnanimous *intention*. We ascertain, too, very distinctly, from this admirable inscription, the how as well as the where and the what of the great surrender in question. As to the *where*, it was Yorktown (wherever that was), and as to the *what*, it was General Cornwallis (no doubt some wealthy dealer in corn). *He* was surrendered. The inscription commemorates the surrender of… what?… why, "of Lord Cornwallis". The only question is what could the savages wish him surrendered for. But when we remember that these savages were undoubtedly cannibals, we are led to the conclusion that they intended him for sausage. As to the *how* of the surrender, no language can be more explicit. Lord Cornwallis was surrendered (for sausage) "under the auspices of the Washington Monument Association" – no doubt a charitable institution for the depositing of cornerstones… But, Heaven bless me! What is the matter? Ah, I see… the balloon has collapsed, and we shall have a tumble into the sea. I have, therefore, only time enough to add that, from a hasty inspection of the facsimiles of newspapers, etc., etc., I find that *the* great men in those days among the Amriccans, were one John, a smith,* and one Zacchary, a tailor.*

Goodbye, until I see you again. Whether you ever get this letter or not is point of little importance, as I write altogether for my own amusement. I shall cork the MS up in a bottle, however, and throw it into the sea.

Yours everlastingly,

PUNDITA

THE MAN THAT WAS USED UP*

A TALE OF THE LATE BUGABOO AND KICKAPOO CAMPAIGN*

Pleurez, pleurez, mes yeux, et fondez vous en eau!
*La moitié de ma vie a mis l'autre au tombeau.**
– Corneille

I cannot just now remember when or where I first made the acquaintance of that truly fine-looking fellow, Brevet Brigadier General John A.B.C. Smith. Someone *did* introduce me to the gentleman, I am sure… at some public meeting, I know very well… held about something of great importance, no doubt… at some place or other, I feel convinced – whose name I have unaccountably forgotten. The truth is… that the introduction was attended, upon my part, with a degree of anxious embarrassment which operated to prevent any definite impressions of either time or place. I am constitutionally nervous – this, with me, is a family failing, and I can't help it. In especial, the slightest appearance of mystery – of any point I cannot exactly comprehend – puts me at once into a pitiable state of agitation.

There was something, as it were, remarkable – yes, *remarkable*, although this is but a feeble term to express my full meaning – about the entire individuality of the personage in question. He was, perhaps, six feet in height, and of a presence singularly commanding. There was an *air distingué** pervading the whole man, which spoke of high breeding and hinted at high birth. Upon this topic – the topic of Smith's personal appearance – I have a kind of melancholy satisfaction in being minute. His head of hair would have done honour to a Brutus* – nothing could be more richly flowing or possess a brighter gloss. It was of a jetty black – which was also the colour (or, more properly, the no-colour) of his unimaginable whiskers.

You perceive I cannot speak of these latter without enthusiasm: it is not too much to say that they were the handsomest pair of whiskers under the sun. At all events, they encircled, and at times partially overshadowed, a mouth utterly unequalled. Here were the most entirely even and the most brilliantly white of all conceivable teeth. From between them, upon every proper occasion, issued a voice of surpassing clearness, melody and strength. In the matter of eyes, also, my acquaintance was pre-eminently endowed. Either one of such a pair was worth a couple of the ordinary ocular organs. They were of a deep hazel exceedingly large and lustrous, and there was perceptible about them, ever and anon, just that amount of interesting obliquity which gives pregnancy to expression.

The bust of the general was unquestionably the finest bust I ever saw. For your life you could not have found a fault with its wonderful proportion. This rare peculiarity set off to great advantage a pair of shoulders which would have called up a blush of conscious inferiority into the countenance of the marble Apollo.* I have a passion for fine shoulders, and may say that I never beheld them in perfection before. The arms altogether were admirably modelled. Nor were the lower limbs less superb. These were, indeed, the *ne plus ultra** of good legs. Every connoisseur in such matters admitted the legs to be good. There was neither too much flesh nor too little – neither rudeness nor fragility. I could not imagine a more graceful curve than that of the *os femoris*,* and there was just that due gentle prominence in the rear of the *fibula** which goes to the conformation of a properly proportioned calf. I wish to God my young and talented friend Chiponchipino, the sculptor, had but seen the legs of Brevet Brigadier General John A.B.C. Smith.

But although men so absolutely fine-looking are neither as plenty as reasons* or blackberries, still I could not bring myself to believe that *the remarkable* something to which I alluded just now – that the odd air of *je ne sais quoi** which hung about my new acquaintance – lay altogether, or indeed at all, in the supreme excellence of his bodily endowments. Perhaps it might be traced to the *manner* – yet here again I could not pretend to be positive. There *was* a primness (not to say stiffness) in his carriage, a degree of measured and, if I may so express it, of rectangular precision attending his every movement, which, observed in a more diminutive figure, would have had the least little savour in the world of affectation, pomposity or constraint, but which, noticed in a gentleman of his undoubted dimensions, was readily placed to the account of reserve, *hauteur* – of a commendable sense, in short, of what is due to the dignity of colossal proportion.

The kind friend who presented me to General Smith whispered in my ear some few words of comment upon the man. He was a *remarkable* man, a *very* remarkable man – indeed, one of the *most* remarkable men of the age. He was an especial favourite, too, with the ladies – chiefly on account of his high reputation for courage.

"In *that* point he is unrivalled – indeed, he is a perfect desperado, a downright fire-eater, and no mistake," said my friend, here dropping his voice excessively low, and thrilling me with the mystery of his tone. "A downright fire-eater, and *no* mistake. Showed *that*, I should say, to some purpose, in the late tremendous swamp fight, away down south, with the Bugaboo and Kickapoo Indians." Here my friend opened his eyes to some extent. "Bless my soul!… Blood and thunder, and all that!… *Prodigies* of valour!… Heard of him of course?… You know he's the man—"

"Man alive, how *do* you do? Why, how *are* ye? *Very* glad to see ye, indeed!" here interrupted the general himself, seizing my companion by the hand as he drew near, and bowing stiffly but profoundly as I was presented. I then thought (and I think so still) that I never heard a clearer nor a stronger voice, nor beheld a finer set of teeth – but I *must* say that I was sorry for the interruption just at that moment, as, owing to the whispers and insinuations aforesaid, my interest had been greatly excited in the hero of the Bugaboo and Kickapoo campaign.

However, the delightfully luminous conversation of Brevet Brigadier General John A.B.C. Smith soon completely dissipated this chagrin. My friend leaving us immediately, we had quite a long tête-à-tête, and I was not only pleased but *really*… instructed. I never heard a more fluent talker, or a man of greater general information. With becoming modesty, he forbore, nevertheless, to touch upon the theme I had just then most at heart – I mean the mysterious circumstances attending the Bugaboo war – and, on my own part, what I conceive to be a proper sense of delicacy forbade me to broach the subject, although in truth I was exceedingly tempted to do so. I perceived, too, that the gallant soldier preferred topics of philosophical interest, and that he delighted especially in commenting upon the rapid march of mechanical invention. Indeed, lead him where I would, this was a point to which he invariably came back.

"There is nothing at all like it," he would say. "We are a wonderful people, and live in a wonderful age. Parachutes and railroads – mantraps and spring guns! Our steamboats are upon every sea, and the Nassau balloon packet is about to run regular trips (fare either way only twenty pounds sterling) between London and Timbuctoo.*

And who shall calculate the immense influence upon social life… upon arts… upon commerce… upon literature… which will be the immediate result of the great principles of electromagnetics! Nor is this all, let me assure you! There is really no end to the march of invention. The most wonderful… the most ingenious… and, let me add, Mr… Mr… Thompson, I believe, is your name… let me add, I say the most *useful*… the most truly *useful*… mechanical contrivances are daily springing up like mushrooms, if I may so express myself, or, more figuratively, like… ah… grasshoppers… like grasshoppers, Mr Thompson… about us and ah… ah… ah… around us!"

Thompson, to be sure, is not my name, but it is needless to say that I left General Smith with a heightened interest in the man, with an exalted opinion of his conversational powers and a deep sense of the valuable privileges we enjoy in living in this age of mechanical invention. My curiosity, however, had not been altogether satisfied, and I resolved to prosecute immediate enquiry among my acquaintances touching the Brevet Brigadier General himself, and particularly respecting the tremendous events *quorum pars magna fuit*,* during the Bugaboo and Kickapoo campaign.

The first opportunity which presented itself, and which (*horresco referens*)* I did not in the least scruple to seize, occurred at the church of the Revd Dr Drummummupp, where I found myself established, one Sunday, just at sermon time, not only in the pew, but by the side of that worthy and communicative little friend of mine, Miss Tabitha T. Thus seated, I congratulated myself, and with much reason, upon the very flattering state of affairs. If any person knew anything about Brevet Brigadier General John A.B.C. Smith, that person, it was clear to me, was Miss Tabitha T. We telegraphed a few signals, and then commenced, *sotto voce*, a brisk tête-à-tête.

"Smith!" said she, in reply to my very earnest enquiry. "Smith!… Why, not General A.B.C.? Bless me, I thought you *knew* all about *him*! This is a wonderfully inventive age! Horrid affair, that!… A bloody set of wretches, those Kickapoos!… Fought like a hero… prodigies of valour… immortal renown. Smith!… Brevet Brigadier General John A.B.C.!… Why, you know he's the man—"

"Man," here broke in Dr Drummummupp at the top of his voice, and with a thump that came near knocking the pulpit about our ears, "man that is born of a woman hath but a short time to live – he cometh up and is cut down like a flower!"* I started to the extremity of the pew, and perceived by the animated looks of the divine that the wrath which had nearly proved fatal to the pulpit had been excited by the whispers of the lady and myself. There was no help for it – so I submitted with a good grace and listened, in all the martyrdom of dignified silence, to the balance of that very capital discourse.

Next evening found me a somewhat late visitor at the Rantipole Theatre, where I felt sure of satisfying my curiosity at once by merely stepping into the box of those exquisite specimens of affability and omniscience, the Misses Arabella and Miranda Cognoscenti. That fine tragedian, Climax, was doing Iago to a very crowded house, and I experienced some little difficulty in making my wishes understood – especially as our box was next the slips,* and completely overlooked the stage.

"Smith!" said Miss Arabella, as she at length comprehended the purport of my query. "Smith!... Why, not General John A.B.C.?"

"Smith?" enquired Miranda musingly. "God bless me, did you ever behold a finer figure?"

"Never, madam, but *do* tell me—"

"Or so inimitable grace?"

"Never, upon my word! But pray, inform me—"

"Or so just an appreciation of stage effect?"

"Madam!"

"Or a more delicate sense of the true beauties of Shakespeare? Be so good as to look at that leg!"

"The devil!" and I turned again to her sister.

"Smith!" said she. "Why, not General John A.B.C.? Horrid affair that, wasn't it?... Great wretches, those Bugaboos... savage and so on... but we live in a wonderfully inventive age!... Smith!... Oh, yes! Great man!... Perfect desperado... immortal renown!... Prodigies of valour! *Never heard!*" This was given in a scream. "Bless my soul!... Why, he's the man—"

> "...Mandragora
> Nor all the drowsy syrups of the world
> Shall ever medicine thee to that sweet sleep
> Which thou ow'dst yesterday!"*

here roared our Climax just in my ear, and shaking his fist in my face all the time, in a way that I *couldn't* stand, and I *wouldn't*. I left the Misses Cognoscenti immediately, went behind the scenes forthwith, and gave the beggarly scoundrel such a thrashing as I trust he will remember to the day of his death.

At the soirée of the lovely widow, Mrs Kathleen O'Trump, I was confident that I should meet with no similar disappointment. Accordingly, I was no sooner seated at the card table with my pretty hostess for a vis-à-vis than I propounded those questions the solution of which had become a matter so essential to my peace.

"Smith!" said my partner. "Why, not General John A.B.C.? Horrid affair, that, wasn't it?... Diamonds, did you say?... Terrible wretches those Kickapoos!... We are playing *whist*, if you please, Mr Tattle... however, this is the age of invention, most certainly *the* age, one may say... *the* age par excellence... speak French?... oh, quite a hero... perfect desperado!... *No hearts*, Mr Tattle? I don't believe it!... Immortal renown and all that!... Prodigies of valour! *Never heard!...* Why, bless me, he's the man—"

"Mann?... *Captain* Mann!" here screamed some little feminine interloper from the farthest corner of the room. "Are you talking about Captain Mann and the duel?... Oh, I *must* hear... do tell... go on, Mrs O'Trump!... Do now go on!" And go on Mrs O'Trump did – all about a certain Captain Mann, who was either shot or hung, or should have been both shot and hung. Yes! Mrs O'Trump, she went on, and I... I went off. There was no chance of hearing anything further that evening in regard to Brevet Brigadier General John A.B.C. Smith.

Still I consoled myself with the reflection that the tide of ill luck would not run against me for ever, and so determined to make a bold push for information at the rout* of that bewitching little angel, the graceful Mrs Pirouette.

"Smith!" said Mrs P. as we twirled about together in a *pas de zephyr*,* "Smith!... Why, not General John A.B.C.? Dreadful business that of the Bugaboos, wasn't it?... Dreadful creatures, those Indians!... *Do* turn out your toes! I really am ashamed of you... Man of great courage, poor fellow!... But this is a wonderful age for invention... Oh dear me, I'm out of breath... Quite a desperado... prodigies of valour... *Never heard!...* Can't believe it... I shall have to sit down and enlighten you... Smith! Why, he's the man—"

"Man-*Fred*, I tell you!" here bawled out Miss Bas-Bleu,* as I led Mrs Pirouette to a seat. "Did ever anybody hear the like? It's Man-*Fred*, I say, and not at all by any means Man-*Friday*."* Here Miss Bas-Bleu beckoned to me in a very peremptory manner – and I was obliged, willy-nilly, to leave Mrs P. for the purpose of deciding a dispute touching the title of a certain poetical drama of Lord Byron's. Although I pronounced, with great promptness, that the true title was Man-*Friday*, and not by any means Man-*Fred*, yet when I returned to seek Mrs Pirouette she was not to be discovered, and I made my retreat from the house in a very bitter spirit of animosity against the whole race of the Bas-Bleus.

Matters had now assumed a really serious aspect, and I resolved to call at once upon my particular friend, Mr Theodore Sinivate – for I knew that here at least I should get something like definite information.

"Smith!" said he, in his well-known peculiar way of drawling out his syllables. "Smith!... Why, not General John A.B.C.? Savage affair that with the Kickapo-o-o-os, wasn't it? Say, don't you think so?... Perfect despera-a-ado... Great pity, 'pon my honour!... Wonderfully inventive age!... Pro-o-odigies of valour! By the by, did you ever hear about Captain Ma-a-a-a-nn?"

"Captain Mann be d——d!" said I. "Please to go on with your story."

"Hem!... Oh well!... Quite *la même cho-o-ose*,* as we say in France. Smith, eh? Brigadier General John A. B. C.? I say" – here Mr S. thought proper to put his finger to the side of his nose – "I say, you don't mean to insinuate now, really and truly, and conscientiously, that you don't know all about that affair of Smith's as well as I do, eh? Smith? John A. B. C.? Why, bless me, he's the ma-a-an—"

"*Mr* Sinivate," said I imploringly, "*is* he the Man in the Mask?"*

"No-o-o!" said he, looking wise. "Nor the Man in the Mo-o-on."

This reply I considered a pointed and positive insult, and so left the house at once in high dudgeon, with a firm resolve to call my friend, Mr Sinivate, to a speedy account for his ungentlemanly conduct and ill breeding.

In the mean time, however, I had no notion of being thwarted touching the information I desired. There was one resource left me yet. I would go to the fountainhead. I would call forthwith upon the general himself, and demand, in explicit terms, a solution of this abominable piece of mystery. Here, at least, there should be no chance for equivocation. I would be plain, positive, peremptory – as short as pie-crust, as concise as Tacitus or Montesquieu.*

It was early when I called, and the general was dressing, but I pleaded urgent business, and was shown at once into his bedroom by an old Negro valet, who remained in attendance during my visit. As I entered the chamber, I looked about, of course, for the occupant, but did not immediately perceive him. There was a large and exceedingly odd-looking bundle of something which lay close by my feet on the floor, and, as I was not in the best humour in the world, I gave it a kick out of the way.

"Hem! Ahem! Rather civil that, I should say!" said the bundle, in one of the smallest and altogether the funniest little voices, between a squeak and a whistle, that I ever heard in all the days of my existence.

"Ahem! Rather civil that, I should observe."

I fairly shouted with terror, and made off, at a tangent, into the farthest extremity of the room.

"God bless me, my dear fellow!" here again whistled the bundle. "What... what... what... why, what *is* the matter? I really believe you don't know me at all."

What *could* I say to all this – what *could* I? I staggered into an armchair, and, with staring eyes and open mouth, awaited the solution of the wonder.

"Strange you shouldn't know me, though, isn't it?" presently resqueaked the nondescript, which I now perceived was performing, upon the floor, some inexplicable evolution, very analogous to the drawing-on of a stocking. There was only a single leg, however, apparent.

"Strange you shouldn't know me, though, isn't it? Pompey, bring me that leg!" Here Pompey handed the bundle a very capital cork leg, already dressed, which it screwed on in a trice – and then it stood up before my eyes.

"And a bloody action it *was*," continued the thing, as if in a soliloquy. "But then one mustn't fight with the Bugaboos and Kickapoos and think of coming off with a mere scratch. Pompey, I'll thank you now for that arm. Thomas" – turning to me – "is decidedly the best hand at a cork leg, but if you should ever want an arm, my dear fellow, you must really let me recommend you to Bishop." Here Pompey screwed on an arm.

"We had rather hot work of it – that you may say. Now, you dog, slip on my shoulders and bosom. Pettitt makes the best shoulders, but for a bosom you will have to go to Ducrow."

"Bosom!" said I.

"Pompey, will you *never* be ready with that wig? Scalping is a rough process, after all – but then you can procure such a capital scratch at De L'Orme's."

"Scratch!"

"Now, you Nigger, my teeth!" For a *good* set of these you had better go to Parmly's at once – high prices, but excellent work. I swallowed some very capital articles, though, when the big Bugaboo rammed me down with the butt end of his rifle."

"Butt end! Ram down! My eye!"

"Oh yes... by the by, my eye... here, Pompey, you scamp, screw it in! Those Kickapoos are not so very slow at a gouge – but he's a belied man, that Dr Williams, after all: you can't imagine how well I see with the eyes of his make."

I now began very clearly to perceive that the object before me was nothing more nor less than my new acquaintance, Brevet Brigadier General John A.B.C. Smith. The manipulations of Pompey had made, I must confess, a very striking difference in the personal appearance of the man.* The voice, however, still puzzled me no little – but even this apparent mystery was speedily cleared up.

"Pompey, you black rascal," squeaked the general, "I really do believe you would let me go out without my palate."

Hereupon, the Negro, grumbling out an apology, went up to his master, opened his mouth with the knowing air of a horse jockey and adjusted therein a somewhat singular-looking machine in a very dextrous manner, that I could not altogether comprehend. The alteration, however, in the entire expression of the general's countenance was instantaneous and surprising. When he again spoke, his voice had resumed all that rich melody and strength which I had noticed upon our original introduction.

"D—n the vagabonds!" said he, in so clear a tone that I positively started at the change. "D—n the vagabonds! They not only knocked in the roof of my mouth, but took the trouble to cut off at least seven eighths of my tongue. There isn't Bonfanti's equal, however, in America,* for really good articles of this description. I can recommend you to him with confidence" – here the general bowed – "and assure you that I have the greatest pleasure in so doing."

I acknowledged his kindness in my best manner, and took leave of him at once, with a perfect understanding of the true state of affairs – with a full comprehension of the mystery which had troubled me so long. It was evident. It was a clear case. Brevet Brigadier General John A.B.C. Smith was the man... was *the man that was used up*.

THE BUSINESSMAN*

Method is the soul of business.
– Old saying

I am a businessman. I am a methodical man. Method is *the* thing, after all. But there are no people I more heartily despise than your eccentric fools who prate about method without understanding it, attending strictly to its letter and violating its spirit. These fellows are always doing the most out-of-the-way things in what they call "an orderly manner". Now here, I conceive, is a positive paradox. True method appertains to the ordinary and the obvious alone, and cannot be applied to the outré.* What definite idea can a body attach to such expressions as "methodical Jack o' Dandy" or "a systematical Will o' the Wisp"?

My notions upon this head might not have been so clear as they are but for a fortunate accident which happened to me when I was a very little boy. A good-hearted old Irish nurse (whom I shall not forget in my will) took me up one day by the heels, when I was making more noise than was necessary, and, swinging me round two or three times, d——d my eyes for "a screaking little spalpeen", and then knocked my head into a cocked hat against the bedpost. This, I say, decided my fate, and made my fortune. A bump arose at once on my sinciput,* and turned out to be as pretty an organ of *order** as one shall see on a summer's day. Hence that positive appetite for system and regularity which has made me the distinguished man of business that I am.

If there is anything on earth I hate, it is a genius. Your geniuses are all arrant asses – the greater the genius, the greater the ass – and to this rule there is no exception whatever. Especially, you cannot make a man of business out of a genius any more than money out of a Jew or the best nutmegs out of pine knots.* The creatures are always going off at a tangent into some fantastic employment or ridiculous speculation entirely at variance with the "fitness of things", and having no business whatever to be considered as a business at all. Thus you may tell these characters immediately by the nature of their occupations. If you ever perceive a man setting up as a merchant or a manufacturer; or going into the cotton or tobacco trade, or any of those eccentric pursuits; or getting to be a dry-goods dealer or soap-boiler, or something of that kind; or pretending to be a lawyer or a blacksmith, or a physician, anything out of the usual way – you may set him down at once as a genius, and then, according to the rule of three,* he's an ass.

Now, I am not in any respect a genius, but a regular businessman. My daybook and ledger will evince this in a minute. They are well kept, though I say it myself – and, in my general habits of accuracy and punctuality, I am not to be beat by a clock. Moreover, my occupations have been always made to chime in with the ordinary habitudes of my fellow men. Not that I feel the least indebted, upon this score, to my exceedingly weak-minded parents, who, beyond doubt, would have made an arrant genius of me at last if my guardian angel had not come, in good time, to the rescue. In biography the truth is everything, and in autobiography it is especially so – yet I scarcely hope to be believed when I state, however solemnly, that my poor father put me, when I was about fifteen years of age, into the counting house of what he termed "a respectable hardware and commission merchant doing a capital bit of business"! A capital bit of fiddlestick! However, the consequence of this folly was that, in two or three days, I had to be sent home to my button-headed family in a high state of fever and with a most violent and dangerous pain in the sinciput, all round about my organ of order. It was nearly a gone case with me then – just touch and go for six weeks, the physicians giving me up and all that sort of thing. But, although I suffered much, I was a thankful boy in the main. I was saved from being a "respectable hardware and commission merchant, doing a capital bit of business", and I felt grateful to the protuberance which had been the means of my salvation, as well as to the kind-hearted female who had originally put these means within my reach.

The most of boys run away from home at ten or twelve years of age, but I waited till I was sixteen. I don't know that I should have gone even then, if I had not happened to hear my old mother talk about setting me up on my own hook in the grocery way. The *grocery* way! – only think of that! I resolved to be off forthwith, and try and establish myself in some *decent* occupation, without dancing attendance any longer upon the caprices of these eccentric old people and running the risk of being made a genius of in the end. In this project I succeeded perfectly well at the first effort, and, by the time I was fairly eighteen, found myself doing an extensive and profitable business in the Tailor's Walking-Advertisement line.

I was enabled to discharge the onerous duties of this profession only by that rigid adherence to system which formed the leading feature of my mind. A scrupulous *method* characterized my actions as well as my accounts. In my case, it was method, not money, which made the man – at least all of him that was not made by the tailor whom I served. At nine, every morning, I called upon that individual for the clothes of the day. Ten o'clock found me in some fashionable promenade or other place of public amusement. The precise regularity with which I turned my handsome person about, so as to bring successively into view every portion of the suit upon my back, was the admiration of all the knowing men in the trade. Noon never passed without my bringing home a customer to the house of my employers, Messrs Cut and Comeagain. I say this proudly, but with tears in my eyes – for the firm proved themselves the basest of ingrates. The little account about which we quarrelled and finally parted cannot, in any item, be thought overcharged by gentlemen really conversant with the nature of the business. Upon this point, however, I feel a degree of proud satisfaction in permitting the reader to judge for himself. My bill ran thus:

Messrs Cut and Comeagain, Merchant Tailors,

	To Peter Proffit, Walking Advertiser,*	Drs.
JULY 10	To promenade, as usual, and customer brought home	\$0 25
JULY 11	To do. do. do.	25
JULY 12	To one lie, second class; damaged black cloth sold for invisible green	25
JULY 13	To one lie, first class, extra quality and size; recommending milled satinet as broadcloth	75
JULY 20	To purchasing brand-new paper shirt collar or dicky, to set off grey Petersham*	2
AUG. 15	To wearing double-padded bobtail frock (thermometer 206* in the shade)	25
AUG. 16	Standing on one leg three hours, to show off new-style strapped pants at 12½ cents per leg per hour	37½
AUG. 17	To promenade, as usual, and large customer brought (fat man)	50
AUG. 18	To do. do. (medium size)	25
AUG. 19	To do. do. (small man and bad pay)	6
		\$2 95½

The item chiefly disputed in this bill was the very moderate charge of two pennies for the dicky. Upon my word of honour, this *was not* an unreasonable price for that dicky. It was one of the cleanest and prettiest little dickies I ever saw – and I have good reason to believe that it effected the sale of three Petershams. The elder partner of the firm, however, would allow me only one penny* of the charge, and took it upon himself to show in what manner four of the same-sized conveniences could be got out of a sheet of foolscap. But it is needless to say that I stood upon the *principle* of the thing. Business is business, and should be done in a business way. There was no *system whatever* in swindling me out of a penny – a clear fraud of fifty per cent – no *method* in any respect. I left at once the employment of Messrs Cut and Comeagain, and set up in the Eyesore line by myself – one of the most lucrative, respectable and independent of the ordinary occupations.

My strict integrity, economy and rigorous business habits here again came into play. I found myself driving a flourishing trade, and soon became a marked man upon 'Change.* The truth is, I never dabbled in flashy matters, but jogged on in the good old sober routine of the calling – a calling in which I should no doubt have remained to the present hour but for a little accident which happened to me in the prosecution of one of the usual business operations of the profession. Whenever a rich old hunks* or prodigal heir or bankrupt corporation gets into the notion of putting up a palace, there is no such thing in the world as stopping either of them, and this every intelligent person knows. The fact in question is indeed the basis of the Eyesore trade. As soon, therefore, as a building project is fairly afoot by one of these parties, we merchants secure a nice corner of the lot in contemplation, or a prime little situation just adjoining or right in front. This done, we wait until the palace is halfway up, and then we pay some tasty architect to run us up an ornamental mud hovel right against it, or a Down-East or Dutch Pagoda, or a pigsty, or an ingenious little bit of fancy work, either Eskimo, Kickapoo or Hottentot.* Of course we can't afford to take these structures down under a bonus of five hundred per cent upon the prime cost of our lot and plaster. *Can* we? I ask the question. I ask it of businessmen. It would be irrational to suppose that we can. And yet there was a rascally corporation which asked me to do this very thing – this *very thing*! I did not reply to their absurd proposition, of course, but I felt it a duty to go that same night and lamp-black* the whole of their palace. For this the unreasonable villains clapped me into jail – and the gentlemen of the Eyesore trade could not well avoid cutting my connection when I came out.

The Assault-and-Battery business into which I was now forced to adventure for a livelihood was somewhat ill adapted to the delicate nature of my constitution, but I went to work in it with a good heart, and found my account here, as heretofore, in those stern habits of methodical accuracy which had been thumped into me by that delightful old nurse – I would indeed be the basest of men not to remember her well in my will. By observing, as I say, the strictest system in all my dealings, and keeping a well-regulated set of books, I was enabled to get over many serious difficulties, and, in the end, to establish myself very decently in the profession. The truth is that few individuals, in any line, did a snugger little business than I. I will just copy a page or so out of my daybook, and this will save me the necessity of blowing my own trumpet – a contemptible practice of which no high-minded man will be guilty. Now, the daybook is a thing that don't lie.

JAN. 1. New Year's Day. Met Snap in the street, groggy. Mem. – he'll do. Met Gruff shortly afterwards, blind drunk. Mem. – he'll answer, too. Entered both gentlemen in my ledger, and opened a running account with each.

JAN. 2. Saw Snap at the Exchange, and went up and trod on his toe. Doubled his fist and knocked me down. Good!... Got up again. Some trifling difficulty with Bag, my attorney. I want the damages at a thousand, but he says that for so simple a knock-down we can't lay them at more than five hundred. Mem. – must get rid of Bag: no *system* at all.

JAN. 3. Went to the theatre, to look for Gruff. Saw him sitting in a side box, in the second tier, between a fat lady and a lean one. Quizzed the whole party through an opera glass, till I saw the fat lady blush and whisper to G. Went round, then, into the box, and put my nose within reach of his hand. Wouldn't pull it – no go. Blew it, and tried again – no go. Sat down then, and winked at the lean lady, when I had the high satisfaction of finding him lift me up by the nape of the neck and fling me over into the pit. Neck dislocated, and right leg capitally splintered. Went home in high glee, drank a bottle of champagne and booked the young man for five thousand. Bag says it'll do.

FEB. 15. Compromised the case of Mr Snap. Amount entered in journal (fifty cents), which see.

FEB. 16. Cast by that villain, Gruff, who made me a present of five dollars. Costs of suit: four dollars and twenty-five cents. Net profit (see journal): seventy-five cents.

Now, here is a clear gain, in a very brief period, of no less than one dollar and twenty-five cents – this is in the mere cases of Snap and Gruff, and I solemnly assure the reader that these extracts are taken at random from my daybook.

It's an old saying, and a true one, however, that money is nothing in comparison with health. I found the exactions of the profession somewhat too much for my delicate state of body – and, discovering at last that I was knocked all out of shape, so that I didn't know very well what to make of the matter, and so that my friends, when they met me in the street, couldn't tell that I was Peter Proffit at all, it occurred to me that the best expedient I could adopt was to alter my line of business. I turned my attention, therefore, to Mud-Dabbling, and continued it for some years.

The worst of this occupation is that too many people take a fancy to it, and the competition is in consequence excessive. Every ignoramus of a fellow who finds that he hasn't brains in sufficient quantity to make his way as a walking advertiser or an eyesore prig or a salt-and-batter* man, thinks, of course, that he'll answer very well as a dabbler of mud. But there never was entertained a more erroneous idea than that it requires no brains to mud-dabble. Especially, there is nothing to be made in this way without *method*. I did only a retail business myself, but my old habits of *system* carried me swimmingly along. I selected my street crossing, in the first place, with great deliberation, and I never put down a broom in any part of the town *but that*. I took care, too, to have a nice little puddle at hand, which I could get at in a minute. By these means I got to be well known as a man to be trusted – and this is one half the battle, let me tell you, in trade. Nobody ever failed to pitch *me* a copper, and got over *my* crossing with a clean pair of pantaloons. And, as my business habits, in this respect, were sufficiently understood, I never met with any attempt at imposition. I wouldn't have put up with it, if I had. Never imposing upon anyone myself, I suffered no one to play the possum* with me. The frauds of the banks of course I couldn't help. Their suspension* put me to ruinous inconvenience. These, however, are not individuals, but corporations – and corporations, it is very well known, have neither bodies to be kicked nor souls to be damned.

I was making money at this business when, in an evil moment, I was induced to merge it in the Cur-Spattering – a somewhat analogous but by no means so respectable a profession. My location, to be sure, was an excellent one, being central, and I had capital blacking and brushes. My little dog, too, was quite fat and up to all varieties of snuff. He had been in the trade a long time, and, I may say, understood it. Our general routine was this. Pompey, having rolled himself well in the mud, sat upon end at the shop door, until he observed a dandy approaching in bright boots. He then proceeded to meet him, and gave the Wellingtons a rub or two with his wool. Then the dandy swore very much, and looked about for a bootblack. There I was, full in his view, with blacking and brushes. It was only a minute's work, and then came a sixpence. This did moderately well for a time – in fact, I was not avaricious, but my dog was. I allowed him a third of the profit, but he was advised to insist upon half. This I couldn't stand – so we quarrelled and parted.

I next tried my hand at the Organ-Grinding for a while, and may say that I made out pretty well. It is a plain, straightforward business, and requires no particular abilities. You can get a music mill* for a mere song, and to put it in order you have but to open the works and give them three or four smart raps with a hammer. It improves the tone of the thing, for business purposes, more than you can imagine. This done, you have only to stroll along with the mill on your back until you see tanbark* in the street and a knocker wrapped up in buckskin. Then you stop and grind, looking as if you meant to stop and grind till doomsday. Presently a window opens and somebody pitches you a sixpence, with a request to "Hush up and go on", etc. I am aware that some grinders have actually afforded to "go on" for this sum, but for my part I found the necessary outlay of capital too great to permit of my "going on" under a shilling.

At this occupation I did a good deal – but, somehow, I was not quite satisfied, and so finally abandoned it. The truth is, I laboured under the disadvantage of having no monkey – and American streets are *so* muddy, and a Democratic rabble is *so* obstrusive and so full of demnition* mischievous little boys.

I was now out of employment for some months, but at length succeeded, by dint of great interest, in procuring a situation in the Sham Post. The duties, here, are simple, and not altogether unprofitable. For example: very early in the morning I had to make up my packet of sham letters. Upon the inside of each of these I had to scrawl a few lines, on any subject which occurred to me as sufficiently mysterious – signing all the epistles "Tom Dobson" or "Bobby Tompkins", or anything in that way. Having folded and sealed all, and stamped them with sham postmarks – New Orleans, Bengal, Botany Bay or any other place a great way off – I set out, forthwith, upon my daily route, as if in a very great hurry. I always called at the big houses to deliver the letters and receive the postage.* Nobody hesitates at paying for a letter, especially for a double one – people are *such* fools – and it was no trouble to get round a corner before there was time to open the epistles. The worst of this profession was that I had to walk so much and so fast, and so frequently to vary my route. Besides, I had serious scruples of conscience. I can't bear to hear innocent individuals abused – and the way the whole town took to cursing Tom Dobson and Bobby Tompkins was really awful to hear. I washed my hands of the matter in disgust.

My eighth and last speculation has been in the Cat-Growing way. I have found this a most pleasant and lucrative business, and, really, no trouble at all. The country, it is well known, has become infested with cats – so much so, of late, that a petition for relief, most numerously and respectably signed, was brought before the legislature at its late memorable session. The assembly, at this epoch, was unusually well informed, and, having passed many other wise and wholesome enactments, it crowned all with the Cat Act. In its original form, this law offered a premium for cat heads (fourpence a piece), but the Senate succeeded in amending the main clause, so as to substitute the word "*tails*" for "heads." This amendment was so obviously proper that the House concurred in it *nem. con.**

As soon as the governor had signed the bill, I invested my whole estate in the purchase of Toms and Tabbies. At first I could only afford to feed them upon mice (which are cheap), but they fulfilled the scriptural injunction* at so marvellous a rate that I at length considered it my best policy to be liberal, and so indulged them in oysters and turtle.* Their tails, at a legislative price, now bring me in a good income, for I have discovered a way in which, by means of Macassar oil,* I can force three crops in a year. It delights me to find, too, that the animals soon get accustomed to the thing, and would rather have the appendages cut off than otherwise. I consider myself, therefore, a made man, and am bargaining for a country seat on the Hudson.

THE POWER OF WORDS*

OINOS: Pardon, Agathos, the weakness of a spirit new-fledged with immortality!

AGATHOS: You have spoken nothing, my Oinos, for which pardon is to be demanded. Not even here is knowledge a thing of intuition. For wisdom, ask of the angels freely, that it may be given!

OINOS: But in this existence I dreamt that I should be at once cognizant of all things, and thus at once be happy in being cognizant of all.

AGATHOS: Ah, not in knowledge is happiness, but in the acquisition of knowledge! In for ever knowing we are for ever blessed – but to know all were the curse of a fiend.

OINOS: But does not the Most High know all?

AGATHOS: *That* (since he is the Most Happy) must be still the *one* thing unknown even to HIM.

OINOS: But, since we grow hourly in knowledge, must not *at last* all things be known?

AGATHOS: Look down into the abysmal distances!... Attempt to force the gaze down the multitudinous vistas of the stars, as we sweep slowly through them thus... and thus... and thus! Even the spiritual vision, is it not at all points arrested by the continuous golden walls of the universe – the walls of the myriads of the shining bodies that mere number has appeared to blend into unity?

OINOS: I clearly perceive that the infinity of matter is no dream.

AGATHOS: There are *no* dreams in Aidenn* – but it is here whispered that, of this infinity of matter, the *sole* purpose is to afford infinite springs, at which the soul may allay the thirst *to know* which is for ever unquenchable within it, since to quench it would be to extinguish the soul's self. Question me then, my Oinos, freely and without fear. Come! We will leave to the left the loud harmony of the Pleiades and swoop outwards from the throne into the starry meadows beyond

Orion, where, for pansies and violets and heart's-ease,* are the beds of the triplicate and triple-tinted suns.

OINOS: And now, Agathos, as we proceed, instruct me!... Speak to me in the earth's familiar tones. I understood not what you hinted to me, just now, of the modes or of the methods of what, during mortality, we were accustomed to call "Creation". Do you mean to say that the Creator is not God?

AGATHOS: I mean to say that the Deity does not create.

OINOS: Explain!

AGATHOS: In the beginning *only*, he created. The seeming creatures which are now, throughout the universe, so perpetually springing into being, can only be considered as the mediate or indirect, not as the direct or immediate results of the Divine creative power.

OINOS: Among men, my Agathos, this idea would be considered heretical in the extreme.

AGATHOS: Among angels, my Oinos, it is seen to be simply true.

OINOS: I can comprehend you thus far – that certain operations of what we term "Nature", or the natural laws, will, under certain conditions, give rise to that which has all the *appearance* of creation. Shortly before the final overthrow of the earth, there were, I well remember, many very successful experiments in what some philosophers were weak enough to denominate "the creation of animalcula".

AGATHOS: The cases of which you speak were, in fact, instances of the secondary creation – and of the *only* species of creation which has ever been since the first word spoke into existence the first law.

OINOS: Are not the starry worlds that from the abyss of nonentity burst hourly forth into the heavens – are not these stars, Agathos, the immediate handiwork of the King?

AGATHOS: Let me endeavour, my Oinos, to lead you, step by step, to the conception I intend. You are well aware that, as no thought can perish, so no act is without infinite result. We moved our hands, for example, when we were dwellers on the earth, and, in so doing, we gave vibration to the atmosphere which engirdled it. This vibration was indefinitely extended, till it gave impulse to every particle of the earth's air, which thenceforward, *and for ever*, was actuated by the one movement of the hand. This fact the mathematicians of our globe well knew. They made the special effects, indeed, wrought in the fluid by special impulses, the subject of exact calculation – so that it became easy to determine in what precise period an impulse of given extent would engirdle the orb, and impress (for ever) every atom of the atmosphere circumambient. Retrograding, they found no difficulty, from a given effect, under given conditions, in determining the value of the original impulse. Now, the mathematicians who saw that the results of any given impulse were absolutely endless, and who saw that a portion of these results were accurately traceable through the agency of algebraic analysis – who saw, too, the facility of the retrogradation – these men saw, at the same time, that this species of analysis itself had within itself a capacity for indefinite progress, that there were no bounds conceivable to its advancement and applicability except within the intellect of him who advanced or applied it. But at this point our mathematicians paused.

OINOS: And why, Agathos, should they have proceeded?

AGATHOS: Because there were some considerations of deep interest beyond. It was deducible from what they knew that to a being of infinite understanding, one to whom the *perfection* of the algebraic analysis lay unfolded, there could be no difficulty in tracing every impulse given the air – and the ether through the air – to the remotest consequences at any even infinitely remote epoch of time. It is indeed demonstrable that every such impulse *given the air*, must, *in the end*, impress every individual thing that exists *within the universe*, and the being of infinite understanding, the being whom we have imagined, might trace the remote undulations of the impulse, trace them upwards and onwards in their influences upon all particles of all matter – upwards and onwards for ever in their modifications of old forms, or, in other words, *in their creation of new*, until he found them reflected (unimpressive *at last*) back from the throne of the Godhead. And not only could such a being do this, but at any epoch, should a given result be afforded him: should one of these numberless comets, for example, be presented to his inspection, he could have no difficulty in determining, by the analytic retrogradation, to what original impulse it was due. This power of retrogradation in its absolute fullness and perfection, this faculty of referring at *all* epochs *all* effects to *all* causes, is of course the prerogative of the Deity alone – but in every variety of degree short of the absolute perfection is the power itself exercised by the whole host of the Angelic intelligences.

OINOS: But you speak merely of impulses upon the air.

AGATHOS: In speaking of the air, I referred only to the earth, but the general proposition has reference to impulses upon the ether – which, since it pervades (and alone pervades) all space, is thus the great medium of *creation*.

OINOS: Then all motion, of whatever nature, creates?

AGATHOS: It must: but a true philosophy has long taught that the source of all motion is thought – and the source of all thought is—

OINOS: God.

AGATHOS: I have spoken to you, Oinos, as to a child of the fair Earth which lately perished – of impulses upon the atmosphere of the earth.

OINOS: You did.

AGATHOS: And while I thus spoke, did there not cross your mind some thought of the *physical power of words*? Is not every word an impulse on the air?

OINOS: But why, Agathos, do you weep – and why, oh why do your wings droop as we hover above this fair star, which is the greenest and yet most terrible of all we have encountered in our flight? Its brilliant flowers look like a fairy dream – but its fierce volcanoes like the passions of a turbulent heart.

AGATHOS: They *are*!... They *are*! This wild star, it is now three centuries since, with clasped hands and with streaming eyes, at the feet of my beloved, I spoke it – with a few passionate sentences – into birth. Its brilliant flowers *are* the dearest of all unfulfilled dreams, and its raging volcanoes *are* the passions of the most turbulent and unhallowed of hearts.

THE COLLOQUY OF MONOS AND UNA*

Μέλλοντα ταῦτα.*

"These things are in the near future."
– SOPHOCLES – *Antig.*

UNA: "Born again?"

MONOS: Yes, fairest and best beloved Una, "born again". These were the words upon whose mystical meaning I had so long pondered, rejecting the explanations of the priesthood, until Death himself resolved for me the secret.

UNA: Death!

MONOS: How strangely, sweet Una, you echo my words! I observe, too, a vacillation in your step – a joyous inquietude in your eyes. You are confused and oppressed by the majestic novelty of the Life Eternal. Yes, it was of Death I spoke. And here how singularly sounds that word which of old was wont to bring terror to all hearts – throwing a mildew upon all pleasures!

UNA: Ah, Death, the spectre which sat at all feasts! How often, Monos, did we lose ourselves in speculations upon its nature! How mysteriously did it act as a check to human bliss – saying unto it "thus far, and no farther!" That earnest mutual love, my own Monos, which burned within our bosoms – how vainly did we flatter ourselves, feeling happy in its first upspringing, that our happiness would strengthen with its strength! Alas, as it grew, so grew in our hearts the dread of that evil hour which was hurrying to separate us for ever! Thus, in time, it became painful to love. Hate would have been mercy then.

MONOS: Speak not here of these griefs, dear Una – mine, mine for ever now!

UNA: But the memory of past sorrow... is it not present joy? I have much to say yet of the things which have been. Above all, I burn to know the incidents of your own passage through the dark Valley and Shadow.*

MONOS: And when did the radiant Una ask anything of her Monos in vain? I will be minute in relating all – but at what point shall the weird narrative begin?

UNA: At what point?

MONOS: You have said.

UNA: Monos, I comprehend you. In Death we have both learnt the propensity of man to define the indefinable. I will not say, then, commence with the moment of life's cessation, but commence with that sad, sad instant when, the fever having abandoned you, you sank into a breathless and motionless torpor, and I pressed down your pallid eyelids with the passionate fingers of love.

MONOS: One word first, my Una, in regard to man's general condition at this epoch. You will remember that one or two of the wise among our forefathers – wise in fact, although not in the world's esteem – had ventured to doubt the propriety of the term "improvement" as applied to the progress of our civilization. There were periods in each of the five or six centuries immediately preceding our dissolution when arose some vigorous intellect, boldly contending for those principles whose truth appears now, to our disenfranchised reason, so utterly obvious – principles which should have taught our race to submit to the guidance of the natural laws rather than attempt their control. At long intervals some masterminds appeared, looking upon each advance in practical science as a retrogradation in the true utility. Occasionally the poetic intellect – that intellect which we now feel to have been the most exalted of all, since those truths which to us were of the most enduring importance could only be reached by that *analogy* which speaks in proof tones to the imagination alone, and to the unaided reason bears no weight – occasionally did this poetic intellect proceed a step further in the evolving of the vague idea of the philosophic, and find in the mystic parable that tells of the tree of knowledge and of its forbidden fruit, death-producing, a distinct intimation that knowledge was not meet for man in the infant condition of his soul. And these men, the poets, living and perishing amid the scorn of the "utilitarians" – of rough pedants who arrogated to themselves a title which could have been properly applied only to the scorned – these men, the poets, pondered piningly, yet not unwisely, upon the ancient days when our wants were not more simple than our enjoyments were keen, days when *mirth* was a word unknown, so solemnly deep-toned was happiness – holy, august and blissful days, when blue rivers ran undammed between hills unhewn, into far forest solitudes, primeval, odorous and unexplored.

Yet these noble exceptions from the general misrule served but to strengthen it by opposition. Alas, we had fallen upon the most evil of all our evil days! The great "movement" (that was the cant term) went on: a diseased commotion, moral and physical. Art – the Arts – arose supreme, and, once enthroned, cast chains upon the intellect which had elevated them to power. Man, because he could not but acknowledge the majesty of Nature, fell into childish exultation at his acquired and still-increasing dominion over her elements. Even while he stalked a God in his own fancy, an infantine imbecility came over him. As might be supposed from the origin of his disorder, he grew infected with system and with abstraction. He enwrapped himself in generalities. Among other odd ideas, that of universal equality gained ground, and in the face of analogy and of God – in despite of the loud warning voice of the laws of *gradation* so visibly pervading all things in Earth and Heaven – wild attempts at an omniprevalent Democracy were made. Yet this evil sprang necessarily from the leading evil: Knowledge. Man could not both know and succumb. Meantime, huge smoking cities arose, innumerable. Green leaves shrank before the hot breath of furnaces. The fair face of Nature was deformed as with the ravages of some loathsome disease. And methinks, sweet Una, even our slumbering sense of the forced and of the far-fetched might have arrested us here. But now it appears that we had worked out our own destruction in the perversion of our *taste*, or rather in the blind neglect of its culture in the schools. For, in truth, it was at this crisis that taste alone, that faculty which, holding a middle position between the pure intellect and the moral sense, could never safely have been disregarded – it was now that taste alone could have led us gently back to Beauty, to Nature and to Life. But alas for the pure contemplative spirit and majestic intuition of Plato! Alas for μουσική, which he justly regarded as an all-sufficient education for the soul! Alas for him and for it! – since both were most desperately needed when both were most entirely forgotten or despised.*

Pascal, a philosopher whom we both love, has said (how truly!) "*que tout notre raisonnement se réduit à céder au sentiment*"* – and it is not impossible that the sentiment of the natural, had time permitted it, would have regained its old ascendancy over the harsh mathematical reason of the schools. But this thing was not to be. Prematurely induced by intemperance of knowledge, the old age of the world drew on. This the mass of mankind saw not – or, living lustily although unhappily, affected not to see. But, for myself, the earth's records had taught me to look for widest ruin as the price of highest civilization. I had imbibed a prescience of our Fate from comparison of China the simple and enduring, with Assyria the architect, with Egypt the astrologer, with Nubia, more crafty than either, the turbulent mother of all Arts. In history* of these regions I met with a ray from the Future. The individual artificialities of the three latter were local diseases of the earth, and in their individual overthrows we had seen local remedies applied – but for the infected world at large I could anticipate no regeneration save in death. That man, as a race, should not become extinct, I saw that he must be "*born again*".

And now it was, fairest and dearest, that we wrapped our spirits, daily, in dreams. Now it was that, in twilight, we discoursed of the days to come, when the Art-scarred surface of the earth, having undergone that purification* which alone could efface its rectangular obscenities, should clothe itself anew in the verdure and the mountain slopes and the smiling waters of Paradise, and be rendered at length a fit dwelling place for man – for man the Death purged, for man to whose now-exalted intellect there should be poison in knowledge no more, for the redeemed, regenerated, blissful and now immortal, but still for the *material*, man.

UNA: Well do I remember these conversations, dear Monos, but the epoch of the fiery overthrow was not so near at hand as we believed and as the corruption you indicate did surely warrant us in believing. Men lived, and died individually. You yourself sickened, and passed into the grave – and thither your constant Una speedily followed you. And though the century which has since elapsed, and whose conclusion brings us thus together once more, tortured our slumbering senses with no impatience of duration, yet, my Monos, it was a century still.

MONOS: Say, rather, a point in the vague infinity. Unquestionably, it was in the Earth's dotage that I died. Wearied at heart with anxieties which had their origin in the general turmoil and decay, I succumbed to the fierce fever. After some few days of pain, and many of dreamy delirium replete with ecstasy, the manifestations of which you mistook for pain, while I longed but was impotent to undeceive you – after some days, there came upon me, as you have said, a breathless and motionless torpor, and this was termed *Death* by those who stood around me.

Words are vague things. My condition did not deprive me of sentience. It appeared to me not greatly dissimilar to the extreme quiescence of him who, having slumbered long and profoundly, lying motionless and fully prostrate in a midsummer noon, begins to steal slowly back into consciousness through the mere sufficiency of his sleep, and without being awakened by external disturbances.

I breathed no longer. The pulses were still. The heart had ceased to beat. Volition had not departed, but was powerless. The senses were unusually active, although eccentrically so – assuming often each other's functions at random. The taste and the smell were inextricably confounded, and became one sentiment, abnormal and intense. The rose-water with which your tenderness had moistened my lips to the last affected me with sweet fancies of flowers – fantastic flowers, far more lovely than any of the old Earth, but whose prototypes we have here blooming around us. The eyelids, transparent and bloodless, offered no complete impediment to vision. As volition was in abeyance, the balls could not roll in their sockets – but all objects within the range of the visual hemisphere were seen with more or less distinctness, the rays which fell upon the external retina or into the corner of the eye producing a more vivid effect than those which struck the front or interior surface. Yet, in the former instance, this effect was so far anomalous that I appreciated it only as *sound* – sound sweet or discordant as the matters presenting themselves at my side were light or dark in shade, curved or angular in outline. The hearing, at the same time, although excited in degree, was not irregular in action – estimating real sounds with an extravagance of precision not less than of sensibility. Touch had undergone a modification more peculiar. Its impressions were tardily received, but pertinaciously retained, and resulted always in the highest physical pleasure. Thus the pressure of your sweet fingers upon my eyelids, at first only recognized through vision, at length, long after their removal, filled my whole being with a sensual delight immeasurable. I say "with a sensual delight". *All* my perceptions were purely sensual. The materials furnished the passive brain by the senses were not in the least degree wrought into shape by the deceased understanding. Of pain there was some little, of pleasure there was much – but of moral pain or pleasure none at all. Thus your wild sobs floated into my ear with all their mournful cadences, and were appreciated in their every variation of sad tone, but they were soft musical sounds and no more: they conveyed to the extinct reason no intimation of the sorrows which gave them birth, while the large and constant tears which fell upon my face, telling the bystanders of a heart which broke, thrilled every fibre of my frame with ecstasy alone. And this was in truth the *Death* of which these bystanders spoke reverently, in low whispers – you, sweet Una, gaspingly, with loud cries.

They attired me for the coffin – three or four dark figures which flitted busily to and fro. As these crossed the direct line of my vision, they affected me as *forms*, but upon passing to my side their images impressed me with the idea of shrieks, groans and other dismal expressions of terror, of horror or of woe. You alone, habited in a white robe, passed in all directions musically about me.

The day waned, and, as its light faded away, I became possessed by a vague uneasiness, an anxiety such as the sleeper feels when sad real sounds fall continuously within his ear – low distant bell tones, solemn, at long but equal intervals, and commingling with melancholy dreams. Night arrived, and with its shadows a heavy discomfort. It oppressed my limbs with the oppression of some dull weight, and was palpable. There was also a moaning sound, not unlike the distant reverberation of surf, but more continuous – which, beginning with the first twilight, had grown in strength with the darkness. Suddenly lights were brought into the room, and this reverberation became forthwith interrupted into frequent unequal bursts of the same sound, but less dreary and less distinct. The ponderous oppression was in a great measure relieved – and, issuing from the flame of each lamp (for there were many), there flowed unbrokenly into my ears a strain of melodious monotone. And when now, dear Una, approaching the bed upon which I lay outstretched, you sat gently by my side, breathing odour from your sweet lips and pressing them upon my brow, there arose tremulously within my bosom, and mingling with the merely physical sensations which circumstances had called forth, a something akin to sentiment itself, a feeling that, half appreciating, half responded to your earnest love and sorrow – but this feeling took no root in the pulseless heart, and seemed indeed rather a shadow than a reality, and faded quickly away, first into extreme quiescence and then into a purely sensual pleasure as before.

And now, from the wreck and the chaos of the usual senses, there appeared to have arisen within me a sixth, all perfect. In its exercise I found a wild delight – yet a delight still physical, inasmuch as the understanding had in it no part. Motion in the animal frame had fully ceased. No muscle quivered, no nerve thrilled, no artery throbbed. But there seemed to have sprung up in the brain *that* of which no words could convey to the merely human intelligence even an indistinct conception. Let me term it "a mental pendulous pulsation". It was the moral embodiment of man's abstract idea of Time. By the absolute equalization of this movement – or of such as this – had the cycles of the firmamental orbs themselves been adjusted. By its aid I measured the irregularities of the clock upon the mantel, and of the watches of the attendants. Their tickings came sonorously to my ears. The slightest deviations from the true proportion (and these deviations were omniprevalent) affected me just as violations of abstract truth were wont, on earth, to affect the moral sense. Although no two of the timepieces in the chamber struck the individual seconds accurately together, yet I had no difficulty in holding steadily in mind the tones and the respective momentary errors of each. And this – this keen, perfect, self-existing sentiment of *duration*, this sentiment existing (as man could not possibly have conceived it to exist) independently of any succession of events, this idea, this sixth sense, upspringing from the ashes of the rest, was the first obvious and certain step of the intemporal soul upon the threshold of the temporal Eternity.

It was midnight, and you still sat by my side. All others had departed from the chamber of Death. They had deposited me in the coffin. The lamps burned flickeringly – for this I knew by the tremulousness of the monotonous strains. But suddenly these strains diminished in distinctness and in volume. Finally they ceased. The perfume in my nostrils died away. Forms affected my vision no longer. The oppression of the Darkness uplifted itself from my bosom. A dull shock like that of electricity pervaded my frame, and was followed by total loss of the idea of contact. All of what man has termed "sense" was merged in the sole consciousness of entity, and in the one abiding sentiment of duration. The mortal body had been at length stricken with the hand of the deadly *Decay*.

Yet had not all of sentience departed, for the consciousness and the sentiment remaining supplied some of its functions by a lethargic intuition. I appreciated the direful change now in operation upon the flesh, and, as the dreamer is sometimes aware of the bodily presence of one who leans over him, so, sweet Una, I still dully felt that you sat by my side. So, too, when the noon of the second day came, I was not unconscious of those movements which displaced you from my side, which confined me within the coffin, which deposited me within the hearse, which bore me to the grave, which lowered me within it, which heaped heavily the mould upon me, and which thus left me, in blackness and corruption, to my sad and solemn slumbers with the worm.

And here, in the prison house which has few secrets to disclose, there rolled away days and weeks and months, and the soul watched narrowly each second as it flew, and, without effort, took record of its flight – without effort and without object.

A year passed. The consciousness of being had grown hourly more indistinct, and that of mere *locality* had, in great measure, usurped its position. The idea of entity was becoming merged in that of *place*. The narrow space immediately surrounding what had been the body was now growing to be the body itself. At length, as often happens to the sleeper (by sleep and its world alone is *Death* imaged) – at length, as sometimes happened on earth to the deep slumberer when some flitting light half startled him into awaking, yet left him half enveloped in dreams – so to me, in the strict embrace of the *Shadow*, came *that* light which alone might have had power to startle: the light of enduring *Love*. Men toiled at the grave in which I lay darkling. They upthrew the damp earth. Upon my mouldering bones there descended the coffin of Una.

And now again all was void. That nebulous light had been extinguished. That feeble thrill had vibrated itself into quiescence. Many *lustra* had supervened. Dust had returned to dust. The worm had food no more. The sense of being had at length utterly departed, and there reigned in its stead – instead of all things – dominant and perpetual, the autocrats *Place* and *Time*. For *that* which *was not*, for that which had no form, for that which had no thought, for that which had no sentience, for that which was soulless, yet of which matter formed no portion – for all this nothingness, yet for all this immortality, the grave was still a home, and the corrosive hours co-mates.*

THE CONVERSATION OF EIROS AND CHARMION*

Πῦρ σοι προσοίσω.*

"I will bring fire to thee."
– EURIPIDES, *Androm.*

EIROS: Why do you call me Eiros?

CHARMION: So henceforward will you always be called. You must forget, too, *my* earthly name, and speak to me as Charmion.

EIROS: This is indeed no dream!

CHARMION: Dreams are with us no more – but of these mysteries anon. I rejoice to see you looking lifelike and rational. The film of the shadow has already passed from off your eyes. Be of heart and fear nothing. Your allotted days of stupor have expired, and tomorrow I will myself induct you into the full joys and wonders of your novel existence.

EIROS: True – I feel no stupor, none at all. The wild sickness and the terrible darkness have left me, and I hear no longer that mad, rushing, horrible sound, like the "voice of many waters".* Yet my senses are bewildered, Charmion, with the keenness of their perception of *the new*.

CHARMION: A few days will remove all this – but I fully understand you, and feel for you. It is now ten earthly years since I underwent what you undergo, yet the remembrance of it hangs by me still. You have now suffered all of pain, however, which you will suffer in Aidenn.*

EIROS: In Aidenn?

CHARMION: In Aidenn.

EIROS: Oh God!... Pity me, Charmion!... I am overburdened with the majesty of all things... of the unknown now known... of the speculative Future merged in the august and certain Present.

CHARMION: Grapple not now with such thoughts. Tomorrow we will speak of this. Your mind wavers, and its agitation will find relief in the exercise of simple memories. Look not around, nor forward – but back. I am burning with anxiety to hear the details of that stupendous event which threw you among us. Tell me of it. Let us converse of familiar things in the old familiar language of the world which has so fearfully perished.

EIROS: Most fearfully, fearfully!... This is indeed no dream.

CHARMION: Dreams are no more. Was I much mourned, my Eiros?

EIROS: Mourned, Charmion?... Oh, deeply. To that last hour of all, there hung a cloud of intense gloom and devout sorrow over your household.

CHARMION: And that last hour... speak of it. Remember that, beyond the naked fact of the catastrophe itself, I know nothing. When, coming out from among mankind, I passed into Night through the Grave – at that period, if I remember aright, the calamity which overwhelmed you was utterly unanticipated. But, indeed, I knew little of the speculative philosophy of the day.

EIROS: The individual calamity was, as you say, entirely unanticipated, but analogous misfortunes had been long a subject of discussion with astronomers. I need scarce tell you, my friend, that, even when you left us, men had agreed to understand those passages in the most holy writings which speak of the final destruction of all things by fire as having reference to the orb of the earth alone.* But in regard to the immediate agency of the ruin, speculation had been at fault from that epoch in astronomical knowledge in which the comets were divested of the terrors of flame. The very moderate density of these bodies had been well established. They had been observed to pass among the satellites of Jupiter without bringing about any sensible alteration either in the masses or in the orbits of these secondary planets. We had long regarded the wanderers as vapoury creations of inconceivable tenuity, and as altogether incapable of doing injury to our substantial globe, even in the event of contact. But contact was not in any degree dreaded, for the elements of all the comets were accurately known. That among *them* we should look for the agency of the threatened fiery destruction had been for many years considered an inadmissible idea. But wonders and wild fancies had been, of late days, strangely rife among mankind – and, although it was only with a few of the ignorant that actual apprehension prevailed, upon the announcement by astronomers of a *new* comet, yet this announcement was generally received with I know not what of agitation and mistrust.

The elements of the strange orb were immediately calculated, and it was at once conceded by all observers that its path, at perihelion,* would bring it into very close proximity with the earth. There were two or three astronomers of secondary note who resolutely maintained that a contact was inevitable. I cannot very well express to you the effect of this intelligence upon the people. For a few short days they would not believe an assertion which their intellect, so long employed among worldly considerations, could not in any manner grasp. But the truth of a vitally important fact soon makes its way into the understanding of even the most stolid. Finally, all men saw that astronomical knowledge lied not, and they awaited the comet. Its approach was not, at first, seemingly rapid – nor was its appearance of very unusual character. It was of a dull red, and had little perceptible train. For seven or eight days we saw no material increase in its apparent diameter, and but a partial alteration in its colour. Meantime, the ordinary affairs of men were discarded, and all interests absorbed in a growing discussion, instituted by the philosophic, in respect to the cometary nature. Even the grossly ignorant aroused their sluggish capacities to such considerations. The learned *now* gave their intellect – their soul – to no such points as the allaying of fear or to the sustenance of loved theory. They sought, they panted for right views. They groaned for perfected knowledge. *Truth* arose in the purity of her strength and exceeding majesty, and the wise bowed down and adored.

That material injury to our globe or to its inhabitants would result from the apprehended contact was an opinion which hourly lost ground among the wise – and the wise were now freely permitted to rule the reason and the fancy of the crowd. It was demonstrated that the density of the comet's *nucleus* was far less than that of our rarest gas, and the harmless passage of a similar visitor among the satellites of Jupiter was a point strongly insisted upon, and which served greatly to allay terror. Theologists with an earnestness fear-enkindled dwelt upon the biblical prophecies, and expounded them to the people with a directness and simplicity of which no previous instance had been known. That the final destruction of the earth must be brought about by the agency of fire was urged with a spirit that enforced everywhere conviction – and that the comets were of no fiery nature (as all men now knew) was a truth which relieved all, in a great measure, from the apprehension of the great calamity foretold. It is noticeable that the popular prejudices and vulgar errors in regard to pestilences and wars – errors which were wont to prevail upon every appearance of a comet – were now altogether unknown. As if by some sudden convulsive exertion, reason had at once hurled superstition from her throne. The feeblest intellect had derived vigour from excessive interest.

What minor evils might arise from the contact were points of elaborate question. The learned spoke of slight geological disturbances, of probable alterations in climate, and consequently in vegetation – of possible magnetic and electric influences. Many held that no visible or perceptible effect would in any manner be produced. While such discussions were going on, their subject gradually approached, growing larger in apparent diameter, and of a more brilliant lustre. Mankind grew paler as it came. All human operations were suspended.

There was an epoch in the course of the general sentiment when the comet had attained, at length, a size surpassing that of any previously recorded visitation. The people now, dismissing any lingering hope that the astronomers were wrong, experienced all the certainty of evil. The chimerical aspect of their terror was gone. The hearts of the stoutest of our race beat violently within their bosoms. A very few days sufficed, however, to merge even such feelings in sentiments more unendurable. We could no longer apply to the strange orb any *accustomed* thoughts. Its *historical* attributes had disappeared. It oppressed us with a hideous *novelty* of emotion. We saw it not as an astronomical phenomenon in the heavens, but as an incubus upon our hearts, and a shadow upon our brains. It had taken, with inconceivable rapidity, the character of a gigantic mantle of rare flame extending from horizon to horizon.

Yet a day, and men breathed with greater freedom. It was clear that we were already within the influence of the comet – yet we lived. We even felt an unusual elasticity of frame and vivacity of mind. The exceeding tenuity of the object of our dread was apparent, for all heavenly objects were plainly visible through it. Meantime, our vegetation had perceptibly altered, and we gained faith, from this predicted circumstance, in the foresight of the wise. A wild luxuriance of foliage utterly unknown before burst out upon every vegetable thing.

Yet another day – and the evil was not altogether upon us. It was now evident that its nucleus would first reach us. A wild change had come over all men – and the first sense of *pain* was the wild signal for general lamentation and horror. This first sense of pain lay in a rigorous constriction of the breast and lungs, and an insufferable dryness of the skin. It could not be denied that our atmosphere was radically affected – the conformation of this atmosphere and the possible modifications to which it might be subjected were now the topics of discussion. The result of investigation sent an electric thrill of the intensest terror through the universal heart of man.

It had been long known that the air which encircled us was a compound of oxygen and nitrogen gases, in the proportion of twenty-one measures of oxygen and seventy-nine of nitrogen, in every one hundred of the atmosphere. Oxygen, which was the principle of combustion and the vehicle of heat, was absolutely necessary to the support of animal life, and was the most powerful and energetic agent in nature. Nitrogen, on the contrary, was incapable of supporting either animal life or flame. An unnatural excess of oxygen would result, it had been ascertained, in just such an elevation of the animal spirits as we had latterly experienced. It was the pursuit, the extension of the idea, which had engendered awe. What would be the result of *a total extraction of the nitrogen*? A combustion irresistible, all-devouring, omniprevalent, immediate – the entire fulfilment, in all their minute and terrible details, of the fiery and horror-inspiring denunciations of the prophecies of the Holy Book.

Why need I paint, Charmion, the now disenchained frenzy of mankind? That tenuity in the comet which had previously inspired us with hope was now the source of the bitterness of despair. In its impalpable gaseous character we clearly perceived the consummation of Fate. Meantime, a day again passed, bearing away with it the last shadow of Hope. We gasped in the rapid modification of the air. The red blood bounded tumultuously through its strict channels. A furious delirium possessed all men – and, with arms rigidly outstretched towards the threatening heavens, they trembled and shrieked aloud. But the nucleus of the destroyer was now upon us, even here in Aidenn – I shudder while I speak. Let me be brief – brief as the ruin that overwhelmed. For a moment there was a wild, lurid light alone, visiting and penetrating all things. Then… let us bow down, Charmion, before the excessive majesty of the great God!… Then, there came a shouting and pervading sound, as if from the mouth itself of HIM, while the whole incumbent mass of ether in which we existed burst at once into a species of intense flame, for whose surpassing brilliancy and all-fervid heat even the angels in the high heaven of pure knowledge have no name. Thus ended all.

SHADOW*

A PARABLE

Yea, though I walk through the valley of the *Shadow*.*
– Psalm of David

Ye who read are still among the living, but I who write shall have long since gone my way into the region of shadows. For indeed strange things shall happen, and secret things be known, and many centuries shall pass away, ere these memorials be seen of men. And, when seen, there will be some to disbelieve and some to doubt, and yet a few who will find much to ponder upon in the characters here graven with a stylus of iron.

The year had been a year of terror, and of feelings more intense than terror for which there is no name upon the earth. For many prodigies and signs had taken place, and far and wide, over sea and land, the black wings of the Pestilence were spread abroad. To those, nevertheless, cunning in the stars, it was not unknown that the heavens wore an aspect of ill – and to me, the Greek Oinos,[n] among others, it was evident that now had arrived the alternation of that seven hundred and ninety-fourth year when, at the entrance of Aries, the planet Jupiter is conjoined with the red ring of the terrible Saturnus.* The peculiar spirit of the skies, if I mistake not greatly, made itself manifest not only in the physical orb of the earth, but in the souls, imaginations and meditations of mankind.

Over some flasks of the red Chian wine,* within the walls of a noble hall, in a dim city called Ptolemais, we sat at night, a company of seven. And to our chamber there was no entrance save by a lofty door of brass, and the door was fashioned by the artisan Corinnos – and, being of rare workmanship, was fastened from within. Black draperies, likewise, in the gloomy room, shut out from our view the moon, the lurid stars and the peopleless streets – but the boding and the memory of Evil, they would not be so excluded. There were things around us and about of which I can render no distinct account – things material and spiritual: heaviness in the atmosphere, a sense of suffocation, anxiety – and, above all, that terrible state of existence which the nervous experience when the senses are keenly living and awake, and meanwhile the powers of thought lie dormant. A dead weight hung upon us. It hung upon our limbs, upon the household furniture, upon the goblets from which we drank – and all things were depressed, and borne down thereby, all things save only the flames of the seven iron lamps which illumined our revel. Uprearing themselves in tall slender lines of light, they thus remained burning all pallid and motionless, and in the mirror which their lustre formed upon the round table of ebony at which we sat, each of us there assembled beheld the pallor of his own countenance, and the unquiet glare in the downcast eyes of his companions. Yet we laughed and were merry in our proper way, which was hysterical, and sang the songs of Anacreon,* which are madness – and drank deeply, although the purple wine reminded us of blood. For there was yet another tenant of our chamber in the person of young Zoilus. Dead, and at full length he lay, enshrouded – the genius and the demon of the scene. Alas, he bore no portion in our mirth, save that his countenance, distorted with the plague, and his eyes, in which Death had but half extinguished the fire of the pestilence, seemed to take such interest in our merriment as the dead may haply take in the merriment of those who are to die. But although I, Oinos, felt that the eyes of the departed were upon me, still I forced myself not to perceive the bitterness of their expression, and, gazing down steadily into the depths of the ebony mirror, sang with a loud and sonorous voice the songs of the son of Teios.* But gradually my songs they ceased, and their echoes, rolling afar off among the sable draperies of the chamber, became weak and undistinguishable, and so faded away. And lo! from among those sable draperies where the sounds of the song departed, there came forth a dark and undefined shadow, a shadow such as the moon, when low in heaven, might fashion from the figure of a man – but it was the shadow neither of man nor of God, nor of any familiar thing. And quivering awhile among the draperies of the room, it at length rested in full view upon the surface of the door of brass. But the shadow was vague and formless, and indefinite, and was the shadow neither of man nor of God – neither God of Greece nor God of Chaldea,* nor any Egyptian God. And the shadow rested upon the brazen doorway, and under the arch of the entablature of the door, and moved not, nor spoke any word, but there became stationary and remained. And the door whereupon the shadow rested was, if I remember aright, over against the feet of the young Zoilus enshrouded. But we, the seven there assembled, having seen the shadow as it came out from among the draperies, dared not steadily behold it, but cast down our eyes and gazed continually into the depths of the mirror of ebony. And at length I, Oinos, speaking some low words, demanded of the shadow its dwelling and its appellation. And the shadow answered, "I am SHADOW, and my dwelling is near to the Catacombs of Ptolemais, and hard by those dim plains of Helusion which border upon the foul Charonian canal."* And then did we, the seven, start from our seats in horror, and stand trembling and shuddering and aghast, for the tones in the voice of the shadow were not the tones of any one being, but of a multitude of beings – and, varying in their cadences from syllable to syllable, fell duskily upon our ears in the well-remembered and familiar accents of many thousand departed friends.

SILENCE*

A FABLE

Εὕδουσιν δ' ὀρέων κορυφαί τε καὶ φάραγγες,
πρώονές τε καὶ χαράδραι.*

"The mountain pinnacles slumber; valleys, crags
And caves *are silent*."

— ALCMAN

"Listen to *me*," said the Demon as he placed his hand upon my head. "The region of which I speak is a dreary region in Libya, by the borders of the river Zaïre. And there is no quiet there, nor silence.

"The waters of the river have a saffron and sickly hue, and they flow not onwards to the sea, but palpitate forever and forever beneath the red eye of the sun with a tumultuous and convulsive motion. For many miles on either side of the river's oozy bed is a pale desert of gigantic water lilies. They sigh one unto the other in that solitude, and stretch towards the heaven their long and ghastly necks, and nod to and fro their everlasting heads. And there is an indistinct murmur which cometh out from among them like the rushing of subterrene* water. And they sigh one unto the other.

"But there is a boundary to their realm: the boundary of the dark, horrible, lofty forest. There, like the waves about the Hebrides, the low underwood is agitated continually. But there is no wind throughout the heaven. And the tall primeval trees rock eternally hither and thither with a crashing and mighty sound. And from their high summits, one by one, drop everlasting dews. And at the roots strange poisonous flowers lie writhing in perturbed slumber. And overhead, with a rustling and loud noise, the grey clouds rush westwardly forever, until they roll, a cataract, over the fiery wall of the horizon. But there is no wind throughout the heaven. And by the shores of the river Zaïre there is neither quiet nor silence.

"It was night, and the rain fell – and, falling, it was rain, but, having fallen, it was blood. And I stood in the morass among the tall lilies, and the rain fell upon my head – and the lilies sighed one unto the other in the solemnity of their desolation.

"And, all at once, the moon arose through the thin ghastly mist, and was crimson in colour. And mine eyes fell upon a huge grey rock which stood by the shore of the river and was lighted by the light of the moon. And the rock was grey, and ghastly, and tall – and the rock was grey. Upon its front were characters engraven in the stone – and I walked through the morass of water lilies, until I came close unto the shore, that I might read the characters upon the stone. But I could not decipher them. And I was going back into the morass when the moon shone with a fuller red, and I turned and looked again upon the rock, and upon the characters – and the characters were 'DESOLATION'.

"And I looked upwards, and there stood a man upon the summit of the rock – and I hid myself among the water lilies, that I might discover the actions of the man. And the man was tall and stately in form, and was wrapped up from his shoulders to his feet in the toga of old Rome. And the outlines of his figure were indistinct – but his features were the features of a deity, for the mantle of the night, and of the mist, and of the moon, and of the dew, had left uncovered the features of his face. And his brow was lofty with thought, and his eye wild with care – and, in the few furrows upon his cheek, I read the fables of sorrow and weariness, and disgust with mankind, and a longing after solitude.

"And the man sat upon the rock, and leant his head upon his hand, and looked out upon the desolation. He looked down into the low unquiet shrubbery, and up into the tall primeval trees, and up higher at the rustling heaven, and into the crimson moon. And I lay close within shelter of the lilies, and observed the actions of the man. And the man trembled in the solitude – but the night waned and he sat upon the rock.

"And the man turned his attention from the heaven, and looked out upon the dreary river Zaïre, and upon the yellow ghastly waters, and upon the pale legions of the water lilies. And the man listened to the sighs of the water lilies, and to the murmur that came up from among them. And I lay close within my covert and observed the actions of the man. And the man trembled in the solitude – but the night waned and he sat upon the rock.

"Then I went down into the recesses of the morass, and waded afar in among the wilderness of the lilies, and called unto the hippopotami which dwelt among the fens in the recesses of the morass. And the hippopotami heard my call, and came, with the behemoth, unto the foot of the rock, and roared loudly and fearfully beneath the moon. And I lay close within my covert and observed the actions of the man. And the man trembled in the solitude – but the night waned and he sat upon the rock.

"Then I cursed the elements with the curse of tumult, and a frightful tempest gathered in the heaven where, before, there had been no wind. And the heaven became livid with the violence of the tempest, and the rain beat upon the head of the man, and the floods of the river came down, and the river was tormented into foam, and the water lilies shrieked within their beds, and the forest crumbled before the wind, and the thunder rolled, and the lightning fell, and the rock rocked to its foundation. And I lay close within my covert and observed the actions of the man. And the man trembled in the solitude – but the night waned and he sat upon the rock.

"Then I grew angry and cursed with the curse of *silence*, the river, and the lilies, and the wind, and the forest, and the heaven, and the thunder, and the sighs of the water lilies. And they became accursed, and *were still*. And the moon ceased to totter up its pathway to heaven, and the thunder died away, and the lightning did not flash, and the clouds hung motionless, and the waters sunk to their level and remained, and the trees ceased to rock, and the water lilies sighed no more, and the murmur was heard no longer from among them, nor any shadow of sound throughout the vast, illimitable desert. And I looked upon the characters of the rock, and they were changed – and the characters were 'SILENCE'.

"And mine eyes fell upon the countenance of the man, and his countenance was wan with terror. And, hurriedly, he raised his head from his hand and stood forth upon the rock and listened. But there was no voice throughout the vast, illimitable desert, and the characters upon the rock were 'SILENCE'. And the man shuddered, and turned his face away, and fled afar off, in haste, so that I beheld him no more."

* * * * * * *

Now, there are fine tales in the volumes of the Magi – in the iron-bound, melancholy volumes of the Magi. Therein, I say, are glorious histories of the Heaven, and of the Earth, and of the mighty sea – and of the Genii that overruled the sea, and the earth, and the lofty heaven. There was much lore too in the sayings which were said by the Sibyls – and holy, holy things were heard of old by the dim leaves that trembled around Dodona* – but, as Allah liveth, that fable which the Demon told me as he sat by my side in the shadow of the tomb, I hold to be the most wonderful of all! And as the Demon made an end of his story, he fell back within the cavity of the tomb and laughed. And I could not laugh with the Demon, and he cursed me because I could not laugh. And the lynx which dwelleth forever in the tomb came out therefrom, and lay down at the feet of the Demon, and looked at him steadily in the face.

A TALE OF JERUSALEM*

Intonsos rigidam in frontem ascendere canos
*Passus erat…**

– LUCAN, *De Catone**

…a bristly *bore.*

Translation

"Let us hurry to the walls," said Abel-Phittim to Buzi-Ben-Levi and Simeon the Pharisee, on the tenth day of the month Thammuz, in the year of the world three thousand nine hundred and forty-one,* "let us hasten to the ramparts adjoining the Gate of Benjamin, which is in the City of David,* and overlooking the camp of the uncircumcised, for it is the last hour of the fourth watch, being sunrise, and the idolaters, in fulfilment of the promise of Pompey, should be awaiting us with the lambs for the sacrifices."

Simeon, Abel-Phittim and Buzi-Ben-Levi were the Gizbarim,* or sub-collectors of the offering, in the holy city of Jerusalem.

"Verily," replied the Pharisee, "let us hasten, for this generosity in the heathen is unwonted, and fickle-mindedness has ever been an attribute of the worshippers of Baal."*

"That they are fickle-minded and treacherous is as true as the Pentateuch,"* said Buzi-Ben-Levi, "but that is only towards the people of Adonai.* When was it ever known that the Ammonites proved wanting to their own interests? Methinks it is no great stretch of generosity to allow us lambs for the altar of the Lord, receiving in lieu thereof thirty silver shekels per head!"

"Thou forgettest, however, Ben-Levi," replied Abel-Phittim, "that the Roman Pompey, who is now impiously besieging the city of the Most High,* has no assurity that we apply not the lambs thus purchased for the altar to the sustenance of the body, rather than of the spirit."

"Now, by the five corners of my beard!" shouted the Pharisee, who belonged to the sect called "the Dashers" (that little knot of saints whose manner of *dashing* and lacerating the feet against the pavement was long a thorn and a reproach to less zealous devotees – a stumbling block to less gifted perambulators) – "by the five corners of that beard which, as a priest, I am forbidden to shave!… Have we lived to see the day when a blaspheming and idolatrous upstart of Rome shall accuse us of appropriating to the appetites of the flesh the most holy and consecrated elements? Have we lived to see the day when—"

"Let us not question the motives of the Philistine,"* interrupted Abel-Phittim, "for today we profit for the first time by his avarice or by his generosity, but rather let us hurry to the ramparts, lest offerings should be wanting for that altar whose fire the rains of heaven cannot extinguish, and whose pillars of smoke no tempest can turn aside."

That part of the city to which our worthy Gizbarim now hastened, and which bore the name of its architect, King David, was esteemed the most strongly fortified district of Jerusalem, being situated upon the steep and lofty hill of Zion. Here, a broad, deep circumvallatory trench,* hewn from the solid rock, was defended by a wall of great strength erected upon its inner edge. This wall was adorned, at regular interspaces, by square towers of white marble – the lowest sixty, and the highest one hundred and twenty cubits in height. But, in the vicinity of the Gate of Benjamin, the wall arose by no means from the margin of the fosse.* On the contrary, between the level of the ditch and the basement of the rampart, sprang up a perpendicular cliff of two hundred and fifty cubits, forming part of the precipitous Mount Moriah.* So that when Simeon and his associates arrived on the summit of the tower called Adoni-Bezek – the loftiest of all the turrets round about Jerusalem, and the usual place of conference with the besieging army – they looked down upon the camp of the enemy from an eminence excelling by many feet that of the Pyramid of Cheops, and by several that of the Temple of Belus.*

"Verily," sighed the Pharisee as he peered dizzily over the precipice, "the uncircumcised are as the sands by the seashore* – as the locusts in the wilderness! The Valley of the King hath become the Valley of Adommin."

"And yet," added Ben-Levi, "thou canst not point me out a Philistine – no, not one… from aleph to tau… from the wilderness to the battlements – who seemeth any bigger than the letter jod!"*

"Lower away the basket with the shekels of silver!" here shouted a Roman soldier in a hoarse, rough voice, which appeared to issue from the regions of Pluto* – "lower away the basket with the accursed coin which it has broken the jaw of a noble Roman to pronounce! Is it thus you evince your gratitude to our master Pompeius, who, in his condescension, has thought fit to listen to your idolatrous importunities? The god Phoebus, who is a true god, has been charioted for an hour* – and were you not to be on the ramparts by sunrise? *Ædepol!** Do you think that we, the conquerors of the world, have nothing better to do than stand waiting by the walls of every kennel to traffic with the dogs of the earth? Lower away, I say! – and see that your trumpery be bright in colour and just in weight!"

"El Elohim!"* ejaculated the Pharisee as the discordant tones of the centurion rattled up the crags of the precipice and fainted away against the temple. "El Elohim!... Who is the god Phoebus?... *Whom* doth the blasphemer invoke? Thou, Buzi-Ben-Levi, who art read in the laws of the Gentiles and hast sojourned among them who dabble with the teraphim!...* Is it Nergal of whom the idolater speaketh?... Or Ashimah?... Or Nibhaz... Or Tartak?... Or Adramalech?... Or Anamalech?... Or Succoth-Benith?... Or Dagon?... Or Belial?... Or Baal-Perith?... Or Baal-Peor?... Or Baal-Zebub?"*

"Verily it is neither – but beware how thou lettest the rope slip too rapidly through thy fingers, for should the wickerwork chance to hang on the projection of yonder crag, there will be a woeful outpouring of the holy things of the sanctuary."

By the assistance of some rudely constructed machinery, the heavily laden basket was now carefully lowered down among the multitude, and, from the giddy pinnacle, the Romans were seen gathering confusedly round it – but owing to the vast height and the prevalence of a fog, no distinct view of their operations could be obtained.

Half an hour had already elapsed.

"We shall be too late!" sighed the Pharisee as at the expiration of this period he looked over into the abyss. "We shall be too late! We shall be turned out of office by the Katholim."*

"No more," responded Abel-Phittim, "no more shall we feast upon the fat of the land...* no longer shall our beards be odorous with frankincense, our loins girded up with fine linen from the Temple."

"Raca!"* swore Ben-Levi. "Raca! Do they mean to defraud us of the purchase money? Or, Holy Moses, are they weighing the shekels of the tabernacle?"

"They have given the signal at last!" cried the Pharisee. "They have given the signal at last!... Pull away, Abel-Phittim! – and thou, Buzi-Ben-Levi, pull away! – for verily the Philistines have either still hold upon the basket, or the Lord hath softened their hearts to place therein a beast of good weight!" And the Gizbarim pulled away, while their burden swung heavily upwards through the still-increasing mist.

* * * * * * *

"Booshoh he!" – as, at the conclusion of an hour, some object at the extremity of the rope became indistinctly visible. "Booshoh he!" was the exclamation which burst from the lips of Ben-Levi.

"Booshoh he!… For shame!… It is a ram from the thickets of Engedi, and as rugged as the Valley of Jehoshaphat!"

"It is a firstling of the flock," said Abel-Phittim. "I know him by the bleating of his lips and the innocent folding of his limbs. His eyes are more beautiful than the jewels of the pectoral, and his flesh is like the honey of Hebron."

"It is a fatted calf from the pastures of Bashan," said the Pharisee. "The heathen have dealt wonderfully with us… Let us raise up our voices in a psalm – let us give thanks on the shawm and on the psaltery… on the harp and on the huggab… on the cythern and on the sackbut!"*

It was not until the basket had arrived within a few feet of the Gizbarim that a low grunt betrayed to their perception a *hog* of no common size.

"Now, El Emanu!" slowly and with upturned eyes ejaculated the trio as, letting go their hold, the emancipated porker tumbled headlong among the Philistines. "El Emanu!… God be with us – *it is the unutterable flesh!*"

"THOU ART THE MAN"*

I will now play the Oedipus to the Rattleborough enigma.* I will expound to you, as I alone can, the secret of the enginery* that effected the Rattleborough miracle – the one, the true, the admitted, the undisputed, the indisputable miracle which put a definite end to infidelity among the Rattleburghers and converted to the orthodoxy of the grandames all the carnal-minded who had ventured to be sceptical before.

This event, which I should be sorry to discuss in a tone of unsuitable levity, occurred in the summer of 18—. Mr Barnabas Shuttleworthy – one of the wealthiest and most respectable citizens of the borough – had been missing for several days under circumstances which gave rise to suspicion of foul play. Mr Shuttleworthy had set out from Rattleborough very early one Saturday morning, on horseback, with the avowed intention of proceeding to the city of ———, about fifteen miles distant, and of returning the night of the same day. Two hours after his departure, however, his horse returned without him, and without the saddlebags which had been strapped on his back at starting. The animal was wounded, too, and covered with mud. These circumstances naturally gave rise to much alarm among the friends of the missing man – and when it was found, on Sunday morning, that he had not yet made his appearance, the whole borough arose en masse to go and look for his body.

The foremost and most energetic in instituting this search was the bosom friend of Mr Shuttleworthy, a Mr Charles Goodfellow – or, as he was universally called, "Charley Goodfellow", or "Old Charley Goodfellow". Now, whether it is a marvellous coincidence or whether it is that the name itself has an imperceptible effect upon the character I have never yet been able to ascertain, but the fact is unquestionable that there never yet was any person named Charles who was not an open, manly, honest, good-natured and frank-hearted fellow, with a rich, clear voice that did you good to hear it, and an eye that looked you always straight in the face, as much as to say: "I have a clear conscience myself, am afraid of no man, and am altogether above doing a mean action." And thus all the hearty, careless, "walking gentlemen" of the stage* are very certain to be called Charles.

Now, "Old Charley Goodfellow", although he had been in Rattleborough not longer than six months or thereabouts, and although nobody knew anything about him before he came to settle in the neighbourhood, had experienced no difficulty in the world in making the acquaintance of all the respectable people in the borough. Not a man of them but would have taken his bare word for a thousand at any moment – and as for the women, there is no saying what they would not have done to oblige him. And all this came of his having been christened Charles, and of his possessing, in consequence, that ingenuous face which is proverbially the very "best letter of recommendation".

I have already said that Mr Shuttleworthy was one of the most respectable, and, undoubtedly, he was the most wealthy man in Rattleborough, while "Old Charley Goodfellow" was upon as intimate terms with him as if he had been his own brother. The two old gentlemen were next-door neighbours, and, although Mr Shuttleworthy seldom, if ever, visited "Old Charley", and never was known to take a meal in his house, still this did not prevent the two friends from being exceedingly intimate, as I have just observed, for "Old Charley" never let a day pass without stepping in three or four times to see how his neighbour came on, and very often he would stay to breakfast or tea, and almost always to dinner – and then the amount of wine that was made way with by the two cronies at a sitting, it would really be a difficult thing to ascertain. Old Charley's favourite beverage was Château Margaux,* and it appeared to do Mr Shuttleworthy's heart good to see the old fellow swallow it, as he did, quart after quart, so that one day, when the wine was *in* and the wit, as a natural consequence, somewhat *out*, he said to his crony, as he slapped him upon the back: "I tell you what it is, Old Charley: you are, by all odds, the heartiest old fellow I ever came across in all my born days – and, since you love to guzzle the wine at that fashion, I'll be darned if I don't have to make thee a present of a big box of the Château Margaux. Od rot me" – Mr Shuttleworthy had a sad habit of swearing, although he seldom went beyond "Od rot me" or "By Gosh" or "By the Jolly Golly" – "Od rot me," says he, "if I don't send an order to town this very afternoon for a double box of the best that can be got, and I'll make ye a present of it – I will!… ye needn't say a word now… I *will*, I tell ye, and there's an end of it – so look out for it: it will come to hand some of these fine days, precisely when ye are looking for it the least!" I mention this little bit of liberality on the part of Mr Shuttleworthy just by way of showing you how *very* intimate an understanding existed between the two friends.

Well, on the Sunday morning in question, when it came to be fairly understood that Mr Shuttleworthy had met with foul play, I never saw anyone so profoundly affected as "Old Charley Goodfellow". When he first heard that the horse had come home without his master and without his master's saddlebags, and all bloody from a pistol shot that had gone clean through and through the poor animal's chest without quite killing him – when he heard all this, he turned as pale as if the missing man had been his own dear brother or father, and shivered and shook all over as if he had had a fit of the ague.

At first he was too much overpowered with grief to be able to do anything at all, or to decide upon any plan of action, so that for a long time he endeavoured to dissuade Mr Shuttleworthy's other friends from making a stir about the matter, thinking it best to wait awhile – say for a week or two, or a month or two – to see if something wouldn't turn up, or if Mr Shuttleworthy wouldn't come in the natural way and explain his reasons for sending his horse on before. I dare say you have often observed this disposition to temporize, or to procrastinate, in people who are labouring under any very poignant sorrow. Their powers of mind seem to be rendered torpid, so that they have a horror of anything like action, and like nothing in the world so well as to lie quietly in bed and "nurse their grief", as the old ladies express it – that is to say, ruminate over their trouble.

The people of Rattleborough had, indeed, so high an opinion of the wisdom and discretion of "Old Charley" that the greater part of them felt disposed to agree with him and not make a stir in the business "until something should turn up", as the honest old gentleman worded it – and I believe that, after all, this would have been the general determination but for the very suspicious interference of Mr Shuttleworthy's nephew, a young man of very dissipated habits and otherwise of rather bad character. This nephew, whose name was Pennifeather, would listen to nothing like reason in the matter of "lying quiet", but insisted upon making immediate search for the "corpse of the murdered man". This was the expression he employed – and Mr Goodfellow acutely remarked at the time that it was "a *singular* expression, to say no more". This remark of Old Charley's, too, had great effect upon the crowd – and one of the party was heard to ask, very impressively, "how it happened that young Mr Pennifeather was so intimately cognizant of all the circumstances connected with his wealthy uncle's disappearance as to feel authorized to assert, distinctly and unequivocally, that his uncle *was* 'a murdered man'". Hereupon some little squibbing* and bickering occurred among various members of the crowd, and especially between "Old Charley" and Mr Pennifeather, although this latter occurrence was indeed by no means a novelty, for goodwill had subsisted between the parties for the last three or four months – and matters had even gone so far that Mr Pennifeather had actually knocked down his uncle's friend for some alleged excess of liberty that the latter had taken in the uncle's house, of which the nephew was an inmate. Upon this occasion, "Old Charley" is said to have behaved with exemplary moderation and Christian charity. He arose from the blow, adjusted his clothes and made no attempt at retaliation at all, merely muttering a few words about "taking summary vengeance at the first convenient opportunity" – a natural and very justifiable ebullition of anger, which meant nothing, however, and, beyond doubt, was no sooner given vent to than forgotten.

However these matters may be (which have no reference to the point now at issue), it is quite certain that the people of Rattleborough, principally through the persuasion of Mr Pennifeather, came at length to the determination of dispersing over the adjacent country in search of the missing Mr Shuttleworthy. I say they came to this determination in the first instance. After it had been fully resolved that a search should be made, it was considered almost a matter of course that the seekers should disperse – that is to say, distribute themselves in parties – for the more thorough examination of the region round about. I forget, however, by what ingenious train of reasoning it was that "Old Charley" finally convinced the assembly that this was the most injudicious plan that could be pursued. Convince them, however, he did – all except Mr Pennifeather – and, in the end, it was arranged that a search should be instituted, carefully and very thoroughly, by the burghers en masse, "Old Charley" himself leading the way.

As for the matter of that, there could have been no better pioneer than "Old Charley", whom everybody knew to have the eye of a lynx – but, although he led them into all manner of out-of-the-way holes and corners, by routes that nobody had ever suspected of existing in the neighbourhood, and although the search was incessantly kept up day and night for nearly a week, still no trace of Mr Shuttleworthy could be discovered. When I say no trace, however, I must not be understood to speak literally – for trace, to some extent, there certainly was. The poor gentleman had been tracked, by his horse's shoes (which were peculiar), to a spot about three miles to the east of the borough, on the main road leading to the city. Here the track made off into a bypath through a piece of woodland – the path coming out again into the main road and cutting off about half a mile of the regular distance. Following the shoe marks down this lane, the party came at length to a pool of stagnant water, half hidden by the brambles, to the right of the lane, and opposite this pool all vestige of the track was lost sight of. It appeared, however, that a struggle of some nature had here taken place, and it seemed as if some large and heavy body, much larger and heavier than a man, had been drawn from the bypath to the pool. This latter was carefully dragged* twice, but nothing was found – and the party were upon the point of going away, in despair of coming to any result, when Providence suggested to Mr Goodfellow the expediency of draining the water off altogether. This project was received with cheers and many high compliments to "Old Charley" upon his sagacity and consideration. As many of the burghers had brought spades with them, supposing that they might possibly be called upon to disinter a corpse, the drain was easily and speedily effected – and no sooner was the bottom visible than right in the middle of the mud that remained was discovered a black silk velvet waistcoat which nearly everyone present immediately recognized as the property of Mr Pennifeather. This waistcoat was much torn and stained with blood, and there were several persons among the party who had a distinct remembrance of its having been worn by its owner on the very morning of Mr Shuttleworthy's departure for the city – while there were others, again, ready to testify upon oath, if required, that Mr P. did *not* wear the garment in question at any period during the *remainder* of that memorable day – nor could anyone be found to say that he had seen it upon Mr P.'s person at any period at all subsequent to Mr Shuttleworthy's disappearance.

Matters now wore a very serious aspect for Mr Pennifeather, and it was observed, as an indubitable confirmation of the suspicions which were excited against him, that he grew exceedingly pale, and, when asked what he had to say for himself, was utterly incapable of saying a word. Hereupon, the few friends his riotous mode of living had left him deserted him at once to a man, and were even more clamorous than his ancient and avowed enemies for his instantaneous arrest. But, on the other hand, the magnanimity of Mr Goodfellow shone forth with only the more brilliant lustre through contrast. He made a warm and intensely eloquent defence of Mr Pennifeather, in which he alluded more than once to his own sincere forgiveness of that wild young gentleman – "the heir of the worthy Mr Shuttleworthy" – for the insult which he (the young gentleman) had, no doubt in the heat of passion, thought proper to put upon him (Mr Goodfellow). He forgave him for it, he said, "from the very bottom of his heart" – and for himself (Mr Goodfellow), so far from pushing the suspicious circumstances to extremity, which, he was sorry to say, really *had* arisen against Mr Pennifeather, he (Mr Goodfellow) would make every exertion in his power, would employ all the little eloquence in his possession, to… to… to… soften down, as much as he could conscientiously do so, the worst features of this really exceedingly perplexing piece of business.

Mr Goodfellow went on for some half-hour longer in this strain, very much to the credit both of his head and of his heart, but your warm-hearted people are seldom apposite in their observations: they run into all sorts of blunders, *contretemps* and malaproposisms* in the hot-headedness of their zeal to serve a friend – thus, often with the kindest intentions in the world, doing infinitely more to prejudice his cause than to advance it.

So, in the present instance, it turned out with all the eloquence of "Old Charley" – for, although he laboured earnestly in behalf of the suspected, yet it so happened, somehow or other, that every syllable he uttered of which the direct but unwitting tendency was not to exalt the speaker in the good opinion of his audience had the effect of deepening the suspicion already attached to the individual whose cause he pled,* and of arousing against him the fury of the mob.

One of the most unaccountable errors committed by the orator was his allusion to the suspected as "the heir of the worthy old gentleman Mr Shuttleworthy". The people had really never thought of this before. They had only remembered certain threats of disinheritance uttered a year or two previously by the uncle (who had no living relative except the nephew), and they had, therefore, always looked upon this disinheritance as a matter that was settled, so single-minded a race of beings were the Rattleburghers – but the remark of "Old Charley" brought them at once to a consideration of this point, and thus gave them to see the possibility of the threats having been nothing *more* than a threat. And straightway hereupon arose the natural question of "*cui bono?*"* – a question that tended even more than the waistcoat to fasten the terrible crime upon the young man. And here, lest I be misunderstood, permit me to digress for one moment merely to observe that the exceedingly brief and simple Latin phrase which I have employed is invariably mistranslated and misconceived. "*Cui bono?*" in all the crack novels and elsewhere – in those of Mrs Gore, for example (the author of *Cecil*), a lady who quotes all tongues from the Chaldean to Chickasaw, and is helped to her learning, "as needed", upon a systematic plan, by Mr Beckford* – in *all* the crack novels, I say, from those of Bulwer* and Dickens to those of Turnapenny and Ainsworth,* the two little Latin words "*cui bono*" are rendered "to what purpose?" – or (as if "*quo bono*") "to what good?" Their true meaning, nevertheless, is "for whose advantage". "*Cui*", "to whom" – "*bono?*", "is it for a benefit?" It is a purely legal phrase, and applicable precisely in cases such as we have now under consideration, where the probability of the doer of a deed hinges upon the probability of the benefit accruing to this individual or to that from the deed's accomplishment. Now, in the present instance, the question "*cui bono?*" very pointedly implicated Mr Pennifeather. His uncle had threatened him, after making a will in his favour, with disinheritance. But the threat had not been actually kept: the original will, it appeared, had not been altered. *Had* it been altered, the only supposable motive for murder on the part of the suspected would have been the ordinary one of revenge – and even this would have been counteracted by the hope of reinstation* into the good graces of the uncle. But the will being unaltered, while the threat to alter remained suspended over the nephew's head, there appears at once the very strongest possible inducement for the atrocity, and so concluded, very sagaciously, the worthy citizens of the borough of Rattle.

Mr Pennifeather was, accordingly, arrested upon the spot, and the crowd, after some further search, proceeded homeward, having him in custody. On the route, however, another circumstance occurred tending to confirm the suspicion entertained. Mr Goodfellow, whose zeal led him to be always a little in advance of the party, was seen suddenly to run forward a few paces, stoop and then apparently to pick up some small object from the grass. Having quickly examined it, he was observed, too, to make a sort of half-attempt at concealing it in his coat pocket, but this action was noticed, as I say, and consequently prevented, when the object picked up was found to be a Spanish knife which a dozen persons at once recognized as belonging to Mr Pennifeather. Moreover, his initials were engraved upon the handle. The blade of this knife was open and bloody.

No doubt now remained of the guilt of the nephew, and immediately upon reaching Rattleborough he was taken before a magistrate for examination.

Here matters again took a most unfavourable turn. The prisoner, being questioned as to his whereabouts on the morning of Mr Shuttleworthy's disappearance, had absolutely the audacity to acknowledge that on that very morning he had been out with his rifle deer-stalking in the immediate neighbourhood of the pool where the bloodstained waistcoat had been discovered through the sagacity of Mr Goodfellow.

This latter now came forward, and, with tears in his eyes, asked permission to be examined. He said that a stern sense of the duty he owed his Maker, not less than his fellow men, would permit him no longer to remain silent. Hitherto, the sincerest affection for the young man (notwithstanding the latter's ill treatment of himself, Mr Goodfellow) had induced him to make every hypothesis which imagination could suggest, by way of endeavouring to account for what appeared suspicious in the circumstances that told so seriously against Mr Pennifeather, but these circumstances were now altogether *too* convincing – *too* damning: he would hesitate no longer – he would tell all he knew, although his heart (Mr Goodfellow's) should absolutely burst asunder in the effort. He then went on to state that, on the afternoon of the day previous to Mr Shuttleworthy's departure for the city, that worthy old gentleman had mentioned to his nephew, in *his* hearing (Mr Goodfellow's), that his object in going to town on the morrow was to make a deposit of an unusually large sum of money in the "Farmers' and Mechanics' Bank" – and that, then and there, the said Mr Shuttleworthy had distinctly avowed to the said nephew his irrevocable determination of rescinding the will originally made, and of cutting him off with a shilling. He (the witness) now solemnly called upon the accused to state whether what he (the witness) had just stated was or was not the truth in every substantial particular. Much to the astonishment of everyone present, Mr Pennifeather frankly admitted that *it was*.

The magistrate now considered it his duty to send a couple of constables to search the chamber of the accused in the house of his uncle. From this search they almost immediately returned with the well-known steel-bound, russet-leather pocketbook which the old gentleman had been in the habit of carrying for years. Its valuable contents, however, had been abstracted, and the magistrate in vain endeavoured to extort from the prisoner the use which had been made of them, or the place of their concealment. Indeed, he obstinately denied all knowledge of the matter. The constables also discovered, between the bed and sacking of the unhappy man, a shirt and neck-handkerchief both marked with the initials of his name, and both hideously besmeared with the blood of the victim.

At this juncture, it was announced that the horse of the murdered man had just expired in the stable from the effects of the wound he had received, and it was proposed by Mr Goodfellow that a *post-mortem* examination of the beast should be immediately made, with the view, if possible, of discovering the ball. This was accordingly done – and, as if to demonstrate beyond a question the guilt of the accused, Mr Goodfellow, after considerable searching in the cavity of the chest, was enabled to detect and to pull forth a bullet of very extraordinary size, which, upon trial, was found to be exactly adapted to the bore of Mr Pennifeather's rifle, while it was far too large for that of any other person in the borough or its vicinity. To render the matter even surer yet, however, this bullet was discovered to have a flaw or seam at right angles to the usual suture – and, upon examination, this seam corresponded precisely with an accidental ridge or elevation in a pair of moulds acknowledged by the accused himself to be his own property. Upon the finding of this bullet, the examining magistrate refused to listen to any further testimony, and immediately committed the prisoner for trial – declining resolutely to take any bail in the case, although against this severity Mr Goodfellow very warmly remonstrated, and offered to become surety in whatever amount might be required. This generosity on the part of "Old Charley" was only in accordance with the whole tenor of his amiable and chivalrous conduct during the entire period of his sojourn in the borough of Rattle. In the present instance, the worthy man was so entirely carried away by the excessive warmth of his sympathy that he seemed to have quite forgotten, when he offered to go bail for his young friend, that he himself (Mr Goodfellow) did not possess a single dollar's worth of property upon the face of the earth.

The result of the committal may be readily foreseen. Mr Pennifeather, amid the loud execrations of all Rattleborough, was brought to trial at the next criminal sessions, when the chain of circumstantial evidence (strengthened as it was by some additional damning facts, which Mr Goodfellow's sensitive conscientiousness forbade him to withhold from the court) was considered so unbroken and so thoroughly conclusive that the jury, without leaving their seats, returned an immediate verdict of "*Guilty of murder in the first degree*". Soon afterwards, the unhappy wretch received sentence of death, and was remanded to the county jail to await the inexorable vengeance of the law.

In the mean time, the noble behaviour of "Old Charley Goodfellow" had doubly endeared him to the honest citizens of the borough. He became ten times a greater favourite than ever, and, as a natural result of the hospitality with which he was treated, he relaxed, as it were, perforce the extremely parsimonious habits which his poverty had hitherto impelled him to observe, and very frequently had little *réunions** at his own house, when wit and jollity reigned supreme – dampened a little, *of* *course*, by the occasional remembrance of the untoward and melancholy fate which impended over the nephew of the late lamented bosom friend of the generous host.

One fine day, this magnanimous old gentleman was agreeably surprised at the receipt of the following letter:

> Charles Goodfellow, Esq., Rattleborough
> From H.F.B. & Co.,
> Chat. Mar. A – No. 1 – 6 doz. bottles ($\frac{1}{2}$ Gross)
>
> CHARLES GOODFELLOW, ESQUIRE,
>
> Dear Sir,
>
> In conformity with an order transmitted to our firm about two months since by our esteemed correspondent, Mr Barnabas Shuttleworthy, we have the honour of forwarding this morning, to your address, a double box of Château Margaux, of the antelope brand, violet seal. Box numbered and marked as per margin.
>
> We remain, sir,
>
> Your most ob'nt ser'ts,
>
> HOGGS, FROGS, BOGS, & CO.
>
> City of ———, June 21, 18—
>
> PS: The box will reach you by wagon on the day after your receipt of this letter. Our respects to Mr Shuttleworthy.
>
> H. F. B. & CO.

The fact is that Mr Goodfellow had, since the death of Mr Shuttleworthy, given over all expectation of ever receiving the promised Château Margaux – and he, therefore, looked upon it *now* as a sort of especial dispensation of Providence in his behalf. He was highly delighted, of course, and in the exuberance of his joy invited a large party of friends to a *petit souper** on the morrow, for the purpose of broaching the good old Mr Shuttleworthy's present. Not that he *said* anything about "the good old Mr Shuttleworthy" when he issued the invitations. The fact is, he thought much and concluded to say nothing at all. He did *not* mention to anyone – if I remember aright – that he had received a *present* of Château Margaux. He merely asked his friends to come and help him drink some of a remarkably fine quality and rich flavour that he had ordered up from the city a couple of months ago, and of which he would be in the receipt upon the morrow. I have often puzzled myself to imagine *why* it was that "Old Charley" came to the conclusion to say nothing about having received the wine from his old friend, but I could never precisely understand his reason for the silence, although he had *some* excellent and very magnanimous reason no doubt.

The morrow at length arrived, and with it a very large and highly respectable company at Mr Goodfellow's house. Indeed, half the borough was there (I myself among the number) – but, much to the vexation of the host, the Château Margaux did not arrive until a late hour, and when the sumptuous supper supplied by "Old Charley" had been done very ample justice by the guests. It came at length, however – a monstrously big box of it there was, too – and as the whole party were in excessively good humour, it was decided, *nem. con.*,* that it should be lifted upon the table and its contents disembowelled forthwith.

No sooner said than done. I lent a helping hand – and, in a trice, we had the box upon the table, in the midst of all the bottles and glasses, not a few of which were demolished in the scuffle. "Old Charley", who was pretty much intoxicated and excessively red in the face, now took a seat, with an air of mock dignity, at the head of the board, and thumped furiously upon it with a decanter, calling upon the company to keep order "during the ceremony of disinterring the treasure".

After some vociferation, quiet was at length fully restored, and, as very often happens in similar cases, a profound and remarkable silence ensued. Being then requested to force open the lid, I complied, of course, "with an infinite deal of pleasure". I inserted a chisel, and, giving it a few slight taps with a hammer, the top of the box flew suddenly off – and, at the same instant, there sprang up into a sitting position, directly facing the host, the bruised, bloody and nearly putrid corpse of the murdered Mr Shuttleworthy himself. It gazed for a few moments, fixedly and sorrowfully, with its decaying and lacklustre eyes, full into the countenance of Mr Goodfellow – uttered slowly, but clearly and impressively, the words "Thou art the man!" and then, falling over the side of the chest as if thoroughly satisfied, stretched out its limbs quiveringly upon the table.

The scene that ensued is altogether beyond description. The rush for the doors and windows was terrific, and many of the most robust men in the room fainted outright through sheer horror. But after the first wild, shrieking burst of affright, all eyes were directed to Mr Goodfellow. If I live a thousand years, I can never forget the more than mortal agony which was depicted in that ghastly face of his, so lately rubicund with triumph and wine. For several minutes he sat rigidly as a statue of marble, his eyes seeming, in the intense vacancy of their gaze, to be turned inward and absorbed in the contemplation of his own miserable, murderous soul. At length their expression appeared to flash suddenly out into the external world, when, with a quick leap, he sprang from his chair and, falling heavily with his head and shoulders upon the table, and in contact with the corpse, poured out rapidly and vehemently a detailed confession of the hideous crime for which Mr Pennifeather was then imprisoned and doomed to die.

What he recounted was in substance this. He followed his victim to the vicinity of the pool; there shot his horse with a pistol; dispatched the rider with its butt end; possessed himself of the pocketbook; and, supposing the horse dead, dragged it with great labour to the brambles by the pond. Upon his own beast he slung the corpse of Mr Shuttleworthy, and thus bore it to a secure place of concealment a long distance off through the woods.

The waistcoat, the knife, the pocketbook and bullet had been placed by himself where found, with the view of avenging himself upon Mr Pennifeather. He had also contrived the discovery of the stained handkerchief and shirt.

Towards the end of the blood-chilling recital, the words of the guilty wretch faltered and grew hollow. When the record was finally exhausted, he arose, staggered backwards from the table and fell… *dead*.

* * * * * * *

The means by which this happily timed confession was extorted, although efficient, were simple indeed. Mr Goodfellow's excess of frankness had disgusted me, and excited my suspicions from the first. I was present when Mr Pennifeather had struck him, and the fiendish expression which then arose upon his countenance, although momentary, assured me that his threat of vengeance would, if possible, be rigidly fulfilled. I was thus prepared to view the *manoeuvring* of "Old Charley" in a very different light from that in which it was regarded by the good citizens of Rattleborough. I saw at once that all the criminating* discoveries arose either directly or indirectly from himself. But the fact which clearly opened my eyes to the true state of the case was the affair of the bullet, *found* by Mr G. in the carcass of the horse. I had not forgotten, although the Rattleburghers *had*, that there was a hole where the ball had entered the horse and another where it *went out*. If it were found in the animal then, after having made its exit, I saw clearly that it must have been deposited by the person who found it. The bloody shirt and handkerchief confirmed the idea suggested by the bullet, for the blood upon examination proved to be capital claret and no more. When I came to think of these things, and also of the late increase of liberality and expenditure on the part of Mr Goodfellow, I entertained a suspicion which was none the less strong because I kept it altogether to myself.

In the mean time, I instituted a rigorous private search for the corpse of Mr Shuttleworthy, and, for good reasons, searched in quarters as divergent as possible from those to which Mr Goodfellow conducted his party. The result was that, after some days, I came across an old dry well, the mouth of which was nearly hidden by brambles – and here, at the bottom, I discovered what I sought.

Now, it so happened that I had overheard the colloquy between the two cronies when Mr Goodfellow had contrived to cajole his host into the promise of a box of Châteaux Margaux. Upon this hint I acted. I procured a stiff piece of whalebone, thrust it down the throat of the corpse and deposited the latter in an old wine box – taking care so to double the body up as to double the whalebone with it. In this manner I had to press forcibly upon the lid to keep it down while I secured it with nails – and I anticipated, of course, that as soon as these latter were removed, the top would fly *off* and the body *up*.

Having thus arranged the box, I marked, numbered and addressed it as already told – and then, writing a letter in the name of the wine merchants with whom Mr Shuttleworthy dealt, I gave instructions to my servant to wheel the box to Mr Goodfellow's door in a barrow at a given signal from myself. For the words which I intended the corpse to speak, I confidently depended upon my ventriloquial abilities – for their effect, I counted upon the conscience of the murderous wretch.

I believe there is nothing more to be explained. Mr Pennifeather was released upon the spot, inherited the fortune of his uncle, profited by the lessons of experience, turned over a new leaf and led happily ever afterwards a new life.

FOUR BEASTS IN ONE*

THE HOMO-CAMELEOPARD

*Chacun a ses vertus.**
– Crébillon's *Xerxes*

Antiochus Epiphanes* is very generally looked upon as the Gog of the prophet Ezekiel.* This honour is, however, more properly attributable to Cambyses, the son of Cyrus.* And, indeed, the character of the Syrian monarch does by no means stand in need of any adventitious embellishment. His accession to the throne (or, rather, his usurpation of the sovereignty) a hundred and seventy-one* years before the coming of Christ, his attempt to plunder the Temple of Diana at Ephesus, his implacable hostility to the Jews, his pollution of the Holy of Holies and his miserable death at Taba, after a tumultuous reign of eleven years, are circumstances of a prominent kind, and therefore more generally noticed by the historians of his time than the impious, dastardly, cruel, silly and whimsical achievements which make up the sum total of his private life and reputation.

* * * * * * *

Let us suppose, gentle reader, that it is now the year of the world three thousand eight hundred and thirty,* and let us, for a few minutes, imagine ourselves at that most grotesque habitation of man, the remarkable city of Antioch. To be sure there were, in Syria and other countries, sixteen cities of that appellation, besides the one to which I more particularly allude. But *ours* is that which went by the name of Antiochia Epidaphne, from its vicinity to the little village of Daphne, where stood a temple to that divinity. It was built (although about this matter there is some dispute) by Seleucus Nicanor, the first king of the country after Alexander the Great, in memory of his father Antiochus,* and became immediately the residence of the Syrian monarchy. In the flourishing times of the Roman Empire it was the ordinary station of the prefect of the eastern provinces, and many of the emperors of the Queen City* (among whom may be mentioned, especially, Verus and Valens)* spent here the greater part of their time. But I perceive we have arrived at the city itself. Let us ascend this battlement and throw our eyes upon the town and neighbouring country.

"What broad and rapid river is that which forces its way, with innumerable falls, through the mountainous wilderness and finally through the wilderness of buildings?"

That is the Orontes, and it is the only water in sight, with the exception of the Mediterranean, which stretches, like a broad mirror, about twelve miles off to the southward. Everyone has seen the Mediterranean – but let me tell you, there are few who have had a peep at Antioch. By "few", I mean few who, like you and me, have had, at the same time, the advantages of a modern education. Therefore cease to regard that sea, and give your whole attention to the mass of houses that lie beneath us. You will remember that it is now the year of the world three thousand eight hundred and thirty. Were it later – for example, were it the year of our Lord eighteen hundred and forty-five – we should be deprived of this extraordinary spectacle. In the nineteenth century, Antioch is – that is to say, Antioch *will be* – in a lamentable state of decay. It will have been, by that time, totally destroyed, at three different periods, by three successive earthquakes. Indeed, to say the truth, what little of its former self may then remain will be found in so desolate and ruinous a state that the patriarch shall have removed his residence to Damascus. This is well. I see you profit by my advice and are making the most of your time in inspecting the premises – in...

> ...satisfying your eyes
> With the memorials and the things of fame
> That most renown this city...*

I beg pardon – I had forgotten that Shakespeare will not flourish for seventeen hundred and fifty years to come. But does not the appearance of Epidaphne justify me in calling it *grotesque*?

"It is well fortified – and in this respect is as much indebted to nature as to art."

Very true.

"There are a prodigious number of stately palaces."

There are.

"And the numerous temples, sumptuous and magnificent, may bear comparison with the most lauded of antiquity."

All this I must acknowledge. Still there is an infinity of mud huts and abominable hovels. We cannot help perceiving abundance of filth in every kennel, and, were it not for the overpowering fumes of idolatrous incense, I have no doubt we should find a most intolerable stench. Did you ever behold streets so insufferably narrow, or houses so miraculously tall? What a gloom their shadows cast upon the ground! It is well the swinging lamps in those endless colonnades are kept burning throughout the day – we should otherwise have the darkness of Egypt in the time of her desolation.*

"It is certainly a strange place! What is the meaning of yonder singular building? See! It towers above all others, and lies to the eastward of what I take to be the royal palace!"

That is the new Temple of the Sun, who is adored in Syria under the title of Elah Gabalah. Hereafter a very notorious Roman emperor will institute this worship in Rome, and thence derive a cognomen, Heliogabalus.* I dare say you would like to take a peep at the divinity of the temple. You need not look up at the heavens: His Sunship is not there – at least not the Sunship adored by the Syrians. *That* deity will be found in the interior of yonder building. He is worshipped under the figure of a large stone pillar terminating at the summit in a cone or *pyramid*, whereby is denoted "Fire".

"Hark... behold!... Who *can* those ridiculous beings be, half naked, with their faces painted, shouting and gesticulating to the rabble?"

Some few are mountebanks. Others more particularly belong to the race of philosophers. The greatest portion, however – those especially who belabour the populace with clubs – are the principal courtiers of the palace, executing, as in duty bound, some laudable comicality of the king's.

"But what have we here? Heavens! The town is swarming with wild beasts! How terrible a spectacle!... how dangerous a peculiarity!"

Terrible, if you please, but not in the least degree dangerous. Each animal, if you will take the pains to observe, is following, very quietly, in the wake of its master. Some few, to be sure, are led with a rope about the neck, but these are chiefly the lesser or timid species. The lion, the tiger and the leopard are entirely without restraint. They have been trained without difficulty to their present profession, and attend upon their respective owners in the capacity of *valets-de-chambre*.* It is true, there are occasions when Nature asserts her violated dominion – but then the devouring of a man-at-arms or the throttling of a consecrated bull is a circumstance of too little moment to be more than hinted at in Epidaphne.

"But what extraordinary tumult do I hear? Surely this is a loud noise even for Antioch! It argues some commotion of unusual interest."

Yes… undoubtedly. The king has ordered some novel spectacle – some gladiatorial exhibition at the hippodrome… or perhaps the massacre of the Scythian prisoners… or the conflagration of his new palace… or the tearing-down of a handsome temple… or, indeed, a bonfire of a few Jews. The uproar increases. Shouts of laughter ascend the skies. The air becomes dissonant with wind instruments, and horrible with the clamour of a million throats. Let us descend, for the love of fun, and see what is going on! This way… be careful! Here we are in the principal street, which is called "the Street of Timarchus". The sea of people is coming this way, and we shall find a difficulty in stemming the tide. They are pouring through the Alley of Heraclides,* which leads directly from the palace – therefore the king is most probably among the rioters. Yes… I hear the shouts of the herald proclaiming his approach in the pompous phraseology of the East. We shall have a glimpse of his person as he passes by the Temple of Ashimah.* Let us ensconce ourselves in the vestibule of the sanctuary – he will be here anon. In the mean time, let us survey this image. What is it? Oh, it is the god Ashimah in proper person! You perceive, however, that he is neither a lamb nor a goat, nor a satyr – neither has he much resemblance to the Pan of the Arcadians. Yet all these appearances have been given (I beg pardon – *will* be given) by the learned of future ages to the Ashimah of the Syrians. Put on your spectacles, and tell me what it is. What is it?

"Bless me! It is an ape!"

True… a baboon – but by no means the less a deity. His name is a derivation of the Greek *simia* – what great fools are antiquarians! But see!… see!… yonder scampers a ragged little urchin. Where is he going? What is he bawling about? What does he say? Oh! He says the king is coming in triumph; that he is dressed in state; that he has just finished putting to death, with his own hand, a thousand chained Israelitish prisoners! For this exploit the ragamuffin is lauding him to the skies! Hark! Here comes a troop of a similar description. They have made a Latin hymn upon the valour of the king, and are singing it as they go:

Mille, mille, mille,
Mille, mille, mille,
Decollavimus, unus homo!
Mille, mille, mille, mille, decollavimus!
Mille, mille, mille,
Vivat qui mille mille occidit!
Tantum vini habet nemo
*Quantum sanguinis effudit!**

Which may be thus paraphrased:

A thousand, a thousand, a thousand,
A thousand, a thousand, a thousand,
We, with one warrior, have slain!
A thousand, a thousand, a thousand, a thousand.
Sing a thousand over again!
Soho!... Let us sing
Long life to our king,
Who knocked over a thousand so fine!
Soho!... Let us roar,
He has given us more
Red gallons of gore
Than all Syria can furnish of wine!

"Do you hear that flourish of trumpets?"

Yes... the king is coming! See! The people are aghast with admiration, and lift up their eyes to the heavens in reverence! He comes!... He is coming!... There he is!

"Who?... Where?... The king?... Do not behold him – cannot say that I perceive him."

Then you must be blind.

"Very possible. Still, I see nothing but a tumultuous mob of idiots and madmen who are busy in prostrating themselves before a gigantic camel-eopard and endeavouring to obtain a kiss of the animal's hoofs. See! The beast has very justly kicked one of the rabble over... and another... and another... and another. Indeed, I cannot help admiring the animal for the excellent use he is making of his feet."

Rabble, indeed!... Why, these are the noble and free citizens of Epidaphne! Beasts, did you say?... Take care that you are not overheard. Do you not perceive that the animal has the visage of a man? Why, my dear sir, that cameleopard is no other than Antiochus Epiphanes – Antiochus the Illustrious, King of Syria, and the most potent of all the autocrats of the East! It is true that he is entitled, at times, Antiochus Epimanes – Antiochus the Madman – but that is because all people have not the capacity to appreciate his merits. It is also certain that he is at present ensconced in the hide of a beast, and is doing his best to play the part of a cameleopard – but this is done for the better sustaining his dignity as king. Besides, the monarch is of gigantic stature, and the dress is therefore neither unbecoming nor overlarge. We may, however, presume he would not have adopted it but for some occasion of especial state. Such, you will allow, is the massacre of a thousand Jews. With how superior a dignity the monarch perambulates on all fours! His tail, you perceive, is held aloft by his two principal concubines, Elline and Argelais,* and his whole appearance would be infinitely prepossessing were it not for the protuberance of his eyes, which will certainly start out of his head, and the queer colour of his face, which has become nondescript from the quantity of wine he has swallowed. Let us follow him to the hippodrome, whither he is proceeding, and listen to the song of triumph which he is commencing:

Who is king but Epiphanes?
  Say – do you know?
Who is king but Epiphanes?
  Bravo!… Bravo!
There is none but Epiphanes,
  No – there is none:
So tear down the temples,
  And put out the sun!

Well and strenuously sung! The populace are hailing him "Prince of Poets" as well as "Glory of the East", "Delight of the Universe" and "Most Remarkable of Cameleopards". They have encored his effusion, and – do you hear? – he is singing it over again. When he arrives at the hippodrome, he will be crowned with the poetic wreath, in anticipation of his victory at the approaching Olympics.

"But, good Jupiter! What is the matter in the crowd behind us?"

Behind us, did you say?… Oh! Ah!… I perceive. My friend, it is well that you spoke in time. Let us get into a place of safety as soon as possible. Here!... Let us conceal ourselves in the arch of this aqueduct, and I will inform you presently of the origin of the commotion. It has turned out as I have been anticipating. The singular appearance of the cameleopard with the head of a man has, it seems, given offence to the notions of propriety entertained in general by the wild animals domesticated in the city. A mutiny has been the result – and, as is usual upon such occasions, all human efforts will be of no avail in quelling the mob. Several of the Syrians have already been devoured, but the general voice of the four-footed patriots seems to be for eating up the cameleopard. "The Prince of Poets", therefore, is upon his hinder legs, running for his life. His courtiers have left him in the lurch, and his concubines have followed so excellent an example. "Delight of the Universe", thou art in a sad predicament! "Glory of the East", thou art in danger of mastication! Therefore never regard so piteously thy tail – it will undoubtedly be draggled in the mud, and for this there is no help. Look not behind thee, then, at its unavoidable degradation, but take courage, ply thy legs with vigour and scud for the hippodrome! Remember that thou art Antiochus Epiphanes. Antiochus the Illustrious!... also "Prince of Poets", "Glory of the East", "Delight of the Universe" and "Most Remarkable of Cameleopards!" Heavens! What a power of speed thou art displaying! What a capacity for leg bail* thou art developing! Run, Prince!... Bravo, Epiphanes!... Well done, Cameleopard!... Glorious Antiochus!... He runs!... he leaps!... he flies! Like an arrow from a catapult he approaches the hippodrome! He leaps!... he shrieks!... he is there! This is well, for hadst thou, "Glory of the East", been half a second longer in reaching the gates of the amphitheatre, there is not a bear's cub in Epidaphne that would not have had a nibble at thy carcass. Let us be off – let us take our departure! – for we shall find our delicate modern ears unable to endure the vast uproar which is about to commence in celebration of the king's escape! Listen! It has already commenced. See!... The whole town is topsy-turvy.

"Surely this is the most populous city of the East! What a wilderness of people! What a jumble of all ranks and ages! What a multiplicity of sects and nations! What a variety of costumes! What a Babel of languages! What a screaming of beasts! What a tinkling of instruments! What a parcel of philosophers!"

Come, let us be off.

"Stay a moment! I see a vast hubbub in the hippodrome – what is the meaning of it, I beseech you?"

That?… Oh, nothing! The noble and free citizens of Epidaphne being, as they declare, well satisfied of the faith, valour, wisdom and divinity of their king, and having, moreover, been eyewitnesses of his late superhuman agility, do think it no more than their duty to invest his brows (in addition to the poetic crown) with the wreath of victory in the foot race – a wreath which it is evident he *must* obtain at the celebration of the next Olympiad, and which, therefore, they now give him in advance.

WHY THE LITTLE FRENCHMAN WEARS HIS HAND IN A SLING*

It's on my wisiting cards sure enough (and it's them that's all o' pink satin paper) that inny gintleman that plases may behould the intheristhin' words "Sir Pathrick O'Grandison, Barronitt, 39 Southampton Row, Russell Square, Parrish o' Bloomsbury". And shud ye be wantin' to diskiver who is the pink of purliteness* quite, and the laider of the hot tun* in the houl city o' Lonon – why, it's jist mesilf. And fait that same is no wonder at all at all (so be plased to stop curlin' your nose), for every inch o' the six wakes that I've been a gintleman and left aff wid the bog-throthing to take up wid the barronissy, it's Pathrick that's been living like a houly imperor, and gitting the iddication and the graces. Och! And wouldn't it be a blessed thing for your sperrits if ye cud lay your two peepers jist upon Sir Pathrick O'Grandison, Barronitt, when he is all riddy-drissed for the hopperer or stipping into the brisky* for the drive into the Hyde Park? But it's the iligant big figgur that I 'ave, for the rason o' which all the ladies fall in love wid me. Isn't it my own swate silf now that'll missure the six fut, and the three inches more nor that, in me stockings, and that am excadingly will proportioned all over to match? And is it ralelly more than three fut and a bit that there is, innyhow, of the little ould furrener Frinchman that lives jist over the way, and that's a-oggling and a-goggling the houl day (and bad luck to him) at the purty widdy Misthress Tracle that's my own nixt-door neighbour (God bliss her!) and a most particuller frind and acquaintance? You percave the little spalpeen is summat down in the mouth, and wears his lift hand in a sling – and it's for that same thing, by yur lave, that I'm going to give you the good rason.

The truth of the houl matter is jist simple enough: for the very first day that I com'd from Connaught and showd my swate little silf in the strait to the widdy who was looking through the windy, it was a gone case althegither wid the heart o' the purty Misthress Tracle. I percaved it, ye see, all at once, and no mistake – and that's God's thruth. First of all, it was up wid the windy in a jiffy, and thin she threw open her two peepers to the itmost, and thin it was a little gould spyglass that she clapped tight to one o' them, and divil may burn me if it didn't spake to me as plain as a peeper cud spake, and says it, through the spyglass: "Och! The tip o' the mornin' to ye, Sir Pathrick O'Grandison, Barronitt, mavourneen* – and it's a nate gintleman that ye are, sure enough, and it's mesilf and me forten jist that'll be at yur sarvice, dear, inny time o' day at all at all for the asking." And it's not mesilf ye wud have to be bate in the purliteness, so I made her a bow that wud ha' broken yur heart althegither to behould, and thin I pulled aff me hat with a flourish, and thin I winked at her hard wid both eyes, as much as to say: "True for you, yer a swate little crature, Mrs Tracle, me darlint, and I wish I may be drownthed dead in a bog if it's not mesilf, Sir Pathrick O'Grandison, Barronitt, that'll make a houl bushel o' love to Yur Leddyship in the twinkling o' the eye of a Londonderry purraty."

And it was the nixt mornin', sure, jist as I was making up me mind whither it wouldn't be the purlite thing to sind a bit o' writin' to the widdy by way of a love litter, when up cum'd the delivery sarvant wid an illigant card, and he tould me that the name on it (for I niver cud rade the copperplate printin', on account of being lift-handed) was all about Mounseer, the Count, A Goose, Look-aisy, Maiter-di-dauns, and that the houl of the divilish lingo was the spalpeeny long name of the little ould furrener Frinchman as lived over the way.

And jist wid that in cum'd the little willain himself, and thin he made me a broth of a bow, and thin he said he had ounly taken the liberty of doing me the honour of the giving me a call, and thin he went on to palaver at a great rate, and divil the bit did I comprehind what he wud be afther the tilling me at all at all, excipting and saving that he said "pulley wou, woolly wou", and tould me, among a bushel o' lies, bad luck to him, that he was mad for the love o' my widdy Misthress Tracle, and that my widdy Mrs Tracle had a puncheon* for *him*.

At the hearin' of this, ye may swear, though, I was as mad as a grasshopper, but I remimbered that I was Sir Pathrick O'Grandison, Barronitt, and that it wasn't althegither gentaal to lit the anger git the upper hand o' the purliteness, so I made light o' the matter and kipt dark, and got quite sociable wid the little chap, and afther a while what did he do but ask me to go wid him to the widdy's, saying he wud give me the feshionable inthroduction to Her Leddyship.

"Is it there ye are?" said I thin to mesilf. "And it's thrue for you, Pathrick, that ye're the fortunnittest mortal in life. We'll soon see now whither it's your swate silf or whither it's little Mounseer Maiter-di-dauns that Misthress Tracle is head and ears in the love wid."

Wid that we wint aff to the widdy's next door, and ye may well say it was an illigant place – so it was. There was a carpet all over the floor, and in one corner there was a forty-pinny and a jew's harp and the divil knows what ilse, and in another corner was a sofy, the beautifullest thing in all natur, and sitting on the sofy, sure enough, there was the swate little angel, Misthress Tracle.

"The tip o' the mornin' to ye," says I, "Mrs Tracle" – and thin I made sich an illegant obaysance that it wud ha quite althegither bewildered the brain o' ye.

"Wully woo, pulley woo, plump in the mud,"* says the little furrenner Frinchman, "and sure Mrs Tracle," says he, that he did, "isn't this gintleman here jist His Reverence Sir Pathrick O'Grandison, Barronitt, and isn't he althegither and entirely the most purticular frind and acquintance that I have in the houl world?"

And wid that the widdy, she gits up from the sofy and makes the swatest curtchy nor iver was seen – and thin down she sits like an angel, and thin, by the powers, it was that little spalpeen Mounseer Maiter-di-dauns that plumped his silf right down by the right side of her. Och hon! I ixpicted the two eyes o' me wud ha cum'd out of my head on the spot, I was so dispirate mad! Howiver, "Bait who!" says I, after a while. "Is it there ye are, Mounseer Maiter-di-dauns?" – and so down I plumped on the lift side of Her Leddyship, to be aven wid the willain. Botheration! It wud ha' done your heart good to percave the illigant double wink that I gived her jist thin right in the face wid both eyes.

But the little ould Frinchman, he niver beginned to suspict me at all at all, and disperate hard it was he made the love to Her Leddyship. "Woully wou," says he, "pulley wou," says he, "plump in the mud," says he.

"That's all to no use, Mounseer Frog, mavourneen," thinks I – and I talked as hard and as fast as I could all the while, and throth it was mesilf jist that divarted Her Leddyship complately and intirely, by rason of the illigant conversation that I kipt up wid her all about the dear bogs of Connaught. And by and by she gived me such a swate smile, from one ind of her mouth to the ither, that it made me as bould as a pig, and I jist took hould of the ind of her little finger in the most dillikittest manner in natur, looking at her all the while out o' the whites of my eyes.

And then ounly percave the cuteness of the swate angel, for no sooner did she obsarve that I was afther the squazing of her flipper* than she up wid it in a jiffy and put it away behind her back, jist as much as to say, "Now thin, Sir Pathrick O'Grandison, there's a bitther chance for ye, mavourneen, for it's not althegither the gentaal thing to be afther the squazing of my flipper right full in the sight of that little furrenner Frinchman, Mounseer Maiter-di-dauns."

Wid that I giv'd her a big wink jist to say "Lit Sir Pathrick alone for the likes o' them thricks", and thin I wint aisy to work, and you'd have died wid the divarsion to behould how cliverly I slipped my right arm betwane the back o' the sofy and the back of Her Leddyship – and there, sure enough, I found a swate little flipper all a-waiting to say, "The tip o' the mornin' to ye, Sir Pathrick O'Grandison, Barronitt." And wasn't it mesilf, sure, that jist giv'd it the laste little bit of a squaze in the world, all in the way of a commincement, and not to be too rough wid Her Leddyship? And och, botheration, wasn't it the gentaalest and dilikittest of all the little squazes that I got in return? "Blood and thunder, Sir Pathrick, mavourneen," thinks I to mesilf, "fait it's jist the mother's son of you, and nobody else at all at all, that's the handsomest and the fortunittest young bog-throtter that ever cum'd out of Connaught!" And wid that I giv'd the flipper a big squaze – and a big squaze it was, by the powers, that Her Leddyship giv'd to me back. But it would ha' split the seven sides of you wid the laffin' to behould, jist then all at once, the consated behaviour of Mounseer Maiter-di-dauns. The likes o' sich a-jabbering and a-smirking and a-parly-wouing as he begin'd wid Her Leddyship niver was known before upon arth – and divil may burn me if it wasn't me own very two peepers that cotch'd him tipping her the wink out of one eye. Och hon, if it wasn't mesilf thin that was mad as a Kilkenny cat, I shud like to be tould who it was!

"Let me infarm you, Mounseer Maiter-di-dauns," said I, as purlite as iver ye seed, "that it's not the gintaal thing at all at all, and not for the likes o' you innyhow, to be afther the oggling and a-goggling at Her Leddyship in that fashion" – and jist wid that such another squaze as it was I giv'd her flipper, all as much as to say, "Isn't it Sir Pathrick now, my jewel, that'll be able to the protectin' o' you, my darlint?" And then there cum'd another squaze back, all by way of the answer. "Thrue for you, Sir Pathrick," it said as plain as iver a squaze said in the world, "thrue for you, Sir Pathrick, mavourneen, and it's a proper nate gintleman ye are – that's God's truth" – and wid that she opened her two beautiful peepers till I belaved they wud ha' com'd out of her hid althegither and intirely, and she looked first as mad as a cat at Mounseer Frog, and thin as smiling as all out o' doors at mesilf.

"Thin," says he, the willain, "och hon, and a wolly-wou, pulley-wou" – and then wid that he shoved up his two shoulders till the divil the bit of his hid was to be diskivered, and then he let down the two corners of his purraty-trap, and thin not a haporth more of the satisfaction could I git out o' the spalpeen.

Belave me, my jewel, it was Sir Pathrick that was unrasonable mad thin, and the more by token that the Frinchman kipt an wid his winking at the widdy – and the widdy, she kipt an wid the squazing of my flipper, as much as to say, "At him again Sir Pathrick O'Grandison, mavourneen" – so I just ripped out wid a big oath, and says I:

"Ye little spalpeeny frog of a bog-throtting son of a bloody noun!" – and jist thin what d'ye think it was that Her Leddyship did? Troth she jumped up from the sofy as if she was bit and made off through the door, while I turned my head round afther her, in a complete bewilderment and botheration, and followed her wid me two peepers. You percave I had a reason of my own for knowing that she couldn't git down the stares althegither and intirely, for I knew very well that I had hould of her hand, for divil the bit had I iver lit it go. And says I:

"Isn't it the laste little bit of a mistake in the world that ye've been afther the making, Yer Leddyship? Come back now, that's a darlint, and I'll give ye yur flipper." But aff she wint down the stairs like a shot, and thin I turned round to the little Frinch furrenner. Och hon, if it wasn't his spalpeeny little paw that I had hould of in my own... why thin... thin it wasn't... that's all.

And maybe it wasn't mesilf that jist died then outright wid the laffin' to behould the little chap when he found out that it wasn't the widdy at all at all that he had had hould of all the time, but only Sir Pathrick O'Grandison. The ould divil himself niver behild sich a long face as he pet an! As for Sir Pathrick O'Grandison, Barronitt, it wasn't for the likes of His Riverence to be afther the minding of a thrifle of a mistake. Ye may jist say though (for it's God's thruth) that afore I lift hould of the flipper of the spalpeen (which was not till afther Her Leddyship's futman had kicked us both down the stairs), I gived it such a nate little broth of a squaze as made it all up into raspberry jam.

"Wouly-wou," says he, "pulley-wou," says he. "Cot tam!"

And that's jist the thruth of the rason why he wears his lift hand in a sling.

BON-BON*

Quand un bon vin meuble mon estomac
Je suis plus savant que Balzac –
Plus sage que Pibrac;
Mon bras seul faisant l'attaque
De la nation Cossaque,
La mettroit au sac.
De Charon je passerois le lac
En dormant dans son bac;
J'irois au fier Eac,
Sans que mon cœur fit tic ni tac,
*Présenter du tabac.**

– French vaudeville

That Pierre Bon-Bon was a restaurateur of uncommon qualifications, no man who during the reign of ——— frequented the little café in the cul-de-sac Le Febvre at Rouen will, I imagine, feel himself at liberty to dispute. That Pierre Bon-Bon was, in an equal degree, skilled in the philosophy of that period is, I presume, still more especially undeniable. His *pâtés à la fois** were beyond doubt immaculate – but what pen can do justice to his essays *sur la Nature** – his thoughts *sur l'Âme** – his observations *sur l'Esprit?** If his omelettes, if his fricandeaux* were inestimable, what *littérateur** of that day would not have given twice as much for an "*idée de Bon-Bon*"* as for all the trash of all the "*idées*" of all the rest of the savants? Bon-Bon had ransacked libraries which no other man had ransacked, had read more than any other would have entertained a notion of reading, had understood more than any other would have conceived the possibility of understanding, and although, while he flourished, there were not wanting some authors at Rouen to assert "that his dicta evinced neither the purity of the Academy nor the depth of the Lyceum"* – although, mark me, his doctrines were by no means very generally comprehended, still it did not follow that they were difficult of comprehension. It was, I think, on account of their self-evidency that many persons were led to consider them abstruse. It is to Bon-Bon (but let this go no further) – it is to Bon-Bon that Kant* himself is mainly indebted for his metaphysics. The former was indeed not a Platonist, nor strictly speaking an Aristotelian – nor did he, like the modern Leibnitz,* waste those precious hours which might be employed in the invention of a fricassée or, *facili gradu*,* the analysis of a sensation, in frivolous attempts at reconciling the obstinate oils and waters of ethical discussion. Not at all. Bon-Bon was Ionic – Bon-Bon was equally Italic.* He reasoned a priori – he reasoned a posteriori. His ideas were innate – or otherwise. He believed in George of Trebizond – he believed in Bessarion.* Bon-Bon was emphatically a… Bon-Bonist.

I have spoken of the philosopher in his capacity of restaurateur. I would not, however, have any friend of mine imagine that, in fulfilling his hereditary duties in that line, our hero wanted a proper estimation of their dignity and importance. Far from it. It was impossible to say in which branch of his profession he took the greater pride. In his opinion, the powers of the intellect held intimate connection with the capabilities of the stomach. I am not sure, indeed, that he greatly disagreed with the Chinese, who hold that the soul lies in the abdomen. The Greeks at all events were right, he thought, who employed the same word for the mind and the diaphragm.* By this I do not mean to insinuate a charge of gluttony, or indeed any other serious charge to the prejudice of the metaphysician. If Pierre Bon-Bon had his failings (and what great man has not a thousand?), if Pierre Bon-Bon, I say, had his failings, they were failings of very little importance – faults indeed which, in other tempers, have often been looked upon rather in the light of virtues. As regards one of these foibles, I should not even have mentioned it in this history but for the remarkable prominency – the extreme *alto rilievo** – in which it jutted out from the plane of his general disposition. He could never let slip an opportunity of making a bargain.

Not that he was avaricious – no. It was by no means necessary to the satisfaction of the philosopher that the bargain should be to his own proper advantage. Provided a trade could be effected – a trade of any kind, upon any terms, or under any circumstances – a triumphant smile was seen for many days thereafter to enlighten his countenance, and a knowing wink of the eye to give evidence of his sagacity.

At any epoch it would not be very wonderful if a humour so peculiar as the one I have just mentioned should elicit attention and remark. At the epoch of our narrative, had this peculiarity *not* attracted observation, there would have been room for wonder indeed. It was soon reported that, upon all occasions of the kind, the smile of Bon-Bon was wont to differ widely from the downright grin with which he would laugh at his own jokes or welcome an acquaintance. Hints were thrown out of an exciting nature; stories were told of perilous bargains made in a hurry and repented of at leisure; and instances were adduced of unaccountable capacities, vague longings and unnatural inclinations implanted by the author of all evil for wise purposes of his own.

The philosopher had other weaknesses – but they are scarcely worthy our serious examination. For example, there are few men of extraordinary profundity who are found wanting in an inclination for the bottle. Whether this inclination be an exciting cause or rather a valid proof of such profundity, it is a nice thing to say. Bon-Bon, as far as I can learn, did not think the subject adapted to minute investigation – nor do I. Yet, in the indulgence of a propensity so truly classical, it is not to be supposed that the restaurateur would lose sight of that intuitive discrimination which was wont to characterize, at one and the same time, his *essais** and his omelettes. In his seclusions, the Vin de Bourgogne had its allotted hour, and there were appropriate moments for the Côtes du Rhône. With him Sauternes was to Médoc what Catullus* was to Homer. He would sport with a syllogism in sipping Saint-Péray, but unravel an argument over Clos de Vougeot, and upset a theory in a torrent of Chambertin.* Well had it been if the same quick sense of propriety had attended him in the peddling propensity to which I have formerly alluded – but this was by no means the case. Indeed, to say the truth, *that* trait of mind in the philosophic Bon-Bon *did* begin at length to assume a character of strange intensity and mysticism, and appeared deeply tinctured with the *diablerie** of his favourite German studies.

To enter the little café in the cul-de-sac Le Febvre was, at the period of our tale, to enter the sanctum of a man of genius. Bon-Bon was a man of genius. There was not a *sous-cuisinier** in Rouen who could not have told you that Bon-Bon was a man of genius. His very cat knew it, and forbore to whisk her tail in the presence of the man of genius. His large water dog* was acquainted with the fact, and upon the approach of his master betrayed his sense of inferiority by a sanctity of deportment, a debasement of the ears and a dropping of the lower jaw not altogether unworthy of a dog. It is, however, true that much of this habitual respect might have been attributed to the personal appearance of the metaphysician. A distinguished exterior will, I am constrained to say, have its weight even with a beast – and I am willing to allow much in the outward man of the restaurateur calculated to impress the imagination of the quadruped. There is a peculiar majesty about the atmosphere of the little great (if I may be permitted so equivocal an expression) which mere physical bulk alone will be found at all times inefficient in creating. If, however, Bon-Bon was barely three feet in height, and if his head was diminutively small, still it was impossible to behold the rotundity of his stomach without a sense of magnificence nearly bordering upon the sublime. In its size both dogs and men must have seen a type of his acquirements – in its immensity, a fitting habitation for his immortal soul.

I might here (if it so pleased me) dilate upon the matter of habiliment and other mere circumstances of the external metaphysician. I might hint that the hair of our hero was worn short, combed smoothly over his forehead and surmounted by a conical-shaped white flannel cap and tassels; that his pea-green jerkin was not after the fashion of those worn by the common class of restaurateurs at that day; that the sleeves were something fuller than the reigning costume permitted; that the cuffs were turned up, not as usual in that barbarous period, with cloth of the same quality and colour as the garment, but faced in a more fanciful manner with the particoloured velvet of Genoa; that his slippers were of a bright purple, curiously filigreed, and might have been manufactured in Japan but for the exquisite pointing of the toes and the brilliant tints of the binding and embroidery; that his breeches were of the yellow satin-like material called *aimable*;* that his, sky-blue cloak, resembling in form a dressing wrapper and richly bestudded all over with crimson devices, floated cavalierly upon his shoulders like a mist of the morning; and that his *tout ensemble** gave rise to the remarkable words of Benevenuta, the improvisatrice of Florence, "that it was difficult to say whether Pierre Bon-Bon was indeed a bird of Paradise or the rather a very Paradise of perfection". I might, I say, expatiate upon all these points if I pleased – but I forbear: merely personal details may be left to historical novelists – they are beneath the moral dignity of matter of fact.

I have said that "to enter the café in the cul-de-sac Le Febvre was to enter the sanctum of a man of genius" – but then it was only the man of genius who could duly estimate the merits of the sanctum. A sign consisting of a vast folio swung before the entrance. On one side of the volume was painted a bottle, on the reverse a pâté. On the back were visible in large letters *Œuvres de Bon-Bon*.* Thus was delicately shadowed forth the twofold occupation of the proprietor.

Upon stepping over the threshold, the whole interior of the building presented itself to view. A long, low-pitched room of antique construction was indeed all the accommodation afforded by the café. In a corner of the apartment stood the bed of the metaphysician. An array of curtains, together with a canopy *à la grecque*,* gave it an air at once classic and comfortable. In the corner diagonally opposite appeared, in direct family communion, the properties of the kitchen and the *bibliothèque*.* A dish of polemics stood peacefully upon the dresser. Here lay an ovenful of the latest ethics – there a kettle of duodecimo *mélanges*.* Volumes of German morality were hand and glove with the gridiron; a toasting fork might be discovered by the side of Eusebius;* Plato reclined at his ease in the frying pan; and contemporary manuscripts were filed away upon the spit.

In other respects, the Café de Bon-Bon might be said to differ little from the usual *restaurants* of the period. A large fireplace yawned opposite the door. On the right of the fireplace, an open cupboard displayed a formidable array of labelled bottles.

It was here, about twelve o'clock one night, during the severe winter of ——, that Pierre Bon-Bon, after having listened for some time to the comments of his neighbours upon his singular propensity – that Pierre Bon-Bon, I say, having turned them all out of his house, locked the door upon them with an oath and betook himself in no very pacific mood to the comforts of a leather-bottomed armchair and a fire of blazing faggots.

It was one of those terrific nights which are only met with once or twice during a century. It snowed fiercely, and the house tottered to its centre with the floods of wind that, rushing through the crannies of the wall and pouring impetuously down the chimney, shook awfully the curtains of the philosopher's bed and disorganized the economy of his pâté pans and papers. The huge folio sign that swung without, exposed to the fury of the tempest, creaked ominously, and gave out a moaning sound from its stanchions of solid oak.

It was in no placid temper, I say, that the metaphysician drew up his chair to its customary station by the hearth. Many circumstances of a perplexing nature had occurred during the day to disturb the serenity of his meditations. In attempting *des œufs à la princesse*, he had unfortunately perpetrated an *omelette à la reine*;* the discovery of a principle in ethics had been frustrated by the overturning of a stew; and, last not least, he had been thwarted in one of those admirable bargains which he at all times took such especial delight in bringing to a successful termination. But in the chafing of his mind at these unaccountable vicissitudes there did not fail to be mingled some degree of that nervous anxiety which the fury of a boisterous night is so well calculated to produce. Whistling to his more immediate vicinity the large black water dog we have spoken of before, and settling himself uneasily in his chair, he could not help casting a wary and unquiet eye towards those distant recesses of the apartment whose inexorable shadows not even the red firelight itself could more than partially succeed in overcoming. Having completed a scrutiny whose exact purpose was perhaps unintelligible to himself, he drew close to his seat a small table covered with books and papers, and soon became absorbed in the task of retouching a voluminous manuscript intended for publication on the morrow.

He had been thus occupied for some minutes when "I am in no hurry, Monsieur Bon-Bon," suddenly whispered a whining voice in the apartment.

"The Devil!" ejaculated our hero, starting to his feet, overturning the table at his side and staring around him in astonishment.

"Very true," calmly replied the voice.

"Very true!... What is very true?... How came you here?" vociferated the metaphysician as his eye fell upon something which lay stretched at full length upon the bed.

"I was saying..." said the intruder, without attending to the interrogatories,* "I was saying that I am not at all pushed for time... that the business upon which I took the liberty of calling is of no pressing importance – in short, that I can very well wait until you have finished your exposition."

"My exposition!... There now!... How do *you* know?... How came *you* to understand that I was writing an exposition?... Good God!"

"Hush!" replied the figure in a shrill undertone – and, arising quickly from the bed, he made a single step towards our hero, while an iron lamp that depended overhead swung convulsively back from his approach.

The philosopher's amazement did not prevent a narrow scrutiny of the stranger's dress and appearance. The outlines of his figure, exceedingly lean but much above the common height, were rendered minutely distinct by means of a faded suit of black cloth which fitted tight to the skin, but was otherwise cut very much in the style of a century ago. These garments had evidently been intended for a much shorter person than their present owner. His ankles and wrists were left naked for several inches. In his shoes, however, a pair of very brilliant buckles gave the lie to the extreme poverty implied by the other portions of his dress. His head was bare and entirely bald, with the exception of the hinder part, from which depended a queue* of considerable length. A pair of green spectacles with side glasses protected his eyes from the influence of the light, and at the same time prevented our hero from ascertaining either their colour or their conformation. About the entire person there was no evidence of a shirt – but a white cravat of filthy appearance was tied with extreme precision around the throat, and the ends, hanging down formally side by side, gave (although I dare say unintentionally) the idea of an ecclesiastic. Indeed, many other points both in his appearance and demeanour might have very well sustained a conception of that nature. Over his left ear he carried, after the fashion of a modern clerk, an instrument resembling the stylus of the ancients. In a breast pocket of his coat appeared conspicuously a small black volume fastened with clasps of steel. This book, whether accidentally or not, was so turned outwardly from the person as to discover the words "*Rituel Catholique*"* in white letters upon the back. His entire physiognomy was interestingly saturnine – even cadaverously pale. The forehead was lofty, and deeply furrowed with the ridges of contemplation. The corners of the mouth were drawn down into an expression of the most submissive humility. There was also a clasping of the hands, as he stepped towards our hero, a deep sigh and altogether a look of such utter sanctity as could not have failed to be unequivocally prepossessing. Every shadow of anger faded from the countenance of the metaphysician as, having completed a satisfactory survey of his visitor's person, he shook him cordially by the hand and conducted him to a seat.

There would however be a radical error in attributing this instantaneous transition of feeling in the philosopher to any one of those causes which might naturally be supposed to have had an influence. Indeed, Pierre Bon-Bon, from what I have been able to understand of his disposition, was of all men the least likely to be imposed upon by any speciousness of exterior deportment. It was impossible that so accurate an observer of men and things should have failed to discover, upon the moment, the real character of the personage who had thus intruded upon his hospitality. To say no more, the conformation of his visitor's feet was sufficiently remarkable; he maintained lightly upon his head an inordinately tall hat; there was a tremulous swelling about the hinder part of his breeches; and the vibration of his coat-tail was a palpable fact. Judge, then, with what feelings of satisfaction our hero found himself thrown thus at once into the society of a person for whom he had at all times entertained the most unqualified respect. He was, however, too much of the diplomatist to let escape him any intimation of his suspicions in regard to the true state of affairs. It was not his cue to appear at all conscious of the high honour he thus unexpectedly enjoyed, but, by leading his guest into conversation, to elicit some important ethical ideas which might, in obtaining a place in his contemplated publication, enlighten the human race and at the same time immortalize himself – ideas which, I should have added, his visitor's great age and well-known proficiency in the science of morals might very well have enabled him to afford.

Actuated by these enlightened views, our hero bade the gentleman sit down, while he himself took occasion to throw some faggots upon the fire and place upon the now re-established table some bottles of *mousseux*.* Having quickly completed these operations, he drew his chair vis-à-vis to his companion's,* and waited until the latter should open the conversation. But plans even the most skilfully matured are often thwarted in the outset of their application – and the restaurateur found himself *nonplussed* by the very first words of his visitor's speech.

"I see you know me, Bon-Bon," said he. "Ha ha ha!... He he he!... Hi hi hi!... Ho ho ho!... Hu hu hu!" – and the Devil, dropping at once the sanctity of his demeanour, opened to its fullest extent a mouth from ear to ear so as to display a set of jagged and fang-like teeth, and, throwing back his head, laughed long, loudly, wickedly and uproariously, while the black dog, crouching down upon his haunches, joined lustily in the chorus, and the tabby cat, flying off at a tangent, stood up on end and shrieked in the farthest corner of the apartment.

Not so the philosopher: he was too much a man of the world either to laugh like the dog or by shrieks to betray the indecorous trepidation of the cat. It must be confessed, he felt a little astonishment to see the white letters which formed the words "*Rituel Catholique*" on the book in his guest's pocket momently changing both their colour and their import – and in a few seconds, in place of the original title, the words "*Registre des Condamnés*"* blaze forth in characters of red. This startling circumstance, when Bon-Bon replied to his visitor's remark, imparted to his manner an air of embarrassment which probably might not otherwise have been observed.

"Why, sir," said the philosopher, "why, sir, to speak sincerely... I believe you are... upon my word... the d——dest... that is to say, I think... I imagine... I *have* some faint... some *very* faint idea... of the remarkable honour—"

"Oh!... Ah!... Yes!... Very well!" interrupted His Majesty. "Say no more... I see how it is." And hereupon, taking off his green spectacles, he wiped the glasses carefully with the sleeve of his coat and deposited them in his pocket.

If Bon-Bon had been astonished at the incident of the book, his amazement was now much increased by the spectacle which here presented itself to view. In raising his eyes with a strong feeling of curiosity to ascertain the colour of his guest's, he found them by no means black, as he had anticipated – nor grey, as might have been imagined, nor yet hazel nor blue, nor indeed yellow nor red, nor purple, nor white, nor green, nor any other colour in the heavens above or in the earth beneath or in the waters under the earth.* In short, Pierre Bon-Bon not only saw plainly that His Majesty had no eyes whatsoever, but could discover no indications of their having existed at any previous period – for the space where eyes should naturally have been was, I am constrained to say, simply a dead level of flesh.

It was not in the nature of the metaphysician to forbear making some enquiry into the sources of so strange a phenomenon – and the reply of His Majesty was at once prompt, dignified and satisfactory.

"Eyes! My dear Bon-Bon... eyes, did you say?... Oh!... Ah!... I perceive! The ridiculous prints, eh, which are in circulation, have given you a false idea of my personal appearance? Eyes!... true. Eyes, Pierre Bon-Bon, are very well in their proper place... *That*, you would say, is the head?... Right... the head of a worm. To *you*, likewise, these optics are indispensable – yet I will convince you that my vision is more penetrating than your own. There is a cat I see in the corner – a pretty cat... look at her... observe her well. Now, Bon-Bon, do you behold the thoughts – the thoughts, I say... the ideas... the reflections – which are being engendered in her pericranium? There it is, now... you do not! She is thinking we admire the length of her tail and the profundity of her mind. She has just concluded that I am the most distinguished of ecclesiastics, and that you are the most superficial of metaphysicians. Thus you see I am not altogether blind – but to one of my profession, the eyes you speak of would be merely an incumbrance, liable at any time to be put out by a toasting iron or a pitchfork. To you, I allow, these optical affairs are indispensable. Endeavour, Bon-Bon, to use them well... *My* vision is the soul."

Hereupon the guest helped himself to the wine upon the table, and, pouring out a bumper for Bon-Bon, requested him to drink it without scruple and make himself perfectly at home.

"A clever book that of yours, Pierre," resumed His Majesty, tapping our friend knowingly upon the shoulder as the latter put down his glass after a thorough compliance with his visitor's injunction. "A clever book that of yours, upon my honour. It's a work after my own heart. Your arrangement of the matter, I think, however, might be improved, and many of your notions remind me of Aristotle. That philosopher was one of my most intimate acquaintances. I liked him as much for his terrible ill temper as for his happy knack at making a blunder. There is only one solid truth in all that he has written, and for that I gave him the hint out of pure compassion for his absurdity. I suppose, Pierre Bon-Bon, you very well know to what divine moral truth I am alluding?"

"Cannot say that I—"

"Indeed!… Why, it was I who told Aristotle that, by sneezing, men expelled superfluous ideas through the proboscis."*

"Which is – hiccup! – undoubtedly the case," said the metaphysician, while he poured out for himself another bumper of *mousseux* and offered his snuffbox to the fingers of his visitor.

"There was Plato, too," continued His Majesty, modestly declining the snuffbox and the compliment it implied, "there was Plato, too, for whom I, at one time, felt all the affection of a friend. You knew Plato, Bon-Bon?… Ah, no, I beg a thousand pardons. He met me at Athens, one day, in the Parthenon, and told me he was distressed for an idea. I bade him write down that ο νους εστιν αυλος. He said that he would do so and went home, while I stepped over to the pyramids. But my conscience smote me for having uttered a truth, even to aid a friend, and, hastening back to Athens, I arrived behind the philosopher's chair as he was inditing the 'αυλος'.

"Giving the lambda a fillip with my finger, I turned it upside down. So the sentence now read 'ο νους εστιν αυγος' – and is, you perceive, the fundamental doctrine in his metaphysics."*

"Were you ever at Rome?" asked the restaurateur as he finished his second bottle of *mousseux* and drew from the closet a larger supply of Chambertin.

"But once, Monsieur Bon-Bon, but once. There was a time," said the Devil, as if reciting some passage from a book, "there was a time when occurred an anarchy of five years, during which the Republic, bereft of all its officers, had no magistracy besides the tribunes of the people, and these were not legally vested with any degree of executive power…* At that time, Monsieur Bon-Bon, at that time *only* I was in Rome, and I have no earthly acquaintance, consequently, with any of its philosophy."*

"What do you think of… what do you think of – hiccup! – Epicurus?"*

"What do I think of *whom*?" said the Devil, in astonishment. "You surely mean to find any fault with Epicurus! What do I think of Epicurus! Do you mean 'me', sir?… *I* am Epicurus! I am the same philosopher who wrote each of the three hundred treatises commemorated by Diogenes Laertes."*

"That's a lie!" said the metaphysician, for the wine had gotten a little into his head.

"Very well!… Very well, sir!… Very well, indeed, sir!" said His Majesty, apparently much flattered.

"That's a lie!" repeated the restaurateur dogmatically. "That's a – hiccup! – a lie!"

"Well, well… have it your own way!" said the Devil pacifically, and Bon-Bon, having beaten His Majesty at an argument, thought it his duty to conclude a second bottle of Chambertin.

"As I was saying," resumed the visitor, "as I was observing a little while ago, there are some very outré notions in that book of yours, Monsieur Bon-Bon. What, for instance, do you mean by all that humbug about the soul? Pray, sir, what *is* the soul?"

"The – hiccup! – soul," replied the metaphysician, referring to his MS, "is undoubtedly—"

"No, sir!"

"Indubitably—"

"No, sir!"

"Indisputably—"

"No, sir!"

"Evidently—"

"No, sir!"

"Incontrovertibly—"

"No, sir!"

"Hiccup!—"

"No, sir!"

"And beyond all question, a—"

"No sir, the soul is no such thing!" Here the philosopher, looking daggers, took occasion to make an end, upon the spot, of his third bottle of Chambertin.

"Then – hiccup! – pray, sir… what… what is it?"

"That is neither here nor there, Monsieur Bon-Bon," replied His Majesty musingly. "I have tasted – that is to say, I have known – some very bad souls, and some too… pretty good ones." Here he smacked his lips, and, having unconsciously let fall his hand upon the volume in his pocket, was seized with a violent fit of sneezing.

He continued.

"There was the soul of Cratinus… passable; Aristophanes… racy; Plato… exquisite – not *your* Plato, but Plato the comic poet… your Plato would have turned the stomach of Cerberus... faugh! Then, let me see! There were Naevius and Andronicus, and Plautus, and Terentius. Then there were Lucilius and Catullus, and Naso, and Quintus Flaccus... 'dear Quinty', as I called him when he sung a *seculare* for my amusement, while I toasted him, in pure good humour, on a fork. But they want *flavour*, these Romans. One fat Greek is worth a dozen of them, and besides will *keep*, which cannot be said of a Quirite. Let us taste your Sauternes."*

Bon-Bon had by this time made up his mind to the *nil admirari*,* and endeavoured to hand down the bottles in question. He was, however, conscious of a strange sound in the room, like the wagging of a tail. Of this, although extremely indecent in His Majesty, the philosopher took no notice – simply kicking the dog and requesting him to be quiet. The visitor continued:

"I found that Horace tasted very much like Aristotle – you know I am fond of variety. Terentius I could not have told from Menander.* Naso, to my astonishment, was Nicander* in disguise. Virgilius had a strong twang of Theocritus. Martial put me much in mind of Archilochus – and Titus Livius was positively Polybius and none other."*

"Hiccup!" here replied Bon-Bon, and His Majesty proceeded:

"But if I *have* a *penchant*, Monsieur Bon-Bon – if I *have* a *penchant*, it is for a philosopher. Yet, let me tell you, sir, it is not every dev... I mean, it is not every gentleman who knows how to *choose* a philosopher. Long ones are *not* good – and the best, if not carefully shelled, are apt to be a little rancid on account of the gall."

"Shelled!"

"I mean, taken out of the carcass."

"What do you think of a – hiccup! – physician?"

"*Don't* mention them!... Ugh! Ugh!" Here His Majesty retched violently. "I never tasted but one – that rascal Hippocrates!...* Smelt of asafoetida... Ugh! Ugh! Ugh!... caught a wretched cold washing him in the Styx* – and, after all, he gave me the cholera morbus."*

"The – hiccup – wretch!" ejaculated Bon-Bon. "The – hiccup! – abortion of a pillbox!" – and the philosopher dropped a tear.

"After all," continued the visitor, "after all, if a dev... if a gentleman wishes to *live*, he must have more talents than one or two – and with us a fat face is an evidence of diplomacy."

"How so?"

"Why, we are sometimes exceedingly pushed for provisions. You must know that, in a climate so sultry as mine, it is frequently impossible to keep a spirit alive for more than two or three hours – and after death, unless pickled immediately (and a pickled spirit is *not* good), they will... smell... you understand, eh? Putrefaction is always to be apprehended when the souls are consigned to us in the usual way."

"Hiccup!... Hiccup!... Good God! How *do* you manage?"

Here the iron lamp commenced swinging with redoubled violence, and the Devil half-started from his seat – however, with a slight sigh, he recovered his composure, merely saying to our hero in a low tone: "I tell you what, Pierre Bon-Bon, we *must* have no more swearing."

The host swallowed another bumper, by way of denoting thorough comprehension and acquiescence, and the visitor continued:

"Why, there are *several* ways of managing. The most of us starve: some put up with the pickle – for my part, I purchase my spirits *vivente corpore*,* in which case I find they keep very well."

"But the body – hiccup! – the body!"

"The body, the body... well, what of the body?... Oh! Ah! I perceive. Why, sir, the body is not *at all* affected by the transaction. I have made innumerable purchases of the kind in my day, and the parties never experienced any inconvenience. There were Cain and Nimrod, and Nero, and Caligula, and Dionysius, and Pisistratus,* and... and a thousand others who never knew what it was to have a soul during the latter part of their lives... Yet, sir, these men adorned society. Why, isn't there A——— now, whom you know as well as I? Is *he* not in possession of all his faculties, mental and corporeal? Who writes a keener epigram? Who reasons more wittily? Who... but stay! I have his agreement in my pocketbook."

Thus saying, he produced a red leather wallet and took from it a number of papers. Upon some of these Bon-Bon caught a glimpse of the letters "Machi—", "Maza—", "Robesp—",* with the words Caligula, George, Elizabeth.* His Majesty selected a narrow slip of parchment, and from it read aloud the following words:

> In consideration of certain mental endowments which it is unnecessary to specify, and in further consideration of one thousand louis d'or, I being aged one year and one month, do hereby make over to the bearer of this agreement all my right, title and appurtenance in the shadow called my soul. (Signed) A———

Here his Majesty repeated a name which I did not feel myself justified in indicating more unequivocally.*

"A clever fellow that," resumed he, "but, like you, Monsieur Bon-Bon, he was mistaken about the soul. The soul a shadow – truly! The soul a shadow! Ha ha ha!... He he he!... Hu hu hu!... Only think of a fricasséed shadow!"

"*Only* think – hiccup! – of a fricasséed shadow!" exclaimed our hero, whose faculties were becoming much illuminated by the profundity of His Majesty's discourse.

"Only think of a – hiccup! – fricasséed shadow! Now, damme! – hiccup! – humph! If *I* would have been such a – hiccup! – nincompoop! *My* soul, Mr... humph!"

"*Your* soul, Monsieur Bon-Bon?"

"Yes, sir – hiccup! – *my* soul is—"

"What, sir?"

"*No* shadow, damme!"

"Did you mean to say—"

"Yes, sir, *my* soul is – hiccup! – humph!... Yes, sir."

"Did you not intend to assert—"

"*My* soul is – hiccup! – peculiarly qualified for – hiccup! – a..."

"What, sir?"

"Stew."

"Ha!"

"Soufflée."

"Eh!"

"Fricassée."

"Indeed!"

"Ragout and fricandeau* – and see here, my good fellow! I'll let you have it – hiccup! – a bargain." Here the philosopher slapped His Majesty upon the back.

"Couldn't think of such a thing," said the latter calmly, at the same time rising from his seat. The metaphysician stared.

"Am supplied at present," said His Majesty.

"Hic-cup!... e-h?" said the philosopher.

"Have no funds on hand."

"What?"

"Besides, very unhandsome in me—"

"Sir!"

"To take advantage of—"

"Hic-cup!"

"Your present disgusting and ungentlemanly situation."

Here the visitor bowed and withdrew – in what manner could not precisely be ascertained, but, in a well-concerted effort to discharge a bottle at "the villain", the slender chain was severed that depended from the ceiling, and the metaphysician prostrated by the downfall of the lamp.

THE DOMAIN OF ARNHEIM*

OR THE LANDSCAPE GARDEN

The garden like a lady fair was cut
  That lay as if she slumbered in delight,
And to the open skies her eyes did shut.
  The azure fields of heaven were sembled right
  In a large round, set with the flowers of light.
The flowers de luce and the round sparks of dew
That hung upon their azure leaves did shew
Like twinkling stars that sparkle in the evening blue.*
– Giles Fletcher

From his cradle to his grave, a gale of prosperity bore my friend Ellison along. Nor do I use the word "prosperity" in its mere worldly sense. I mean it as synonymous with happiness. The person of whom I speak seemed born for the purpose of foreshadowing the doctrines of Turgot, Price, Priestley and Condorcet* – of exemplifying by individual instance what has been deemed the chimera of the perfectionists. In the brief existence of Ellison I fancy that I have seen refuted the dogma that in man's very nature lies some hidden principle, the antagonist of bliss. An anxious examination of his career has given me to understand that, in general, from the violation of a few simple laws of humanity arises the wretchedness of mankind; that as a species we have in our possession the as yet unwrought elements of content; and that, even now, in the present darkness and madness of all thought on the great question of the social condition, it is not impossible that man, the individual, under certain unusual and highly fortuitous conditions, may be happy.

With opinions such as these my young friend, too, was fully imbued, and thus it is worthy of observation that the uninterrupted enjoyment which distinguished his life was, in great measure, the result of preconcert.* It is indeed evident that with less of the instinctive philosophy which, now and then, stands so well in the stead of experience, Mr Ellison would have found himself precipitated, by the very extraordinary success of his life, into the common vortex of unhappiness which yawns for those of pre-eminent endowments. But it is by no means my object to pen an essay on happiness. The ideas of my friend may be summed up in a few words. He admitted but four elementary principles – or, more strictly, conditions of bliss. That which he considered chief was (strange to say!) the simple and purely physical one of free exercise in the open air. "The health," he said, "attainable by other means is scarcely worth the name." He instanced the ecstasies of the fox hunter, and pointed to the tillers of the earth, the only people who, as a class, can be fairly considered happier than others. His second condition was the love of woman. His third, and most difficult of realization, was the contempt of ambition. His fourth was an object of unceasing pursuit – and he held that, other things being equal, the extent of attainable happiness was in proportion to the spirituality of this object.

Ellison was remarkable in the continuous profusion of good gifts lavished upon him by fortune. In personal grace and beauty he exceeded all men. His intellect was of that order to which the acquisition of knowledge is less a labour than an intuition and a necessity. His family was one of the most illustrious of the empire. His bride was the loveliest and most devoted of women. His possessions had been always ample – but, on the attainment of his majority, it was discovered that one of those extraordinary freaks of fate had been played in his behalf which startle the whole social world amid which they occur, and seldom fail radically to alter the moral constitution of those who are their objects.

It appears that, about a hundred years before Mr Ellison's coming of age, there had died, in a remote province, one Mr Seabright Ellison. This gentleman had amassed a princely fortune, and, having no immediate connections, conceived the whim of suffering his wealth to accumulate for a century after his decease. Minutely and sagaciously directing the various modes of investment, he bequeathed the aggregate amount to the nearest of blood bearing the name of Ellison who should be alive at the end of the hundred years. Many attempts had been made to set aside this singular bequest – their ex-post-facto* character rendered them abortive – but the attention of a jealous government was aroused, and a legislative act finally obtained, forbidding all similar accumulations. This act, however, did not prevent young Ellison from entering into possession, on his twenty-first birthday, as the heir of his ancestor Seabright, of a fortune of *four hundred and fifty millions of dollars.**

When it had become known that such was the enormous wealth inherited, there were, of course, many speculations as to the mode of its disposal. The magnitude and the immediate availability of the sum bewildered all who thought on the topic. The possessor of any *appreciable* amount of money might have been imagined to perform any one of a thousand things. With riches merely surpassing those of any citizen, it would have been easy to suppose him engaging to supreme excess in the fashionable extravagances of his time, or busying himself with political intrigue, or aiming at ministerial power, or purchasing increase of nobility, or collecting large museums of virtu,* or playing the munificent patron of letters, of science, of art – or endowing and bestowing his name upon extensive institutions of charity. But for the inconceivable wealth in the actual possession of the heir, these objects and all ordinary objects were felt to afford too limited a field. Recourse was had to figures, and these but sufficed to confound. It was seen that, even at three per cent, the annual income of the inheritance amounted to no less than thirteen millions and five hundred thousand dollars – which was one million and one hundred and twenty-five thousand per month, or thirty-six thousand nine hundred and eighty-six per day, or one thousand five hundred and forty-one per hour, or six-and-twenty dollars for every minute that flew. Thus the usual track of supposition was thoroughly broken up. Men knew not what to imagine. There were some who even conceived that Mr Ellison would divest himself of at least one half of his fortune as of utterly superfluous opulence – enriching whole troops of his relatives by division of his superabundance. To the nearest of these he did, in fact, abandon the very unusual wealth which was his own before the inheritance.

I was not surprised, however, to perceive that he had long made up his mind on a point which had occasioned so much discussion to his friends. Nor was I greatly astonished at the nature of his decision. In regard to individual charities, he had satisfied his conscience. In the possibility of any improvement, properly so called, being effected by man himself in the general condition of man, he had (I am sorry to confess it) little faith. Upon the whole, whether happily or unhappily, he was thrown back, in very great measure, upon self.

In the widest and noblest sense he was a poet. He comprehended, moreover, the true character, the august aims, the supreme majesty and dignity of the poetic sentiment. The fullest, if not the sole proper satisfaction of this sentiment, he instinctively felt to lie in the creation of novel forms of beauty. Some peculiarities, either in his early education or in the nature of his intellect, had tinged with what is termed materialism all his ethical speculations – and it was this bias, perhaps, which led him to believe that the most advantageous at least, if not the sole legitimate field for the poetic exercise, lies in the creation of novel moods of purely *physical* loveliness. Thus it happened he became neither musician nor poet – if we use this latter term in its everyday acceptation. Or it might have been that he neglected to become either, merely in pursuance of his idea that in contempt of ambition is to be found one of the essential principles of happiness on earth. Is it not indeed possible that, while a high order of genius is necessarily ambitious, the highest is above that which is termed ambition? And may it not thus happen that many far greater than Milton have contentedly remained "mute and inglorious"?* I believe that the world has never seen (and that, unless through some series of accidents goading the noblest order of mind into distasteful exertion, the world will never see) that full extent of triumphant execution, in the richer domains of art, of which the human nature is absolutely capable.

Ellison became neither musician nor poet – although no man lived more profoundly enamoured of music and poetry. Under other circumstances than those which invested him, it is not impossible that he would have become a painter. Sculpture, although in its nature rigorously poetical, was too limited in its extent and consequences to have occupied, at any time, much of his attention. And I have now mentioned all the provinces in which the common understanding of the poetic sentiment has declared it capable of expatiating. But Ellison maintained that the richest, the truest and most natural, if not altogether the most extensive province, had been unaccountably neglected. No definition had spoken of the landscape gardener as of the poet – yet it seemed to my friend that the creation of the landscape garden offered to the proper Muse the most magnificent of opportunities. Here, indeed, was the fairest field for the display of imagination in the endless combining of forms of novel beauty, the elements to enter into combination being, by a vast superiority, the most glorious which the earth could afford. In the multiform and multicolour of the flowers and the trees, he recognized the most direct and energetic efforts of Nature at physical loveliness. And in the direction or concentration of this effort – or, more properly, in its adaptation to the eyes which were to behold it on earth – he perceived that he should be employing the best means, labouring to the greatest advantage, in the fulfilment not only of his own destiny as poet, but of the august purposes for which the Deity had implanted the poetic sentiment in man.

"Its adaptation to the eyes which were to behold it on earth." In his explanation of this phraseology, Mr Ellison did much towards solving what has always seemed to me an enigma – I mean the fact (which none but the ignorant dispute) that no such combination of scenery exists in nature as the painter of genius may produce. No such paradises are to be found in reality as have glowed on the canvas of Claude.* In the most enchanting of natural landscapes, there will always be found a defect or an excess – many excesses and defects. While the component parts may defy, individually, the highest skill of the artist, the arrangement of these parts will always be susceptible of improvement. In short, no position can be attained on the wide surface of the *natural* earth from which an artistical eye, looking steadily, will not find matter of offence in what is termed the "composition" of the landscape. And yet how unintelligible is this! In all other matters we are justly instructed to regard Nature as supreme. With her details we shrink from competition. Who shall presume to imitate the colours of the tulip, or to improve the proportions of the lily of the valley? The criticism which says, of sculpture or portraiture, that here Nature is to be exalted or idealized rather than imitated is in error. No pictorial or sculptural combinations of points of human loveliness do more than approach the living and breathing beauty. In landscape alone is the principle of the critic true – and, having felt its truth here, it is but the headlong spirit of generalization which has led him to pronounce it true throughout all the domains of art. Having, I say, *felt* its truth here, for the feeling is no affectation or chimera. The mathematics afford no more absolute demonstrations than the sentiment of his art yields the artist. He not only believes, but positively knows that such and such apparently arbitrary arrangements of matter constitute and alone constitute the true beauty. His reasons, however, have not yet been matured into expression. It remains for a more profound analysis than the world has yet seen fully to investigate and express them. Nevertheless, he is confirmed in his instinctive opinions by the voice of all his brethren. Let a "composition" be defective, let an emendation be wrought in its mere arrangement of form, let this emendation be submitted to every artist in the world: by each will its necessity be admitted. And even far more than this: in remedy of the defective composition, each insulated member of the fraternity would have suggested the identical emendation.

I repeat that in landscape arrangements alone is the physical Nature susceptible of exaltation, and that, therefore, her susceptibility of improvement at this one point was a mystery I had been unable to solve. My own thoughts on the subject had rested in the idea that the primitive intention of Nature would have so arranged the earth's surface as to have fulfilled at all points man's sense of perfection in the beautiful, the sublime or the picturesque, but that this primitive intention had been frustrated by the known geological disturbances – disturbances of form and colour-grouping, in the correction or allaying of which lies the soul of art. The force of this idea was much weakened, however, by the necessity which it involved of considering the disturbances abnormal and unadapted to any purpose. It was Ellison who suggested that they were prognostic of *death*. He thus explained: admit the earthly immortality of man to have been the first intention. We have then the primitive arrangement of the earth's surface adapted to his blissful estate as not existent, but designed. The disturbances were the preparations for his subsequently conceived deathful condition.

"Now," said my friend, "what we regard as exaltation of the landscape may be really such as respects only the mortal* or human *point of view*. Each alteration of the natural scenery may possibly effect a blemish in the picture if we can suppose this picture viewed at large, in mass, from some point distant from the earth's surface, although not beyond the limits of its atmosphere. It is easily understood that what might improve a closely scrutinized detail may at the same time injure a general or more distantly observed effect. There *may* be a class of beings, human once but now invisible to humanity, to whom, from afar, our disorder may seem order, our unpicturesqueness picturesque – in a word, the earth-angels, for whose scrutiny more especially than our own, and for whose death-refined appreciation of the beautiful, may have been set in array by God the wide landscape gardens of the hemispheres."

In the course of discussion, my friend quoted some passages from a writer on landscape gardening who has been supposed to have well treated his theme:

> There are properly but two styles of landscape gardening, the natural and the artificial. One seeks to recall the original beauty of the country by adapting its means to the surrounding scenery; cultivating trees in

harmony with the hills or plain of the neighbouring land; detecting and bringing into practice those nice relations of size, proportion and colour which, hid from the common observer, are revealed everywhere to the experienced student of nature. The result of the natural style of gardening is seen rather in the absence of all defects and incongruities – in the prevalence of a healthy harmony and order – than in the creation of any special wonders or miracles. The artificial style has as many varieties as there are different tastes to gratify. It has a certain general relation to the various styles of building. There are the stately avenues and retirements of Versailles; Italian terraces; and a various mixed old-English style which bears some relation to the domestic Gothic or English Elizabethan architecture. Whatever may be said against the abuses of the artificial landscape gardening, a mixture of pure art in a garden scene adds to it a great beauty. This is partly pleasing to the eye, by the show of order and design, and partly moral. A terrace with an old moss-covered balustrade calls up at once to the eye the fair forms that have passed there in other days. The slightest exhibition of art is an evidence of care and human interest.*

"From what I have already observed," said Ellison, "you will understand that I reject the idea, here expressed, of recalling the original beauty of the country. The original beauty is never so great as that which may be introduced. Of course, everything depends on the selection of a spot with *capabilities*.* What is said about detecting and bringing into practice nice relations of size, proportion and colour is one of those mere vaguenesses of speech which serve to veil inaccuracy of thought. The phrase quoted may mean anything or nothing, and guides in no degree. That the true result of the natural style of gardening is seen rather in the absence of all defects and incongruities than in the creation of any special wonders or miracles is a proposition better suited to the grovelling apprehension of the herd than to the fervid dreams of the man of genius. The negative merit suggested appertains to that hobbling criticism which, in letters, would elevate Addison* into apotheosis. In truth, while that virtue which consists in the mere avoidance of vice appeals directly to the understanding, and can thus be circumscribed in *rule*, the loftier virtue, which flames in creation, can be apprehended in its results alone. Rule applies but to the merits of denial – to the excellencies which refrain. Beyond these, the critical art can but suggest. We may be instructed to build a *Cato*, but we are in vain told *how* to conceive a Parthenon or an *Inferno*. The thing done, however, the wonder accomplished, and the capacity for apprehension becomes universal. The sophists of the negative school who, through inability to create, have scoffed at creation are now found the loudest in applause. What in its chrysalis condition of principle affronted their demure reason never fails, in its maturity of accomplishment, to extort admiration from their instinct of beauty.

"The author's observations on the artificial style," continued Ellison, "are less objectionable. A mixture of pure art in a garden scene adds to it a great beauty. This is just – as also is the reference to the sense of human interest. The principle expressed is incontrovertible – but there *may* be something beyond it. There may be an object in keeping with the principle – an object unattainable by the means ordinarily possessed by individuals, yet which, if attained, would lend a charm to the landscape garden far surpassing that which a sense of merely human interest could bestow. A poet, having very unusual pecuniary resources, might, while retaining the necessary idea of art or culture (or, as our author expresses it, of interest), so imbue his designs at once with extent and novelty of beauty as to convey the sentiment of spiritual interference. It will be seen that, in bringing about such result, he secures all the advantages of interest or *design*, while relieving his work of the harshness or technicality of the worldly *art*. In the most rugged of wildernesses, in the most savage of the scenes of pure nature, there is apparent the *art* of a creator – yet this art is apparent to reflection only: in no respect has it the obvious force of a feeling. Now, let us suppose this sense of the Almighty design to be *one step depressed*, to be brought into something like harmony or consistency with the sense of human art, to form an intermedium between the two – let us imagine, for example, a landscape whose combined vastness and definitiveness, whose united beauty, magnificence and *strangeness*, shall convey the idea of care or culture, or superintendence, on the part of beings superior yet akin to humanity – then the sentiment of *interest* is preserved, while the art intervolved is made to assume the air of an intermediate or secondary nature, a nature which is not God nor an emanation from God, but which still is nature in the sense of the handiwork of the angels that hover between man and God."

It was in devoting his enormous wealth to the embodiment of a vision such as this, in the free exercise in the open air ensured by the personal superintendence of his plans, in the unceasing object which these plans afforded, in the high spirituality of the object, in the contempt of ambition which it enabled him truly to feel, in the perennial springs with which it gratified, without possibility of satiating, that one master passion of his soul, the thirst for beauty – above all, it was in the sympathy of a woman not unwomanly, whose loveliness and love enveloped his existence in the purple atmosphere of paradise – that Ellison thought to find, *and found*, exemption from the ordinary cares of humanity with a far greater amount of positive happiness than ever glowed in the rapt daydreams of De Staël.*

I despair of conveying to the reader any distinct conception of the marvels which my friend did actually accomplish. I wish to describe, but am disheartened by the difficulty of description, and hesitate between detail and generality. Perhaps the better course will be to unite the two in their extremes.

Mr Ellison's first step regarded, of course, the choice of a locality, and scarcely had he commenced thinking on this point when the luxuriant nature of the Pacific Islands arrested his attention. In fact, he had made up his mind for a voyage to the South Seas when a night's reflection induced him to abandon the idea. "Were I misanthropic," he said, "such a locale would suit me. The thoroughness of its insulation and seclusion, and the difficulty of ingress and egress, would in such case be the charm of charms – but as yet I am not Timon.* I wish the composure but not the depression of solitude. There must remain with me a certain control over the extent and duration of my repose. There will be frequent hours in which I shall need, too, the sympathy of the poetic in what I have done. Let me seek, then, a spot not far from a populous city – whose vicinity, also, will best enable me to execute my plans."

In search of a suitable place so situated, Ellison travelled for several years, and I was permitted to accompany him. A thousand spots with which I was enraptured he rejected without hesitation, for reasons which satisfied me, in the end, that he was right. We came at length to an elevated tableland of wonderful fertility and beauty, affording a panoramic prospect very little less in extent than that of Etna, and, in Ellison's opinion, as well as my own, surpassing the far-famed view from that mountain in all the true elements of the picturesque.

"I am aware," said the traveller, as he drew a sigh of deep delight after gazing on this scene, entranced, for nearly an hour, "I know that here, in my circumstances, nine tenths of the most fastidious of men would rest content. This panorama is indeed glorious, and I should rejoice in it but for the excess of its glory. The taste of all the architects I have ever known leads them, for the sake of 'prospect', to put up buildings on hilltops. The error is obvious. Grandeur in any of its moods, but especially in that of extent, startles, excites... and then fatigues, depresses. For the occasional scene nothing can be better – for the constant view, nothing worse. And, in the constant view, the most objectionable phase of grandeur is that of extent – the worst phase of extent, that of distance. It is at war with the sentiment and with the sense of *seclusion* – the sentiment and sense which we seek to humour in 'retiring to the country'. In looking from the summit of a mountain we cannot help feeling *abroad* in the world. The heartsick avoid distant prospects as a pestilence."

It was not until towards the close of the fourth year of our search that we found a locality with which Ellison professed himself satisfied. It is, of course, needless to say *where* was the locality. The late death of my friend, in causing his domain to be thrown open to certain classes of visitors, has given to Arnheim a species of secret and subdued if not solemn celebrity – similar in kind, although infinitely superior in degree, to that which so long distinguished Fonthill.*

The usual approach to Arnheim was by the river. The visitor left the city in the early morning. During the forenoon he passed between shores of a tranquil and domestic beauty, on which grazed innumerable sheep, their white fleeces spotting the vivid green of rolling meadows. By degrees, the idea of cultivation subsided into that of merely pastoral care. This slowly became merged in a sense of retirement – this again in a consciousness of solitude. As the evening approached, the channel grew more narrow, the banks more and more precipitous – and these latter were clothed in rich, more profuse and more sombre foliage. The water increased in transparency. The stream took a thousand turns, so that at no moment could its gleaming surface be seen for a greater distance than a furlong. At every instant the vessel seemed imprisoned within an enchanted circle, having insuperable and impenetrable walls of foliage, a roof of ultramarine satin, and *no* floor, the keel balancing itself with admirable nicety on that of a phantom bark which, by some accident having been turned upside down, floated in constant company with the substantial one, for the purpose of sustaining it. The channel now became a *gorge* – although the term is somewhat inapplicable, and I employ it merely because the language has no word which better represents the most striking, not the most distinctive feature, of the scene. The character of gorge was maintained only in the height and parallelism of the shores: it was lost altogether in their other traits. The walls of the ravine (through which the clear water still tranquilly flowed) arose to an elevation of a hundred and occasionally of a hundred and fifty feet, and inclined so much towards each other as, in a great measure, to shut out the light of day, while the long, plume-like moss which depended densely from the intertwining shrubberies overhead gave the whole chasm an air of funereal gloom. The windings became more frequent and intricate, and seemed often as if returning in upon themselves, so that the voyager had long lost all idea of direction. He was, moreover, enwrapped in an exquisite sense of the strange. The thought of Nature still remained, but her character seemed to have undergone modification: there was a weird symmetry, a thrilling uniformity, a wizard propriety in these her works. Not a dead branch, not a withered leaf, not a stray pebble, not a patch of the brown earth was anywhere visible. The crystal water welled up against the clean granite or the unblemished moss with a sharpness of outline that delighted while it bewildered the eye.

Having threaded the mazes of this channel for some hours, the gloom deepening every moment, a sharp and unexpected turn of the vessel brought it suddenly, as if dropped from heaven, into a circular basin of very considerable extent when compared with the width of the gorge. It was about two hundred yards in diameter, and girt in at all points but one – that immediately fronting the vessel as it entered – by hills equal in general height to the walls of the chasm, although of a thoroughly different character. Their sides sloped from the water's edge at an angle of some forty-five degrees, and they were clothed from base to summit – not a perceptible point escaping – in a drapery of the most gorgeous flower blossoms, scarcely a green leaf being visible among the sea of odorous and fluctuating colour. This basin was of great depth, but so transparent was the water that the bottom, which seemed to consist of a thick mass of small round alabaster pebbles, was distinctly visible by glimpses – that is to say, whenever the eye could permit itself *not* to see, far down in the inverted heaven, the duplicate blooming of the hills. On these latter, there were no trees, nor even shrubs of any size. The impressions wrought on the observer were those of richness, warmth, colour, quietude, uniformity, softness, delicacy, daintiness, voluptuousness and a miraculous extremeness of culture that suggested dreams of a new race of fairies – laborious, tasteful, magnificent and fastidious – but as the eye traced upward the myriad-tinted slope, from its sharp junction with the water to its vague termination amid the folds of overhanging cloud, it became indeed difficult not to fancy a panoramic cataract of rubies, sapphires, opals and golden onyxes rolling silently out of the sky.

The visitor, shooting suddenly into this bay from out the gloom of the ravine, is delighted but astounded by the full orb of the declining sun, which he had supposed to be already far below the horizon, but which now confronts him, and forms the sole termination of an otherwise limitless vista seen through another chasm-like rift in the hills.

But here the voyager quits the vessel which has borne him so far and descends into a light canoe of ivory, stained with arabesque devices in vivid scarlet, both within and without. The poop and beak of this boat arise high above the water with sharp points, so that the general form is that of an irregular crescent. It lies on the surface of the bay with the proud grace of a swan. On its ermined floor reposes a single feathery paddle of satinwood, but no oarsman or attendant is to be seen. The guest is bidden to be of good cheer – that the fates will take care of him. The larger vessel disappears, and he is left alone in the canoe, which lies apparently motionless in the middle of the lake. While he considers what course to pursue, however, he becomes aware of a gentle movement in the fairy bark. It slowly swings itself around until its prow points towards the sun. It advances with a gentle but gradually accelerated velocity, while the slight ripples it creates seem to break about the ivory side in divinest melody – seem to offer the only possible explanation of the soothing yet melancholy music for whose unseen origin the bewildered voyager looks around him in vain.

The canoe steadily proceeds, and the rocky gate of the vista is approached, so that its depths can be more distinctly seen. To the right arise a chain of lofty hills rudely and luxuriantly wooded. It is observed, however, that the trait of exquisite *cleanness* where the bank dips into the water still prevails. There is not one token of the usual river debris. To the left, the character of the scene is softer and more obviously artificial. Here the bank slopes upwards from the stream in a very gentle ascent, forming a broad sward of grass of a texture resembling nothing so much as velvet, and of a brilliancy of green which would bear comparison with the tint of the purest emerald. This plateau varies in width from ten to three hundred yards, reaching from the riverbank to a wall fifty feet high, which extends in an infinity of curves, but following the general direction of the river, until lost in the distance to the westward. This wall is of one continuous rock, and has been formed by cutting perpendicularly the once-rugged precipice of the stream's southern bank, but no trace of the labour has been suffered to remain. The chiselled stone has the hue of ages, and is profusely overhung and overspread with the ivy, the coral honeysuckle, the eglantine and the clematis. The uniformity of the top and bottom lines of the wall is fully relieved by occasional trees of gigantic height, growing singly or in small groups, both along the plateau and in the domain behind the wall, but in close proximity to it, so that frequent limbs (of the black walnut especially) reach over and dip their pendent extremities into the water. Further back within the domain, the vision is impeded by an impenetrable screen of foliage.

These things are observed during the canoe's gradual approach to what I have called "the gate of the vista". On drawing nearer to this, however, its chasm-like appearance vanishes: a new outlet from the bay is discovered to the left – in which direction the wall is also seen to sweep, still following the general course of the stream. Down this new opening the eye cannot penetrate very far, for the stream, accompanied by the wall, still bends to the left, until both are swallowed up by the leaves.

The boat, nevertheless, glides magically into the winding channel – and here the shore opposite the wall is found to resemble that opposite the wall in the straight vista. Lofty hills, rising occasionally into mountains and covered with vegetation in wild luxuriance, still shut in the scene.

Floating gently onwards, but with a velocity slightly augmented, the voyager, after many short turns, finds his progress apparently barred by a gigantic gate or rather door of burnished gold, elaborately carved and fretted, and reflecting the direct rays of the now fast-sinking sun with an effulgence that seems to wreath the whole surrounding forest in flames. This gate is inserted in the lofty wall, which here appears to cross the river at right angles. In a few moments, however, it is seen that the main body of the water still sweeps in a gentle and extensive curve to the left, the wall following it as before, while a stream of considerable volume, diverging from the principal one, makes its way, with a slight ripple, under the door, and is thus hidden from sight. The canoe falls into the lesser channel and approaches the gate. Its ponderous wings are slowly and musically expanded. The boat glides between them, and commences a rapid descent into a vast amphitheatre entirely begirt with purple mountains, whose bases are laved by a gleaming river throughout the full extent of their circuit. Meantime, the whole paradise of Arnheim bursts upon the view. There is a gush of entrancing melody, there is an oppressive sense of strange, sweet odour... there is a dreamlike intermingling to the eye of tall, slender Eastern trees... bosky shrubberies... flocks of golden and crimson birds... lily-fringed lakes... meadows of violets, tulips, poppies, hyacinths and tuberoses... long intertangled lines of silver streamlets... and, upspringing confusedly from amid all, a mass of semi-Gothic, semi-Saracenic architecture sustaining itself by miracle in mid-air, glittering in the red sunlight with a hundred oriels, minarets and pinnacles, and seeming the phantom handiwork, conjointly, of the sylphs, of the fairies, of the genii and of the gnomes.

THE SPECTACLES*

Many years ago, it was the fashion to ridicule the idea of "love at first sight", but those who think (not less than those who feel deeply) have always advocated its existence. Modern discoveries, indeed, in what may be termed "ethical magnetism", or "magneto-aesthetics", render it probable that the most natural (and, consequently, the truest and most intense) of the human affections are those which arise in the heart as if by electric sympathy – in a word, that the brightest and most enduring of the psychal fetters are those which are riveted by a glance. The confession I am about to make will add another to the already almost innumerable instances of the truth of the position.

My story requires that I should be somewhat minute. I am still a very young man – not yet twenty-two years of age. My name, at present, is a very usual and rather plebeian one: Simpson. I say "at present", for it is only lately that I have been so called, having legislatively adopted this surname within the last year in order to receive a large inheritance left me by a distant male relative, Adolphus Simpson, Esq. The bequest was conditioned upon my taking the name of the testator – the family, not the Christian name: my Christian name is Napoleon Bonaparte (or, more properly, these are my first and middle appellations).

I assumed the name Simpson with some reluctance, as in my true patronym, Froissart, I felt a very pardonable pride – believing that I could trace a descent from the immortal author of the *Chronicles*.* While on the subject of names, by the by, I may mention a singular coincidence of sound attending the names of some of my immediate predecessors. My father was a Monsieur Froissart of Paris. His wife – my mother, whom he married at fifteen – was a Mademoiselle Croissart, eldest daughter of Croissart the banker, whose wife, again, being only sixteen when married, was the eldest daughter of one Victor Voissart. Monsieur Voissart, very singularly, had married a lady of similar name – a Mademoiselle Moissart.

She, too, was quite a child when married – and her mother also, Madame Moissart, was only fourteen when led to the altar. These early marriages are usual in France. Here, however, are Moissart, Voissart, Croissart and Froissart all in the direct line of descent. My own name though, as I say, became Simpson by act of legislature, and with so much repugnance on my part that, at one period, I actually hesitated about accepting the legacy with the useless and annoying proviso attached.

As to personal endowments, I am by no means deficient. On the contrary, I believe that I am well made and possess what nine tenths of the world would call "a handsome face". In height I am five feet eleven. My hair is black and curling. My nose is sufficiently good. My eyes are large and grey – although, in fact, they are weak to a very inconvenient degree, still no defect in this regard would be suspected from their appearance. The weakness itself, however, has always much annoyed me, and I have resorted to every remedy – short of wearing glasses. Being youthful and good-looking, I naturally dislike these, and have resolutely refused to employ them. I know nothing, indeed, which so disfigures the countenance of a young person or so impresses every feature with an air of demureness, if not altogether of sanctimoniousness and of age. An eyeglass, on the other hand, has a savour of downright foppery and affectation. I have hitherto managed as well as I could without either. But something too much of these merely personal details – which, after all, are of little importance. I will content myself with saying, in addition, that my temperament is sanguine, rash, ardent, enthusiastic – and that all my life I have been a devoted admirer of the women.

One night last winter, I entered a box at the P—— Theatre* in company with a friend, Mr Talbot. It was an opera night, and the bills presented a very rare attraction, so that the house was excessively crowded. We were in time, however, to obtain the front seats which had been reserved for us, and into which, with some little difficulty, we elbowed our way.

For two hours my companion, who was a musical *fanatico*,* gave his undivided attention to the stage – and, in the mean time, I amused myself by observing the audience, which consisted, in chief part, of the very elite of the city. Having satisfied myself upon this point, I was about turning my eyes to the prima donna when they were arrested and riveted by a figure in one of the private boxes which had escaped my observation.

If I live a thousand years, I can never forget the intense emotion with which I regarded this figure. It was that of a female, the most exquisite I had ever beheld. The face was so far turned towards the stage that, for some minutes, I could not obtain a view of it, but the form was *divine* – no other word can sufficiently express its magnificent proportion – and even the term "divine" seems ridiculously feeble as I write it.

The magic of a lovely form in woman – the necromancy of female gracefulness – was always a power which I had found it impossible to resist, but here was grace personified, incarnate, the *beau idéal** of my wildest and most enthusiastic visions. The figure, almost all of which the construction of the box permitted to be seen, was somewhat above the medium height, and nearly approached, without positively reaching, the majestic. Its perfect fullness and *tournure** were delicious. The head, of which only the back was visible, rivalled in outline that of the Greek Psyche,* and was rather displayed than concealed by an elegant cap of *gaze aérienne*,* which put me in mind of the *ventum textilem* of Apuleius.* The right arm hung over the balustrade of the box, and thrilled every nerve of my frame with its exquisite symmetry. Its upper portion was draperied by one of the loose open sleeves now in fashion. This extended but little below the elbow. Beneath it was worn an under one of some frail material, close-fitting, and terminated by a cuff of rich lace, which fell gracefully over the top of the hand, revealing only the delicate fingers, upon one of which sparkled a diamond ring, which I at once saw was of extraordinary value. The admirable roundness of the wrist was well set off by a bracelet which encircled it, and which also was ornamented and clasped by a magnificent aigrette of jewels – telling, in words that could not be mistaken, at once of the wealth and fastidious taste of the wearer.

I gazed at this queenly apparition for at least half an hour, as if I had been suddenly converted to stone – and, during this period, I felt the full force and truth of all that has been said or sung concerning "love at first sight". My feelings were totally different from any which I had hitherto experienced in the presence of even the most celebrated specimens of female loveliness. An unaccountable, and what I am compelled to consider a *magnetic* sympathy of soul for soul seemed to rivet not only my vision, but my whole powers of thought and feeling upon the admirable object before me. I saw... I felt... I knew that I was deeply, madly, irrevocably in love – and this even before seeing the face of the person beloved. So intense, indeed, was the passion that consumed me that I really believe it would have received little if any abatement had the features, yet unseen, proved of merely ordinary character, so anomalous is the nature of the only true love – of the love at first sight – and so little really dependent is it upon the external conditions which only seem to create and control it.

While I was thus wrapped in admiration of this lovely vision, a sudden disturbance among the audience caused her to turn her head partially towards me, so that I beheld the entire profile of the face. Its beauty even exceeded my anticipations – and yet there was something about it which disappointed me without my being able to tell exactly what it was. I said "disappointed", but this is not altogether the word. My sentiments were at once quieted and exalted. They partook less of transport and more of calm enthusiasm – of enthusiastic repose. This state of feeling arose, perhaps, from the Madonna-like and matronly air of the face – and yet I at once understood that it could not have arisen entirely from this. There was something else – some mystery which I could not develop, some expression about the countenance which slightly disturbed me while it greatly heightened my interest. In fact, I was just in that condition of mind which prepares a young and susceptible man for any act of extravagance. Had the lady been alone, I should undoubtedly have entered her box and accosted her at all hazards, but fortunately she was attended by two companions: a gentleman and a strikingly beautiful woman, to all appearance a few years younger than herself.

I revolved in my mind a thousand schemes by which I might obtain, hereafter, an introduction to the elder lady, or, for the present, at all events, a more distinct view of her beauty. I would have removed my position to one nearer her own, but the crowded state of the theatre rendered this impossible, and the stern decrees of Fashion had, of late, imperatively prohibited the use of the opera glass in a case such as this, even had I been so fortunate as to have one with me – but I had not, and was thus in despair.

At length I bethought me of applying to my companion.

"Talbot," I said, "*you* have an opera glass. Let me have it."

"An opera glass!... No!... What do you suppose *I* would be doing with an opera glass?" Here he turned impatiently towards the stage.

"But, Talbot," I continued, pulling him by the shoulder, "listen to me, will you? Do you see the stage box?... There!... No, the next... Did you ever behold as lovely a woman?"

"She is very beautiful, no doubt," he said.

"I wonder who she can be?"

"Why, in the name of all that is angelic, don't you *know* who she is? 'Not to know her argues yourself unknown.'* She is the celebrated Madame Lalande* – the beauty of the day par excellence, and the talk of the whole town. Immensely wealthy too... a widow, and a great match... has just arrived from Paris."

"Do you know her?"

"Yes – I have the honour."

"Will you introduce me?"

"Assuredly – with the greatest pleasure... When shall it be?"

"Tomorrow, at one, I will call upon you at B——'s."

"Very good – and now *do* hold your tongue, *if* you can."

In this latter respect, I was forced to take Talbot's advice, for he remained obstinately deaf to every further question or suggestion, and occupied himself exclusively for the rest of the evening with what was transacting upon the stage.

In the mean time, I kept my eyes riveted on Madame Lalande, and at length had the good fortune to obtain a full front view of her face. It was exquisitely lovely – this, of course, my heart had told me before, even had not Talbot fully satisfied me upon the point, but still the unintelligible something disturbed me. I finally concluded that my senses were impressed by a certain air of gravity, sadness or, still more properly, of weariness which took something from the youth and freshness of the countenance, only to endow it with a seraphic tenderness and majesty, and thus, of course, to my enthusiastic and romantic temperament, with an interest tenfold.

While I thus feasted my eyes, I perceived, at last, to my great trepidation, by an almost imperceptible start on the part of the lady, that she had become suddenly aware of the intensity of my gaze. Still, I was absolutely fascinated, and could not withdraw it, even for an instant. She turned aside her face, and again I saw only the chiselled contour of the back portion of the head. After some minutes, as if urged by curiosity to see if I was still looking, she gradually brought her face again around and again encountered my burning gaze. Her large dark eyes fell instantly, and a deep blush mantled her cheek. But what was my astonishment at perceiving that she not only did not a second time avert her head, but that she actually took from her girdle a double eyeglass, elevated it, adjusted it, and then regarded me through it, intently and deliberately, for the space of several minutes!

Had a thunderbolt fallen at my feet, I could not have been more thoroughly astounded – astounded *only*, not offended or disgusted in the slightest degree, although an action so bold in any other woman would have been likely to offend or disgust. But the whole thing was done with so much quietude, so much nonchalance, so much repose – with so evident an air of the highest breeding, in short – that nothing of mere effrontery was perceptible, and my sole sentiments were those of admiration and surprise.

I observed that, upon her first elevation of the glass, she had seemed satisfied with a momentary inspection of my person, and was withdrawing the instrument when, as if struck by a second thought, she resumed it, and so continued to regard me with fixed attention for the space of several minutes – for five minutes at the very least, I am sure.

This action, so remarkable in an American theatre, attracted very general observation, and gave rise to an indefinite movement, or *buzz*, among the audience, which for a moment filled me with confusion, but produced no visible effect upon the countenance of Madame Lalande.

Having satisfied her curiosity (if such it was), she dropped the glass and quietly gave her attention again to the stage, her profile now being turned towards myself, as before. I continued to watch her unremittingly, although I was fully conscious of my rudeness in so doing. Presently I saw the head slowly and slightly change its position, and soon I became convinced that the lady, while pretending to look at the stage, was in fact attentively regarding myself. It is needless to say what effect this conduct, on the part of so fascinating a woman, had upon my excitable mind.

Having thus scrutinized me for perhaps a quarter of an hour, the fair object of my passion addressed the gentleman who attended her, and, while she spoke, I saw distinctly, by the glances of both, that the conversation had reference to myself.

Upon its conclusion, Madame Lalande again turned towards the stage, and, for a few minutes, seemed absorbed in the performances. At the expiration of this period, however, I was thrown into an extremity of agitation by seeing her unfold, for the second time, the eyeglass which hung at her side, fully confront me as before, and, disregarding the renewed buzz of the audience, survey me, from head to foot, with the same miraculous composure which had previously so delighted and confounded my soul.

This extraordinary behaviour, by throwing me into a perfect fever of excitement – into an absolute delirium of love – served rather to embolden than to disconcert me. In the mad intensity of my devotion, I forgot everything but the presence and the majestic loveliness of the vision which confronted my gaze. Watching my opportunity, when I thought the audience were fully engaged with the opera, I at length caught the eyes of Madame Lalande, and, upon the instant, made a slight but unmistakable bow.

She blushed very deeply, then averted her eyes, then slowly and cautiously looked around, apparently to see if my rash action had been noticed – then leant over towards the gentleman who sat by her side.

I now felt a burning sense of the impropriety I had committed, and expected nothing less than instant exposure, while a vision of pistols upon the morrow floated rapidly and uncomfortably through my brain. I was greatly and immediately relieved, however, when I saw the lady merely hand the gentleman a playbill without speaking, but the reader may form some feeble conception of my astonishment – of my *profound* amazement, my delirious bewilderment of heart and soul – when, instantly afterwards, having again glanced furtively around, she allowed her bright eyes to set fully and steadily upon my own, and then, with a faint smile disclosing a bright line of her pearly teeth, made two distinct, pointed and unequivocal affirmative inclinations of the head.

It is useless, of course, to dwell upon my joy, upon my transport, upon my illimitable ecstasy of heart. If ever man was mad with excess of happiness, it was myself at that moment. I loved. This was my *first* love – so I felt it to be. It was love supreme – indescribable. It was "love at first sight" – and at first sight, too, it had been appreciated and *returned*.

Yes, returned. How and why should I doubt it for an instant? What other construction could I possibly put upon such conduct on the part of a lady so beautiful, so wealthy, evidently so accomplished, of so high breeding, of so lofty a position in society – in every regard so entirely respectable as I felt assured was Madame Lalande? Yes, she loved me: she returned the enthusiasm of my love with an enthusiasm as blind, as uncompromising, as uncalculating, as abandoned and as utterly unbounded as my own! These delicious fancies and reflections, however, were now interrupted by the falling of the drop-curtain. The audience arose, and the usual tumult immediately supervened. Quitting Talbot abruptly, I made every effort to force my way into closer proximity with Madame Lalande. Having failed in this on account of the crowd, I at length gave up the chase and bent my steps homeward, consoling myself for my disappointment in not having been able to touch even the hem of her robe by the reflection that I should be introduced by Talbot, in due form, upon the morrow.

This morrow at last came – that is to say, a day finally dawned upon a long and weary night of impatience – and then the hours until "one" were snail-paced, dreary and innumerable. But even Stamboul,* it is said, shall have an end, and there came an end to this long delay. The clock struck. As the last echo ceased, I stepped into B——'s and enquired for Talbot.

"Out," said the footman – Talbot's own.

"Out!" I replied, staggering back half a dozen paces. "Let me tell you, my fine fellow, that this thing is thoroughly impossible and impracticable – Mr Talbot is *not* out. What do you mean?"

"Nothing, sir – only, Mr Talbot is not in, that's all. He rode over to S—— immediately after breakfast, and left word that he would not be in town again for a week."

I stood petrified with horror and rage. I endeavoured to reply, but my tongue refused its office. At length I turned on my heel, livid with wrath, and inwardly consigning the whole tribe of the Talbots to the innermost regions of Erebus.* It was evident that my considerate friend, *il fanatico*, had quite forgotten his appointment with myself – had forgotten it as soon as it was made. At no time was he a very scrupulous man of his word. There was no help for it – so, smothering my vexation as well as I could, I strolled moodily up the street, propounding futile enquiries about Madame Lalande to every male acquaintance I met. By report she was known, I found, to all – to many by sight – but she had been in town only a few weeks, and there were very few, therefore, who claimed her personal acquaintance. These few, being still comparatively strangers, could not or would not take the liberty of introducing me through the formality of a morning call. While I stood thus in despair, conversing with a trio of friends upon the all-absorbing subject of my heart, it so happened that the subject itself passed by.

"As I live, there she is!" cried one.

"Surpassingly beautiful!" exclaimed a second.

"An angel upon earth!" ejaculated a third.

I looked – and, in an open carriage which approached us, passing slowly down the street, sat the enchanting vision of the opera, accompanied by the younger lady who had occupied a portion of her box.

"Her companion also wears remarkably well," said the one of my trio who had spoken first.

"Astonishingly," said the second. "Still quite a brilliant air – but art will do wonders. Upon my word, she looks better than she did at Paris five years ago. A beautiful woman still – don't you think so, Froissart?… Simpson, I mean."

"*Still!*" said I. "And why shouldn't she be? But compared with her friend she is as a rushlight to the evening star – a glow-worm to Antares."*

"Ha ha ha!… Why, Simpson, you have an astonishing tact at making discoveries – original ones, I mean." And here we separated, while one of the trio began humming a gay vaudeville, of which I caught only the lines

Ninon, Ninon, Ninon à bas –
*À bas Ninon de l'Enclos!**

During this little scene, however, one thing had served greatly to console me, although it fed the passion by which I was consumed. As the carriage of Madame Lalande rolled by our group, I had observed that she recognized me – and, more than this, she had blessed me by the most seraphic of all imaginable smiles, with no equivocal mark of the recognition.

As for an introduction, I was obliged to abandon all hope of it until such time as Talbot should think proper to return from the country. In the mean time, I perseveringly frequented every reputable place of public amusement – and, at length, at the theatre, where I first saw her, I had the supreme bliss of meeting her and of exchanging glances with her once again. This did not occur, however, until the lapse of a fortnight. Every day, in the interim, I had enquired for Talbot at his hotel, and every day had been thrown into a spasm of wrath by the everlasting "Not come home yet" of his footman.

Upon the evening in question, therefore, I was in a condition little short of madness. Madame Lalande, I had been told, was a Parisian, had lately arrived from Paris... Might she not suddenly return? Return before Talbot came back? And might she not be thus lost to me for ever? The thought was too terrible to bear. Since my future happiness was at issue, I resolved to act with a manly decision. In a word, upon the breaking-up of the play, I traced the lady to her residence, noted the address and the next morning sent her a full and elaborate letter, in which I poured out my whole heart.

I spoke boldly, freely – in a word, I spoke with passion. I concealed nothing – nothing even of my weakness. I alluded to the romantic circumstances of our first meeting – even to the glances which had passed between us. I went so far as to say that I felt assured of her love, while I offered this assurance, and my own intensity of devotion, as two excuses for my otherwise unpardonable conduct. As a third, I spoke of my fear that she might quit the city before I could have the opportunity of a formal introduction. I concluded the most wildly enthusiastic epistle ever penned with a frank declaration of my worldly circumstances – of my affluence – and with an offer of my heart and of my hand.

In an agony of expectation I awaited the reply. After what seemed the lapse of a century, it came.

Yes, *actually came*. Romantic as all this may appear, I really received a letter from Madame Lalande – the beautiful, the wealthy, the idolized

Madame Lalande. Her eyes – her magnificent eyes – had not belied her noble heart. Like a true Frenchwoman as she was, she had obeyed the frank dictates of her reason – the generous impulses of her nature – despising the conventional pruderies of the world. She had *not* scorned my proposals. She had *not* sheltered herself in silence. She had *not* returned my letter unopened. She had even sent me, in reply, one penned by her own exquisite fingers. It ran thus:

> Monsieur Simpson vill pardonne me for not compose de butefulle tong of his contrée so vell as might. It is only de late dat I am arrive, and not yet ave do opportunité for to… l'étudier.
>
> Vid dis apologie for the manière, I vill now say dat, hélas!… Monsieur Simpson ave guess but de too true. Need I say de more? Hélas! Am I not ready speak de too moshe?
>
> EUGÉNIE LALANDE

This noble-spirited note I kissed a million times, and committed no doubt, on its account, a thousand other extravagances that have now escaped my memory. Still Talbot *would* not return. Alas! Could he have formed even the vaguest idea of the suffering his absence had occasioned his friend, would not his sympathizing nature have flown immediately to my relief? Still, however, he came *not*. I wrote. He replied. He was detained by urgent business – but would shortly return. He begged me not to be impatient, to moderate my transports, to read soothing books, to drink nothing stronger than hock* – and to bring the consolations of philosophy to my aid. The fool! If he could not come himself, why, in the name of everything rational, could he not have enclosed me a letter of presentation? I wrote him again, entreating him to forward one forthwith. My letter was returned by *that* footman with the following endorsement in pencil. The scoundrel had joined his master in the country:

> Left S—— yesterday for parts unknown… did not say where… or when be back… so thought best to return letter, knowing your handwriting, and as how you is always, more or less, in a hurry.
>
> Yours sincerely, STUBBS

After this, it is needless to say that I devoted to the infernal deities both master and valet – but there was little use in anger, and no consolation at all in complaint.

But I had yet a resource left in my constitutional audacity. Hitherto it had served me well, and I now resolved to make it avail me to the end. Besides, after the correspondence which had passed between us, what act of mere informality *could* I commit, within bounds, that ought to be regarded as indecorous by Madame Lalande? Since the affair of the letter, I had been in the habit of watching her house, and thus discovered that, about twilight, it was her custom to promenade, attended only by a Negro in livery, in a public square overlooked by her windows. Here, amid the luxuriant and shadowing groves, in the grey gloom of a sweet midsummer evening, I observed my opportunity and accosted her.

The better to deceive the servant in attendance, I did this with the assured air of an old and familiar acquaintance. With a presence of mind truly Parisian, she took the cue at once, and, to greet me, held out the most bewitchingly little of hands. The valet at once fell into the rear, and now, with hearts full to overflowing, we discoursed long and unreservedly of our love.

As Madame Lalande spoke English even less fluently than she wrote it, our conversation was necessarily in French. In this sweet tongue, so adapted to passion, I gave loose to the impetuous enthusiasm of my nature, and, with all the eloquence I could command, besought her to consent to an immediate marriage.

At this impatience she smiled. She urged the old story of decorum – that bugbear which deters so many from bliss until the opportunity for bliss has for ever gone by. I had most imprudently made it known among my friends, she observed, that I desired her acquaintance – thus that I did not possess it... thus, again, there was no possibility of concealing the date of our first knowledge of each other. And then she adverted, with a blush, to the extreme recency of this date. To wed immediately would be improper... would be indecorous... would be outré. All this she said with a charming air of *naïveté* which enraptured while it grieved and convinced me. She went even so far as to accuse me, laughingly, of rashness – of imprudence. She bade me remember that I really even knew not who she was – what were her prospects, her connections, her standing in society. She begged me, but with a sigh, to reconsider my proposal, and termed my love an infatuation... a will o' the wisp... a fancy or fantasy of the moment... a baseless and unstable creation rather of the imagination than of the heart. These things she uttered as the shadows of the sweet twilight gathered darkly and more darkly around us – and then, with a gentle pressure of her fairy-like hand, overthrew, in a single sweet instant, all the argumentative fabric she had reared.

I replied as best I could – as only a true lover can. I spoke at length and perseveringly of my devotion, of my passion – of her exceeding beauty, and of my own enthusiastic admiration. In conclusion, I dwelt, with a convincing energy, upon the perils that encompass the course of love – that course of true love that never did run smooth* – and thus deduced the manifest danger of rendering that course unnecessarily long.

This latter argument seemed finally to soften the rigour of her determination. She relented, but there was yet an obstacle, she said, which she felt assured I had not properly considered. This was a delicate point – for a woman to urge, especially so: in mentioning it, she saw that she must make a sacrifice of her feelings – still, for *me*, every sacrifice should be made. She alluded to the topic of *age*. Was I aware – was I fully aware of the discrepancy between us? That the age of the husband should surpass by a few years – even by fifteen or twenty – the age of the wife was regarded by the world as admissible, and, indeed, as even proper, but she had always entertained the belief that the years of the wife should never exceed in number those of the husband. A discrepancy of this unnatural kind gave rise – too frequently, alas! – to a life of unhappiness. Now she was aware that my own age did not exceed two-and-twenty – and I, on the contrary, perhaps, was *not* aware that the years of my Eugénie extended very considerably beyond that sum.

About all this there was a nobility of soul, a dignity of candour, which delighted, which enchanted me – which eternally riveted my chains. I could scarcely restrain the excessive transport which possessed me.

"My sweetest Eugénie," I cried, "what is all this about which you are discoursing? Your years surpass in some measure my own. But what then? The customs of the world are so many conventional follies. To those who love as ourselves, in what respect differs a year from an hour? I am twenty-two, you say – granted: indeed, you may as well call me, at once, twenty-three. Now, you yourself, my dearest Eugénie, can have numbered no more than… can have numbered no more than… no more than… than… than… than—"

Here I paused for an instant, in the expectation that Madame Lalande would interrupt me by supplying her true age. But a Frenchwoman is seldom direct, and has always, by way of answer to an embarrassing query, some little practical reply of her own. In the present instance, Eugénie, who for a few moments past had seemed to be searching for something in her bosom, at length let fall upon the grass a miniature, which I immediately picked up and presented to her.

"Keep it!" she said, with one of her most ravishing smiles. "Keep it for my sake – for the sake of her whom it too flatteringly represents. Besides, upon the back of the trinket you may discover, perhaps, the very information you seem to desire. It is now, to be sure, growing rather dark – but you can examine it at your leisure in the morning. In the mean time, you shall be my escort home tonight. My friends are about holding a little musical levee. I can promise you, too, some good singing. We French are not nearly so punctilious as you Americans, and I shall have no difficulty in smuggling you in, in the character of an old acquaintance."

With this, she took my arm, and I attended her home. The mansion was quite a fine one, and, I believe, furnished in good taste. Of this latter point, however, I am scarcely qualified to judge, for it was just dark as we arrived, and in American mansions of the better sort lights seldom, during the heat of summer, make their appearance at this, the most pleasant period of the day. In about an hour after my arrival, to be sure, a single shaded solar lamp was lit in the principal drawing room, and this apartment, I could thus see, was arranged with unusual good taste and even splendour, but two other rooms of the suite, and in which the company chiefly assembled, remained, during the whole evening, in a very agreeable shadow. This is a well-conceived custom, giving the party at least a choice of light or shade, and one which our friends over the water could not do better than immediately adopt.

The evening thus spent was unquestionably the most delicious of my life. Madame Lalande had not overrated the musical abilities of her friends; and the singing I here heard I had never heard excelled in any private circle out of Vienna. The instrumental performers were many and of superior talents. The vocalists were chiefly ladies, and no individual sang less than well. At length, upon a peremptory call for "Madame Lalande", she arose at once, without affectation or demur, from the chaise longue upon which she had sat by my side, and, accompanied by one or two gentlemen and her female friend of the opera, repaired to the piano in the main drawing room. I would have escorted her myself, but felt that, under the circumstances of my introduction to the house, I had better remain unobserved where I was. I was thus deprived of the pleasure of seeing, although not of hearing, her sing.

The impression she produced upon the company seemed electrical – but the effect upon myself was something even more. I know not how adequately to describe it.* It arose in part, no doubt, from the sentiment of love with which I was imbued, but chiefly from my conviction of the extreme sensibility of the singer. It is beyond the reach of art to endow either air or recitative with more impassioned *expression* than was hers. Her utterance of the romance in *Otello*,* the tone with which she gave the words "*Sul mio sasso*" in the *Capuleti** – is ringing in my memory yet. Her lower tones were absolutely miraculous. Her voice embraced three complete octaves, extending from the contralto D to the D upper soprano, and, though sufficiently powerful to have filled the San Carlo,* executed, with the minutest precision, every difficulty of vocal composition – ascending and descending scales, cadences or *fioriture*.* In the finale of the *Sonnambula*, she brought about a most remarkable effect at the words:

> *Ah, non giunge uman pensiero*
> *Al contento ond'io son piena!**

Here, in imitation of Malibrán, she modified the original phrase of Bellini, so as to let her voice descend to the tenor G, when, by a rapid transition, she struck the G above the treble stave, springing over an interval of two octaves.

Upon rising from the piano after these miracles of vocal execution, she resumed her seat by my side, when I expressed to her, in terms of the deepest enthusiasm, my delight at her performance. Of my surprise I said nothing, and yet was I most unfeignedly surprised, for a certain feebleness, or rather a certain tremulous indecision of voice in ordinary conversation, had prepared me to anticipate that, in singing, she would not acquit herself with any remarkable ability.

Our conversation was now long, earnest, uninterrupted and totally unreserved. She made me relate many of the earlier passages of my life, and listened with breathless attention to every word of the narrative. I concealed nothing – felt that I had a right to conceal nothing – from her confiding affection. Encouraged by her candour upon the delicate point of her age, I entered, with perfect frankness, not only into a detail of my many minor vices, but made full confession of those moral and even of those physical infirmities the disclosure of which, in demanding so much higher a degree of courage, is so much surer an evidence of love. I touched upon my college indiscretions, upon my extravagances, upon my carousals, upon my debts, upon my flirtations. I even went so far as to speak of a slightly hectic cough with which, at one time, I had been troubled, of a chronic rheumatism, of a twinge of hereditary gout – and, in conclusion, of the disagreeable and inconvenient, but hitherto carefully concealed, weakness of my eyes.

"Upon this latter point," said Madame Lalande laughingly, "you have been surely injudicious in coming to confession – for, without the confession, I take it for granted that no one would have accused you of the crime. By the by," she continued, "have you any recollection" – and here I fancied that a blush, even through the gloom of the apartment, became distinctly visible upon her cheek – "have you any recollection, *mon cher ami,** of this little ocular assistant which now depends from my neck?"

As she spoke, she twirled in her fingers the identical double eyeglass which had so overwhelmed me with confusion at the opera.

"Full well – alas! – do I remember it," I exclaimed, pressing passionately the delicate hand which offered the glasses for my inspection. They formed a complex and magnificent toy, richly chased and filigreed, and gleaming with jewels which, even in the deficient light, I could not help perceiving were of high value.

"*Eh bien, mon ami*,"* she resumed with a certain *empressement** of manner that rather surprised me, "*eh bien, mon ami*, you have earnestly besought of me a favour which you have been pleased to denominate 'priceless'. You have demanded of me my hand upon the morrow. Should I yield to your entreaties – and, I may add, to the pleadings of my own bosom – would I not be entitled to demand of you a very... a very little boon in return?"

"Name it!" I exclaimed with an energy that had nearly drawn upon us the observation of the company, and restrained by their presence alone from throwing myself impetuously at her feet. "Name it, my beloved, my Eugénie, my own!... Name it!... But, alas, it is already yielded ere named!"

"You shall conquer, then, *mon ami*," said she, "for the sake of the Eugénie whom you love, this little weakness which you have at last confessed, this weakness more moral than physical, and which, let me assure you, is so unbecoming the nobility of your real nature, so inconsistent with the candour of your usual character – and which, if permitted further control, will assuredly involve you, sooner or later, in some very disagreeable scrape. You shall conquer, for my sake, this affectation which leads you, as you yourself acknowledge, to the tacit or implied denial of your infirmity of vision. For this infirmity you virtually deny in refusing to employ the customary means for its relief. You will understand me to say, then, that I wish you to wear spectacles... ah, hush!... you have already consented to wear them, *for my sake*. You shall accept the little toy which I now hold in my hand, and which, though admirable as an aid to vision, is really of no very immense value as a gem. You perceive that, by a trifling modification thus – or thus – it can be adapted to the eyes in the form of spectacles, or worn in the waistcoat pocket as an eyeglass. It is in the former mode, however, and habitually, that you have already consented to wear it *for my sake*."

This request – must I confess it? – confused me in no little degree. But the condition with which it was coupled rendered hesitation, of course, a matter altogether out of the question.

"It is done!" I cried, with all the enthusiasm that I could muster at the moment. "It is done – it is most cheerfully agreed. I sacrifice every feeling for your sake. Tonight I wear this dear eyeglass *as* an eyeglass, and upon my heart – but with the earliest dawn of that morning which gives me the pleasure of calling you wife, I will place it upon my... upon my nose... and there wear it ever afterwards, in the less romantic and less fashionable, but certainly in the more serviceable, form which you desire."

Our conversation now turned upon the details of our arrangements for the morrow. Talbot, I learnt from my betrothed, had just arrived in town. I was to see him at once, and procure a carriage. The soirée would scarcely break up before two, and by this hour the vehicle was to be at the door, when, in the confusion occasioned by the departure of the company, Madame L. could easily enter it unobserved. We were then to call at the house of a clergyman who would be in waiting – there be married, drop Talbot and proceed on a short tour to the East, leaving the fashionable world at home to make whatever comments upon the matter it thought best.

Having planned all this, I immediately took leave and went in search of Talbot, but, on the way, I could not refrain from stepping into a hotel for the purpose of inspecting the miniature – and this I did by the powerful aid of the glasses. The countenance was a surpassingly beautiful one! Those large luminous eyes!... That proud Grecian nose!... Those dark luxuriant curls!... "Ah," said I, exultingly to myself, "this is indeed the speaking image of my beloved!" I turned the reverse, and discovered the words "Eugénie Lalande – aged twenty-seven years and seven months".

I found Talbot at home, and proceeded at once to acquaint him with my good fortune. He professed excessive astonishment, of course, but congratulated me most cordially, and proffered every assistance in his power. In a word, we carried out our arrangement to the letter – and, at two in the morning, just ten minutes after the ceremony, I found myself in a close carriage with Madame Lalande – with Mrs Simpson, I should say – and driving at a great rate out of town in a direction north-east by north, half-north.

It had been determined for us by Talbot that, as we were to be up all night, we should make our first stop at C——, a village about twenty miles from the city, and there get an early breakfast and some repose before proceeding upon our route. At four precisely, therefore, the carriage drew up at the door of the principal inn. I handed my adored wife out and ordered breakfast forthwith. In the mean time, we were shown into a small parlour and sat down.

It was now nearly if not altogether daylight – and, as I gazed enraptured at the angel by my side, the singular idea came all at once into my head that this was really the very first moment since my acquaintance with the celebrated loveliness of Madame Lalande that I had enjoyed a near inspection of that loveliness by daylight at all.

"And now, *mon ami*," said she, taking my hand, and so interrupting this train of reflection, "and now, *mon cher ami*, since we are indissolubly one, since I have yielded to your passionate entreaties and performed my portion of our agreement, I presume you have not forgotten that you also have a little favour to bestow – a little promise which it is your intention to keep. Ah, let me see! Let me remember! Yes, full easily do I call to mind the precise words of the dear promise you made to Eugénie last night. Listen! You spoke thus: 'It is done!... It is most cheerfully agreed! I sacrifice every feeling for your sake. Tonight I wear this dear eyeglass *as* an eyeglass, and upon my heart – but with the earliest dawn of that morning which gives me the privilege of calling you wife, I will place it upon my... upon my nose... and there wear it ever afterwards in the less romantic and less fashionable but certainly in the more serviceable form which you desire.' These were the exact words, my beloved husband, were they not?"

"They were," I said. "You have an excellent memory – and assuredly, my beautiful Eugénie, there is no disposition on my part to evade the performance of the trivial promise they imply. See! Behold! They are becoming... rather – are they not?" And here, having arranged the glasses in the ordinary form of spectacles, I applied them gingerly in their proper position, while Madame Simpson, adjusting her cap and folding her arms, sat bolt upright in her chair in a somewhat stiff and prim, and indeed in a somewhat undignified position.

"Goodness gracious me!" I exclaimed, almost at the very instant that the rim of the spectacles had settled upon my nose. "*My!* Goodness gracious me!… Why, what *can* be the matter with these glasses?" – and taking them quickly off, I wiped them carefully with a silk handkerchief and adjusted them again.

But if, in the first instance, there had occurred something which occasioned me surprise, in the second this surprise became elevated into astonishment, and this astonishment was profound, was extreme – indeed, I may say it was horrific. What, in the name of everything hideous, did this mean? Could I believe my eyes?… *Could* I?… That was the question. Was that… was that… was that *rouge*? And were those… and were those… were those *wrinkles* upon the visage of Eugénie Lalande? And oh, Jupiter and every one of the gods and goddesses, little and big!… What… what… what… *what* had become of her teeth? I dashed the spectacles violently to the ground and, leaping to my feet, stood erect in the middle of the floor, confronting Mrs Simpson with my arms set akimbo and grinning and foaming, but, at the same time, utterly speechless with terror and with rage.

Now, I have already said that Madame Eugénie Lalande – that is to say, Simpson – spoke the English language but very little better than she wrote it, and for this reason she very properly never attempted to speak it upon ordinary occasions. But rage will carry a lady to any extreme, and in the present case it carried Mrs Simpson to the very extraordinary extreme of attempting to hold a conversation in a tongue that she did not altogether understand.

"Vell, Monsieur," said she, after surveying me, in great apparent astonishment, for some moments, "well, Monsieur?… And vat den?… Vat de matter now? Is it de dance of de Saint Vitusse dat you ave? If not like me, vat for vy buy de pig in the poke?"*

"You wretch!" said I, catching my breath. "You… you… you villainous old hag!"

"Ag?… Ole?… Me not so *ver* ole, after all! Me not one single day more dan de eighty-doo."

"Eighty-two!" I ejaculated, staggering to the wall. "Eighty-two hundred thousand baboons! The miniature said twenty-seven years and seven months!"

"To be sure!… Dat is so!… Ver true! But den de portraite has been take for dese fifty-five year. Ven I go marry my segonde usbande, Monsieur Lalande, at dat time I had de portraite take for my daughter by my first usbande, Monsieur Moissart!"

"Moissart!" said I.

"Yes, Moissart," said she, mimicking my pronunciation – which, to speak the truth, was none of the best. "And vat den? Vat *you* know about de Moissart?"

"Nothing, you old fright!... I know nothing about him at all – only, I had an ancestor of that name, once upon a time."

"Dat name! And vat you ave for say to dat name? 'Tis ver *goot* name, and so is Voissart – dat is ver goot name too. My daughter, Mademoiselle Moissart, she marry von Monsieur Voissart, and de name is bote *ver* respectaable name."

"Moissart?" I exclaimed. "And Voissart! Why, what is it you mean?"

"Vat I mean?... I mean Moissart and Voissart – and for de matter of dat, I mean Croissart and Froissart too, if I only tink proper to mean it. My daughter's daughter, Mademoiselle Voissart, she marry von Monsieur Croissart, and den agin, my daughter's grande-daughter, Mademoiselle Croissart, she marry von Monsieur Froissart – and I suppose you say dat *dat* is not von *ver* respectaable name."

"Froissart!" said I, beginning to faint. "Why, surely you don't say Moissart, and Voissart, and Croissart, and Froissart?"

"Yes," she replied, leaning fully back in her chair and stretching out her lower limbs at great length. "Yes, Moissart, and Voissart, and Croissart, and Froissart. But Monsieur Froissart, he vas von *ver* big vat you call fool... he vas von ver great big donce like yourself... for he lef *la belle France** for come to dis stupide Amérique... and ven he get here, he vent and ave von *ver* stupide, von *ver, ver* stupide sonn, so I hear, dough I not yet av de plaisir to meet vid him – neither me nor my companion, de Madame Stephanie Lalande. He is name de Napoleon Bonaparte Froissart, and I suppose you say dat *dat*, too, is not von *ver* respectable name."

Either the length or the nature of this speech had the effect of working up Mrs Simpson into a very extraordinary passion indeed – and as she made an end of it, with great labour she jumped up from her chair like somebody bewitched, dropping upon the floor an entire universe of bustle as she jumped. Once upon her feet, she gnashed her gums, brandished her arms, rolled up her sleeves, shook her fist in my face and concluded the performance by tearing the cap from her head, and with it an immense wig of the most valuable and beautiful black hair, the whole of which she dashed upon the ground with a yell, and there trampled and danced a fandango upon it, in an absolute ecstasy and agony of rage.

Meantime, I sank aghast into the chair which she had vacated. "Moissart and Voissart!" I repeated thoughtfully as she cut one of her pigeon wings,* and "Croissart and Froissart!" as she completed another… "Moissart and Voissart and Croissart and Napoleon Bonaparte Froissart!… Why, you ineffable old serpent, that's *me*… that's *me*… d'ye hear?… that's *me*…" – here I screamed at the top of my voice – "that's *me-e-e! I* am Napoleon Bonaparte Froissart! And if I haven't married my great-great-grandmother, I wish I may be everlastingly confounded!"

Madame Eugénie Lalande, *quasi* Simpson – formerly Moissart – was, in sober fact, my great-great-grandmother. In her youth she had been beautiful, and even at eighty-two retained the majestic height, the sculptural contour of head, the fine eyes and the Grecian nose of her girlhood. By the aid of these, of pearl powder, of rouge, of false hair, false teeth and false *tournure*, as well as of the most skilful modistes of Paris, she contrived to hold a respectable footing among the beauties *un peu passées** of the French metropolis. In this respect, indeed, she might have been regarded as little less than the equal of the celebrated Ninon de l'Enclos.

She was immensely wealthy, and being left, for the second time, a widow without children, she bethought herself of my existence in America, and for the purpose of making me her heir paid a visit to the United States, in company with a distant and exceedingly lovely relative of her second husband's – a Madame Stephanie Lalande.

At the opera, my great-great-grandmother's attention was arrested by my notice – and, upon surveying me through her eyeglass, she was struck with a certain family resemblance to herself. Thus interested, and knowing that the heir she sought was actually in the city, she made enquiries of her party respecting me. The gentleman who attended her knew my person, and told her who I was. The information thus obtained induced her to renew her scrutiny – and this scrutiny it was which so emboldened me that I behaved in the absurd manner already detailed. She returned my bow, however, under the impression that, by some odd accident, I had discovered her identity. When, deceived by my weakness of vision and the arts of the toilet in respect to the age and charms of the strange lady, I demanded so enthusiastically of Talbot who she was, he concluded that I meant the younger beauty, as a matter of course, and so informed me, with perfect truth, that she was "the celebrated widow, Madame Lalande".

In the street, next morning, my great-great-grandmother encountered Talbot, an old Parisian acquaintance, and the conversation, very naturally, turned upon myself. My deficiencies of vision were then explained, for these were notorious, although I was entirely ignorant of their notoriety – and my good old relative discovered, much to her chagrin, that she had been deceived in supposing me aware of her identity, and that I had been merely making a fool of myself in making open love, in a theatre, to an old woman unknown. By way of punishing me for this imprudence, she concocted with Talbot a plot. He purposely kept out of my way to avoid giving me the introduction. My street enquiries about "the lovely widow, Madame Lalande" were supposed to refer to the younger lady, of course, and thus the conversation with the three gentlemen whom I encountered shortly after leaving Talbot's hotel will be easily explained, as also their allusion to Ninon de l'Enclos. I had no opportunity of seeing Madame Lalande closely during daylight – and, at her musical soirée, my silly weakness in refusing the aid of glasses effectually prevented me from making a discovery of her age. When "Madame Lalande" was called upon to sing, the younger lady was intended – and it was she who arose to obey the call, my great-great-grandmother, to further the deception, arising at the same moment and accompanying her to the piano in the main drawing room. Had I decided upon escorting her thither, it had been her design to suggest the propriety of my remaining where I was – but my own prudential views rendered this unnecessary. The songs which I so much admired, and which so confirmed my impression of the youth of my mistress, were executed by Madame Stephanie Lalande. The eyeglass was presented by way of adding a reproof to the hoax – a sting to the epigram of the deception. Its presentation afforded an opportunity for the lecture upon affectation with which I was so especially edified. It is almost superfluous to add that the glasses of the instrument, as worn by the old lady, had been exchanged by her for a pair better adapted to my years. They suited me, in fact, to a T.

The clergyman who merely pretended to tie the fatal knot was a boon companion of Talbot's, and no priest. He was an excellent "whip", however, and having doffed his cassock to put on a greatcoat, he drove the hack which conveyed the "happy couple" out of town. Talbot took a seat at his side. The two scoundrels were thus "in at the death",* and through a half-open window of the back parlour of the inn amused themselves in grinning at the denouement of the drama. I believe I shall be forced to call them both out.

Nevertheless, I am *not* the husband of my great-great-grandmother, and this is a reflection which affords me infinite relief, but I *am* the husband of Madame Lalande – of Madame Stephanie Lalande – with whom my good old relative, besides making me her sole heir when she dies (if she ever does) has been at the trouble of concocting me a match. In conclusion: I am done for ever with billets-doux, and am never to be met without SPECTACLES.

THE DUC DE L'OMELETTE*

And stepped at once into a cooler clime.*
– Cowper

Keats fell by a criticism.* Who was it died of *The Andromache*?* Ignoble souls!... De L'Omelette perished of an ortolan.* *L'histoire en est brève.** Assist me, Spirit of Apicius!*

A golden cage bore the little winged wanderer, enamoured, melting, indolent, to the Chaussée-d'Antin* from its home in far Peru. From its queenly possessor La Bellissima* to the Duc de l'Omelette, six peers of the empire conveyed the happy bird.

That night the duc was to sup alone. In the privacy of his bureau he reclined languidly on that ottoman for which he sacrificed his loyalty in outbidding his king – the notorious ottoman of Cadêt.*

He buries his face in the pillow. The clock strikes! Unable to restrain his feelings, His Grace swallows an olive. At this moment the door gently opens to the sound of soft music – and lo! the most delicate of birds is before the most enamoured of men! But what inexpressible dismay now overshadows the countenance of the duc! "*Horreur!... Chien!... Baptiste!... L'oiseau! Ah, bon Dieu! Cet oiseau modeste que tu as déshabillé de ses plumes, et que tu as servi sans papier!*"* It is superfluous to say more: the duc expired in a paroxysm of disgust.

* * * * * * *

"Ha ha ha!" said His Grace on the third day after his decease.

"He he he!" replied the Devil faintly, drawing himself up with an air of hauteur.

"Why, surely you are not serious," retorted de l'Omelette. "I have sinned – *c'est vrai** – but, my good sir, consider!... You have no actual intention of putting such... such... barbarous threats into execution."

"No *what*?" said His Majesty. "Come, sir, strip!"

"Strip, indeed! Very pretty, i' faith! No, sir, I shall *not* strip. Who are you, pray, that I, Duc de l'Omelette, Prince de Foie-Gras, just come of age, author of the *Mazurkiad*, and Member of the Academy, should divest myself at your bidding of the sweetest pantaloons ever made by Bourdon, the daintiest *robe de chambre** ever put together by Rombêrt – to say nothing of the taking my hair out of paper... not to mention the trouble I should have in drawing off my gloves?"

"Who am I?... Ah, true! I am Baal-Zebub, Prince of the Fly.* I took thee, just now, from a rosewood coffin inlaid with ivory. Thou wast curiously scented, and labelled as per invoice. Belial sent thee – my Inspector of Cemeteries. The pantaloons which thou sayest were made by Bourdon are an excellent pair of linen drawers, and thy *robe de chambre* is a shroud of no scanty dimensions."

"Sir!" replied the duc. "I am not to be insulted with impunity!... Sir! I shall take the earliest opportunity of avenging this insult!... Sir! You shall hear from me! In the mean time, *au revoir*!"* – and the duc was bowing himself out of the Satanic presence when he was interrupted and brought back by a gentleman in waiting. Hereupon His Grace rubbed his eyes, yawned, shrugged his shoulders, reflected. Having become satisfied of his identity, he took a bird's-eye view of his whereabouts.

The apartment was superb. Even de l'Omelette pronounced it *bien comme il faut*.* It was not its length nor its breadth, but its height... ah, that was appalling!... There was no ceiling – certainly none – but a dense whirling mass of fiery-coloured clouds. His Grace's brain reeled as he glanced upward. From above hung a chain of an unknown blood-red metal – its upper end lost, like the city of Boston, *parmi les nues*.* From its nether extremity swung a large cresset. The duc knew it to be a ruby, but from it there poured a light so intense, so still, so terrible, Persia never worshipped such... Guebre never imagined such...* Mussulman never dreamt of such when, drugged with opium, he has tottered to a bed of poppies, his back to the flowers and his face to the god Apollo.* The duc muttered a slight oath, decidedly approbatory.

The corners of the room were rounded into niches. Three of these were filled with statues of gigantic proportions. Their beauty was Grecian, their deformity Egyptian, their *tout ensemble** French. In the fourth niche the statue was veiled – it was *not* colossal. But then there was a taper ankle, a sandalled foot. De l'Omelette pressed his hand upon his heart, closed his eyes, raised them and caught His Satanic Majesty... in a blush.

But the paintings!... Kupris! Astarte! Ashtoreth!...* A thousand and the same! And Raphael* has beheld them! Yes, Raphael has been here, for did he not paint the ——? And was he not consequently damned? The paintings!... The paintings! Oh, luxury! Oh, love!... Who, gazing on those forbidden beauties, shall have eyes for the dainty devices of the golden frames that besprinkled, like stars, the hyacinth and the porphyry walls?

But the duc's heart is fainting within him. He is not, however, as you suppose, dizzy with magnificence, nor drunk with the ecstatic breath of those innumerable censers. "*C'est vrai que de toutes ces choses il a pensé beaucoup... mais!*"* The Duc de l'Omelette is terror-stricken, for, through the lurid vista which a single uncurtained window is affording, lo! gleams the most ghastly of all fires!

*Le pauvre duc!** He could not help imagining that the glorious, the voluptuous, the never-dying melodies which pervaded that hall, as they passed filtered and transmuted through the alchemy of the enchanted window panes, were the wailings and the howlings of the hopeless and the damned! And there, too!... there!... upon the ottoman!... who could *he* be?... he, the *petit-maître*... no, the Deity... who sat as if carved in marble, *et qui sourit*, with his pale countenance, *si amèrement?**

*Mais il faut agir** – that is to say, a Frenchman never faints outright. Besides, His Grace hated a scene... De l'Omelette is himself again. There were some foils upon a table – some points also. The duc had studied under B——: *il avait tué ses six hommes.** Now, then, *il peut s'échapper.** He measures two points, and, with a grace inimitable, offers His Majesty the choice. *Horreur!* His Majesty does not fence!

*Mais il joue!...** How happy a thought!... But His Grace had always an excellent memory. He had dipped in the *Diable* of Abbé Gaultier.* Therein it is said "*que le Diable n'ose pas refuser un jeu d'écarté*".*

But the chances... the chances! True... desperate – but scarcely more desperate than the duc. Besides, was he not in the secret?... Had he not skimmed over Père Le Brun?...* Was he not a member of the Club Vingt-un? "*Si je perds,*"* said he, "*je serai deux fois perdu*" – "I shall be doubly damned" – "*voilà tout!*"* Here His Grace shrugged his shoulders. "*Si je gagne, je reviendrai à mes ortolans – que les cartes soient préparées!*"*

His Grace was all care, all attention – His Majesty all confidence. A spectator would have thought of Francis and Charles.* His Grace thought of his game. His Majesty did not think – he shuffled. The duc cut.

The cards are dealt. The trump is turned... it is... it is... the king! No... it was the queen. His Majesty cursed her masculine habiliments. De l'Omelette placed his hand upon his heart.

They play. The duc counts. The hand is out. His Majesty counts heavily, smiles and is taking wine. The duc slips a card.

"*C'est à vous à faire*,"* said His Majesty, cutting. His Grace bowed, dealt and arose from the table *en presentant le roi*.*

His Majesty looked chagrined.

Had Alexander not been Alexander, he would have been Diogenes* – and the duc assured his antagonist, in taking leave, "*que s'il n'eût été de l'Omelette, il n'aurait point d'objection d'être le Diable*".*

KING PEST*

A TALE CONTAINING AN ALLEGORY

> The gods do bear and well allow in kings
> The things which they abhor in rascal routs.*
> – Buckhurst's *Tragedy of Ferrex and Porrex*

About twelve o'clock one night in the month of October, and during the chivalrous reign of the third Edward,* two seamen belonging to the crew of the *Free and Easy*, a trading schooner plying between Sluys* and the Thames, and then at anchor in that river, were much astonished to find themselves seated in the taproom of an alehouse in the parish of St Andrews, London* – which alehouse bore for sign the portraiture of a "Jolly Tar".*

The room, although ill contrived, smoke-blackened, low-pitched and in every other respect agreeing with the general character of such places at the period, was nevertheless, in the opinion of the grotesque groups scattered here and there within it, sufficiently well adapted to its purpose.

Of these groups, our two seamen formed, I think, the most interesting, if not the most conspicuous.

The one who appeared to be the elder, and whom his companion addressed by the characteristic appellation of "Legs", was at the same time much the taller of the two. He might have measured six feet and a half, and an habitual stoop in the shoulders seemed to have been the necessary consequence of an altitude so enormous. Superfluities in height were, however, more than accounted for by deficiencies in other respects. He was exceedingly thin – and might, as his associates asserted, have answered, when drunk, for a pennant at the masthead, or, when sober, have served for a jib-boom.* But these jests, and others of a similar nature, had evidently produced, at no time, any effect upon the cachinnatory muscles* of the tar. With high cheekbones, a large hawk nose, retreating chin, fallen underjaw and huge protruding white eyes, the expression of his countenance, although tinged with a species of dogged indifference to matters and things in general, was not the less utterly solemn and serious beyond all attempts at imitation or description.

The younger seaman was, in all outward appearance, the converse of his companion. His stature could not have exceeded four feet. A pair of stumpy bow legs supported his squat, unwieldy figure, while his unusually short and thick arms, with no ordinary fists at their extremities, swung off dangling from his sides like the fins of a sea turtle. Small eyes of no particular colour twinkled far back in his head. His nose remained buried in the mass of flesh which enveloped his round, full and purple face – and his thick upper lip rested upon the still thicker one beneath with an air of complacent self-satisfaction, much heightened by the owner's habit of licking them at intervals. He evidently regarded his tall shipmate with a feeling half wondrous, half quizzical – and stared up occasionally in his face as the red setting sun stares up at the crags of Ben Nevis.

Various and eventful, however, had been the peregrinations of the worthy couple in and about the different tap-houses of the neighbourhood during the earlier hours of the night. Funds even the most ample are not always everlasting, and it was with empty pockets our friends had ventured upon the present hostelry.

At the precise period, then, when this history properly commences, Legs and his fellow, Hugh Tarpaulin, sat each with both elbows resting upon the large oaken table in the middle of the floor and with a hand upon either cheek. They were eyeing, from behind a huge flagon of unpaid-for "humming stuff"* the portentous words "No Chalk"* which to their indignation and astonishment were scored over the doorway by means of that very mineral whose presence they purported to deny. Not that the gift of deciphering written characters – a gift among the commonalty* of that day considered little less cabalistical than the art of inditing – could, in strict justice, have been laid to the charge of either disciple of the sea, but there was, to say the truth, a certain twist in the formation of the letters – an indescribable lee lurch about the whole – which foreboded, in the opinion of both seamen, a long run of dirty weather, and determined them at once, in the allegorical words of Legs himself, to "pump ship, clew up all sail and scud before the wind".*

Having accordingly disposed of what remained of the ale and looped up the points of their short doublets, they finally made a bolt for the street. Although Tarpaulin rolled twice into the fireplace, mistaking it for the door, yet their escape was at length happily effected – and half after twelve o'clock found our heroes ripe for mischief and running for life down a dark alley in the direction of St Andrew's Stair,* hotly pursued by the landlady of the Jolly Tar.

At the epoch of this eventful tale, and periodically for many years before and after, all England, but more especially the metropolis, resounded with the fearful cry of "Plague!" The city was in a great measure depopulated – and in those horrible regions in the vicinity of the Thames, where amid the dark, narrow and filthy lanes and alleys the Demon of Disease was supposed to have had his nativity, Awe, Terror and Superstition were alone to be found stalking abroad.

By authority of the king, such districts were placed *under ban*, and all persons forbidden, under pain of death, to intrude upon their dismal solitude. Yet neither the mandate of the monarch nor the huge barriers erected at the entrances of the streets, nor the prospect of that loathsome death which, with almost absolute certainty, overwhelmed the wretch whom no peril could deter from the adventure prevented the unfurnished and untenanted dwellings from being stripped, by the hand of nightly rapine, of every article such as iron, brass or leadwork which could in any manner be turned to a profitable account.

Above all, it was usually found, upon the annual winter opening of the barriers, that locks, bolts and secret cellars had proved but slender protection to those rich stores of wines and liquors which, in consideration of the risk and trouble of removal, many of the numerous dealers having shops in the neighbourhood had consented to trust, during the period of exile, to so insufficient a security.

But there were very few of the terror-stricken people who attributed these doings to the agency of human hands. Pest spirits, plague goblins and fever demons were the popular imps of mischief – and tales so blood-chilling were hourly told that the whole mass of forbidden buildings was, at length, enveloped in terror as in a shroud, and the plunderer himself was often scared away by the horrors his own depredations had created, leaving the entire vast circuit of prohibited district to gloom, silence, pestilence and death.

It was by one of the terrific barriers already mentioned, and which indicated the region beyond to be under the pest ban, that, in scrambling down an alley, Legs and the worthy Hugh Tarpaulin found their progress suddenly impeded. To return was out of the question, and no time was to be lost, as their pursuers were close upon their heels. With thoroughbred seamen to clamber up the roughly fashioned plankwork was a trifle – and, maddened with the twofold excitement of exercise and liquor, they leapt unhesitatingly down within the enclosure, and, holding on their drunken course with shouts and yellings, were soon bewildered in its noisome and intricate recesses.

Had they not, indeed, been intoxicated beyond moral sense, their reeling footsteps must have been palsied by the horrors of their situation. The air was cold and misty. The paving stones, loosened from their beds, lay in wild disorder amid the tall, rank grass which sprang up around the feet and ankles. Fallen houses choked up the streets. The most fetid and poisonous smells everywhere prevailed – and, by the aid of that ghastly light which, even at midnight, never fails to emanate from a vapoury and pestilential atmosphere, might be discerned lying in the bypaths and alleys, or rotting in the windowless habitations, the carcass of many a nocturnal plunderer arrested by the hand of the plague in the very perpetration of his robbery.

But it lay not in the power of images or sensations, or impediments such as these, to stay the course of men who, naturally brave and, at that time especially, brimful of courage and of "humming stuff", would have reeled, as straight as their condition might have permitted, undauntedly into the very jaws of Death. Onwards, still onwards stalked the grim Legs, making the desolate solemnity echo and re-echo with yells like the terrific war whoop of the Indian – and onwards, still onwards rolled the dumpy Tarpaulin, hanging on to the doublet of his more active companion, and far surpassing the latter's most strenuous exertions in the way of vocal music by bull roarings *in basso*,* from the profundity of his stentorian lungs.

They had now evidently reached the stronghold of the pestilence. Their way at every step or plunge grew more noisome and more horrible – the paths more narrow and more intricate. Huge stones and beams falling momently from the decaying roofs above them gave evidence, by their sullen and heavy descent, of the vast height of the surrounding houses – and while actual exertion became necessary to force a passage through frequent heaps of rubbish, it was by no means seldom that the hand fell upon a skeleton or rested upon a more fleshly corpse.

Suddenly, as the seamen stumbled against the entrance of a tall and ghastly-looking building, a yell more than usually shrill from the throat of the excited Legs was replied to from within in a rapid succession of wild, laughter-like and fiendish shrieks. Nothing daunted at sounds which, of such a nature, at such a time and in such a place might have curdled the very blood in hearts less irrevocably on fire, the drunken couple rushed headlong against the door, burst it open and staggered into the midst of things with a volley of curses.

The room within which they found themselves proved to be the shop of an undertaker, but an open trapdoor in a corner of the floor near the entrance looked down upon a long range of wine cellars, whose depths the occasional sound of bursting bottles proclaimed to be well stored with their appropriate contents. In the middle of the room stood a table – in the centre of which again arose a huge tub of what appeared to be punch. Bottles of various wines and cordials, together with jugs, pitchers and flagons of every shape and quality, were scattered profusely upon the board. Around it, upon coffin tressels, was seated a company of six. This company I will endeavour to delineate one by one.

Fronting the entrance, and elevated a little above his companions, sat a personage who appeared to be the president of the table. His stature was gaunt and tall, and Legs was confounded to behold in him a figure more emaciated than himself. His face was as yellow as saffron – but no feature excepting one alone was sufficiently marked to merit a particular description. This one consisted in a forehead so unusually and hideously lofty as to have the appearance of a bonnet or crown of flesh superadded upon the natural head. His mouth was puckered and dimpled into an expression of ghastly affability, and his eyes, as indeed the eyes of all at table, were glazed over with the fumes of intoxication. This gentleman was clothed from head to foot in a richly embroidered black silk-velvet pall, wrapped negligently around his form after the fashion of a Spanish cloak. His head was stuck full of sable hearse plumes, which he nodded to and fro with a jaunty and knowing air – and, in his right hand, he held a huge human thigh-bone, with which he appeared to have been just knocking down some member of the company for a song.

Opposite him, and with her back to the door, was a lady of no whit the less extraordinary character. Although quite as tall as the person just described, she had no right to complain of his unnatural emaciation. She was evidently in the last stage of a dropsy, and her figure resembled nearly that of the huge puncheon of October beer* which stood, with the head driven in, close by her side in a corner of the chamber. Her face was exceedingly round, red and full, and the same peculiarity, or rather want of peculiarity, attached itself to her countenance which I before mentioned in the case of the president – that is to say, only one feature of her face was sufficiently distinguished to need a separate characterization: indeed, the acute Tarpaulin immediately observed that the same remark might have applied to each individual person of the party: every one of whom seemed to possess a monopoly of some particular portion of physiognomy. With the lady in question, this portion proved to be the mouth. Commencing at the right ear, it swept with a terrific chasm to the left – the short pendants which she wore in either auricle continually bobbing into the aperture. She made, however, every exertion to keep her mouth closed and look dignified, in a dress consisting of a newly starched and ironed shroud coming up close under her chin, with a crimpled ruffle of cambric muslin. At her right hand sat a diminutive young lady whom she appeared to patronize. This delicate little creature, in the trembling of her wasted fingers, in the livid hue of her lips and in the slight hectic spot which tinged her otherwise leaden complexion, gave evident indications of a galloping consumption. An air of extreme *haut ton*,* however, pervaded her whole appearance; she wore in a graceful and dégagé manner a large and beautiful winding sheet of the finest India lawn; her hair hung in ringlets over her neck; a soft smile played about her mouth; but her nose, extremely long, thin, sinuous, flexible and pimpled, hung down far below her under lip – and, in spite of the delicate manner in which she now and then moved it to one side or the other with her tongue, gave to her countenance a somewhat equivocal expression.

Over against her, and upon the left of the dropsical lady, was seated a little puffy, wheezing and gouty old man whose cheeks reposed upon the shoulders of their owner like two huge bladders of Oporto wine. With his arms folded and with one bandaged leg deposited upon the table, he seemed to think himself entitled to some consideration. He evidently prided himself much upon every inch of his personal appearance, but took more especial delight in calling attention to his gaudy-coloured surtout. This, to say the truth, must have cost him no little money, and was made to fit him exceedingly well – being fashioned from one of the curiously embroidered silken covers appertaining to those glorious escutcheons which, in England and elsewhere, are customarily hung up in some conspicuous place upon the dwellings of departed aristocracy.

Next to him, and at the right hand of the president, was a gentleman in long white hose and cotton drawers. His frame shook in a ridiculous manner with a fit of what Tarpaulin called "the horrors". His jaws, which had been newly shaved, were tightly tied up by a bandage of muslin, and his arms, being fastened in a similar way at the wrists, prevented him from helping himself too freely to the liquors upon the table – a precaution rendered necessary, in the opinion of Legs, by the peculiarly sottish and wine-bibbing cast of his visage. A pair of prodigious ears, nevertheless, which it was no doubt found impossible to confine, towered away into the atmosphere of the apartment, and were occasionally pricked up in a spasm at the sound of the drawing of a cork.

Fronting him, sixthly and lastly, was situated a singularly stiff-looking personage, who, being afflicted with paralysis, must, to speak seriously, have felt very ill at ease in his unaccommodating habiliments. He was habited, somewhat uniquely, in a new and handsome mahogany coffin. Its top or headpiece pressed upon the skull of the wearer, and extended over it in the fashion of a hood, giving to the entire face an air of indescribable interest. Armholes had been cut in the sides for the sake not more of elegance than of convenience, but the dress, nevertheless, prevented its proprietor from sitting as erect as his associates – and as he lay reclining against his tressel at an angle of forty-five degrees, a pair of huge goggle eyes rolled up their awful whites towards the ceiling in absolute amazement at their own enormity.

Before each of the party lay a portion of a skull, which was used as a drinking cup. Overhead was suspended a human skeleton by means of a rope tied round one of the legs and fastened to a ring in the ceiling. The other limb, confined by no such fetter, stuck off from the body at right angles, causing the whole loose and rattling frame to dangle and twirl about at the caprice of every occasional puff of wind which found its way into the apartment. In the cranium of this hideous thing lay a quantity of ignited charcoal, which threw a fitful but vivid light over the entire scene – while coffins and other wares appertaining to the shop of an undertaker were piled high up around the room and against the windows, preventing any ray from escaping into the street.

At sight of this extraordinary assembly, and of their still more extraordinary paraphernalia, our two seamen did not conduct themselves with that degree of decorum which might have been expected. Legs, leaning against the wall near which he happened to be standing, dropped his lower jaw still lower than usual, and spread open his eyes to their fullest extent, while Hugh Tarpaulin, stooping down so as to bring his nose upon a level with the table and spreading out a palm upon either knee, burst into a long, loud and obstreperous roar of very ill-timed and immoderate laughter.

Without, however, taking offence at behaviour so excessively rude, the tall president smiled very graciously upon the intruders, nodded to them in a dignified manner with his head of sable plumes and, arising, took each by an arm and led him to a seat which some others of the company had placed in the mean time for his accommodation. Legs to all this offered not the slightest resistance, but sat down as he was directed, while the gallant Hugh, removing his coffin tressel from its station near the head of the table to the vicinity of the little consumptive lady in the winding sheet, plumped down by her side in high glee, and, pouring out a skull of red wine, quaffed it to their better acquaintance. But at this presumption the stiff gentleman in the coffin seemed exceedingly nettled, and serious consequences might have ensued had not the president, rapping upon the table with his truncheon, diverted the attention of all present to the following speech:

"It becomes our duty, upon the present happy occasion—"

"Avast* there!" interrupted Legs, looking very serious. "Avast there a bit, I say, and tell us who the devil ye all are, and what business ye have here, rigged off like the foul fiends, and swilling the snug blue ruin* stowed away for the winter by my honest shipmate, Will Wimble the undertaker!"

At this unpardonable piece of ill breeding, all the original company half-started to their feet and uttered the same rapid succession of wild fiendish shrieks which had before caught the attention of the seamen. The president, however, was the first to recover his composure, and at length, turning to Legs with great dignity, recommenced:

"Most willingly will we gratify any reasonable curiosity on the part of guests so illustrious, unbidden though they be. Know then that in these dominions I am monarch, and here rule with undivided empire under the title of 'King Pest the First'.

"This apartment, which you no doubt profanely suppose to be the shop of Will Wimble the undertaker – a man whom we know not, and whose plebeian appellation has never before this night thwarted our royal ears – this apartment, I say, is the dais chamber* of our palace, devoted to the councils of our kingdom and to other sacred and lofty purposes.

"The noble lady who sits opposite is Queen Pest, our serene consort. The other exalted personages whom you behold are all of our family, and wear the insignia of the blood royal under the respective titles of 'His Grace the Archduke Pest-Iferous', 'His Grace the Duke Pest-Ilential', 'His Grace the Duke Tem-Pest' and 'Her Serene Highness the Archduchess Ana-Pest.'

"As regards," continued he, "your demand of the business upon which we sit here in council, we might be pardoned for replying that it concerns, and concerns *alone*, our own private and regal interest, and is in no manner important to any other than ourself. But in consideration of those rights to which as guests and strangers you may feel yourselves entitled, we will furthermore explain that we are here this night, prepared by deep research and accurate investigation, to examine, analyse and thoroughly determine the indefinable spirit – the incomprehensible qualities and nature – of those inestimable treasures of the palate, the wines, ales and liquors of this goodly metropolis: by so doing, to advance not more our own designs than the true welfare of that unearthly sovereign whose reign is over us all, whose dominions are unlimited, and whose name is 'Death'."

"Whose name is Davy Jones!"* ejaculated Tarpaulin, helping the lady by his side to a skull of liquor, and pouring out a second for himself.

"Profane varlet!" said the president, now turning his attention to the worthy Hugh. "Profane and execrable wretch!... We have said that, in consideration of those rights which, even in thy filthy person, we feel no inclination to violate, we have condescended to make reply to thy rude and unseasonable enquiries. We nevertheless, for your unhallowed intrusion upon our councils, believe it our duty to mulct thee and thy companion in each a gallon of blackstrap* – having imbibed which to the prosperity of our kingdom at a single draught, and upon your bended knees, ye shall be forthwith free either to proceed upon your way or remain and be admitted to the privileges of our table, according to your respective and individual pleasures."

"It would be a matter of utter impossibility," replied Legs, whom the assumptions and dignity of King Pest the First had evidently inspired with some feelings of respect, and who arose and steadied himself by the table as he spoke, "it would, please Your Majesty, be a matter of utter impossibility to stow away in my hold even one fourth part of that same liquor which Your Majesty has just mentioned. To say nothing of the stuffs placed on board in the forenoon by way of ballast, and not to mention the various ales and liquors shipped this evening at various seaports, I have, at present, a full cargo of 'humming stuff' taken in and duly paid for at the sign of the Jolly Tar. You will, therefore, please Your Majesty, be so good as to take the will for the deed, for by no manner of means either can I or will I swallow another drop – least of all a drop of that villainous bilge-water that answers to the hail of 'blackstrap'."

"Belay that!"* interrupted Tarpaulin, astonished not more at the length of his companion's speech than at the nature of his refusal. "Belay that, you lubber!… And I say, Legs, none of your palaver! *My* hull is still light, although I confess you yourself seem to be a little top-heavy – and, as for the matter of your share of the cargo, why, rather than raise a squall, I would find stowage room for it myself, but—"

"This proceeding," interposed the president, "is by no means in accordance with the terms of the mulct or sentence, which is in its nature median, and not to be altered or recalled. The conditions we have imposed must be fulfilled to the letter, and that without a moment's hesitation – in failure of which fulfilment, we decree that you do here be tied neck and heels together, and duly drowned as rebels in yon hogshead of October beer!"

"A sentence!… A sentence!… A righteous and just sentence!… A glorious decree!… A most worthy and upright and holy condemnation!" shouted the Pest family all together. The king elevated his forehead into innumerable wrinkles; the gouty little old man puffed like a pair of bellows; the lady of the winding sheet waved her nose to and fro; the gentleman in the cotton drawers pricked up his ears; she of the shroud gasped like a dying fish; and he of the coffin looked stiff and rolled up his eyes.

"Ugh ugh ugh!" chuckled Tarpaulin, without heeding the general excitation. "Ugh ugh ugh!… Ugh ugh ugh! Ugh!… Ugh ugh ugh!… I was saying," said he, "I was saying when Mr King Pest poked in his marlinspike,* that as for the matter of two or three gallons more or less of blackstrap, it was a trifle to a tight seaboat like myself not overstowed – but when it comes to drinking the health of the Devil (whom God assoilzie)* and going down upon my marrowbones to His ill-favoured Majesty there, whom I know as well as I know myself to be a sinner, to be nobody in the whole world but Tim Hurlygurly the stage player… why, it's quite another guess sort of a thing, and utterly and altogether past my comprehension!"

He was not allowed to finish this speech in tranquillity. At the name Tim Hurlygurly, the whole assembly leapt from their seats.

"Treason!" shouted His Majesty King Pest the First.

"Treason!" said the little man with the gout.

"Treason!" screamed the Archduchess Ana-Pest.

"Treason!" muttered the gentleman with his jaws tied up.

"Treason!" growled he of the coffin.

"Treason! Treason!" shrieked Her Majesty of the mouth, and, seizing by the hinder part of his breeches the unfortunate Tarpaulin, who had just commenced pouring out for himself a skull of liquor, she lifted him high into the air and let him fall without ceremony into the huge open puncheon of his beloved ale. Bobbing up and down for a few seconds like an apple in a bowl of toddy, he at length finally disappeared amid the whirlpool of foam which, in the already effervescent liquor, his struggles easily succeeded in creating.

Not tamely, however, did the tall seaman behold the discomfiture of his companion. Jostling King Pest through the open trap, the valiant Legs slammed the door down upon him with an oath and strode towards the centre of the room. Here, tearing down the skeleton which swung over the table, he laid it about him with so much energy and goodwill that, as the last glimpses of light died away within the apartment, he succeeded in knocking out the brains of the little gentleman with the gout. Rushing then with all his force against the fatal hogshead full of October ale and Hugh Tarpaulin, he rolled it over and over in an instant. Out burst a deluge of liquor so fierce, so impetuous, so overwhelming, that the room was flooded from wall to wall, the loaded table was overturned, the tressels were thrown upon their backs, the tub of punch into the fireplace – and the ladies into hysterics. Piles of death furniture floundered about. Jugs, pitchers and carboys mingled promiscuously in the mêlée, and wicker flagons encountered desperately with bottles of junk. The man with the horrors was drowned upon the spot, the little stiff gentleman floated off in his coffin, and the victorious Legs, seizing by the waist the fat lady in the shroud, rushed out with her into the street and made a beeline for the *Free and Easy*, followed under easy sail by the redoubtable Hugh Tarpaulin, who, having sneezed three or four times, panted and puffed after him with the Archduchess Ana-Pest.

THREE SUNDAYS IN A WEEK*

"You hard-hearted, dunderheaded, obstinate, rusty, crusty, musty, fusty old savage!" said I, in fancy, one afternoon, to my grand-uncle Rumgudgeon, shaking my fist at him in imagination.

Only in imagination. The fact is, some trivial discrepancy *did* exist, just then, between what I said and what I had not the courage to say – between what I did and what I had half a mind to do.

The old porpoise, as I opened the drawing-room door, was sitting with his feet upon the mantelpiece and a bumper of port in his paw, making strenuous efforts to accomplish the ditty

Remplis ton verre vide!
*Vide ton verre plein!**

"My *dear* uncle," said I, closing the door gently and approaching him with the blandest of smiles, "you are always so *very* kind and considerate, and have evinced your benevolence in so many... so *very* many ways... that... that I feel I have only to suggest this little point to you once more to make sure of your full acquiescence."

"Hem!" said he. "Good boy! Go on!"

"I am sure, my dearest uncle" – (you confounded old rascal!) – "that you have no design really, seriously, to oppose my union with Kate. This is merely a joke of yours, I know – Ha ha ha! – how very pleasant you are at times!"

"Ha ha ha!" said he. "Curse you! Yes!"

"To be sure... of course! I *knew* you were jesting. Now, uncle, all that Kate and myself wish at present is that you would oblige us with your advice as... as regards the *time*... *you* know, uncle... in short, when will it be most convenient for yourself that the wedding shall... shall... come off, you know?"

"Come off, you scoundrel!... What do you mean by that?... Better wait till it goes on."

"Ha ha ha!... He he he!... Hi hi hi!... Ho ho ho!... Hu hu hu!... Oh, that's good!... Oh, that's capital... *such* a wit! But all we want just *now*, you know, uncle, is that you would indicate the time precisely."

"Ah!... Precisely?"

"Yes, uncle – that is, if it would be quite agreeable to yourself."

"Wouldn't it answer, Bobby, if I were to leave it at random – sometime within a year or so, for example?... *Must* I say precisely?"

"*If* you please, uncle – precisely."

"Well, then, Bobby, my boy... you're a fine fellow, aren't you?... Since you *will* have the exact time, I'll... why, I'll oblige you for once."

"Dear uncle!"

"Hush, sir!" – drowning my voice. "I'll oblige you for once. You shall have my consent – and the *plum*,* we mus'n't forget the plum... Let me see! When shall it be? Today's Sunday, isn't it? Well, then, you shall be married precisely... *precisely*, now mind!... *when three Sundays come together in a week!* Do you hear me, sir? *What* are you gaping at? I say, you shall have Kate and her plum when three Sundays come together in a week... but not *till* then... you young scapegrace... not *till* then, if I die for it. You know me... *I'm a man of my word*... now be off!" Here he swallowed his bumper of port, while I rushed from the room in despair.

A very "fine old English gentleman" was my grand-uncle Rumgudgeon, but, unlike him of the song,* he had his weak points. He was a little, pursy, pompous, passionate semicircular somebody with a red nose, a thick skull, a long purse and a strong sense of his own consequence. With the best heart in the world, he contrived, through a predominant whim of *contradiction*, to earn for himself, among those who only knew him superficially, the character of a curmudgeon. Like many excellent people, he seemed possessed with a spirit of *tantalization* which might easily, at a casual glance, have been mistaken for malevolence. To every request, a positive "No!" was his immediate answer, but in the end – in the long, long end – there were exceedingly few requests which he refused. Against all attacks upon his purse, he made the most sturdy defence, but the amount extorted from him, at last, was generally in direct ratio with the length of the siege and the stubbornness of the resistance. In charity no one gave more liberally or with a worse grace.

For the fine arts, and especially for the belles-lettres, he entertained a profound contempt. With this he had been inspired by Casimir Périer, whose pert little query, "*À quoi un poète est-il bon?*", he was in the habit of quoting, with a very droll pronunciation, as the *ne plus ultra* of logical wit.* Thus my own inkling for the Muses had excited his entire displeasure. He assured me one day, when I asked him for a new copy of Horace, that the translation of "*Poeta nascitur, non fit*"* was "a nasty poet for nothing fit" – a remark which I took in high dudgeon. His repugnance to "the humanities" had, also, much increased of late by an accidental bias in favour of what he supposed to be natural science. Somebody had accosted him in the street, mistaking him for no less a personage than Doctor Dubble L. Dee,* the lecturer upon quack physics. This set him off at a tangent, and just at the epoch of this story – for story it is getting to be after all – my grand-uncle Rumgudgeon was accessible and pacific only upon points which happened to chime in with the caprioles of the hobby he was riding.* For the rest, he laughed with his arms and legs, and his politics were stubborn and easily understood. He thought, with Horsley, that "the people have nothing to do with the laws but to obey them".*

I had lived with the old gentleman all my life. My parents, in dying, had bequeathed me to him as a rich legacy. I believe the old villain loved me as his own child, nearly if not quite as well as he loved Kate – but it was a dog's existence that he led me, after all. From my first year until my fifth, he obliged me with very regular floggings. From five to fifteen, he threatened me, hourly, with the House of Correction. From fifteen to twenty, not a day passed in which he did not promise to cut me off with a shilling. I was a sad dog, it is true – but then it was a part of my nature – a point of my faith. In Kate, however, I had a firm friend, and I knew it. She was a good girl, and told me very sweetly that I might have her (plum and all) whenever I could badger my grand-uncle Rumgudgeon into the necessary consent. Poor girl!... She was barely fifteen, and, without this consent, her little amount in the funds was not come-at-able until five immeasurable summers had "dragged their slow length along".* What, then, to do? At fifteen, or even at twenty-one (for I had now passed my fifth olympiad),* five years in prospect are very much the same as five hundred. In vain we besieged the old gentleman with importunities. Here was a *pièce de résistance* (as Messieurs Ude and Carême would say)* which suited his perverse fancy to a T. It would have stirred the indignation of Job himself to see how much like an old mouser he behaved to us two poor wretched little mice. In his heart he wished for nothing more ardently than our union. He had made up his mind to this all along. In fact, he would have given ten thousand pounds from his own pocket (Kate's plum was *her own*) if he could have invented anything like an excuse for complying with our very natural wishes. But then we had been so imprudent as to broach the subject *ourselves*. Not to oppose it under such circumstances, I sincerely believe, was not in his power.

I have said already that he had his weak points – but, in speaking of these, I must not be understood as referring to his obstinacy, which was one of his strong points – "*assurement ce n'était pas sa foible*".* When I mention his weakness, I have allusion to a *bizarre* old-womanish superstition which beset him. He was great in dreams, portents *et id genus omne** of rigmarole. He was excessively punctilious, too, upon small points of honour, and, after his own fashion, was a man of his word, beyond doubt. This was, in fact, one of his hobbies. The *spirit* of his vows he made no scruple of setting at naught, but the *letter* was a bond inviolable. Now it was this latter peculiarity in his disposition, of which Kate's ingenuity enabled us one fine day, not long after our interview in the dining room, to take a very unexpected advantage – and, having thus, in the fashion of all modern bards and orators, exhausted in prolegomena all the time at my command and nearly all the room at my disposal, I will sum up in a few words what constitutes the whole pith of the story.

It happened then – so the Fates ordered it – that among the naval acquaintances of my betrothed were two gentlemen who had just set foot upon the shores of England after a year's absence each in foreign travel. In company with these gentlemen, my cousin and I, preconcertedly, paid uncle Rumgudgeon a visit on the afternoon of Sunday, October the tenth – just three weeks after the memorable decision which had so cruelly defeated our hopes. For about half an hour, the conversation ran upon ordinary topics, but at last we contrived, quite naturally, to give it the following turn.

CAPT. PRATT: Well, I have been absent just one year. Just one year today, as I live – let me see!… yes! – this is October the tenth. You remember, Mr Rumgudgeon, I called, this day year to bid you goodbye. And by the way, it *does* seem something like a coincidence, does it not, that our friend, Captain Smitherton here, has been absent exactly a year also – a year today!

SMITHERTON: Yes! Just one year to a fraction. You will remember, Mr Rumgudgeon, that I called with Captain Pratt on this very day last year to pay my parting respects.

UNCLE: Yes, yes, yes... I remember it very well... very queer indeed! Both of you gone just one year. A very strange coincidence, indeed! Just what Doctor Dubble L. Dee would denominate an extraordinary concurrence of events. Doctor Dub—

KATE (*interrupting*): To be sure, Papa, it is something strange – but then Captain Pratt and Captain Smitherton didn't go altogether the same route, and that makes a difference, you know.

UNCLE: I don't know any such thing, you huzzy! How should I? I think it only makes the matter more remarkable, Doctor Dubble L. Dee...

KATE: Why, Papa, Captain Pratt went round Cape Horn, and Captain Smitherton doubled the Cape of Good Hope.

UNCLE: Precisely!... The one went east and the other went west, you jade, and they both have gone quite round the world. By the by, Doctor Dubble L. Dee...

MYSELF (*hurriedly*): Captain Pratt, you must come and spend the evening with us tomorrow... you and Smitherton... you can tell us all about your voyage, and we'll have a game of whist and—

PRATT: Whist, my dear fellow... you forget. Tomorrow will be Sunday. Some other evening—

KATE: Oh, no, fie!... Robert's not *quite* so bad as that. *Today's* Sunday.

UNCLE: To be sure... to be sure!

PRATT: I beg both your pardons – but I can't be so much mistaken. I know tomorrow's Sunday, because—

SMITHERTON (*much surprised*): What *are* you all thinking about? Wasn't *yesterday* Sunday, I should like to know?

ALL: Yesterday indeed! You *are* out!

UNCLE: Today's Sunday, I say – don't *I* know?

PRATT: Oh no!... Tomorrow's Sunday.

SMITHERTON: You are *all* mad – every one of you. I am as positive that yesterday was Sunday as I am that I sit upon this chair.

KATE (*jumping up eagerly*): I see it – I see it all. Papa, this is a judgement upon you, about... about you know what. Let me alone, and I'll explain it all in a minute. It's a very simple thing, indeed. Captain Smitherton says that yesterday was Sunday – so it was: he is right. Cousin Bobby and uncle and I say that today is Sunday – so it is: we are right. Captain Pratt maintains that tomorrow will be Sunday – so it will: he is right, too. The fact is, we are all right, and thus *three Sundays have come together in a week.*

SMITHERTON (*after a pause*): By the by, Pratt, Kate has us completely. What fools we two are! Mr Rumgudgeon, the matter stands thus: the earth, you know, is twenty-four thousand miles in circumference. Now, this globe of the earth turns upon its own axis… revolves… spins round… these twenty-four thousand miles of extent, going from west to east, in precisely twenty-four hours. Do you understand, Mr Rumgudgeon?…

UNCLE: To be sure… to be sure… Doctor Dub—

SMITHERTON (*drowning his voice*): Well, sir – that is at the rate of one thousand miles per hour. Now, suppose that I sail from this position a thousand miles east. Of course I anticipate the rising of the sun here at London by just one hour. I see the sun rise one hour before you do. Proceeding, in the same direction, yet another thousand miles, I anticipate the rising by two hours – another thousand, and I anticipate it by three hours, and so on, until I go entirely round the globe and back to this spot, when, having gone twenty-four thousand miles east, I anticipate the rising of the London sun by no less than twenty-four hours, that is to say, I am a day *in advance* of your time. Understand, eh?

UNCLE: But Double L. Dee—

SMITHERTON (*speaking very loud*): Captain Pratt, on the contrary, when he had sailed a thousand miles west of this position, was an hour, and when he had sailed twenty-four thousand miles west, was twenty-four hours, or one day, *behind* the time at London. Thus, with me, yesterday was Sunday… thus, with you, today is Sunday… and thus, with Pratt, tomorrow will be Sunday. And, what is more, Mr Rumgudgeon, it is positively clear that we are *all right*, for there can be no philosophical reason assigned why the idea of one of us should have preference over that of the other.

UNCLE: My eyes!… Well, Kate… well, Bobby!… this is a judgement upon me, as you say. But I am a man of my word – *mark that!* You shall have her, boy (plum and all), when you please. Done up, by Jove! Three Sundays all in a row! I'll go and take Dubble L. Dee's opinion upon *that*.

LIONIZING*

> …all people went
> Upon their ten toes in wild wonderment.*
> – Bishop Hall's *Satires*

I am – that is to say, I *was* – a great man, but I am neither the author of Junius nor the man in the mask,* for my name, I believe, is Robert Jones, and I was born somewhere in the city of Fum-Fudge.

The first action of my life was the taking hold of my nose with both hands. My mother saw this and called me a genius – my father wept for joy and presented me with a treatise on Nosology.* This I mastered before I was breeched.

I now began to feel my way in the science, and soon came to understand that, provided a man had a nose sufficiently conspicuous, he might, by merely following it, arrive at a lionship.* But my attention was not confined to theories alone. Every morning I gave my proboscis a couple of pulls and swallowed a half-dozen of drams.

When I came of age, my father asked me, one day, if I would step with him into his study.

"My son," said he, when we were seated, "what is the chief end of your existence?"

"My father," I answered, "it is the study of Nosology."

"And what, Robert," he enquired, "is Nosology?"

"Sir," I said, "it is the Science of Noses."

"And can you tell me," he demanded, "what is the meaning of a nose?"

"A nose, my father," I replied, greatly softened, "has been variously defined by about a thousand different authors." Here I pulled out my watch. "It is now noon or thereabouts – we shall have time enough to get through with them all before midnight. To commence, then: the nose, according to Bartholinus,* is that protuberance… that bump… that excrescence… that—"

"Will do, Robert," interrupted the good old gentleman. "I am thunderstruck at the extent of your information… I am positively… upon my soul." Here he closed his eyes and placed his hand upon his heart. "Come here!" Here he took me by the arm. "Your education may now be considered as finished: it is high time you should scuffle for yourself – and you cannot do a better thing than merely follow your nose… so… so… so…" – here he kicked me downstairs and out of the door – "so get out of my house, and God bless you!"

As I felt within me the divine afflatus, I considered this accident rather fortunate than otherwise. I resolved to be guided by the paternal advice. I determined to follow my nose. I gave it a pull or two upon the spot, and wrote a pamphlet on Nosology forthwith.

All Fum-Fudge was in an uproar.

"Wonderful genius!" said the *Quarterly*.

"Superb physiologist!" said the *Westminster*.

"Clever fellow!" said the *Foreign*.

"Fine writer!" said the *Edinburgh*.

"Profound thinker!" said the *Dublin*.

"Great man!" said *Bentley*.

"Divine soul!" said *Fraser*.

"One of us!" said *Blackwood*.

"Who can he be?" said Mrs Bas-Bleu.*

"What can he be?" said big Miss Bas-Bleu.

"Where can he be?" said little Miss Bas-Bleu. But I paid these people no attention whatever – I just stepped into the shop of an artist.

The Duchess of Bless-my-Soul* was sitting for her portrait; the Marquis of So-and-So was holding the Duchess's poodle; the Earl of This-and-That was flirting with her salts; and His Royal Highness of Touch-me-Not was leaning upon the back of her chair.

I approached the artist and turned up my nose.

"Oh, beautiful!" sighed Her Grace.

"Oh my!" lisped the Marquis.

"Oh, shocking!" groaned the Earl.

"Oh, abominable!" growled His Royal Highness.

"What will you take for it?" asked the artist.

"For his *nose*!" shouted Her Grace.

"A thousand pounds," said I, sitting down.

"A thousand pounds?" enquired the artist musingly.

"A thousand pounds," said I.

"Beautiful!" said he, entranced.

"A thousand pounds," said I.

"Do you warrant it?" he asked, turning the nose to the light.

"I do," said I, blowing it well.

"Is it *quite* original?" he enquired, touching it with reverence.

"Humph!" said I, twisting it to one side.

"Has *no* copy been taken?" he demanded, surveying it through a microscope.

"None," said I, turning it up.

"*Admirable!*" he ejaculated, thrown quite off his guard by the beauty of the manoeuvre.

"A thousand pounds," said I.

"A *thousand* pounds?" said he.

"Precisely," said I.

"A thousand *pounds*?" said he.

"Just so," said I.

"You shall have them," said he. "What a piece of virtu!"* So he drew me a cheque upon the spot, and took a sketch of my nose. I engaged rooms in Jermyn Street,* and sent Her Majesty the ninety-ninth edition of the *Nosology*, with a portrait of the proboscis... That sad little rake, the Prince of Wales, invited me to dinner.

We were all lions and *recherchés*.*

There was a modern Platonist. He quoted Porphyry, Iamblichus, Plotinus, Proclus, Hierocles, Maximus Tyrius and Syrianus.*

There was a human-perfectibility man. He quoted Turgot, Price, Priestley, Condorcet,* De Staël* and the "Ambitious Student in Ill Health".*

There was Sir Positive Paradox. He observed that all fools were philosophers, and that all philosophers were fools.

There was Aestheticus Ethix. He spoke of fire, unity and atoms; bipart and pre-existent soul; affinity and discord; primitive intelligence and homoeomeria.*

There was Theologos Theology. He talked of Eusebius and Arianus; heresy and the Council of Nice;* Puseyism and consubstantialism;* *homoousios* and *homoiousios*.*

There was fricassée from the Rocher de Cancale.* He mentioned Muriton of red tongue;* cauliflowers with velouté sauce; veal *à la Sainte-Menehould*;* marinade *à la Saint-Florentin*;* and orange jellies *en mosaïque*.*

There was Bibulus O'Bumper. He touched upon Latour* and Markbrünnen;* upon *mousseux* and Chambertin;* upon Richebourg and Saint-Georges;* upon Haubrion,* Leonville* and Médoc;* upon Barac and Preignac;* upon Graves, upon Sauternes, upon Lafite and upon Saint-Péray. He shook his head at Clos de Vougeot,* and told, with his eyes shut, the difference between sherry and amontillado.

There was Signor Tintontintino from Florence. He discoursed of Cimabue, Arpino, Carpaccio* and Argostino* – of the gloom of Caravaggio,* of the amenity of Albano,* of the colours of Titian, of the vrows of Rubens,* and of the waggeries of Jan Steen.*

There was the president of the Fum-Fudge University. He was of opinion that the moon was called Bendis in Thrace, Bubastis in Egypt, Dian in Rome and Artemis in Greece.* There was a Grand Turk from Stamboul.* He could not help thinking that the angels were horses, cocks and bulls; that somebody in the sixth heaven had seventy thousand heads; and that the earth was supported by a sky-blue cow with an incalculable number of green horns.*

There was Delphinus Polyglott. He told us what had become of the eighty-three lost tragedies of Aeschylus;* of the fifty-four orations of Isaeus; of the three hundred and ninety-one speeches of Lysias;* of the hundred and eighty treatises of Theophrastus;* of the eighth book of the conic sections of Apollonius;* of Pindar's hymns and dithyrambics;* and of the five-and-forty tragedies of Homer Junior.*

There was Ferdinand Fitz-Fossillus Feltspar. He informed us all about internal fires and tertiary formations; about aeriforms, fluidiforms and solidiforms; about quartz and marl; about schist and schorl; about gypsum and trap; about talc and calc; about blende and hornblende; about mica slate and puddingstone; about cyanite and lepidolite; about haematite and tremolite; about antimony and calcedony; about manganese and whatever you please.

There was myself. I spoke of myself... of myself, of myself, of myself... of Nosology, of my pamphlet and of myself. I turned up my nose and I spoke of myself.

"Marvellous clever man!" said the prince.

"Superb!" said his guests – and next morning Her Grace of Bless-my-Soul paid me a visit.

"Will you go to Almack's,* pretty creature?" she said, tapping me under the chin.

"Upon honour," said I.

"Nose and all?" she asked.

"As I live," I replied.

"Here then is a card, my life. Shall I say you *will* be there?"

"Dear duchess, with all my heart."

"Pshaw, no!... But with all your nose?"

"Every bit of it, my love," said I. So I gave it a twist or two, and found myself at Almack's.

The rooms were crowded to suffocation.

"He is coming!" said somebody on the staircase.

"He is coming!" said somebody further up.

"He is coming!" said somebody further still.

"He is come!" exclaimed the duchess. "He is come, the little love!" – and, seizing me firmly by both hands, she kissed me thrice upon the nose.

A marked sensation immediately ensued.

"*Diavolo!*" cried Count Capricornuti.*

"*Dios guarda!*"* muttered Don Stiletto.

"*Mille tonnerres!*"* ejaculated the Prince de Grenouille.*

"*Tausend Teufel!*"* growled the Elector of Bluddennuff.

It was not to be borne. I grew angry. I turned short upon Bluddennuff.

"Sir!" said I to him. "You are a baboon."

"Sir," he replied, after a pause, "*Donner und Blitzen!*"*

This was all that could be desired. We exchanged cards. At Chalk Farm, the next morning, I shot off his nose* – and then called upon my friends.

"*Bête!*"* said the first.

"Fool!" said the second.

"Dolt!" said the third.

"Ass!" said the fourth.

"Ninny!" said the fifth.

"Noodle!" said the sixth.

"Be off!" said the seventh.

At all this I felt mortified, and so called upon my father.

"Father," I asked, "what is the chief end of my existence?"

"My son," he replied, "it is still the study of Nosology – but in hitting the elector upon the nose you have overshot your mark. You have a fine nose, it is true, but then Bluddennuff has none. You are damned, and he has become the hero of the day. I grant you that in Fum-Fudge the greatness of a lion is in proportion to the size of his proboscis, but – good Heavens! – there is no competing with a lion who has no proboscis at all."

ABBREVIATIONS

EUR Edgar Allan Poe, *Eureka* (London: Alma Classics, 2018)

JLG (Also known as the "J. Lorimer Graham copy of *Tales*") Poe's personal copy of TA1, with pencil corrections in his hand

PW1 *The Works of the Late Edgar Allan Poe*, ed. Rufus Wilmot Griswold, Vol. 1, *Tales* (New York: J.S. Redfield, 1850)

PW2 *The Works of the Late Edgar Allan Poe*, ed. Rufus Wilmot Griswold, Vol. 2, *Poems and Miscellanies* (New York: J.S. Redfield, 1850)

PW4 *The Works of the Late Edgar Allan Poe*, ed. Rufus Wilmot Griswold, Vol. 4, *Arthur Gordon Pym, etc.* (New York: Redfield, 1856)

TA1 Edgar Allan Poe, *Tales* (New York: Wiley and Putnam, 1845)

TGA Edgar Allan Poe, *Tales of the Grotesque and Arabesque* (Philadelphia: Lea and Blanchard, 1840)

TH Edgar Allan Poe, *Tales of Horror* (London: Alma Classics, 2016)

NOTES

p. 3, *The Unparalleled Adventure of One Hans Pfaall*: First published in the *Southern Literary Messenger* (June 1835) and later revised by the author and reprinted in PW1, from where our text is taken. Poe derived most of the astronomical details – at times quoting verbatim – from *The Cyclopædia, or Universal Dictionary of Arts, Sciences, and Literature* (1802–20), a thirty-nine-volume encyclopedia compiled by Abraham Rees (1743–1825), and from Sir John Herschel's (1792–1871) *Treatise on Astronomy* (1833), as well as other scientific works and journals of the time.

p. 3, *Tom O'Bedlam's Song*: The epigraph is from the last stanza of an anonymous poem composed at the beginning of the seventeenth century, which Poe appears to have taken from Isaac D'Israeli's (1766–1848) work *Curiosities of Literature*, originally published in five volumes between 1791 and 1823.

p. 3, *the Exchange in the well-conditioned city of Rotterdam*: The Rotterdam Old Stock Exchange (Beurs), which stood from 1736 to 1940 on Westnieuwland, on the north bank of the Blaak canal. The square in front of its eastern entrance was called Beursplein.

p. 4, *Mynheer*: A polite or respectful form of address to a Dutchman; "Mister".

p. 4, *to the tune of 'Betty Martin'*: A reference to 'Hey Betty Martin' (also known as 'High Betty Martin' and 'Pretty Betty Martin', among other titles), an American song from the mid-eighteenth century sung and played by the drummers in the War of 1812 between the United States and the United Kingdom and its allies.

p. 5, *vrow*: A Dutch matron or goodwife.

p. 7, *Duns*: Debt collectors.

p. 8, *Professor Encke of Berlin*: The German astronomer Johann Franz Encke (1791–1865), director of the Berlin observatory.

p. 9, *a moiety*: A half, one of two equal parts.

p. 9, *caoutchouc*: Unvulcanized natural rubber.

p. 10, *slow match*: "Material, such as hempen cord, that is made or treated so as to burn very slowly" (*OED*).

p. 10, *M. Grimm's improvements... atmospheric air*: The reference to Grimm is fictional.

p. 11, *It was the first of April*: As in 'Mellonta Tauta' (see p. 183), the balloon ride start on April Fool's Day.

p. 12, *unslacked lime*: Another name for calcium oxide, or quicklime, an alkaline powder obtained by heating limestone. When it is "slaked", that is, mixed with water, the resulting exothermic reaction would, for instance, enable Pfaall to heat water and provisions without an open flame.

p. 12, *pemmican*: A paste made from pounded dried meat with melted fat and other ingredients, and condensed into a cake. It was originally made by some North American tribes and was later adopted by explorers due to its high nutritional value and transportability.

p. 14, *stupid*: Stupefied.

p. 15, *close-hauled*: That is, with its sails set as close to the wind as possible, typically at an angle of between thirty and forty-five degrees relative to the wind direction.

p. 15, *perigee*: The point in the orbit of the moon (or other celestial body) at which it is nearest to the earth.

p. 16, *Cotopaxi*: A volcanic mountain in Ecuador, reaching a height of 5,897 m.

p. 16, *ponderable*: Having detectable weight or mass.

p. 16, *the aeronautic expedition of Messieurs Gay-Lussac and Biot*: In July 1804, Joseph Louis Gay-Lussac (1778–1850) and Jean-Baptiste Biot (1774–1862) made a widely publicized hydrogen-balloon ascent to measure how the earth's magnetic field varies with elevation. Later that year, Gay-Lussac took a solo ride in a balloon to investigate the earth's atmosphere, reaching a height of 7,016 m (23,018 ft).

p. 17, *perihelion*: The point in the orbit of a comet (or other celestial body) at which it is closest to the sun; the opposite of aphelion.

p. 17, *justified*: Amended from "justifiable".

p. 17, *M. Valz*: The French astronomer Benjamin Valz (1787–1867), known for his study of comets.

p. 17, *"the zodiacal light"*: The zodiacal light is probably what the ancients called *trabes*. "*Emicant trabes quos docos vocant*" (Pliny, lib. 2, p. 26) [POE'S NOTE]. Poe appears to have taken the note from Rees's *Cyclopædia* (see first note to p. 3), which differs from Pliny, who has: "*Emicant et trabes simili modo, quas δοκοὺς vocant*" ("The *trabes* also, which are named δοκοὶ, shine in the same manner"), *Natural History* II, 26. It is supposed that the *trabes* for the most part refer to the aurora borealis.

p. 19, *It has been observed... the altitude observed*: Since the original publication of 'Hans Pfaall', I find that Mr Green, of Nassau-balloon notoriety, and other late aeronauts, deny the assertions of Humboldt in this respect, and speak of a decreasing inconvenience – precisely in accordance with the theory here urged [POE'S NOTE]. The references are to Charles Green (1785–1870), the most famous British balloonist of the nineteenth century, who set a long-distance record of 480 miles in 1836 by flying overnight in his balloon from London to the German town of Weilburg in the Duchy of Nassau, and to the German naturalist and explorer Alexander von Humboldt (1769–1859), who in 1802, in the company of the French explorer Aimé Bonpland (1773–1858) the Ecuadorian nobleman Carlos Montúfar (1780–1816) and a party of indigenous guides, climbed the extinct volcano Chimborazo, reaching an altitude of almost 20,000 feet, a world record at the time – higher even than the heights attained by balloon ascensions.

p. 21, *rencontre*: "Rencounter" (French).

p. 24, *gum-elastic bag*: That is, a bag made of gum elastic, or caoutchouc (see second note to p. 9).

p. 33, *whose apparent diameter subtended... sixty-five seconds*: That is, from the perspective of the balloon, the angle that would be formed at the intersection of two straight lines drawn from opposite points on the circumference of the circle would be a tiny fraction of a single degree. (A second is one sixtieth of a minute, which in turn is one sixtieth of a degree.)

p. 35, *the line of apsides*: The apsides are the two points on the orbit of a celestial body that are nearest to (perigee) or farthest from (apogee) the body round which it moves.

p. 37, *bouleversement*: "Upheaval" (French).

p. 37, *the Campi Phlegræi*: The Latin name (literally meaning "Burning Fields") for the Phlegraean Fields, a large volcanic area west of Naples.

p. 38, *Mr Schröter, of Lilienthal*: The German astronomer Johann Hieronymus Schröter (1745–1816), who was chief magistrate and district governor of Lilienthal, a town in Lower Saxony.

p. 38, *Paris feet*: A Paris foot was the equivalent of 12.785 English inches.

p. 38, *My ideas... near the limb*: Hevelius writes that he has several times found, in skies perfectly clear, when even stars of the sixth and seventh magnitude were conspicuous, that at the same altitude of the moon, at the same elongation from the earth, and with one and the same excellent telescope, the moon and its *maculæ* did not appear equally lucid at all times. From the circumstances of the observation, it is evident that the cause of this phenomenon is not either in our air, in the tube, in the moon or in the eye of the spectator, but must be looked for in something (an atmosphere?) existing about the moon.

Cassini frequently observed Saturn, Jupiter and the fixed stars, when approaching the moon to occultation, to have their circular figure changed into an oval one – and, in other occultations, he found no alteration of figure at all. Hence it might be supposed that at some times, and not at others, there is a dense matter encompassing the moon wherein the rays of the stars are refracted [POE'S NOTE]. *Philosophical Transactions* is a scientific journal published by London's Royal Society since 1665. The German astronomer Johannes Hevelius (1611–87) was the founder of lunar topography; the Italian-French mathematician and astronomer Giovanni Domenico Cassini (1625–1712) was the first to create a scientific map of the moon. "*Maculæ*" (Latin for "spots"), more commonly known as "*maria*" (Latin plural of "*mare*" – "sea"), are dark plains on the surface of the moon.

p. 40, *in vacuo*: "In a vacuum" (Latin).

p. 42, *bottle conjuror*: A fraudster. The term refers to a famous theatrical hoax perpetrated in January 1749 at London's Haymarket Theatre, where an unnamed magician who claimed to be able to insert himself into an empty wine bottle failed to appear for a widely advertised performance, resulting in a riot that all but destroyed the theatre.

p. 42, *the celebrated 'Moon Story' of Mr Locke... New York Sun*: A reference to the "Great Moon Hoax" of 1835, a series of articles published in the columns of the New York *Sun* in August and September 1835 about the supposed discovery of life on the moon by the English astronomer Sir John Herschel (and his fictitious companion Andrew Grant) through an immense telescope whose lens measured 24 feet. The articles were later attributed to a *Sun* reporter, Richard Adams Locke (1800–71). Poe's first version of 'Hans Pfaall' was published in the *Southern Literary Messenger* in June 1835.

p. 43, *Papaver rhoeas*: The scientific name of the common poppy.

p. 43, *glasshouse*: Glassworks.

p. 43, *Blunt's Lunar Chart*: This cannot be traced, and is most probably part of Locke's hoax, Edmund March Blunt (1770–1862) being a renowned hydrographer and navigator who published numerous charts of the American coasts.

p. 44, *Mare Nubium, Mare Tranquillitatis, Mare Fœcunditatis*: "Sea of Clouds, Sea of Tranquillity, Sea of Fecundity" (Latin).

p. 44, *a literal copy of Peter Wilkins's account... flying islanders*: A reference to *The Life and Adventures of Peter Wilkins, a Cornish Man*, a 1751 work by Robert Paltock (1697–1767), in which the hero, after being shipwrecked near the South Pole, visits the land of Normnbdsgrsutt, the country of the Glumms and Gawrys, flying men and women, respectively.

p. 44, *Edinburgh Journal of Science*: A scientific journal founded in 1824, later published, between 1832 and 1840, under the title *The London and Edinburgh Philosophical Magazine and Journal of Science*.

p. 45, *Brewster*: The English scientist and inventor Sir David Brewster (1781–1868).

p. 45, *The Earl of Rosse telescope, lately constructed in England*: The so-called "Leviathan of Parsonstown", or "Rosse six-foot telescope", a reflective telescope with a 72-inch (*c.*1.83 m) aperture, was built between 1842 and 1845 by William Parsons, 3rd Earl of Rosse (1800–67), on his estate, Birr Castle, at Parsonstown (now Birr) in Ireland. It remained the largest telescope in the world until the construction of the 100-inch Hooker Telescope in California in 1917.

p. 45, *L'HOMME DANS LA LVNE... Consultations*: "The Man in the Moon, or The Chimeric Voyage to the Country of the Moon, recently discovered by Dominique Gonzales, Spanish Adventurer, also known as 'The Flying Horserider'. Translated by J.B.D. [Published] At Paris, by François Piot, near the Fontaine Saint-Benoît; and by J. Guignard, by the first column of the Grand-Salle du Palais [de la Cité], near the Rooms for [legal] Consultation". The book is a 1648 French translation, by Jean Baudoin (1590–1650), of *The Man in the Moone, or A Discourse of a Voyage Thither, by Domingo Gonsales*, a work by the English historian Francis Godwin (1562–1633) but purporting to be by the individual named in the title, probably written during the 1620s. The French quotations have been slightly amended to match the text of the original title page and translator's note.

p. 46, *I'en ay eu... de la mienne*: "I had the original from Mr D'Avisson, a doctor, among those best versed today in the field of literature and, above all, of natural philosophy. I owe him this favour, among others: of having entrusted into my hands not only this book in English, but also a manuscript by Sir Thomas d'Anan, a Scottish Gentleman commendable for his virtue, on whose version I confess to have drawn the plan for my own" (French).

p. 46, *Gil Blas*: A picaresque novel by the French author Alain-René Lesage (1668–1747) published between 1715 and 1735 – one of the most popular books of the eighteenth century.

p. 46, *Señor*: Changed, here and elsewhere in the story, from "Signor" in the original.

p. 47, *For I admit the opinion of Copernicus... those of the zodiac*: The distinction made is between rotation on the earth's polar axis and on the axis of an imaginary sphere extrapolated from the circle created by the sun's apparent path through the skies during the course of a year, known as the ecliptic. (The "zodiac" is the belt of stars and other celestial bodies within around 8° either side of the ecliptic; hence, "poles of the zodiac".) In the former (true) case, the planet is tilted at an angle of 23.4° from the perpendicular represented by the latter. For reasons that are unclear, the author evidently believes that, in the former scenario, he would remain stationary while the earth revolved beneath him; the fact that he is moving with the earth confirms his belief in rotation around the ecliptic axis. He attributes a belief in rotation around the "poles of the zodiac" to the Polish astronomer Nicolaus Copernicus (1473–1543), who in fact believed that the earth rotated daily on its polar axis, as well as that it orbited the sun (the discovery for which he is most famous).

p. 47, *"I must now declare... have since forgotten"*: For the French text, see pp. 76–79 of the above-mentioned 1648 edition of *L'Homme dans la Lune*.

p. 47, *That of Bergerac*: *L'Autre Monde: ou les États et Empires de la Lune* ("The Other World, or The States and Empires of the Moon"), a work by the French novelist and playwright Cyrano de Bergerac (1619–55), published posthumously in 1657.

p. 47, *In the third volume... of the kind in question*: A reference to an article published in the *American Quarterly Review* (Vol. 3, March and June 1828, pp. 62–88), a literary journal published in Philadelphia between 1827 and 1837. The piece is a criticism of *A Voyage to the Moon, with Some Account of the Manners and Customs, Science and Philosophy, of the People of Morosofia, and Other Lunarians*, an 1827 science-fiction novel by the American author George Tucker (1775–1861), published under the pseudonym "Joseph Atterley".

p. 47, *'The Flight of Thomas O'Rourke'*: A slightly incorrect reference to 'Daniel O'Rourke's Wonderful Voyage to the Moon', a short story by the Irish journalist William Maginn (1794–1842), first appearing in an anonymous 1825 collection, *The Fairy Legends and Traditions of the South of Ireland*, published in London by John Murray.

p. 49, *Mesmeric Revelation*: First published in the *Columbian Magazine* (August 1844) and later reprinted in TA1, from where our text is taken. According to the theory of animal magnetism, or mesmerism, developed by the German physician Franz Anton Mesmer (1734–1815), all living creatures possess an invisible natural fluid, identifiable with magnetic-field forces, which can be influenced and controlled, for example by hypnosis.

p. 49, *sleepwaker*: A mesmerized (hypnotized) person.

p. 49, *phthisis*: Pulmonary tuberculosis.

p. 49, *instant*: Of the current month.

p. 50, *psychal*: Spiritual.

p. 50, *Cousin*: A reference to the works of the French spiritualist philosopher Victor Cousin (1792–1867).

p. 50, *Charles Elwood of Mr Brownson*: *Charles Elwood, or The Infidel Converted*, an 1840 semi-autobiographical novel by the American activist and preacher Orestes Augustus Brownson (1803–76).

p. 50, *the government of Trinculo*: In Shakespeare's *Tempest*, Antonio says of Gonzalo's (not Trinculo's) description of his ideal society: "The latter end of his commonwealth forgets the beginning" (Act II, Sc. 1, l. 164).

p. 55, *the worm and the butterfly*: A metaphor for body and soul: in Greek the word "psyche" means both "butterfly" and "soul".

p. 57, *from Azrael's hand*: In the Islamic tradition, Azrael is the angel of death.

p. 59, *The Thousand-and-Second Tale of Scheherazade*: First published in *Godey's Lady's Book* (February 1845) and later reprinted, with some authorial changes, in PW1, from where our text is taken. Scheherazade is the heroine of the frame story for a cycle of Arabic tales known as the *Thousand and One Nights* or *Arabian Nights*, which includes those of Aladdin, Ali Baba and Sinbad the Sailor. As Poe goes on to explain in his long preamble, the frame story tells how Scheherazade, newly married to a king who killed each of his wives on the first night of their marriage, defers her own execution night after night by beginning an exotic story of love, magic, adventure or suchlike one evening and refusing to finish it till the next. After a thousand and one nights, the king, enchanted by the stories, agrees to lift the death sentence.

p. 59, *the Tellmenow Isitsöornot... Zohar of Simeon Jochaides*: The first title (a humorous compression of the words "Tell me now, Is it so or not") is fictional, whereas the *Zohar*, a foundational thirteenth-century work of cabbala, is a collection of esoteric material attributed to Shimon bar Yochai (Jochaides), who is thought to have lived between 90 and 160 AD.

p. 59, *"Curiosities of American Literature"*: A work compiled by the American poet, anthologist and editor Rufus Wilmot Griswold (1815–57), a lifelong literary rival of Poe, and published as an appendix to an 1844 American edition of D'Israeli's *Curiosities of Literature* (see second note to p. 3).

p. 60, *bowstrung*: That is, strangled using a bowstring, as capital offenders were traditionally executed in Turkey.

p. 61, *being lineally descended... garden of Eden*: The reference here is ultimately to a passage in the Babylonian Talmud, an ancient collection of Jewish laws and traditions compiled by rabbinic scholars around the fifth century AD. The section concerning marriage laws, called Kiddushin, contains a debate about the way in which various traits were distributed across the world: "Ten kabs of speech descended to the world: women took nine, and the rest of the world, one" (49b). ("Kab" was an ancient Hebrew measure of volume, roughly equivalent to two quarts.) There is evidence from the periodicals of Poe's day that this had become something of a running joke. See, for example, "The Ladies", an article published in the *New-York Mirror* on 30th May 1835: "The Rabbins ought to be ashamed of themselves for their scandalous libel, in saying that ten baskets of chatter were let down from heaven, and that the women appropriated nine of them."

p. 61, *"Le mieux...est l'ennemi du bien"*: "Perfect is the enemy of good" (French). The expression can be found in *La Bégueule* ("The Prudish Woman", l. 2), a 1772 moral poem by the French philosopher Voltaire (pseudonym of François-Marie Arouet, 1694–1778).

p. 65, *a colony of little things like caterpillars*: The corallites [POE'S NOTE]. Corallites are fossil corals.

p. 66, *the forests were of solid stone... to cut them down*: "One of the most remarkable natural curiosities in Texas is a petrified forest near the head of

Pasigono River. It consists of several hundred trees, in an erect position, all turned to stone. Some trees, now growing, are partly petrified. This is a startling fact for natural philosophers, and must cause them to modify the existing theory of petrification." – Kennedy.

This account, at first discredited, has since been corroborated by the discovery of a completely petrified forest near the head waters of the Cheyenne, or Chienne, River, which has its source in the Black Hills of the Rocky chain.

There is scarcely, perhaps, a spectacle on the surface of the globe more remarkable, either in a geological or picturesque point of view, than that presented by the petrified forest near Cairo. The traveller, having passed the tombs of the caliphs, just beyond the gates of the city, proceeds to the southward, nearly at right angles to the road across the desert to Suez, and, after having travelled some ten miles up a low, barren valley, covered with sand, gravel and seashells, fresh as if the tide had retired but yesterday, crosses a low range of sandhills which has for some distance run parallel to his path. The scene now presented to him is beyond conception singular and desolate. A mass of fragments of trees, all converted into stone, and, when struck by his horse's hoof, ringing like cast iron, is seen to extend itself for miles and miles around him, in the form of a decayed and prostrate forest. The wood is of a dark-brown hue, but retains its form in perfection, the pieces being from one to fifteen feet in length, and from half a foot to three feet in thickness, strewed so closely together, as far as the eye can reach, that an Egyptian donkey can scarcely thread its way through amongst them, and so natural that, were it in Scotland or Ireland, it might pass without remark for some enormous drained bog on which the exhumed trees lay rotting in the sun. The roots and rudiments of the branches are, in many cases, nearly perfect, and in some the wormholes eaten under the bark are readily recognizable. The most delicate of the sap vessels, and all the finer portions of the centre of the wood, are perfectly entire, and bear to be examined with the strongest magnifiers. The whole are so thoroughly silicified as to scratch glass, and are capable of receiving the highest polish. – *Asiatic Magazine* [POE'S NOTE]. The first paragraph is from *Texas: The Rise, Progress, and Prospects of the Republic of Texas* (Book I, Chapter 5) by the Irish author William Kennedy (1799–1871), first published in London in 1841, although Poe's source was an article headed "Prairie and Mountain Life: The Petrified Forest", published in the *St Louis Weekly Reveille* on 18th November 1844, for which Kennedy's quotation served as an epigraph. The information in Poe's second paragraph was also taken from this article. The third paragraph is taken verbatim from the *Asiatic Journal*, series 3, Vol. 3, No. 359 (August 1844).

p. 66, *a cave… fish that had no eyes*: The Mammoth Cave of Kentucky [POE'S NOTE]. Mammoth Cave, in Kentucky, is the longest known cave system in the world.

p. 66, *a lofty mountain... sixty miles long*: In Iceland, 1783 [POE'S NOTE]. The reference is to the largest recorded lava flow in history, produced by the Laki volcanic fissure in Iceland in 1783.

p. 66, *so vast a quantity of ashes... our eyes*: "During the eruption of Hecla in 1766, clouds of this kind produced such a degree of darkness that, at Glaumba, which is more than fifty leagues from the mountain, people could only find their way by groping. During the eruption of Vesuvius in 1794, at Caserta, four leagues distant, people could only walk by the light of torches. On the first of May 1812, a cloud of volcanic ashes and sand, coming from a volcano in the island of St Vincent, covered the whole of Barbadoes, spreading over it so intense a darkness that, at midday, in the open air, one could not perceive the trees or other objects near him, or even a white handkerchief placed at the distance of six inches from the eye." – Murray, p. 215, Phil. Edit. [POE'S NOTE]. The information contained in this note (as well as the previous one and the next one) is from *An Encyclopaedia of Geography* ("Philadelphia Edition", 1843) by the Scottish geographer Hugh Murray (1779–1846).

p. 66, *a great lake... luxuriant trees*: "In the year 1790, in the Caraccas, during an earthquake, a portion of the granite soil sank and left a lake eight hundred yards in diameter, and from eighty to a hundred feet deep. It was a part of the forest of Aripao, which sank, and the trees remained green for several months under the water." Murray, p. 221 [POE'S NOTE]. For Murray, see previous note. Major earthquakes struck Caracas in Venezuela in 1766 and 1812, but not in 1790.

p. 66, *so dense as to sustain iron or steel... does feathers*: The hardest steel ever manufactured may, under the action of a blowpipe, be reduced to an impalpable powder, which will float readily in the atmospheric air [POE'S NOTE].

p. 66, *the most magnificent region in the whole world*: The region of the Niger. See *Simmond's Colonial Magazine* [POE'S NOTE]. Poe's source for this passage is a series of articles by Richard Mouat entitled "A Narrative of the Niger Expedition", published in *Simmond's Colonial Magazine* between June and September 1844.

p. 67, *myriads of monstrous animals... "the caverns of death"*: The *Myrmeleon* – lion-ant. The term "monster" is equally applicable to small abnormal things and to great, while such epithets as "vast" are merely comparative. The cavern of the myrmeleon is *vast* in comparison with the hole of the common red ant. A grain of silex is, also, a "rock" [POE'S NOTE].

p. 67, *vegetables that grew... in the air*: The *Epidendron*, *Flos Aeris*, of the family of the *Orchideæ*, grows with merely the surface of its roots attached to a tree or other object, from which it derives no nutriment – subsisting altogether upon air [POE'S NOTE]. Poe means *Epidendrum flos-aeris*, known today as *Arachnis flos-aeris*, and popularly called the "scorpion orchid".

p. 67, *others that sprang from the substance of other vegetables*: The parasites, such as the wonderful *Rafflesia arnaldii* [POE'S NOTE]. The correct spelling is *Rafflesia arnoldii*.

p. 67, *others that derived their substance from the bodies of living animals*: Schouw advocates a class of plants that grow upon living animals – the *Plantæ epizoæ*. Of this class are the *Fuci* and *Algæ*.

Mr J.B. Williams, of Salem, Mass., presented the National Institute with an insect from New Zealand, with the following description: "The Hotté, a decided caterpillar, or worm, is found growing at the foot of the Rata tree, with a plant growing out of its head. This most peculiar and most extraordinary insect travels up both the Rata and Perriri trees, and, entering into the top, eats its way, perforating the trunk of the tree until it reaches the root; it then comes out of the root and dies, or remains dormant, and the plant propagates out of its head; the body remains perfect and entire, of a harder substance than when alive. From this insect the natives make a colouring for tattooing" [POE'S NOTE]. The references are to the Danish botanist Joakim Frederik Schouw (1789–1852) and to the American diplomat John Brown Williams (1810–60).

p. 67, *there were others that glowed all over with intense fire*: In mines and natural caves we find a species of cryptogamous fungus that emits an intense phosphorescence [POE'S NOTE].

p. 67, *others that moved from place to place at pleasure*: The orchis, seabius and valisneria [POE'S NOTE].

p. 67, *flowers... tasks*: "The corolla of this flower (*Aristolochia clematitis*), which is tubular but terminating upwards in a ligulate limb, is inflated into a globular figure at the base. The tubular part is internally beset with stiff hairs, pointing downwards. The globular part contains the pistil, which consists merely of a germen and stigma, together with the surrounding stamens. But the stamens, being shorter than even the germen, cannot discharge the pollen so as to throw it upon the stigma, as the flower stands always upright till after impregnation. And hence, without some additional and peculiar aid, the pollen must necessarily fall down to the bottom of the flower. Now, the aid that nature has furnished in this case is that of the *Tiputa pennicornis*, a small insect, which, entering the tube of the corolla in quest of honey, descends to the bottom and rummages about till it becomes quite covered with pollen – but, not being able to force its way out again, owing to the downward position of the hairs, which converge to a point like the wires of a mousetrap, and being somewhat impatient of its confinement, it brushes backwards and forwards, trying every corner, till, after repeatedly traversing the stigma, it covers it with pollen sufficient for its impregnation, in consequence of which the flower soon begins to droop, and the hairs to shrink to the side of the tube, effecting an easy passage for the escape of the insect" – Revd P. Keith, *System of Physiological Botany* [POE'S NOTE].

The quotation is from *A System of Physiological Botany*, Vol. 2 (London: Baldwin, Cradock and Joy, 1816), p. 354, by Patrick Keith (1769–1840).

p. 67, *in which the bees and the birds are mathematicians... birds*: The bees – ever since bees were – have been constructing their cells with just such sides, in just such number and at just such inclinations as it has been demonstrated (in a problem involving the profoundest mathematical principles) are the very sides, in the very number and at the very angles which will afford the creatures the most room that is compatible with the greatest stability of structure.

During the latter part of the last century, the question arose among mathematicians "to determine the best form that can be given to the sails of a windmill according to their varying distances from the revolving vanes, and likewise from the centres of the revolution". This is an excessively complex problem, for it is, in other words, to find the best possible position at an infinity of varied distances, and at an infinity of points on the arm. There were a thousand futile attempts to answer the query on the part of the most illustrious mathematicians – and when, at length, an undeniable solution was discovered, men found that the wing of a bird had given it with absolute precision ever since the first bird had traversed the air [POE'S NOTE].

p. 68, *another... several millions of millions of fowl*: "He observed a flock of pigeons passing betwixt Frankfurt and the Indiana territory, one mile at least in breadth; it took up four hours in passing – which, at the rate of one mile per minute, gives a length of 240 miles; and, supposing three pigeons to each square yard, gives 2,230,272,000 pigeons" – *Travels in Canada and the United States* by Lieut. F. Hall [POE'S NOTE]. The quotation is from Francis Hall's (1797–1833) *Travels in Canada, and the United States, in 1816 and 1817* (London: Longman, Hurst, Rees, Orme and Brown, 1819), p. 13. Hall is in his turn quoting from the Scottish-American ornithologist and illustrator Alexander Wilson's (1766–1813) *American Ornithology* (1808–14), a nine-volume collection of illustrations of all the birds of North America.

p. 68, *rocs*: The roc is a gigantic mythological bird described in the *Arabian Nights*.

p. 68, *a fowl of another kind... filled with sand!*: The monster is a balloon, and the sack filled with sand is ballast.

p. 68, *a continent... four hundred horns*: "The earth is upheld by a cow of a blue colour, having horns four hundred in number" – Sale's *Koran* [POE'S NOTE]. This is likely to be a tongue-in-cheek joke by Poe, as the quotation cannot be found in George Sale's (1697–1736) 1734 translation of the Koran, nor in any other edition of the sacred Islamic text.

p. 68, *powerful magicians, who lived with worms in their brain*: "The *Entozoa*, or intestinal worms, have repeatedly been observed in the muscles and in the cerebral substance of men" – see Wyatt's *Physiology*, p. 143 [POE'S NOTE]. The correct reference should be to *A Synopsis of Natural History* (Philadelphia: Thomas Wardle, 1839), by Louis-Céran Lemmonnier (b. 1810), translated into English by Thomas Wyatt, p. 143.

p. 69, *a huge horse… most birds*: On the Great Western railway, between London and Exeter, a speed of 71 miles per hour has been attained. A train weighing 90 tons was whirled from Paddington to Didcot (53 miles) in 51 minutes [POE'S NOTE].

p. 69, *a hen without feathers… their mother*: The eccaleobion [POE'S NOTE]. The eccaleobion is a device for hatching eggs by artificial heat.

p. 69, *a man out of brass and wood and leather… the great caliph Harun al-Rashid*: Mälzel's automaton chess player [POE'S NOTE]. The reference is to an automaton, referred to as "The Turk", invented by Wolfgang von Kempelen (1734–1804) in 1769 and brought to the United States in 1825 by Johann Nepomuk Mälzel (1772–1838). Poe wrote an essay entitled 'Maelzel's Chess Player' (1836), in which he proved that the automaton was activated fraudulently by a chess master hidden in its lower cavity. Harun al-Rashid (763–809) was the fifth Abbasid caliph of Baghdad (786–809); his reign saw the transformation of the city into an intellectual, cultural and trade hub, and is regarded as the beginning of the Islamic Golden Age.

p. 69, *a creature… for a year*: Babbage's calculating machine [POE'S NOTE]. The reference it to an automatic mechanical calculator, the so-called "difference engine", developed by the English mathematician Charles Babbage (1791–1871) between 1822 and the mid-1830s.

p. 69, *a still more wonderful conjuror… for evil and for good*: The "thing" described by Poe is the printing press.

p. 69, *one who had in his veins… upon its floor*: Chabert, and, since him, a hundred others [POE'S NOTE]. For this and many of the following notes, Poe drew the information from *Course of Lectures*, an 1842 work by the Irish scientific writer Dionysius Lardner (1793–1859). The story of stage magician and fire eater John Xavier Chabert (1792–1859) is from the beginning of Lecture IV, under the heading "Popular Fallacies": "He had an oven, which he was accustomed to have heated to such a degree that he could broil a beef steak by its heat while he quietly sat in the oven and cooked and ate his steak. But Chabert did not stand upon the bottom of the oven: he took care to have between his feet and the iron which formed its bottom, and on which the steak was cooked, some non-conducting substance. Air not being a good conductor, and by being careful to have a carpet or piece of cork upon which to stand, he could quietly remain in the oven without injury."

p. 69, *Another had the faculty… during the process*: Electrotype [POE'S NOTE]. Electrotype is a copy in metal of an engraved or moulded surface made by a process involving the electrolytic deposition of copper or other metal.

p. 69, *Another... invisible*: Wollaston made of platinum for the field of views in a telescope a wire one eighteen-thousandth part of an inch in thickness. It could be seen only by means of the microscope [POE'S NOTE]. The reference is to the English scientist William Hyde Wollaston (1766–1828).

p. 69, *Another... in a second*: Newton demonstrated that the retina, beneath the influence of the violet ray of the spectrum, vibrated 900,000,000 of times in a second [POE'S NOTE].

p. 70, *Another of these magicians... dance at his will*: The voltaic pile [POE'S NOTE]. The voltaic pile, invented by Alessandro Volta (1745–1827) towards the end of the eighteenth century, was based on Luigi Galvani's (1737–98) discovery that a circuit of two metals and a frog's leg can cause the frog's leg to move.

p. 70, *Another... one end of the world to the other*: The electro-telegraph transmits intelligence instantaneously – at least so far as regards any distance upon the earth [POE'S NOTE].

p. 70, *Another... any distance whatsoever*: The electro-telegraph printing apparatus [POE'S NOTE].

p. 70, *Another commanded... out of two brilliant lights*: Common experiments in natural philosophy. If two red rays from two luminous points be admitted into a dark chamber so as to fall on a white surface, and differ in their length by 0.0000258 of an inch, their intensity is doubled. So also if the difference in length be any whole-number multiple of that fraction. A multiple by 2¼, 3¼, etc. gives an intensity equal to one ray only, but a multiple by 2½, 3½, etc. gives the result of total darkness. In violet rays similar effects arise when the difference in length is 0.000157 of an inch, and with all other rays the results are the same – the difference varying with a uniform increase from the violet to the red.

Analogous experiments in respect to sound produce analogous results [POE'S NOTE].

p. 70, *Another made ice in a red-hot furnace*: Place a platina crucible over a spirit lamp and keep it a red heat; pour in some sulphuric acid – which, though the most volatile of bodies at a common temperature, will be found to become completely fixed in a hot crucible, and not a drop evaporates: being surrounded by an atmosphere of its own, it does not, in fact, touch the sides. A few drops of water are now introduced, when the acid, immediately coming in contact with the heated sides of the crucible, flies off in sulphurous acid vapour, and so rapid is its progress that the caloric of the water passes off with it, which falls a lump of ice to the bottom. By taking advantage of the moment before it is allowed to re-melt, it may be turned out a lump of ice from a red hot vessel [POE'S NOTE]. "Platina" is platinum.

p. 70, *Another directed the sun to paint his portrait, and the sun did*: The daguerreotype [POE'S NOTE]. One of the earliest photographic processes, invented by Louis Daguerre (1787–1851) in 1839.

p. 70, *this luminary*: The sun.

p. 70, *Another took this luminary... the face of creation*: Although light travels 167,000 miles in a second, the distance of 61 Cygni (the only star whose distance is ascertained) is so inconceivably great that its rays would require more than ten years to reach the earth. For stars beyond this, 20 – or even 1,000 years – would be a moderate estimate. Thus, if they had been annihilated 20 or 1,000 years ago, we might still see them today by the light which started from their surfaces 20 or 1,000 years in the past time. That many which we see daily are really extinct is not impossible – not even improbable.

The elder Herschel maintains that the light of the faintest nebulae seen through his great telescope must have taken 3,000,000 years in reaching the earth. Some, made visible by Lord Rosse's instrument, must then have required at least 20,000,000 [POE'S NOTE]. For the Herschel and Earl of Rosse telescopes, see p. 45. For Herschel, see first note to p. 3; for the Earl of Rosse, see second note to p. 45.

p. 70, *crotchet*: A perverse or unfounded belief or notion; a whimsical fancy.

p. 73, *The Mystery of Marie Rogêt*: Upon the original publication of 'Marie Rogêt', the footnotes now appended were considered unnecessary, but the lapse of several years since the tragedy upon which the tale is based renders it expedient to give them, and also to say a few words in explanation of the general design. A young girl, Mary Cecilia Rogers, was murdered in the vicinity of New York – and, although her death occasioned an intense and long-enduring excitement, the mystery attending it had remained unsolved at the period when the present paper was written and published (November 1842). Herein, under pretence of relating the fate of a Parisian grisette, the author has followed, in minute detail, the essential, while merely paralleling the inessential facts of the real murder of Mary Rogers. Thus all argument founded upon the fiction is applicable to the truth, and the investigation of the truth was the object.

The 'Mystery of Marie Rogêt' was composed at a distance from the scene of the atrocity, and with no other means of investigation than the newspapers afforded. Thus much escaped the writer of which he could have availed himself had he been upon the spot and visited the localities. It may not be improper to record, nevertheless, that the confessions of two persons (one of them the Madame Deluc of the narrative) made, at different periods, long subsequent to the publication, confirmed in full not only the general conclusion, but absolutely all the chief hypothetical details by which that conclusion was attained [POE'S NOTE]. First serialized in the *Ladies' Companion* between November 1842 and February 1843; republished, with corrections, in TA1 and later reprinted in PW1, from where our text is taken. Poe's manuscript corrections in his personal copy of TA1 (from now on referred to as JLG), dating from 1846–49, are indicated in the notes. As explained by the author himself, the story, presented as "A Sequel to 'The Murders in the Rue Morgue'", was inspired by the murder of a well-known New York beauty, Mary Rogers (born *c.*1820), whose body was found in the Hudson River on 28th July 1841. Poe transposes her story to Paris, indicating most of the real-life names and New York toponyms in the notes, and, through the reasoning of detective Dupin, claims to have found an explanation for the unresolved crime. The "second confession" (in addition to Madame Deluc's) confirming the truth of Dupin's theory is, of course, Poe's mystification for the sake of the denouement. For 'The Murders in the Rue Morgue' (1841), an unrelated story about the double murder of Madame L'Espanaye and her daughter Camille, which shares its main character with 'The Mystery of Marie Rogêt', the fictional detective C. Auguste Dupin, see TH, pp. 106–38.

p. 73, *Es giebt eine Reihe... Novalis, Moralische Ansichten*: The epigraph is one of the fragmentary observations for which the German poet Novalis (1772–1801), "The nom de plume of [Georg Philipp Friedrich] Von Hardenberg" [POE'S NOTE], is best remembered today. Poe found it in a book he reviewed for *Graham's Magazine* for December 1841, *Fragments from German Prose Writers*, tr. Sarah Austin (1793–1867) (New York: D. Appleton and Company, 1841), although he made some changes to the translation. We have amended the German text provided by Poe to match that in modern editions of Novalis's works. *Moralische Ansichten* (corrected editorially from "*Moral Ansichten*" in Poe) is German for "Moral Views".

p. 73, *such sentiments*: These two words are deleted in JLG.

p. 74, *'The Murders in the Rue Morgue'... the Chevalier C. Auguste Dupin*: See the headnote to this story.

p. 74, *thoroughly*: Deleted in JLG.

p. 74, *wild*: Deleted in JLG.

p. 74, *the cynosure*: The centre of attention.

p. 75, *"cigar girl"*: Marie Rogers was referred to, in reports of her murder, as the "Beautiful Cigar Girl".

p. 75, *Rue Pavée-Saint-Andrée*: Nassau Street [POE'S NOTE].

p. 75, *Le Blanc*: Anderson [POE'S NOTE].

p. 75, *three years*: Amended from "five months" in PW1, based on Poe's own change in JLG, correcting an error of continuity. Mary Rogers's second disappearance did in fact occur around three years after the first one.

p. 75, *the Seine*: The Hudson [POE'S NOTE].

p. 75, *Barrière du Roule*: Weehawken [POE'S NOTE].

p. 76, *émeutes*: "Riots" (French).

p. 77, *abroad*: Out of doors.

p. 77, *Jacques Saint-Eustache*: Payne [POE'S NOTE].

p. 77, *Rue des Drômes*: The fictional equivalent of Jane Street in New York.

p. 78, *Monsieur Beauvais*: Crommelin [POE'S NOTE].

p. 79, *A weekly paper*: The NY *Mercury* [POE'S NOTE]. The murder was first brought to public attention by a piece in the *Sunday Mercury* of 1st August 1841.

p. 79, *L'Étoile*: The NY *Brother Jonathan*, edited by H. Hastings Weld, Esq. [POE'S NOTE]. This and the following two "translations" are in fact almost verbatim transcriptions (with the exception of the substitution of fictional for actual names and dates) from the *Brother Jonathan* (a Saturday weekly) of 28th August 1841, which reprinted excerpts from its daily version, the *Tattler*. Horatio Hastings Weld (1811–88), the *Brother Jonathan* editor, later became an Episcopalian minister, and was the author of several religious books.

p. 80, *Even where a cannon... if let alone*: In the eighteenth and nineteenth centuries it was popularly believed that the acoustic shock wave or concussion produced by the firing of a cannon would rupture the gall bladder of a submerged corpse and cause it to rise to the surface. See, for instance, Mark Twain's *Adventures of Huckleberry Finn* (1884): "You see, they was firing cannon over the water, trying to make my carcass come to the top" (Chapter 7).

p. 81, *In a subsequent number of the paper*: It is in fact from the same issue of the *Brother Jonathan* (28th August 1841), but a "subsequent issue" of the daily *Tattler* (25th August 1841), which had published the first two excerpts on 23rd August 1841.

p. 82, *Le Commerciel*: NY *Journal of Commerce* [POE'S NOTE]. The quoted extract is an almost verbatim transcription of a piece published in the *Journal of Commerce* of 23rd August 1841.

p. 82, *that*: Amended from "when" (see Dupin's quotation of this excerpt on p. 95).

p. 83, *pocket handkerchiefs*: Amended, for consistency with later mentions of this passage, from "pocket handkerchief".

p. 83, *Madame Deluc*: The fictional equivalent of Frederica Loss, alias Kellenbarack, an innkeeper from Weehawken.

p. 83, *Le Soleil*: Phil. *Sat. Evening Post*, edited by C.J. Peterson, Esq. [POE'S NOTE]. The quoted extract is a verbatim transcription of a piece published in the Philadelphia *Saturday Evening Post* of 25th September 1841.

p. 83, *she keeps a roadside inn opposite the Barrière du Roule*: Frederica Loss's Weehawken inn was called Nick Moore's House.

p. 84, *Valence*: Adam [POE'S NOTE]. The name of the omnibus driver was given in full by other papers as "Adam Wall".

p. 85, *In the investigations at the house of Madame L'Espanaye*: See 'Murders in the Rue Morgue' [POE'S NOTE].

p. 87, *ex parte*: A legal term meaning, literally, "from a side" (Latin), and used to refer to something that is done or said in the interests of one side only.

p. 87, *Le Moniteur*: The NY *Commercial Advertiser*, edited by Col. Stone [POE'S NOTE]. "Colonel Stone" was the name under which the journalist and publisher William Leete Stone senior (1792–1844) was better known.

p. 91, *sequitur*: Inference or conclusion.

p. 93, *de lunatico inquirendo*: "Inquiry into one's sanity of mind" (Latin). This legal expression describes an official order commanding an inquiry to determine if a person is of unsound mind. *The Commissioner, or De Lunatico Inquirendo* is also the title of a novel by the English writer George Payne Rainsford James (1799–1860), serialized in 1842 and published in volume form in 1843.

p. 93, *rectangular*: "Formal, stiff, rigid" (*OED*).

p. 93, *booked*: That is, recorded in books (as legal precedents are).

p. 93, *I would here observe... individual error*: "A theory based on the qualities of an object will prevent its being unfolded according to its objects, and he who arranges topics in reference to their causes will cease to value them according to their results. Thus the jurisprudence of every nation will show that, when law becomes a science and a system, it ceases to be justice. The errors into which a blind devotion to principles of classification has led the common law will be seen by observing how often the legislature has been obliged to come forward to restore the equity its scheme had lost" – Landor [POE'S NOTE]. The quotation is from the novel *Stanley, or The Recollections of a Man of the World* (published anonymously in 1838), by the lawyer and critic Horace Binney Wallace (1817–52), whom Poe knew under his pseudonym "William Landor". Poe has omitted the words "arbitrary and theoretical" before "principles".

p. 95, *discursive*: Unpredictable.

p. 96, *vast*: Deleted in JLG.

p. 97, *cotemporary*: Contemporary.

p. 97, *comptoir*: "Counter" (French).

p. 98, *Evening Paper, Monday, June 23*: NY *Express* [POE'S NOTE].

p. 98, *Le Mercurie, Tuesday Morning, June 24*: NY *Herald* [POE'S NOTE].

p. 98, *Morning Paper, June 25*: NY *Courier and Enquirer* [POE'S NOTE].

p. 98, *Mennais*: Mennais was one of the parties originally suspected and arrested, but discharged through total lack of evidence [POE'S NOTE].

p. 98, *Morning Paper, June 28*: NY *Courier and Enquirer* [POE'S NOTE].

p. 98, *Evening Paper, Tuesday, June 30*: NY *Evening Post* [POE'S NOTE].

p. 99, *Le Diligence, Thursday, June 26*: NY *Standard* [POE'S NOTE].

p. 103, *single*: Deleted in JLG.

p. 103, *the unwashed*: The lower classes.

p. 104, *within a few rods*: The rod is a unit of length equal to around five metres.

p. 104, *in search of the bark of the sassafras*: The bark of the sassafras tree is used to make root beer.

p. 106, *collectedly*: Collectively.

p. 109, *Et hinc illæ iræ?*: "And hence that anger?" (Latin). The expression is modelled on "*Hinc illæ lacrimæ*" ("Hence those tears"), a famous line from the first scene (l. 126) of *Andria*, a comedy by the Latin poet Terence (*c.*195–*c.*159 BC).

p. 110, *King's evidence*: That is, state's evidence.

p. 111, *MS*: Abbreviation of "manuscript" (plural: MSS) – that is, specimens of handwriting.

p. 113, *Eds.*: Of the magazine in which the article was originally published [POE'S NOTE]. "Eds." is an abbreviation for "Editors". For the magazine in which 'The Mystery of Marie Rogêt' was first published, see the headnote.

p. 115, *The Island of the Fay*: First published in *Graham's Magazine* (June 1841) and later reprinted, with two small authorial changes, in PW1, from where our text is taken.

p. 115, *Nullus enim locus sine genio est*: The epigraph, a slightly incorrect quotation from a commentary on Virgil's *Aeneid* by the Latin grammarian Servius (*fl.* late fourth–early fifth century AD), was taken by Poe from the end of Book 7, Chapter 5, of *Notre-Dame de Paris* (usually translated into English as *The Hunchback of Notre-Dame*), an 1831 novel by Victor Hugo (1802–85), and can be translated as "No place is without its spirit".

p. 115, *Contes moraux... spirit*: "*Moraux*" is here derived from *mœurs*, and its meaning is "fashionable" – or, more strictly, "of manners" [POE'S NOTE]. The *Contes moraux*, a series of pictures of French society under King Louis XV written between 1755 and 1759, are among the works of the French historian and *encyclopédiste* Jean-François Marmontel (1723–99).

p. 115, *la musique... des témoins*: "Music is the only talent that finds enjoyment in itself – all others must have partakers." The quote is from the "moral tale" 'La Bergère des Alpes' ("The Shepherdess of the Alps").

p. 116, *animalculæ*: "Animalcules" (Latin) – microscopic creatures.

p. 116, *"clod of the valley"*: See Job 21:33: "The clods of the valley shall be sweet unto him, and every man shall draw after him, as there are innumerable before him."

p. 116, *to which he denies a soul... in operation*: Speaking of the tides, Pomponius Mela, in his treatise *De situ orbis*, says "either the world is a great animal, or", etc. [POE'S NOTE]. The quote, from *De situ orbis* (III, 1) by the Roman geographer Pomponius Mela (d. *c.*45 AD), was probably taken by Poe from *An Encyclopaedia of Geography* (see fourth note to p. 66): "Either the world is a great animal whose breathings excite in its breast these alternate movements, or it contains deep caves into which the waters are alternately absorbed and ejected" (Part I, Book I, Chapter 5).

p. 117, *What flippant Frenchman was it... belle chose"*: Balzac – in substance – I do not remember the words [POE'S NOTE]. The quotation, which means

"Solitude is a fine thing, but you need someone to say that solitude is a fine thing", is a slightly misremembered passage from the *Dissertations chrétiennes et morales* ("Christian and Moral Dissertations") by Jean-Louis Guez de Balzac (1597–1654): "Solitude is certainly a fine thing, but it is pleasant to have someone who can reply, whom we can tell from time to time that it is a fine thing" (Dissertation XVIII, "The Pleasures of a Retired Life"). Balzac could not have said those words "in allusion to the well-known work of Zimmerman", since the essay referred to, *Über die Einsamkeit* ("On Solitude"), published by the Swiss philosopher and naturalist Johann Georg Ritter von Zimmermann (1728–95) in 1756, appeared well after Balzac's death. Poe may have confused the author of the quote with his more famous namesake, the French novelist Honoré de Balzac (1799–1850).

p. 117, *tarns*: Small mountain lakes.

p. 117, *So blended bank... pendulous in air*: The two lines can be found, in a slightly different form – "So blend the turrets and shadows there / That all seem pendulous in air" – in Poe's poem 'The Doomed City' (ll. 41–42) and in his later reworking of it, 'The City in the Sea' (ll. 26–27).

p. 117, *asphodel-interspersed*: The asphodel is both a flowering plant in the lily family and, in Greek mythology, an immortal flower that covered the Elysian Fields, the final resting place of the dead in the underworld.

p. 117, *that might have been mistaken for tulips with wings*: *Florem putares nare per liquidum æthera.* – P. Commire [POE'S NOTE]. The Latin quotation ("You would think a flower was floating through the liquid air") is from 'Papilio et apis' ("The Butterfly and the Bee", l. 11), a poem by the Jesuit author Jean Commire (also known as "Père Commire", 1625–1702).

p. 118, *whelmed*: Engulfed, submerged.

p. 121, *The Assignation*: First published in *Godey's Lady's Book* (January 1834); later revised and collected in PW1, from where our text is taken.

p. 121, *Stay for me there!... hollow vale*: The epigraph is from 'The Exequy' (ll. 88–89), a poem written by the English poet Henry King, Bishop of Chichester (1592–1669), on the death of his wife Anne (1600–24).

p. 121, *the Genius of Romance... the narrow canal*: Possibly an allusion to the poem 'To the Genius of Romance' by the English poet Henry Kirk White (1785–1806): "O thou who, in my early youth, / When fancy wore the garb of truth, / Wert wont to win my infant feet / To some retired, deep fabled seat, / Where, by the brooklet's secret tide, / The midnight ghost was known to glide" (ll. 1–6).

p. 121, *the Piazza*: Piazza San Marco, with its famous Campanile.

p. 121, *the old Ducal Palace*: Also known as "the Doge's Palace".

p. 121, *Piazzetta*: Literally "Little Square", an extension of Piazza San Marco towards the Lagoon.

p. 122, *Canal San Marco*: This was sometimes used as another name for the Grand Canal, but, from the description that follows, Poe appears to be referring to the Rio di Palazzo (or Rio della Canonica), the narrow canal to the east of Piazza San Marco and the Doge's Palace that flows under the Bridge of Sighs.

p. 122, *intriguing*: Scheming.

p. 122, *the Niobe*: Niobe is a figure in Greek mythology who, according to Homer's *Iliad*, boasted of her six sons and six daughters to the Titan Leto, whose son Apollo and daughter Artemis punished her for her pride by murdering all twelve of her children. The reference here is to a statue of Niobe sheltering one of her daughters, one of a group depicting the story held at the Uffizi Gallery in Florence. They are Roman copies of Greek originals by Scopas or Praxiteles, two sculptors who flourished in the fourth century BC.

p. 122, *The Prison of the Old Republic*: The Prisons' Palace (Palazzo delle Prigioni), linked to the Doge's Palace by the Bridge of Sighs.

p. 123, *ennuyé*: "Bored" (French).

p. 123, *"soft and almost liquid"*: The quotation is from the *Epistulæ* (v, 6) of Pliny the Younger (61–*c.*113 AD).

p. 124, *Emperor Commodus*: Commodus (161–92 AD), Roman emperor from 177 AD until his death, was the subject of many statues, the most famous of which is the bust of *Commodus as Hercules*, housed at the Musei Capitolini in Rome.

p. 125, *decora*: "Proprieties" (Latin).

p. 125, *keeping*: A technical term from painting, referring to the harmonious distance and relation between the various objects in a composition.

p. 125, *grotesques*: Grotesque figures.

p. 125, *Chile gold*: Chile was a large producer of gold in the eighteenth and early nineteenth centuries.

p. 126, *bienséance*: "Etiquette" (French).

p. 126, *Sir Thomas More died laughing, you remember*: It is reported, in a biography of Sir Thomas More (1478–1535) written by his son-in-law William Roper (*c.*1496–1578) and published in 1626 (*The Mirrour of Vertue in Worldly Greatnes, or The Life of Sir Thomas More*), that when he ascended the scaffold to be beheaded, he said jokingly: "I pray you, Master Lieutenant, see me safe up, and for my coming down let me shift for myself." Then, after saying his prayers, he knelt down and, turning to the executioner with a cheerful countenance, said: "Pluck up thy spirits, man, and be not afraid to do thine office: my neck is very short – take heed, therefore, thou strike not awry, for saving of thine honesty."

p. 126, *in the Absurdities of Ravisius Textor... the same magnificent end*: The reference is to the chapter "De gaudio et risu mortui" ("Of the Joy and Laughter of the Dead") in the encyclopedic work *Officina* by the humanist

French writer Jean Tixier de Ravisi ("Johannes Textor Ravisius", *c.*1470–1542), which Poe (or the speaker in the story) irreverently or mistakenly refers to as *Absurdities*.

p. 126, *Palæochori*: Palæochori (literally, in Greek, "the Old City") is the name of a number of villages in Greece, but not the modern-day name of Sparta. In his *Itinéraire de Paris à Jérusalem* ("A Journey from Paris to Jerusalem", 1811), François-René de Chateaubriand (1768–1848) recounts how, as he struggled to locate the site of ancient Sparta, his Greek guide suggested: "Your Lordship is perhaps looking for Palæochori?" To which Chateaubriand, remembering a passage he had read in a work by the French cartographer Jean-Baptiste Bourguignon d'Anville (1697–1782), replied: "Yes, Palæochori! The old city! Where is it, Palæochori?" – which allowed his cicerone to guide him to Sparta's citadel. Poe read Chateaubriand's book in the 1812 translation by the English journalist Frederic Shoberl (1775–1853): *Travels in Greece, Palestine, Egypt, and Barbary, during the Years 1806 and 1807*.

p. 126, *at Sparta, I say, to the west of the citadel... survived all the others!*: Chateaubriand's book (see previous note) is also the source for this passage about the inscription on the "*socle*", or "pedestal": "There were, at Sparta, a host of altars and statues consecrated to Sleep, Death and Beauty (Venus-Morpho), deities to all men – and to Fear in arms, apparently that which the Lacedaemonians inspired in their enemies: none of these remain, but I read on a kind of pedestal these four letters: ΛΑΣΜ. Should we read ΓΕΛΑΣΜΑ, *Gelasma*? Could this be the pedestal of the statue of Laughter that Lycurgus erected among the austere descendants of Hercules? An altar to Laughter standing alone in the middle of Sparta's ruins offers a glorious subject to Democritus's philosophy!" The information about the statues consecrated to Venus-Morpho (Aphrodite-Beauty) is from Pausanias's *Description of Greece* (III, 15, 10–11); that about the statue of Laughter erected by Lycurgus, the legendary lawgiver of Sparta, is from Plutarch's *Lives* ('Lycurgus', XXV); according to legend, the Spartans (or Lacedaemonians) were descendants of the hero Heracles (Hercules); the pre-Socratic philosopher Democritus (*c.*460–*c.*370 BC) was known as "the laughing philosopher", as he regarded good humour as essential for human happiness. In Chateaubriand's original (but not in Shoberl's translation) the four letters on the pedestal are "ΛΑΣΑ" rather than "ΛΑΣΜ". In PW4, the "Σ" (Sigma) has been incorrectly replaced with a "Ξ" (Xi).

p. 126, *ultras*: "Ultras" are people who go to the extreme of fashion. Here the meaning appears to be "extravagances".

p. 126, *bedizened*: Dressed up (in a vulgar or gaudy fashion).

p. 126, *Cimabue*: The Italian painter Cimabue (*c.*1240–1302), often considered one of the first modern painters after the classical era.

p. 126, *Virtù*: "Virtue" (Italian).

p. 127, *"It is Guido's own!"*: The reference is to the Italian baroque painter Guido Reni (1575–1642), whose religious, mythological and allegorical paintings were particularly popular in the nineteenth century. His depictions of women were regarded as the epitome of classical beauty. Poe may be alluding to one of his most famous works, the *Pietà dei Mendicanti* (1616), commissioned by the Bolognese senate for the Church of Santa Maria della Pietà, and now at Bologna's Pinacoteca Nazionale. A *pietà* is a representation in art of the Virgin Mary holding the dead body of Christ.

p. 127, *Venus of the Medici... gilded hair*: The *Venus de' Medici*, a first-century-BC Roman marble copy of a Greek bronze dating from the 4th century BC, now housed in the Uffizi Gallery in Florence, is often considered the nonpareil of classical beauty.

p. 127, *Give me the Canova!*: That is, the Canova *Venus*, or *Pauline Bonaparte as Venus Victrix*, another celebrated depiction of classical beauty, sculpted by the Italian artist Antonio Canova (1757–1822).

p. 127, *The Apollo*: The so-called *Apollo Belvedere*, a second-century-AD Roman marble copy of a Greek bronze dating from between 330 and 320 BC.

p. 127, *the Antinous*: Antinous (*c.*110–30 AD) was the Greek lover of the Roman emperor Hadrian (76–138 AD). When he died, the emperor, stricken by grief, celebrated his memory lavishly: he ordered numerous artistic depictions of him to be made, and even temples to be built in his honour, raising him to the level of godhood. Many of these works survive, and he is now seen as the Roman ideal of youthful beauty. Poe is probably referring here to one of the most famous representations of the youth, the so-called *Antinous Farnese*, a marble statue sculpted between 130 and 137 AD.

p. 127, *Socrates who said... the block of marble*: In his *Lives and Opinions of Eminent Philosophers*, the third-century-AD biographer Diogenes Laertius writes: "[Socrates] often said that he wondered at those who made stone statues when he saw how careful they were that the stone should be like the man it was intended to represent, but how careless they were of themselves as to guarding against being like the stone" (Book II, "Socrates", tr. C.D. Yonge).

p. 127, *Non ha l'ottimo artista... circonscriva*: "There is no idea by the best of artists / That isn't already contained in a block of marble" – the first two lines of a famous sonnet by Michelangelo Buonarroti (1475–1564).

p. 127, *Persepolis*: The capital of the Achaemenid Empire (*c.*550–330 BC) in Persia and, in modern times, a major archaeological site.

p. 128, *Politian's beautiful tragedy, The Orfeo... a passage towards the end of the third act*: The *Fabula di Orfeo* ("Fable of Orpheus") is a dramatic poem written by the Italian humanist Angelo (or Agnolo) Poliziano ("Politian", 1454–94) between 1479 and 1480. It is considered the first non-religious dramatic work in the Italian language. Politian's drama is based on the story of the mythical poet and musician Orpheus, who, according to Greek legend, was said to be able to charm living and inanimate things with his music, and descended into the underworld to recover his lost wife, Eurydice. The "passage underlined in pencil" probably refers to Orpheus's lament: "Let us weep now, O disconsolate lyre, / because the erstwhile song is not befitting: / Let us weep as heaven revolves around the poles, / And let Philomel give way to our dirge. / Oh, heaven! Oh, earth! Oh, sea! Oh dire fate! / How can I bear so much misery? / My beautiful Eurydice – my very life! – / Without you, it is not worth staying in this world." Some old editions of Politian's poem, such as *Poesie italiane di messer Angelo Poliziano* (Milan: Giovanni Silvestri, 1825), divide it into five acts, and Orpheus's lament can be found in these towards the end of Act III.

p. 130, *Chapman's Bussy D'Ambois... made him marble!*: An adapted quotation from *Bussy D'Ambois*, a 1607 tragedy by George Chapman (*c.*1559–1634): "I am up. / Here, like a Roman statue, I will stand / Till death hath made me marble" (Act V, Sc. 4, ll. 96–98).

p. 130, *Johannisberger*: A fine white wine from the Rhine region of Germany.

p. 130, *decorist*: A person attached to artistic proprieties.

p. 131, *Stay for me there!... that hollow vale*: See second note to p. 121.

p. 131, *upon a cracked and blackened goblet*: Venetian glass was thought to fracture or burst when filled with poison.

p. 133, *The System of Doctor Tarr and Professor Fether*: First published in *Graham's Magazine* (November 1845) and later reprinted, with minor authorial changes, in PW4, from where our text is taken.

p. 134, *Bellini*: The Italian opera composer Vincenzo Bellini (1801–35).

p. 135, *reductio ad absurdum*: "Reduction to absurdity" (Latin), the carrying through of a premise to its logical extreme.

p. 137, *à la Menehould*: That is, *à la Sainte-Menehould*, referring to a method of slow-cooking veal or pig's feet.

p. 137, *Clos de Vougeot*. Clos Vougeot is a grand cru from the northern part of Burgundy's Côte-d'Or.

p. 137, *salle à manger*: "Dining room" (French).

p. 137, *vieille cour*: "Old court" (French).

p. 138, *the Anakim*: A race of giants mentioned in the Bible (see Numbers 13:33).

p. 138, *nil admirari*: "Marvel at nothing" (Latin).

p. 138, *Britannia-ware teapot*: Britannia ware (or Britannia metal) is a type of pewter alloy.

p. 139, *mon ami*: "My friend" (French).

p. 139, *"monstrum horrendum... ademptum"*: "Horrible, malformed, huge monster deprived of light" (Latin). The words, referring to the Cyclops blinded by Ulysses, are a quotation from Virgil's *Aeneid* (III, l. 658).

p. 139, *morceau*: "Titbit" (French).

p. 141, *Demosthenes's from the top... and Lord Brougham's from the mouth to the chin*: The British statesman Henry Brougham, 1st Baron Brougham and Vaux (1778–1868), was the author of a translation of *On the Crown*, a speech delivered in 330 BC by the Athenian statesman and orator Demosthenes (384–322 BC). The translation, titled *The Oration of Demosthenes upon the Crown*, appeared in 1840. In July 1839, Poe reviewed for *Burton's Gentleman's Magazine* Brougham's *Sketches of Public Characters, Discourses, and Essays*, which included some of his translations from Demosthenes.

p. 141, *for he was a man of great eloquence*: Cicero, Brougham and Demosthenes were all famed orators.

p. 141, *teetotum*: "A small four-sided disk or die having an initial letter inscribed on each of its sides and a spindle passing down through it by which it could be twirled or spun with the fingers like a small top, the letter which lay uppermost, when it fell, deciding the fortune of the player" (*OED*).

p. 142, *"Mon Dieu!"*: "My God!" (French).

p. 142, *the Medicean Venus*: The Venus de' Medici (see second note to p. 127).

p. 144, *Sauternes*: A French dessert wine.

p. 144, *row-de-dowed*: Produced a din.

p. 144, *brazen bulls of Phalaris*: Phalaris (d. *c*.554 BC), the notoriously cruel tyrant of the city of Acragas in Sicily, is said to have had built a bronze bull in which his victims were roasted alive, their agonized cries resembling the creature's bellowing.

p. 144, *a sort of Pandaemonium in petto*: That is, a Pandaemonium in miniature, on a small scale. Pandaemonium, literally meaning "[the place of] all the devils", is the capital of hell in Milton's *Paradise Lost*.

p. 146, *gammoned*: Deceived.

p. 147, *'Yankee Doodle'*: A traditional American song, very popular in Poe's time.

p. 147, *the catastrophe of the drama*: The denouement of a classical tragedy.

p. 147, *pêle-mêle*: "Pell-mell" (French).

p. 148, *were first well tarred, then carefully feathered*: Tarring and feathering was a humiliating form of punishment inflicted on outlaws in Europe from the Middle Ages, and very common in the British colonies in North America and the early American Frontier.

p. 149, *The Literary Life of Thingum Bob, Esq.*: First published in the *Southern Literary Messenger* (December 1844); reprinted, with corrections, in the *Broadway Journal* (26th July 1845) and later collected in PW4, from where our text is taken. A "thingumbob" or "thingamabob" is a "thingummy", or "what-you-may-call-it".

p. 149, *Mr Emmons*: The American poet Richard Emmons (1788–1834), author of *The Fredoniad, or Independence Preserved: An Epick Poem on the Late*

War of 1812 (1827) and *The Battle of Bunker Hill, or The Temple of Liberty*, published posthumously in 1839. One critic described him as "unrivalled in the art of bathos", and his poetry was the subject of Poe's lampooning on several occasions.

p. 150, *"Oil-of-Bob" (so called... my father)*: Perhaps humorously modelled on the "oil of ben", oil obtained from the ben-nut. See also fourth note to p. 162.

p. 150, *a trump*: A first-rate fellow.

p. 151, *a man named Ugolino, who had a parcel of brats*: The tragic story of Count Ugolino della Gherardesca (*c.*1214–1289) and his sons, who were starved to death in the Muda Tower in Pisa under the orders of Archbishop Ruggieri degli Ubaldini (d. 1295), is narrated in Canto XXXIII of Dante's *Inferno*.

p. 151, *a great number of lines about "angels"... and more besides of that sort*: An allusion to *Hamlet*, Act 1, Sc. 4, ll. 20–21: "Angels and ministers of grace defend us! / Be thou a spirit of health or goblin damned".

p. 151, *Choctaw*: One of the indigenous peoples of the Southeastern Woodlands of the United States, based in what is now Louisiana.

p. 151, *I took about fifty verses... and something else*: From the first line of Alexander Pope's (1688–1744) translation of Homer's *Iliad*: "Achilles' wrath, to Greece the direful spring". According to tradition, Homer was blind.

p. 151, *From a fourth... sufficiently good in their way*: The fourth book is *Paradise Lost* by John Milton, who spent the last two decades of his life in total blindness. The quotations are from the first line of Book III: "Hail, holy light, offspring of heaven first-born".

p. 151, *"Oppodeldoc"*: Opodeldoc is an alcoholic solution of soap and camphor, with some added essential oils, used as an ointment. See also fourth note to p. 162.

p. 151, *afterlife*: Later life.

p. 151, *the city of the transcendentals*: Transcendentalism was a philosophical and literary school that developed in New England in the 1830s as a reaction against rationalism, and that included prominent figures such as Ralph Waldo Emerson (1803–82) and Henry David Thoreau (1817–62). The "city of the transcendentals" is probably Boston, where Emerson hailed from.

p. 151, *using-up*: Lambasting.

p. 151, *Rowdy-Dow*: Noise, din.

p. 152, *Nat Lee*: The English playwright Nathaniel Lee (*c.*1653–1692), who wrote pompous historical tragedies and spent five years in St Mary Bethlehem psychiatric hospital (Bedlam).

p. 152, *Achilles' wrath... etc., etc.*: From the first two lines of Alexander Pope's translation of Homer's *Iliad*. See fourth note to p. 151.

p. 152, *printer's devil*: An errand boy or apprentice in a printing office.

p. 153, *Hail, holy light, offspring of heaven first-born*: See fifth note to p. 151.

p. 153, *verbatim et literatim*: "Word for word and literally" (Latin).

p. 154, *The putting them... gigantic capitals!*: "Minion" is a size of type equivalent to 7 point. (A point is 0.351 mm.) There is a degree of hyperbole here: the entire quotation, including the capitalized "WE", is set at a consistent size.

p. 154, *Edinburgh Review*: An influential Whig-aligned literary journal published in Edinburgh between 1802 and 1929.

p. 154, *Quarterly*: The *Quarterly Review*, an influential liberal-conservative literary journal, and the primary rival of the *Edinburgh Review* (see previous note), published in London between 1809 and 1967.

p. 155, *acknowledge*: Amended from "acknowledged" in PW4, based on the *Southern Literary Messenger* text.

p. 155, *upon the tapis*: Under discussion or consideration.

p. 156, *my third lustrum*: That is, fifteen years.

p. 157, *argent comptant*: "Cash" (French).

p. 157, *note at nine months*: A promissory note to pay in nine months' time.

p. 157, *'burst-up'*: Failure, bankruptcy.

p. 157, *"I awoke and found myself famous"*: A quotation attributed to Byron in *Letters and Journals of Lord Byron: With Notices of His Life* (1830) by the poet's close friend Thomas Moore (1779–1852). It refers to Byron's overnight success after the publication of his poem *Childe Harold's Pilgrimage* (1812). Moore claims to be quoting Byron's 'Memoranda' – his unpublished memoir, the manuscript of which was famously destroyed in 1824 by a group including Moore and John Murray (1778–1843), Byron's publisher.

p. 157, *"Sep. 15 – 1 t"*: The "hieroglyphical marks" indicate a paid advert to be inserted "1 t[ime]" only on "Sep. 15", which is the date when most October magazines appeared.

p. 157, *as Hyperion with satyr*: The comparison between the godly Titan Hyperion, often identified with the sun, and a satyr is an echo of *Hamlet*, Act 1, Sc. 2, ll. 139–40: "So excellent a king – that was to this / Hyperion to a satyr".

p. 158, *nom de guerre*: An assumed name under which a person engages in combat or some other activity such as publishing.

p. 158, *bijou*: "Jewel" (French).

p. 159, *prononcés*: "Pronounced, conspicuous" (French).

p. 159, *Mr Fatquack... the Dish-Clout*: Possibly a jeer at *The Autobiography of a Pocket Handkerchief* by James Fenimore Cooper (1789–1851), serialized in *Graham's Magazine* in 1843. A "dish-clout" is a "dishcloth".

p. 159, "BOZ": A pen name used in his early career by Charles Dickens (1812–70), deriving from a nickname he had given his younger brother Augustus (1827–66).

p. 161, *"damning with faint praise"*: The expression, which is now an English idiom, derives from Alexander Pope's 'Epistle to Doctor Arbuthnot' (1734): "Damn with faint praise, assent with civil leer, / And, without sneering, teach the rest to sneer" (ll. 201–2).

p. 162, *cartel*: A written challenge, a letter of defiance.

p. 162, *Lord Brougham's Speeches*: *Speeches of Henry Lord Brougham upon Questions Relating to Public Rights, Duties and Interests* (1838). For Lord Brougham, see first note to p. 141.

p. 162, *Cobbett's Complete Works*: *Selections from Cobbett's Political Works, Being a Complete Abridgement of the 100 Volumes Which Comprise the Writings of "Porcupine" and the "Weekly Political Register"* (1835), a six-volume collection of essays and journalism by the English politician and pamphleteer William Cobbett (1763–1835).

p. 162, *Lewis G. Clark on Tongue*: The American literary critic and editor Lewis Gaylord Clark (1808–73) was the editor and publisher of *The Knickerbocker* from 1834 to 1861, and an adversary of Edgar Allan Poe. Clark's twin brother Willis (1808–41) wrote a series of pieces for *The Knickerbocker*, between March 1835 and April 1840, under the heading "Ollapodiana", a name that was intended to reflect the familiar chat or gossip of Doctor Ollapod, a character in the 1801 comedy *The Poor Gentleman* by George Colman the Younger (1762–1836). Lewis Gaylor Clark published his late brother's *Literary Remains*, including the "Ollapodiana" papers, in 1844, and it is possible that Poe intended to parody the Clark brothers by using the similar-sounding "Oil-of-Bob" and "Oppodeldoc" in this story. Among the miscellaneous papers published in the *Literary Remains* is an essay on 'Language'.

p. 162, *curry-comb*: A metal instrument used to groom ("curry") a horse.

p. 163, *aper*: "Wild boar" (Latin).

p. 164, *rem... modo*: The allusion is to "*rem facias, rem, / si possis, recte; si non, quocumque modo*" ("Make a fortune – a fortune, if you can, honestly; if not, a fortune by any means"), a quotation from Horace's *Epistles* (I, I, ll. 65–66).

p. 165, *bouleversement*: See first note to p. 37.

p. 165, *to say, with Chateaubriand... "J'ai fait l'histoire"*: Chateaubriand (see fourth note to p. 126) wrote this remark in his *Mémoires d'Outre-Tombe* ("Memoirs from Beyond the Grave"), published posthumously in 1849–50. Poe probably read it in excerpts that were published in the *New-York Mirror* on 24th May 1834.

p. 166, *I agree with Buffon – with Hogarth: it is but diligence, after all*: The French naturalist Georges-Louis Leclerc, Comte de Buffon (1707–88), is reported to have said once to the politician Marie-Jean Hérault de Séchelles (1759–94): "*La génie n'est qu'une plus grande aptitude à la patience*" ("Genius is only a greater aptitude for patience"); the English painter and engraver William Hogarth (1697–1764) is reported to have said once to the poet John Gilbert Cooper (1722–69): "Genius is nothing but labour and diligence." Poe probably derived both quotes from the chapter on "Buffon" in Vol. 2 of *Biographiana*, a 1799 collection of anecdotes by William Seward (1747–99).

p. 166, *tête baissée*: "Head down" (French).

p. 166, *the Kickapoo*: An indigenous people of North America formerly living in what is now Wisconsin.

p. 167, *X-ing a Paragrab*: First published in *Flag of Our Union* (12th May 1849), and later reprinted in PW4, from where our text is taken.

p. 167, *the "wise men" came "from the East"*: See Matthew 2:1: "Now when Jesus was born in Bethlehem of Judaea in the days of Herod the king, behold, there came wise men from the east to Jerusalem." The "wise men" are the Magi.

p. 167, *Mr Touch-and-Go Bullet-Head*: "Mr Touchandgo, the great banker" is a character from *Crotchet Castle*, an 1831 novel by Thomas Love Peacock (1785–1866); in a piece headed "The Literati of New York City – No. V" published in *Godey's Lady's Book* in September 1846, Poe says of Lewis Gaylord Clark (see fourth note to p. 162): "His forehead is, phrenologically, bad – round and what is termed 'bullety'"; in a letter to F.W. Thomas of 8th September 1844 he had described another of his old adversaries, the poet and politician Thomas Dunn English (1819–1902), editor of the *Aurora*, as "a bullet-headed and malicious villain".

p. 167, *Brownson*: See third note to p. 50.

p. 167, *Nopolis*: Literally "No city" in Greek.

p. 168, *in the light of a salamander*: Salamanders were thought to be able to endure fire.

p. 168, *Oh, tempora! Oh, Moses!*: A garbled variation on the famous words pronounced by Cicero in four different speeches, the most famous of which is his first oration against Catiline: "*O tempora! O mores!*" ("Oh, what times! Oh, what customs!").

p. 168, *"O, it is pitiful!"*: A quotation from 'The Bridge of Sighs' (l. 46) by the English poet and humorist Thomas Hood (1799–1845).

p. 168, *the eel-skinning principle*: Poe may be alluding to the fact that if an eel is too small, it cannot be skinned – and therefore Bullet-Head cannot feel the insult, since his sense of integrity is too small.

p. 168, *Frogpondium*: Boston, from the name of its famous Frog Pond.

p. 169, *"So much for Buckingham!"*: From the end of Act IV of *The Tragical History of King Richard III*, a 1699 adaptation of Shakespeare's play by Colley Cibber (1671–1757): "CATESBY: My Liege, the Duke of Buckingham is taken. / RICHARD: Off with his head – so much for Buckingham."

p. 169, *homo*: "Man" (Latin).

p. 170, *his MS to the devil*: That is, his manuscript to the printer's devil (see third note to p. 152).

p. 170, *"case"*: "On a compositor's frame: either of two shallow trays divided into compartments in order to hold printing type" (*OED*).

p. 170, *izzards*: Zeds.

p. 170, *else there'll be... not a bit of pitch hot*: "The devil to pay and no pitch hot" is a proverb describing a situation in which one has a difficult and unpleasant task to perform without the necessary materials. The expression is nautical in origin, meaning, literally, "the longest seam on the ship to caulk without the necessary sealant". ("Pitch" is a kind of tar.)

p. 172, *riding him on a rail*: "Riding on a rail" was a form of mob justice commonly administered in the United States in the eighteenth and nineteenth centuries, consisting of parading an offender around town astraddle a fence rail held on the shoulders of two or more bearers.

p. 173, *The Angel of the Odd*: First published in *Columbian Magazine* (October 1844), and later reprinted in PW4, from where our text is taken.

p. 173, *truffe*: "Truffle" (French).

p. 173, *Glover's Leonidas... Griswold's "Curiosities"*: References to *Leonidas*, a 1737 poem by the English poet and politician Richard Glover (1712–85), about the Battle of Thermopylae of 480 BC; *The Epigoniad*, a 1757 poem in heroic couplets by the Church of Scotland minister and poet William Wilkie (1721–72), based on the story of the Seven against Thebes, as recounted in the fourth book of the *Iliad*; *Voyage en Orient* ("Journey to the Orient"), published in English in 1835 under the title *A Pilgrimage to the Holy Land*, a three-volume travelogue by the French author and statesman Alphonse de Lamartine (1790–1869); *The Columbiad*, an 1807 patriotic poem by the American diplomat and author Joel Barlow (1754–1812); *Isabel, or Sicily: A Pilgrimage*, an 1839 novel by the American author Henry Theodore Tuckerman (1813–71). For Griswold's "Curiosities", see third note to p. 59. All the above books are given by Poe as examples of literary dullness, turgidness and tediousness.

p. 173, *stupid*: Dazed – but obviously playing on the other meaning of the word.

p. 173, *Lafite*: A French claret produced at Château Lafite, in the Médoc district of the Gironde.

p. 173, *This folio... critics criticize*: From *The Task*, IV, ll. 50–51, by the English poet and hymn writer William Cowper (1731–1800).

p. 174, *Cockaigne*: Both the land of plenty in medieval folklore and (with punning allusion to "cockney") London.

p. 174, *Mein Gott!*: "My God!" (German).

p. 174, *pipe*: A large container for storing solids or liquids.

p. 174, *puncheon*: A large cask for liquids.

p. 174, *a truly Falstaffian air*: Shakespeare's Falstaff was famously corpulent.

p. 174, *one of those Hessian canteens*: A metal canteen like those carried by Hessian (that is, German) soldiers, so called because a large proportion of them hailed from Hesse in Germany. Hessian soldiers served as auxiliaries to the British army in several wars in the eighteenth century, such as the American Independence War (1775–83).

p. 175, *head-teuffel*: A portmanteau word composed of the English "head" and the German "Teufel" ("devil").

p. 176, *Kirschwasser*: Also known as "kirsch", kirschwasser (spelt "Kirschenwässer" and ""Kirschenwasser" by Poe) is brandy distilled from the fermented juice of cherries.

p. 176, *"beaucoup de bonheur et un peu plus de bon sens"*: "Much happiness and a little more common sense." The actual quote from *Gil Blas* (VII, iv) reads: "*toutes sortes de prospérités avec un peu plus de goût*" ("all kind of success with a little bit more good taste". For *Gil Blas*, see second note to p. 46.

p. 177, *The Omnipresence of the Deity*: An 1828 religious poem in three parts by the English poet and minister Robert Montgomery (1807–55).

p. 178, *Grandjean*: The New York hairdresser and wig maker Auguste Grandjean (1804–70).

p. 179, *I had a drop in it*: "To have a drop in the eye" is "to be tipsy".

p. 179, *brandy-saturated corn*: That is, a corn mash from which whiskey is distilled.

p. 179, *guide rope*: "A long rope hung from a balloon [...] so as to trail along the ground and to preserve altitude automatically by the drag of the rope without loss of ballast or gas" (*OED*).

p. 179, *depended*: Hung down.

p. 179, *meerschaum*: A tobacco pipe with a bowl made from meerschaum, a soft, white, claylike material.

p. 181, *Schiedam*: A large Dutch town west of Rotterdam.

p. 183, *Mellonta Tauta*: First published in *Godey's Lady's Book* (February 1849) and later reprinted in PW4, from where our text is taken. The story had been written before 17th January 1848, and was accepted at once for publication in *Godey's Lady's Book*, but was only published a year later. On 3rd February 1848, Poe delivered a lecture on 'The Universe' at the New York Society Library, and for the occasion quoted material from the story which had been rewritten and expanded. The lecture was later further reworked into *Eureka*, a book published in July 1848, which contains 'A Remarkable Letter', a substantially revised version of a section of 'Mellonta Tauta' (see EUR, pp. 3–11). "Mellonta Tauta" ("Μέλλοντα ταύτα") is Greek for "These are the things the future holds", a quotation from the end of Sophocles's tragedy *Antigone* (l. 1334), which Poe also used as the epigraph for 'The Colloquy of Monos and Una' (see p. 217). The *Godey's Lady's Book* version of the story includes the following short introductory letter by the author:

> TO THE EDITORS OF THE LADY'S BOOK,
>
> I have the honour of sending you, for your magazine, an article which I hope you will be able to comprehend rather more distinctly than I do myself. It is a translation by my friend, Martin Van Buren Mavis (sometimes called

the "Toughkeepsie Seer") of an odd-looking MS which I found, about a year ago, tightly corked up in a jug floating in the *Mare Tenebrarum* – a sea well described by the Nubian geographer, but seldom visited nowadays, except by the transcendentalists and divers for crotchets.

Truly yours,

EDGAR A. POE

"Martin Van Buren Mavis" the "Toughkeepsie Seer" is a reference to the American spiritualist Andrew Jackson Davis (1826–1910), called the "Poughkeepsie Seer" because he came to perceive himself as being endowed with clairvoyant powers after attending a series of lectures on mesmerism (see first note to p. 49) in Poughkeepsie in 1843 (it is not clear if the spelling "Toughkeepsie" is a compositor's error or authorial mystification). Poe substitutes the name of the former US president Martin Van Buren (1782–1862), who served from 1837 to 1841, for that of his predecessor, Andrew Jackson (1767–1845), who served from 1829 to 1837. Together, Van Buren and Jackson founded the Democratic Party in 1828. *Mare Tenebrarum*, Latin for "Sea of Shadows", is a medieval name for the southern Atlantic Ocean. The "Nubian geographer" is the cartographer and scholar Muhammad al-Idrisi (1100–65), author of a compendium of geographical knowledge usually known in English under the title *The Book of Pleasant Journeys into Faraway Lands*, an abridged Latin version of which was published in 1619 under the title *Geographia nubiensis*. For transcendentalism, see eighth note to p. 151.

p. 183, *April 1*: April Fool's Day. See note to p. 11.

p. 183, *the canaille*: The rabble, the populace.

p. 184, *drag rope*: Another name for "guide rope" (see third note to p. 179).

p. 184, *euphorbium... "milkweed"*: *Euphorbia corollata* is the scientific name for milkweed.

p. 184, *"silk-buckingham"*: A parodic allusion to the English author, traveller and politician James Silk Buckingham (1786–1855).

p. 184, *caoutchouc*: See second note to p. 9.

p. 184, *gutta-percha*: "A tough plastic substance obtained from the latex of various Malaysian trees" (*Oxford Concise Dictionary*).

p. 184, *an Irish philosopher called Furrier*: A garbled reference to the French socialist thinker Charles Fourier (1772–1837), one of the founders of utopian socialism.

p. 184, *the Hindoo Aries Tottle*: Another garbled reference, this time to the Greek philosopher Aristotle.

p. 184, *"Thus must we say... among men"*: The quotation is from Aristotle's *Meteorologia* (I, 3).

p. 185, *Horse*: Garbled reference to Samuel Morse (1791–1872), the inventor of the electric telegraph.

p. 185, *Tempora mutantur*: "Times change" (Latin).

p. 185, *Yellow... who is supposed to have been the first aeronaut*: Charles Green (see note to p. 19).

p. 186, *Neuclid*: Euclid.

p. 186, *Cant*: The German philosopher Immanuel Kant (1724–1804).

p. 186, *Hog, surnamed the "Ettrick Shepherd"... inductive*: The Scottish poet and novelist James Hogg (1770–1835), who was nicknamed ("surnamed") the "Ettrick Shepherd" (having been born in Ettrick, Selkirkshire), a name under which he published a number of his works. Poe, playing on the meaning of the word "hog" ("pig", and by extension its flesh used as food, "bacon"), jokingly attributes to him the main tenets of Francis Bacon's (1561–1626) philosophy, including the so-called "Baconian method" based on inductive, *a posteriori* reasoning, in opposition to the traditional Aristotelian method.

p. 186, *instantiæ naturæ*: "Occurrences of nature" (Latin).

p. 186, *noumena*: Objects knowable only by the mind or intellect, not by the senses.

p. 186, *bullet-headed*: See third note to p. 167.

p. 187, *"Ex nihilo nihil fit"*: "Nothing comes from nothing" (Latin) – an ancient dictum.

p. 187, *the cleverest ancient work... Mill*: A reference to the English philosopher and political economist John Stuart Mill (1806–73) and his 1843 work *A System of Logic*.

p. 187, *mill horse called Bentham*: Mill's mill horse is jokingly given the name of another famous English philosopher, Jeremy Bentham (1748–1832).

p. 188, *Kepler*: The German astronomer Johannes Kepler (1571–1630).

p. 188, *his three laws*: Kepler's three laws of planetary motion.

p. 188, *Champollion... his deciphering the Hieroglyphics*: A reference to the French philologist Jean-François Champollion (1790–1832), famous for deciphering Egyptian hieroglyphs.

p. 189, *unique*: Consisting of a single thing.

p. 189, *"prairie dogs" that we read of in fable*: "Prairie dogs" (which are, in fact, a kind of herbivorous rodent similar to a squirrel) are the subject of a chapter (XXXII) entitled "A Republic of Prairie Dogs" in *A Tour on the Prairies*, an 1835 work by the American author Washington Irving (1783–1859).

p. 190, *the fabulous Zeros and Hellofagabaluses*: A garbled reference to despotic tyrants such as Nero and Heliogabalus (or "Elagabalus", originally meaning "God of the Mountain" but later connected to "Helios", the sun, and interpreted as "God of the Sun"), the name by which the Roman emperor Marcus Aurelius Antoninus (r. 218–22 AD) was known posthumously. "Fabulous" here means "fabled", "legendary".

p. 190, *Alpha Lyrae*: The star Vega.

p. 190, *subtends an angle of half a degree*: See note to p. 33.

p. 191, *Alcyone in the Pleiades*: Alcyone is the brightest star in the Pleiades, part of the constellation Taurus.

p. 191, *one Mudler*: A garbled reference to the German astronomer Johann Heinrich von Mädler (1794–1874), who, in his 1846 work *Die Centralsonne* ("The Central Sun"), proposed that all the solar systems of the galaxy revolve about a central orb.

p. 192, *Neptunian*: Amended from "Nepturian" in PW4.

p. 192, *an island*: The island is Manhattan.

p. 192, *Knickerbocker tribe*: A "Knickerbocker" is a descendant of the original Dutch settlers in New York – hence, a New Yorker.

p. 192, *Recorder Riker, a knight of the Golden Fleece*: An allusion to the American lawyer and politician Richard Riker (1773–1842), who was Recorder of New York City from 1815 to 1819. The Distinguished Order of the Golden Fleece is a Catholic order of chivalry founded in 1430. Poe may be jokingly hinting at the fact that Riker had "fleeced" his fellow citizens of their "gold".

p. 193, *The women... a dromedary*: See 'The Thousand-and-Second Tale of Scheherazade', p. 70.

p. 193, *This Cornerstone... the City of New York*: Poe is alluding to the much-publicized laying of the cornerstone for a proposed monument to George Washington in Hamilton Square, New York City, on 19th October 1847, which was accompanied by a military parade, cannon salvoes, speeches and other ceremonies, and attended by vast crowds of New Yorkers (see, for example, the report in the *New-York Daily Tribune* of 20th October 1847, p. 2). The project, however, was abandoned through lack of funds, and came to fruition only several years later, when an equestrian bronze statue of George Washington was unveiled in Union Square in 1856. The British general Charles Cornwallis (1738–1805) surrendered his garrison of 7,000 troops at Yorktown on 19th October 1781, after a siege by a combined Franco-American force, resulting in negotiations between the United States and Great Britain that led to the Treaty of Paris of 1783 and the end of the American War of Independence. The inscription given by Poe is exactly as it appears in the *New-York Daily Tribune* report mentioned above.

p. 194, *"solitary and alone"... the great Amriccan poet Benton!*: The American politician Thomas Hart Benton (1782–1858), senator for Missouri from 1821 to 1851, famously used this expression in a statement before a Senate vote on 17th January 1837: "Solitary and alone I set this ball in motion!"

p. 194, *John, a smith*: John Smith, the commonest name, which Poe also used in 'X-ing a Paragrab' and 'The Man That Was Used Up'.

p. 194, *Zacchary, a tailor*: The American military officer and statesman Zachary Taylor (1784–1850), the recently elected twelfth president of the United States, who served from March 1849 until his death in July 1850.

p. 195, *The Man That Was Used Up*: First published in *Burton's Gentleman's Magazine* (August 1839) and later reprinted, with some authorial changes, in PW4, from where our text is taken. "Used up" was a term used to describe soldiers who were maimed or disabled to such an extent as to be unfit for combat.

p. 195, *A Tale of the Late Bugaboo and Kickapoo Campaign*: For the Kickapoo, see third note to p. 166. Their humorously named allies, the Bugaboo, are fictional.

p. 195, *Pleurez... tombeau*: From the 1636 play *Le Cid* (Act III, Sc. 3, ll. 7–8) by the French dramatist Pierre Corneille (1606–84): "Weep, weep, my eyes, and melt into water! / Half of my life has been buried by the other half."

p. 195, *air distingué*: "Air of distinction" (French).

p. 195, *His head of hair would have done honour to a Brutus*: Likely a reference to the "*coiffure à la Titus*", a hairstyle for men and, later, women, in which the hair was curled and cut short in the manner of a Roman bust. It was popularized at the end of the eighteenth century by the French actor François-Joseph Talma (1763–1826), who pioneered the fashion while portraying Titus Junius Brutus, son of Lucius Junius Brutus (*fl.* sixth century BC), the semi-legendary founder of the Roman Republic, in a 1791 production of Voltaire's *Brutus* in Paris.

p. 196, *the marble Apollo*: See fourth note to p. 127.

p. 196, *ne plus ultra*: "The furthest attainable point" (Latin) – that is, perfection.

p. 196, *os femoris*: "Thigh bone" (Latin).

p. 196, *fibula*: "Calf bone" (Latin).

p. 196, *reasons*: Punning on the near-homophone "raisins".

p. 196, *je ne sais quoi*: "An indescribable something" (French).

p. 197, *Nassau balloon packet... Timbuctoo*: For the balloon ride from London to Weilburg in the Duchy of Nassau, see note to p. 19. General Smith imagines a "balloon packet" – that is, a balloon travelling at regular intervals between two ports, carrying mail, goods and passengers.

p. 198, *quorum pars magna fuit*: "Of which he was a great part" – an adapted quotation from *Aeneid* II, l. 6.

p. 198, *horresco referens*: "I shudder to relate" – another quotation from the second book of the *Aeneid* (l. 204).

p. 198, *"man that is born of a woman... cut down like a flower!"*: From 'The Order for the Burial of the Dead', as contained in the Book of Common Prayer, the official service book of the Church of England, first issued in 1549. The words are an adaptation of Job 14:1–2.

p. 199, *the slips*: The sides of the gallery in a theatre.

p. 199, *Mandragora... yesterday!*: *Othello*, Act III, Sc. 3, ll. 334–37.
p. 200, *rout*: A large evening party or soirée.
p. 200, *pas de zephyr*: A ballet step – literally "Zephyr-like step" (French).
p. 200, *Miss Bas-Bleu*: A "bas-bleu" is a "bluestocking", a woman with literary pretensions.
p. 200, *Man-Fred... Man-Friday*: *Manfred* is the title of a dramatic poem written in 1816–17 by Lord Byron (1788–1824); "Man Friday" is the name given by Robinson Crusoe to his servant in Daniel Defoe's (*c.*1660–1731) famous novel.
p. 201, *la même cho-o-ose*: "La même chose" is French for "the same thing".
p. 201, *the Man in the Mask*: The "Man in the Mask" (or, more commonly, the "Man in the Iron Mask") was a political prisoner in France during the reign of Louis XIV (1643–1715) whose identity was protected by a black-velvet mask (misreported by Voltaire as being made of iron).
p. 201, *as concise as Tacitus or Montesquieu*: The Roman historian Tacitus (*c.*56–*c.*120 AD) and the French philosopher and historian Montesquieu (1689–1755), both renowned for their conciseness.
p. 203, *in the personal appearance of the man*: Amended, for sense, from "in the appearance of the personal man" (the wording in PW4 and the *Burton's Gentleman's Magazine* version).
p. 203, *There isn't Bonfanti's equal... America*: Joseph Bonfanti (1788–1838) was the owner of a well-known "fancy store" situated at 279 Broadway, New York.
p. 205, *The Businessman*: First published, under the title 'Peter Pendulum, the Business Man', in *Burton's Gentleman's Magazine* (February 1840); later revised for publication in the *Broadway Journal* (2nd August 1845) and collected, under the title 'The Business Man', in PW4, from where our text is taken. The "Peter Pendulum" in the original title of this story derives from the name of a character in sketches by the American journalist Joseph Dennie (1768–1812) that appeared in the *Farmer's Weekly Museum*, a New Hampshire newspaper, in the 1790s.
p. 205, *outré*: Eccentric.
p. 205, *sinciput*: The front of the skull from the forehead to the crown.
p. 205, *organ of order*: In phrenology, the organ of order, supposedly located in the forehead, was said to house the faculties communicating the love of physical arrangement.
p. 205, *pine knots*: Knots of pinewood.
p. 206, *the rule of three*: An arithmetic method of finding an unknown number in the same ratio to a given number as exists between two other given numbers.
p. 207, *To Peter Proffit*: In the original version of the story published in *Burton's Gentleman's Magazine*, the bill is made out to "Peter Pendulum" (see first note to p. 205). The total of the bill has been amended from "$2 96½", as it appears in PW4, to the correct amount. The notation "do." stands for "ditto".
p. 207, *Petersham*: A kind of greatcoat.

p. 207, *206*: Amended from "706" in PW4, based on the original version published in *Burton's Gentleman's Magazine*. "206 F" (around 97° C), close to the top reading of a traditional Fahrenheit thermometer, is near the standard boiling point of water.

p. 208, *penny*: Cent.

p. 208, *'Change*: The (Stock) Exchange.

p. 208, *hunks*: Miser.

p. 208, *Hottentot*: A name used by European colonists to refer to the Khoikhoi people of southern Africa, now considered offensive.

p. 208, *lamp-black*: Smear with lamp-black, a pigment made by collecting the soot produced by burning oil.

p. 210, *salt-and-batter*: That is, "assault-and-batter", punning on "salt-and-butter".

p. 210, *to play the possum*: That is, to feign ignorance of danger.

p. 210, *Their suspension*: The allusion is to the frequent suspension of banks during the administrations of President Andrew Jackson (1829–37) and President Martin Van Buren (1837–41).

p. 211, *a music mill*: A barrel organ.

p. 211, *tanbark*: The bark of oak and other trees, used to obtain tannin.

p. 211, *demnition*: Damnedly, utterly.

p. 211, *to deliver the letters and receive the postage*: At the time, the postage fee was paid by the recipient on delivery of the mail.

p. 212, *nem. con.*: An abbreviation of the Latin phrase "*nemine contradicente*" ("with no one dissenting") – that is, unanimously.

p. 212, *the scriptural injunction*: See Genesis 1:22: "Be fruitful, and multiply, and fill the waters in the seas, and let fowl multiply in the earth."

p. 212, *turtle*: Turtle meat, used to make turtle soup, was regarded as a delicacy.

p. 212, *Macassar oil*: An oil used at the time by men to make their hair shine and lie flat.

p. 213, *The Power of Words*: First published in *Democratic Review* (June 1845); later revised for publication in the *Broadway Journal* (25th October 1845) and collected in PW2, from where our text is taken. The tale is an imaginary dialogue between two angelic spirits in heaven, Oinos and Agathos, whose names derive from the Greek for "One" and "Good", respectively.

p. 213, *Aidenn*: Poe uses the name Aidenn (from the Arabic *Adn*, "Eden") for Heaven.

p. 214, *heart's-ease*: The wild pansy.

p. 217, *The Colloquy of Monos and Una*: First published in *Graham's Magazine* (August 1841) and later reprinted, with minor authorial revisions, in TA1, from where our text is taken. This is another imaginary dialogue between two angelic spirits in heaven, Monos and Una, whose names derive from the Greek masculine and Latin feminine for "One", respectively.

p. 217, *Μέλλοντα ταῦτα*: See first note to p. 183.

p. 218, *your own passage through the dark Valley and Shadow*: See Psalm 23:4: "Yea, though I walk through the valley of the shadow of death, I will fear no evil: for thou art with me; thy rod and thy staff they comfort me."

p. 219, *But alas... despised*: "It will be hard to discover a better [method of education] than that which the experience of so many ages has already discovered – and this may be summed up as consisting in gymnastics for the body and *music* for the soul." – *Repub*. lib. 2. "For this reason is a musical education most essential, since it causes Rhythm and Harmony to penetrate most intimately into the soul, taking the strongest hold upon it, filling it with beauty and making the man *beautiful-minded*. [...] He will praise and admire *the beautiful*, will receive it with joy into his soul, will feed upon it and *assimilate his own condition with it*." – Ibid. lib. 3. Music (μουσική) had, however, among the Athenians, a far more comprehensive signification than with us. It included not only the harmonies of time and of tune, but the poetic diction, sentiment and creation, each in its widest sense. The study of *music* was with them, in fact, the general cultivation of the taste – of that which recognizes the beautiful – in contradistinction from reason, which deals only with the true [POE'S NOTE]. The quotations are from Plato's *Republic* (II, 376e and III, 401d–402a, respectively).

p. 219, *Pascal... au sentiment*: A quotation from the *Pensées* ("Thoughts") by the French philosopher and mathematician Blaise Pascal (1623–62): "All our reasoning reduces itself to yielding to feeling" (I, 10, 4).

p. 220, *history*: From ιστορεῖν, to contemplate [POE'S NOTE]. It is in fact widely accepted today that the word derives from the ancient Greek word ἱστορία ("enquiry").

p. 220, *purification*: The word "purification" seems here to be used with reference to its root in the Greek πῦρ, "fire" [POE'S NOTE].

p. 224, *co-mates*: Companions.

p. 225, *The Conversation of Eiros and Charmion*: First published in *Burton's Gentleman's Magazine* (December 1839) and later reprinted, with minor authorial revisions, in TA1, from where our text is taken. This is another imaginary dialogue between two angelic spirits in heaven, Eiros and Charmion, whose names derive from those of Cleopatra's handmaids (see, for example, Plutarch's *Lives*, "Antony", LX, 1), although the former (Εἰράς in Greek) is usually transliterated "Iras".

p. 225, *Πῦρ σοι προσοίσω*: The epigraph is a quotation from Euripides's *Andromache* (l. 257).

p. 225, *like the "voice of many waters"*: See Revelation 14:2: "And I heard a voice from heaven, as the voice of many waters, and as the voice of a great thunder: and I heard the voice of harpers harping with their harps."

p. 225, *Aidenn*: See second note to p. 213.

p. 226, *those passages in the most holy writings... the orb of the earth alone*: See 2 Peter 3:10: "But the day of the Lord will come as a thief in the night; in the which the heavens shall pass away with a great noise, and the elements shall melt with fervent heat, the earth also and the works that are therein shall be burned up."

p. 227, *perihelion*: See first note to p. 17.

p. 231, *Shadow*: First published in the *Southern Literary Messenger* (September 1835) and later reprinted, with some authorial corrections, in PW2, from where our text is taken.

p. 231, *Yea, though I walk through the valley of the Shadow*: See note to p. 218.

p. 231, *Oinos*: See first note to p. 213.

p. 231, *now had arrived the alternation... the terrible Saturnus*: Poe appears to have derived this astrological information from *Les Premier traits de l'Érudition universelle* (Vol. 1, Chapter 49, Section 78), a 1767 work by the German statesman and science writer Jakob Friedrich von Bielfeld (1717–70), translated into English in 1770 as *The Elements of Universal Erudition*.

p. 231, *red Chian wine*: Wine from the Greek island of Chios.

p. 232, *the songs of Anacreon*: Anacreon was a Greek lyric poet (*c.*582–*c.*485 BC) famous for his drinking songs.

p. 232, *the son of Teios*: Anacreon (see previous note) was from the Greek city of Teos on the western coast of Asia Minor.

p. 232, *Chaldea*: Chaldea was an ancient state and region of lower Mesopotamia.

p. 233, *those dim plains of Helusion... the foul Charonian canal*: Poe appears to have lifted the description from *A New System, or An Analysis of Ancient Mythology* (1774–76) by the English scholar and mythographer Jacob Bryant (1715–1804): "The Elysian plain, near the Catacombs in Egypt, stood upon the foul Charonian canal." "Helusion" is "Elysium", also known as the "Elysian Fields" or "Elysian Plains". In Greek mythology, the "Charonian canal" is the Styx, across which the boatman Charon ferries the souls of the dead to their final abode, Hades. According to the myth, the souls of heroic and righteous people were allowed to sojourn in the Elysian Fields for eternity and enjoy a blissful afterlife.

p. 235, *Silence*: First published, under the title 'Siope – A Fable' (with the subtitle "In the manner of the Psychological Autobiographists"), in *The Baltimore Book: A Christmas and New-Year's Present* (Baltimore: Bayly and Burns, 1838), and later reprinted under the current title, with some authorial corrections, in PW2, from where our text is taken. "Psychological Autobiographists" is an allusion to the English writer and politician Edward Bulwer-Lytton (1803–73) and the English author and literary critic Thomas De Quincey (1785–1859).

p. 235, *Εὕδουσιν... τε καὶ χαράδραι*: The epigraph is a poetry fragment by the Greek lyric poet Alcman, who flourished in the seventh century BC.

p. 235, *subterrene*: Subterranean; underground.

p. 238, *the Sibyls… Dodona*: Dodona was an ancient sanctuary in Epirus, Greece, home to the oldest Hellenic oracle, where Zeus's will was divined by sibyls from the rustling of a sacred oak's leaves or the cooing of doves.

p. 239, *A Tale of Jerusalem*: First published in the *Saturday Courier* (9th June 1832); later reprinted with authorial corrections in the *Broadway Journal* (20th September 1845) and collected in PW2, from where our text is taken. The story draws many of its elements and details from *Zillah, A Tale of the Holy City* (1828), a historical novel by the English poet and novelist Horace Smith (1779–1849). Its main incident is inspired by an anecdote narrated in Chapter VII of Smith's book.

p. 239, *Intensos rigidam… Passus erat*: A slightly adapted quote from *Pharsalia* (II, ll. 375–76) by the Latin poet Lucan (39–65 AD). In the original, which has "*descendere*" instead of "*ascendere*", Lucan tells how, from the outbreak of the civil war (49–45 BC) between the factions led by Caesar and Pompey (Gnæus Pompeius Magnus, 106–48 BC), Cato ("the Younger", 95–46 BC) "had let the grey hair hang over his stern brow". Presumably Poe's substitution is intended as a joke, as if to say that Cato "had let the grey hair stand on end above his stern brow". We have silently corrected Poe's "Intensos" for "Intonsos".

p. 239, *De Catone*: "On Cato" (Latin).

p. 239, *in the year of the world three thousand nine hundred and forty-one*: That is, 3,941 years since the creation of the world, calculated as having occurred in 4004 BC by the Irish churchman James Ussher (1581–1656) in his work *Annales veteris testamenti, a prima mundi origine deducti* (a title meaning "Annals of the Old Testament, deduced from the first origins of the world"), published in 1650, based on a literal reading of the Bible. In Ussher's chronology – one of many "Anno Mundi" ("year of the world") calendars – the year 3941 corresponds to 63 BC.

p. 239, *the City of David*: Jerusalem.

p. 239, *Gizbarim*: "Cashiers" (Hebrew). According to most ancient sources, three Gizbarim handled the money deposited into the treasury of Jerusalem's Temple, under the supervision of seven Amarkol, or trustees, above whom were two Catholici ("Katholikin" in Horace Smith's *Zillah*), or overseers of the treasury, themselves under the direction of the high priest.

p. 239, *Baal*: Baal, or Ba'al (a generic name applied to many gods, and literally meaning "Lord"), was the chief god of the Canaanites.

p. 239, *the Pentateuch*: The first five books of the Old Testament (Genesis, Exodus, Leviticus, Numbers and Deuteronomy).

p. 239, *the people of Adonai*: The Jews, who use the word "Adonai" ("Lord") for God.

p. 239, *the Roman Pompey... the city of the Most High*: Pompey's siege of Jerusalem, part of his campaigns in the East, took place in 63 BC.

p. 240, *the Philistine*: "A member of a non-Semitic people occupying the southern coast of Palestine in biblical times, who came into conflict with the Israelites during the 12th and 11th centuries BC" (*OED*). Here the word is used simply as a derogatory term for an enemy.

p. 240, *circumvallatory trench*: A trench with ramparts.

p. 240, *fosse*: A long, narrow trench.

p. 240, *Mount Moriah*: The site of Jerusalem's Temple.

p. 240, *the Temple of Belus*: The temple consecrated to the god Belus at Babylon.

p. 240, *are as the sands by the seashore*: See Genesis 22:17: "That in blessing I will bless thee, and in multiplying I will multiply thy seed as the stars of the heaven, and as the sand which is upon the seashore; and thy seed shall possess the gate of his enemies."

p. 240, *from aleph to tau... the letter jod*: Aleph, tau and jod are the first, last and smallest letters of the Hebrew alphabet, respectively.

p. 241, *the regions of Pluto*: In Roman mythology, Pluto was the ruler of the underworld.

p. 241, *The god Phoebus... charioted for an hour*: That is, it is an hour since sunrise. Phoebus (from the Greek Φοῖβος, "bright") was an epithet of the god Apollo, often identified with the sun, who was imagined as driving his golden chariot across the sky.

p. 241, *Ædepol*: A contracted Latin oath: "By the god Pollux!"

p. 241, *"El Elohim!"*: "Ye Gods!" (Hebrew).

p. 241, *teraphim*: Deities.

p. 241, *Nergal... Baal-Zebub*: For the first seven gods, see 2 Kings 17:30–31: "And the men of Babylon made Succothbenoth, and the men of Cuth made Nergal, and the men of Hamath made Ashima, / And the Avites made Nibhaz and Tartak, and the Sepharvites burned their children in fire to Adrammelech and Anammelech, the gods of Sepharvaim." The others are derived by Poe from Horace Smith's novel *Zillah* (for which see first note to p. 239): Dagon was a god worshipped in ancient Syria; Belial is the name of a demon in the Hebrew Bible, later identified with the Devil; Baal-Berith, Baal-Peor and Baal-Zebub (literally, "Lord of the Flies") were titles of the god Baal worshipped by the Canaanites (see seventh note to p. 239).

p. 241, *Katholim*: "Catholics" (Hebrew). Poe meant "Katholikin" (see sixth note to p. 239).

p. 241, *the fat of the land*: See Genesis 45:18: "And take your father and your households, and come unto me: and I will give you the good of the land of Egypt, and ye shall eat the fat of the land."

p. 241, *Raca*: A Hebrew oath. See Matthew 5:22: "But I say unto you that whosoever is angry with his brother without a cause shall be in danger of the judgement: and whosoever shall say to his brother 'Raca' shall be in danger of the council: but whosoever shall say 'Thou fool' shall be in danger of hellfire."

p. 242, *shawm... sackbut*: The names of these musical instruments are all derived from Smith's *Zillah*. The Hebrew "shawm" is translated, in the King James Version, as "cornet"; the huggab is a kind of panpipe.

p. 243, *"Thou Art the Man"*: First published in *Godey's Lady's Book* (November 1844) and later reprinted, with minor authorial changes, in PW2, from where our text is taken. The title is a quotation from 2 Samuel 12:7: "And Nathan said to David, 'Thou art the man. Thus saith the Lord God of Israel, I anointed thee king over Israel, and I delivered thee out of the hand of Saul.'"

p. 243, *play the Oedipus to the Rattleborough enigma*: Oedipus, the mythical king of Thebes, famously solved the riddle of the Sphinx. Rattleborough (or Rattle) is a fictional town.

p. 243, *enginery*: Machinery.

p. 244, *"walking gentlemen" of the stage*: Male actors playing small parts with little or no speaking.

p. 244, *Château Margaux*: A premier cru from the Bordeaux region of France.

p. 246, *squibbing*: Lampooning.

p. 247, *dragged*: That is, searched using a drag, an apparatus for recovering objects from the bottom of a body of water.

p. 248, *malaproposisms*: Slips, or involuntary deviations from the speaker's intention.

p. 248, *pled*: Pleaded.

p. 248, *cui bono?*: "For whose benefit?" (Latin).

p. 249, *Mrs Gore... Mr Beckford*: The reference is to the prolific English novelist Catherine Gore (1798–1861), whose best-known novel was *Cecil, or The Adventures of a Coxcomb* (1841). Poe is paraphrasing an accusation of plagiarism levelled at her by the English poet and critic Richard Henry Horne (1802–84) in his 1844 work *A New Spirit of the Age*: "It is well known in the literary circles that Mrs Gore is the author of that clever but surpassingly impudent book, *Cecil*. We believe she has never avowed it, and has rather, on the contrary, kept up a little mystification about it. But there is really no doubt on the subject. She wrote the story, and Mr Beckford helped her to the learning. The public have been often perplexed by Mrs Gore's Greek and Latin, which, although they were never paraded so impertinently as the polyglot pretensions of Lady Morgan, were still remote enough from the ordinary course of female accomplishments to startle the public. Where they came from on former occasions we know not, but in this instance they may be referred to Mr Beckford, together with the still more recondite scraps of far-off tongues that are scattered through the work" (Chapter 7). The English author William Beckford (1760–1844) is best known for the Gothic novel *Vathek* (1786). Sydney, Lady Morgan (*c.*1778–1859), was an Irish novelist. Chaldean is the language of Chaldea (see third note to p. 232); the Chickasaw language was spoken by the Chickasaw, one of the indigenous peoples of the Southeastern Woodlands of the United States, based in what is now northern Mississippi, north-western and northern Alabama, western Tennessee and south-western Kentucky.

p. 249, *Bulwer*: See first note to p. 235.

p. 249, *Turnapenny and Ainsworth*: "Turnapenny" is a made-up name for a hack; William Harrison Ainsworth (1805–82) was an English historical novelist.

p. 249, *reinstation*: Reinstatement.

p. 251, *réunions*: "Get-togethers" (French).

p. 252, *petit souper*: A little supper; a small, informal dinner.

p. 253, *nem. con.*: See first note to p. 212.

p. 254, *criminating*: Incriminating.

p. 257, *Four Beasts in One*: First published, under the title 'Epimanes', in the *Southern Literary Messenger* (March 1836); later revised and reprinted, under the current title, in PW2, from where our text is taken. The "four beasts" in the title are man ("homo"), camel, lion ("leo") and panther ("pard"). "Epimanes" ("Furious", or "Raving-Mad") refers to the nickname given by the Jews to Antiochus IV Epiphanes ("Illustrious"), for whom see third note to this page. "Camelopard" is an antiquated name for the giraffe.

p. 257, *Chacun a ses vertus*: The epigraph is a quotation from *Xerxes*, a 1714 tragedy by the French playwright Prosper Jolyot de Crébillon (1674–1762): "Everyone has his good qualities" (Act IV, Sc. 2, l. 4).

p. 257, *Antiochus Epiphanes*: Antiochus IV Epiphanes (*c.*215–164 BC) was king of the Seleucid Empire – and often referred to as "King of Syria", since the Seleucids ruled that entire region – from 175 BC until his death. He is remembered for his persecutions of the Jews of Judea and Samaria, and for a revolt of the Jewish people against his rule, the so-called "Maccabean Revolt" (167–160 BC). According to ancient sources, during his final campaign in Persia, he tried to plunder the Temple of Artemis in Elymais in Persia (not Ephesus in Ionia), but the citizens knew of his approach, and were able to defend their city; he captured Jerusalem in 167 BC and desecrated its Temple (the "Holy of Holies") by offering the sacrifice of a pig on an altar to Zeus; he died a miserable death (at Tabae in Persia), as recounted in 2 Maccabees 9:5–29.

p. 257, *the Gog of the prophet Ezekiel*: "Gog, of the land of Magog, the chief prince of Meshek and Tubal", according to Ezekiel 38–39.

p. 257, *Cambyses, the son of Cyrus*: Cambyses II, the elder son of Cyrus the Great (d. *c.*530 BC), was King of Persia between 530 and 522 BC. According to the *Histories* of the ancient Greek historian Herodotus (b. *c.*484 BC), Cambyses was regarded as a despot by his subjects due to his being "harsh and arrogant" (III, 89).

p. 257, *a hundred and seventy-one*: It should, in fact, be "a hundred and seventy-five".

p. 257, *the year of the world three thousand eight hundred and thirty*: 174 BC. (See fourth note to p. 239.)

p. 258, *Seleucus Nicanor... Antiochus*: The Macedonian Greek general Seleucus I Nicator (*c.*358–281 BC), not "Nicanor". He was son of Antiochus (*fl.* fourth century BC), successor to Alexander the Great and founder of the Seleucid Empire.

p. 258, *the Queen City*: Rome.

p. 258, *Verus and Valens*: The Roman emperors Lucius Verus (130–69 AD) and Valens (328–78 AD).

p. 258, *satisfying your eyes... this city*: A quotation from *Twelfth Night*, Act III, Sc. 3, ll. 22–24.

p. 259, *the darkness of Egypt in the time of her desolation*: An allusion to Exodus 10:21: "And the Lord said unto Moses, 'Stretch out thine hand towards heaven, that there may be darkness over the land of Egypt, even darkness which may be felt.'"

p. 259, *Elah Gabalah... Heliogabalus*: See first note to p. 190.

p. 260, *valets-de-chambre*: "Valets" (French).

p. 260, *Timarchus... Heraclides*: Timarchus and his brother Heracleides were influential Greek noblemen, possibly from Miletus, during the early part of the second century BC, serving under Antiochus IV Epiphanes.

p. 260, *Ashimah*: See sixth note to p. 241. Poe's etymology from "the Greek *simia*" is of course fictitious.

p. 261, *Mille... effudit*: Flavius Vopiscus says that the hymn here introduced was sung by the rabble upon the occasion of Aurelian, in the Sarmatic War, having slain with his own hand nine hundred and fifty of the enemy [POE'S NOTE]. The Latin verse is taken from the chapter "Divus Aurelianus, by Flavius Vopiscus (of Syracuse)" of *Historiæ augustæ scriptores*, a late-Roman collection of biographies by various authors, including Vopiscus, of the Roman emperors. Specifically, Poe's source was the 1620 edition of this work produced by the French classical scholar Claude de Saumaise ("Claudius Salmasius", 1588–1653). The Roman emperor Aurelian reigned from 270 to 275 AD. He repulsed an invasion by the Sarmatians in 270 AD.

p. 262, *Elline and Argelais*: Fictional.

p. 263, *leg bail*: Unauthorized absence or departure.

p. 265, *Why the Little Frenchman Wears His Hand in a Sling*: First published in TGA and later reprinted, with authorial corrections, in PW2, from where our text is taken.

p. 265, *the pink of purliteness*: The flower (that is, the epitome) of politeness.

p. 265, *hot tun*: *Haut ton*, that is, "high fashion".

p. 265, *brisky*: Britzka (or britchka), an open carriage with a folding hood and space for people to recline.

p. 266, *mavourneen*: "My darling" (Irish).

p. 266, *puncheon*: That is, a "penchant".

p. 267, *Wully woo, pulley woo, plump in the mud*: Poe took this sequence of three phrases from the novel *Jacob Faithful* (1834) by the English novelist Captain Frederick Marryat (1792–1848), about Thames watermen: "And if we had tumbled, Father, we should have just died betwixt and between, not water enough to float us. It would have been *woolez wous parlez wous*, plump in the mud, as you say sometimes" (Chapter XVII). He perhaps did not realize that only the first two are intended as crude phonetic renderings of spoken French: respectively, of "*voulez-vous*" ("do you want") and "*parlez-vous*" ("do you speak"). See Kevin J. Hayes, 'Poe's "Little Frenchman" and Marryat's *Jacob Faithful*', *Notes and Queries*, Vol. 59 (2012), pp. 394–95.

p. 268, *flipper*: Hand.

p. 271, *Bon-Bon*: First published, under the title 'The Bargain Lost', in the *Saturday Courier* (1st December 1832); later revised and reprinted under the title 'Bon-Bon' in the *Southern Literary Messenger* (August 1835), TGA and in the *Broadway Journal* (19th April 1845); collected, after further authorial corrections, under the title 'Bon-Bon', in PW2, from where our text is taken.

p. 271, *Quand un bon vin… Présenter du tabac*: The epigraph, a French vaudeville that Poe took from Bielfeld's *Les Premier traits de l'Érudition universelle* (see fourth note to p. 231), can be translated: "When a good wine fills my stomach, / I am more learned than Balzac, / Wiser than Pibrac. / If I attacked the Cossack nation, / I'd ransack it / With just one arm; / I would cross Charon's lake / Sleeping in his bark; / I would go to fierce Aeacus / Without my heart going ding-dong, / And offer him some snuff" (Vol. 2, Chapter 7, Section 29). For Jean-Louis Guez de Balzac, see first note to p. 117; Guy Du Faur, Seigneur de Pibrac (1529–84) was a French jurist and poet; for Charon, see note to p. 233; in Greek mythology, Aeacus was, with Minos and Rhadamanthus, one of the judges of the underworld.

p. 271, *pâtés à la fois*: Possibly a garbled reference to *pâté de foie*, or liver pâté, made from ground pork liver and lard.

p. 271, *sur la Nature*: "On Nature" (French).

p. 271, *sur l'Âme*: "On the Soul" (French).

p. 271, *sur l'Esprit*: "On the Mind" (French).

p. 271, *fricandeaux*: Braised and larded fillets of veal.

p. 271, *littérateur*: "Man of letters" (French).

p. 271, *"idée de Bon-Bon"*: "A Bon-Bon idea" (French).

p. 271, *"Academy... Lyceum"*: A reference to the Academy school of philosophy founded by Plato and the Lyceum, the Athenian Temple to Apollo Lyceus where Aristotle's Peripatetic school was founded.

p. 272, *Kant*: See second note to p. 186.

p. 272, *Leibnitz*: The German philosopher and mathematician Gottfried Wilhelm Leibniz (1646–1716).

p. 272, *facili gradu*: "By an easy progression" (Latin).

p. 272, *Bon-Bon was Ionic – Bon-Bon was equally Italic*: A reference to the pre-Socratic Ionic and Italian schools of philosophy: the former included philosophers such as Thales, Anaximander, Heraclitus and Anaxagoras, the latter Pythagoras (and his followers), Parmenides, Zeno and Empedocles, among others.

p. 272, *George of Trebizond – he believed in Bessarion*: The Byzantine Greek humanists George of Trebizond (1395–1486) and Bessarion (1403–72) had conflicting philosophical views: when the former published *Comparatio Aristotelis et Platonis* ("A Comparison between Aristotle and Plato", 1458), in which he attacked Plato's philosophy, the latter responded, in 1469, with a virulent rebuttal, *In calumniatorem Platonis* ("Against Plato's Slanderer").

p. 272, *The Greeks... the same word for the mind and the diaphragm*: Φρένες [POE'S NOTE]. The term was used by the Greek to refer both to the "midriff" and the "heart" or "mind". We have corrected Poe's "θζενες", either an authorial or a compositor's error.

p. 272, *alto rilievo*: "High relief" (Italian).

p. 273, *essais*: "Essays" (French).

p. 273, *Catullus*: The Roman poet Catullus (*c.*84–*c.*54 BC).

p. 273, *Vin de Bourgogne... Chambertin*: "Vin de Bourgogne" is burgundy; for Sauternes see first note to p. 144; Côtes du Rhône and Médoc are renowned French wines; Saint-Péray is a sparkling white wine from the southernmost part of the northern Rhône region; for Clos de Vougeot see second note to p. 137; Chambertin is a celebrated grand cru.

p. 273, *diablerie*: "Devilishness" (French).

p. 273, *sous-cuisinier*: "Sub-chef" (French).

p. 273, *water dog*: "A dog that swims well, and is habituated to or not shy of the water"; in particular, "a dog trained to retrieve waterfowl" (*OED*).

p. 274, *aimable*: "Amiable" (French). There is no fabric of this name.

p. 274, *tout ensemble*: "All the parts taken together" (French).

p. 274, *Œuvres de Bon-Bon*: "Works by Bon-Bon" (French).

p. 275, *à la grecque*: "After the Greek fashion" (French) – but, as a culinary expression, "served in a sauce made of olive oil, lemon juice and several seasonings, such as fennel, coriander, sage and thyme" (*Merriam-Webster*).

p. 275, *bibliothèque*: "Library" (French).

p. 275, *mélanges*: A "mélange" is both a "miscellany" and, as a culinary term, a "mixture", a "hotchpotch".

p. 275, *Eusebius*: The Roman historian, Christian exegete and polemicist Eusebius of Caesarea (*c.*260–339 AD).

p. 275, *des œufs à la princesse, he had unfortunately perpetrated an omelette à la reine*: "Eggs princess-style" and "omelette queen-style", respectively (French). As culinary terms, "*À la princesse*" indicates a way of preparing certain dishes, so called because of the delicacy or richness of the ingredients used, whereas "*à la reine*" indicates a way of preparing chicken stew or purée.

p. 276, *interrogatories*: Questions.

p. 276, *queue*: A pigtail.

p. 277, *"Rituel Catholique"*: "Catholic Rites" (French).

p. 278, *mousseux*: "Sparkling (wine)" (French).

p. 278, *vis-à-vis to his companion's*: That is, facing his companion.

p. 278, *"Registre des Condamnés"*: "Register of Convicted Persons" (French).

p. 279, *in the heavens above… or in the waters under the earth*: See Exodus 20:4: "[A]ny thing that is in heaven above, or that is in the earth beneath, or that is in the water under the earth."

p. 280, *it was I who told Aristotle… through the proboscis*: Aristotle often talks about the causes and origins of sneezing (as well as "hiccuping"), especially in Book XXXIII of his *Problems*, but he never said that through sneezing "men expelled superfluous ideas".

p. 280, *He met me at Athens… the fundamental doctrine in his metaphysics*: A slightly amended version of a story Poe found in *The Posthumous Works of a Late Celebrated Genius* (later republished as *The Koran, or Essays, Sentiments, Characters, and Callimachies, of Tria Juncta in Uno, M.N.A., Master of No Arts*), a 1770 work of mystification by one Richard Griffith (d. 1788): "Even so late as near the beginning of the sixteenth century, a certain priest, having met with this passage in some Greek author, ὁ νοῦς ἐστιν ἄϋλος, *mens humana immaterialis est*, and finding, in his Lexicon, that αὐλός signified a flute or pipe, brought no less than fifteen arguments, in an academic exercise, to prove the human soul to be a whistle." The letter lambda (λ), transliterated *l*, if inverted, looks like a gamma (γ), transliterated *g* (in PW2, the γ is replaced by an actual inverted λ). Poe humorously changes the second "αυλος" in Griffith's story to "αυγος", Greek for "morning light", which certainly does not form part of Plato's "fundamental doctrine in his metaphysics". The original title of Griffith's book points to the supposed posthumous writings of the Irish novelist Laurence Sterne (1713–68), in fact a spurious work by Griffith himself.

p. 280, *an anarchy of five years… any degree of executive power*: The period alluded to by the Devil is that of the Roman civil war (86–82 BC) between the factions led by Roman general Gaius Marius (*c.*157–86 BC) and consul Lucius

Cornelius Cinna (before 130–84 BC) on the one hand, and the Roman general Sulla (138–78 BC) on the other, which resulted in the victorious Sulla becoming dictator of the Roman Republic.

p. 280, *I have no earthly acquaintance... with any of its philosophy*: "*Ils écrivaient sur la philosophie (Cicero, Lucretius, Seneca), mais c'etait la philosophie grecque*" – Condorcet [POE'S NOTE]. The French here means: "They wrote about philosophy (Cicero, Lucretius, Seneca), but it was Greek philosophy" – Poe's point being that Roman civilization had no philosophy of its own. It is a paraphrase of a passage in the "Fifth Epoch" of *Esquisse d'un tableau historique des progrès de l'esprit humain* (*Outlines of a Historical View of the Progress of the Human Mind*), a 1795 work by the French philosopher the Marquis de Condorcet (1743–94), in which the author discusses the inferiority of Roman culture to that of the Greeks: "*Cicéron, Lucrèce et Sénèque écrivirent éloquemment dans leur langue sur la philosophie; mais c'était sur celle des Grecs*" ("Cicero, Lucretius and Seneca wrote eloquently about philosophy in their native tongue, but the philosophy they discussed was Greek").

p. 280, *Epicurus*: The Greek philosopher Epicurus (341–270 BC) taught that pleasure should be the aim of life, and reputedly led a life of luxury and sensuality.

p. 280, *Diogenes Laertes*: A reference to the Greek biographer Diogenes Laertius (*fl.* third century AD), who talks about Epicurus's voluminous body of work in Book x of his *Lives and Opinions of Eminent Philosophers*.

p. 282, *There was the soul of Cratinus... your Sauternes*: The names mentioned by the Devil are the Greek poet Cratinus (*c.*519–*c.*422 BC), the Greek comediographer Aristophanes (*c.*446–*c.*386 BC) and his contemporary, the comic poet Plato (*fl.* 410–390 BC), the Roman epic poet and dramatist Gnaeus Naevius (*c.*270–*c.*201 BC), the Greco-Roman poet and dramatist Livius Andronicus (*c.*284–*c.*204 BC), the Roman comediographers Plautus (*c.*254–184 BC) and Terentius (or Terence in English – see note to p. 109), the Roman satirist Gaius Lucilius (*c.*148–103 BC), the Roman poet Catullus (see second note to p. 273) and the Roman poets Publius Ovidius Naso (better known in English as Ovid, 43 BC–17/18 AD) and Quintus Horatius Flaccus (better known in English as Horace, 65–8 BC). A "Quirite" is a Roman citizen.

p. 282, *nil admirari*: See second note to p. 138.

p. 282, *Menander*: The Greek dramatist Menander (*c.*341–*c.*290 BC).

p. 282, *Nicander*: The Greek poet Nicander of Colophon (*fl.* second century BC).

p. 282, *Virgilius... Polybius and none other*: Virgilius (Publius Vergilius Maro) is the Latin name of the Roman poet Virgil (70–19 BC). The other names mentioned by the Devil are the Greek poet Theocritus (*c.*300–after 260 BC), the Roman epigrammatist Martial (*c.*38–*c.*104 AD), the Greek poet Archilochus (*c.*680–*c.*645 BC), the Roman historian Titus Livius (better known in English as Livy, 59 BC–17 AD) and the Greek historian Polybius (*c.*200–*c.*118 BC).

p. 282, *Hippocrates*: The Greek physician Hippocrates (*c*.460–377 BC), regarded as the father of medicine.

p. 282, *Styx*: See note to p. 233.

p. 282, *cholera morbus*: The name used in Poe's time to refer to cholera, to differentiate it from was then called "Asiatic cholera", associated with the second cholera pandemic of 1826–37.

p. 283, *vivente corpore*: "As a living body" (Latin).

p. 283, *Cain... Pisistratus*: Famous examples of wickedness. In the Book of Genesis, Cain, son of Adam and Eve, kills his brother Abel, thereby becoming the first murderer. Nimrod, the "mighty hunter before the Lord" of Genesis 10:9, is traditionally held to be responsible for the building of the Tower of Babel and the subsequent confusion of tongues (described in Genesis 11:1–9, though Nimrod is not mentioned), and is associated with slaughter and cruelty. Nero and Caligula were notoriously cruel Roman emperors. Dionysius of Syracuse (*c*.432–367 BC) and Pisistratus of Athens (*c*.600–527 BC) were infamous Greek tyrants.

p. 283, *"Machi—", "Maza—", "Robesp—"*: The incomplete names are those of the Italian historian and author Niccolò Machiavelli (1469–1527), the Italian-born French statesman Cardinal Jules Mazarin (1602–61) and Maximilien de Robespierre (1758–94), the leader of the radical Jacobins during the Reign of Terror.

p. 283, *George, Elizabeth*: Presumably the English monarchs George IV (1762–1830) and Elizabeth I (1533–1603).

p. 283, *a name... indicating more unequivocally*: Quere: Arouet? [POE'S NOTE]. The Latin term "*quere*" can here be translated "question". For François-Marie Arouet (real name of the French philosopher and author Voltaire), whose anti-Catholic ideas gained him a sulphurous reputation, see second note to p. 61.

p. 284, *fricandeau*: See seventh note to p. 271.

p. 287, *The Domain of Arnheim*: First published, under the title 'The Landscape Garden', in *The Ladies' Companion* (October 1842); extensively revised by the author and reprinted, under the current title, in the *Columbian Magazine* (March 1847); later collected in PW1, from where our text is taken. Arnheim is the name of the ancestral home of the heroine of *Anne of Geierstein, or The Maiden of the Mist*, an 1829 novel by Sir Walter Scott (1771–1832), a book that Poe had read.

p. 287, *The garden... the evening blue*: The epigraph is a quotation from *Christ's Victory and Triumph in Heaven and Earth, over and after Death* (Part II, "Christ's Victory on Earth", stanza 42), a 1610 allegorical poem by the English poet and cleric Giles Fletcher (*c*.1585–1623). The word "sembled" here means "represented", "pictured"; the "flowers de luce" are purple irises.

p. 287, *Turgot, Price, Priestley and Condorcet*: Enlightenment thinkers who believed in the perfectibility of human nature and society. The first three are the French economist and statesman Anne Robert Jacques Turgot (1727–81), the Welsh philosopher and Nonconformist minister Richard Price (1723–91) and the English chemist and natural philosopher Joseph Priestley (1733–1804). For Condorcet, see fourth note to p. 280.

p. 288, *preconcert*: A pre-existing arrangement.

p. 288, *ex-post-facto*: "Retrospective" (Latin).

p. 289, *This act... dollars*: An incident similar in outline to the one here imagined occurred, not very long ago, in England. The name of the fortunate heir was Thelluson. I first saw an account of this matter in the *Tour* of Prince Pückler-Muskau, who makes the sum inherited ninety millions of pounds, and justly observes that "in the contemplation of so vast a sum and of the services to which it might be applied, there is something even of the sublime". To suit the views of this article, I have followed the prince's statement, although a grossly exaggerated one. The germ (and, in fact, the commencement) of the present paper was published many years ago – previous to the issue of the first number of Sue's admirable *Juif errant*, which may possibly have been suggested to him by Muskau's account [POE'S NOTE]. As Poe states in this note, he drew inspiration from a story recounted in *Tour in England, Ireland, and France, in the Years 1826, 1827, 1828, and 1829* (1831–32), by the German nobleman Hermann, Fürst von Pückler-Muskau (1785–1871), an expert in landscape gardening: "You have no doubt heard that an ancestor of the Thelluson family made a will according to which his property was to accumulate for a hundred and fifty years, interest upon interest, and the then existing young Thelluson to come into possession of the whole. In twenty years this term will expire, and I saw the present Mr Thelluson, a man of forty, who has very little, and his son, a pretty boy of eight, who is probably destined in his twenty-eighth year to be master of twelve millions sterling – ninety-four millions of our money. An act of parliament has prohibited all such wills for the future, but could not invalidate this, though great efforts were made to do so. So enormous a fortune certainly invests a private man with a very unnatural degree of power. However, I could not help heartily wishing good luck to the little fellow, with his splendid hopes. There is really something grand in having such enormous wealth, for it cannot be denied that money is the representative of most things in the world. What marvellous objects might be attained by such a fortune well applied!" (Vol. 4, Letter VIII). *Le Juif errant* (*The Wandering Jew*) is a novel by the prolific French writer Eugène Sue (1804–57), published in instalments between 25th June 1844 and 26th August 1845.

p. 289, *virtu*: Fine art.

p. 290, *many far greater than Milton… "mute and inglorious"*: See Thomas Gray's (1716–71) 'Elegy Written in a Country Churchyard': "Some mute inglorious Milton here may rest" (l. 59).

p. 291, *Claude*: The French artist Claude Lorrain (*c*.1600–1682), famous for his landscape paintings.

p. 292, *mortal*: Amended from "moral" in PW1, based on the reading of the corresponding passage in 'The Landscape Garden'.

p. 293, *There are properly… human interest*: The quotation is from a review of *A Treatise on the Theory and Practice of Landscape Gardening, Adapted to North America*, an 1841 work by the American landscape designer Andrew Jackson Downing (1815–52), that appeared in the June 1841 issue of the New York literary journal *Arcturus*.

p. 293, *a spot with capabilities*: An obvious allusion to the English landscape designer Lancelot Brown (1716–83), nicknamed "Capability" for his habit of pointing out to his clients "capabilities" for improvement on their properties.

p. 293, *Addison*: The English writer and politician Joseph Addison (1672–1719), famous among other things for the tragedy *Cato* (1712), alluded to later in the paragraph.

p. 295, *De Staël*: The French writer and intellectual Madame de Staël (1766–1817), here cited as the epitome of literary Romanticism.

p. 295, *Timon*: The misanthropic Athenian who, according to Plutarch's *Lives* ('Antony', LXX), lived during the era of the Peloponnesian War (431–404 BC)

p. 296, *Fonthill*: The Wiltshire estate where William Beckford (see first note to p. 249) built a Gothic Revival country house known as "Fonthill Abbey" or "Beckford's Folly".

p. 301, *The Spectacles*: First published in the *Dollar Newspaper* (27th March 1844); later reprinted in the *Broadway Journal* (22nd November 1845) and collected in PW2, from where our text is taken.

p. 301, *Froissart… the immortal author of the Chronicles*: A reference to the *Chronicles*, a prose history of the Hundred Years War (1337–1453) by the French court historian Jean Froissart (*c*.1337–*c*.1405).

p. 302, *the P—— Theatre*: Probably a reference to the Park Theatre, at the time New York's leading playhouse.

p. 302, *fanatico*: "Fanatic" (Italian).

p. 303, *beau idéal*: "Ideal beauty" (French).

p. 303, *tournure*: "Bearing" (French).

p. 303, *the Greek Psyche*: Poe may have had in mind the Psyche of Capua, a famous Roman marble sculpture from the first century BC, after a Greek original by Scopas.

p. 303, *gaze aérienne*: "Ethereal gauze" (French).

p. 303, *the ventum textilem of Apuleius*: The expression "*ventum textilem*" ("a breeze-like garment") is in fact not by Apuleius (*c*.124–after 170 AD), but can be found in the *Satyricon* (LV), a novel by the Roman author Petronius (*c*.27–*c*.66 AD).

p. 304, *Not to know her argues yourself unknown*: An adapted quote from *Paradise Lost* IV, l. 830: "Not to know me argues yourselves unknown."

p. 304, *Madame Lalande*: The name is derived from that of a famous singer of the time, the French operatic soprano Henriette Méric-Lalande (1799–1867). She is mentioned in a biography of the singer María Malibrán Poe had read (see note to p. 313).

p. 307, *Stamboul*: Constantinople.

p. 308, *Erebus*: In Greek mythology, another name for the underworld.

p. 308, *Antares*: The brightest star in the constellation Scorpius.

p. 309, *Ninon… de l'Enclos*: The lines – which allude to the French courtesan Ninon de l'Enclos (1620–1705), famous for her beauty even in old age – can be translated "Down with Ninon, Ninon, Ninon – / Down with Ninon de l'Enclos!"

p. 310, *hock*: A dry white wine from the German Rhineland.

p. 312, *that course of true love that never did run smooth*: "Ay me! For aught that I could ever read, / Could ever hear by tale or history, / The course of true love never did run smooth" (*A Midsummer Night's Dream*, Act I, Sc. 1, ll. 134–46).

p. 313, *I know not how adequately to describe it*: Poe lifted a large part of the subsequent description of Lalande's singing from *Memoirs and Letters of Madame Malibran* (Vol. 2, p. 110), an 1840 biography of the celebrated Spanish opera singer María Malibrán (1808–36) by the Cuban writer María de las Mercedes Santa Cruz y Montalvo, Countess de Merlin (1789–1852).

p. 314, *the romance in Otello*: Probably the aria 'Ave Maria, piena di grazia' sung by Desdemona in Act IV, Sc. 2 of *Otello*, an 1816 opera by Gioachino Rossini (1792–1868).

p. 314, *the words "Sul mio sasso" in the Capuleti*: The words are in fact sung by Romeo in a duet with Giulietta from Act II, Sc. 3 of *I Capuleti e i Montecchi*, an 1830 opera by Vincenzo Bellini.

p. 314, *the San Carlo*: The main royal opera theatre in Naples (amended from "San Carlos" in PW2).

p. 314, *fioriture*: "Embellishments" (Italian). Amended from "*fiorituri*" in PW2.

p. 314, *the Sonnambula… ond'io son piena!*: The quotation is from Act II, Sc. 10 of *La Sonnambula*, an 1831 opera by Vincenzo Bellini. The Italian means: "Human thought cannot conceive of the happiness that fills me."

p. 315, *mon cher ami*: "My dear friend" (French).

p. 315, *"Eh bien, mon ami"*: "Oh well, my friend" (French).

p. 315, *empressement*: "Eagerness" (French).

p. 318, *buy de pig in the poke*: "To buy a pig in a poke" means to buy something without inspecting or assessing it first.

p. 319, *la belle France*: "Beautiful France" (French).

p. 319, *pigeon wings*: A pigeon wing is "a dance step performed by jumping up and striking the legs together whilst in the air" (*OED*).

p. 320, *un peu passées*: "A little past their prime" (French).

p. 321, *"at the death"*: A hunting expression, meaning "at the point when game is caught and killed".

p. 323, *The Duc de l'Omelette*: First published in the *Saturday Courier* (3rd March 1832); later reprinted in the *Broadway Journal* (11th October 1845) and collected in PW2, from where our text is taken. The story was intended in part as a parody of *The Young Duke*, an 1831 novel by the English statesman and writer Benjamin Disraeli (1804–81).

p. 323, *And stepped at once into a cooler clime*: The epigraph is a quote from Cowper's *The Task* (I, l. 337). For Cowper, see sixth note to p. 173.

p. 323, *Keats fell by a criticism*: Following Lord Byron's famous quip – "John Keats, who was kill'd off by one critique" (*Don Juan* XI, 60, l. 1) – it was widely believed that the disappointment caused by the *Quarterly Review*'s April 1818 review of his poem *Endymion* had led the English poet John Keats (1795–1821) to an early death.

p. 323, *Who was it died of The Andromache?*: Montfleury. The author of the *Parnasse Réformé* makes him speak in Hades: "*L'homme donc qui voudrait savoir ce dont je suis mort, qu'il ne demande pas si'l fût de fièvre ou de podagre ou d'autre chose, mais qu'il entende que ce fût de* L'Andromache" [POE'S NOTE]. Montfleury was the stage name of Zacharie Jacob (d. 1667), a renowned French actor and playwright. The anecdote has been lifted by Poe from D'Israeli's *Curiosities of Literature* (Vol. 1, "Tragic Actors"), for which see second note to p. 3. The *Parnasse Réformé* ("The Reform of Parnassus") is a 1668 satirical work by the French lawyer and writer Gabriel Guéret (1641–88). Montfleury's words (which Poe translated back into French from D'Israeli's book) can be translated: "Whoever wanted to know the cause of my death should not ask if it was a fever or gout or some other disease: it was *The Andromache*!"

p. 323, *an ortolan*: The migratory bunting, a songbird related to the finches.

p. 323, *L'histoire en est brève*: "This is but a short story" (French).

p. 323, *Apicius*: Caelius Apicius, the supposed author of *De re culinaria* ("On Cooking"), a collection of ancient Roman cookery recipes thought to date from the fifth century AD.

p. 323, *Chaussée-d'Antin*: Rue de la Chaussée-d'Antin, a fashionable street in the 9th *arrondissement* of Paris.

p. 323, *La Bellissima*: "The Most Beautiful" (Italian).

p. 323, *that ottoman… the notorious ottoman of Cadêt*: The allusion is obscure. In the original *Saturday Courier* version (3rd March 1832) "Cadêt" is spelt "Cadet". Poe was an officer cadet at West Point from October 1830 to February 1831, and this could well be an in-joke, as suggested by some critics.

p. 323, *"Horreur!… servi sans papier!"*: "Oh, horror!… You cur!… Baptiste!… The bird!… Ah, good God! You have stripped that modest bird of its feathers and served it without paper!" (French).

p. 323, *c'est vrai*: "It's true" (French).

p. 324, *robe de chambre*: "Dressing gown" (French).

p. 324, *Baal-Zebub, Prince of the Fly*: See sixth note to p. 241.

p. 324, *au revoir*: "Goodbye" (French).

p. 324, *bien comme il faut*: "Pretty good" (French).

p. 324, *parmi les nues*: "Among the clouds" (French).

p. 324, *Persia never worshipped such… Guebre never imagined such*: The Guebres were a Persian sect of fire-worshippers, the remnant of the ancient Zoroastrians.

p. 324, *the god Apollo*: See second note to p. 241.

p. 324, *tout ensemble*: See second note to p. 274.

p. 325, *Kupris! Astarte! Ashtoreth!*: Kupris is another Greek name for Aphrodite (Venus); Ashtoreth (or Astarte) was a Middle Eastern goddess of fertility and war.

p. 325, *Raphael*: The Italian Renaissance painter Raffaello Sanzio (1483–1520), who depicted Venus (Aphrodite) in many of his paintings.

p. 325, *"C'est vrai… il a pensé beaucoup… mais!"*: "It's true that he thought a great deal about all these things… but!" (French).

p. 325, *Le pauvre duc!*: "Poor duke!" (French).

p. 325, *the petit-maître… et qui sourit… si amèrement*: "The fop… and who smiles… so bitterly" (French).

p. 325, *Mais il faut agir*: "But something must be done" (French).

p. 325, *il avait tué ses six hommes*: "He had killed half a dozen men" (French).

p. 325, *il peut s'échapper*: "He might escape" (French).

p. 325, *Mais il joue!*: "But he plays cards!" (French).

p. 325, *the Diable of Abbé Gaultier*: A fictional work by the French Catholic priest Louis Gaultier (*c.*1745–1818), who wrote a number of books advocating the pedagogic use of games for children.

p. 325, *"que le Diable n'ose pas refuser un jeu d'écarté"*: "That the Devil dare not refuse a game of écarté" (French). Écarté is a game of cards for two persons, similar to whist.

p. 325, *Père Le Brun*: The allusion is to the French painter Charles Le Brun (1619–90), who was interested in physiognomy and the ability to describe or read people's states of mind using their facial expressions.

p. 325, *"Si je perds"*: "If I lose" (French).

p. 325, *"voilà tout!"*: "That's all" (French).

p. 325, *"Si je gagne... soient préparées!"*: "If I win, I'll return to my ortolan – let the cards be shuffled!" (French).

p. 325, *Francis and Charles*: Two famous rivals: Francis I of France (1494–1547) and the Holy Roman Emperor Charles V (1500–58), who waged war against each other for over two decades.

p. 326, *"C'est à vous à faire"*: "Your turn" (French).

p. 326, *en presentant le roi*: "Laying down the king" (French).

p. 326, *Had Alexander not been Alexander... Diogenes*: According to a story in Plutarch's *Lives* ("Life of Alexander", XIV, 1–5), when Alexander the Great (356–323 BC), king of Macedon, visited Diogenes the Cynic (*c.*400–*c.*325 BC) to enquire why he had not congratulated him on being proclaimed the leader of a forthcoming expedition against Persia, the philosopher replied by requesting that Alexander step aside so as not to block the sun. Impressed by the insouciance of this response, the king later told his followers that if he were not Alexander, he would choose to be Diogenes.

p. 326, *"que s'il n'eût été de l'Omelette... d'être le Diable"*: "That, had he not been de l'Omelette, he would have had no objection to being the Devil" (French).

p. 327, *King Pest*: First published in the *Southern Literary Messenger* (September 1835); later reprinted with authorial corrections in the *Broadway Journal* (18th October 1845) and collected in PW2, from where our text is taken. The story was inspired by a number of contemporary sources, including an article in the *New-York Mirror* (21st June 1832) about a man attending a masked ball in Paris in the character of the Cholera and the party described in Book VI, Chapter 1, of *Vivian Grey*, an 1826 novel by Benjamin Disraeli (see first note to p. 323).

p. 327, *The gods... in rascal routes*: The epigraph is a quotation from Act II, Sc. 1, of *The Tragedie of Gorboduc* (also titled *The Tragedie of Ferrex and Porrex*), a 1561 play by Thomas Norton (1532–84) and Thomas Sackville, Lord Buckhurst (1536–1608). The word "routs" here means "gatherings", "groups of people".

p. 327, *the third Edward*: Edward III (1312–77), king of England from 1327 until his death. It was during his reign that the Black Death of 1348 struck England, causing the death of a third or more of its inhabitants.

p. 327, *Sluys*: Sluis, a town in the south-western Dutch province of Zeeland.

p. 327, *the parish of St Andrews, London*: Probably St Andrew-by-the-Wardrobe, in the City of London.

p. 327, *"Jolly Tar"*: A "tar" is a seaman. "Jolly tar" was also used to refer to a cooper who crafted barrels on ships.

p. 327, *jib-boom*: "A spar run out from the end of the bowsprit, to which the tack of the jib is lashed" (*OED*).

p. 328, *the cachinnatory muscles*: The facial muscles used to cachinnate – that is, to laugh.

p. 328, *"humming stuff"*: That is, "very strong stuff".

p. 328, *"No Chalk"*: That is, "no credit" – a reference to the old custom at alehouses of writing up with chalk an account of credit given to customers.

p. 328, *the commonalty*: Ordinary people.

p. 328, *"pump ship, clew up all sail and scud before the wind"*: That is, prepare for a hasty departure. "Pump ship" was, among sailors, an established euphemism for "urinate", referring originally to the removal of bilge water from a vessel. To "clew up all sail" is to "draw the lower ends (clews) of all sails up to the upper yard or the mast in preparation for furling"; to "scud before the wind" is to "run before a gale with little or no sail".

p. 329, *St Andrew's Stair*: No stairs of that name appear to have ever existed along the north bank of the Thames.

p. 330, *in basso*: "In a bass voice" (Italian).

p. 331, *October beer*: Strong beer.

p. 332, *haut ton*: See third note to p. 265.

p. 334, *Avast*: "Stop" (nautical slang).

p. 334, *"blue ruin"*: Gin.

p. 334, *dais chamber*: A chamber at the dais end of a hall.

p. 335, *Davy Jones*: In nautical slang, Davy Jones is "the evil spirit of the sea" (*OED*).

p. 335, *to mulct thee and thy companion in each a gallon of blackstrap*: That is, they are to be punished by each being forced to imbibe a gallon of blackstrap, a drink made by mixing rum and molasses.

p. 336, *"Belay that!"*: "Hang on a moment!" – literally, to "belay", in nautical slang, is to "coil a running rope round a cleat, belaying pin or kevel so as to fasten or secure it" (*OED*).

p. 336, *marlinspike*: A pointed metal tool used by sailors to separate strands of rope.

p. 336, *whom God assoilzie*: Whom God absolve (from sin).

p. 339, *Three Sundays in a Week*: First published in the *Saturday Evening Post* (27th November 1841); later reprinted with authorial corrections in the *Broadway Journal* (10th May 1845) and collected in PW2, from where our text is taken. The story was likely inspired by an unsigned article entitled "Three Thursdays in One Week" published in the *Philadelphia Public Ledger* of 29th October 1841, which begins: "Of all the paradoxes there, is none more surprising or more calculated to disturb the mind than that which asserts the possibility of having three Thursdays in one week. It is, notwithstanding, possible, and during the last century it was demonstrated more than once. Circumnavigators, in their voyages round the world, have discovered the fact."

p. 339, *Remplis... ton verre plein!*: "Refill your empty glass, / Empty your full glass!" (French).

p. 340, *the plum*: The fortune.

p. 340, *"fine old English gentleman"... him of the song*: The allusion is to the traditional ballad 'The Old English Gentleman', whose first stanza reads: "I'll sing you an old ballad that was made by an old pate, / Of a poor old English gentleman who had an old estate. / He kept a brave old mansion at a bountiful old rate / With a good old porter to relieve the old poor at this gate. / Like a fine old English gentleman of the olden time."

p. 341, *Casimir Périer... logical wit*: The French quotation attributed by Poe to the French banker, mine owner and statesman Casimir Périer (1777–1832) can be translated: "What is a poet good for?" For "*ne plus ultra*", see second note to p. 196.

p. 341, *"Poeta nascitur, non fit"*: "A poet is born, not made" – a Latin adage, not a quotation from Horace.

p. 341, *Doctor Dubble L. Dee*: A caricature of Dionysius Lardner (for whom, see sixth note to p. 69), who was a Doctor of Laws (*legum doctor*, abbreviation LL D).

p. 341, *caprioles... riding*: In horse-riding, a "capriole" is "a high leap made by a horse without advancing". A "hobby" is a small horse or pony – here Poe is playing on its other meaning of "*idée fixe*".

p. 341, *"the people have nothing to do with the laws but to obey them"*: The English churchman Samuel Horsley (1733–1806), who was Dean of Westminster and Bishop of Rochester between 1793 and 1802, made this remark during a debate in the House of Lords on 11th November 1795.

p. 341, *"dragged their slow length along"*: An adapted quote from Alexander Pope's 1711 poem *An Essay on Criticism*: "That, like a wounded snake, drags its slow length along" (II, l. 157). For Pope, see fourth note to p. 151.

p. 341, *my fifth olympiad*: That is, my twentieth year (an "olympiad" is a period of four years between the Olympic Games, used by the ancient Greeks in dating events).

p. 341, *a pièce de résistance (as Messieurs Ude and Carême would say)*: A "*pièce de résistance*" is the most substantial dish of a meal; Louis-Eustache Ude (*c.*1769–1846) and Marie-Antoine Carême (*c.*1783–1833) were French chefs and writers of cookbooks. Poe is probably punning on the literal interpretation of the expression "piece of resistance" – that is, "stumbling block".

p. 342, *"assurement ce n'était pas sa foible"*: "Certainly it was not his weak point" (French).

p. 342, *et id genus omne*: "And all that sort" (Latin).

p. 345, *Lionizing*: First published, under the title 'Lion-izing: A Tale', in the *Southern Literary Messenger* (May 1835); extensively revised and reprinted, under the title 'Some Passages in the Life of a Lion', in the *Broadway Journal* (15th March 1845) and later collected, under the title 'Lionizing', in TA1, from where our text is taken. The story was intended in part as a parody of 'Too Handsome for Anything', a short story by Edward Bulwer-Lytton (see first note to p. 235), collected in *Conversations with an Ambitious Student in Ill Health, with Other Pieces* (1832), and as a gentle mockery of one of Poe's friends, the American poet and editor Nathaniel Parker Willis (1806–67), who wrote a series of letters about his travels in France, Italy, Greece and London that were published in the *New-York Mirror* and later collected in the volume *Pencillings by the Way* (1835).

p. 345, *all people went... in wild wonderment*: A misquotation from *Virgidemiarum*, a 1597 satirical work by the English cleric and moralist John Hall, Bishop of Norwich (1574–1656): "Genus and Species long since barefoot went / Upon their ten toes in wild wanderment" (II, 3, ll. 19–20).

p. 345, *neither the author of Junius nor the man in the mask*: Junius was the pseudonym used by an anonymous English writer who penned a series of letters that appeared, between January 1769 and January 1772, in London's *Public Advertiser*, and were later collected, along with other, private correspondence, in *Letters of Junius* (1772). For "the man in the mask", see second note to p. 201.

p. 345, *Nosology*: Properly, the branch of medical science dealing with the classification of diseases, but here used humorously as the "Science of Noses".

p. 345, *arrive at a lionship*: Become a personality, a celebrity.

p. 346, *Bartholinus*: The Danish anatomist Caspar Bartholin the Younger (1655–1738), author of, among other works, *De olfactus organo disquisitio anatomica* ("An Anatomical Examination of the Olfactory Organ", 1679) and *De respiratione animalium disputatio* ("A Debate on the Breathing of Animals", 1700).

p. 346, *Quarterly... Mrs Bas-Bleu*: For the *Quarterly Review* and the *Edinburgh Review*, see third and second notes to p. 154, respectively. The other periodicals mentioned in this dialogue are the *Westminster Review*, the *Foreign Quarterly Review*, the *Dublin Review*, *Bentley's Miscellany*, *Fraser's Magazine* and *Blackwood's Edinburgh Magazine*. For "Bas-Bleu", see third note to p. 200.

p. 346, *Duchess of Bless-my-Soul*: An allusion to the Irish novelist and literary hostess Marguerite Gardiner, Countess of Blessington (1789–1849). In his letters for the *New-York Mirror*, Nathaniel Parker Willis describes meeting some of London's most renowned literati at her dinner soirées (see *Pencillings by the Way*, CXVI, CXVIII, CXXI).

p. 347, *virtu*: See second note to p. 289.

p. 347, *Jermyn Street*: A fashionable street in the St James's area of London.

p. 347, *recherchés*: "Very refined" (French).

p. 347, *a modern Platonist... and Syrianus*: The list of Neoplatonist philosophers (who flourished between the second and fifth centuries AD) is lifted from Disraeli's *Vivian Grey* (see first note to p. 327): "Father! I wish to make myself master of the latter Platonists. I want Plotinus, and Porphyry, and Iamblichus, and Syrianus, and Maximus Tyrius, and Proclus, and Hierocles, and Sallustius, and Damascius" (Chapter VI). Describing a soirée at Lady Blessington's, Willis wrote: "The conversation turned on Platonism, and Disraeli (who seemed to have remembered the shelf on which Vivian Grey was to find 'the latter Platonists' in his father's library) 'flared up', as a dandy would say. [...] He gave us an account of Taylor, almost the last of the celebrated Platonists" (CXXI). Thomas Taylor (1758–1835) was a renowned translator and latter-day Neoplatonist.

p. 347, *Turgot, Price, Priestley, Condorcet*: See third note to p. 287.

p. 347, *De Staël*: See first note to p. 295.

p. 347, *the "Ambitious Student in Ill Health"*: For Bulwer-Lytton, one of the literati Willis met at Lady Blessington's, and the "Ambitious Student in Ill Health", see first note to p. 235 and first note to p. 345, respectively.

p. 347, *homoeomeria*: The theory propounded by the philosopher Anaxagoras (*c.*500–*c.*428 BC) that the ultimate particles of matter are homogeneous, or of the same kind.

p. 347, *Eusebius and Arianus... Nice*: Eusebius of Nicomedia (d. *c.*342 AD) was a supporter of Arius (*c.*250–336 AD), the founder of Arianism (the doctrine that Jesus Christ is not of the same substance as God), a heresy condemned at the First Council of Nicaea (May to July 325 AD).

p. 347, *Puseyism and consubstantialism*: A reference to the Anglican cleric Edward Bouverie Pusey (1800–82), a prominent figure in the high-church Oxford Movement, who promoted the doctrine of consubstantiation, the belief in the real presence of the body and blood of Christ together with the bread and wine in the Eucharist.

p. 347, *homoousios and homoiousios*: Greek for "of the same essence" (consubstantial) and "of a similar essence", terms used in connection with disquisitions about the true nature of Christ in relation to God the Father – the first being the accepted Christian tenet, the second a heretical belief.

p. 347, *Rocher de Cancale*: A Parisian restaurant mentioned by Willis in *Pencillings by the Way* (XIV) as "the first eating house in Paris". Its name derives by that of a large rock off the Brittany coast.

p. 347, *Muriton of red tongue*: "Miroton" is a French dish consisting of leftover meat, usually beef, cooked slowly in a sauce with onions.

p. 347, *à la Sainte-Menehould*: See first note to p. 137.

p. 347, *marinade à la Saint-Florentin*: Saint-Florentin is a cheese from Burgundy.

p. 347, *en mosaïque*: "(Laid out) as a mosaic" (French).

p. 348, *Latour*: Château Latour.

p. 348, *Markbrünnen*: Marcobrunnen is a Riesling wine.

p. 348, *mousseux and Chambertin*: See first note to p. 378 and third note to p. 273, respectively.

p. 348, *Richebourg and Saint-Georges*: Richebourg and Saint-Georges are two fine wines from the Côte de Nuits subregion of Burgundy.

p. 348, *Haubrion*: Perhaps Château Haut-Brion.

p. 348, *Leonville*: Perhaps Château Léoville.

p. 348, *Médoc*: See third note to p. 273.

p. 348, *Barac and Preignac*: Barsac (not "Barac") and Preignac are towns in the Sauternes wine region.

p. 348, *Graves... Clos de Vougeot*: Graves is a subregion of the Bordeaux wine region. For the other wines, see first note to p. 144, fifth note to p. 173, third notes to p. 273 and second note to p. 137.

p. 348, *Cimabue... Carpaccio*: The Italian painters Cimabue (*c.*1240–1302); Cavalier d'Arpino (1568–1640) and Vittore Carpaccio (*c.*1460–*c.*1525).

p. 348, *Argostino*: Probably fictional. The most famous "Agostino" is the Italian painter Agostino Beltrano (1607–56), nicknamed "Agostiniello". Poe may have also been punning on "Aragostino", "Little Lobster".

p. 348, *Caravaggio*: The Italian painter Michelangelo Merisi da Caravaggio (1571–1610), better known as "Caravaggio".

p. 348, *Albano*: The Italian painter Francesco Albani (or Albano, 1578–1660). The "amenity" could be an allusion to Willis's description of the "pretty village of Albano" in his *Pencillings by the Way* (LIV).

p. 348, *Titian... Rubens*: The Italian painter Tiziano Vecellio (better known in English as "Titian", *c.*1488–1576) and the Dutch painter Peter Paul Rubens (1577–1640). For "vrow", see note to p. 5.

p. 348, *Jan Steen*: The Dutch painter Jan Steen (*c.*1626–1679).

p. 348, *the moon was called Bendis... Artemis in Greece*: The passage is again lifted from Disraeli's *Vivian Grey* (see first note to p. 327): "Here to thee, Queen of the Night! In whatever name thou most delightest! Or Bendis, as they hailed thee in rugged Thrace; or Bubastis, as they howled to thee in mysterious Egypt; or Diana, as they sacrificed to thee in gorgeous Rome; or Artemis, as they sighed to thee on the bright plains of ever glorious Greece!" (Chapter VI).

p. 348, *Stamboul*: See note to p. 307.

p. 348, *a sky-blue cow with an incalculable number of green horns*: See fourth note to p. 68.

p. 348, *Aeschylus*: The Greek tragedian Aeschylus (*c.*525–*c.*455 BC).

p. 348, *Isaeus... Lysias*: The Greek orators Isaeus (*fl.* early fourth century BC) and Lysias (*c.*445–*c.*380 BC).

p. 348, *Theophrastus*: The Greek philosopher and naturalist Theophrastus (*c.*371–*c.*287 BC).

p. 348, *Apollonius*: The Greek geometer and astronomer Apollonius of Perga (*c.*240–*c.*190 BC).

p. 348, *Pindar's hymns and dithyrambics*: The reference is to the Greek lyric poet Pindar (*c.*518–*c.*438 BC).

p. 348, *Homer Junior*: A tragedian who is said to have flourished in the third century BC. All his works have been lost.

p. 348, *Almack's*: Socially exclusive assembly rooms on King Street, St James's, central London, founded by William Almack (1741–81).

p. 349, *"Diavolo!" cried Count Capricornuti*: "Diavolo" is Italian for "Devil"; "Capricornuti" literally means "Horned Billy Goats".

p. 349, *"Dios guarda!"*: "God protect (us)!" (Spanish).

p. 349, *"Mille tonnerres!"*: "A thousand thunders!" (French).

p. 349, *Grenouille*: "Frog" (French).

p. 349, *"Tausend Teufel!"*: "A thousand devils!" (German).

p. 349, *"Donner und Blitzen!"*: "Thunder and lightning!" (German).

p. 349, *At Chalk Farm, the next morning, I shot off his nose*: Chalk Farm, north-west of central London, was a notorious spot for duelling, since it was located beyond the outskirts of the city. After the publication of *Pencillings by the Way*, Willis fought a bloodless duel with the English novelist Captain Frederick Marryat, following a hostile correspondence between the two caused by a virulent attack on Willis and his book in the *Metropolitan Magazine*, then under the editorship of Marryat. For Marryat, see note to p. 267.

p. 349, *"Bête!"*: "Fool!" (French).

Extra Material on Edgar Allan Poe's

The Mystery of Marie Rogêt

and Other Tales

Edgar Allan Poe's Life

Early Life and Family

Edgar Allan Poe was born in a lodging house in Boston, Massachusetts, on 19th January 1809. His mother, Eliza (née Arnold, 1787–1811), an actress and a celebrated beauty, had arrived in the United States from England in 1796, going on to play more than two hundred parts in the theatre over the course of her brief career. On 14th March 1806 she had married an aspiring actor, David Poe, Jr (1784–*c.*1811), in Richmond, Virginia – her first husband, Charles Hopkins, another thespian, having died the previous year. Her new husband failed to match Eliza's success on the stage, however, and was a heavy drinker. Their first child, Henry, was born in January 1807. Due to his parents' itinerant lifestyle, at the age of two the young boy was sent to be cared for by his paternal grandparents, Elizabeth (1756–1835) and "General" David Poe (1743–1816), in Baltimore, Maryland. (The senior David Poe was not in fact a general, although he had served as deputy quartermaster general for the city of Baltimore during the War of American Independence.) After his own birth, Edgar too was cared for by his paternal grandparents for several months, returning to his parents in Richmond in the summer of 1809. A third child, Rosalie, was born in December 1810. By this time, both of Edgar's parents were suffering from tuberculosis, and the family's financial situation was dire.

In spring 1811 David Poe abandoned his family. The reason for his disappearance is unclear, although there was speculation that Rosalie was not his. Then, in November, Eliza died. Later in his life, Poe reported in a letter that his father passed away only a few weeks after his mother – whether this is true or not, the three children were now in effect orphans. "I have many occasional dealings with adversity," he wrote, "but the want of parental affection has been the heaviest of my trials."

After their mother's death, the children were separated: Rosalie was thereafter raised by a family named the Mackenzies, while Edgar was taken in by the twenty-five-year-old Frances ("Fanny") Allan (1784–1829), who had visited the dying Eliza in response to a plea for help that had appeared in the *Richmond Enquirer* during her final illness, and had taken an interest in the young boy. She was the wife of John Allan (1779–1834), a Scottish-born merchant, who resided above the premises of Ellis & Allan on the corner of Thirteenth Street and Main Street in Richmond. The Allans proved to be kindly foster parents – Fanny, in particular, pampered her new charge. The change in Edgar's circumstances was reflected in the name he was christened with on 7th January 1812: Edgar Allan Poe.

London In June 1815, in a move made necessary by a decline in John Allan's fortunes, the family left for Liverpool aboard the *Lothair*, arriving in England on 29th July. After a tour of Scotland, they reached London in October, taking lodgings on Southampton Row. In April 1816, Edgar began attending a boarding school in Sloane Street, where he proved an able learner: "Edgar is a fine boy and reads Latin pretty sharply," wrote John Allan in June 1818. In July of the same year, he was moved to the Manor House School in Stoke Newington, then a rural village north-east of the capital, whose headmaster, the Reverend John Bransby, later described Edgar as "quick and clever", claiming that he "would have been a very good boy if he had not been spoilt by his parents" – evidence of the doting affection that Fanny Allan had for her foster son. Edgar's time at the Manor House School – which he subsequently described as "sad, lonely and unhappy" – later inspired the short story 'William Wilson' (1839).

Return to Richmond

Due to a drop in tobacco prices in London, the Allans returned to Richmond in the summer of 1820, lodging initially with John Allan's business partner, Charles Ellis, who was perhaps instrumental in persuading him to remain in his post and not to abandon trade in favour of a career in farming, as he had planned to do. Edgar was sent to a local school, Richmond Academy, where, as well as acquitting himself capably in both his academic work and as a sportsman, he proved himself, in the words of one teacher, to be a "born poet", whose verses were written "*con amore* and not as mere tasks". According to one contemporary, however, he was "self-willed, capricious, inclined to be imperious, and though of generous impulses, not steadily kind, or even amiable"; another remarked that he was "retiring in disposition and singularly unsociable in manner". During this period Edgar began to form his first romantic attachments: first to the mother of a school friend, the thirty-year-old Jane Stanard, who inspired the poem 'To Helen' ("Helen, thy beauty is to me"), which appeared in the 1831 collection *Poems*, and whose death in spring 1824 affected him profoundly, and then to the fifteen-year-old Elmira Royster, who lived opposite his school. Meanwhile, Edgar had to contend with new-found domestic difficulties, as Fanny's health deteriorated and relations with his foster father began to show signs of strain. John Allan complained that Edgar "possesses not a spark of affection for us, not a particle of gratitude for all my care and kindness towards him", while Edgar later described his surrogate parent as "a man of gross and brutal temperament".

University; First Book of Poems

In February 1826, Edgar began attending the schools of Ancient Languages and Modern Languages at the newly founded University of Virginia in Charlottesville. Though he excelled in his scholarly endeavours, he once again showed himself to be somewhat aloof, forming no close friendships with his fellow students, one of whom remembered him as having "a sad, melancholy face always – and even a smile... seemed to be forced". The same student also referred to Edgar's tendency to "put himself under the influence" of alcohol as a means of medicating the "nervous excitability" that plagued him, while another described his "passion" for gambling.

Increasingly resentful of his errant charge, who had by now amassed debts of $2,000, at the end of 1826 John Allan announced that he would no longer subsidize Edgar's university career, as a consequence of which relations between foster father and son reached a new low. In the following March, the disgruntled and penniless young man – his mood worsened by the revelation that Elmira Royster was engaged to be married to another man – left the home of the Allans and travelled to Boston. It was here that, with the help of a young printer, Calvin Frederick Stephen Thomas, he published fifty copies of his first book of verse, *Tamerlane and Other Poems*.

The Army

Failing to secure any stable employment in Boston, in May 1826 Poe elected to enlist in the US Army, which he did under the pseudonym "Edgar A. Perry". Over the next two years he served first in an artillery battery off Boston Harbor, then at Fort Moultrie on Sullivan's island off the coast of South Carolina, and finally at Fortress Monroe on the Virginia Peninsula, where, in early 1829, he was made regimental sergeant major, the highest non-commissioned rank. By this time tiring of life as a common soldier, however, he sought his foster father's consent in securing a discharge, in order that he might then apply to West Point, the officers' academy on the west bank of the Hudson River in New York State. His request coincided with the final illness of Fanny Allan, however – Poe learnt of her death on 1st March and returned to Richmond the following day, only to find that the funeral had already taken place. He later wrote to Allan: "*Your* love I never valued – but she I believed loved me as her own child." His resolve perhaps weakened by his loss, John Allan acceded to Poe's entreaty, and in April the young man left the army, submitting his application to West Point soon afterwards.

Meeting with Virginia Clemm; Second Book of Poems

In May 1829 Poe travelled to Baltimore to visit his elder brother, Henry, in order to become more closely acquainted with his paternal grandfather's family. "General" Poe was now dead; his widow, along with Henry, Poe's aunt Maria Clemm (1790–1871) and her six-year-old daughter Virginia (1822–47), were living in poverty. Henry, according to Poe's account a drunkard, was dying of consumption; both his grandmother and Maria Clemm were also in poor health. Nevertheless, Poe formed a profound attachment to both Maria and Virginia. From Baltimore Poe travelled by steamer to Philadelphia, where he presented the manuscript of a new collection of poems to Isaac Lea of the publishing house Carey, Lea & Carey, only to receive a standard rejection letter a few weeks later. He therefore offered it instead to the Baltimore firm of Hatch & Dunning, who published *Al Aaraaf, Tamerlane and Minor Poems*, by "Edgar A. Poe", in December 1829.

West Point

The parlous state of Poe's finances compelled him to return to Richmond in early 1830. Then, in May, he left for West Point, where he lodged with three fellow cadets at 28 South Barracks. A contemporary remembered him as "shy, proud, sensitive and unsociable… He spent more time in reading than in study." Another, Cadet Gibson, stated: "Very early in his brief career at the Point he established a high reputation for genius, and poems and squibs of local interest were daily issued from Number 28." Characteristically, however, Poe quickly grew weary of life as an officer cadet – but his efforts to resign were thwarted by John Allan, whose parental permission was required if his wayward foster son was to receive an honourable discharge. Newly remarried, and eager to free himself of the burden that Edgar had become, Allan went so far as to attempt to sever relations with him – something that, in a letter to his surrogate parent, Poe responded to with predictable self-pity: "It was my crime to have no one on earth who cared for me or loved me." In the absence of Allan's blessing, therefore, from early 1831 Poe set about deliberately attempting to provoke his superiors into expelling him from the academy. His persistent heavy drinking, combined with his failure to attend to his duties, led to a court martial at the end of January, as a result of which he was charged with "gross neglect of duty" and "disobedience of orders", and dismissed.

Third Book of Poems; Early Fiction

On 19th February he left for New York, where – miserable, impecunious and plagued by ill health – he stayed for three months. It was here, in April, that his third book of poetry, entitled simply *Poems* – financed in part by some of his West Point colleagues, each of whom contributed seventy-five cents towards the cost – was published, by the printer Elam Bliss. In May, Poe returned to Baltimore, where his brother Henry died in August. During this time he became increasingly dependent on his aunt, Maria Clemm, nicknamed "Muddy", who shouldered the burden of keeping the household together (she was later described as the "ever-vigilant guardian of the home" by a neighbour), and deepened his attachment to the eight-year-old Virginia, whom he called "Sis" or "Sissie". Unable to find work, and receiving no answer to the begging letters he sent to his erstwhile guardian, John Allan, he now turned his hand to fiction as a means of earning a living – Poe always believed that his true vocation was as a poet – with the result that 'Metzengerstein', a Gothic tale "in imitation of the German" appeared in Philadelphia's *Saturday Courier* in January 1832. Despite this, and the four further sensational or supernatural tales that appeared in the same publication over the course of the year, plus an unknown quantity of journalistic hack work, Poe was forced to turn to his foster father for help one final time, in April 1833. "For God's sake pity me," he wrote, "and save me from destruction." Allan did not reply, and communication between the two ceased for ever.

In autumn 1833 Poe won a competition in the weekly periodical the *Baltimore Saturday Visiter* for his story 'MS Found in a Bottle', a nautical tale with a supernatural flavour, and was awarded fifty dollars. It was published in the magazine in October. As a result, he made the acquaintance of John P. Kennedy, one of the *Visiter*'s editorial committee, who became his de facto patron. In the month in which this story was printed, it was announced in the *Visiter* that a collection entitled *Tales of the Folio Club*, containing seventeen pieces by Poe – satires on various literary styles – was to be published by subscription. The proposed volume never in fact materialized, however, due to the unwillingness of American publishers to take on work by one of their compatriots – the lack of copyright legislation ensuring that it was more profitable to produce pirated editions of works by British authors. Nevertheless, the individual tales – including 'The Duc de L'Omelette', 'Lionizing' and 'King Pest' – appeared in the *Philadelphia Saturday Courier* and the *Southern Literary Messenger* between 1832 and 1836.

Death of John Allan; the Southern Literary Messenger

In March 1834 John Allan died, leaving nothing to Poe in his will, provoking a typically resentful and self-indulgent response from his former charge in which he bemoaned his poverty and friendlessness. Penniless as ever, Poe turned for help to Kennedy, who, in the spring of 1835, recommended him to Thomas Willis White, the editor of the new monthly *Southern Literary Messenger*, based in Richmond, who agreed to publish a characteristically macabre new story, 'Berenice'. In correspondence Poe told White that he believed that the best stories contained "the ludicrous heightened into the grotesque, the fearful coloured into the horrible, the witty exaggerated into the burlesque, the singular wrought out into the strange and mystical", as well as offering him a great deal of unsolicited editorial advice. As a consequence, in June White offered Poe a job as a staff writer and critic on the magazine – his first ever secure employment – at sixty dollars per month. After some prevarication, Poe accepted and returned to Richmond. However, White was soon complaining about his "rather dissipated" and unreliable new employee. Meanwhile, Poe's stories continued to appear – including 'Morella' (April 1835) and 'Hans Phaall – A Tale' (June 1835).

Poe abandoned his new post in September on learning to his horror that his beloved Virginia, now thirteen, was to be taken in by his cousin, Neilson Poe. Fearful of losing his "darling little wifey" – who was half his age – he returned to Baltimore, where it is conjectured that he married her in secret. Either way, Virginia's proposed relocation to the home of her relative did not take place. He then requested of White that he be allowed to return to his job on the *Messenger*. White agreed so long as Poe promised to abstain from alcohol. "No man is safe who drinks before breakfast," he warned him.

Marriage to Virginia

Poe returned to Richmond in October, bringing with him Maria and Virginia, the trio presenting themselves as a mother and daughter accompanied by their unmarried cousin. No longer tormented by the prospect of losing Virginia, Poe temporarily gave up drinking, and was made editor of the *Messenger* by White. In the spring of 1836, in a service performed by the Presbyterian minister Amasa Converse, Poe married Virginia formally, lying about her age – one witness stated on oath that she was twenty-one. By September, Poe had fallen back into the habit of immoderate drinking, and was given notice by White, but was able to persuade the editor to reconsider. White imposed certain conditions, but Poe proved unable to keep them, and so was finally dismissed in January 1837 – the same month in which the first instalment of a novel, *The Narrative of Arthur Gordon Pym of Nantucket*, appeared in the *Messenger*. "I am as sick of his writings as I am of him," White wrote.

Philadelphia; the Burton's Gentleman's Magazine

At the end of February 1837, Poe and his family left for New York, where they stayed for an unhappy year, during which Poe succeeded in publishing only two stories. Furthermore, serialization of *Arthur Gordon Pym* in the *Messenger* ceased after only two instalments. At the beginning of 1838, therefore, Poe, accompanied as ever by his wife and Maria, relocated to Philadelphia, at the time the largest city in the United States as well as the hub of the country's publishing industry. The family were now desperately poor. That summer, *Arthur Gordon Pym* was published in volume form by Harper & Brothers, but received mixed reviews and made no money – Poe himself dismissed it as "a very silly book". 'Ligeia', a story inspired by a dream, was published in September in the *American Museum of Literature and the Arts* – Poe later called it "my *best* tale".

Still in straitened circumstances, in the spring of 1839 Poe offered his services as assistant to William E. Burton, a comic actor from England who was editor of the eponymously named and Philadelphia-based *Burton's Gentleman's Magazine*. Burton accepted, proposing to pay him ten dollars a day for two hours' work. He was formally employed in June, and quickly gained a reputation for the vicious, scathing reviews he wrote of the work of other writers. "I intend to put up with nothing that I can *put down*," he wrote to a correspondent in August. Many of his finest stories appeared in the *Burton's Gentleman's Magazine* in this period, including 'The Fall of the House of Usher' (September 1839) and 'William Wilson' (October 1839). At the end of the year, twenty-five of Poe's tales, including these two, were collected as *Tales of the Grotesque and Arabesque*, published in two volumes by Lea & Blanchard (the successor firm of Carey, Lea & Carey, who had previously rejected Poe's second book of poetry). The two volumes did not sell well, however, and Poe received no payment.

Plans for the Penn Magazine

The perennial problem of Poe's heavy drinking continued to interfere with his working life, however, resulting in the breakdown in his relationship with Burton and his dismissal in May 1840. In response Poe hatched a plan to establish his own journal, the *Penn Magazine*, which he said would inhabit "the loftiest regions of literature", and thus began to contact editors, publishers and journalists in order to build up a subscription list. The first edition was planned for early 1841; however, in late 1840 Poe was bedridden for a month with what he described as a "severe illness", and so publication was pushed back to March – but then a financial crisis in February forced him to abandon the project altogether.

Poe once again offered his services to the *Burton's Gentleman's Magazine*, now under the ownership of George Rex Graham, a Philadelphia lawyer with little journalistic experience, and retitled *Graham's Lady's and Gentleman's Magazine*. He consequently became editor of the book reviews in spring 1841 at a salary of eight hundred dollars per year. Over the next two years nine more of his stories appeared in the magazine, including the pioneering detective tale 'The Murders in the Rue Morgue' (April 1841) and 'A Descent into the Maelstrom' (May 1841). Despite now enjoying the highest income he had ever received, he considered the appointment a temporary one, and after a few months tried – with the help of the writer Frederick W. Thomas, one of his few close friends – to secure a position with the Department of the Treasury in Washington DC. This plan foundered, however, and in autumn 1841 he agreed to stay in his role with *Graham's* – whose circulation had increased from five to twenty-five thousand, due in no small part to the presence in its pages of Poe's fiction and journalism – for a further year. At this time he proposed to Lea & Blanchard another collection of his short fiction, which would comprise the contents of *Tales of the Grotesque and Arabesque* plus eight newer stories, and was to be called *Phantasy Pieces*. Lea & Blanchard, however, declined, on the basis that they were still burdened with unsold copies of the former work.

Resignation from Graham's Magazine

In January 1842 Virginia began to cough up blood, a sign of the tuberculosis that would eventually claim her life. "Mrs Poe is again dangerously ill with haemorrhage from the lungs. It is folly to hope," Poe despaired. He later wrote that "at each accession of the disorder I loved her more dearly and clung to her life with more desperate pertinacity". In his misery he turned to drink once more, and, in the spring, resigned from *Graham's*, claiming to be disgusted with the "namby-pamby character" of the magazine – although in reality he was forced to leave because of the irregularity of his own behaviour. In the summer he went to New York, ostensibly to look for journalistic work. The expedition, however, degenerated into a drinking "spree" (his own term for such binges), during which he went missing. In the words of Mary Devereaux, an old flame he had decided in his inebriation to visit, Poe was eventually found "in the woods on the outskirts of Jersey City, wandering about like a crazy man". Despite his misfortunes, he produced some of his greatest stories during this year: 'The Masque of the Red Death' (published in May 1842), 'The Mystery of Marie Rogêt' (published in November 1842) and 'The Tell-Tale Heart' (published in January 1843).

In the next year, 1843, with his drinking now the gossip of Philadelphia and his family once again in dire financial straits, Poe sought to secure a clerkship at the Philadelphia Custom House, something that he hoped would give him the security he needed to launch his journal, now to be called *The Stylus* – which, he claimed, would "far surpass all American journals of its kind". The attempt to secure an administrative position came to nothing, although at this time Poe was fortunate enough to make the acquaintance of Thomas C. Clarke, editor of the Philadelphia *Saturday Museum*, who agreed to finance the proposed magazine. Poe travelled to Washington to look for subscribers – while there, he also entertained the fanciful notion of securing an audience with the US president, John Tyler, as part of his ongoing efforts to obtain an administrative position with the federal government. As before, however, in practice the trip was nothing more than another humiliating alcoholic "spree".

Back in Philadelphia, Poe began writing 'The Raven'. Meanwhile, his adventure yarn 'The Gold Bug' won a prize of one hundred dollars in the city's *Dollar Newspaper*, and was published in two instalments on 21st and 28th June. The story was described in the *Saturday Museum* as "the most remarkable piece of American fiction that has been published within the last fifteen years". Other major stories were written at this time but published later, including 'The Premature Burial' (published in July 1844) and 'The Purloined Letter' (published in December 1844). In November Poe began a series of lectures, the first of which was held at the Julianna Street Church in Philadelphia on the subject of "American poetry". He was typically acerbic in his pronouncements, singling out the poet Rufus Wilmot Griswold, his successor at *Graham's* and already a literary rival, whose anthology *Poets and Poetry of America* (1842) was, he said, the best of those available, but still showed a "miserable want of judgement – the worst specimens being chosen instead of the best". This contributed to a literary feud that continued to rage even after Poe's death.

New York; 'The Raven'

In April 1844, Poe and Virginia moved again to New York, staying at a boarding house on Greenwich Street, where they were joined a short while later by Maria. Almost immediately on arrival, Poe sold a story to the *New York Sun* about a man, Monck Mason – the name of a real-life balloonist – who had apparently crossed the Atlantic in three days aboard a hot-air balloon. The story, a hoax, appeared on 13th April, but was retracted two days later. In June the family moved to a farmhouse five miles outside the city, where it was hoped that the country air might improve Virginia's health. With the family as indigent as ever, Maria Clemm took it upon herself to find work for Poe, travelling into the city and calling on Nathaniel P. Willis, editor of the new *Evening Mirror*. As a result, Poe became a "mechanical paragraphist" on the newspaper, a relatively lowly copy-writing position. In the winter, the family moved back to Greenwich Street in order that Poe might be closer to his place of work.

'The Raven' was published in the *Evening Mirror* on 29th January 1845, and quickly became a sensation. The *New York Express* claimed that it transcended "anything that has been done even by the best poets of the age". It earned Poe the acclaim he had craved all his life. He began to appear at New York literary salons, and for the time being succeeded in remaining sober. Poe himself became known as "the Raven" – not least because of his custom of dressing entirely in black. For its author, the poem was calculated to achieve commercial success: "'The Raven' has had a great 'run'," he wrote to Frederick W. Thomas, "but I wrote it for the express purpose of running." He also wrote an essay, 'The Philosophy of Composition', published in April 1846, in which he elucidated in great technical detail the poetic processes involved in bringing the poem into existence.

The Broadway Journal; the "Longfellow War"

Buoyed by this success, Poe left his job on the *Evening Mirror* and joined the *Broadway Journal* as editor soon afterwards (February 1845). In its pages he repeatedly attacked the eminent American poet Henry Wadsworth Longfellow, accusing him, not for the first time, of plagiarism, calling him a "determined imitator and a dextrous adapter of the ideas of other people" (specifically Tennyson). Although Longfellow did not respond, and while such diatribes may have been merely a publicity stunt designed to draw attention to the *Broadway Journal*, Poe's repeated assaults on his literary contemporary came to be known as "the Longfellow War", one of the most notorious literary feuds in American history. Poe levelled the accusation of plagiarism at other poets during this period, including James Russell Lowell and Richard Henry Stoddard.

Soon, however, Poe – complaining of being "dreadfully unwell" – expressed a desire to give up his post on the *Broadway Journal*, where, once again, his drinking had made him unreliable. Although his partner, Charles Frederick Briggs – who had come to regard Poe as a liability, describing him as "a drunken sot" and the "most purely selfish of human beings" – was more than happy to see him go, Poe quickly changed his mind, desiring instead to be given "entire control" of the magazine in order to turn it into "the great literary journal of the future". Thus in October he bought Briggs out and became proprietor, with full editorial authority. Only six weeks later, however, he sold half his interest to a man named Thomas H. Lane, and, after another month, went on one of his debauched "sprees". Lane closed the magazine in January 1846. Appropriately enough, Poe's story 'The Imp of the Perverse' – about the impulse to perform self-destructive actions "merely because we feel we should not" – was published during this period (in the July 1845 issue of *Graham's*).

Frances Sargent Osgood and Elizabeth F. Ellet

Meanwhile, in March 1845, Poe made the acquaintance of the poet Frances Sargent Osgood, whom he had praised in his lecture on American poetry, and with whom he embarked on what seemed to be a romantic dalliance. Poe printed several of her poems in the *Broadway Journal*, responding with some of his own, including 'To F—s S. O—d' and 'To F—', both of which had originally been written for other women. 'For Her These Lines Are Penned…' – which appeared in the *Evening Mirror* on 21st February 1846 – even contained within it the name "Frances Sargent Osgood", obtained by taking the first letter of the first line, the second of the second line, and so on. The admiration was clearly mutual – one writer remembered how Osgood had been put under Poe's "wizard spell" – although it is unlikely that the relationship was sexual: indeed, it may even have been purely platonic, not least because it was conducted with the knowledge of Virginia, who seemed in fact to approve of the association on the basis that it kept her husband sober, as well as of Osgood's spouse, the painter Samuel Stillman Osgood.

Scandal ensued in early 1846, however, when Elizabeth F. Ellet, another poet and perhaps Osgood's rival for Poe's attentions, claimed that Virginia had shown her an indiscreet letter from Osgood to Poe, and advised Ellet to retrieve her correspondence from him. When two other literary women, Margaret Fuller and Anne Lynch, subsequently demanded that Poe return Osgood's letters, Poe retaliated by suggesting that Ellet "look after her *own* letters". Poe was then threatened by Ellet's brother, Colonel William Lummis, who did not believe the former's claim to have already returned his sister's letters. In response Poe attempted to borrow a pistol – to use in self-defence – from the writer Thomas Dunn English, but the conversation devolved into a fist fight when English stated that he did not believe that Poe had ever possessed any correspondence from Ellet. Poe subsequently persuaded his doctor to write an apologetic letter to Ellet in which he attributed his behaviour to temporary insanity. In July, under threat of legal action from Osgood's husband, Ellet sent a letter of apology to Osgood, in which she said that the note she had seen must have been a forgery created by Poe himself. The scandal abated, although the flirtation between Poe and Osgood – as well as between Poe and Ellet – was at an end.

Move to Fordham

1845 also saw the publication first of *Tales* (June) and then of *The Raven and Other Poems* (November), the first poetry collection published by Poe since 1831. Then, in the spring of 1846, Poe began to publish a series of critical articles under the title 'The Literati of New York

City' for the magazine *Godey's Lady's Book*, in which he attacked many of the prominent literary figures of the day with typical brutality. Some of his targets were minded to reciprocate, including Thomas Dunn English, who responded with a piece in the *New York Mirror* in which he accused Poe of, among other things, forgery and plagiarism. In turn, Poe set about suing the newspaper for libel. At this time he and his family moved to a cottage in the village of Fordham, thirteen miles north of New York, where their poverty was acute enough to compel Maria to dig up and cook the turnips that were intended as fodder for the cattle. Meanwhile, Poe's claim of temporary insanity during the Ellet affair had become the subject of gossip, leading to much speculation in the press, with the Baltimore *Saturday Visiter* claiming that he was suffering from "mental derangement" and had been consigned to an asylum in Utica. Poe's physical well-being also became the focus of attention, with New York's *Morning Express* stating on 15th December that the writer and his wife were both "dangerously ill with the consumption" and so poor as to be "barely able to obtain the necessaries of life". Several papers – including the *Mirror*, the publication being sued by Poe – appealed for financial contributions on his family's behalf. Such publicity brought Poe's plight to the attention of a woman named Marie Louise Shew, who became Virginia's nurse during her final days.

Death of Virginia

Virginia Poe died on 30th January 1847. Several weeks later Poe wrote: "I was overwhelmed by a sorrow so poignant as to deprive me for several weeks of all power of thought or action." Shew, believing Poe to be suffering from madness produced by a lesion on the brain, nursed him back to health. The day before Virginia's funeral, Poe's libel case against the *Mirror* was heard before the New York Superior Court. During the hearing English called Poe "a notorious liar" and "a common drunkard" – nevertheless, the court found in Poe's favour, and he was awarded $225.06 in damages and $101.42 in costs.

Thereafter, with Shew's help, his health slowly recovered from the blow dealt by his wife's death, to the extent that by the summer he was able to visit Washington and Philadelphia in yet another attempt to launch *The Stylus*. As so often, however, he resorted to the bottle when separated from the restraining influences of home.

Eureka

On 3rd February 1848, Poe gave a lecture on the subject of "The Cosmography of the Universe" at the Society Library on Leonard Street and Broadway, in which he expounded on his theories about the origins and nature of the cosmos to sixty somewhat bemused audience members (inclement weather having ensured only sparse attendance). The lecture put a strain on Poe's relationship with Shew, who, considering the ideas it described to be heretical, left him in the early summer. Poe subsequently adapted the lecture into *Eureka: A Prose Poem*, published in March 1848 by George P. Putnam. Around this time Poe also composed 'Ulalume' and 'The Bells', two of his best-known poems.

Annie Richmond and Sarah Helen Whitman

Poe's behaviour became increasingly erratic in the period following Virginia's death, as demonstrated by his somewhat hysterical and simultaneous pursuit of two unobtainable women. In summer 1848, while visiting a married friend named Jane E. Locke (yet another woman to whom he had written passionate letters) in Lowell, Massachusetts, he was introduced to, and immediately smitten with, a married woman named Nancy Locke ("Annie") Richmond. Very soon afterwards, in September, he proposed marriage to a widow named Sarah Helen Whitman, a poet and spiritualist from Providence, Rhode Island, who had come to his attention by writing him a Valentine's poem earlier in the year. Whitman declined – on the basis that she was responsible for the care of her elderly mother – but Poe persisted, only to be met with further refusal, or at any rate prevarication. When Richmond, aware of Poe's relationship with the other woman, recommended that he marry Whitman, he was grief-stricken by her apparent willingness to countenance his romantic attachment to another – thus, in November, in an apparent bid to end his life, Poe purchased two ounces of laudanum before boarding a train from Lowell to Boston. The suicide attempt succeeded only in making Poe severely ill, and two days later he travelled to Providence to visit Whitman, apparently in a state of mental disorder. After he had recuperated, Whitman finally agreed to marry him – on the condition that he stop drinking. However, when, during a visit made by the couple to a Providence library, an anonymous note was handed to Whitman notifying her that Poe had reneged on his promise to stay sober, she broke off the engagement.

Richmond; Engagement to Elmira Shelton

In early 1849 Poe completed the poem 'The Bells' and began writing 'Annabel Lee', but by April had become unwell and depressed once more: "My life seems wasted – the future looks a dreary blank," he wrote. On 29th June he set off on a steamboat to Philadelphia, en route to Richmond, where he was to deliver a series of lectures, but relapsed into dipsomaniacal ways on the journey. The events of the following two or three days in the former city – where he mislaid the suitcase containing his lecture notes – are obscured by an alcoholic miasma. For instance, he told Maria Clemm that he had been arrested for drunkenness, although there is no record of this having taken place. Meanwhile George Lippard, a Philadelphia journalist, reported that a penniless Poe had visited him wearing only one shoe. Poe attributed his erratic behaviour on this occasion to "*mania a potu*" – that is, delirium tremens. He eventually made it to Richmond, where he recovered somewhat, as well as reacquainting himself with his sister Rosalie. He also called on his boyhood sweetheart Elmira Royster, now Elmira Shelton and a widow. Rumours began to circulate that they were engaged, although Shelton later denied that this was the case. As is often the case with Poe, it is difficult to determine the truth of what happened.

Griswold's Obituary and 'Memoir of the Author'

Last Days and Mysterious Death

In September, Poe, still in Richmond, was invited to travel to Philadelphia to edit a volume of poems by the wife of a piano manufacturer, an uncongenial job he accepted for the money, with the intention of then travelling on to New York, where he planned to make further preparations for the launch of *The Stylus*. He expected to be away from Richmond for a total of two weeks. The day before his departure he visited Shelton, who judged that he was too ill to travel. Nevertheless, early the next morning, 27th September, he boarded the steamboat for Baltimore – forgetting to take his luggage with him. The next six days are shrouded in mystery. As his cousin, Neilson Poe, subsequently wrote to Maria Clemm: "At what time he arrived in [Baltimore], where he spent the time he was here, or under what circumstances, I have been unable to ascertain." Poe was found insensible in a Baltimore inn called Gunner's Hall, clad in a straw hat and strange clothes (not those he had been wearing on leaving Richmond) on 3rd October. The inn was at that time doubling as a polling station for congressional elections that were taking place in Maryland on that day. One popular theory is that Poe, in his inebriated state, had somehow become involved in electoral fraud by being persuaded to don a different set of garments in order to vote more than once for a particular candidate. Whatever the explanation, Poe – after his cousin, Henry Herring, who coincidentally arrived on the scene, had refused to take responsibility for him – was removed from the tavern to the city's Washington College Hospital, where, delirious and full of self-reproach, he died four days later. The official cause of death was given as "phrenitis" – inflammation of the brain. A funeral was held the next day, 8th October, attended by only four mourners, including Herring and Neilson Poe.

An obituary appeared in the *New York Tribune* on 9th October 1849, signed "Ludwig", the pseudonym of Poe's long-standing adversary Rufus Wilmot Griswold, which stated that "few will be grieved" by Poe's death since "he had few or no friends". At this time Griswold also claimed that it was Poe's wish that he (Griswold) be made his literary executor – whether this is the case or not, it is true that Maria Clemm transferred power of attorney to Griswold on 20th October. As a result, a three-volume collection of Poe's works was published from January 1850, edited by Griswold, James Russell Lowell and Nathaniel Parker Willis. The third volume was prefaced by a vituperative 'Memoir of the Author' written by Griswold, which contained many fabrications – including that Poe was expelled from the University of Virginia and that he attempted to seduce his foster father John Allan's second wife – and in which he represented the author as a lunatic, a drug addict and a drunkard. Although it was denounced by many who had known Poe, including Sarah Helen Whitman, Charles Frederick Briggs and George Rex Graham, Griswold's character assassination coloured the writer's posthumous reputation throughout the nineteenth century.

Edgar Allan Poe's Works

Tamerlane and Other Poems

Poe published his first, forty-page book of verse, entitled *Tamerlane and Other Poems*, at his own expense in June or July 1827, with the help of a Boston printer named Calvin Frederick Stephen Thomas, about whom little is known. Only fifty copies were printed, and the volume received no critical attention during the author's lifetime. Indeed, so small was the volume's print run, and so limited was its distribution, that, writing in 1850 – the year after Poe's death – the editor and critic Rufus Wilmot Griswold questioned whether it had existed at all. (A copy was eventually found in 1859.) The book contained ten poems, including the long title piece, about the Turko-Mongol conqueror Tamerlane (1336–1405). In the book's preface the anonymous author (called simply "a Bostonian" on the cover), referring to himself in the third person, asserted that "failure will not at all influence him in a resolution already adopted".

The author's second collection, *Al Aaraaf, Tamerlane and Minor Poems*, which included revised versions of five of the poems from the first volume, was published by the Baltimore firm of Hatch & Dunning in December 1829 and ascribed to "Edgar A. Poe". The extent of the print run is unknown, although it is likely that five hundred copies or fewer were produced. The book contains the first published version of Poe's longest poem, 'Al Aaraaf' (422 lines), which took as its inspiration the discovery in 1572 by the Danish astronomer Tycho Brahe of a supernova, which Poe equated with Al Aaraaf, a place described in the Koran as, in Poe's words, "a medium between Heaven and Hell". Critics mostly reacted negatively to the volume, although John Neal, editor of the *Yankee and Boston Literary Gazette*, opined that if the author "would but do himself justice he might make a beautiful and perhaps a magnificent poem". *Al Aaraaf, Tamerlane and Minor Poems*

Al Aaraaf, Tamerlane and Minor Poems was followed just over a year later, in the spring of 1831, by a third collection of poetry, entitled simply *Poems*, printed by Elam Bliss of New York, probably in a run of between five hundred and a thousand copies. Poe dedicated it to his former colleagues in "the US Corps of Cadets" – some of whom had contributed seventy-five cents each towards the cost. The book described itself as a "second edition", since it contained many poems that had appeared in previous collections, notably 'Tamerlane' and 'Al Aaraaf', as well as six previously unpublished pieces, including early versions of 'To Helen' and 'Israfel'. The volume also included a preface, 'Letter to Mr —', in which Poe outlined his belief that a poem "is opposed to a work of science by having, for its immediate object, *pleasure*, not truth". *Poems*

Having switched his attention to fiction in the early 1830s, partly for pragmatic reasons, Poe had begun to devise a plan for a volume of short stories under the title *Tales of the Folio Club*. However, the collection *The Narrative of Arthur Gordon Pym of Nantucket* was turned down by the publishers Harper & Brothers, who suggested to Poe that "a single work" – that is, a novel – might appeal to "the ordinary comprehension of the generality of readers". Thus he began composing what would be his only novel – a seafaring adventure yarn with supernatural elements about a stowaway aboard a whaling ship – arranging with his employer, Thomas Willis White, editor of the Richmond-based *Southern Literary Messenger*, to have the story, titled *The Narrative of Arthur Gordon Pym of Nantucket*, serialized in the periodical. However, only two instalments appeared before Poe was fired from his position on the *Messenger* in January 1837. Economic necessity later forced Poe to complete the novel, which was published in two volumes by Harper & Brothers in July 1838, presented as an account by Pym himself – Poe's name did not appear. Contemporary reviewers were unimpressed, with many criticizing its violence as well as the attempt to trick readers into believing it was a true story. Poe himself called it "a very silly book". Nevertheless, *Arthur Gordon Pym* has proven to be a highly influential work, with eminent authors such as Jorge Luis Borges, H.G. Wells and Arthur Conan Doyle among its admirers.

Tales of the Grotesque and Arabesque

In late 1839, the Philadelphia firm Lea & Blanchard produced a collection of twenty-five of Poe's short stories, comprising those that were to have been included in the abandoned *Tales of the Folio Club* – including 'MS Found in a Bottle' and 'Metzengerstein' – plus several more, notably 'The Fall of the House of Usher', 'William Wilson' and 'Ligeia'. All of the pieces included in the two volumes, titled *Tales of the Grotesque and Arabesque* and dated 1840, had previously appeared in print, in a variety of publications including the *Southern Literary Messenger* and *Burton's Gentleman's Magazine*. "If in many of my productions terror has been the thesis, I maintain that terror is not of Germany, but of the soul," Poe wrote in his preface, responding to the criticisms of "'Germanism' and gloom" in his fiction. The author was beginning to receive considerable praise for his own work at this time, something that he craved, and many of the reviews of the collection were positive: Poe had "placed himself in the foremost rank of American writers", according to the reviewer of *Alexander's Weekly*. The book failed to sell, however, and Poe received no payment. A year later he approached Lea & Blanchard with a proposal for a second, expanded edition – to be titled *Phantasy Pieces* and incorporating newer stories such as 'The Murders in the Rue Morgue' and 'A Descent into the Maelstrom' – but the publisher declined.

Tales

The next collection of Poe's fiction to be published was *Tales*, which appeared in June 1845 under the imprint of the New York-based Wiley & Putnam. The selection of twelve stories – which, as well as 'The Murders in the Rue Morgue', included two other adventures featuring Poe's detective C. Auguste Dupin, 'The Mystery of Marie Rogêt' and 'The Purloined Letter', as well as now-famous pieces such as 'The Gold-Bug' and 'The Black Cat' – was made by an editor, Evert Augustus Duyckinck, although Poe expressed dissatisfaction with the choices, believing that they represented an insufficient "diversity of subject, thought and especially tone and manner of handling". Nevertheless, the collection was a critical success, with the *American Review* hailing it as "one of the most original and peculiar [volumes] ever published in the United States".

The Raven and Other Poems

Only four months later, in November 1845, *The Raven and Other Poems*, the first collection of Poe's verse to be published for fourteen years, appeared, courtesy again of Wiley & Putnam. The title work had appeared in the New York *Evening Mirror* on 29th January 1845, and had proved wildly popular, enabling Poe to enjoy a taste of the popular and critical approbation he felt so keenly that he needed. The new volume, which contained thirty poems, reprinted several works that had appeared in previous collections, notably 'Tamerlane' and 'Al Aaraaf', alongside a number of hitherto unpublished pieces. In his preface Poe wrote: "With me poetry has been not a purpose, but a passion." Anticipating brisk sales following the success of *Tales*, the publisher increased the print run of *The Raven and Other Poems* from 750 to about 1,500 copies. The collection, however, failed to make a significant commercial impact.

Eureka The last of Poe's works to be issued in his lifetime was *Eureka: A Prose Poem*, which appeared in July 1848, published by George P. Putnam (the successor firm of Wiley & Putnam). A work of non-fiction, it was based on a lecture titled "The Cosmography of the Universe" that Poe gave at New York's Society Library on 3rd February of the same year. Two months after the lecture, Poe approached Putnam with a proposal to adapt its contents into a treatise on the origins, expansion and ultimate collapse of the cosmos, a work whose impact would eclipse that of Newton's theory of gravitation. Putnam was impressed, and agreed to print five hundred copies (a tenth of the quantity suggested by Poe). Poe presented it in his preface "as an art product alone: let us say as a romance – or, if I be not urging too lofty a claim, as a poem". Despite its eccentricity, and the fact that Poe had no formal scientific training to draw on, some see *Eureka* – and the lecture – as predicting aspects of modern cosmology, including the Big Bang theory (in Poe's description of a "primordial particle" created by God) and relativity (in Poe's claim that "space and duration are one"). Poe considered it his greatest work, although the critics failed to agree, with many dismissing it as baffling and absurd.

Edgar Allan Poe's Works

Correspondence:

The Collected Letters of Edgar Allan Poe, ed. J.W. Ostrom, B.R. Pollin and J.A. Savoye, 2 vols., 3rd edn. (New York: Gordian Press, 2008)

Biographies:

Peter Ackroyd, *Poe: A Life Cut Short* (London: Chatto & Windus, 2008)

Hervey Allen, *Israfel: The Life and Times of Edgar Allan Poe*, 2 vols. (New York: George H. Doran, 1927)

Jeffrey Meyers, *Edgar Allan Poe: His Life and Legacy* (New York: Charles Scribner's Sons, 1992)

Una Pope-Hennessy, *Edgar Allan Poe, 1809–1849: A Critical Biography* (New York: Haskell House, 1934)

Arthur Hobson Quinn, *Edgar Allan Poe: A Critical Biography* (New York: D. Appleton–Century, 1941)

Additional Recommended Background Material:

Kevin J. Hayes, ed., *The Cambridge Companion to Edgar Allan Poe* (Cambridge: Cambridge University Press, 2002)

I.M. Walker, ed., *Edgar Allan Poe: The Critical Heritage* (London: Routledge, 1986)

Websites:

The Edgar Allan Poe Society of Baltimore, available at eapoe.org

The Poe Museum, available at poemuseum.org

EVERGREENS SERIES

Beautifully produced classics, affordably priced

Alma Classics is committed to making available a wide range of literature from around the globe. Most of the titles are enriched by an extensive critical apparatus, notes and extra reading material, as well as a selection of photographs. The texts are based on the most authoritative editions and edited using a fresh, accessible editorial approach. With an emphasis on production, editorial and typographical values, Alma Classics aspires to revitalize the whole experience of reading classics.

On the Origin of Species
Charles Darwin
Daniel Defoe
Moll Flanders
Charles Dickens
A Christmas Carol
David Copperfield
Charles Dickens
Great Expectations
Charles Dickens
Hard Times
Charles Dickens
Charles Dickens
Oliver Twist
Charles Dickens
A Tale of Two Cities
The Double
Fyodor Dostoevsky
Fyodor Dostoevsky
The Gambler
The Idiot
Fyodor Dostoevsky
Notes from Underground
Fyodor Dostoevsky
Middlemarch
George Eliot
The Mill on the Floss
George Eliot
Praise of Folly
Erasmus
The Beautiful and Damned
F. Scott Fitzgerald
The Great Gatsby
F. Scott Fitzgerald
Tender is the Night
F. Scott Fitzgerald
Gustave Flaubert
Madame Bovary
North and South
Elizabeth Gaskell
The Sorrows of Young Werther
Goethe
Dead Souls
Nikolai Gogol
Nikolai Gogol
Petersburg Tales
Thomas Hardy
Far from the Madding Crowd
Thomas Hardy
Jude the Obscure
Thomas Hardy
Tess of the d'Urbervilles
Nathaniel Hawthorne
The Scarlet Letter
The Portrait of a Lady
Henry James
Three Men in a Boat
Jerome K. Jerome
Dubliners
James Joyce
Ulysses
James Joyce
Franz Kafka
Metamorphosis
Franz Kafka
The Trial
Lady Chatterley's Lover
D.H. Lawrence
Sons and Lovers
D.H. Lawrence
Mikhail Lermontov
A Hero of Our Time

The PRINCE
Machiavelli
MOBY DICK OR THE WHALE BY HERMAN MELVILLE
UTOPIA
THOMAS MORE
POE
TALES OF HORROR
Eugene ONEGIN
Alexander Pushkin
PANTAGRUEL & GARGANTUA
SONNETS
FRANKENSTEIN
MARY SHELLEY
THE EXPEDITION OF HUMPHRY CLINKER
TOBIAS SMOLLETT
The LIFE and OPINIONS of Tristram SHANDY Gentleman
LAURENCE STERNE
STRANGE CASE OF
Dr Jekyll & MR HYDE
ROBERT LOUIS STEVENSON
THE ART OF WAR
SUN TZU
GULLIVER'S TRAVELS
Jonathan SWIFT
JOURNEY BY MOONLIGHT
ANTAL SZERB
VANITY FAIR
THACKERAY
LEO TOLSTOY
ANNA KARENINA
Fathers AND Children
Ivan Turgenev
ADVENTURES OF HUCKLEBERRY FINN
Mark Twain
ADVENTURES OF TOM SAWYER
TOM SAWYER, DETECTIVE
Mark Twain
H.G. WELLS
THE INVISIBLE MAN
H.G. WELLS
THE ISLAND OF DR MOREAU
H.G. WELLS
THE TIME MACHINE
H.G. WELLS
THE WAR OF THE WORLDS
the Age of Innocence
EDITH WHARTON
OSCAR WILDE
DORIAN GRAY
TO THE LIGHTHOUSE
VIRGINIA WOOLF
MRS DALLOWAY
VIRGINIA WOOLF
VIRGINIA WOOLF
THE WAVES
ZAMYATIN
WE
THE GAME OF CHESS AND OTHER STORIES
BY STEFAN ZWEIG

ALMA CLASSICS

ALMA CLASSICS aims to publish mainstream and lesser-known European classics in an innovative and striking way, while employing the highest editorial and production standards. By way of a unique approach the range offers much more, both visually and textually, than readers have come to expect from contemporary classics publishing.

LATEST TITLES PUBLISHED BY ALMA CLASSICS

473. Sinclair Lewis, *Babbitt*
474. Edith Wharton, *The House of Mirth*
475. George Orwell, *Burmese Days*
476. Virginia Woolf, *The Voyage Out*
477. Charles Dickens, *Pictures from Italy*
478. Fyodor Dostoevsky, *Crime and Punishment*
479. Anton Chekhov, *Small Fry and Other Stories*
480. George Orwell, *Homage to Catalonia*
481. Carlo Collodi, *The Adventures of Pinocchio*
482. Virginia Woolf, *Between the Acts*
483. Alain Robbe-Grillet, *Last Year at Marienbad*
484. Charles Dickens, *The Pickwick Papers*
485. Wilkie Collins, *The Haunted Hotel*
486. Ivan Turgenev, *Parasha and Other Poems*
487. Arthur Conan Doyle, *His Last Bow*
488. Ivan Goncharov, *The Frigate Pallada*
489. Arthur Conan Doyle, *The Casebook of Sherlock Holmes*
490. Alexander Pushkin, *Lyrics Vol. 4*
491. Arthur Conan Doyle, *The Valley of Fear*
492. Gottfried Keller, *Green Henry*
493. Grimmelshausen, *Simplicius Simplicissimus*
494. Edgar Allan Poe, *The Raven and Other Poems*
495. Sinclair Lewis, *Main Street*
496. Prosper Mérimée, *Carmen*
497. D.H. Lawrence, *Women in Love*
498. Albert Maltz, *A Tale of One January*
499. George Orwell, *Coming Up for Air*
500. Anton Chekhov, *The Looking Glass and Other Stories*
501. Ivan Goncharov, *An Uncommon Story*
502. Paul Éluard, *Selected Poems*
503. Ivan Turgenev, *Memoirs of a Hunter*
504. Albert Maltz, *A Long Day in a Short Life*
505. Edith Wharton, *Ethan Frome*
506. Charles Dickens, *The Old Curiosity Shop*
507. Fyodor Dostoevsky, *The Village of Stepanchikovo*
508. George Orwell, *The Clergyman's Daughter*
509. Virginia Woolf, *The New Dress and Other Stories*
510. Ivan Goncharov, *A Serendipitous Error and Two Incidents at Sea*
511. Beatrix Potter, *Peter Rabbit*